Just Jenny and Scout –

The Collective Works

by

Dani Haviland
USA Today Bestselling Author

Please Read Me First

Jenny and Scout's tale is part of several – but not all – of the fifteen stories in THE FAIRIES SAGA series. I decided to create a box set *just* about them and their lives in Early America (1780s North Carolina). That involved some creative editing.

You see…

Jenny and Scout first show up in the last six chapters of NAKED IN THE WINTER WIND (NITWW), a very long book narrated by Evie, a 'rejuvenated' time traveler from the 21st century. The rest of Jenny and Scout's story follows, either as complete novels or as extended excerpts from other books in The Fairies Saga series.

After each chapter heading, I inserted the parent book's abbreviated name and chapter number in parentheses:

Chapter 1: The Fifth Fourth (NITWW Chapter 44)

If you want to know more about the other people in that storyline, check out that book to read later.

NITWW: Naked in the Winter Wind (partial novel, full chapters)

H'PJ: Ha'Penny Jenny (complete novel)

AYE: Aye, I am a Fairy (partial novel)

TGBF: The Great Big Fairy (partial novel, full chapters)

CC: Chasing Christmas (complete novel)

LDB: Little Drummer Boy (complete novel)

NTY: Never Too Young (complete novel)

For now, here is *Just Jenny and Scout – The Collective Works*, beginning with the excerpt from the first novel I ever wrote, Naked in the Winter Wind.

Oh, and a handy **Cast of Characters** list is on the last page, the easiest place to find it.

Contents

Extended excerpt from

Naked in the Winter Wind

The Fairies Saga Book Three

(First book in Chronological Order)

Copyright ©2011 by Dani Haviland
Published by Chill Out!
ISBN 978-1-946752-48-2

Naked in the Winter Wind and *The Fairies Saga* are works of fiction. Names, places, characters, and incidents are the product of the author's imagination or used fictitiously for the reader's entertainment. Any resemblance to persons living, dead, or fictional, events, business establishments, or locales, is entirely coincidental.

Chapter 1: The Fifth Fourth (NITWW Ch 44)

July 4, 1781

Today was a day of celebration for many of us and just another summer day for the Tories and Loyalists. Independence Day number five was an affirmation and show of unity for all of us who had kept the faith and persevered, and who were still striving to win the conflict with England. Tonight, all up and down the eastern seaboard and in all thirteen colonies, American patriots would observe the fifth anniversary of the signing of the Declaration of Independence with parties, drinking, banners, and bragging. There would be cannons blasting, guns saluting, and rockets painting the night sky with festive fire, acknowledging our gratefulness to God, our soldiers, and the Continental Congress for working together toward our deliverance from English tyranny.

We were still at war, but I knew beyond a hiccup of a doubt that we would win this. My faith was contagious to others, too. Jody was aware of the outcome before I showed up because of Sarah and her knowledge of English and American 'history,' but he was absolutely passionate about our new form of government, as if he had discovered it himself.

I felt privileged to be able to observe his finesse in promoting the push for our new country's independence. He was easily wound up and preached whenever he saw an opportunity. He knew how to use his size, bearing, and voice to great advantage. He would start low, just a comment or an aside, to someone in town. "Better a free mouse than a slaved cat," he was fond of saying.

The crowd would grow as people curious about the tall red-haired man would stop, watch him gesticulate with those long arms and broad hands, and listen to his booming voice hawk the merits of self-rule. The crescendo moved into an awesome finale, a passionate speech, sweeping all within earshot of him into a roaring fever of patriotism and hope. Then, to make sure they understood the concept, he would give his short comprehensive summary of what we were fighting for.

"We will make this a great country. We will have the right to say how we govern ourselves; we will elect our own people to *enact* the laws, *interpret* the laws, and *enforce* the laws. This will be the greatest

1

nation on earth: one nation, under God, indivisible, with liberty and justice for all!"

His powerful speeches and the boldness of Angus and other printers to publish booklets and broadsheets to spread the word even further enabled the masses to understand how great our potential was. There were other great speakers around, and I'm sure glad they were all Americans. The Loyalists evidently didn't feel as if they had to support or prove their side of the conflict. I guess the fine art of political debate would have to wait a few generations until broader venues were available.

Not all of the well-spoken American patriots made it, or will make it, through this war, though. "I regret that I have but one life to give for my country," were powerful words spoken by a very young twenty-one-year-old, Nathan Hale, just before he was executed by the British in 1776. These words helped inspire the fight for a new nation. Jody's words may not be remembered 230 years into the future, but he didn't—oh, my God, I hope he doesn't—die a martyr.

Maybe the pen *is* mightier than the sword. If Hale's affirmation and the words of others had never been written down and shared within this fledgling nation, would we have been as brave and fearless? Young America was certainly underpowered as far as weapons, money, and a navy were concerned. Yes, the American spirit, shared in voice and spread in ink, was definitely what won—will win—the war for independence.

I couldn't—wouldn't—live in fear for my life or the lives of my family. Our future Constitution and Bill of Rights would be to protect us from fear. But today, right here, right now, lingering Loyalist factions were still pressing their interests, both personal and respective to the Crown, into our lives.

Word came through the usual local news network—paranoid gossip with a smattering of fact thrown in—that a motley crew of disgruntled Loyalists was roaming the area, collecting taxes without regard to who the property owners were or their delinquency status. As far as we knew, the 'maybe they were, maybe they weren't British soldiers' had no valid basis for the tax they were collecting. These bandits were working solely by intimidation. If the landowner couldn't pay hard cash, they would take anything of value they could put their hands on. If the landowner refused, bloodshed ensued. There was a term for this course of action in my time: extortion.

We had heard the rumors and were cautious, and never left our little homestead unattended. Today Wallace was the sentinel, staying home with me and the babies.

Jody and Sarah had gone into the little big town of Gibsonville for the latest news, salt, and a few other staples. Sarah had insisted on bringing the wagon, hoping that they would be able to bring home some of those flat stones that were down by the creek. I guessed what she wanted were what I called flagstones.

"I want a solid floor, Jody, and one without splinters, one that I can cover with rugs in the winter and have cool to my feet in the summer. Nothing can stay clean with this hard-packed earth as a floor. Pretty soon the babies will be crawling, and we don't want them scooting around on this, do we?"

She had a good argument, and he knew it. Julian said that José had more rugs than they could use at their house. Evidently, his mother, Señora Rojas, had been quite the collector. José, although he probably would have given them to us just to be rid of them, was glad that he could offer them as gifts for the babies. He had only seen the wee'uns once, when he had come to bring Julian back to the ranch the week after they were born, and had fallen in love with them at first sight.

"Tres, um, three? At the same time?" he asked.

José had taken to heart my suggestion and was speaking English as much as possible. He looked at the petite crew, sleeping in one heap on the middle of Sarah and Jody's bed. I had only made two little baskets for use as bassinets when I was pregnant—not knowing I would need three—but they slept better when snuggled up together and fussed when separated. I guessed they had lived in close quarters for eight months and weren't quite ready to be apart.

Julian had just about completed their new bed. "Wally, can you finish this for me? I thought I'd be done by now, but I didn't plan on, ahem, doing other things," he carped, then grinned. Julian had been roped into doing all of the cooking. Sarah's hands were still tender, and I was always busy tending to the input or output of the babies.

"I'll be glad to cook, Julian," I teased. "You just come over here and whip out your boob and feed these little guys." He glared at me and went back to cracking eggs for our dinner omelet. His eggs were always good, too. Why did men always make the best omelets? Maybe it was because that was the only dish they ever cooked. Practice makes perfect and all that, you know.

So, Julian was back with José, and Sarah and Jody were out harvesting river rock flooring, possibly until tomorrow. Wallace and I had time to ourselves. Well, sort of—we still had the babies to tend to. I took out the little Bible. "Is it okay if I get a head start on finishing the birth records? I…well, I want to give them their last names now, if it's okay with you. You see, in my time, a baby can be given any last name, not just the mother's or father's surname. You might think I'm a bit twisted, but I think it would be kind of cute if they had your last name before I did."

"I would be honored to give them my name," he said proudly. He sighed then added, almost apologetically, "The way the country is now; it's only the name of Urquhart I can give them. I think I have forfeited my title and the Falls Church estate as a result of changing allegiances. It looks as if we will all be wearing homespun for a long time."

I looked up to see if I could read anything in his face after his last soft-spoken remark. I could. The love he was radiating was undeniable. He saw the insecure look in my eyes and said, "A small price to pay for a bit of heaven on earth, I say. Even without the babies, you alone are worth it."

"Wow, um, thank you." I put down the mini Bible and reached up, clasping my arms around his neck, to give him a smooch worthy of Burt Lancaster and Deborah Kerr in 'From Here to Eternity.' I composed myself after the kiss but couldn't manage—and really didn't want—to get rid of my huge grin of satisfaction. "I'd better be careful; if I don't stop smiling so big, my face will freeze like this forever."

"That would be fine by me. I like seeing you happy. Now let me see that Bible."

A card fell out as I handed it to him: a business card. I hadn't seen it when I put the babies' birth date in the book; it must have been stuck between the pages. He picked it up and glanced at it, then stared at it, as if he couldn't believe what he was seeing. "Where did you get this?" he asked coolly.

"I don't know. It's new to me, which really isn't saying much. Here, let me see."

He let me take it but didn't move his hand to offer it to me. He was shocked—at it or something on it.

"It's just a business card—see," I said and waved it in the air, showing off how harmless it was. "I guess it was in my backpack and…oh, my," I looked at the card, "isn't your uncle Lord Melbourne?"

"Yes, and that's the family's coat of arms. But my uncle's name isn't James. I've never seen a card like this. The paper is so smooth and shiny, the letters are raised, and the printing is so, so perfect. What do all these numbers mean?"

"Those are phone numbers. Remember when I told you about telephones? Phone numbers are how we kept everyone indexed, sorted, and how we accessed them, I mean… Well, there are also faxes, which need numbers, too, and emails, which use letters and/or numbers. And gosh, look at that—he even has his own website."

I set the card down. This wasn't working, and it wasn't because I had overloaded him with my rambling about numbers and modern technology. This twenty-first-century business card was from someone with his family name, actually his kin by the use of the coat of arms and title. And I must have had it in my possession since…well, at least since a minute before I arrived here from the twenty-first century.

I lifted my suddenly insecure fiancé's chin and fixed my eyes on his half-closed ones. "Wallace, I think this is from one of your relatives, or rather your relative's descendants. But I swear I don't know how I got this. I don't have any feelings for or about this card, or this 'James Melbourne' person, at all!"

I hadn't started out to be emotional or excited about a silly old slip of thick paper. Good grief, it was just a business card. I received cards like this all the time in my previous life. I think. But this was 'when' I was, here and now. It should be no big deal after seeing the smartphone a few weeks ago, but this had something to do with Wallace and Julian's heritage. Or whatever the opposite of heritage was: *descentage*?

Wallace's head was bowed and still. I looked at the card again, then gave it back to him. He rubbed his thumb over the embossed lettering. "Oh, well," he remarked nonchalantly, then lifted his head to gaze at me with a weak smile, "another mystery."

"Like bumblebees," I said with a one-shoulder shrug of agreement.

He raised one eyebrow and looked down his nose, asking me wordlessly, "Explain, please."

"Aerodynamically, bumblebees aren't supposed to be able to fly, but they do. You know, fat little bodies and itty-bitty wings? An eagle soaring, that's easy to see, but those chunky little buggers popping from flower to flower, mathematically and scientifically shouldn't be able to fly. A mystery, but real; something we accept and don't try to explain."

"Okay, a bumblebee," he said and shoved the card back into the Bible.

"Maybe we can do the names a little later," I mumbled, suddenly feeling insecure.

He looked over at me and saw that my big happy smile had managed to totally disappear and was now approaching a frown. "We have the first and last names. Why don't we figure out a few middle names before we enter them in the Bible? After all, we aren't going anywhere."

"Okay," I chirped, popping right out of my funk, "fine by me."

And it was. Now what were some good middle names, and how many should I give each child? Those were happy posers for me to consider and didn't even begin to drag me down into curiosity about my unknown past.

***

Wallace went to the barn to continue with his woodworking. He was finishing the babies' playpen/crib that Julian had started. I was hoping to get a few minutes to myself before a baby woke up. I grabbed a clean cloth and filled a small pot with fresh water. I sat on the porch and untied my shirt. I felt icky, covered with baby spit-up and sweat. I wet the cloth and wiped from my forehead down to my neck. I rinsed the cloth and washed the top of my breasts then rinsed again. Ah, now the best part. I lifted one of my heavy breasts and washed away the perspiration and spilled milk. The babies all nursed well, as in vigorously, but they all seemed to fall asleep with a mouthful of milk. It dribbled out their lips, and down and underneath my breasts. It wasn't always possible to clean up after each feeding. There was always another one waiting to be fed or changed.

My little sponge bath was just the pick-me-up I needed. I felt almost as clean as if I'd taken a whole bath. Maybe I'd be able to do that later on tonight.

It was still early but looked like it was going to be another miserably hot day. There wasn't a white spot in the sky, which was good. I didn't mind the heat, but I hated the humidity that came with the clouds and haze. I decided to be brazen and leave my shirt open so I could thoroughly dry out. I knew I'd be able to hear anyone coming before they could see me, so I put my legs up and kicked back on the porch bench, ready to catch some rays and vitamin D.

I looked up at the north end of the porch through squinted eyes and visualized a swing. I'd have to show Wallace how they were made where I came from—or would that be when I came from? It would be nice to have one wide enough for two adults to share. And it shouldn't take much more effort to hang three little swings from the porch beam.

I was fantasizing about swinging and fresh air when someone threw a cloth over my chest. I looked down and saw it was a diaper off of the clothesline.

"Cover up, quick," a husky voice ordered.

I did, hurriedly tying together my blouse underneath the cloth—at the same time, looking for my modesty policeman. I didn't see him but did see a rider coming in at a fast pace, kicking up a twisty, tan dust cloud, followed by a wagon with three men.

I searched again for the cloth-tosser but didn't see anyone. I called for Wallace, but he didn't answer. Something fishy was going on, and I was starting to get scared.

The rider, a scruffy-looking British soldier, jerked back hard on the reins when he saw me, and came to a gravel-crunching stop. He had kicked his horse hard and repeatedly to get her to the house so quickly. Fresh blood was oozing from the gouges in the long-legged black mare's flanks. I looked over and saw that, although the man was dressed in a tattered and filthy British officer's uniform, he was wearing Spanish spurs—mean, ugly, sharp ones that would give the SPCA and PETA fits.

I walked to the edge of the porch to greet the stranger. "Can I help you, sir," I said in my bravest voice. My knees felt watery, but gratefully, they still held me up. I reached out and held onto the porch post in order to give myself more stability. My courageous demeanor would mean nothing if I passed out from fright right in front of him.

"I'm the new tax collector and I see that," he pulled out a little booklet that looked like one of those cheap dirty novels that made the circuit, "this household has not paid any taxes this year."

I leaned in closer to see if I could see the name of his little novella. He quickly pulled it close to his chest and shoved it back into his jacket pocket.

He was lying, and I wasn't the least bit subtle with my distrustful leer, letting him know that I knew he did not have a tax-roll book in his jacket.

"I think you're mistaken, sir," I said with a newfound confidence, "we are current on our taxes. Someone must have given you the wrong book." Then I glared at him, daring him to challenge me.

That was probably a bad move. He was not a nice man by the looks of his horse's bleeding flesh. I quickly backpedaled, "I'm sure it wasn't your mistake though, sir." I batted my eyelashes, hoping to cover my tough northern girl persona with a charming young southern belle flirtation. "Good help is so hard to find nowadays," I added demurely.

I should have continued with the engaging debutante role and asked if he would like a drink of water, but I really wanted him gone. Just as I was wondering what to do next, my decision was made for me. The creepy soldier jumped up onto the porch and literally got in my face.

"What's a sweet young thing like you doing out here all alone? Did your menfolk go out and get themselves killed by the mean old British soldiers?"

His breath reeked of rum and rotten teeth. I took two steps back to get away from him, but he advanced three.

"If you're lonely, I can be real friendly," he cooed.

His hands reached for my hair, but my reflexes were fast, and he didn't get a chance to touch me. Instead, it was I who reached out. I instinctively slapped him across his stubble-whiskered cheek before I could think.

"Oh, you shouldn't have done that, little lady. I don't take to violence. At least *I* don't like being hit. I do like to inflict a little pain every now and then, though. I find it—rather, arousing…"

He dragged the last word out in a most perverse manner. I had ducked and drawn away from him with the slap, but he was closing in on me, making sure I didn't have an escape route. He was between me and the steps now. I could hear his heavy breathing and smell his rummy breath. He reached down and grabbed the front of his pants. "Give the taxman his due, little lady, and maybe he won't take too much from your little bitty home. The wagon is fairly full already, but what I'd really like..."

"Mama, Mama," the little boy said as he popped up between the extortionist and me. "I'm back. Did ye miss me?"

I reached down and clutched the unknown dark-haired boy to me, and hugged him hard. "Oh, I did miss you," I said sincerely, keeping hold of this little person who had just stopped an assault. He was about ten years old and wiry—hard, skinny, and definitely clever.

"Father says that he'll be right back. He and uncle and cousin and all the men from the...the...the store will be here any minute. He says he loves ye and misses ye."

The little boy stammered on where the menfolk were, and I hoped the taxman—or whoever he was—had missed his little sign of lying.

"Thank you, dear," I said as I brushed his wayward hair out of his eyes.

I gasped, glad that my back was toward the soldier. I suddenly realized who this boy must be, and I was sure the look of shock showed on my face. He had to be Ian's son! His features, that hair that wouldn't go where it was supposed to, and those soft brown eyes—if he wasn't Ian's son, I was a rhinoceros.

My momentary trance was broken by the sound of a baby crying. It was little Danielle. If I didn't get to her soon, she'd have her brothers awake and screaming with her. "I need to take care of my daughter," I said as I excused myself, not waiting to see if he had any objections. No one was going to keep me from my babies.

The little boy followed me inside. He literally stood guard at the door as I sat on a kitchen chair and bared a breast to both quiet and feed her.

"Get out of here," growled the little boy. "This house is for family only."

There wasn't any sign of fear in his voice, and I realized why. I think he knew I was feeding his sister; she *was* his family.

My back was turned away from the opened door—I wanted at least a modicum of privacy in nursing—and I didn't see it coming.

"Move out of the way, boy. I wanna see what we have here." I heard

9

the shuffle of bodies in contention and turned around just in time to see Little Ian fly through the air. The taxman had lifted him bodily and tossed him into the corner like a dirty shirt.

I stood up and backed away from the man as he neared me with a lusty smirk. "Ooh, a little one, but she's *too* little right now. Give her a couple of years, and she'll be just right."

"Keep away, you bastard," I hissed, controlling the urge to scream—I didn't want to startle the baby. I saw movement out of the corner of my eye. Little Ian had come to his wits, and was inching our way.

"Now lookie there; she is a fresh one, isn't she? I'll bet you and your husband—if there even is a husband—haven't had relations since she was born."

He reached up to brush my breasts with his huge, filthy hand, but I feigned right and dodged him. Now I was on the other side of him and could easily run outside. But I couldn't leave him in the house with my other two babies. One of them was sure to awaken soon.

He glared at me, angry at my clever escape. It was a stare-down, and I won. Sort of. His eyes changed focus and peered down, leering at the opening of my blouse. Then he looked up to my gold nugget necklace, and another kind of lust appeared.

"Aarrgghh!" I caught sight of the tanned buckskinned-clad boy just as he tackled the taxman behind the legs, effectively knocking the much bigger man flat on his back…and evidently the wind out of his lungs. The man's mouth was moving, but his chest was still. He couldn't draw a breath.

"Hmph," I snorted. I didn't care if he ever breathed again.

Little Ian stood above his prey, a dirk in his hand, his foot ready to stomp on the man's windpipe if he should try to rise. "Shall I cut him?" he asked.

"Yes," I answered angrily in emotional reflex. "Cut him? Oh, no," I said as I suddenly realized what he meant.

"Too late," he said.

I was afraid that he had meant kill him, but he hadn't. Nevertheless, he really had cut him. The taxman had a 'Y' cut into his cheek. He still couldn't breathe, though, and was beginning to turn blue. Little Ian stepped back and kicked him hard under the ribcage. The man gasped, and his color started to return with the intake of air.

I heard a noise in the doorway, saw that it was Wallace, and was relieved.

And then it was terror time all over again.

I noticed the look in Wallace's eyes and the knife at his neck—he was being held hostage. Three men were standing behind him, grinning like cats at an overstocked fishpond. The taxman's reinforcements had arrived.

Judah and Leo chose that moment to wake up and call for their lunch. I let them scream. I knew an infant's cry was irritating to a human male's eardrum. The high pitch actually caused men physical pain...or so I recalled reading or hearing...somewhere. If I could irritate the intruders in an unobtrusive manner, maybe they wouldn't be able to think clearly. Then Wallace, the boy, and I could find a way out of this mess.

The boy! If Ian's son was here—and how in the hell did he have a son that he didn't, or wouldn't, tell me about—then Ian was around here somewhere. That made me feel better—I had an invisible ally.

Surely Ian would want his prey out in the open where he could see them. Now I felt like I was part of a rescue team, and my partner was out there somewhere, just waiting for me to flush out his quarry.

"How about if we go outside where it isn't so noisy," I suggested as I put Danielle down into the nest of quilts on the bed. I picked up Leo—he was protesting the loudest—turned my back on the men, and let the baby start nursing. There was no reason for him to be deprived of lunch. And right now, I needed him as much as he needed me.

Leo and I followed the gruesome foursome outside. I hoped Wallace, the boy, the babies, and I had someone—my modesty policeman maybe—to help us.

The taxman was a bit loopy from his assault, but managed to grasp onto one of his cronies, and made it to the porch bench. Little Ian—or should that be Wee Ian—had picked up little Judah and brought him outside to be with me. He was cooing and cuddling the baby; actually doing a great job of distracting the little two-week-old—oh my, Judah was his little brother!

I took a deep breath to compose myself. Too much had just happened, and I couldn't handle it, even with the aid of my little dark-haired champion. "Lord, help us," I prayed softly to the man upstairs.

11

"Who you talkin' to," asked the skinny man who still had a knife to Wallace's neck.

"God," I answered with self-assurance. I suddenly felt braver because I knew He would help us. "You know, the man who gave us 'thou shalt not kill' and 'thou shalt not steal' and about eight other good 'thou shalt nots' to live by."

"Hmph," was the monosyllabic reply from the man who looked like he had a single digit IQ.

Okay, maybe I could work this in my favor. The taxman was evidently the head honcho in this little extortion ring. Right now, he was pretty much out of commission. His three apes were apparently trying to keep up the intimidation and theft gambit and weren't quite sure about what to do next.

"Would you believe that you have a knife to the neck of General William Howe's son?" I asked. "You do know who General Howe is, don't you?"

Skinny looked at the other two, and they all shrugged shoulders.

Gee, maybe these guys were too dumb to fool. "General Howe is a big time British general, and his brother is 'Admiral' Richard Howe. You know him, of course. *Everybody* knows him," I said dramatically.

Skinny started bobbing his head, then the others did, too. "Yeah, we know 'em; *everybody* knows him," the bald one said enthusiastically. He was lying and I knew it.

Of course, I wasn't lying. I hadn't said that Wallace was the general's son. I had said 'Would you believe?' and they did.

"Now," I continued with great sincerity, "if the Howe family found out that you hurt one of their own kin... My, my, there would be, pardon the vulgarity, hell to pay."

The boys were getting nervous now. "But we can't leave without takin' somethin'," the bald one—evidently the new leader—said.

"Now, how are you going to get your—captain, is he—home with all of this 'stuff' in the back of your wagon?"

I walked over to the wagon and lifted one edge of the canvas tarp covering it. I couldn't see what was in the little barrels, but I *could* smell it. They had gunpowder. Kegs and kegs of gunpowder. I wasn't a betting person, but still, I'd bet those long boxes under the seat had rifles or muskets in them.

"I'll tell you what, why don't you just unload this wagon here, and then your captain can ride in the b…"

"Shut up, bitch," boomed an angry voice from the porch. Taxman had regained his senses and was reclaiming control. "I'm going to take you for everything you've got. Including that little boy of yours, the bastard," he said as he reached up to feel the wound on his cheek.

I needed to think of what to do next, so I stalled. Leo had finished nursing, so I moved him off the breast and covered myself in one smooth move. As I walked back up the porch steps to be near Danielle, I put him over my shoulder to burp him. Five seconds passed, and I still hadn't had a brainstorm.

Taxman had moved from the bench to the porch post, and was trying to stand up straight by himself, testing his balance without using his cronies as crutches. They were mumbling amongst themselves, but I couldn't hear what they were saying.

I was scared, staring off into space, not knowing what to do next, when I felt the tugging at my elbow, a small hand trying to get my attention.

"Here, Mama, I'll take him," Wee Ian said as he handed me Judah who, although not screaming, was making faces and shaking his fists in frustration. I swapped out babies and saw the boy's eyes shift to the barn.

"Thank you, dear," I said. "You're such a good big brother." I got Judah started on lunch, then turned to face Taxman. He was able to stand alone now, only touching the porch post for security.

I cleared my throat to get the captain's attention. He looked down at me with disgust, but I didn't mind. I'd rather have him look at me like that than with his earlier ogles and leers. "Sir, I don't think you have the situation under control like you think you do."

My confidence level was Rocky Mountain high, and I was letting it shine. I tossed my hair back and stuck out my chin. "You see, right now you are being targeted by a very angry man. He doesn't take too kindly to his kin being threatened. So, I suggest that you let his cousin go…*right now!*" I dipped my head down to accentuate my guttural threat and glared into his eyes, an angry bull daring the toreador to approach.

Skinny let his knife fall away from Wallace's neck, but Taxman interceded. "Not so quick there, mate," he said. Skinny brought the knife up again, straightened his back, and froze, as if he were at attention.

13

"There's still the matter of the taxes, you see," Taxman said as he worked his way toward me.

I sidled around him, keeping eye contact. He had changed his demeanor back to letch mode. With it came that ugly, lustful sneer. His eyes moved from my one covered breast, ignoring the baby actively nursing, to the other side, and then back up my throat to the gold nugget necklace.

"Oh, and I *know* that you're lying about a marksman in the barn," he said. "My men looked in there, and all they found was this wee little patriot," then he poked Wallace in the ribs with his silver-barreled pistol.

I looked toward the barn. I multitasked, holding the suckling baby with my right arm, lifting my left hand straight up to the porch beam to point to a spot two feet above my head. "Right here, Ian," I yelled.

Zing! Twack.

An arrow hit the spot I had pointed to. I looked over at our extortionist and grinned. "Now, let's talk terms, shall we?"

The captain glared at me, obviously thinking of his options. He didn't want to back down to anyone—especially a woman—in front of his men and didn't want to leave empty-handed, either. He would have to let Wallace go, or get himself shot; that was obvious. And I was far enough away now that he couldn't grab me. I wasn't going to let him have two hostages.

Wee Ian had disappeared during all of this and had put Leo on the bed with his sister. He was back now—his knife in hand and a squint in his eye—just daring the captain to make a move.

The tension was smothering. Taxman turned toward Wee Ian and spat on the ground, aiming for the boy's feet. The boy jumped out of the way and stabbed him in the thigh at the same time.

"Do ye really want me to cut ye some more? Jest keep it up, and we willna have to waste an arrow. I'll bleed ye right here and now." Wee Ian snarled with grim satisfaction. "Willna bother me none."

"Goddamn bastard," Taxman swore as he clutched his fresh leg wound. I could tell it was a deep cut, but because of where it was, the blood was only dribbling, not gushing. I was sure he hurt plenty, but the injury couldn't be as painful as the humiliation of being attacked by a child in front of his minions.

I glanced toward the barn and realized that Ian, my first husband,

14

the man who just two weeks earlier I had been wishing was by my side to share in the pain and joy—in that order—of the birth of my children, was less than a hundred feet away. The man who had abandoned me, the one who I had longed for once upon a time, was just across the yard. Flashbacks of the beaten and burned man I had rescued, the weakened man who with his first flush of strength made love to me after promising to never leave me, the man whose seed had spawned my three babies…

Focus, woman, focus! He's just a tool in the woods, a weapon to help resolve this conflict.

I stopped staring and started glaring. Taxman was still grumbling about his leg and tying a handkerchief around his thigh, eyes down on his first aid ministrations. I glanced over and saw that Skinny still had the knife to Wallace's throat. Wallace's eyes were on me but were vacant. He wasn't letting anyone know—including me—what he was thinking.

"Wee Ian, take the baby back to the bed, please. And don't stab anyone unless I say so, okay?" I covered myself up, put my finger in between my son's mouth and my nipple to break the bond, and then offered the bundle of baby to his big brother.

Wee Ian sheathed his knife and walked over to me, but kept his eye on Taxman, his stare somewhere between mocking and sheer hatred. "Asshole," he said, as he looked the bigger man in the eye.

I had to stifle my laugh—it was such an appropriate name for the brigand. Wee Ian took the baby from me and walked backward into the house, throwing a quick glance in my direction, making sure I was still safe. I nodded that I was okay, and then he passed through the doorway, disappearing into the shadows.

As soon as the two boys were safely inside, I squared my shoulders and growled, "Take that effin' knife away from his throat." Skinny dropped his knife—from either shock or obedience—and Wallace stepped away, to stand at my side.

Taxman looked up, one eyebrow raised in satisfaction. He had finished bandaging his leg and figured out his next strategy: humiliation. His acne-scarred face screwed up into a complete sneer as he asked Wallace, "Do you always let the woman do the talking?"

"She seems to be doing all right. If she needs help, she'll ask." Wallace nodded to me to dismiss himself, then moved past the Taxman, intentionally bumping into the man's wounded leg on his way into the house.

"Good job, lad," he said to Wee Ian as he walked inside to check on the boy and the babies. Wallace knew he wasn't leaving me alone—the master archer was still watching over me—and, as he said, I'd ask for help if I needed it.

"Okay, Captain Asshole, is it?" I asked, not really wanting an answer.

He glared at me. He had no intention of replying and I knew it. I'm sure he didn't want me to know who he was. I was definitely the type who had no qualms about spreading the name of the crooked British officer who illegally collected taxes. And I'd also let everyone know that the dirtbag had been overtaken and marked by a boy not even old enough to have a whisker.

"So you want to collect some 'taxes' from us, even though we're current?" I asked sarcastically.

His reply was to stare at me, to try to intimidate me with his clenched jaws and barely audible growl.

It wasn't working. I grinned in response, just to make sure he knew it.

"Well, what I want is for you to be gone, and never to return again." I paused for effect—and for the muscle strength to return to my shaky legs. I shook my head at him with disgust, "And since you are wearing a British uniform, you should be under some sort of code of ethics."

A snarl escaped his raised lip at my remark, but I ignored it and continued. "So, I'll let you go with a bargain. You see, if you take anything from us, it would be considered stealing since your 'tax record' is, shall we say, out of date. If I *voluntarily* give you the taxes for the next ten years in advance, you'll never come back. Sound like a deal?"

Wallace was standing in the doorway now, pale at my words, but quiet out of respect for my negotiating. Captain Asshole, the taxman, nodded.

I continued, letting a slight grin of superiority escape. "But you have something I want, and if I am to pay with this," I fingered my gold nugget necklace, and his eyes widened, "I want a full measure of compensation."

"Yes, ma'am," he said. His threw his shoulders back and straightened his spine. His whole attitude had changed with the promise of the nugget necklace without a fight. He was now respectful and at full attention. He was looking at my upper body again, but not even glancing at my bosom—his eyes were fixed on the gold.

"So, I'll take that wagon, all of its contents, and your horse. You can have the necklace, but I want your word as an officer and a subject of the Crown that you will never tax or bother this property, or its residents, ever again…or suggest to or order anyone else to do the same."

"Yes, ma'am," he said, his tongue literally licking his lips in anticipation of getting the gold, his eyes still fixed on the necklace.

"Oh, and one other thing I'll be wanting. You can consider this compensation for the harassment and duress you have inflicted on members of this household."

His face froze—the transaction wasn't going as smoothly as he had hoped.

"I want those spurs," I said. "You can ride the wagon horse back to whatever privy-hole you came out of, but you have to do it without spurs. Deal?"

"Yes, ma'am," he said and stuck out his hand.

I didn't know if the hand was to seal the transaction or to claim the necklace, but I didn't want to touch it either way. "Wallace," I said as I looked over to the doorway. My betrothed walked up to me and waited while I took the necklace off my neck with a jerk. It was a tricky clasp, and I hoped I had broken it. I put it in Wallace's hand and looked toward the captain.

Wallace held the necklace in his left hand and stuck out his right. The captain was gazing at the gold, and then realized that Wallace was waiting for him to shake his hand. Wallace took the hand offered him and squeezed hard, barely shaking it at all, until the man winced and squeaked from the pain. He let Asshole's hand go at the squeal, then dropped the necklace into the waiting, throbbing palm.

Skinny and Baldy were standing by, fidgeting, not knowing what to do. The captain saw Wallace walking over to the wagon and extended a bit of unexpected courtesy. "Curly, help him with the gear. I'm riding the bay out. I got the tax payment. We'll be leaving the wagon here. We can make good time getting back to New Bern now," he said with a voice of authority.

The bald man—ironically, he must be Curly—walked up to the

horse and started removing the harness and reins, throwing them onto the wagon seat. He grabbed a little bag from the back, and was going to take it with him, when I hollered, "The wagon, and all that's in it, stays here. All you get is the horse," I said.

I was taking a liberty here. It was probably just their rations, but I didn't care. I made a point of catching the captain's eye, and then looked to the barn, a subtle reminder that my marksman was still watching them.

The Taxman saw my gesture and ordered his men, "Leave it there." I think he started to say, 'Do as she says,' but bit off the words, his pride stopping him. He looked over to me and asked, "I do get my saddle, don't I?"

"Sure," I said and turned to sit down on the porch bench. I was getting weak all over now and wanted to conserve enough energy to at least keep my voice strong.

"Put my saddle on the bay," he told the third man. I noticed he had a limp but still managed to get the job done.

It took a long five minutes, but they were finally ready to leave. "Good day, ma'am," the captain said as he sat tall on the swaybacked wagon horse.

"Not so fast," I said, "You're forgetting something." I looked down at his boot.

"Pardon me," he said sarcastically, and bent down to remove one, then the other, of his spurs. "You'll need these," he said as he waved the shiny metal and leather devices. "The horse may look fine," he grinned like he knew how the deck of cards was marked, "but she won't break a run; she won't get past a trot." He tossed the spurs to the ground in front of me and said, "Let's get the hell out of here, boys," and was gone with a gallop, his three stooges obediently following behind him.

Wallace reached down to get the spurs. "It was just gold," I said, "and it never had any sentimental value for me. I don't even know where it came from."

"You know I don't care about material goods—were you harmed? I couldn't tell what was going on from the barn," he said.

I wasn't sure if it was embarrassment or an apology, but he definitely felt inadequate about not protecting me.

"Not a scratch on me or the babies, but Wee Ian," I asked my little protector, "are you okay?"

The young man was standing in the doorway, watching the bandits as they disappeared into a trail of dust. "Aye, I'm fine, but why do ye call me Wee Ian?"

"Well, because you look like your father and his name is Ian. Actually, when he was young, he was called Wee Ian because his father's name was Ian, too."

All of a sudden, I remembered that Ian was in the barn or in the woods or somewhere where he had a good shot at the house and its enemies. I looked up and saw that Wallace was already walking toward the barn. I patted the boy's hand, put it down, and followed after Wallace. Wee Ian ran after me, reached out, and retook my hand, escorting me as if the two of us walked hand in hand every day.

Wee Ian and I caught up, the three of us undoubtedly a very intimidating triad. Wallace called out coolly, "Cousin, you can come out now."

Ian jumped down from the rafter of the barn, but neither Wallace nor I got a chance to speak. Wee Ian strutted up to him purposefully and stopped three feet in front of him, his hand on the dirk in its sheath. Wallace and I looked at each other, then back to the confrontation.

"She says yer my father; is that right?" the young man demanded. After what he had just been through, it was easier to think of him as a young man rather than as a prepubescent boy who was not much more than four feet tall.

Ian closed his eyes and brought his hand up in front of his brow. He squeezed his forehead with long, knobby fingers, thinking about his answer. He dropped his hand to his chin and brought his forehead down in a gesture of shame. His hand remained at his chin momentarily. He sighed, lifted his head, and then dropped his hand to his side—limp—no fight or resistance left in the sentinel.

"Aye, I suppose I am yer father," he said. "At least that's what yer grandmother said, and I was marrit to yer mother when…weel, I dinna ken ye were even born until three moons ago!"

"When were ye gonna tell me?" the boy demanded, his fists on his hips, making Ian look the child who had just been caught shaving the cat.

Wallace walked up to Wee Ian and put his hand on his shoulder. "It's a funny thing about this family. Some of the men are a bit slow to admit that they're a father. It happened to me, too. But, at least we did

19

find out. I'm sure it's just that Ian didn't want you to care less about your other father. You mother, uh, remarried, right?"

Wee Ian had been glaring at Ian during Wallace's little chat but let his shoulders slump at the last remark. "Aye, she did, and I have two wee sisters. They're with her now. But my other father, their father, is deid. That's why I went with Star Walker." Wee Ian stopped and squinted at Ian. "So, what am I supposed to call ye now?" he asked.

Ian chewed on his lower lip a couple of times, then said, "Ye can call me Da, if ye like. I mean, I'd like it if ye did."

I could see Ian's eyes getting moist, as if he wanted to cry. All of a sudden, I had bucket loads of compassion for him. His father was probably dead, and now he was waiting to find out if this 'surprise' son—the boy he had known of for only three months—could, or would, acknowledge him. And I had named this bright and brave young man Wee Ian after him.

Wee Ian thought about it for a moment. "Okay—Da," he said in a stilted manner, as if this was the first time the name had crossed his lips. He looked up from Wallace to me, and then said to his father, "I think they want to talk to ye, too."

Wallace nodded at the boy, and then fixed his eyes on Ian. He said, "Thank you," and turned away to escort me back to the house.

And that was that.

Apparently, Wallace felt that he didn't need to say anything else.

We were halfway to the house when we heard Ian yell after us. "The bairns: there were two of 'em. Did ye have twins?"

Wallace stopped. He looked at me, his back still turned away from the man who he had only recently found out was his cousin. "I can't do this to him," he told me. He took a deep breath and turned halfway around.

"No, we did not have twins," he said.

I could hear the smile in his tone and was concerned. Was he being cruel? I looked at him and saw that he was not being mean but was teasing.

"But there were two! Do they belong to someone else? Evie, I saw ye feedin' 'em…"

Ian, the tough mountain man who had lived for years as an Indian, was distraught—his voice squeaking with his plea, anxious to find out about the babies.

I was still mad at him for leaving me, but I would get over it. I had Wallace and was happy, happier, the happiest that I could ever be because of him. There really wasn't a reason to punish Ian for the rest of his life, or for even the next five minutes.

I grinned at him and shook my head. "Oh, you saw two of them, all right, but they're not twins, not really. You saw two of them, but there's one more. Wallace and I had triplets! Come on in and see."

I grabbed Wee Ian with one hand and kept hold of Wallace with the other. Ian ran to catch up with us, but stayed six feet away, off to the side of us. I guessed any closer than that would have made him uncomfortable.

The babies were still asleep in the clutter of quilts. They hadn't suffered through the day's ordeal, and I was grateful for that. Actually, the only wounded one, besides Wee Ian's possible bruising from being tossed across the room, was Captain Asshole. And nobody cared about him.

Ian stayed outside, just beyond the porch steps. I remembered how it felt to have a roof over my head after being in the open for so long. He probably didn't have claustrophobia, but I didn't want him to feel uneasy either. I picked up Leonardo and brought him out to the porch.

"Here's Leonardo, he was the first one born," I said.

Ian took slow deliberate steps up to the bench and sat down. He held his breath as I handed him the bundle of sleeping baby boy. "He's got red hair!" he exclaimed in a soft whisper.

"They all do," I replied, "just like their Grandpa Jody."

His eyebrows crowded together in a frown as he realized that I hadn't said great-uncle Jody. Then he looked up at Wallace. Wallace cocked his head and shrugged his shoulder as in, 'Yeah, I found out your Uncle Jody is my father,' and then brought Judah to him for inspection.

Ian now had a baby tucked into the crook of each elbow. He looked from one to the other. "These two look jest alike! How do ye tell them apart?"

Wallace pointed to the cowlicks on their foreheads, mirrored images of each other, and said, "They'll be a handful, but I think they're worth it."

I came up with the last swaddled infant. "It's easy to tell this one

21

apart from the others," I said as I pulled back the clout, "She's a girl. Our little bonus baby was a big surprise. I thought I was finished, and then boom! There she was."

Ian handed off the boys to Wallace, and I gave him Danielle. "Weel, thank ye fer lettin' me see 'em. I woulda understood if ye dinna ever want to see me again, here or anywhere else." Ian's head was bowed down, his long finger stroking Danielle's fine pink hair, ashamed of his previous actions, but fascinated with the baby girl, the first living daughter he had ever seen.

Wallace said to his cousin, "Thank you for them," he nodded to each of the babies, "and for Evie. She and I will be married in front of a preacher next month. I just thought you should hear it from me." Wallace said it sincerely, without a trace of malice, and by the blinking of Ian's eyes as he looked at him, he could tell.

"Aye, thank ye fer tellin' me. I wish ye both well," Ian said sincerely, almost embarrassed at his admission. He swallowed, closed his eyes in deep thought, then opened them again, looking at Wallace as if to ask a favor. "So does this mean I can come see 'em every once in a while, since they're my cousin's children?" he asked.

Wallace looked at me to see if I had any objection to having Ian back in my life, even if only on a very limited basis. I shrugged one shoulder. It was okay with me. Now that I had seen Ian in the flesh, my flesh was neither craving him nor hating him. That was a relief, and a reaction I hadn't expected.

"There's one more thing," Wallace said, "If it's all right with you, Evie. We were talking of middle names earlier today. Wow, it was only today, wasn't it? Anyway, if it's all right with you," he nodded to me, "could we use Kincaid as a middle name for the boys? I mean, he was their protector, and the protector of their parents, too."

"Sounds like a good idea to me, a very good way to say thank you forever. As long as it isn't Danielle's middle name," I said, giving Wallace an exaggerated scowl wrapped around a grin.

"How about Wren?" asked Wee Ian. "She has a pretty cry, like a wren, not a crow."

Wallace and I looked at each other. "Well, it's better than Magpie," he said. "Okay, then her name's Danielle Wren Urquhart, unless we find another name to throw in with those three."

22

I looked over at Ian and smiled. "Oh, and since we're saying our thank you's—thank you for being the sperm donor, Ian."

"Sperm donor? What's a sperm donor?" asked Wee Ian.

Wallace and I couldn't help but laugh. "Welcome to fatherhood, Ian. You get to explain that one to him, not me," said Wallace.

***

I was famished, so decided to bring out the leftover noodles I had set aside for a pasta salad. All I needed were a few more items to stretch the meal. "Ian," I called.

"Yes, ma'am," came the quick response from both of the Ians. They looked at each other and grinned.

"Okay, Ians, would one or both of you go into the garden and bring me three ripe tomatoes? I saw some turning red a couple of days ago, and they should be ready."

"Red already?" and "What's a tomato?" were the questions from both of the Ians at the same time.

"Come on, and I'll show ye," said Ian the elder as he led the way to the garden.

"And ye can tell me what a sperm donor is while we're out here," said the younger Ian as he hurried to catch up.

***

Wallace and I, and the babies of course, were alone and not under duress for the first time in hours, or so it seemed. I took a deep breath and strolled up to him, ready for a big hug and a long kiss. He was ready, too. The soft kiss sealed the contentment that we both deserved. I sighed as he pulled away, the dreamy look warm on my face.

"I have to ask you," Wallace said softly, trying to hide his embarrassment. "I've never heard that word before. What does effin' mean?"

"Um," I stalled and glanced around the room, avoiding his gaze. The blush that had begun on his face was spreading and was now rising to a full bloom on mine. "I really, really wanted to say another word, but just said the first letter instead. It's nasty and crude—and I did almost say it—but I wasn't going to let anyone make me mad enough to use *that* word."

"Oh, I think I know which one you mean," Wallace said and swallowed a smirk. He reached up and pushed a stray hair behind my

23

ear. "What about Ian? I thought you wanted to—how did you say it, 'punch him out'?"

"Nah, that would take an intense emotion and, believe it or not, I don't have any strong feelings for him either way. I mean, I don't hate him, and I don't love him. I'm grateful for the babies, and very glad that he at least had the courtesy to leave me with Sarah and Jody. He didn't just drop me under a spreading chestnut tree or something. No, I think I'm worthy and well, he just blew it!"

"Blue it?" asked the confused young man standing in the doorway. "And he left ye? And those bairns are my brothers and sister? And, and ye dinna hate him fer leavin' ye?"

Wee Ian looked at me, then at Wallace, still very closely linked. I stepped away. "Come here and see the babies again," I said.

He followed and sat on the edge of the bed next to me. 'Lord, give me the right words,' I prayed silently. Okay, start small and work up to the big stuff.

"Blew it means he made a big mistake. Have you ever seen anything swell up really big, then bigger still, and then 'kaboom!'—it blows up? Well, if that occurred in the past, it 'blew' is what happened."

Wee Ian was listening intently to my explanation. "I saw a raccoon once that had been deid for a long time. Its belly was swelled up real big, and when I poked it with a stick, the belly popped, and there were stinky innards all over the place. Is that what ye mean when ye say 'blew it'?"

"Exactly. And if you 'blew it,' it's like a dead raccoon's exploded bloated belly. It's kind of hard to, no, it's impossible to put it back together again like it was, right?"

Wee Ian nodded that he understood, so I continued. "Well, your Da 'blew it' with me, but it's okay. It all turned out fine. As a matter of fact, if Ian hadn't left me, he never would have found you or your mother and grandmother. And then you would never have met me or your, um, kin," I said and pointed to the babies.

"So are these my brothers and sister or my cousins?" he asked.

"Yes," I answered. I paused, wanting to end it there, but the brokenhearted frown made me feel guilty for my short, succinct response. I amended my answer, "Both, but that might be confusing to other people, so let's just say they're your kin. Wallace is your kin, too, and he's their father now, and Ian, well, he kind of gave up the right to

24

be their father, but he's a cousin and kin, too. It's nobody's business how we're kin. Kin is a good enough explanation for anybody, all right?"

"Okay. Does this mean yer my kin, too?"

"Oh," I paused to think about it for the first time. "Aye, I am." I grinned. "Now, where are those tomatoes?" I said, effectively ending the thread of the awkward, but revealing conversation.

I cut up the tomatoes and tossed them together with some salt, onions, garlic, dried blueberries, and herbs. I threw in a healthy dash of vinegar and oil, stirred, and added them to the leftover egg noodles. It was red, white, and blue pasta salad for our Fourth of July lunch, with forgiveness for dessert. It was turning out to be a spectacular day.

***

After lunch, we passed around the babies for closer examination and appreciation by their new family. Wee Ian couldn't keep his hands off of his newfound kin. He seemed to know all about babies. He held them correctly, could get the burps out without spit-up, and made funny faces that amused me as much as them.

It naturally progressed that we began to share stories. Wallace bragged about my stoic composure during delivery.

"Ye mean she dinna yell or even curse?" asked Ian, eyes wide and jaw slack.

Wallace beamed as he recalled that day. "She made us all proud," he said. "She's a very brave and strong young woman. But you probably noticed that this afternoon," he added with a gimlet eye to Ian, waiting for, but not necessarily expecting, an answer. Ian gave a brief, embarrassed nod, and Wallace continued.

"Danielle, Wren," he corrected as he nodded to Wee Ian, "surprised us with her appearance after her twin brothers' births."

I interrupted at this point, "Yeah, I hollered for the chamber pot because I had thought I had to, well, you know, but realized it was another baby coming out. Wallace got to me just as I yelled 'catch!' She plopped right out, into his hands." I was smiling all over again, remembering that moment when he and I were joined by a little girl and an umbilicus. I glanced over and saw that Wallace was radiant all over again, too. Could it have only been two weeks ago? It seemed like at least a year had passed.

I looked over at Ian. He was fingering the cloth of little Wren's

25

clout, pensive, and probably feeling guilty that he hadn't been there for her birth. Personally, I really didn't want him to feel bad. I wasn't mean, and it *was* in the past. And socially, well, I was still the hostess, and in charge of the good will and comfort of my guests.

"So what's been going on in your life," I asked. I wasn't just being polite; I was truly curious.

Ian's eyes fixed on a distant point in the sky above the barn. He stared off into nothingness as he began an obviously planned dissertation about how after he had left me with Sarah, some unsavory sorts caught up with him. I was only half listening. I was mad that he was lying to me, to all of us. I couldn't help but glare at him and would have shot rubber bands or thrown marshmallows at him instead if I had had them.

"I was injured and so dinna think I should come back…" He looked up as he continued—probably ready to add in the old sympathy lie about getting castrated—but stopped cold at the sight of me.

My jaws clenched, I shook my head slowly, as if to say, 'Don't go there, dude,' so he didn't. He knew I didn't approve of his personal vendetta with the gang that had captured and tortured him and his dog, Rocky. He was a cad for his single-minded vengeance, but he could at least be respectful and not speak of taboo subjects—and certainly not lie—while a guest in my, rather his uncle's, home.

I swallowed the bile that was rising with my rage. "How about if you tell us how you found Wee Ian," I suggested. I didn't want to hear fabrications, and hopefully there was nothing in this recent event that needed to be distorted or embellished.

He had gone back to check on Robin—his first wife—he said. He wasn't returning to the village to reclaim her—he was only going for a short visit to see her. He had heard she had remarried and had a child and went back to make sure it was true. He thought he had ruined her by giving her two dead babies. The grief at the loss of their bairns was terrible, but the guilt of her not being able to have more children with another man was even worse.

He found Robin in a Cherokee village three days journey from here. She was very polite, showed him her new home, and verified that she now had three children, but she was also distant. There was nothing left of the relationship between the two of them. As he was leaving the village, a young boy approached him. He said he was Robin's son. They talked for a short time. The lad knew all about him; he had heard about Star Walker from his grandmother, his mother's mother. The boy said his grandmother told him that he had Star Walker's—Ian's—spirit.

"It was too much to hope for—that this sharp and fast young lad," he said as he looked over at Wee Ian with pride, "was my son, so I dinna ask. I left the village and returned to my...er...um, business, and tried to forget about him."

Ian looked away as he continued with his recent history. "I had been *hunting*," he glanced over at me to see my reaction to his new word for vengeance, "fer two months when I heard that Robin's husband had been kilt by a bear. It was a brave way to die, but still hard on a woman with three wee 'uns.

"By the time I had made it back to her home, she had found another husband. The man was fond of the two daughters, but dinna want another man's son in the house. The boy was sent to live with his grandmother, even though she was verra old and in poor health. I went to visit the grandmother," he paused to take a drink of the whisky I had brought out for the reunion. I recalled that this was the woman who had made Ian leave Robin, her daughter, after the death of their second child.

Ian settled back on the porch step and continued. "She was blind but recognized me as soon as I came to her side.

"'I was wrong to send ye away, Star Walker,' she said. 'I canna change what has happened, but I would ask yer forgiveness and a favor. Take the boy with ye. Teach him the ways of the Indian, and the White Man, too. Teach him yer language. He's a fast learner. He will need to ken the White Man's world, but should ken what is right, too. The world as I kent it will soon be gone. He still needs to be taught more of our ways, the true ways, and our stories. Of how to hunt and fish, he already knows much, but there are things only a father can teach."

"I dinna talk while the old woman spoke. I let her finish. She closed her eyes, and I found the courage to ask: is he my son? I looked at her and saw her smile. She was happier than I had ever seen her. But she wasna breathin'. She died givin' me a young lad to watch over. I could only hope that he was mine."

Ian leaned forward, and then looked over at me. "And it wasna until today when ye called him Wee Ian that I kent fer sure that he was mine. But I had no right to claim him after what I had done to ye and the

27

bairns; the leavin' and all…"

Now I was uncomfortable, and didn't feel like I should be, so I changed the subject. "Why were you here today?" I asked. Ian hadn't expected that, nor did anyone else on the porch, although it was a valid question.

"I was followin' those three men," was all he said, then rose to stand, looking as if he were going to excuse himself.

"Those are some of the…the…*them*, aren't they?" I accused.

He looked guilty but didn't answer.

I was persistent, though. "And you're going back after them, aren't you?" I asked, not really wanting to hear the answer that I knew was coming.

"Aye, the last three," he said almost apologetically. "Come on, let's go, lad," he said to Wee Ian.

The boy looked up at him, and then over at me nursing one of his brothers, and then back to his father. "We can stay here longer, maybe a day or two. I nicked a mark in the horse's hoof, and then put camphor on it. If we canna smell 'em, we can see 'em. It has my mark on it."

"Your mark?" I asked.

"Aye, the lizard's tongue," he said simply.

"The lizard's tongue?" Then it dawned on me. "You didn't carve a 'Y' into the Captain's cheek, did you? It was a lizard's tongue?"

"Aye, that's my mark," he said proudly.

"Well, I thought it was a 'Y' for yellow, as in cowardly." I popped right back into mommy mode and dared to ask, "Ian, if you want to go on your 'hunt,' that's your business. But it's okay with me, and I'm sure it's okay with everyone else in this household, if Wee Ian stays here until you've completed your *business*." I couldn't help but add with a black splash of nastiness, "Because you know how I feel about that *business*…"

"He comes with me," Ian said with a coldness that was flat scary. He had his 'possessed by an alien hate force' face on. He was back in vengeance mode.

I couldn't stand the thought of Wee Ian becoming like his father, callus and jaded about taking another human's life. I wanted him to retain at least some of his innocence and humanity. "Well, he's our kin, too, and I think we have a right to want to keep him safe," I argued.

28

"Safe?" Ian yelled. His face was red, and he was breathing so hard, he was almost snorting.

Well, at least he wasn't cold and emotionless…

"Ye call what went on here today, safe? If I hadna come by, ye would be dead…or worse!"

"And who's to say that you didn't drive them here on purpose, huh?" It was a totally irrational question, but I didn't care. My maternal hormones were raging again; I had a child to protect. I felt Wallace's hand on my shoulder, his gentle pressure urging me to back down.

"I'm sure he didn't send anyone here, Evie. At least, not on purpose," he added with a stern look at his cousin. "Wee Ian is kin, and he is more than welcome to wait here for you to finish your blood feud. I understand that he is your responsibility, but he *is* still only a lad."

"I'll go with Da," Wee Ian said solemnly, his chin out, hands behind his back like a patriarch watching over his family. He stepped next to his father and said, "Someone has to watch out for him, so he doesn't 'blew it' again." He looked right at me as he used the colloquialism incorrectly, but accurately.

I couldn't help it. I rushed over and grabbed Wee Ian with Judah still at my breast. I squeezed the two of them to me, not wanting to let the elder boy leave to watch his father kill people in retaliation for deeds done months ago.

I looked up to Wallace for help, knowing there was nothing he could do. But he tried. He looked right at Ian and said, "Vengeance is mine, sayeth the Lord."

"Not this time, cousin, not this time," Ian said right back at him, and then headed down the porch steps toward the woods.

Wee Ian went over to his little sister and kissed her on the head. "Good-bye, Wren. Watch out fer yer brothers, hear?" Then he ran outside, and caught up to his father who looked down, made sure the boy was with him, and with a definite relief shown in his bearing, continued down the path the horse and the men had taken.

***

"You don't think I'm a coward, do you?" Wallace asked.

His question took me completely off guard. "No; why would you ask, or even think, that?" I replied, truly baffled.

"Because I don't fight, didn't fight, when the taxman came, and when the…those…um..."

I didn't want him to fumble, so I just popped in, "the incident in the woods?"

He nodded sheepishly.

"Well, if I remember correctly, you came armed with nothing but a draw knife, ready to fight three men for me. I have no doubt that if they hadn't had a blade to my face, you would have—shall we say—taken out every one of them. You risked your life to protect me; you suffered a hideous indignation worse than bodily death rather than allow me to be hurt. I'm just glad I was able to get you back." I walked up to him and put my hand on his face and looked deep into his heart by way of his eyes. He saw I was speaking the truth and smiled weakly.

"And as far as Captain Asshole, I was the one dealing with the situation first, and you let me continue until it was resolved. I think the greatest thing you did for me today was to let him know that you had complete faith in me and my abilities. And you were right; I would have asked for help if I needed it. Well, I did ask for help, but I asked Him," I said as I looked up. "And He is the One who gave you to me—and I always thank Him for that. You're always there when I need you. Besides, any man with a hand can make a fist and throw a punch. Not many know when and how to deal with situations so that a punch or an arrow or a gun isn't needed. That is where you excel."

Another weak smile appeared, but I could tell he still wasn't mollified. "Okay, what do you want to tell me?" I asked.

"I almost killed someone once, actually four someones. Papa had been very diligent in teaching me the many ways to fight—properly, of course. I could fence, use a broadsword—which isn't an easy task, by the way—shoot a pistol, and he even had a man from the Orient show me some unusual ways to use my body to disarm and even kill a man. But Papa was also insistent that I knew that being able to tactfully avoid physical or armed confrontation—while at the same time having all parties satisfied with the arrangement—was much more valuable than fighting. Diplomacy is the civilized man's warfare, he'd say. I did listen to him, but I was young, and didn't really understand what he meant.

"I was sixteen years old and full of myself. I was tall and proud of it. My classmates weren't even up to my shoulders. The girls had just started to notice me and were fluttering around me like pigeons after breadcrumbs. The other boys didn't like that at all. They knew that they couldn't beat me. I was too big. Fighting would get us all expelled from school, too, and our fathers wouldn't care for that…" he looked at me and grinned.

"So, they lay an ambush for me when school was out for the holidays. It was Christmas Eve, and I wanted to get Papa one of those brandy-soaked cakes; you know, the kind you light on fire just before eating it? Well, I heard there was a shop in town that still had some of them left. I left Uncle Tony's house early in the afternoon—we often spent the holidays with him—and hoped that the shop was still open. Somehow they found out where I was going, because when I got there, four of my classmates were waiting for me.

"I ignored them as I went in. They didn't like that. They started calling me names, but I was determined not to let them bother me. 'Boot-licker,' 'bollocks-breath' and 'shite-pile'—they were just frustrated teenagers, trying to sound big, saying all the nasty sounding words they could think of. But when I heard the name 'bastard,' I froze. Evie, I could take just about any name but that one. I'd heard it since I was old enough to—no, even before I knew what it meant. When I came to London to attend school, I thought that stigma would stay at Richwood Hall, but it didn't. In retrospect, they probably didn't know about any of the rumors. It was probably just a dirty name to them. But I let them get me angry. Then someone threw a snowball with a rock in it. It caught me in the head, right here," he said, and parted the hair in front of his left ear to show me the scar.

"Between the pain in my head, and the rage at hearing that name again, I lost it. I was livid and, well, it was as if I was somewhere above my body, watching this frenzied madman beat four of his peers until they stopped moving. I stopped swinging and kicking because…well, maybe it was because I was tired of not getting any reaction when a punch or kick landed. I regained my senses—slowly at first—and then saw the pile of muddy, bloody bodies I had created, all because I had let my mouthy classmates make me mad.

"Evie, it was just me, unarmed, and I almost killed those boys. I didn't know what to do, so I ran. I forgot all about the plum pudding cake. When I got home, I asked to be excused for my disheveled appearance, saying that I had fallen down and hit my head," Wallace pointed to the same scarred spot near his ear, "and I was sorry that the dessert had been spoiled. Papa never called me out over it. I was sure he suspected something was amiss, though. You see, I never was a good liar.

"Well, the four boys recovered and never called me names again. Actually, they never talked to me at all, and would walk to the other side of the courtyard rather than come near me. They spread the story that they had been waylaid on Christmas Eve by a gang of ten highwaymen, were beaten and robbed, but were still able to inflict grave bodily injuries on their assailants."

Wallace grinned weakly at the memory of his attackers' fabrication. "But I received my punishment with the guilt I had to carry. It would have been easier if I had been whipped for it, but Papa didn't believe in the belt. I never hit anyone in anger again. I knew I couldn't control my rage once I started. But if you hadn't been under Gimpy's knife, I would have, oh…" Wallace's words stopped as he sucked in a deep breath to compose himself, jaws clenched in recollection.

I put my arms around his neck and brought myself as close to his body as our clothes would allow. "Let's hope we never get in a situation like that again, all right?" I gave him a quick, sisterly kiss. "You've received the fighting blood from the Pomeroys, and the tutelage and temperance from Julian. Now, I think you've managed to overcome the reaction to fight with knowledge of when it is appropriate, and the smarts to know how to avoid it all together. I think you're quite well-balanced."

I purposely tilted off center to force him to catch me and bring me back to center, still in his arms. "Well-balanced and practically perfect in every way," I said in a dead-on imitation of Mary Poppins. Then I planted a long, very un-sisterly kiss on, in, and around his mouth. "Perfect."

Chapter 2: Wedding Day Blues (NITWW Ch. 45)

August 3, 1781

I'm getting married.

Again.

I wasn't sure if my marriage to Ian was actually legal since we hadn't had any witnesses. Jody assured me, though, that since Ian and I had performed the traditional rite of handfast, we were indeed wed, but the marriage was only valid for a year and a day. Ian's surprise visit last month sped things up a couple of months or so—I didn't want to do the math because I really didn't like reflecting on the past. But it didn't make any difference because he essentially 'released' me from the handfasting and wished Wallace and me well in our upcoming marriage. I was no longer obligated to wait for the entire 366 days to pass before having a proper wedding. I didn't care if this was my first or fourth wedding; it was going to be my last. I had met Mr. Right and he was mine.

The babies were six weeks old now, and Sarah said I should be able to resume—or in the case of marrying Wallace—commence 'relations.' Resume, commence, either way, I was more than ready for my wedding night—I was eager.

Sarah hadn't examined me since the babies were two weeks old, and I wasn't looking forward to another one of what I called 'those physical indignations.' She wanted to give me the customary six-week postpartum checkup to make sure I had completely healed.

"Thanks for the offer, but honestly, Sarah, my modesty has returned. A pregnant woman doesn't seem to be shy that way, and when she's in labor, well; she'll let anybody check her bottom end if it means getting the baby out faster."

"All right, but would you at least let me feel your belly? I want to make sure you haven't developed any abnormal masses. Your uterus expanding big enough to carry three babies could cause problems with clots…and you wouldn't necessarily feel any pain or discomfort."

Sarah had asked my permission in a clinical, sisterly, and pleading manner. The last two aspects of her request, and the furrowed forehead of extreme concern, persuaded me to let her poke and thump my tummy.

I sat down on my chaise and pulled off my winter shawl, tacky with sweat, which had stuck to my bare skin. The air moving across my damp neck and shoulders immediately produced an evaporative cooling effect. I sighed at the brief, blissful moment of feeling cool, if only on a few inches of skin.

I had decided to spend the day covered with my shawl, in self-imposed misery, because I didn't want to appear semi-decent or offensive to our guests. I refused to wear a corset and didn't want my unbound body shape offending anyone. Uncorseted women were called 'loose' women, and although they meant it literally, its connotation was the same now as it would be in the future. I knew Sarah and the men didn't mind that I wouldn't wear stays, but we had company coming soon, and I wanted to be courteous.

I kicked off my slippers, lay back, and tried to relax. Another sigh escaped as I felt that same wonderful cooling on my bared feet. Lying down in the middle of the day felt great. Why should I stress over whether I needed the exam or not? I decided to give in to it and enjoy the rare, and guilt-free, moments of idleness.

Sarah helped me hike up the skirt of my new green calico gown. She chuckled when she saw them. "You still like those white cotton briefs, I see."

I growled at her like a dog at a stranger. She grabbed a handful of skirt, playfully threw it over my face, and then got down to business. She pulled my panties down to just above my pubic bone and started kneading my flesh with two fingers, as if she were looking for lumps of flour in bread dough. I peeked over my skirting as she worked over my much smaller, but still mushy, belly.

"I don't see how you swelled up as big as," she looked around for a comparison, "well, as big as this house, and still didn't get any stretch marks. I only had one child at a time, and my belly looked like a road map."

"Good genes, I suppose," I said as I worked the rest of the skirt out of my face with my chin. "It certainly wasn't because I used fancy designer creams or lotions." I unbuttoned the top two buttons of my blouse and looked down at my huge breasts. "Looks like I'm going to have candy-striped boobs, though. These red lines will fade to silver ones, right?"

Loud footfalls, boots stomping up the porch steps, interrupted our

34

conversation. I yanked up my underwear and the two of us tugged at my clothing to get me presentable. I buttoned up as I sat up, sucking in deep breaths of composure, then relaxed—it was Wallace.

It had become a standard, unspoken protocol that when one of the men approached the house, he was to walk heavy as he came up the porch steps to the door. If I was nursing—and it seemed as if I always had at least one baby feeding—I would have a chance to cover up. It might have been different if it was winter, but this was July. Our small, un-air-conditioned southern home had only one small window. It was hot enough inside to bake bread by late morning—or at least it felt that way to me. The skin-to-skin contact necessary to feed the babies was hot and sticky for me and for them. As a result, the red blush of prickly heat spread from their cheeks to my breasts. When alone, or only in the company of people under ten pounds, I tried cooling down by baring as much of my upper body as I could.

It was impossible to keep our home environment comfortable. Still, I did my best, stealing random moments of bareness for me, keeping the babies in their sleeveless little green calico gowns and skimpy clouts rather than swaddled. The babies were small and didn't fill their diapers with much output. For right now, I'd rather suffer a wet spot in my lap than deal with diaper rashes on their behinds. I still wasn't brave enough to hold and feed them bare-bottomed though.

Wallace and Julian had constructed and set up what I called a playpen. The men laughed at the name but agreed that it was an apt description. Right now, since they were still small and didn't move much more than a fist or a foot, the child container was perched atop sawhorses. With this arrangement, I didn't have to bend down to floor level to pick up the babies, and the airflow was better for cooling them. I had to admit, I was a little jealous of their life of leisure. When they were hungry, they got their hot dinner brought right to them on the second or third screech or cry.

"Ye canna be feedin' them at the first wail. Ye need to let them work up an appetite," Jody said. "At least that's what my sister Elly told me. Otherwise, ye'll be feedin' them all day and all night. Ye need yer rest and time to yerself too, ye ken."

Jody was careful about speaking of his family. I knew Jody's sister, Elly, was Ian's mother. I didn't know if he had written to her to let her know that she was a grandmother again, and that Ian had fathered three babies at the same time—and with the same woman.

I snorted at the very idea. Fathered; I guess I should say he sired three children because he sure didn't take to fathering. Oh, well, his loss, Wallace's and my gain. I stamped my foot and twisted the sole of my handmade slipper into the ground. Sarah looked over at me like 'am I supposed to know what you're doing there?'

I repeated the stamp and squish into the ground movement. "Bad thought, struck down and buried," I said.

She tipped her head back, sucking in a sigh of understanding, and nodded. Yes, she knew what I was talking about. It was cool to have someone around who was like me. It was also nice that I didn't have to over-explain my idiosyncrasies.

Wallace—my betrothed and the man I loved—was a great father. His fathers, Julian and Jody, were both delighted with their grandchildren. Julian had never been a grandfather, had never even been a father to a baby before, so infants were new to him. Jody had been close to his nieces and nephews in Scotland, and then lived right next door to his daughter Mona's children. Those first grandchildren were a cherished part of his daily life until they time traveled with their parents, back to the late 20th century for medical support. Jody loved babies and spent as much time as he could spare with his new wee kinfolk.

The men were all tuned into their own godchild's cry, too. Jody, who was essentially tone deaf, could differentiate Leonardo's cry from the other two's, but couldn't tell the difference between Judah's and Wren's squalls. Julian would know if his godson was the one fussing. He'd be on edge, trying not to interfere, but would give me 'the look' if I didn't attend to his godson, Judah, right away. He even asked if I needed help on occasion. I knew he didn't want to change diapers, and he certainly wasn't equipped to feed the baby, but he was definitely little Judah's advocate and quite good at settling him down for sleep after a feeding.

Wallace was still partial to Wren but was on hand to help with all of the children. He was more attentive and helpful than most men of this time. I take that back, he was probably more helpful than most men of any time. He told me that he hadn't had any brothers or sisters and had always wanted them. He was lonely as a child, with only adults and animals for company. He knew early on that he wanted a big family but hadn't been in a hurry because he wanted to make sure he had a good wife. "I didn't know I would find the perfect woman and get a big family all at the same time. God sure has been good to me," he said as he rubbed little Wren's back. He kissed her on top of her pink fuzzy head. "He's been verra good to me."

***

Jody and Julian had stayed outside at the corral fence when Wallace went into the house to check on Evie and the babies. The morning was hot, and a break sounded good. The two of them were leaning on the fence, not doing anything but waiting for a bit of breeze to blow across their sweat-soaked bodies.

Julian was deep in thought, going over and over it in his mind. Why had he not talked to Wallace sooner? He had planned on telling him the basics of human reproduction and how it was accomplished when he was entering puberty, but that window of opportunity had long since passed. He should have taken Wallace to see Mrs. Abbott when he caught him with his classmate's book, London's Women of Pleasure. Surely one of the girls in her employ could have delicately and tastefully shown an innocent yet inquisitive lad of sixteen the basic mechanics of heterosexual sex. He, or someone, would have to tell Wally today, before the wedding, how it was between a man and a woman. After the ceremony, there might not be a chance to speak with him in private before his wedding night, as it were.

"If this fence gets any harder to hold down, we'll have to call Wallace to help us," Jody joked.

Julian pushed together a small pile of stones next to the base of the fence post. He was smiling at Jody's joke but didn't say anything. Jody looked over and said, "Are my jokes that bad, or is there somethin' botherin' ye?"

"I want to ask you a favor," Julian said with a large intake of air, finishing with a gust that could have blown out a candle at twenty paces. Yes, Jody could tell Wallace how it was between a man and a woman much better than he could, that was for sure. He took another deep breath, paused, blew it out, breathed in deeply, and then said, "I'd appreciate it if you would talk with Wallace about his wedding night and what to do." He paused, kicking the pebbles hard across the yard, trying

37

to gather courage. "I know the ladies liked him, but I really don't think he's—how should I say—experienced? I've not been married in a long time, and you're still married, and well…"

Julian was fumbling for words, getting red faced with frustration and embarrassment. He looked at the ground for inspiration and couldn't find it. He took another deep breath as if to say something, but no words came out. Not only did he not know the right words to use, he didn't know how to put even the wrongs ones together into a coherent request. He was also starting to get light-headed from all the deep breathing. Then he felt the heavy hand on his shoulder.

"I'd be glad to help with this, shall we say, responsibility?" Jody gave an expression that was half grin and half grimace. He was proud of the fatherly task he had been asked to undertake, but was also scared, unsure of what he was going to say.

"Ye ken, the men who told me about what to do and what to expect on my wedding night werena exactly right. My father dinna get the chance to give me the talk. He died before he could see me with a wife, or even a girlfriend. I dinna ken exactly what to say to the lad, but I do ken a few things not to say," he said, laughing.

The blush of tension was gone from Julian's face, and the start of a smile was on Jody's. "I'm verra glad that Evie has been marrit before. She'll ken what to do, but I dinna want him goin' to his marriage bed without an idea of how it should be done. I," Jody faltered, then regained his composure, chin out and spine straight, ready to shoulder the responsibility. "I had better have that talk with him now, before I lose my nerve. You can stay here and hold the fence down or move some fresh straw into the stalls. We willna be havin' too many people over this afternoon, but there's no need to have a foul-smellin' barn fer their horses. Besides, if some of them take to drinkin' too much, they can jest sleep it off on the clean beddin'."

Jody reached over and grabbed the wooden pitchfork, propped against the fence. "Use it well, my friend. Ye have the easy task." Jody wiped the sweat off of his upper lip with the back of his hand. "Aye, ye have the easy task," he mumbled as he walked away.

***

Jody stomped his feet as he climbed the steps, trying, but not succeeding, to crush his childish insecurity about discussing sex.

I could tell the difference between Jody and Julian's footfalls, but not between his and Wallace's. Since Wallace had just come in, it had to be Jody. "Come on in, Jody, I'm decent," I hollered.

"Of course, yer decent. Who said ye werena decent?" Jody asked, truly confused. Then it dawned on him what I had meant. "Oh, all right. Weel, ahem, I came to ask Wallace to come help me outside fer jest a bit. I need a hand movin' a couple of fence rails, and Julian is busy with a…another chore." He smiled at the mental image of Julian holding down the fence as his other chore.

"I'll be right there," Wallace said. "I just came in to see how my little family was doing." He turned from looking at Wren to me. "Do you need anything before I go?" his hand still stroking little Wren's forehead.

"Yes," I replied, "please send in a cool, gentle breeze, but not too gentle. I want to be able to feel it, but I don't want to get knocked down either."

"I'll do my best," he said, smiling, then turned to Jody. "Ready?" he asked.

Jody took a deep breath, held it, and then blew it out in a huff. "Ready as I'll ever be, I guess."

Wallace and I stared at him, both of us wondering how much trouble setting fence rails could be. He repeated it again, softly this time, and without the hurricane blast. "Ready as I'll ever be."

***

Julian saw the two tall men coming out of the house, picked up the pitchfork, hailed them with it, and then walked around the back to the haystack, relieved that Jody doing the deed, not him.

Jody walked up to the same spot where he and Julian had been standing. A slight smile appeared—now it was Wallace's turn to help him hold down the fence.

"Where are we going to put in the rails? This one looks fine." Wallace saw the slightly contorted scowl on his father's face. "Are you all trigh? You look like you're choking on a bone or…"

Jody snorted and said, "No, we dinna need to be changin' out perfectly fine fence rails, and I'm not chokin' on anythin' but words. Ye see, yer other father wanted me to have a talk with ye about yer, um, yer…"

39

"Wedding night?" Wallace suggested, an open, inquiring look on his face.

Oh my God, Jody thought; he doesn't have any idea of what's going to happen! He looked at Wallace again and saw that he had the most innocent, pleading look on his face. He had a 'please tell me, father, I need to know: will it hurt, will she bite me, am I going to explode' expression of a scared three-year-old.

Wallace burst out laughing. "I got you, didn't I?" he said. He kept laughing as his father's face changed from shock, to anger at being made fun of, to laughing right along with him.

"Aye, ye got me," Jody conceded. His laughter turned into light seriousness. "Now, yer father said that he never had the talk with ye. He wanted to make sure ye dinna have some wrong ideas about…weel, ye ken, the weddin' night. And, weel, it will be more than jest one night if ye have a good wife, and I'm sure Evie will make ye a good wife."

"I'm sure she will. And for the rest of it, I was reared around horses and other animals. It can't be that much different, can it?" Wallace asked with total sincerity.

Jody rolled his eyes, leaned back against the fence with a small thud, and said, "Yes, it can and is that much different." He looked into his son's eyes, trying to gauge if he was teasing again. "Ye really dinna ken, do ye?"

"Well, no, I've never 'been' with a woman, although I have kissed a few. Things 'happened' when Evie and I, well, we got carried away kissing, but we had our clothes on the whole time. I know what a woman looks like without clothes, sort of, but I never touched one all over. What I did touch felt mighty good, though," Wallace said with alacrity, indicating that he was definitely looking forward to being married.

Wallace came out of his reverie and asked bluntly, "So what's different with what happens between a man and a woman, and between two other mammals?"

"Weel, first off, ye do it face to face, mostly. Ye can do it jest about any way the, um, parts will fit together, but fer the first time, I suggest face to face." Jody was flustered but didn't want to leave Wallace ignorant on his first encounter. "And use yer elbows. Ye dinna need to be squeezin' the air out of yer new bride, after all. And if she makes a verra ugly face and little squeakin' noises, that's a good thing. Make sure she

40

makes the faces and squeaks before ye, er—before ye finish…"

Jody looked over at Wallace to see if he understood. At first, there was a blank stare of uncertainty. Then, all of a sudden, his eyes widened—he knew.

"I've seen that look!" Wallace said. "One time when Evie and I were…kissing, she made this horrid face, and then she went limp, almost collapsed. And she was grinning…" His focus drifted off with the memory of their encounter in the garden. "She said she got hers first, and then I got mine. Well, I know what I got, but now it makes sense. Women get that, too?"

"Aye, they do, if yer doin' it right."

Father and son became silent, looking away from each other into the woods, neither of them ready to return to the awkward discussion. Then they both spoke at the same time. "If ye have any questions," Jody began, just as Wallace said, "If I have any questions…"

They both laughed and stared at each other's shoulders, still too embarrassed because of the topic of their conversation to look each other in the face. Then Jody put his hand on his son's shoulder, looked him in the eye, and said, "Dinna worry; jest love her, respect her and protect her, and ye'll have a wonderful marriage. It worked fer me, and I'm sure it'll work fer ye."

Wallace said, "Thank you, father, thank you very much," and started to walk past him to the haystack, intending to help Julian with the straw redistribution task.

Jody's face flashed recall, and he raised his hand to stop his son from leaving. "I have somethin' fer ye. I ken ye canna get yer hands on yer money to buy yer wife a proper ring, but ye'll be wantin' to give yer bride a token of yer marriage. So here, Sarah gave me a bit of ribbon to use as a necklace fer it."

Wallace opened his hand and Jody put a length of black silk ribbon with an ancient silver coin attached to it. "I think that's Athena," he said as he pointed to the face on the coin, "and I'm sure this is Pegasus on the back." He turned over the coin to reveal the struck impression of a flying horse. "See, someone punched a couple of holes here, so the ribbon went right through to make a lovely necklace."

Wallace looked carefully at the coin, and then up to Jody with a raised eyebrow, asking 'where did you get this?' without words.

"It's a long story, but whether it's worth lots of money or nae, there isna anyone here in this land who could change this coin into anythin' but a pretty piece of jewelry. Jest dinna let one of the bairns put it in his mouth when he gets older. It's a bit messy gettin' it back," he said with a smile of remembrance.

***

I decided that a salad would be good for lunch. It was too hot to cook inside, and I had just been given two fish as a wedding present by our neighbor Hannah's younger brother, Jedediah. The fish could be wrapped in mud and set in the fire outside to slow-bake. It wouldn't be tuna salad, but flaked trout mixed with mayonnaise on greens sounded yummy. Jedediah said he wanted to give me a present because I was so pretty, but I think he just wanted an excuse to come see the babies.

"You had them all at once?" he asked.

"Well, not exactly. It was kind of like a cat having kittens. They came out one right after the other," I said.

"Did it hurt?" He looked over the edge of the playpen at the babies who were getting their air bath in the late morning shade. "Hannah says the ladies always scream somethin' terrible when the babes are comin'. She puts wadding in her ears, it gets so bad."

Just then, Jody hopped up the steps to the porch. "Weel, some women screech and holler so bad, ye'd think they were dyin', but Miss Evie here, she was quiet as a…as a fish in the water."

"Really?" asked Jedediah. "Do you mean that it doesn't hurt when you have three at a time?"

"Oh, it hurts, all right," I said. "I just found out that it hurt more when I yelled."

"Oh, oh, oh, I almost forgot. Da would give me a whippin' for sure if I didn't tell you. Mr. Pomeroy, Da said that there was some soldiers muckin' around the mill yesterday afternoon. He didn't know who they was but he figured they was up to no good, and that I should tell you right away. Except that I forgot about the right away part. I wanted to bring Miss Evie and the babies something, so I stopped and caught these fish. It's okay, isn't it? That I didn't come here right away, I mean." Poor Jedediah looked as if he could feel the spanking on his bottom while he was talking about it.

Jody said, "Ach, its fine. You had better go on home and tell yer da that ye told me, and that I'll look onto it. And ye dinna have to tell him about the fish, aye?"

"Yes, sir, thank you, sir," he said as he walked backwards away from the house toward the trail. "Thank you very much," he said again, and then turned around and began his race home, sprinting like a short distance runner in an heroic attempt to make up the time lost with the fishing expedition.

Jody looked at me, shrugged, and explained, "No use the boy gettin' whipped fer doin' a good deed fer ye. I canna go back in time and start checkin' on the soldiers sooner. I dinna think the lad will be makin' the same mistake again—with or without the strap. I'll leave with Julian now to see to it. You stay here and let the others ken what's goin on."

I watched dejectedly as Jody strode purposefully toward the barn. He stopped suddenly and turned around sharply. I could tell by his face that he had just remembered something. He came back to where I was, wearing a grin like the fox that had just found the key to the chicken coop. He patted his sporran, and then opened it. "Jest fer the ceremony, here, take the somethin' borrowed. That is, of course, unless ye want to consider it somethin' new. I'll be sure to take it back after the weddin' so it wilna be hauntin' ye. I heard someone is comin' by later with the somethin' blue, and I ken ye have a somethin' old comin' yer way soon. Dinna fash," he consoled, "We'll be back before ye can miss us."

"But…" I started to say something but thought better of it. I'd heard that phrase 'be back before ye can miss me' one too many times. "God bless," I said instead, hoping that Jody hadn't heard the fear in my voice.

He was halfway to the barn when he called back to me, "Oh, and tell Wallace that we'll be back fer the weddin'. We wouldna want to miss that."

I pulled apart the rag-wrapped parcel he had given me. Jody had 'gifted' me the smartphone he had been holding onto for the last couple months. Now I would have it as a something borrowed, or ironically, something new, 'jest for the ceremony.' Funny man. It was new as in 'this cell phone is so new that it hasn't even been thought of yet, much less created.'

I stashed it in my pocket. I really didn't want it. I didn't like to be reminded of the life I used to have but knew nothing about. At least I didn't have to clean it, feed it, or worry about it giving me fleas. "Nice pocket," I said softly, "you just stay here in this nice pocket, wee black box, and don't give me any reason to toss you down the privy."

Chapter 3: Clyde Returns (NITWW Ch 46)

Wallace and Evie's wedding day

All the major chores had been completed in time for the big celebration. Wallace was behind the house, musing while he busied himself with the never-ending project. The steady tug, tug of clearing out the weeds in Evie's vegetable garden was soothing. He really didn't mind the task; it was actually therapeutic. Yanking and pulling out the bad stuff and seeing immediate results for his effort—if only life was that straightforward.

However, no matter how much time he spent on gardening, the weeds always found their way back. Wedding and weeding. Evie would be sure to have a joke or a pun about how he was burning hours on one, waiting for the other. "Wally weeding while waiting for the wedding?" he recited to his audience, the magpies in the tree, eating the last of the mulberries. "I'll have to try that one out on her and see what she thinks. Even if it is a groaner, she'll smile for me. Helen of Troy may have had the face that launched a thousand ships, but Evie has the face that lights up this whole colony."

He hoped that there were enough weeds to keep him busy until the wedding. He had been waiting for this day for months. Well, not so much the wedding day, as the wedding night. The warm glow he felt was more than just the weather, exercise, and thinking about his first day and night of being married. He realized that after this evening, he and Evie would be together forever—a well-matched and contented husband and wife like Sarah and his father, Jody.

The summer's heat had really kicked the garden into high production mode. Those tiny seeds Evie had salvaged from the tomatoes and dried peppers from José's ranch really took off after she planted them outside. She had sowed the seeds early, when the garden was still frozen in places. She insisted on keeping her little dirt-filled rag pots in the house so her tomato and pepper plants could get an early start. He had extended the windowsill for her so she could set the seedlings in the sun. "Besides, the soil has to be warm for the seeds to germinate. When it stops freezing at night, I'll plant them in the garden. I'll bet we have tomatoes by the Fourth of July." And she was right; they had tomatoes by the Fourth of July and dozens, scores, more every day.

He had brought along one of the large woven baskets she had made when pregnant to collect today's harvest. That seemed so long ago. Back then, he had been dubious about eating a tomato, but she assured him they were not poisonous, and actually had lots of vitamins and antioxidants in them. He had been a bit embarrassed because he didn't know what those were. "Oh, they're just fancy words that mean they're good for you. You won't get scurvy if you eat one of these every day."

Wallace was contentedly picking the red fruit—what he had been told once upon a time were love apples—when he looked up and saw Jody and Julian quickly and quietly saddling their horses. It was obvious by the sharpness of their movements that they were in a hurry. Something must be wrong for them to be leaving so soon before the wedding.

Wallace sprinted toward them, hurdling over the rail fence like a two-legged jumper horse. Jody saw him approaching and pulled Aries around so they could speak before he left, motioning for Julian to proceed.

Julian nodded in acknowledgment, then turned back to look at Evie. She was on the porch, arms crossed in front of her chest, helpless and frustrated that she couldn't assist her friends and family. The frown on her face was almost enough to pull the brightness from the sunshine. Julian waved his arm to her with a wide goodbye. She grimaced in reply; his false smile hadn't fooled either one of them. He kicked his horse's flanks and swiftly took off to investigate the commotion, hoping that whatever was wrong was easy to repair.

Wallace grabbed the halter of Jody's skittish horse and didn't even get a chance to ask 'why?' when Jody volunteered the answer. "Wee Jedediah jest said his father was concerned about a fuss at the mill. He asked if we would make sure that there was nothin' amiss. Julian and I will look into it and be back in plenty of time fer yer weddin'."

"Don't worry about us; we'll be fine. And I hope you know that we wouldn't think of starting the ceremony without the two of you."

"Aye, we'll be quick about it then," Jody said and turned the horse around.

"Godspeed," Wallace said, slapping Aries on the flank, hoping it would make a difference in the horse's swiftness and getting the situation resolved.

Wallace stood with his knuckles on his hips, helplessly watching the backs of his two fathers disappear into the trees. It could be nothing, or it could be a major confrontation that they were riding into. Nowadays, nothing was safe or simple.

Of course, they wouldn't—couldn't—have the wedding without the two fathers. After all, someone would have to give Evie away, and it looked like that was going to be the responsibility—no, make that the privilege—of her father-in-law, Jody. Papa was also part of the wedding party. Even though he was legally Wallace's stepfather, Julian was offered, and had accepted, the honor of being his best man.

***

I was trying to suppress an intense negative emotion as I stood on the porch and watched Wallace walk back. He didn't look too happy about the men taking off, either. I didn't want to be mad at Jody and Julian for leaving because I knew it was what they had to do; it was a matter of duty. What I had was a case of intense frustration—there was so much going on with this war, and I couldn't help, or do a darned thing about it.

I was sure the two fathers didn't want to leave, but they were soldiers. To them, answering the call to duty was as natural and essential as, well, eating. The gut feeling of frustration that I had was good in a way, though. I didn't have any anxiety or worries that they weren't coming back. At least Sarah and Wallace were still here. If I got to feeling too bad, I could always whine at them.

I wiped my brow with the back of my hand and tried to compose myself. We had guests coming soon—mostly women and children. They probably wouldn't like it either, but would understand about the delay. Young Hannah, who was now acting as au pair to the four young Donaldson girls and the twin baby boys, was coming along with Mrs. Donaldson. The amiable teenager had decided it was safer to stay with the Donaldson family than to follow Sarah around, learning the doctoring trade, at least for the time being. Sarah had agreed it would be best for her to continue her medical training when 'things settled down'— meaning when the war was over.

Wallace hadn't come back to the house but had returned to the barn and was finishing the clean hay exchange. I could really use a hug but

47

didn't want to call him back just for that. My frustration was beginning to segue into moping: I hated the idea that I had become so selfish, clingy, and needy.

Darn it! The wedding ceremony wasn't set up to be a huge or lavish affair, but it was still supposed to be our day! Ergh! Not now, woman... I shook my head and tried to find a positive outlook. Nope, I couldn't find one.

I had fed the boys before the hullabaloo, and now *I* was hungry. I didn't feel like making a sandwich, so settled for polishing off a few tomatoes waiting to be sliced for our celebration meal. I heard one of the babies start to fuss and, sure enough, little Wren was winding up her little pink fists, getting ready for her lioness roar of 'feed me now!'

I scooped her up into my arms, hopped up the steps, and in three long strides was inside the house, settled back on my chaise, having managed to unbutton my dress and bare a breast as I did so.

As soon as she smelled skin, she latched on. It was a phenomenon that never failed to occur; as soon as a baby started to suckle, I would get thirsty. I tried to make sure that I either had a cup of water or milk within reach when I sat down to feed a baby. I had been drinking lots of water today, but water didn't give me the calories I needed to make breakfast, lunch, dinner, and snacks for my three little redheads. I got up and grabbed the pitcher with my free arm. Not bothering with a cup, I slugged down nearly a quart of still-warm goat's milk without stopping for a breath. I wiped off my milk mustache with my quilt and wished that I had a big bowl of fruit salad loaded with bananas for dessert. Even an apple would do. Maybe Sarah knew of a good substitute. I was craving fruit big time, and the endless supply of tomatoes wasn't cutting it.

I laid Wren down on the bed and reached up as high as I could. My fingertips weren't even close to touching the tall ceiling, but I tried to, just the same. I didn't want to get round-shouldered as so many women did, from hunching over babies and chores all day and night. I raised my other arm high, dropped it, then repeated the exercise on the other side. Yoda—at least, I think that's what this was called—was part of my daily routine now.

My workout session was interrupted by light footsteps coming up the porch. It wasn't the normal stomping the men used to announce their arrival. My blouse was still unbuttoned. I had been airing out as I worked out; damp nipples soon developed into cracked and bleeding nipples. I quickly threw my shawl over my shoulders and stood up straight, ready to look any stranger in the eye.

It wasn't a stranger, though; it was Wallace. "I didn't walk heavy coming up the steps because I didn't want to wake the babies if they were asleep. I figured you'd know it was me. Sorry if I frightened you."

I hadn't realized how staid I must have looked, straight-backed, wearing a shawl in this insufferable heat, the milk pitcher in my hand, readied as a weapon. I put down the pitcher, turned around, and buttoned up under the shawl. I looked over my shoulder at my betrothed, gave him a mischievous grin, spun around, and with a grandiose flourish, flung the shawl onto the chair. "Better?" I asked.

His head literally flipped back at my almost obscene gesture. I guessed if it had been anyone other than a husband—or a soon-to-be one—that gesture would have been outright nasty for this time, even though I was flashing a fully-covered bosom.

His mouth worked around a smirk, trying to clean it up to a smile. He hadn't responded to my question but knew he didn't have to.

"I have something to give you," he said, his eyes shining, dimples stretching. "It's not as pretty as your *ravishing* neck and shoulders," Wallace paused as he took in my shocked expression, "or any of the rest of you."

I couldn't believe that he had just made me blush, especially since I had just been playing the vixen, but he had.

"Oh, you are beautiful, all over: nose, elbows, toes... I'm sorry if I haven't told you enough." He gave me a quick kiss on the end of my nose. "Nothing can come close, but I thought this might suit you since you had to give up your pretty gold nugget necklace to…well, we don't need to talk about that now, do we?"

"No, we don't," I agreed sheepishly. "But you really think I'm beautiful? Beautiful all over?"

"I always have and always will. Here," Wallace got down on one knee and put out his closed hand. He slowly opened out his fingers, and the ribbon expanded like one of those Fourth of July black carbon snakes after it had been lit. My mind raced through thoughts of Independence Day, fighting, gunpowder, and then slammed shut. Nope, not today. I hoped. I didn't want to think about any kind of war or explosions, *especially* today.

"Are you all right?" Wallace asked.

I guessed my eyes had glazed over, fearing armed confrontations. "Aye," I brightened up, and replied in a Scottish accent, "its jest the lack of sleep. I'll bide fine in a wee bit." I changed back to the appropriate voice for the occasion. "What do you have there?"

"It's something for you until I can get you a proper ring. I'd like you to have a gold setting with lots of big diamonds around another, bigger diamond, or maybe you'd prefer a ruby or sapphire in the center. But for now, would you accept this as a token of my love? I'd like you to wear it for our wedding ceremony."

I looked down at the ribbon that was pulling away from the coin in an unplanned, but stunning, animated formal presentation. Wallace had threaded the shiny disc onto a black ribbon, which offset the silver of the pendant beautifully. I picked up the coin and walked through the doorway to see it better in the bright sunlight. "Oh, my," I said, unable to contain the low groan of dread. I lost my legs and sat down quickly on the porch bench.

I looked up and saw the shocked expression on Wallace's face. "Oh, my," I repeated, but with an inflection of adoration rather than recognition. "This is beautiful, so beautiful that it took my breath away."

I doubted that I had fooled Wallace, but he probably would rather believe a lie than ask me more about it. I recognized the coin, sort of, but didn't remember from where. I sucked down the enigma and asked, "Would you put it on me? I'm afraid I can't tie a good bow or knot behind my neck, and I don't want to lose this—ever."

Wallace took the black and silver treasure from my hand. I twisted my hair into a rope and pulled it up into a knot. We did a tiny tango, turning around each other until we were positioned so my neck was presented to his slightly trembling, but warm hands. "It's beautiful, Wallace. And I don't care if I ever get a gold ring. I have the biggest treasure right here," I said as I turned around and put my arms around his neck. "I'm serious, you know. I can't lose you."

I buried my face into his chest. I wasn't brave enough to look up at him. My tears were brimming, being held back by the rise of my bottom eyelashes. I sucked in a breath of bravery and pulled away to look up into his face. His eyes were every bit as full of tears as mine. I jumped up to kiss him just as he leaned down to kiss me, and we bumped noses.

"Ouch," we both squawked at the same time. I reached up and wiped away the tears in his eyes that had spilled over, and he did the same for me. "Love hurts," I giggled.

"Hold still," he said. I grinned and let him lift my chin, my eyes shut in anticipation of a long, warm kiss.

But nothing happened. I opened one eye. He was bent over to kiss me but was looking away, his eyes focused on something in the distance. I turned my head and saw a cloud of dust heading up the road to our place.

"Now you hold still," I said. I put my hands on his shoulders and tip-toed up to get my kiss. It wasn't much of a kiss, though, because he was preoccupied with the thought of company. "It'll be a while before they get here," I reminded him softly.

He turned me away from the distracting view of the road, literally sweeping me off my feet, and gave me a kiss commensurate with the giving of an engagement token. "Much better," I said and smiled. He gave me a quick reassuring hug, and then turned both of us around to face the incoming company.

Wallace took a couple of steps forward to see better, his eyes squinting, searching the distance. I came up beside him and looked. I knew who it was. "That's the Donaldsons," I said. "I recognize the horses. Besides, who else would have that many little people on board?"

I hurried back into the kitchen and got the ewer to refill with fresh water. The gang was sure to be thirsty after the long ride. I also grabbed the plate of oatmeal cookies I had made for the reception. On second thought, "Not a good idea," I said. "We don't want the girls amped on sugar." I reached into the little cooler I had devised and pulled out the veggie tray that had been soaking in chilly water. The radish roses had filled out and the carrot sticks had curled. The cucumbers were just slices, but I told Sarah I was going to call them cucumber coins. The girls would get a kick out of having their own money.

I got the fresh water and cups gathered together while Wallace waited for the wagon, ready to grab the harnesses and bring the horses to the barn. The wagon hadn't even got to him when the girls started trying to climb out.

"Whoa there, young ladies. Wait until the wagon comes to a

complete stop before trying to get out. We don't want anyone to get hurt. Now," he said when he had a hold of the horse's halter, "if you can wait just a wee moment, I'll give you a hand. Let me help the women first."

"Miss Evie!" Miranda squealed, a fistful of blue ribbons in her hand. "Look what I got for you!" She had leaned out so far that she was starting to fall. Wallace saw what was happening and lifted her out the rest of the way.

"Might as well let them out first," said Mrs. Donaldson. "It takes a bit longer to unload us," she observed matter-of-factly. "Miranda, watch out for your sisters, hear?"

"Yes, mum," she replied. She looked toward me and waved, but turned back to her mother, still in the wagon, ready to assume her sisterly duties.

Wallace had all the girls out in three quick lifts and set downs. The Donaldson daughters all held hands as they came running towards me and the house, a chain of calico and curls. "Come on, sisters, I'll bet Miss Evie has more stories to tell us," encouraged Miranda.

Wallace helped Hannah and Mrs. Donaldson out of the wagon, the two women passing the twin boys between them with an ease and familiarity that seemed to be as second nature as scratching an itch.

Within minutes, our little house had added four little girls, two baby boys, and two women, all talking or squawking. I counted Hannah as a woman although she was only about fourteen years old. My babies were used to being around household noises, family talking, or me singing; we didn't pussyfoot around them either. I wanted them to be able to sleep through everyday sounds. However, the addition of eight more voices, and a new octave range, into their lives woke up every one of them at the same time. I had to admit the cacophony was tremendous.

I looked up and saw Wallace through the open door; it was too hot for closed doors today. He was craning his neck, trying to get a peek at me, I think. I picked up the loudest of my babies, little Wren—she had fallen asleep while eating earlier—and fumbled with my buttons to bring out the buffet. As soon as she latched on, I took my free hand and waved at my very, very soon-to-be husband. He waved back and headed to the barn to take care of the horses.

What a wonderful noise I was breathing in. The prattle was like oxygen, feeding my heart and nourishing my spirit. The women were talking on top of each other, admonishing the fidgeting girls, telling their baby boys to hush, while straining to look at my two yowling redheaded sons in green calico diapers. I flashed back to my life before I got here, my trek through the wilderness with Ian and Little Bear. I remembered wanting to be in the presence of another woman and estrogen. Well, I was more than in its presence; I was in an ocean of it now.

I was also surrounded by the smell of babies and what babies do. Only it wasn't my babies.

"I told you it was too soon to be givin' the babies porritch. It jest makes their messes stink," Mrs. Donaldson said to Hannah. "I know you were jest trying to help me, but we'll be fine. See, I got lots of milk now."

The front of Mrs. Donaldson's dress was soaked. "Here, give me one of those we'uns," she told her and pointed to little Judah. "I want to see the difference the three months makes on the sucking."

Judah was squalling and hungry but didn't recognize the source of the milk. His head twisted and turned away from the proffered nipple. "Here," I said as I tossed her my shawl, "throw this over your shoulder, and see if that helps."

She did as I asked and sure enough, Judah shut up and started suckling, his little fist clutching the edge of the shawl. "How about that?" she said. "Ooh, now that feels right nice compared to those little fiends of mine." Hannah handed her little George who was making his wants known, too. Mrs. Donaldson leaned back in the kitchen chair, a babe at each breast, and sighed. I think she was actually enjoying the gentle suckling of my baby boy.

"Here, let me have Leo," I said to Hannah. "We might as well get all of mine fed at once. Hopefully Jody and Julian will be back soon, the babies can take their naps, and we can get on with the wedding. Oh shi… Oh dear, where's the preacher?" I asked as I arranged my two babies so they weren't kicking each other.

"Oh, Pastor Lawrence said he'd be right along. He was going to stop and pick up Mr. Rojas. He wanted to see those horses and goats he's been hearing so much about. By the way, where is Sarah, er, Mrs. Pomeroy?" asked Hannah.

"Well, speaking of goats, she's out in the shed, trying to help little Sharona bring forth her twin kids. Or maybe she's having three. That seems to be the magic," I quickly corrected myself to these superstitious women, "I mean, the special number around here."

The little girls were giggling and dancing around the table, inspecting the colorful vegetable tray I had laid out, hands dutifully held behind their backs. "Did you know I made those radish roses and cucumber coins just for you? Go wash up, and then you can have two of each one." I said.

"Can we buy Da a new gun with the coins?" Miranda asked in complete sincerity. "He's always saying how he could sure use a better one."

"No, these are just pretend coins and roses." All the girls' faces fell with disappointment. I added brightly, "But you can eat them. They taste mighty good." I sighed, exasperated that I couldn't help their father, or anyone else, and said gently, "I'm sure your Da will get a new gun when the time is right."

Lord, when is the right time for hoping or praying for a new, or better, gun? Well, I guess now is the right time with our new country on the brink of becoming either firmly established or totally suppressed. "Lord, give us Your strength and wisdom and the tools needed to ensure the success of the independence of this new country, our home, America. In Jesus's name, Amen."

I looked around and noticed it was suddenly very quiet. I must have been praying out loud. Both the little girls and the big girls were staring at me. "Amen," Hannah and Mrs. Donaldson said solemnly.

"Amen," added all the younger ones, including little Rebecca's, "may men."

Mrs. Donaldson handed little George Washington Donaldson to Hannah, who put him to her shoulder for burping. Then she picked up my little Judah, wiped off the milk dribbling out of his slack mouth, and put him to her shoulder. She gently rubbed his back and said softly, "My husband went to the mill yesterday. He heard that there were soldiers out there, tryin' to take it over, meanin' to keep all of the flour and wheat that was in there still. I guess they're serious about tryin' to starve us out. Anyway, he was supposed to be back by last night, but he never came home. I didn't want the girls to worry so, well, Hannah and I decided we should go ahead and come here for your special day. Maybe that would take their minds off the conflict and their da bein' gone for so long. Do you think we did the right thing?"

"I'm sure that's what Mac would have wanted you to do. Who knows, maybe Jody and Julian will be coming back with him this afternoon. That's where they went, too: to see about a disturbance at the mill. If any two men can help, it would be those two," I told her with exaggerated confidence. "Here, let's see if we can fit all the babies into the playpen. Your boys aren't rolling over yet, are they?"

Changing the subject seemed to help everyone. It was a Kodak moment without a camera: five babies in a homemade playpen. "America, the next generation," I said with pride. 'God willing,' I beseeched silently.

Before the ladies could say anything about my remark, we heard a "Ho, the house," from a man coming up in a wagon. It sounded like José and the new preacher had made it to the festivities. Now, all we needed was the rest of the men.

I wanted to go outside to greet the new arrivals but didn't want to be rude and leave Mrs. Donaldson and Hannah with four little girls and all those babies. Then I thought, 'good grief; they do it all day and night, every day and night, so why should today be any different?' My three were asleep and contained. The girls were proper little duchesses from what I had seen. I didn't think they'd do anything bad on purpose, but I didn't want them pulling the playpen down off the sawhorses for a better look at the five sleeping babies either. I didn't need to worry, though. The girls were well distracted playing with their gourmet cut vegetable *hors d'oeuvres.*

I went outside, eager to meet the preacher who was new in the area. I saw that Wallace had already made it to the wagon, and Sarah was on her way, wiping her hands on her apron. She was radiant, with only a smear of blood on the apron, so I guessed all the kids came out okay. I caught up with her on the way to the wagon and our guests.

"How many?" I asked.

"Three, of course; all healthy, and Sharona's doing fine, too." Sarah's face suddenly fell and I followed her gaze.

There were four men standing next to the wagon parked under the big mulberry tree, their backs to us. I recognized José's fine form right away. Ever the king of courtesy, his hands were already on the horse's halter, ready to assist Wallace. There were two other men, though, not just one in the person of the new preacher who we were expecting. Sarah and I strolled up to the wagon.

The second man turned around. "Good day. I'm Jacob Lawrence the Third," said the dark-skinned man as he extended his hand, "the new preacher."

Everyone was stunned but me. "Hello, glad to meet you," I said as I reached out and shook his hand. "You know, you might get a bit of resistance around here. There's quite the Catholic influence at this house. But, since there isn't a priest anywhere, and I'm the one getting married and not of the Catholic persuasion, I'm glad you could make it. Would you care to come in for refreshments?"

"Yes, yes," added Sarah, "please do come in out of the sun. It's unbearably hot today. But, then again, it seems like it is every day." Sarah started to walk ahead of the new preacher to lead the way to the house, then stopped and turned around. "Master Simon?"

I turned to follow her stare. The sight of a good-looking man—most definitely of African descent—dressed as a white-collared preacher was enough to make anyone in this area stare. It had also been enough to take our attention away from the third man standing by the wagon.

"Simon?" I asked incredulously, wondering why and how I knew that that was his name.

Sarah realized that she had just stopped the new pastor from coming in out of the sun. She looked as bewildered as I felt at the introduction of this new—or was that old?—character of Master Simon into our sheltered life here in the backwoods of North Carolina. "Just a moment, please, Pastor Lawrence. I...I..."

I saw her dilemma. We were both curious about Simon—for different reasons, I'm sure—but wanted to be gracious to our new guest, too. However, we couldn't just lead him into a very small house that was currently overcapacity with little girls, babies, and worried women. In this era, a black man—even a free black man—normally wouldn't interact with white women and children, except as a servant. Sarah and I were both aware of this and stared at each other with the 'what now?' look on our faces.

I knew that slavery was a part of Colonial life, but it hadn't impacted this area. The dirt farmers and tradesmen were too poor to own a slave. By the suffix of Pastor Lawrence's name, I'd say his father or grandfather was a shrewd man who knew, or at least hoped, that being 'the Third' and being a man of the cloth would help protect his heir in this racist region and era. So far, so good.

Then I knew what to do. "Miranda!" I hollered. "Bring me the water and three cups, please." Shouting across the yard was rude, but I knew that little girl was like my magic wand. She would do anything for me, whether it be serving water to our guests or digging privy holes in a rainstorm.

I walked over to our three recent arrivals. "Sorry for the shouting," I said. I looked at Sarah. She looked like a landed fish; she was in some sort of mouth-opening-and-closing shock, and I was beginning to feel a bit overwhelmed, too. "Our house is so small, and right now there are two ladies and nine children in there, five of them under five months old. We haven't had a chance to set up the tables and refreshments yet. It's…"

I didn't get a chance to finish with my excuses. Wallace's hand was on my shoulder, gently telling me with his touch that it was okay. "Sure is hot today, and here she comes," he said as Miranda came up to him with the tray. I noticed that she had eyes for no one but the two of us, and that was a good thing.

"I put some of the Continental coins and other treats on the tray for you. Mum said we couldn't eat them all 'cause there was more company coming."

Wallace took the tray from her and set it on the corner of the wagon. Just then, Miranda spotted the three men. She saw José first and gave him a big grin that bordered on flirting. Then her eyes went to the other two men. She didn't say a word, just stared at the man with cocoa-colored skin. I walked over to her and tapped her on the shoulder.

"Thank you for your help. You'd better go back to the house now, all right? I'll be in later."

I had thought about introducing her but remembered that 'children should be seen and not heard' was the attitude of this time. I never subscribed to that theory, but today, I was glad of it.

The horses and wagon were in the shade, so that's where we stayed to enjoy our little tea party. I served the cups of water then offered the plate of vegetables to our guests. Pastor Lawrence accepted a couple of curled carrot sticks from the plate, commenting on how elegantly I had prepared a simple root vegetable. José said 'thank you' and took a couple of the radish roses.

I was glad that José had not refused to eat the food after a black man had touched the tray. Evidently, segregation was not the way of life in Spain. Simon was mum, just looked constipated and agitated, and ate nothing.

Sarah was beginning to come out of her trance and had accepted a 'Continental coin' cucumber from me. She hadn't stopped staring though. She was just about to say something—profound, I'm sure— when we heard it.

There was a horse coming up to the house at full speed. Wallace walked away from our soirée and stood in the middle of the road, ready to intercept the rider.

The lathered horse came in with a raggedy young man clutching its mane. The spindly roan didn't have a saddle on it, and if it had ever had even a blanket, it was long gone. The man dropped off his ride as soon as it came to a stop. He almost fell down, either from being no-saddle sore or fatigued, but either way, he had lost his legs. Wallace gave him a hand up.

The raggedy man looked up at Wallace and gasped, "It's you!"

Wallace recognized the man immediately and quickly stepped away, rubbing his hand on his pants, as if it was soiled.

It was Clyde, one of the men who had raped Wallace six months before. We had both been attacked, although Wallace much more brutally. We thought that my feral friend, Lady the puma, had devoured or at least killed Clyde. She had killed my attacker, Gimpy, and castrated and possibly killed Clayton, the other rapist. All we ever found of him were the remains of his genitalia.

If looks could kill, Clyde would be dead, but instead, he was on his knees, pleading. "You have a right to punish me, and I'll let you do it later, but please, first, help me! My brother and sister are holed up at the mill with your kin. There's three Redcoats there holdin' 'em with guns. The Captain said as soon as the rest of his men get there tonight, they're gonna line everyone up and shoot 'em all, make an essample of 'em. I knowed the way around the back, so I snuck out to get help. Your kin tole me to get you to come and rescue 'em. The Lobsterbacks didn't see me sneaking out, but I wasn't who they wanted anyhow. They wanted

58

the big man with red hair—your father, I reckon—and anyone that joined up with him. We can sneak back in and blindside 'em if we hurry. There's only the three of 'em right now. Please, help me."

Clyde was prostrate on the ground now, his hands cupped as in prayer on top of Wallace's boots. Wallace took a step back and said, "Get up." He paused and added, "We'll need fresh horses," then turned and headed for the barn.

"I'm coming, too," shouted Sarah as she ran after him.

Wallace stopped and turned on his heel. I saw him take a deep breath, the look of fire ablaze in his eyes. I was sure he was going to tell her to stay put. He blew out his breath in a huff and said, "Then get your bag and let's get on with it."

Wallace took long strides to the barn, grabbed the jackass's reins, and threw them over the hitching post for Clyde. He wasn't going to give him one of our horses to ride and didn't even want the man inside our barn.

I didn't blame him on that one. I looked over and saw Clyde bent over the trough, using both hands to bring water to his face to drink. He felt uncomfortable, and as uncharitable as it was, I was glad. I didn't want to talk to him, nor did anyone else. I shuddered at the thought of him.

I ran after Wallace, my heart ready to tell him that he couldn't go— it was our wedding day—and caught up to him as he swung the saddle over the horse. He just missed my head with a stirrup as I popped up on the other side of him.

"I'm sorry, Evie. What kind of man would I be if I let my fathers be murdered? I have to go."

"I know," I said, as I held the horse's halter for him. Tears were streaming down my face, but I didn't want him to see them. I had left my shawl in the house, so had to settle for wiping my tears on the shoulder of my blouse.

I felt a hand come under my chin and lift it. "Here, blow," said Wallace as he offered me his beige embroidered silk handkerchief. I blew, then quickly tried to wipe away my sadness with the edge of the cloth, only managing to get the wetness removed.

"We may have to delay the wedding a day or two, but I will marry you, I promise," he said. Then he lifted me off the ground and gave me a hard, quick—almost painful, but passionate—kiss. He set me down just as fast as he had lifted me and snorted, his face taut with anger. He turned away and mounted Thor, Jody's latest acquisition, a still not completely broken Arabian mix. "Sarah will have to catch up. Kiss the babies for me, aye?"

"Okay, and I'll save another one for you," I said and pushed his silk handkerchief back into his pocket.

Sarah came running up with her bag in hand. "I hope I have everything," she said frantically as I helped her get her horse ready.

"You always have the best-packed medical bag in the colonies—maybe even the world—and you know it." She shrugged at my remark, her lips tight with frustration. She handed me the bag, then put her foot in the stirrup to climb up. "Let's just hope and pray that you don't need it," I added as I handed it back to her.

It hit me again; I couldn't contain the emotional eruption. I grabbed her leg and clutched tightly, "Bring him home, please, please! I don't want to be a widow before I'm a bride." A huge wail came out of me, then two big hiccups. I sucked it back down and tried to put on my brave-little-soldier mask. "Go, go," I said as I pulled on the horse's rein and led her out of the barn. I slapped Jessie's behind so Sarah had a chance to catch up to Wallace, almost out of sight, and Clyde, just ahead of her, hanging on for dear life on the bare back of that sturdy but ornery jackass, Prince Charles.

Chapter 4: Rescue at the mill (NITWW Ch 47)

I watched the three of them take off, my hopes and dreams for a happy wedding day riding grimly astride Thor's saddle. The unlikely trio was on their way to resolve a disquietingly odd scenario. Wallace, the former victim, was blindly answering his attacker's request, heading into a hostage situation in order to help members of this horrid man's family. Well, Wallace did have a personal interest in the liberation effort, too, so I guessed it wasn't that odd. His fathers were also being held against their will. At least it was a rescue mission and not cold-blooded vengeance. I snorted. "Forever Pollyanna, eh—always looking for the good in a situation—at least it's not vengeance…"

I tried to compose myself and wiped my face on my damp sleeve, only to realize that it was too wet to be of use, so I leaned over and employed my apron. I straightened up, pushed the hair out of my face, and sucked it up, gazing one last time at the vanishing trio. I was standing resolute in my newly recovered respectability when I noticed it. It had flown out of his pocket—the embroidered handkerchief used to wipe away my tears just moments earlier. To hell with respectability and dignity: I ran after that cloth as if it was a lost part of his body. To me, it was, in a way. It was the last object we had shared that I could touch.

I bent over and picked up the now dear and precious memento: my fiancé's crumbled and dusty silk snot rag. I stayed crouched on the ground and shifted side to side on my flat feet, clutching the cloth to me as if it was a pouch of gold coins. I reached in front of me and grabbed a golf-ball-sized stone. I rubbed it hard with my thumb a few strokes, pressing my anger and aggravation into it. I stood up and hurled the rage rock down the road where the three mismatched rescuers had disappeared. "You'd better come back in one big piece!" I shouted at my long-gone fiancé.

I turned around and headed home, angrily kicking stones in front of me. I knew no one had heard my scream. I was still a long distance from the house, and the riders were too far away to hear me, but it felt good to both vent and be bossy.

"Damn…damn…damn…" puffed an angry young voice from the direction where I had just thrown my attitude adjustment rock. For a moment, I thought I was hearing myself curse, but the sounds were coming from behind me.

I turned around quickly and saw a totally naked young girl half-running, half-falling down, on this same trail that Sarah, Wallace, and Slug Mold had just traveled. She must have recently emerged from the brush on the side of the road. I stared at her for a long moment, and then realized that the falling down aspect of her movement was going to win out over the running part. I raced up to her, my skirts pulled high so I could move faster, and caught her just as she stumbled one last time.

What do you say to a naked young lady? In this case, nothing. I could see that she needed water before any questions could be answered. Her lips were swollen and cracked, and it looked as if her tongue was too big for her mouth. "Come here," I said as I bent over and helped her wrap her arms around my neck. "Lift your legs around me and I'll carry you back to the house. We'll get you something to drink and some clothes."

I heard mumbling and crying in my hair. She was wrapped around me like a blonde spider monkey puppet and sobbing, "Damn, damn, damn, damn," over and over again.

The barely lucid young lady—by her budding body parts, I'd say she was about 11—was so lightweight and leggy that it had been no burden to carry her like a toddler. It was a natural progression for me to treat her as one, too.

I stopped at the barn, got her some water to drink, and then gave her a rag I had dipped in the horse trough. Her overheated body was covered in a red flush. "Wipe yourself down with this, and stay put," I said.

I ran over to the clothesline and grabbed a length of the green calico fabric I had prewashed and hung out to dry. It seemed like that bolt of cloth never ended, which was a good thing. I could hear our guests on the porch enjoying themselves. The little girls were teaching Pastor Lawrence some of the songs and stories I had taught them. "One fish, two fish," the girls were chanting. I stayed mum, covert in my laundry retrieval. I didn't want to draw any attention to this new situation.

I rushed back to the barn and saw that Master Simon was looking inside, possibly for me. All of a sudden, his head snapped back, as if he had just been hit on the chin. I couldn't see anyone else, but I realized what had happened: he must have spotted the girl and seen that she wasn't wearing any clothes. A true gentleman, he quickly averted his eyes from the little Lady Godiva, and was now walking my way.

Rather than wait for his questions, I took the proactive approach. "I haven't a clue as to what's going on, but I'll find out once she gets decent. Stick around, though," I said as I turned and walked backward away from him. I shook my finger at him and continued my admonishment, "I want to talk to you, too."

I still wanted to know about Sarah, him, and me, and what we all had to do with each other. Something was niggling at the back of my mind, and it wasn't the current situation, or rather situations, at hand.

I tore three thin strips off the end of the cloth. The girl had cleaned the road dust off herself as best she could. Her frightened blue eyes peered out from behind a wayward tress of long, blond hair. Her face was pink, puffy, and lopsided, and it wasn't that way solely from crying: it looked as if she had been hit recently. The skin was crimson on the left side, although it didn't show any sign of bruising yet.

"Here, hold your arms out like this," I said. I took a hasty measurement, folded the long length of cloth in half then once again sideways. I used the sheep shears to cut out a piece of the double folded corner. I opened out the makeshift dress and threw it over her head. I grabbed two of the short strips, tied them together, and made a belt for the ensemble. The third strip I used as a headband to pull her hair out of her face. The poor girl was shaking as I clothed her, her arms now held close across her belly. She was stunned, possibly in shock, sobbing silently, gulping air, and trying to steady herself.

Simon very gingerly walked over to us. He held the vegetable tray that had been passed around earlier. It had been resupplied with little pinwheel sandwiches and tomato wedges. He held it out to the little girl and waited for her to take one. She looked up at him, wary of his motives. It appeared she wanted to make sure he wasn't going to grab her when she reached for the food. Seeing her distrustful, frightened look, he put the tray down on a barrel top and moved away. She took two cautious steps to the food, then reached out and grabbed the whole plate, clutching it to her chest, cramming the little sandwiches into her mouth as fast as she could.

"Whoa there, little lady," I said and pulled the plate away. I didn't want her to choke. "Don't forget to chew before swallowing, all right?"

She nodded her head twice, then went to the trough and cupped up water with her hands, quickly and efficiently swallowing her big mouthful of food. "It was a trap!" she exclaimed. She started crying again but managed to spit out her words between gulps of air. "I hollered at them as they were riding by, but they didn't hear me," her head dropped low in shame, "or see me."

"Who didn't see you, and what do you mean it was a trap?" I asked, hardly able to contain myself. I wanted to pick her up and shake out the answers but resisted the urge.

"You see, they let my brother Clyde escape so he could come and git the other big one. The first ones was just wantin' the flour and to talk to the big red-haired man, but the captain, he wanted trouble, I could see that. He said he wanted to bring in the Big Red and the son, too, and then arrest 'em both...and anybody else that had been listenin' to 'em."

"So how did you get out?" I asked. If they had let one person escape, maybe this was a trap, too.

The young girl put her head down in embarrassment. She didn't want to talk, but I wanted—needed—to know. I realized I had to get her confidence first. Evidently, feeding and clothing her weren't enough. "What's your name?" I asked.

"Jenny. And don't go makin' jokes about me bein' a female jackass either," she said defensively.

"Okay, Jenny." I paused to savor the name, hoping to earn her trust through flattery. "That's a fine name. Did you know that's the name of Big Red's mother, too? I certainly wouldn't think of teasing you about your name with his mother having the same one. He loves her very much."

"Oh," she paused to think about it. "Really? Okay, I guess I can tell you, seein' as you know him and his kin and all. The Redcoats stopped by the mill yesterday and decided they was gonna take all the flour for theyselves. But the man they called Mac was there, and the miller and Clyde and me and my t'other brother, Clayton, and a couple t'others, too. Well, Mac said they couldn't just be takin' what weren't theirs. I guess he and t'others had been readin' that paper about liberty and stuff. So, the Redcoats, they say they're gonna shoot 'em all, but I don't think they really wanted to do it. So, they just tied 'em up and took all the flour and started loadin' it into a wagon. One of the men that was there at the mill—Mac's friend, I think—he rannned off, and so two of the soldiers took off and chased him, but I don't think they ever caught him.

"Then this afternoon, the Big Red and the one they called the Turncoat—he's a little man, but kinda pretty—they showed up. Clyde took 'em aside and told 'em he knew a way they could all sneak out if one of 'em could addle the soldiers. So Big Red, he just starts talkin' to the Redcoats. And the soldiers, they was about to let everybody go and just keep the flour and the wagon, when another Redcoat come in. He said he was a captain, and he was in charge now. He was mean and ugly, and said they was still gonna keep the flour and the—the sons of liberty, I think he called us—they would have to pay the tax, or they would all get dee ported!

"Well, the first soldiers just wanted the flour, so they took it, and most all of them went off. That only left the two soldiers there with the captain to watch 'em all. Clyde was all set to slip out—he didn't want to get dee ported either—but Big Red asked him if when he left, would he follow this here road," Jenny pointed to the road she had just come down, "and tell his son to come back with help. But he said to make sure he brought back the kegs or cakes or somethin' like that. But I'm not sure Clyde got that part. He's not too bright and can't remember two things at once. But I *know'd* he got out and come down the right road 'cause I just saw him headin' back to the mill. But he musta forgot about t'other part, 'cause he didn't have no cakes with 'em. And, and…"

Little Jenny started crying again and couldn't talk, and I was losing patience. "And what?" I asked sternly.

"After he left, the big ugly captain told one of t'other soldiers to stay outside and watch to make sure Clyde got away. And to let him know when he got back with the, the son, and then they would line 'em up and shoot both the Big Red and his son. And he wasn't just talkin' like t'others, he really meant it!"

I fell back hard against the center post of the barn and slid down in what felt like a controlled faint with consciousness – if there even was such a thing. "Oh, shit," I said.

"Yeah, oh shit is right!" Jenny agreed. "So, I wanted to hurry up and catch Clyde and tell him it was a trap, but I couldn't just run out, me still bein' a prisoner and all. But you see, the ugly captain, he took to starin' at me, wantin' to set real close to me. He came up to me and started runnin' his hand down the side of my face, and then down to my neck

65

and, and... Well, the Big Red told him to take his filthy hands off-a me, but the captain, he just laughed, then kicked him real hard. I thought he hurt him real bad, but he didn't because then there was some scufflin' and next thing ya know, the Big Red has his knee in the captain's throat. But then t'other soldier came by and kicked Big Red in the head, and he rolled over and didn't wake up."

I was even more stunned, wide-eyed with wonder and worry.

Jenny paused to look over at me. "He wasn't dead, though, I checked—you see, they hadn't tied me up." Jenny was concerned about me and made sure I knew that Jody was going to be okay. "But I bet he has a big headache when he wakes up. But then the captain, he starts rubbin' his hands on me again, and then I get an idea."

Jenny's voice changed. She continued but was obviously embarrassed about what she was saying. "I watched a woman do a dance once, and it made the men just stare, and they couldn't even move, except their hands was on their…you know, stuff, and then she took all their money, so I figured that maybe I could do somethin' like that. So, I tell t'other soldier why don't he put down his gun, and I'll do a dance for the both of 'em. But I told him that they can't touch me. The captain, he don't like that much, and he smacks me upside the head for bein' sassy. But t'other soldier, he's got the rifle, and he says he wants to watch, so fer him to keep his paws off-a me.

"So I start dancin' around a little, and my brother Clayton, he starts to holler and tells me don't do it. But then the captain punches him real hard, and then he don't talk no more. I don't think he got killed, though, 'cause he kept groanin'. So, I start doin' the dance, and the miller and Mac just cover their eyes and start prayin', but I tell 'em I'm gonna be all right.

"Then the captain says I have to take off my clothes. So, I take off my dress, and he says I have to take off my shift, too. I can see he's gettin' all worked up, so I tell him he has to take off his clothes, too, if I'm gonna take off mine. Well, he starts to do that, and that's when the other soldier had to hit Mac and the miller to get 'em, get 'em, quiet.

"So, the soldier takes off all his clothes first, and I think he wants to do the nasty with me, but the captain says he has to wait. I didn't want to take off my shift, but the captain smacks me, and says that if I don't, well then, he's gonna do it for me, and cut me, too! So I take off my shift…and he pulls down his pants and, and…"

Jenny paused. I looked up at her, throat tight with terror. It felt like an iron fist was squeezing my heart.

"And I ran like hell!" she bragged. "They had their pants down, and there was only two of them. One of 'em had to stay with the prisoners. I heard 'em yellin' and arguin' as I was runnin' away, about who was gonna do the chasin' and who was gonna do the stayin'. I was flyin' down that road, hopin' to catch up with Clyde on the way back from fetchin' the Big Red's son, but then, then, I got a bit bashful 'cause I didn't have on no clothes, and I hid in the bushes when I heard the horses comin'. I thought they might be more soldiers again 'cause there was more than just two. By the time I got back out on the road and saw it was them with a lady, they was already gone. They was ridin' real fast! I didn't know what to do, and then somebody almost hit me with a rock, and then I saw you. I wasn't afraid of you 'cause you was a woman, and really, I was just too tired and too sad to care about anythin'."

With her last revelation, I realized the need to take quick action. "Okay, so what we have is five men tied up and kicked around. Hey, where was Julian, the pretty Turncoat, during all of this?" I was afraid that something had happened to him that she hadn't revealed.

"Oh, him? The first Redcoats, they stuffed him into a flour sack and said they was gonna beat him with a stick. But they shoved him out back and forgot all about him when they left. It's a good thing, too, I think, or he would be back with those Lobsterbacks, and I don't think they like Turncoats too much."

"Thank you, Lord," I said softly and got up from the barn's dirt floor. I brushed off my skirts, now ready to get back into boss lady mode. "So, right now Julian is safe because they don't even know he's around. That leaves Clayton, Jody, Mac, the miller, and his friend—that's five—and Clyde, Wallace, and Sarah—three more—are on the way." I enumerated the captives, or soon to be captives, on my fingers. "Eight. Ho, boy. But you say that there're only three soldiers?"

"Well, no; that's the bad part," she said. I tipped my head and looked her in the eye, urging her to continue. "I saw six more coming in from t'other way when I was runnin' to catch up with Clyde. That makes ten."

"No, three and six makes nine, but that's still a lot of men for you and me to overpower if Wallace, Sarah, and Clyde get captured."

I paused for a moment, waiting for inspiration. "Cakes; what did you say about Jody and cakes?"

"I don't know if he said cakes or kegs," Jenny said. "Why would he be wantin' food or whisky at a time like this?"

"Oh, oh, oh! Yes!" I burst into grin. "He said kegs! We have lots of kegs: kegs of gunpowder. Simon, we need you to drive us up to the mill in the wagon. Before we actually get there, though, I'm going to do a little sabotage. I may not have C4, but I do have gunpowder, fuses, and a plan. I'm going to do a bit of distraction and diversion while you, little Missy, sneak back in and cut loose the hostages. Those Redcoats won't even know what hit them."

It was first things first, though: I needed to take care of my little family. Right now, that meant I needed to have a talk with Mrs. Donaldson. I walked up to the house and saw that José, Pastor Lawrence, and pretty much everybody who could walk except for Mrs. Donaldson, were outside playing catch with a rag ball. I waved to them, then ventured in through the open front door, my emotions as tangled as an eagle's nest.

"I need to ask a big favor," I said to my bosom buddy, my heart rising to my throat, nearly choking off my words before I could say them. Mrs. Donaldson looked at me as if I was sick, but I held up my hand for her to let me finish. "I have to run a little errand, and I'm not sure how long I'll be. Could you and Hannah take care of my babies? I mean, you'd have to feed them if I didn't get back in time, but…but…"

My words were failing, fumbling out because I was now looking at all three of my babies, sound asleep in their little playpen next to the larger George and Nathanael Donaldson. I sucked it up and continued, "They shouldn't be too much trouble. I just have to take this little girl back to her family. I'm not sure how long I'll be, and she doesn't feel comfortable going with a man, so if the babies need feeding, do you think that you…"

Mrs. Donaldson interrupted me with a compassionate hand on my shoulder. "Of course, my dear; we already know about the shawl trick now, don't we? My boys can have some porritch if they get hungry. It might make their messes stink, but they're gonna have to start eatin' it sooner or later anyhow. You just go on and take care of that little girl.

68

Oh, here she comes now."

I turned around and saw Jenny in the doorway. She glanced sideways then turned her complete attention to the pen full of babies. "Are they all yours?" she asked, her mouth hanging open.

"No, no, only the three little ones; the two bigger ones are hers. Mrs. Donaldson," I nodded the introduction.

"Wow. Are they comin' with us?" Jenny asked, her eyes as big as teacups.

"Oh, no; they'll stay here with me. Are you ready to get back to your family?" asked Mrs. Donaldson.

Jenny looked over at me for an answer, and I dipped my head slightly in acknowledgment. "Yes, ma'am, I'm ready," she replied. She turned to me and asked, "Can we leave now, uh, ma'am?"

I realized that I had never told Jenny my name. I grimaced slightly and tried to recover with the words, "Yes, let's go. Thank you, Mrs. Donaldson."

The two of us scurried out of the house, then almost ran to the barn. "My name is Evie," I said when we got inside. I grabbed two of the long boxes containing the rifles and ammunition from under the loft, set them on the tailgate of the wagon, and pushed them under the seat. I showed Jenny where the kegs of gunpowder were. "Here, these need to go into the back of the wagon."

These kegs were the goods received from my gold nugget necklace trade with Captain Asshole, the taxman. I was pretty sure he knew his lamebrained accomplices had gunpowder in their wagon of stolen goods, but he had let the valuable commodity go in trade. Gold lust will do that to a person. Besides, he probably figured he'd just get more of it down the road. However, I was pretty sure he didn't know that what he had was state of the art—for 1781—ammo propellant. Jody had marveled at the texture of this new powder; it was very consistent and didn't clump. I grunted as I lifted one of the kegs onto the wagon tailgate.

"Simon, would you help her load these?"

Simon had been busy while we were in the house. The team was ready—it never had been unhitched—but he had watered the horses and given them hay. Now, the man with the scholar's soft hands was hefting kegs of gunpowder to the little girl in the wagon. Jenny was strong for her petite size, and was managing quite well, maneuvering the kegs by rolling them on their rims to the front of the wagon. "Don't bump those into each other or anything else," I warned. "And would you ride here in back and make sure they don't move?" I didn't know how explosive the kegs were, but I didn't want to find out until I was ready.

I ran into the corner of the barn and dug out the spool of fuse cord and the lighter from my secret cache. I had left the two items together for rushed times such as this. I patted my pockets and made sure I still had my Leatherman and the smartphone. I grabbed the shovel and carefully placed it next to the six kegs of gunpowder. "I think a six-pack should be enough to get this party rolling. Come on, Simon; let's go."

I climbed into the wagon. "Here, you drive," I said as I handed the reins to him, "I still haven't got the hang of these two-horse powered vehicles."

A cosmic pulse of *déjà vu* throbbed as soon as the words were out of my mouth. It felt as if Simon and I had been out driving around the countryside together once before.

It was too noisy for conversation while riding in the wagon on a rocky road, but I couldn't help staring at him. He must have felt my eyes on him, though, because he turned to look at me. "Later," he said simply, returned his focus forward, and flicked the reins, urging the horses to speed up.

We rode in uncomfortable silence for half an hour. Simon never said a word nor looked in my direction again. Jenny rode quietly, too, scanning the roadside, absorbed in her own thoughts. I made good use of the time cutting fuse cord, and praying—for inspiration, and for the safety of our friends and families.

"Here, here!" Jenny called out suddenly, pointing to a little pullout on the side of the road. "We can't ride up past here or they'll see us." She turned around and looked at the armament, scowling. "Master Simon told me these would explode. How do you make them do that?"

It was a valid question. I guessed Simon—she called him Master Simon, so I supposed he had introduced himself earlier—must have given her a brief lesson on explosives. "Leave that part to me. Now, help me bring those around here."

Just a few yards away was a slightly sloping glen that would be perfect for my pyrotechnics display. If I could get the explosions to shoot up past twenty feet high, they would be in the line of sight of anyone near the mill. Sight, sound, and maybe smell: a perfect distraction so we could rescue the hostages.

The three of us worked in a well-coordinated effort and had the wagon unloaded, the kegs set in more or less a large circle, within minutes.

I turned my attention to Simon. "Give me about fifteen minutes to do my thing, and then very slowly drive up to the mill. You can claim the horse has a sore foot or whatever. I just want them to be watching you as you make your approach. When you get there, ask them if they have your flour ready. Make up some story about how your brother brought in two bushels of wheat or something, and that you want the flour. Just talk, okay? And talk real slow and act stupid."

The indignant look on his face was priceless. I still didn't know who this Master Simon fellow was, but he was definitely a 'master' of something and didn't look the simpleton at all. Maybe this would be harder than I thought.

"Here, unbutton your shirt and re-do it wrong, you know, so you have one button too many left over. And put your hat on crooked." I reached up to shove his hat askew and he pulled back, as if I was trying to wipe a smudge off his face with a spitty finger. That gave me an idea. I reached down and grabbed a juicy weed, pulled it between my thumb and forefinger, then picked up a pinch of dirt. "There," I said, and used my dirty digits to paint the side of his nose and one cheek. "That looks much better."

Jenny was doing the 'me too, me too' dance, eager and more than ready to do anything to help. "Jenny, your job is to sneak around the building and get in the back door. There's probably a guard there, so you'll have to wait until the coast is clear."

I saw her tilt her head in confusion, so I reworded my instructions. "Don't go in until it's safe, and you know you won't get caught. Here, use my knife to cut off the men's bindings. Make sure you tell Jody, that's the Big Red, and his son that I have a *well-stocked wagon* out front. They'll know what that means. Now, this is how it opens up."

I opened up the Leatherman and turned it back on itself to reveal the hidden blades. I debated on whether to show her how to use the wire-cutter feature. That might be too complicated for her. I used my thumbnail to pry the blade up so she could see where it was. "When you're ready, pull it out all the way. It'll lock in place."

I looked up at her face to make sure she understood. She understood, all right. She was about to receive a magnificent piece of equipment and probably thought it was magic. "It's Italian," I explained casually with a shrug of my shoulder.

"Oh, right," she said, nodding politely, but obviously unsure of what I meant. I put the multi-tool in her hand, and she straightened up with pride; she was going to help fight the British. "I can do this, I know I can. But how will I know when it's safe to get out of there?"

"Oh, I'll give a big signal. You just listen for a really loud noise, one like you've never heard before. When you hear it, run like hell. The men will be able to take care of themselves.

"Master Simon," I said as I put my hand on his back. I had true admiration for this man who was putting himself in harm's way for people I didn't even know if he knew. He looked at me with an open face, waiting for his orders, "as soon as you hear the noise, I would suggest you find a good place to hide."

It wasn't showtime yet, and we wouldn't be able to have a dress—or any other kind of—rehearsal for our performance. It was definitely time to set the stage and wire the props, though.

We had spaced the kegs about twenty yards apart. I found a soft spot for each one and quickly dug a hole, buried the keg, inserted the fuse, and covered it. If I couldn't bury it completely, I piled rocks or wood on top of it. I wasn't trying to disguise them—the kegs weren't going to be intact long enough for someone to find them. I needed the added mass for compression, though, so the explosions would be big, loud, and hopefully, distracting.

I heard voices down the road. One was Master Simon, talking slowly and stupidly. Well, at least slowly. I couldn't distinguish his words but could hear the soldier talking to him getting angry. "Spit it out, man," he hollered.

I didn't want to eavesdrop, especially when I realized that I recognized the voice. "It's just some soldier," I mumbled. "It could be someone else."

Yeah, right, I knew better but worked at securing my last bomb, focusing on the task before me rather than speculating as to who was at the mill. That's all I needed—another confrontation with Captain

Asshole.

I had precut all of the fuses on the wagon-ride in, each cord a little shorter than the one before it. This way, after they were inserted into the power kegs, I could light all of them at the same time, but they'd blow up sequentially. I was hoping for at least a two -minute delay between explosions.

"Thank you, Lord, for the lighter," I said softly as I finished lighting the last fuse. "You've given me the ideas, Lord, now if You would just help me execute them, I'd appreciate it. The ideas—not the people," I added to make sure He understood, "In Jesus's name, Amen."

I ran to my next assault position. I was hoping to do a little shock and awe. At least, those were the words that came to mind as I raced to my next site. I didn't know where that phrase came from, but it sounded like a good description for the misdirection I was trying to accomplish.

Sound is an amazing property. If done correctly, it can both reflect and be directed—just like light with a mirror. My plan was to do just this. Hopefully, I had all the factors figured correctly.

I stood behind my shield, a mammoth, odd-shaped boulder with a flat face. It was located at the edge of the clearing, about 100 yards away from the mill. The exterior wall of the building facing me had a tall, flat, uninterrupted surface. When the time came, this would be my sound mirror.

I could see and hear Simon pleading with a soldier. He was getting pretty good at playing dumb. I had had my doubts about his acting ability when we first got started. Now it sounded as if he was immersing himself in the role. "But I have to bring home the flour or my wife will beat me. Please, sir," he whined convincingly.

I dared to peek out and verify that this was indeed the evil Captain Asshole beleaguering our Master Simon. It wasn't. I must have imagined his voice. I knew fear played tricks with the mind, and I guessed mine had just been *abra cadabra'd*.

All of a sudden, we heard a big 'poof,' then the noise of rocks and pebbles raining down from the sky. It sounded like I didn't get that first charge packed tightly enough. Four of the Redcoats came out of the mill and looked down the road at the source of the commotion. They could see a big cloud of dust settling, but no people or animals.

I looked back toward the mill again and saw Jenny's blond hair move through the trees, but not the rest of her. Her little green calico smock was good camouflage. I probably should have covered her whole head. Fortunately, though, the soldiers were all focused on the unusual dusty apparition down the road. They hadn't seen the fair-haired waif running to the back of the building.

"Bang!" The second explosion made a much louder noise. Now two more soldiers came out to see what was going on. That meant that if Jenny really did see six new arrivals, and there were only three of them when she left, there were only two soldiers remaining inside.

I looked at Simon to see how he was reacting to the show. I was glad to see that he was still in character. He had pulled his hat off and was shading his eyes with it, peering off into the area of concern. Just then, a third blast went off, not quite as loud as the second, but much better than the first.

Evidently, three explosions were enough to get the soldiers to take action. I heard orders shouted like 'find out what's going on out there' and 'hurry up' and 'take corporal so and so with you.' Two men mounted up and rode out toward my little Gunpowder Park. It was at this point that the officer came outside.

Captain Asshole.

"Where are the men going?" he barked. "Who said they could leave?" He was angry and wanted answers right away.

"I sent the detail out to check on the source of the explosions, Captain. I'm Sergeant Josef Betz, and these are my men to command," was the quick and concise reply, spoken in a broad German accent by the stocky blonde non-com.

"They may be your men, but I am the superior officer here. You will do as *I* say! Now, I want the men sent out in twos. Take two and head that way, and two back behind, and two up there," he ordered and pointed right to where I was standing.

"Oh, shit," I mumbled and hoped another bomb would go off.

"Right. Now!" Captain Asshole screamed into the sergeant's face.

Sergeant Betz stood his ground, looked the captain right in the eyes, and sneered. "You are not my commanding officer, and my men will do as I tell them. Do you understand *me*?"

I got the feeling that Sergeant Betz believed that the captain was simply an asshole and not a captain of anything. I giggled at the exchange, and boy, was I sorry. No one had been talking, nor were bombs exploding, at that moment. It was dead calm except for the sound of my sniggering. I was sure I had been heard.

I pulled back to the other side of the rock, scurried into the wooded area, and hid behind a low-branched tree. I wanted to climb up and disappear into its lofty branches, but realized that once I was up there, I wouldn't be able to move laterally. I decided it would be better to stay low and mobile.

The captain strode right up to where I *had* been, then another bomb went off. That made four. I looked to the mill and saw Jenny run into the woods, followed by Jody, Wallace, and some of the other men. I needed to move, too, but my escape was cut off by the captain's advance.

Kerboom! Another one of my bombs exploded, and it was the biggest and loudest yet. I really felt the ground shake with that one. I looked back at the captain and saw him spin around, checking behind himself nervously. He acted as if he was being chased, but I think it was only his paranoia catching up with him.

The captain hadn't found me or anyone else, so retraced his steps, going back the same way he had come in. I threaded my way through the trees, making a big loop, and returned to my original location as he headed back toward the mill, his head jerking from right to left, looking for his transparent enemies.

Sergeant Betz and his four men had positioned themselves in front of the mill entrance, an apparent unwelcoming committee for the unpopular captain. It didn't seem to faze him, though; Captain Asshole strode right up to the sergeant. I couldn't see his face, but he was obviously angry by his gait. The sergeant's other men remained stone-faced and at attention. I think they believed that they were still guarding their prisoners: the rabble-rouser Jody Pomeroy and his cohorts. It was too bad—no, it was a good thing—that they hadn't gone inside and found out that all of their prisoners had escaped.

Oh, crap. Sergeant Betz was ignoring the captain's angry approach, turning away from a possible confrontation. He was leaving his men and heading back to the entrance of the mill. Shoot, why was he so smart?

I held my breath and squeezed my eyes shut as he walked through the front door, as if my not seeing what was going on would help. After a long minute and no yelling, I cautiously opened one eye to see the fuming sergeant exit the front door and march toward the captain. Both of my eyes popped open when I saw how mad he was. Sergeant Betz was moving sharply, as if his thigh muscles were made of thunderbolts. I was sure glad he wasn't coming at me!

The sergeant screamed in the captain's face, "You left the prisoners unguarded, and now they've escaped, you fool!"

The captain didn't back down an inch. He snorted and said, "Don't call me a fool, you kraut-eating son of Satan. I was left with only one man, and he just left for a minute to take a piss. I can't do everything by myself!" Apparently, the captain didn't care for people of German descent nor was he fond of being yelled at.

"He only left for a minute? And you didn't ask for a replacement or to be relieved? Don't you have any sense of protocol? I doubt you're even an officer. You are such an asshole!" The sergeant's face was ripe tomato red and looked like it was going to explode.

The sergeant was right, and the captain knew it. He wasn't going to admit it, though, especially since there were other soldiers watching the altercation. So the captain did about the only thing he could do under the circumstances. "Do *not* call me an asshole," he said low and threateningly.

The sergeant pulled himself as tall as his vertically-challenged body could, and glared back. What the man lacked in height, he more than made up for with intensity. "Ass. Hole," he said coldly and clearly, belittling his adversary in front of the other soldiers with the drawn out, emphatic word.

I was really getting into watching their little pissing contest, but before it could get any more intense, a soldier rode in at full speed. He stopped short, right in front of the two adversaries, his horse's hooves kicking up a thick cloud of dust that blocked my view. When the dirt settled, I saw that there was another rider right behind him, his hand atop the green bundle across his lap.

Jenny had been captured.

The first rider gave his report to the sergeant. "Just up the road, it looks like someone rigged six kegs of gunpowder to explode. There's still one left back there. I wasn't sure if it was going to blow up or not, so thought it best to leave it there." The soldier saw the look of scorn on the sergeant's face and added, "Best to leave it there until you told me what

76

you wanted done with it, Sergeant."

"We'll leave it there then," the sergeant agreed. "Did you see any sign of who might have done it?"

"No one was there, sir. But there were lots of footprints there at the site, and a wagon had stopped there recently. There were three sets of footprints including those of a barefoot small person. Apparently they unloaded the gunpowder from a wagon," he said, glancing over at Master Simon and the wagon as he finished his report. The sergeant also looked at the wagon and driver, but before he could say or do anything, a ruckus started.

"Let me go, you rotten Lobsterback!" The green package slung over the front of the other soldier's saddle suddenly burst into screaming, kicking, and writhing.

"Let me have her," ordered Captain Asshole as he strode over to the mounted soldier who was struggling to keep the little dynamo contained. "She's mine," he growled.

The sturdy sergeant stepped between the captain and the squirming young girl. "She is not yours. Here, put her down," he ordered the soldier, who was more than ready to be rid of her. He let loose of her wrists, and Jenny immediately fell to the ground, landing hard on her bottom. The sergeant stepped up to her and congenially offered his hand to help her to her feet.

"Thank you," she said courteously as she rearranged her makeshift dress, shifting it around to re-cover her partially exposed body. She looked over at the captain, sneered, and covertly stuck her tongue out at him. She then turned around to face the sergeant, sporting a sweet smile to match her now polite and ladylike behavior.

"You little bitch!" the captain screamed and grabbed for her.

The sergeant picked her up by the armpits and swung her away, out of the captain's reach. "Men, restrain the captain," he ordered. He set her down and turned back to address the officer held in check. "I think you have forgotten what your mission is," he paused then added, "S*ir*."

Two of the foot soldiers approached to apprehend him, but he ducked and spun around, grabbing Jenny by the hair as he did so. He yanked her hair so hard, he pulled her off her feet, tugging her into his grasp like a trout on a fly line. He held her close and high, so her feet couldn't touch the ground, his inner elbow clamped around her neck. He clutched her so tightly that her face began to turn scarlet. Her little hands clawed at his sleeve, futilely trying to penetrate the thick cloth to get to his skin. She was kicking with the fury of a newly branded mule, but to no effect. She was barefoot, and although she may have inflicted some minor bruising to his shins, the captain was oblivious of anything but keeping her away from the good sergeant and his men.

"Let her go," the sergeant said calmly. "We have a job to do, and she will only be in the way."

Captain Asshole felt her body go slack—she was as limp as a rag doll. He lessened his chokehold to let her get a breath. He didn't want to kill her. Yet. He knew she was either unconscious or pretending to be.

Jenny took a couple of shallow breaths, and then I saw her body tense.

Evidently, the captain felt the change because he resumed his iron-armed hold on her…but not before she had moved her head enough that she could sink her teeth into his bare hand. She wasn't loosening her bite, either. He released his chokehold, and was now batting at her head, using one hand to try to knock her off the other. That didn't work, so he literally swung her away from his body, pivoting in a tight circle, causing her body to fly away from him as if she were on a carnival ride. Even the centrifugal force of her own body weight wasn't enough to cause the little viper to let go, though. Captain Asshole stopped the flinging, reached down, and grabbed the knife out of his boot. "Bite this!" he yelled as he brought the blade to a spot just under her left ear, piercing her skin.

I saw the flow of blood from where I was but didn't know what I could do. I had no idea if Jody and his crew had had a chance to get to the rifles in the wagon yet. This wasn't the distraction that I had planned.

Distraction! That was it! Now was the time!

I squatted down in front of my broad-faced rock pillar and pulled out the smartphone. It was fully charged. I had made sure of it by covertly placing it in the sunlight on the ride in. I pressed the little treble cleft button and the screen lit up. I found the little American flag emblem and tapped on it once. I slid the volume bar all the way to the right, tapped the icon of the fuzzy-haired hippie twice, and set the phone on its little rock stand.

The blare of 'The Star-Spangled Banner' *ala* Woodstock was

deafening to me, and I was off to the side of the speakers with rock amplifiers, not getting the complete effect of the full-tilt volume like those in front of me.

My plan worked. Everyone in the mill are'na was covering his ears and looking at the wall that seemed to be the source of the alien noise, the sound of an electric guitar being put through its paces by the master musician and former US Airborne paratrooper, Jimi Hendrix. Even the captain had loosed his grip on Jenny and dropped his knife away from her neck, at least for a second.

Jenny hadn't been distracted, though. She had been expecting a sound like she had never heard before and had taken advantage of the captain's diversion—she was now running, hauling butt away from the area at top speed.

I looked up and saw Clyde running in to intercept his little sister. Talk about mixed emotions. I was glad she had a protector, but the sight of him still made my stomach churn. It was a gut reaction I had to shut down. I was not willing nor wanting to deal with those feelings now or ever. I scanned the area and saw Jody and Wallace running for the soldiers' horses. My men each had a rifle, and it looked as if they were planning on cutting off the captain's retreat.

Master Simon had wasted no time in leaving. He was already heading back down the road we had come in on. I didn't see anyone else I knew, though, and that worried me. Then again, if I didn't see them, nobody else did either.

But it was too good to be true. One lone soldier was leading Mac and Julian in at gunpoint. Or I guessed that would be at musket muzzle. Either way, they were captured and definitely in harm's way. I didn't recognize the soldier, and then realized that this must be the one who was inside with Captain Asshole and had disappeared to take a leak while on watch. One of Sergeant Betz's men came up beside him to share the captors' duty, so now they each had a prisoner.

At this point, I decided to turn off the noise and listen to the proceedings. Everyone stopped at the sudden sound of silence and looked around, but no one commented. I couldn't help but wonder if they all thought that they had been hallucinating.

Sergeant Betz straightened his shoulders and walked up to the prisoners. "Who are you?" he asked of Mac first.

"Mac Donaldson, sir. I was just here to pick up some flour, when this man," he turned his head back to indicate the first restraining soldier, "and this, this thing in a uniform," he nodded at the captain, "detained me and my neighbors without cause."

Sergeant Betz let a minor smile sneak across his face at the description of Captain Asshole. The prisoner had enough smarts not to call the captain a derogatory name in front of his vanquisher. "And who are you?" he asked Julian.

"My name is Julian Hart, and I am visiting friends and family in the area. I, too, have been detained without cause." Julian's hands were still tied, and it looked as if they had been bound for a long time. They were swollen and deep purple, and if someone didn't remove the bindings soon, it looked as if his hands would fall off.

The sergeant saw his hands, too. "Cut him loose," he commanded the errant soldier. The soldier just looked at him as if he had heard a noise but wasn't sure what it was. I didn't think he wanted to take orders from him.

That didn't sit well with Sergeant Betz. He huffed and strode over to Julian, unsheathed his own knife, and cut the bands off of Julian's hands himself. He looked Julian in the eye—to make sure he was okay, I think—and then flashed recognition. I noticed he recovered quickly, and if Julian had seen it, he didn't react to it. The sergeant looked at Mac's hands and saw that he wasn't bound. He continued with his interrogation.

"By what right are you detaining these men, soldier?" he asked.

The still-nameless soldier looked to the captain for direction. The captain, his child-bitten and bloodied hand held close to his chest, strode over, eyes afire as if he was going to enjoy this confrontation. "This man, *sergeant*," he spat out the title with intense disgust, "is a deserter from His Majesty's Service. He is to be brought in and tried for treason." His smug smile was more tactless than scary.

I had the distinct impression that he was bluffing. Julian certainly didn't look threatened by the accusation. He turned to face the captain with an incredulous look on his face. "What?" was all he said, but with complete innocence. Julian was making his accuser squirm and fidget with his complete lack of distress and fear. Even though his face didn't show it, I was sure Julian was enjoying his captor's backfired ploy. Now I was positive that the captain was bluffing.

The sergeant saw the accusation as a sham, too, and came to the rescue. "I don't think that good manners and proper speech are an indication of either enlistment with or desertion from His Majesty's Service. Are you a deserter, sir?" the sergeant asked Julian with a gleam in his eye.

"No, sir, I am not," replied Julian.

Julian wasn't lying. I remembered him saying that he had just chosen his own retirement time, not deserted. He was answering like the honest and respectable gentleman he was.

"And are you a deserter?" he asked Mac, not even trying to hide the capricious grin on his face.

"No, sir, I am not," replied Mac, using the same words and intonation as Julian had. I could just hear him *not* saying the words 'I wouldn't be a part of your stinkin' army, no way, no how!' but the insinuation of the sentiment was flashing like a neon sign in his eyes.

The sergeant looked as if he was getting ready to dismiss the two prisoners when Captain Asshole spoke up, very dryly. "Then you wouldn't be interested in the reward for catching their friend, the Big Red, then?"

Sergeant Betz glared at him, almost daring him to try and pull a fast one on him, but the captain remained stoic.

None of us in our little community had ever heard of a reward for Jody. He was sometimes a nuisance, but the few British soldiers who were left in the area had pretty much turned a blind eye when Jody took to his patriotic preaching. The British were employing the divide-and-conquer tactic, fighting two distinct campaigns. Most of the battles were being fought either further south or far north of us. That left North Carolina as an area of little interest. The local civil disobedience was so minor that it was easier to ignore it than to respond to it.

The sergeant looked to Julian for his reaction to the reward rumor. I was beginning to believe that these two had a history. Julian's eyes made the slightest twitch indicating the falsehood of the captain's accusation.

The sergeant had seen and believed the answer in Julian's eyes and decided to run with it. Now it was time for him to spin his own web of deception. He walked in a circle around the prisoners and the two soldiers, as if he were pondering his next chess move. "Oh, *that* reward," he deadpanned. "Yes, I did hear that they were paying for the capture of seditious traitors. However, they stopped having any interest in them quite a while back. They are more interested now in catching that scoundrel wearing a British officer's uniform who has been traveling through the area, illegally collecting taxes, and then keeping them for himself. Come to think of it, you fit his description. What unit did you say you were attached to, *sir*?"

Captain Asshole squirmed, chewed his bottom lip, preparing his answer, but before he could reply, Wallace walked out of the woods. All eyes were on the tall, striking young man entering the field of fallacies and fabrications. He stopped ten feet away from the thief who had not only misrepresented himself as a British captain and tax collector, but who had also held him at knifepoint in front of his fiancée.

"Have you turned over the taxes that you extorted from us," Wallace asked as he sauntered in closer, his eyes squinted in an intimidating scowl, until he was two feet away, "or have you decided to keep them for yourself?" Quick as a rattlesnake, Wallace reached out and jerked the gold nugget necklace from around the captain's neck that had been hidden, tucked under his stock, but had fallen out and become visible during his skirmish with Jenny the biter.

The captain lunged forward to take back the necklace, but Wallace took a step to the side, and the thief stumbled forward, landing right in the middle of Jody's chest. "Ach, taxman, are ye?" Jody asked. "Here," he said, and launched an uppercut, landing his fist squarely on the bottom of the captain's chin, knocking him to the ground, senseless. "That's fer hittin' the lass."

Jenny ran up to the prone, momentarily incapacitated molester, and kicked him hard in the head. "Yeah, and this is for hitting Big Red."

"Here, here," the sergeant said, arms spread out defensively, trying to bring order to the mini melee and keep more blows from being struck. "Miss, don't kick a man when he's down, *verstehst?* It is very unladylike. Besides, I think he's had enough."

Sergeant Betz called over four of his men, and then turned his attention to Wallace and Jody. "Is this the man who has been taking goods from the local residents under the guise of a tax for His Majesty?"

Before Wallace could give an affirmative answer, Captain Asshole, flat on his back, sprawled out like a snow angel on a dirt canvas, screamed, "He's lying." He rolled over and scrambled to bring his knees beneath him, so he could stand and face his accuser with some trace of dignity.

But it was too late for that. A quick scan of the gathering crowd showed that all the soldiers were disgusted with him. It was time for a plan B. Captain Asshole looked over and saw that his quick-thinking cohort had come from the back of the group and grabbed little Jenny and was twisting her arm up behind her back.

"Well, I think I'll leave you all to finish this party by yourselves," the captain said as he picked up his black silk-trimmed tricorn hat from the ground, knocking the dust from it onto his britches. He walked tall, full of self-assurance, toward the little beauty, and the beast who had her contorted into submission.

Well, sort of submission. He was controlling her like a marionette by her left arm, but he couldn't control her mouth. "Let go of me, you rotten pig fornicator! I'll have my brothers cut out your liver and eat it for supper, you no-good privy dweller!"

Captain Asshole walked up to her and, without even pausing, swatted her across the face, and continued his trek to the horses. "Let's go, Ronald," he said, "and for God's sake, keep that little bitch quiet!" Then he stopped, waited a moment as if he were making a decision, and turned to face all the soldiers who were standing with the sergeant.

"Any man here who is tired of not getting paid by His Majesty, you're welcome to come with us. There's a lot to be had out there in the way of taxes. Just grab your horse and follow along."

I noticed two of the sergeant's men looking at each other, eyebrows raised, silently deciding to take the offer. I didn't know times were tough for the British, too. I thought the Americans were the only ones starving. They both shouldered their muskets and walked toward their horses.

"Ain't someone gonna do somethin'?" a voice shouted from the back of the mill. It looked like a two-headed monster rushing in to the commotion. It was Clyde, and he was holding up Clayton—or they were holding each other up. Panicked, they were running up to the sergeant like two men in a three-legged race.

"Halt!" the sergeant called to the deserters and the kidnapping thieves who were hauling away Jenny. The erstwhile soldiers ignored his command. They kept walking, not even turning around, confident that they carried the 'get out of trouble free' ticket.

"Take aim, men," the sergeant ordered his remaining squad. They fixed their rifles on the captain and his crew, and waited for their next command.

Captain Asshole stopped and turned to face the militia. Ronald stopped too, his fist held high, still wrapped around Jenny's wrist, controlling her by her dislocated arm. She was in pain, had to be by the way she was almost turned upside down by her captor. Her jaws were clenched in hatred, and tears streaked through the dirt on her face, but there was no sobbing. Her eyes—squinted tight and thin—glared at Private Ronald. She was a time bomb ready to explode.

I was still watching the proceedings from the patch of woods across the way. Wallace, Jody, and Julian were gone—or at least weren't visible. All I could see was the standoff between the sergeant and his loyal men, and the cowards, ready to mount their steeds to unimpeded freedom and larceny. Captain Asshole grabbed Jenny from Ronald. "Go ahead; I'll catch up with you in a minute. This won't take long."

The captain had grabbed Jenny's uninjured arm. He was holding it up and back high behind her, her other arm now hanging limp and useless at her side. "If you want to see her again—alive that is—you'll let us go and not follow." His grinning, greasy face reflected the bloated pride he had in his blank check. He was going to have his freedom and be able to do whatever he wanted with the little girl.

Bang! Bang! Bang! I changed my focus from her to the shots being fired. Evidently the sergeant didn't take too kindly to his men deserting. His remaining soldiers were shooting at the deserters as they tried to get to their horses. I turned back and saw the captain running to join them, dragging the uncooperative and cursing Jenny behind him. He stopped, though, when he heard a voice call out.

Wallace's voice boomed, "Runnin' away like a sissy, are ye?"

I noticed that he had assumed the Highland accent, and then realized why. He was in warrior mode.

I didn't want to think it was vengeance, but it could have been. I preferred to think that it was the fighting Pomeroy blood rising in response to the stimulus of the battle. His fathers and an innocent—weren't they all at that age?—little girl had just been attacked. That would be enough to call up those hormones—or whatever they were. If it had only been pride calling, and he was still angry about being

84

humiliated when the taxman had come to call… Well, I just couldn't believe that's what it was. I knew he was more of a man than that.

Wallace and the captain were the center of everyone's attention now. But what were they going to do? Fight hand to hand? Neither one was armed, as far I could see. The captain's boot knife was still lying on the ground where he had dropped it earlier, when Jimi Hendrix had come to Jenny's rescue. I scanned the trees and saw the flash of a rifle barrel, then another one. It appeared that Julian and Jody had Wallace's back. I'd have to remember later to tell them to put soot on their sights and barrels, so they didn't reflect light.

"Did your wife let you go out all by yourself? Or is she back there," the captain asked, cocking his head to where I was, "making sure you don't do anything to embarrass her? Oh, she's a pretty one, all right, but a little old for my tastes."

He had to be bluffing about knowing where I was. I doubted that he knew I had left our house, much less that I was anywhere near here.

Wallace was grim, and hopefully he wasn't letting the taunts get under his skin. "Let the lass go," he said, his voice low, slow, and commanding. Then he suddenly growled, "Now!" startling everyone.

All but the captain. He was too sure of himself to heed the order from the young, apparently non-military male. "Oh, you want a little of this, do you?" he taunted as he pulled on Jenny's arm, causing her to let out an unintentional squeak. "I don't think so. She's mine, and she's coming with me. And if you try to get her, I'll let you have her, all right. You can have her a little bit at a time." He sneered as he tilted his leg sideways to show off the knife in his other boot. "She won't need all her fingers or toes for what I want her for. Which end do you want me to start on?"

It was now time…time for the second, and hopefully the last, act of this drama. I had no way of knowing whether this would be a victory or a tragedy, but I couldn't stand by and let him take her. A finger slide, a couple of taps, a fast forward, and then the sky was singing, "And I'm proud to be an American, where at least I know I'm free," voiced by 21st century singer Lee Greenwood.

This time there were words, very loud, clear, passionate, and meaningful words, and not just strange noises, coming from the side of the mill. Jenny took advantage of the captain's momentary shock and slackened arm and did a pirouette to face her captor. She pulled back, and with every pound of her body and ton of her anger, head-butted him right in the crotch. He reflexively let go of her hand and grabbed his jewels while she ducked and ran like a rabbit from a fox.

At first, she headed toward the sergeant and his men. Then she saw her brothers pointing towards an opening in the woods. She veered left and took off in that direction, her green calico smock twisted and flying loose, like the tail of a kite.

The words 'God bless the U S AAAay' were now blaring, but the captain was oblivious to everything and everyone around him. He was determined that he would have the little spitfire, Jenny. He gingerly regained his posture and, with eyes focused on his target, began half-limping, half-running toward the fleeing girl. He was obsessed with her, and not even the presence of muskets, men, and loud music distracted him. Jenny tripped on the front of her frock and stumbled, slowing her pace in order to find her feet. "Stop right there," he yelled at her.

Yeah, right, as if she would even consider listening to what he told her to do. I reached over and turned off the music, which was now distracting me in a negative way, and put the smartphone/media player contraption back into my pocket.

I saw the whole scene opening in front of me. The captain was zeroing in on her, like a hawk on a field mouse. She was back on her feet and shifting her weight, side-to-side, trying to decide which was the best escape route. Jody was coming in with nothing but his dirk from the left, and Clyde was running interception from the right. Jenny didn't see Clyde, so ran towards Jody.

Captain Asshole stopped, coolly and vindictively, pulled his silver pistol from his belt, held it over his forearm. Aimed. And fired.

Jody clutched Jenny to his chest. They dropped to the ground just as Clyde lunged out in front of them. All three bodies hit the earth at once.

One shot had been fired, but none of us knew who—if anyone—had been hit. Jody sat up, checked to make sure they were safe, and then unfolded his arms carefully. He looked down to see if Jenny had been hurt. She gazed up at her protector, marveling at his size and closeness, and then turned and saw her brother.

She hadn't seen Clyde leap in front of the shot—she had been enveloped in Jody's arms at the time—but she saw him now, flat on his back, lying still, eyes to heaven.

Blood was gushing out of her brother's neck. She rushed to him, put her hands on the bloody hole, and screamed, "No, no, no! Stop bleeding, you gotta stop!"

His whole bearing changed the moment he saw his little sister above him, working fervently to stop the inevitable. Clyde's pain and anxiety were replaced by pure love.

"No, you can't die, no!" she kept screaming. But it was already too late. The blood had stopped spurting, but only because his heart had stopped beating. Jody came to her side and gently turned her so she wasn't looking into her dead brother's face. He bent down and shut the eyelids that had been staring out in peace, the slight smile frozen on his face.

The captain hadn't moved, but Jody made sure that Jenny stayed behind him, out of the monster's reach. He looked beyond the captain and saw the sergeant approaching with his men.

Sergeant Betz walked up to the scene and glared at the erstwhile captain, who was checking his pistol, looking at the sight, then down the muzzle, frowning, as if there were gremlins inside.

"Who *are* you?" the sergeant asked, holding his potential captive with his gaze.

"I am Captain Atholl MacLeod of His Majesty's Secret Service," he replied. "Now, if you will let me pass, I have work to do," and took steps to leave.

"His Majesty's Secret Service? There is no such division," the sergeant said, and stepped in front of the captain, blocking his retreat. "You know, you really should learn how to lie better if you plan on continuing this ruse. No, on second thought, I don't think you need to expend the effort. You're heading to the gallows. Right. Now." The sergeant turned at the waist, called, "Men," and motioned for his soldiers to apprehend the shooter.

Suddenly, a horrific wail came from the lifeless form of Clyde. It wasn't Clyde, though; it was Clayton. While all the posturing of the captain, the sergeant, and his men had been transpiring, Clayton had come out to mourn his brother, and had been crying softly over his body. But now he was back in the world of the living, and aware of what was going on. His little sister had been assaulted, kidnapped, and nearly raped by their brother's murderer. His rage was at critical mass, and I could see that a nuclear explosion was imminent.

"Aarrggh!" Clayton's cry of vengeance was worthy of any Highlander. But his wisdom of attacking an armed man with nothing but his bare hands was classically stupid Clayton. He pushed Jody and Jenny clear, and charged the captain, tackling his brother's murderer to the ground. He glanced back to make sure that his sister was okay, then pinned the captain's shoulders down and bit off a chunk of his ear. Or maybe he bit off the whole thing if what I saw was the entire appendage being spit out. Either way, Clayton was going back for more.

But Jenny didn't want to be out of the way. She wanted payback, too, and didn't want a champion—she wanted to do it herself. She picked herself up off the ground, and was ready to jump into the fray, when Wallace ordered, "You! Stay!"

She looked up, saw the fire in his eyes, and that long arm pointing at her to remain where she was, and—I was both stunned and happy to see—she stayed put.

Clayton and the captain rolled around on the ground—kicking, scratching, and generally fighting clumsily, but fervently. The captain fumbled for his knife while Clayton, ugh, tried to bite off the man's nose.

Wallace loomed over the wrestling duo, and I thought for sure he was going to break them apart, but he just stayed off to the side, letting the two men beat on each other. He remained neutral, only observing the row—except for the one time he kicked the knife out of the captain's hand.

After ten minutes, it was becoming obvious that both of the combatants were tiring. "Break it up," Wallace said, "he's had enough."

"Yeah, he's beat, and you're next," the captain hissed breathlessly. "Coward."

"I was talking about you, asshole," Wallace replied coolly, looking down at the bloody and beaten pseudo-captain lying on the ground, his child-bitten left hand cradling the spot on the side of his head that used to sport an ear. Wallace glanced up and saw the sergeant observing his four men bringing in the three rogue soldiers. "Sergeant, here's another one for you," he called.

I turned around and saw Sarah rushing toward the wounded, gathering her skirts with one hand, carrying her little black medical bag in the other. It seemed silly to follow her, but I felt as if I needed to protect her, even though there were now half a dozen men fully capable of doing that. I patted my pockets, made sure I had everything I came with, and followed behind her.

Sarah nodded to Wallace and Jody, letting them know that she could handle this. "Sergeant, I'm a healer, and I would like to tend to the, er," she cleared her throat as she tried to assign a name to the phony captain, "the, er, *man's* wounds. I wouldn't want them to get infected."

"Infected? You mean red and full of pus, fevered? I don't see how that will make any difference. He'll probably be hanged in a couple days anyway." The sergeant saw Sarah getting ready to protest, so acquiesced. "Go ahead and see to him if it makes you feel better. Personally, I think he got off easy. You should have let him finish chewing off body parts," he said as he looked over at Wallace. Wallace shrugged his shoulder and escorted Sarah to the captain, still lying on his side.

I hung back; I really didn't want to get too close to that ugly sack of cells with opposable thumbs. Just looking at him literally made my skin crawl. I never knew what that phrase meant until I saw him clutching at Jenny. Ugh, there it goes again. Memo to self: do not think of Captain Asshole ever again, or the sensation of centipede legs marching over limbs and belly will ensue.

Sarah quickly set to her task, focusing on the captain's wounds, totally ignoring Wallace, the sergeant, and the rest of the contingent of good and bad Redcoats. "I want to clean and bandage that hand and ear before you leave. There's no telling if they'll find someone else to take care of it," she said to her patient.

Jenny. I looked up and saw her holding, clutching, Clayton to her chest. She was trying to smooth out his wild hair and was crying. I didn't know whether it was from sorrow about Clyde's death or relief that this incident was over. I wanted to make sure she was okay, but I definitely didn't want to intrude on their private moment. I knew that the brothers were close—ugh, too close—but didn't know much about her. From the fuss she was making about his appearance and comfort, I'd say she was the parent in the relationship.

"I need some water," Sarah said.

"I'll get some for you," I offered.

"There's an empty bucket on the porch," the sergeant told me.

On my way over, I saw that Jody had joined Jenny and Clayton. They were all kneeling beside Clyde's body, and it looked as if Jody was saying a prayer. Wallace was not going near them, and I could understand why on more than one level. He left to go stand with Mac Donaldson and the other man. I passed them on the way to the well. "Are you all right?" I asked.

"Jest a little bruised dignity is all," said Mac. "This is my brother-in-law, Todd Gillespie," he said. We both nodded and smiled.

"Nice to meet you, Todd. Mac, the girls will sure be happy to see you. Everybody is at our place. They came for the wedding. Oh shoot, I have to get water for Sarah. Bye!"

I literally ran to get the water, hoping the tears wouldn't have a chance to catch up with me. "Yeah, wonderful *effin'* wedding day," I grumbled as I filled the pail with water.

I had to get back to Sarah soon, but since it was only to 'help' that creep, I didn't feel as if I should hurry. Besides, I couldn't run with the bucket full of water, so I walked slowly, taking the opportunity to calm down and think about what had just happened.

I still had a groom-to-be, and it could have turned out worse. I looked around at the minimal mess that had ensued. No one in my family had been injured, the phony taxman captain had been apprehended, and Jenny had been saved from the paws of that sadistic pervert. I guessed as dramatic as everything was today, I really hadn't sustained any losses. Maybe we could get home in time for a nighttime wedding. A preacher and plenty of witnesses were already on hand, waiting for us to come back. Yes, it had turned out okay, but I was still pissed off at having to go through all this drama just because of one rotten, greedy asshole!

Oh, Lord. Jenny. I have been so absorbed with how this has impacted me and my wedding day that I haven't even thought about her. She just lost her brother. She still has one more, and I'm sure they'll be fine, but still, darn it, no one needed to die today!

I returned to Sarah with the bucket full of water and a gut full of rage. If she had heard me coming up, she didn't acknowledge it. Her back was to me. She was seated on the ground next to the captain and had already bandaged his hand. By the lack of color in his face, she had used her alcohol blend as the disinfectant. He started to turn his head away so she could assess the damage to where his ear used to be but paused long enough to snort with disdain as he glanced up at me.

My anger flared up again—actually exploded—and I lost control. "Here, let me help," I growled, and impulsively threw half a bucket of water at the captain's head.

The captain bolted upright and grabbed Sarah, all in the same efficient movement, as if he had already had it planned out.

"Oh, shit," I said. I started to set the bucket down but stopped midway when I saw them. The sergeant was coming in, his musket raised, ready to fire. Wallace was racing past him, warrior scowl set, dirk blade shining—it was much scarier than the black powder contraption the sergeant had. I glanced to where Jody had been and saw that he and Clayton were sprinting towards us, too. My spiteful, extemporaneous water toss had just started extreme drama act number three. When would I learn to think before acting!

"I'm sorry, I'm sorry," I said frantically, but I could see it didn't make a difference to the captain. He was purple-faced and furious!

But Sarah was cool, inexplicably mellow for the situation she was in, and then I noticed why—she had a scalpel in her hand. Unfortunately, she didn't know that Captain Asshole had his hand on the pistol in his belt.

I gulped in a quart of courage and changed my attitude right away. "Where did you get that?" I asked and nodded to the pistol, both as a diversion and to let Sarah know that she was under-armed. I could also see Jody approaching in my peripheral vision and wanted him to be able to get closer.

"Oh, our little sauerkraut-sucking sergeant isn't as bright as he thinks. I'll bet he keeps his pistol loaded, right?" he asked, turning around to glare at the sergeant.

Sergeant Betz looked down at his belt and saw that his pistol was missing. The color left his face. He didn't have to say that the pistol was loaded. It showed. "Uh, I'm sorry, miss, ma'am…"

"Ah, don't worry about it, Sarge. I was just waiting for the good missus to finish the bandaging before I took off. Too bad the other one wasn't closer, though. I would have had fun with her, even if she is a bit old," he said, looking straight at me.

I was terrified for the first time today. I had run out of gunpowder and gimmicks and didn't know what to do. I felt deflated, like an empty sack, without substance. Whether this scenario would have played out the same way without my water toss or not, I still felt guilty. Then I remembered the phrase, 'When it doubt, call out.'

Call out to the Man.

And so I did. My heart prayed fervently, but a mumbled, "Help us, Lord," was all I could get out past my lips.

"Oh, so you're one of those religious sorts, are you? I hear they're the lustiest ones. Being repressed all day makes the activities at night much more fun—right, big boy?" he asked Wallace.

Wallace glowered as he slowly walked towards him, ready to put him in his place. Sarah shouted, "Get back," and he froze.

"Oh, so I see you always mind the womenfolk. You have *got* to be the biggest sissy I have ever seen."

Wallace's face turned scarlet, but he breathed slowly and deeply, rearranging the rage within him. Two breaths later, he was totally cool and composed. He grinned as he bragged, "At least I have women in my life who are worthy of listening to."

The captain didn't say a word, but jerked Sarah closer to him and growled, reminding us that he was the one with the hostage.

Wallace's tone and expression quickly changed to that of someone I didn't know: a teasing, cocky, barroom jackass. "What, you don't have a woman? Even your own mother wants nothing to do with you? You have to pay the whores twice the rate, and still they balk. You can't even get one to dance with you? You rob and pillage for months on end, yet can never get enough money for one to sleep with you?"

Now it was time for the captain to turn red. His mouth opened and shut, trying to find words to contradict the accusations, but "Shut up!" was all he managed to say. He shifted his weight, pulling Sarah up with him, clumsily getting to his feet. "Where's your God now, little missy?" he snarled at me.

"Look! Ducks!" Wallace yelled and pointed to a totally empty area in the sky.

It was a totally irrational call, but the ploy worked. The captain dropped his guard, looked up, and Wallace dived in. He wrapped his body around Sarah and rolled away from the kidnapper, depositing her on the ground next to me and the dumbfounded sergeant.

Wallace stood up, casually brushed off his trousers with one hand,

and brandished a shiny pistol with the other, turning it so the sunlight caught its barrel, but keeping it pointed at the captain's chest.

The captain looked down and saw that he was missing his weapon. Wallace grinned at him, "Look familiar?" he asked as he turned it over in his hand. He had not only rescued Sarah, he had grabbed the pistol out of the man's hand in the process.

"Not bad, not bad," the captain replied with a nod of agreement. "But you always should have a backup," he purred, then swiftly drew a pistol from the back of his waistband and fired it right at Sarah.

I saw the intent of his movement and lunged out in front of her, my arms spread wide in the classic gesture of maternal protection.

The musket ball caught me in the left shoulder. I felt an explosion of fiery pain near my heart, and then my whole world was bright white light with no definition.

***

Wallace reached for Evie, and Jody went for his wife. "Get him!" Sarah shouted, pointing at Captain Asshole. She didn't believe in killing people, but Sarah didn't want to let her good-sister's shooter—oh, God don't let him be her assassin—go free. Jody scanned Sarah, made sure she was unhurt, and then joined Wallace in the pursuit of the assailant.

Captain Asshole didn't have a chance of escaping. His four strides were Wallace's two, and he was overtaken even before he had a chance to consider his destination. Wallace stopped right in front of him, blocking his escape. A second later, the sergeant joined them. The captain emitted a nervous laugh when he saw he was both outnumbered and out-weaponed.

"Here, I think this is yours," Wallace said and handed the sergeant his pistol, never taking his eyes from his prisoner.

Captain Asshole studied his options. The pistol he had shot the healer with was spent. The sergeant had his own weapon back now and was already heading back to his men. The big, red-headed man was with the healer, tending to the sassy woman he had shot, and the big sissy in front of him appeared to have dropped his dirk in the chase. No one could hurt him now; he was almost home free. He snorted and looked up at Wallace. "I don't see how you could stand her. She was such a mouthy bitch…"

Wallace swept his boot out in front of him and took the feet right out from underneath the foul-mouthed fiend. The captain landed with a thud, flat on his back. Wallace stood above him, his foot held firmly on the culprit's larynx. "You know, I could fix that rude language of yours. One crunch," he pushed a quick pulse to the voice box, "and you'd never be able to talk, or even whisper, any of your curses or insults again. Or just a bit more pressure," he applied substantially more pressure and held it there, "and your throat would swell shut. You'd die a slow and painful death. Asphyxiation is quite unpleasant, I hear."

Wallace took his foot off the captain's throat, and then offered him his hand. The captain looked at it suspiciously but took it. Wallace pulled him up to his feet, and then quickly twisted his hand up behind his back, turning the captain's arm around so severely that he bent forward, and was nearly standing on his head.

"You know, my fiancée was a very smart woman, and she said that what goes around, comes around." Wallace yanked up so hard on the man's splay-fingered hand that the captain squealed like a piglet and pissed his pants.

"Have mercy! Doesn't your God say you should have mercy?" cried the teary, snot-faced, one-eared monster of a man.

"Aye, He does," sighed Wallace, his shoulders slumped in resignation. "Sergeant, would you please tie up this man and get rid of him?"

As soon as Wallace loosened his grip, the captain snapped back into attack mode. He had hidden one of Sarah's scalpels in his boot. He grabbed the razor-sharp implement and slashed at Wallace's face, aiming for his eyes.

Wallace stepped back from the assault, untouched. "Mercy's done, Asshole!" he growled, then shouted, "*Manu Forti!*" He brought up both fists and quickly spread them out, breaking his assailant's forward attack. One quick uppercut and the scalpel flew into the air, landing far beyond either one's reach. Jenny ran over, picked it up, and held on to it.

Wallace could have knocked out the phony captain in two punches, but drew out the punishment, savoring each well-calculated, painful blow, ignoring the bruising of his own fists.

One two, one two. Wallace was bashing the captain's face beyond recognition with bare-knuckle boxing combinations. The soldiers and most of the men from the mill gathered around the combatants and were urging Wallace to 'hit 'im again.'

But one man watched quietly, waiting for an opportunity to make his way into the are'na. Ronald—the captain's right-hand man—had been detained by the soldiers earlier but had managed to slip away from his guards when the confusion began. He had procured a rifle, but the weapon was empty, and he couldn't find any ammunition to reload it. He decided he'd avenge his captain's beatings with what he had, though: the gun's bayonet. The big, tall, quiet one who was now pummeling his boss wasn't going to die quickly or quietly. Gut stuck was a horrible way to die, and that was how he would take him out.

The watcher had a watcher. Clayton had been following Ronald's movements all afternoon with the intention of killing him as soon as he was away from the soldiers. This man had slapped, twisted, and dragged about his little sister just moments ago, and would have raped her earlier today if it hadn't been for her quick thinking and still quicker feet.

Rape. He had never thought of rape as a personal thing. It was just sex, a form of pleasure—or so he believed. It was true that he and his brother got carried away with Wallace months ago and, although it was fun at the time, they both realized after the incident that it probably hadn't been a good idea. When he saw the way the captain and Ronald had looked at, pawed at, and lusted after his little sister, unwanted sexual attention took on a completely different meaning. It wasn't fun for her, and if it wasn't good for both people, then it wasn't good. Period. All of a sudden, he had intense remorse for the attack on Wallace, this man who today had defended his little sister.

Clayton watched as Ronald began to move amongst the crowd, making his way toward Jenny. He flashed anger, hatred, and revenge— all at the same time. Clayton hadn't come unarmed this time. He had taken a long knife from the wall of the mill. He worked his way around the circle of men to get near Ronald. Maybe he could stab him when no one was looking.

"Hit 'im again, hit 'im again, harder, harder," the crowd chanted. Clayton took his eyes off Ronald momentarily to watch Wallace the punisher wail on his brother's murderer. He grinned. He was glad that the big man was relentless with his pounding on the man who had caused his family so much sorrow. He glanced back just as Ronald lunged forward into the brawl, his bayonet drawn, targeted on Wallace.

Clayton instinctively jumped in front of Wallace, the intended victim, his sister's protector and avenger. He defended him, retaliating by thrusting his own purloined long knife deep into the would-be assailant's belly.

In a bizarre twist of fate, the same man who had raped him months earlier saved Wallace from a potentially mortal assault. But the protection had come at the ultimate price for the defender.

"Arrgh!" Wallace didn't stop the pummeling when he heard two men scream in combat behind him. The sounds of bellies being punctured could have been birds flying overhead. He was focused on his task—the punishment of the man who had killed his fiancée—and nothing else mattered.

Two bodies fell onto Wallace just as he threw his last punch. He didn't let it distract him, but merely moved aside to let them fall, never taking his eyes off of Captain Asshole. He grimaced; he had lost control of his temper, and it would be a long time—if ever—before the captain's face looked like it had even an hour earlier. He took a deep breath of regret, then realized it was a moot point. The man was due to be hanged for murder, insurrection, and illegally taking taxes in the name of the King—and then, in ultimate stupidity, keeping the loot.

Lost in his own reflections of remorse for losing control, Wallace suddenly realized that there was a commotion around him, and it didn't concern him or the beaten prisoner. He kicked over the unconscious captain so he didn't have to look at his mashed and bloody face, and saw the two bodies at his feet. Ronald had a long knife in his stomach, and Clayton—he winced at the thought of him—had a bayonet in his.

Then he heard it: Jenny screaming. The other soldiers were trying to calm her. The sergeant had pulled her away from Clayton, but she was fighting to get back to his side.

"Let her go to him," Wallace said calmly, but with authority. The sergeant looked up and obeyed. He recognized an officer, whether he was in uniform or not. "Now, have someone go and get Sarah, Mrs. Pomeroy, the healer."

Wallace went to Jenny and knelt beside her, knowing that Sarah would be with them soon. It was doubtful that anything could be done for either of the men. He knew about abdominal wounds, and survival was just about impossible. It was supposed to be the most painful way to die and wasn't quick either. Clyde had had it easier, he thought. Then he looked at Jenny, the real victim in all of this. She was a mess, crying and clutching at Clayton's head.

"Here," Wallace said as he lifted Clayton's shoulders, "you can hold him if you'd like."

"Yes, please," she sniffed and scooted under her dying brother. "You're gonna be fine—I'm here now—all right?" she consoled, as if she were a mother, talking to a toddler with a skinned knee.

"Oh, God," Wallace groaned and collapsed next to the little girl. "Mother, no mother," he mumbled in shock. Evie was dead. He had three little children to rear, and no one to feed them. His eyes rolled back in his head, and the sobbing began—this time, his own. He felt a heavy hand drop on his arm and looked over to follow it to its owner. It was Clayton.

"Please forgive me; me and Clyde for, you know. I am so sorry, and I know Clyde was, too, but I am the sorriest, for sure."

Clayton grimaced in pain, then coughed, and yelled out in agony. Jenny was stroking his forehead, pushing the hair out of his eyes, trying to comfort the man. The yelling stopped, but he was still alive. The hand came back to Wallace's arm, beseeching this time. "Can you forgive me, please?"

Wallace sniffed back his tears for Evie and wiped his nose on the back of his shirtsleeve. He looked at his attacker and saw the sincerity and need in his eyes. He started nodding his head slowly, and then moved up to a real assent. "Yes, I forgive you, you and your brother," he said.

Wallace didn't have anything left to give. He rolled over onto his side to face Clayton, his whole world empty except for the dying man and his sister holding him. "If I don't forgive you, how can I expect the Lord to forgive me for the wrongs I've done? That's what it says in the Bible, you know."

Wallace was now the preacher and counselor to the rapist and murderer lying next to him. He reached out and held onto the dying man's hand. He sighed. Now that he had forgiven him and reached out in compassion, his world didn't seem as dreadful as it had moments before.

Then he felt another hand on his. It was Jenny. "Would you say a prayer for him?" she asked, her big blue eyes red-rimmed and pleading.

Wallace looked over and saw the grayness of Clayton's skin. He didn't have long, if he was even still alive. Then he heard another groan and knew the man was still a resident of this realm. He started to say the Gaelic prayer that Jody had taught him but realized that it wouldn't help either of them. "Our Father, who art in heaven, hallowed be Thy name…."

***

The sergeant ushered Sarah to the carnage. "What happened here?" she asked. Three bodies lay on the bloodied ground. Wallace was grim, reciting the Lord's Prayer to a young girl with one of the dying—Clyde's brother—in her lap.

Wallace looked up, tears rolling down his cheeks. "Was she in pain before she…she died?"

"Yes, I mean no, I mean," she took a steadying breath and started all over again. "She's in pain now, but she's not dead. She's…"

Wallace didn't wait to hear the rest of the story. He sprinted to the site where he had last seen his fiancée. He had seen her fall—a musket ball shot into her chest—then saw Sarah bent over her, shaking her head. He was sure she had been killed. But there she was now. Jody was sitting next to her, his hand holding a cloth over the bloody hole in her chest. The wound was on her left side, and it looked as if it had gone straight into her heart.

Jody looked up and said, "She's not deid, but Sarah said she canna fix it. It needs a proper surgeon and tools she doesna have. Weel, she's a proper surgeon, but she doesna have any anestheez, that is, special pain medicine; or lots of other things she needs to get the ball out and sew the vein back together. Wallace, if only we could get her back to her own time some way, she could be healed. She said she dinna know how she got here, so how could she go back, even if she wanted to?"

"I think I can help with that," said a strange, yet familiar, voice behind Wallace. He turned and saw Master Simon walk past him to kneel beside Evie. "We need to take a ride to get you to help. Do you think you can make it?" he asked.

I forced one eye open and saw who it was. "I want to get married first." My eye fell shut—it was too much work to keep it open—and I resumed my slow, gentle breathing regimen. It had worked for labor, and Lamaze breathing was the only respite available for the fiery pain in my chest.

"Ye heard the lady, she wants to get married. Do we have any takers?" asked Jody with a lilt of hope and happiness that was contagious to all who heard it.

"I'd be honored," said Wallace brightly, keeping up the optimism Jody had initiated. "Um, Master Simon, do you have any credentials that would work for performing a marriage ceremony? I mean, you seem to be dressed for it," he said, nodding to Master Simon's black frock coat.

"Er, why, yes, but please, can we make it quick? We have to get to our, um, destination before dawn, and we have a ways to go. Oh, and it would be best if you or your father here would ride in the back of the wagon, just in case... Well, the ride may get bumpy, and I want her to be as comfortable as possible."

"Get on with it," I said, my voice low and eyes still closed. "I hurt like hell."

"Ahem," Simon cleared his throat and motioned for Wallace to scoot next to Evie. "This is the quickest rite that I am accredited to perform. It's a sweet little ceremony they perform in the islands just off the coast of Norway. They do it quickly because of the weather..."

"Hurry. Up," I said.

"Oh, yes, sorry." Master Simon grabbed Wallace's left hand and my right, put them together, and said, "Love, honor, and protect each other, no matter what happens, all right?"

There was silence, and then Wallace realized that Master Simon was waiting for an answer. "All right," Wallace and I said at the same time.

"You're man and wife, and I pity the poor fool who tries to separate you two. The marriage is good with or without, but you may want to wait for the reception and er, wedding night. Now, give your bride a kiss, and let's get going. The wagon is ready, and if you two will help load Miss Evie...oh, my. What *is* her name now?"

"Mrs. Wallace Pomeroy-Hart," Wallace said as he looked towards the still seated Jody. Julian was standing behind him, his hand on his good friend's shoulder. Wallace's two fathers had made it to the wedding ceremony.

Wallace bent down and gave me, the new Mrs. Pomeroy-Hart, a gentle kiss on my lips. He brushed his hand across my forehead. "I'll do better later, I promise," he whispered. I answered with a smile.

"Okay, fathers, let's load my lovely wife into the wagon for a trip to the hospital. Which one of you wants to join us for the ride?"

"Load first, please," Master Simon said. "And make sure she doesn't lose her necklace. She'll need that."

The Pomeroy Hart men looked at each other, confused at the comment, then gathered around, nodding to direct one another to lifting points. Wallace grabbed my shoulders while Julian steadied my head and Jody took my feet.

"Don't let her use her neck muscles," Sarah said. She rushed over to the wagon and climbed in the back, ready to position me in the impromptu ambulance.

I could tell by the feel that she had used a bag of rice to keep my head still, and it was as comfortable as could be under the circumstances, but the quilt had wadded up underneath my hips. "Move, blanket, butt," I said.

"Here, help me," Sarah said to Wallace. "Lift her hiney, and I'll get it straightened out."

Wallace did as instructed then looked at Sarah and asked, "Hiney?"

She shrugged and grinned. "It's a word I learned from your wife."

"Oh," he said, dropping the subject, but glowing with pride. He had a wife.

***

Sarah didn't know what was going on, but assumed, rightfully so, that Master Simon had arranged for a way to take Evie back to her own time for life-saving surgery. Jody walked up to her with Julian at his side and said, "We tossed a coin and he lost—I get to go with the newlyweds. Sarah, take care of Julian, and dinna let him get into too much trouble, aye?"

Julian said, "He's making light of this because he's so concerned. Wallace, you take care of everyone and don't let him get into too much trouble. Evie, I know you can hear us. Be strong, and hurry back home before I get a chance to miss you. Oops, too late—I miss you already, and you haven't even left yet."

I smiled in reply. When I first met Julian, he could barely laugh at a joke, much less make one. Knowing that he would be here when I got back was like cuddling a warm sheet right out of the dryer—or should that be right off the summer clothesline? Either way, he was a warm and fuzzy memory for me to cling to.

Master Simon took command. "We're leaving now. Mister Pomeroy, would you take the honor of driving? Wallace, you need to stay back here with us. Try to keep her from being jostled. Here, drink this," he said as he held a vial to my mouth. "Just a sip, now. It will ease the pain and help you relax. We don't want your muscles to tense and," he paused, obviously making a decision, "here; take another sip, just to make sure."

And that was the last I remembered of my journey, traveling in the back of an 18th century horse-drawn wagon to a 21st century hospital room in Greensboro, North Carolina.

Chapter 5: Voice sweet as chocolate brownies (NITWW Ch 48)

I must have been in a deep sleep because people don't wake up from being dead. And I was awake. Or almost awake.

I didn't know where—or when—I was, but I knew that I wasn't alone. I couldn't make out the words, but her tone was soothing, her voice as sweet and rich as double fudge chocolate brownies. "Mmm, brownies," I cooed.

"Brownies?" she asked. "Do you want a brownie?"

"That would be nice," I answered in a soft, dreamy whisper, "with lots of walnuts; no, pecans would be better. A nice tall glass of milk, too…" I rolled over to embrace my lusty wish and stiffened up with pain. "Oww!"

"Don't move," the velvet-voiced lady said in an authoritative tone, "you'll tear out your stitches. You have to stay on your back." Her hands were chilly, but gentle, as she lifted my upper body, and rearranged the pillows behind me.

"What happened, where am I?" I asked, now completely awake. I couldn't see. I reached up with my right hand and felt a bandage. It covered both my eyes. I patted the gauze and found that it seemed to be wound all the way around my head. I lifted my left hand to check and froze with the piercing pain. "Ow, ow, ow! What in the hell is going on?"

"You were in an accident, I would guess. Let me see your chart. Hmm. This says your name is Jane Doe and that you had a musket ball removed from your left shoulder. It just missed your heart, but it looks like you're going to be good as new. Renaissance Fair accident, it says." The woman paused then added, "They didn't have muskets in the Renaissance. Jane Doe?"

"That isn't my name, it's, uh, oh, shoot. What is my name?" I asked. "Crap!"

"Well, I doubt it's crap. Let's see, it doesn't say anything here about why your eyes are bandaged. Let me check this out."

The nurse unwrapped the gauze strip around my eyes. "I can't see any signs of trauma; there's no blood or seepage." She got all the wrapping off, and then gently pulled off the eye pads one at a time.

"Nothing obvious, and there aren't any notes in your chart about ocular trauma. Open your eyes, please."

I did.

Oh, boy…

I knew her.

"Leah?" I asked.

"Mom?" she answered as a question.

"I think so. What's going on? I don't remember anything," I said. "I mean, really, I don't know why I'm here. Nothing."

I truly didn't remember anything, but I knew that this was Leah—I was absolutely sure of that—and I had the gut feeling that I was her mother.

"You disappeared ten months ago. No body was found; not a trace of you. You look good now except for the hole in your shoulder. You've lost a lot of weight and your wrinkles are, well, they're gone. You dyed your hair, too—no more silver highlights, as you called them. You look good," she repeated, "almost too good."

I was scared beyond words. I slunk back into the pillows and started to hyperventilate, casting my eyes down at my slim midsection. "Thanks," I said softly in response to the compliment. I pressed my lips together and just lay there, stunned, concentrating on my breathing so I wouldn't have to think about this uneasy situation. There was a hole in my memory, and all I could remember was that I had had amnesia before. I didn't know what to say, so I said nothing.

"Well, aren't you going to tell me what happened?" she asked, not even trying to disguise the edge of disgust in her voice.

Just then, the door opened. I looked up and saw a face and body familiar to me, but I couldn't place where this short, odd-looking man fit in my life. He didn't scare me, but I didn't get warm, fuzzy feelings about him either. "How's my patient doing this morning?" he asked cheerily.

"I'm sorry, sir. I don't recognize you. Are you her doctor?" Leah asked in a sharp, indignant tone. I didn't know if she was irritated with him or me, but I suspected both.

"I'm Dr. Em and Ms. Doe is my patient. I've come to see if she is well enough to travel. I would like to get her back to the clinic as soon as possible."

"Dr. Em? I've never heard of a Dr. *Em* at this hospital." Leah picked up the chart and looked it over again. She glanced up at me, then over at the doctor, and then back down at the chart.

"Okay. Dr. Em, first off, this patient isn't a Jane Doe. I think I know who she is." Leah's voice was commanding, as if ready to reveal who murdered whom and with what in a game of Clue. She didn't volunteer any names, though. It was obvious to me that she was testing the man.

"Yes, yes, my dear," he replied in a condescending tone. "We use aliases at the clinic to protect our patient's privacy." Dr. Em looked at me again and realized that he could see my whole face. "Why are the bandages removed from her eyes?" he asked harshly, his knuckles flying to his hips, his body language shouting indignation.

"It's my job to check dressings, sir," Leah answered with self-assurance. "There wasn't anything in the chart about her eyes or why they were bandaged. I wanted to make sure the dressings were clean and that an infection hadn't set in." The confidence in Leah's voice was ebbing. "There didn't seem to be anything wrong with her eyes, so I didn't re-bandage them." Her last words were spoken softly and with just a hint of guilt.

"And are you her doctor? Are you an ophthalmologist? Did it say in her chart to check the bandages? Miss, what is your name? I should report you to the nursing supervisor. This is very inappropriate."

"Sorry, sir, I just thought…" Leah stammered.

"You aren't supposed to think, you're supposed to follow orders, understand?" Dr. Em stuck his chin out, almost hostile toward the young nurse who had taken the initiative. He was short but definitely had a superiority complex.

I stopped listening to the doctor and nurse and their debate on protocol, designated duties, whatever. Young nurse? She looked to be older than me. How could I be her mother?

"Wake up, wake up!" It was the doctor, practically shouting in my stunned face. "Come on, get dressed. We're leaving right now!"

I looked around and Leah was gone. Dr. Em shoved a robe at me and grabbed my good right shoulder, pulling me up into a sitting position. He carefully picked up my left arm—which hurt like hell—and put it into the sleeve. He positioned the plush pink terrycloth robe around my back and helped me put my right arm into the other sleeve.

"My necklace! I won't go anywhere without the necklace Wallace gave me!" I cried.

"Oh, yes, yes. We'll need that. Oh, here it is, in the bureau." Dr. Em pulled the Greek coin necklace laced on black ribbon from the little nightstand drawer. He gently pushed aside my hair, causing a shiver to run up my spine. He quickly tied the ribbon, then let my hair fall back on my neck. "Here, take this," he said and shoved a small bluish bottle to my lips. "It will help ease the pain."

I let him pour some of the liquid into my mouth…but I didn't swallow. As soon as his back was turned, I spit the bitter brew into the pile of gauze that Leah had pulled off. Fortunately, the liquid was clear, so it wasn't obvious that I hadn't swallowed it. My mouth was kind of tingling, though.

"Dr. Em, the head nurse would like to speak with you." Leah was back again, accompanied by a very fat woman in lavender kitty cat-printed scrubs that were at least two sizes too small for her.

"Yes, Dr. Em, Nurse Madigan says she thinks your patient is here under duress. I am going to have to ask you to come with me while we check out your credentials. You're not on our list of doctors authorized to practice at this hospital."

Miss Kitty Nurse was being polite and formal, but she was twice his size. If Dr. Toadface didn't cooperate, she could haul his butt out of here to wherever, if she wanted.

"Nurse, uh," the doctor looked down at her name tag, "Gata, yes, Nurse Gata, my patient is here on a discretionary pass. We do not use our client's names when we come to a public medical facility. We use pseudonyms to protect their privacy. Of course, my patient is not Jane Doe, but her real name is none of your business. Now, if you will kindly move aside, I am ready to transfer my patient to another location."

"Oh, no you don't, mister," Leah said, her cheeks flushed with anger. "I doubt you are even a doctor, and I have reason to suspect that this woman is a victim of kidnapping."

I felt as if I had a front row seat at a mid-morning hospital-themed soap opera: second-rate actors—an obstinate nurse, a clueless supervisor, and the classically-clad doctor—all trying to out-emote each other. My head turned side-to-side as I watched the dimwitted drama unfold. My mouth wasn't tingling anymore, but I probably had been affected by the funny-looking doctor's special medicine. I was feeling very relaxed, definitely more laid back than possible without chemical intervention.

"Out of my way, Ms. Madigan," Dr. Em said as he tried to elbow his way past her.

But Leah wouldn't budge. "I know this woman, and she knows me. She called me by name, and I want her to stay here until this is resolved. Nurse Gata, would you call security, please?"

The matronly supervisor left in a worried waddle, hands in the air as if she was praying to heaven for divine intervention—or she was giving up.

Dr. Em looked both angry and scared at the prospect of more people coming. "Of course, she knows your name; it's right on your name tag," he said and stepped forward to leave. Leah moved away from the door and let him pass.

He hadn't taken me, so she had won.

Or so she thought.

In two blinks of my still befuddled eyes, he was back—he had only left the room to get a wheelchair. He rolled it past Leah and over to the side of my bed, pushing aside the rollaway tray that held my discarded gauze bandages.

I looked up at him and wondered what the drug he had given me was supposed to do. Since I was mellow and not hurting anymore, it was probably both a painkiller and an anti-anxiety medication. But, given that I hadn't swallowed the full dose, maybe it was also intended to make me docile and submissive. I decided to play along, at least until I found a better option.

Leah and her boss didn't seem to be working well together on this. Nurse Kitty was big but was as meek as a melon. Leah was going to have to be both the brains and the brawn in this confrontation.

Evidently, Leah had come to the same conclusion. I looked over at her with awe, wonder, and maternal pride. Awe at how she was taking charge, even though it might mean losing her job by challenging a doctor. Wonder at what her plan was to keep me here, and maternal pride—that I couldn't explain. It was the same innate emotion that I felt when I held my babies.

Dr. Em had been ushering my oblivious body into the wheelchair as

I recalled my babies. I was suddenly aware of how full and hard my breasts were. I hadn't fed them in I don't know long, but I would suspect at least eight hours. I could feel the coolness on my gown where my very large and painfully firm breasts had leaked milk. I looked down and saw the wetness. Leah followed my gaze and her eyes widened.

"Not so fast there, mister," she said. "She called me by my family name, not the name on my tag. We're related, and I'll be damned if I'll let you take her away from me—again."

Dr. Em had been ready for resistance. She was two steps away when he lifted his hand and flung the fluid into her face. She gasped and sunk to her knees. Her head plopped forward and she fell, unable to stop herself, landing on his chest with a thud, her arms limp at her side, unconscious.

He backed away from her and gently, but with mild disgust, laid her on the hospital floor, her face turned to the side. She was alive, breathing shallowly, her eyes glassy and staring into nothingness, but would recover soon. He pulled the privacy curtain around the bed to block the view of her body. Her foot was sticking out, so he knelt down and dragged the leg to the side, essentially bending her body into an "L" shape so she wouldn't be visible to anyone who walked into the room.

I didn't know what to do, so I continued to play the drugged patient. Dr. Em maneuvered me in the wheelchair—stunned, scared, and silent— around her prone body and escorted me out the door.

I wish I knew how I'm supposed to be reacting. Crap! Nurse Gata is coming towards us. Dr. Em sees her, too, and quickly moves us into an alcove. How appropriate; we're in the chapel. "Please help us, Lord," I pray softly: I don't want anyone but God to hear me. I immediately feel a lessening of the tension in the air, and it's not from the drugging. I know I'm going to be okay now.

After a very long thirty seconds, we emerged from our hideout, Dr. Em pushing me in the wheelchair. I felt carefree, as if I was a baby in a stroller, and we were going for a picnic in the park. I started humming for some reason—probably a side effect of the potion. We passed a cart loaded with flowers, balloons, and a fruit basket. I reached out with my good right arm, grabbed a bunch of bananas, and clutched it close to my belly like the golden treasure I felt it was. I started singing, "One banana, two banana, three banana, four…"

"Hush," the doctor said. So I did. Sort of. I couldn't help but keep humming. Between the prayer and the anti-anxiety medicine, I was *very* content.

We made it to the emergency room entrance with hardly a head turned. I say hardly because we did receive a smile from a little boy holding a bouquet of balloons. The balloons were all blue and said, "It's a boy!" He was holding his father's—I guess—hand and waving at us as we passed. I felt moistness in two zones at his smile. I was leaking milk again, and tears were dribbling down my cheeks.

I missed my family, my home in the wilderness, the wildness of the late 18th century. I didn't know who Dr. Em was, but I was sure that he was my ticket back home. I felt sorry and confused about leaving Leah, but my lactating hormones were in charge right now. I needed my babies, and I'm sure they needed me, too.

"Get out, come on, you can do it. Hurry, hurry up." Dr. Em was urging me out of the wheelchair and into the vehicle. I had been oblivious to everything around me while grieving for my babies. I did as I was told, clutching my bunch of bananas as if they were my children, while I waited for the doctor to get in on the other side.

I looked up and saw the seatbelt hanging next to the window of the car door. "Sorry; no way, José," I said. "Ain't gonna put that on with my shoulder torn up and my chest ready to explode."

There was a commotion moving our way. Nurse Kitty was in the lead, speed walking, leading a crowd of uniformed people—male nurse-types in scrubs and a couple of rent-a-cops, or maybe they were real law enforcement officers. Anyhow, they were heading right towards us, looking at the man who had just climbed in next to me. And they didn't look happy.

"Good Lord," Doctor Em exclaimed. "Where's the steering wheel? Oh no, this is America, isn't it? They put the damned operator's station on the wrong side of the conveyance!"

Dr. Em had put me in on the driver's side of the car and was trying to make a getaway by sitting in the passenger's seat. "Drive woman, drive, NOW!"

The mob was getting closer, and I realized that I had just been given the upper hand. "I will," I said, "if you tell me what's going on." I stared at him with narrowed eyes, the medicine's effect was either wearing off or being overridden by adrenaline. "Tell me everything that's going on, or we stay here."

"All right, all right, just go!" he said, his hands flying up in panicked surrender.

The key was already in the ignition. I started the car, dropped it into drive, and floored it.

It was just like buttering toast; it all came back to me. "Where are we going?" I asked as I sped to the end of the parking lot. He could tell me all I wanted—needed—to know later. If the hospital posse caught up with us first, they'd haul him away, and then I would never find out what this last year had been all about.

"Head that way," he said, pointing east. "But go quickly, we don't have much time. They'll be blocking the roads if we don't get out of town soon."

I looked in the rearview mirror and saw that we were in an SUV with an infant car seat and booster seat in the back. There was also a flower arrangement with 'Congratulations' and little blue football and baseball decorations poked in amongst the daisies and carnations. We had just stolen the car that belonged to that smiling little boy's family. Well, they would just have to score another ride home. Something told me that this was my only chance to get away from the hospital authorities and get to wherever it was that I was supposed to go.

"How far?" I asked. I was traveling nine miles an hour above the speed limit. I didn't want to get stopped for a traffic ticket but wanted to get to our destination before the cops figured a way to keep us—me—from going home.

"It's only about 20 miles from here to the exit. After that, it's only six miles on gravel road, and then a mile and a half of walking." Dr. Em was looking around anxiously, rubbing his thumb back and forth over the side of the first joint of his index finger in a nervous manner.

"Chill out, Doc. We'll be fine. I can feel it in my bones, can't you?" I was trying to get him to relax. I wanted to hear the story of me from him and didn't want him distracted when he told it. "Didn't you ever hear that negative energy attracts bad karma?"

"What? Negative energy, bad karma, yes, yes. You are right. How is your shoulder? I'm a bit surprised that you can still talk, much less operate one of these foul-smelling machines."

"My shoulder is fine when I'm not thinking about it. I didn't swallow that elixir you shoved in my face, and it's a good thing, too, or I wouldn't be able to drive. And this may be a foul-smelling conveyance, but it sure is comfortable and fast. At our current rate of speed, we should be at the turnoff in just over 15 minutes. Six miles on a gravel road at 30 miles per hour is about twelve minutes and then, depending on the terrain, a thirty-minute walk. That means you have almost a full hour to tell me why I'm *here*, and why I was *there*."

Dr. Em squirmed in his seat. "Maybe I should have one of these on," he said as he played with the nylon seat belt at his right.

"A seat belt won't protect you from me if you don't start talking. We had an agreement, remember?" I was hoping that this man, this apparent time traveler, had the sense of honesty and integrity that made the men—the gentlemen of earlier eras—so appealing to me.

"Yes, yes, I do owe you that, I suppose. Well, you saved my life, and now I have saved yours. That's it," he said.

A satisfied smug stretched across his face. He didn't know how to smile correctly, though. It looked like his cheeks were going to split—his determined effort to look happy was apparently causing him pain. He gave up on his attempt at a smile, crossed his arms across his chest, and scrunched down in the seat, looking as if he was preparing to take a nap.

"Sorry, Doc, that version's too short to pass as a full and complete explanation. Let's start from the beginning. Who am I?"

"You're Dani Madigan. Next question?"

"You know, you're making this very difficult for me. You said you'd tell me the whole story. Do you want me to pull over here, to the side of this freeway full of fast-moving cars, and wait for roadside assistance from one of our ever-so-vigilant traffic safety officers?"

Dr. Em lost the slouch and scooted back up in his seat, his straight-backed body language practically shouting, 'No, thanks; I'll behave myself.'

"Who are you? I can't believe that Dr. Em is your real name."

"I'm Master Simon and I travel."

"Travel?" I asked. "Here and there, or now and then?"

Master Simon cleared his throat and said, "Yes," with a definite finality. He wasn't going to elaborate.

His answer was good enough for me. I wanted to get down to what concerned me and mine. "Okay, so what did Leah mean when she said she didn't want you to take me away 'again'?"

I figure I had better get as much out of him now as I can. The troopers—or highway patrol, or whatever they are—could still catch up with us even if I don't feint a breakdown. At least we're in a red SUV, and no matter who makes them—Toyota, Chrysler, Ford, Mercedes, Honda, or whoever—they all look alike. That should make tracking us a bit harder. And since this isn't a rental car or an emergency vehicle, there probably isn't a LoJack installed on it either.

I wasn't getting an answer out of Master Simon, so I let my foot off the gas, tapped on the brake, and slowed down. I turned towards him, gave him the evil eye, flipped on the blinker, and headed onto the shoulder of the freeway.

"All right, all right, get back on the road." He huffed in frustration. "Hmph! And hurry."

I turned off the signal and sped back up to my nine miles over the speed limit. He remained mum, so I growled at him, like a dog guarding a purloined steak.

"Sorry, I was just trying to figure out where to start. Let's see, I was going to meet a friend not far from here when you first met me. I had been assaulted and robbed, and you came to my rescue. You helped me retrieve my stolen map, figured out how to read it, and then took me to the park where you were supposed to leave me, and go home. I caught up with my friend there. All was going according to our plan. We were at the nearest high gate to Greensboro and ready to make the jump, but you had followed us. We did our best to, shall we say, sneak past you, but that plan failed. You stepped out over the point when my friend and I weren't watching you. You leaped out—chasing an illusion, I believe— and my friend and I grabbed you. We all fell, but you didn't know how to land. You fractured your skull and broke your back. It didn't look like you were going to survive. I felt a bit guilty; I supposed it was because you had hurt yourself trying to help me. It's not that I needed the help—I knew what I was doing. But I digress. You had major injuries and were 230 years from home and medical attention. So, I gave you some of my FOY water. I was trying to dribble a few drops into your mouth, but you latched onto the bottle and sucked it dry. It was the last of my supply, too. I had to return to Florida to get more so I could get out of this fiasco."

"Uh, okay. But before you go any further, what is FOY water, and what does it do?" I looked down at the steering wheel. There had to be a cruise control button somewhere. I didn't want to trust my reflexes to keep a constant speed with the story that Simon was telling me.

"Fountain of Youth; a couple drops of the water can keep you young or seek out broken body parts to mend. Actually, it replaces the damaged cells in the body, so if you have, say, liver failure, it will repair that. In some cases, it has even shrunk fat cells, and I see that it did that for you, too. I've used it for thous...er... many years with no ill effects. You drank so much, though, that it actually reversed your aging. I hear it also acted as a fertility enhancer in your case. Triplets, I understand."

"Hmm. So I *am* Leah's mother. What was I doing in North Carolina? All of the bits and pieces of memories I have are of Alaska and the desert."

I was only slightly bothered by my lack of personal history, but still very curious about why I was so far from Alaska. I was also glad that the cruise control was now engaged.

"I don't know about you personally. If you remember that you are from both Alaska and the desert, then it is most likely true. Since you met your daughter—I assume she is your daughter—at the hospital, I would surmise that you were there to visit her."

"Brilliant deduction, Dr. Watson. So, I have a daughter who is older than me?"

"No, you are still older in chronological years, but you have had a rewind of your cellular biology. I'd say you are about 18 years old physically. Are all your questions answered, madam?" he asked, looking at me for confirmation.

I turned to him, gave a half-grin, half-grimace, and said, "It'll do for now. Which exit do we take?"

***

About five miles and five minutes later, I had thought of more questions. "So, how did I get hurt? A musket ball wound, Leah said."

"You were in the line of fire, but you should fully recover. My potions can only do so much. Musket balls need to be removed before the healing can begin."

"Why did you bring me back? Couldn't Sarah fix me?" I paused, waiting for the response that didn't come. "She is okay, isn't she?"

"Yes, yes; at least she was when we left. She was afraid to operate so close to your heart. I was willing to bring you back to this time, but your—how do you say, 'menfolk?'— insisted I stay with you at the hospital, and then return you to them. They were *very* insistent," Simon was shuddering at the memory, "that you make it back."

"If you mean Jody, I see what you mean. He can be rather intimidating." I smiled, visualizing Jody lording over the short, squat Master Simon.

"Oh, not just him—it was the both of them. They told me I could bring you here to be mended and then returned to them, or they would pull me apart into so many pieces, that I'd never be whole again, no matter how many stitches were used. I'll get you back to the portal site, but I'd rather not face them another time. Besides, my work there is complete, and I have other places to go. You seemed to manage fine there by yourself before. This time, Sarah, your husband, and father-in-law will be waiting for you."

"My husband and father-in-law? That's right! I remember. You did a little Norwegian wedding ceremony just before the wagon ride. I'm married!" I suddenly felt warm and squishy all over as I realized that I had a husband and was now on my way back to him. A real husband and father for my babies…

My reverie popped shut. "Hey," I said, "Why did you leave me by myself before? I didn't even have any water, much less food or shelter. I could've been eaten by wild animals the first night!"

"Ah, but you weren't, were you?" he said. "You are stronger and smarter than you know."

"Well, you're taking a lot for granted. Oh, my God. Leah! She'll think I've deserted her again. Hey, she said she didn't want you to take me from her *again*. Did she know you were with me the first time I disappeared?"

"No, at least nothing for certain. When we were in the hospital room, I could feel her inside my head. She caught me off guard; I didn't know she was psychic. She couldn't tell much about you, though, because she was so angry with you for being gone. She has your strength and wits. She'll be fine. She's a survivor. Here, take this exit, then turn left at the stop sign."

I followed his directions without any emotion. I didn't know what I wanted to do. I knew I had to go back to my other family, but I also hurt—physically ached all over—when I realized that I was deserting my firstborn. Again. And this time, it was intentional. I had the choice of staying here—or going back.

Master Simon looked over at me and put his hand on my good shoulder, "She's an adult and can take care of herself. You have a new husband and three babies who *need* you. And Sarah could use your help, too. There's a new country that requires support for both its soldiers and citizens. Come on, let's get you back home."

Chapter 6: Back home again with bananas (NITWW Ch 49)

"Now, I'm not going with you this time; you'll have to go by yourself. You probably don't remember how we made the trip yesterday because you were unconscious. I 'carried' you with me. This isn't the same method of transition we used on your first trip either, so don't worry about your landing. Actually, there isn't any kind of drop here—it's a horizontal pass-through. There's a very strong magnetic distortion at this site—marked by those trees—but the coin should help defray the pulses and any potentially harmful static they cause. Take a deep breath before going through, and don't hold your own hands. You don't want to complete a circle with either your hands or feet touching. That could be, well, just don't do it."

"I feel sick," I said. "I think I'm going to throw up."

"No, no; it's just the magnetic field. If you couldn't feel it, you wouldn't be able to go home this way. If we went back to the monadnock—the hanging rock—you'd have too far to walk to get home to your family. Besides, they aren't expecting you to return there. You'd be all alone again. Please, just concentrate on your breathing and…" he looked down at the bundle I held close to my middle, "are you going to take that fruit with you?"

"You bet I am. I've wanted bananas for almost a year. I don't want to eat one of them now and lose it, though," I lifted my yellow potassium-rich booty as if they were trophy-sized trout, "so these guys are coming with me."

"That's fine. Just hold your coin and focus on your family. Do you see them in your head?"

I nodded in acknowledgement, sniffing back my fears and uncertainties.

"Now open your eyes and proceed through there." Master Simon pointed to a gap between two old trees. I walked forward and heard his voice, "Be safe, and I'm sorry I inconvenienced you…"

***

I awoke to someone patting my hand and someone else stroking my hair. "Get away! I need air," I shouted, thrashing my head side to side.

My movement woke me up all the way. "Sarah? Sarah?" I called

115

frantically. I tipped my head back, looked up, and saw it was her. "Oh, sorry. *Déjà vu* all over again. Remember, Sarah?"

"Yes, yes, I remember. But do you remember me, and all of this?"

"Yes, I do," I said with confidence, and smiled at my handsome, hand-holding husband. The pride quickly drained away and frustration took its place. "Damn! I forgot to ask Dr. Em—I mean, Master Simon—how come I couldn't remember anything when I woke up the first time I was here."

"It doesn't matter, does it? You remember us and we remember you, right, Sally?" Wallace asked, grinning.

I snorted at his little joke, then winced in pain. I didn't dare laugh—I still hurt—but kept my smile.

Sarah grinned` and changed the subject, rubbing the edge of my hospital gown between her fingers. "They didn't give you much in the way of a trousseau," she said. "Although they did provide you with a nice traveling cloak," and nodded to the plush pink cotton terrycloth robe, folded beside me.

"Yeah," I said and peeked down the front of the standard issue cotton print smock. I was wearing one frontwards, the other tied on backwards. "But they took my underwear. I guess I'll have to go commando like everyone else."

I got blank stares from both Sarah and Wallace. "No briefs, I mean, small clothes. Never mind, it's just a phrase," I said, and shook my head. If I didn't elaborate on it, I wouldn't get embarrassed.

I put a cautious hand on my tender left shoulder. It wasn't too bad, so I decided to find my limits. I started wiggling, trying to scoot up into a seated position. Wallace saw what I was trying to do, and was right there with me, helping me upright. Sarah moved over to my other side and just kind of hovered, wanting to help, but unneeded. I caught my breath—it was harder to do than I thought—then continued with my challenge. Wallace gently guided me the rest of the way up until I was in a standing position.

I felt all warm and mushy, and I doubt it was from the exercise. My senses were waking up, too. The physical proximity of my husband, his voice, his smell... I looked over at Sarah. "Can you give us a moment, please?"

"Sure, sure; I need to go check on... Well, I'm sure something needs checking on," she said and left in a hurry, her cheeks pink with embarrassment and joy.

I turned into Wallace's firm body and looked up. "I need a hug," I pouted, my bottom lip stuck out in mock drama, and then added, "but be gentle with me. I still have an owie."

His eyebrows crowded together in confusion. It must have been the word 'owie,' but he figured it out. "How about this?" he asked and squatted down so he could hug me at my own, lower altitude. I appreciated his assumption of the awkward posture, so I didn't have to reach up. We were almost in an embrace when he stopped and asked, "What's this?"

I was still clutching the awkward bundle of bananas to my middle, and it was now poking both of us.

"Those are for later. Would you put them over there?"

"Anything for you, Mrs. Pomeroy-Hart."

Wallace put the bananas next to my new, pink robe, and then turned back to me. "Now where were we?" he asked, the glint in his eye letting me know that he knew exactly where we had been.

I didn't say a word; just smiled and did my Groucho Marx double eyebrow pop, adding a 'come hither' purr.

And he did.

The kissing was as good as it could be, considering his awkward position, and my recently assigned status of injured reserved. He was starting to wobble, losing his balance, and reached out to steady himself on the ground. "I think we'd better continue this later," he said. "I think there are others who want to see you."

As if it was his cue, Jody showed up, Sarah at his elbow.

"Hey, Jody. See, I didn't forget to come back. And Sarah, look here: bananas!" I was so excited that I could hardly contain myself.

And then realization hit. I was probably not the only one who had been injured in the confrontation. "Oh, these can wait. Was anyone else hurt?" I asked.

"Yes, but let's not talk about it now. We need to get you back home," Sarah said. "Do you think you can handle the wagon ride back?"

I took Wallace's hand and let him help me into the back of the wagon before I answered. I think I was still in shock at all that had happened.

"Yes, I'm sure I'll be okay. But if it's all the same to you, I think I'll go back to sleep. Traveling 231 years twice in twenty-four hours kind of wore me out." I started to roll onto my left side, was rudely reminded on my recent surgery, and quickly decided to stay flat on my back. I wiggled my head to get my neck comfortable, heard the grains of rice in the burlap bag pillow shift, and then floated back into oblivion and the absence of pain.

***

I awoke to the familiar smells of home: herbs, eggs, and babies. I heard the eggs sizzling and felt someone touching my gown. It was Sarah. "Do you think you could try to feed Leo? We need to get your milk supply going again."

I scooted up on the chaise and gladly took my little boy to my breast. It was frustrating for both of us, though. Both my breasts were hard as brick cheeses from not nursing for so long, and my nipple was too firm for him to latch onto. Sarah handed me a teacup. "Try this," she said.

I must have done it when Leah was a baby. Expressing milk over the edge of a teacup came naturally. I pumped enough off of one breast to allow him to drain the rest. He didn't act as if he was very hungry, though.

"Just before you woke up, Mrs. Donaldson went home to be with the rest of her family. Hannah took all the girls and the twin boys home yesterday so they could be with their father. By the way, he didn't suffer from his ordeal at the mill, and the British soldiers didn't arrest any of the locals. Mrs. Donaldson stayed here to wet nurse your three. She told me you still had plenty of milk, but you need to feed the ones who aren't too hungry first. That way you'll still have some left for the others."

And she was right. I wound up feeding all three of my babies in that first hour of semi-lucidity. I was in my own mini-world, only aware of them and our need for each other. And my world was at peace. No muskets or mean men to ruin my day…or my body.

I looked around and saw that the adult members of my family had divided the childcare duties while I was gone. Sarah changed the diapers, Jody did the burping, and Wallace got them settled back to sleep, rubbing their backs to soothe them into a deep slumber.

Julian had returned to his job as the chef. The four of them had lunched in between cooking and nursery duties but had made sure that there was a hefty portion of omelet left for me. A big mug of buttermilk completed my welcome home dinner. The simple fare was divine and literally restored both my body and soul.

My mind was clearing rapidly. "I'm back," I declared to everyone in the room, "I mean here, too," and pointed to my head. "And, in case any of you were wondering, there was nothing, nobody, here I was running away from. It's just the opposite. There were so many of you here who I cared about, that I was running *to* you!"

"Well, ye did have the bairns to come back to," Jody said. "It's not as if ye had any there."

He saw my face drop. "Lass, did ye have bairns there, back there in yer own time?"

"Well, yes and no," I answered as I looked at Wallace.

He wasn't guarding his feelings at all. He looked afraid, as if he was going to lose me again.

"I have a daughter," I said softly and took his hand. I brought it up to my cheek and held his fingers, so they traced the side of my face from the outside edge of my eye, down my cheek to my neck and collarbone. "Would you love me if I were old?" I asked, making certain I saw his reaction. I was sure he and everyone else thought I was still dopey from my ordeal, and that was fine—actually better.

He smiled and said, "Don't worry; I'll love you forever. We'll grow old together, God willing. Wrinkles won't make any difference to me. Age is just a number. Look at my father," he said as he looked towards Jody. Sarah's hands immediately went up to touch the crow's feet beside her eyes. "Jody doesn't care that Sarah is older than he is, right?"

Sarah saw that he was asking her the question. "Well, biologically I'm older, but chronologically he has me beat by about 200 years," she said with a tinge of sarcasm.

"See," he said, "it never made any difference to them."

"Yeah, well, this is different. You see, I met my daughter when I went back. Actually, she was one of the nurses who took care of me…"

Wallace's eyes widened. He looked over at Jody, Julian, and Sarah and saw that they, too, were as bug-eyed as grasshoppers. He started moving his head from one side to the other, gradually working up to a full-blown head shaking. "But how?"

"Not but how but will. Will you—would you—love me if I were old enough to be your grandmother?"

"I knew it!" exclaimed Julian. "Oh, sorry, it's not my place to speak."

"Go ahead; it looks like everyone else is tongue-tied," I said, and stumbled back to the chaise.

My chaise. I ran my fingers across the little bit of the original fine fabric that was still intact on the side of the chair. "What did you say?" I asked when I realized that Julian had been speaking to me.

"I always knew you had an old soul in that young, nubile body. Well, Wallace, I think you have the perfect woman here. Smart and wise beyond the, shall we say, obvious years of her body. How could you possibly have a problem with that?" Julian was grinning; so proud that he had perceived the real me before I had.

"I'll give you an A-plus in detective work, Julian. I just wish I had found out about it earlier," I said, unable to hide the grumble of regret.

"Why?" asked Wallace. "I mean, yes, I must admit that I'm a little shocked and yes, I definitely want to hear more about my stepdaughter— oops, sorry about using that four-letter word 'step'—but what difference would any of that knowledge make, or have made? I still would have fallen in love with you, and I hope that you would still have loved me. Now what? You think that since you know you're so much older than me that maybe Julian would be a better husband for you?"

I laughed and giggled, and then started coughing from swallowing spit the wrong way. Wallace came over and patted me gingerly on the back to help me stop coughing. I looked over at Julian and saw his frowning, contorted face. "Would that be so bad?" he asked. "I'm not that old," he added indignantly.

I looked over and saw Jody and Sarah rolling their eyes. Both had their hands to their mouths, stifling grins or chuckles, or maybe even belly laughs.

"Julian," I said as I walked over to his side, the coughing fit over, "I love you; I've told you that, but," I leaned in and gave him a kiss on the cheek, "you're not my type." I walked over to Wallace's side and snuggled next to him, still too apprehensive because of the topic of discussion to give him a kiss or a hug. "You're just a little too straight-laced for me," I said as I looked back at him.

120

I turned to look up at Wallace. "I like a man who doesn't have to button up all his buttons." I put my finger under Wallace's chin. His top button was undone. He looked down to see what I was doing. I flipped my finger up, popping him on the nose as I did so. "Gotcha," I said.

"You sure do." He gathered me up in his arms, lifted me by the waist, and gave me a very long welcome home kiss. When we finally broke apart, he set me back on the chaise. "Now tell me about my other daughter," he said, beaming with joy.

His smile was genuine. It was as if I had just announced that he had won a new critter, and he wanted to know all the details. He pulled over the four-legged stool from in front of the hearth, eager to hear stories of his newly discovered daughter.

But I wasn't ready. I still had to find out what had happened at the battle at the mill. I couldn't have been the only one who was injured. There had been muskets, guns, and all sorts of commotions, and I couldn't remember much of anything. "First, tell me who else got hurt."

Wallace rose up from the stool, sat next to me on the chaise, and took my right hand. "I'm afraid that both Clayton and Clyde didn't make it. You were right that there had to be a reason why both of them lived after the…the attack."

Wallace's lips were tight, and it looked as if he were choking. "God, I hated them so much, and I felt like…like Ian had the right idea with vengeance, but I listened to you. Clyde was already dead, but Clayton apologized to me for both of them. I didn't want to accept the apology, but I remembered that part in the Bible that said if I didn't forgive, then how could I ever expect to be forgiven. I don't think I will ever, could ever, do anything that horrid, but, well, they needed to be forgiven, and so I gave it to them—forgiveness."

Wallace looked at me to see how I was reacting to his story. He rubbed my hand, "It actually felt good to forgive them. It wasn't just for them, though. After I forgave them, I found out that it helped me, too."

I gave a weak smile and scooted closer to him, not wanting to stop his recollection of the previous day's events. "Just before the fighting was over, Clayton stepped in front of a bayonet that was meant for me. And earlier, Clyde had jumped in front of an officer who was aiming his pistol at Jody. That bullet hit Clyde in the throat. He died immediately. Clayton didn't fare so well. He had been stabbed in the stomach and held on for nearly an hour. I was by his side at the end. He just kept saying how sorry he was…" Wallace was choked up, the tears slipping down the sides of his red cheeks. "If I had gone out and killed them after they…they…did what they did to me, then they wouldn't have been there to save Father and me. And then where would you and Sarah be?"

A big frown covered me all the way to the ground. I looked over at Sarah and saw she had a similar reaction. I'm sure she was thinking the same thing I was: if our men were gone, would we go back to our former times?

"But that's not what happened, is it?" I asked, not really expecting an answer. "We're all doing fine here in 1781 and ready to take care of the families we have here and now, right?"

"Right!" came the resounding replies, the mood of everyone in the room immediately lifted.

Well, almost everyone.

I looked over and saw Jenny in the corner. I hadn't even noticed that she had come into the house. She had picked up and was now holding and cuddling my baby girl. I was going to have to remember to ask everyone to call her by her middle name, Wren. I didn't know if I was ready to let it be known that I had found out that in my 'other time' I was a Danielle. I had actually grown fond of her new name, and Wren seemed to fit her better anyway.

Neither Wallace nor I realized that Jenny had been in the room when we had spoken of her brothers. I still had a hard time believing that those two degenerates, Clyde and Clayton, were related to her. And now those two were dead. Since she was still here, I had to assume she didn't have any other family.

"Wallace," I called softly. "Do you think we could handle one more?" and nodded to Jenny.

"Absolutely!" he whispered with delight. I tilted my head in her direction again, squinted my eyes, and frowned, giving him the look that said, 'Well, ask her!'

Wallace gently moved away from me and walked over to the girls. "Jenny, would you like Wren to be your little sister?" he asked.

She looked up at him, surprised at his size as much as by the question, I think. I don't know if she had ever been physically that close to him while he was standing. She looked back down at the little red-headed girl in her arms, and then back up to face him. "Could the other two be my brothers then?"

"I wouldn't have it any other way. They're a matched set, you know. They all have the same birthday, parents, and everything."

Jenny's face worked a few emotional twists: a frown, a deep thought, a grin, and then a huge smile. "Does that mean you'd be my father and Evie'd be my mother?"

Wallace nodded, "Yes, that's what that means. Would that be okay with you?"

"A mother, a real mother! And a father, too!" Jenny was beside herself with joy, squealing with excitement. She was still holding onto her new baby sister, and the yelling was upsetting the little one; she started bellowing, too. "You're my new sister, you're my new sister," she sing-songed. "And I'm the big sister to all three of you. Hah!" she said with pride.

"Well grandpas and grandma, it looks like there's another one in the family. Can't say that she was any less pain to get," I said and rubbed my left shoulder, "but the pregnancy was sure a lot shorter."

***

It was evening. The adults were gathered around the kitchen table, sharing stories. Life was starting to settle back into our old routine—with a welcomed modification. Earlier, Sarah had set up a sleeping pallet for Jenny on the floor next to the playpen. The new big sister didn't want to be far away from her new siblings. One of the babies started to fuss. I looked to see who it was, but Jenny lifted her head, saw where the movement was, and placed her hand through the rails and onto Judah's back, rubbing it softly until he went back to sleep.

Jenny had the most contented look on her face. I didn't know if there was a word for it, but what I saw was peaceful satisfaction. Just wait until they're in their terrible twos, I thought. Yes, and now there would be one more person to help me keep them out of trouble. Then I felt that 'peaceful satisfaction' smile come onto my face and welcomed its presence.

***

The next morning started before the sun came up. It was the beginning of my first full day back home. First Wren started squawking. She didn't know how to crow but was still able to wake me with her

123

none-too-subtle wail. There was no hesitation on my part to rise to the call of duty as chuck wagon. I had learned early on to get the first baby 'busted in the mouth' right away, so the other two didn't awaken.

But it was the second loud noise that woke everyone else in the household: my screaming. I hadn't planned on yelling. Then again, pain doesn't always give you that option. When I heard Wren, I immediately sat straight up. I was aware after the fact that I was stiff but still hadn't had any trouble sitting up. But when I reached for Wren with my left arm, all traces of civilized behavior disappeared, and I was a screaming, shoulder-shot banshee.

I had been asleep—totally pain-free—and then risen, half asleep, to a ten plus on the pain scale. It was no wonder that I found it impossible to contain the hysterics. Of course, all of the babies were panicked by mama's screeching, and before I could even think to shut up, three men and two women, one very small, were at my side trying to find out the cause of the uproar. Each one of the men grabbed his godchild, and Jenny grabbed Wallace's leg, trying to make sure her baby sister was okay. Sarah was tending to my shoulder—or trying to. I was thrashing my head back and forth, trying to shake the pain away.

"Whisky," Jody called. "Get whisky down her throat."

"Coming right up; and I'll brew some willow bark tea," said Sarah. "She can use that as a chaser for the whisky."

"Aarrgh! This is worse than labor!" I screamed. I was losing it, and I didn't care.

At least I didn't care for about two whole seconds. One look at the fear on Jenny's face and the concern on Wallace's was enough to shock me back from hysteria to just plain pain and frustration.

I stumbled over to the chaise, panting, clutching my arm. I hadn't screamed with labor pains because I used the Lamaze breathing method. Who was to say that it wouldn't work in this situation? I sat back, and huffed and puffed, eyes focused on the pink bundle on the cold hearth. Slow deep breathing in to the count of five, blow it out to five, and start again.

After a minute or two, I regained my composure. "Sorry 'bout that. It was the pain, you know. God, I wish I had something for it. Here, would you help me with Wren?" I asked Wallace.

He didn't say anything, but brought her to me, her tiny fists clenched as tight as her eyes, little tears making their way down her cheeks. I wiped away her tears and felt them reappear on my cheeks, my feelings of inadequacy manifesting themselves in saline drops. Wallace untied the 21st century hospital gown I had arrived in so I could bare my breast. "You'll be fine; you just have to give it some time. I'm here to help you now." He placed a delicate kiss on top of my head, then walked outside to check on our other children.

Jody and Julian had taken the boys outside and were employing the walk-and-talk infant sedation technique. It must have worked; I didn't hear anything but footsteps and grandpa whispers, the soft sounds of adult men talking to their progeny. I felt Jenny's hand move the hair out of my face. I looked up and saw the fear in her eyes hadn't disappeared.

"I am so sorry. I can't believe I did that. I'm sure I'll be better soon," I apologized.

She leaned forward and her lips brushed my cheek. "Mama. I can call you that, can't I?"

I nodded and smiled. Hearing her say that felt like a warm, moist kiss that covered my whole body all at once. I didn't have to wait a year to hear it from one of the babies; this one could—and did—want to call me by that wonderful name. I felt goose bumps all over and welcomed them.

"When you get better, can you fix my hair? I never had a hairbrush. I have to use my fingers to comb my hair. She," Jenny nodded to Sarah who was pouring a cup of whisky for me, "said that you had a comb and some sweet-smelling soap that you would, uh, probably, maybe, could share with me? I tried to keep clean, all over clean, but we didn't have no soap. You see, I saw that people treated you nicer if you were clean. I tried to tell that to my brothers, but they wouldn't listen. Do you think maybe you could put braids in my hair when…when your arms work better?"

"I would love to do that. But we don't have to wait. You can ask your Grannie. Maybe she can do it today. That is if she has the time," I said and looked at Sarah. She was standing by, waiting for me to finish my little talk with Jenny before handing me the drink. I saw that she had made me a crème liqueur.

"Ah, just what the doctor ordered," I said as I pushed my nose into the cup and inhaled deeply. I took a cautious sip, and then another. The warmth worked its way down my throat, then radiated equilaterally down my shoulders to the inside of my elbows. I set the cup down and let Jenny take Wren. She got a big, very unladylike burp out of her, and then set her back into the playpen.

"Grannie, Grannie, Grrrannie," Jenny was trying out the name of her new grandmother, letting the sounds play on her lips and tongue. I looked at her and couldn't help but think, 'Well, this one will be easy to entertain.' Then I noticed it again, the object of my earlier meditation.

"What's that pink package over there?" It didn't look like it was 18th century vintage, and I couldn't place where I had seen it before.

"That's the robe you had on when you, shall we say, walked back home?" answered Sarah, nodding to Jenny. She picked it up and handed it to Wallace, who had just given me Leo to feed. I settled back on the chaise, happy to be able to cuddle my little rascal again.

"Wallace, do you want to help her with this?" Sarah asked. "It's the only thing she has to wear other than those dreadful hospital gowns. Which, by the way," she said, turning to me, "are going to be reconstructed into useful garments for the babies. There isn't enough fabric in them to make anything decent for you. I think there might still be enough on that bolt of green calico for another dress. We, rather I, can get started on it today unless," she grinned, "someone else shows up with a musket ball in her shoulder."

Even though the fabric was relatively heavy, it would have to suffice for a day of so, even in this August heat. Wallace opened out the robe for me. It was soft and I recognized it as terrycloth cotton. "Look, there's something in the pocket, or rather pockets."

Wallace set the robe down on the table and started pulling items out of the pockets. "What are these?" he asked as he held up little white plastic bottles with color-printed labels on them.

"Oh, my Lord!" I exclaimed. "I don't believe it. Are they all the same, or do they have different names on them?"

"Let's see—here, I'll set them out on the table. Amoxicillin? That sounds Greek. Percocet, Oxycodone, here's a couple of tubes of something: triple antibiotic and Bacatracin?"

Wallace was doing a pretty decent job of pronouncing the names of the medications, but I couldn't help giggle. I worked my way up into joyous laughter and exclaimed, "Sarah, wake up woman! Give me a glass of water and one of those Oxycodones. And we might want to get me started on the antibiotic, just in case. Sarah, Sarah?"

Sarah was in a state of shock, wide-eyed, pawing at the bottles as if they were the priceless commodities that they really were. She looked up at me with the question in her eyes, 'How?'

"I think Master Simon wanted to make sure I recovered completely. But I think there's more than enough here to treat me. Congratulations, Sarah, it's twins: antibiotics and pain killers."

"No," corrected Sarah, "it's triplets: antibiotics, pain killers, and a mystery bottle." She held up a little blue bottle, obviously not twenty-first-century vintage. "Do you know what this is?"

"Uh, oh; my bad," I confessed. "I took it out of Master Simon's pocket, just in case. Well, I was kind of out of my mind and… Oh, shit. He's going to be pissed!"

"Who's gonna be pissed?" asked Jody as he walked in the door. I looked up and saw the full complement of the extended Pomeroy family.

"Oh, just the wagon driver, but don't worry about it. I doubt Master Simon will be coming back, at least anytime soon." I wasn't ready to explain Fountain of Youth water to anyone, except maybe my healer, and that would be done on a one-on-one basis. "Sarah, let's find a safe place for that bottle. It's more precious than gold or diamonds. And even I have a hard time believing what it is, so let's leave this one as a mystery, shall we?"

Everyone in the room looked at each other. Nods and shrugs of agreement bounced back and forth until everyone was satisfied. Everyone, that is, but Jenny. "Are these a mystery, too?" she asked as she held up the bunch of bananas.

"Nope. These are part of a balanced breakfast. Is anyone else hungry?" I asked, and shoved the bunch under my free arm, using the hand cradling Leo to pull free one of the yellow fruits, waving it in the air, showing it off like it was a juicy drumstick. "Let's have a taste of South America, shall we?"

***

August 3, 2013
Moses H. Cone Hospital
Greensboro, North Carolina

The chaos settled down at the hospital after a couple of hours. No

127

one knew of—or could find any history of—a Dr. Em. Leah did find that Dr. Swenson had performed the emergency surgery to remove the musket ball lodged near Jane Doe's heart but didn't know anything about the mysterious young woman other than, yes, she was lactating. Dr. Johnson, the anesthesiologist, confirmed that. He said she kept mumbling, "My babies, I have to get back to my babies," until he had her fully sedated.

"Wow, twins. At least," Leah mumbled as she walked back to the room where her much younger mother had been just hours before. Nurse Gata was there with an orderly who was changing the linens and preparing the room for the next patient.

"Nurse Madigan," the supervisor said formerly. "I need to speak with you in my office, please."

"Oh, crap," mumbled Leah. She'd probably lose her job, or at least get written up, for this debacle. "Yes, ma'am, I'll be right there," she said. She looked around the room one more time and shook her head. 'If I didn't have witnesses, I wouldn't believe it myself,' she thought.

Nurse Gata was waiting for her in her office. "I want to thank you for your help this morning. Your observations about the man were correct. I was told that the police found the stolen car, but the kidnapper and the patient have not yet been found. Now, that being said, didn't you say that the Jane Doe was a relative of yours?"

"I did, ma'am," Leah replied without emotion. She wasn't going to explain how she was related to the missing patient—to her supervisor or anyone else. No one would believe her anyhow. Nurse Gata had said something else. "Excuse me?"

"Here are the belongings that came in with the patient. Since we don't have anyone else to claim these, would you like to take care of them? There's not much for clothing—just her old colonial costume—but she did have a smartphone in her pocket. It's a rather nice one, and since she was family, maybe you can get it back to whoever should have it."

"Yes, ma'am; thank you, ma'am; I'll do that, ma'am," she said mechanically, realizing after the fact that she sounded like an idiot with all of those 'ma'ams' echoing out of her still stunned, empty head.

**

Leah's shift was over, and she was more than ready to be back to that little white-walled apartment she called home. She carried the little beige plastic tub that held the personal effects of the young woman who had been her charge for less than an hour this morning. She was certain that the woman was her mother, but she had no proof, and there was no one whom she could trust to tell her suspicions to. But it was a moot point. The patient was gone, and with her, any evidence she might have had that could connect her with her mother's disappearance.

Was she or wasn't she? Who would believe that the young, mysterious Jane Doe was her sixty-year-old mother? She could hardly believe it herself. She really didn't know for sure whether *she* believed it. Her mind was going in circles. She didn't even remember the ride home. She had been driving solely on response to the stimuli of traffic lights and conditions.

Leah unlocked her front door and went straight to the kitchen cabinet. She grabbed the new bottle of McCallum whisky and the old Flintstones cut-glass cup. It was her favorite cup for drinking. It was the last one left of the set her mother had given her as a house-warming gift for the playhouse she had built for her when she was six. She poured out a healthy splash of the high-dollar-but-worth-it single malt whisky. "*Slante!* Here's to you, Mom, wherever or whenever you are."

Leah pulled the green calico Colonial-style dress out of the plastic bin. She held it up, sniffed it, realized what she was doing, and sniffed it again without reservations. No one was around to make fun of her for the odd behavior. "Yup, smells like Mom all right." She fingered the neckline and noticed the fine hand stitching on the buttonholes. "Bone buttons, hmm, those could be dated. Yeah, but you can buy antique buttons, and it's still possible to make a dress without a sewing machine. What else is there? Ho Kay; talkin' to yerself are ye? Jest like yer mudder. Well, mudder, what did ye leave me besides this sweaty dress."

Leah poured another couple fingers of whisky into the cup before investigating the scant contents of the tub. She took a small sip, enjoying the feel of the cool liquid on her upper lip, before she relaxed her lower jaw and let the sharp yet smooth fluid burn down her throat until it settled warmly in her empty stomach. She set the cup down on the table and nearly knocked it over when she couldn't pull her fingers out of the handle.

She picked up the dress and held it up as if it were a mannequin and danced around the small kitchen-living-and-dining room combination. "Some enchanted evening, you may meet a stranger," she sang. "Yeah right; they don't come much stranger than Dr. Em, do they? Hey, what's this?" she asked of nobody but herself since she was her only company tonight.

"Ooh, a nice, crusty snot rag." She suddenly realized what a treasure it might be. "DNA! Looks like Abby and the forensics lab will get a challenge with this one!"

She ambled over to the chair and plopped down hard. The whisky had definitely relaxed her uptight muscles and was clarifying her muddy-water mind. She put her elbows on the table and dropped her forehead into her hands. She wanted to cry, but the tears wouldn't come. She pulled her head back and sat up with a renewed confidence.

"Well, I didn't cry the first time you disappeared, and I'm not going to cry this time either. You were alive a few hours ago, and I know you're still alive. I can't cry for the living now, can I?"

She looked over at the plastic tote on the table, and there it was: the green-eyed pixie box. The smartphone was identical to the one her mother had when she came to visit ten months ago, the twin of the solar-powered prototype she carried in her pocket now. Could this be the same one?

Leah picked it up and closed her eyes tightly. She rubbed her thumb next to the micro-USB port and found it: the telltale roughness of an engraving. She got up and hurried to the bathroom, nearly tripping over her feet, which seemed to have grown a size with each swallow of her drink. She grabbed the talcum powder and walked back to the table, slower this time, and with one hand on the wall to steady herself. She tipped out a small amount of powder onto the table, dipped her index finger into it, and rubbed some of it into the irregular surface next to the port.

And there they were. The initials DUM were visible, small and now bright white. Danielle Ursula Madigan.

She wiped the excess powder onto the leg of her scrubs and relaxed into the chair, relieved that she wasn't going crazy. She looked back and saw the steady green light was on. The smartphone was charged and hopefully still functional. "Well, what little treasures do you hold, my wee black box?" she asked, holding the phone by the edges. "Talk to me."

**Conclusion of excerpt from *Naked in the Winter Wind* **
HA'PENNY JENNY, the complete story, follows

Complete Book

Ha'Penny Jenny

The Fairies Saga Book Four

Sweet, naïve—and psychic—preadolescent Jenny has just been adopted into a wonderful, yet different family. She knows Mommy and Grannie are from someplace where carriages fly in the air and books have moving pictures, but she doesn't care. Her new family tries to protect her from her past. However, no amount of love can prevent the problems the chatty young girl 'sees.' But she won't stop trying.

Chapter 7: History of Jenny (H'PJ Ch 1)

August 6, 1781

Master Simon may have been the person who physically put the painkillers and antibiotics in the pockets of the pink terrycloth robe I wore from the 21st century back to 1781, but I knew it was God guiding his hands.

"Thank You, Lord," I said, as I downed half an oxycodone.

I didn't like the idea of taking *any* pain medication, but this was for the purpose intended, not for getting high, and was only half a dose. The musket ball had pierced muscle and bone close to my heart, only three days ago. Sarah said the surgeon and surgical nurse were sure to have scrubbed aggressively and that I had both internal and external stitches. The jostling wagon ride home—stretching at all those tender parts— added to the reasons my pain was so great.

I didn't like to admit to myself or anyone else that I needed the chemical help, but the pain was so great, I couldn't focus and could barely function. Dulling the pain with whisky wasn't an option I was willing to take. It would take a substantial amount to work, anyhow. I didn't want my judgment impaired, and besides, I was nursing. I didn't want Jody's 160 proof to pass through my milk to the babies. Sarah insisted that half a pain pill wouldn't bother them.

I was a tough old broad in a young woman's body, and my pain threshold was pretty high, but by all rights, I should still be in a hospital bed, letting others take care of me. Or at the very least, I should be kicked back on my little couch, letting my family take care of my chores and tend to my three babies.

But I was too proud for that. I felt obligated to at least see to the limited tasks my dear sweet husband and good mother-in-law allowed me to perform—feeding my six-week-old babies and changing their clouts. My range of motion was restricted because of the pain. On top of that, I noticed that I was downright cranky if I didn't get at least some relief. Sarah didn't have a problem with me taking the pills—no one did, for that matter—but I felt guilty that I couldn't handle day-to-day tasks without taking 'substances.'

"This isn't like labor," Sarah reminded me. "You did wonderful with that, beyond wonderful. You were perfect as far as how well you handled the contractions, but this is different. With labor, you got a few minutes of relief, more or less, between the pains. This is constant discomfort. Take the pills. I'll make sure you don't take too many, and that I always have willow bark tea brewed to rotate with the painkillers. Eventually, you won't need either one of them. All right?"

"Okay, but I still feel like a failure." I accepted the cup of water, swallowed half a pill, and then realized something. "Hey, just think how much whisky I'm saving! Me taking a pill now and then is better than everyone drinking in order to put up with how crabby I get when I'm hurting, huh?"

Jody had walked in unobserved and responded, "Nah, we'd jest ignore ye either way. We'd drink whether ye were cranky or no." He gave me a fatherly kiss on the top of my head. "Are ye feelin' better today, lass?"

"Yes, much better than yesterday, thank you. You know what I'd like to do—and this may sound crazy—but I want to go outside in the sunshine. I know it's hot, but, well, I guess my body needs it. Vitamin D, right, Sarah?"

"That's true. Speaking of nutrition, there's still one banana left. Do you want it now or later?"

"Where's Jenny? I'll share it with her," I said. "She sure is a good helper."

My adopted pre-adolescent daughter had become my extra set of arms. She even offered to feed me. "No, but thank you for the offer." I saw her face fall. "But when these three start on porritch, I'll definitely need your help," then watched her beam at the prospect.

Just then, Jenny, the lady of the moment, ran through the door, her bounty clutched in her arms. "Look what I got! Daddy said I could pick them, and he even let me use his knife to cut them off so I didn't tear up the plant by pulling on 'em. They're peppers, he said, and José says if you fix them right, they're real good with cheese and eggs, and since we already have those, maybe I can help make dinner tonight. Grannie, do you know how to cook these?" she asked, as she pivoted in place, looking for an empty flat spot to set her harvest.

"Uh, no…" Sarah drew out her answer, then looked at me. "Maybe your mother does."

I almost purred at being called mother again, then felt weepy, and it wasn't because of the presence of what looked like Anaheim green chilies. I was that happy. "Yes, I know a great way to fix them: chiles rellenos." Now my eyes were definitely tearing, but for another reason. "Jenny, put them into that basket, please. Then, would you like to share the last banana with me?"

"Ooh! Ooh! You mean the yellow custard fruit? There's still one left? Are you sure you don't want the whole thing? I mean, Grannie says you have to eat lots of food because your body is making milk to feed all those babies, but if you think there's enough for both of us, yes, yes, yes, I want some, too!" Jenny was literally jumping up and down with excitement.

"Well, while your siblings are quiet, let's go outside for a little walk and talk. I want to know more about my big girl." I nodded to Sarah to make sure she was fine with watching—or rather, listening for—the babies.

"You two go ahead and take those peppers out there with you. I don't have enough room in here as it is."

"Sure, Grannnie!" Jenny trilled.

I cut off the end of the banana, wiped the blade, and put Sarah's paring knife back on the table. I had given Wallace my Leatherman, sort of as a wedding gift. He had always admired it, although I never felt like he coveted it.

"When I get to feeling better, and have more time, maybe I can make a little holster for it," I had told him.

"Well, I'm not too sure how I'd wear a holster, but I can make a little pouch to put it in so it's handy. You know, on second thought, I think I may just have to make a sporran. I'm sure Jody would let me use his as a pattern. He seems to be able to keep everything he needs in there."

Jenny started in on a new subject, breaking my reverie. "So I'm your big girl now? Does that mean that I'm your oldest daughter?" she asked with a mouthful of banana.

"It's not nice to speak with food in your mouth, dear," I said, hoping the subject would change. I didn't want to tell her that she wasn't my eldest. That would be too confusing for her and painful for me. I still missed Leah, the daughter I had left behind in the 21st century.

"But I am your biggest daughter, huh?" she persisted, making sure she had swallowed her food before she spoke.

I rolled my eyes comically and said, "Well, you're the biggest one I see. Now, how old are you?" I asked, redirecting our discussion.

"Uh, I dunno," she practically whispered, her face red in embarrassment. She became unusually quiet and focused on her bare foot as she made circles in the dirt with her big toe. Her energy level was nil and her happiness in the negative zone.

"Ooh! Ooh!" I squealed, mimicking her animated, attention-getting noises. She looked up and smiled at me, genuinely happy to see me acting like her. "Does that mean I get to pick your birthday? I mean, the year and everything?" I was dipping up and down, as if ready to jump. I would have, too, but was afraid the jostling would hurt my shoulder.

"Yeah! Yeah! You and Daddy can pick my birthday, even the year! Should I have the same birthday as Wren and Judah and Leo, or maybe it can be on Christmas or…or…"

Jenny was all wound up, dancing around what I called the family tree, blabbering names of events like Easter that she could share a birthday with.

"Slow down there. First off, Easter wouldn't work because it falls on a different date every year. It has something to do with spring equinox and full moons and Sundays and…" I looked over and saw that I had lost her. "Anyway," I continued, "I want you to have your very own day. But it would be nice to have it in the spring, so when you *do* go to school, your classmates can celebrate with you. We can make a birthday cake and give you a party and…"

I looked down and saw that Jenny was crying. "What's wrong, honey?" I gathered her close. I really had no idea what was wrong. One moody female in the house—me—was already one too many.

"I'm just so happy," she sobbed. "I get to go to school *and* have a party? And a cake? Just for me?" Her upturned faced was searching mine, asking for confirmation that what I had just told her was true.

"Yes, but I'll have to find out if there's a school around here. I don't know if there is one yet. But," I stressed, "if there isn't one, we'll just have to start one ourselves. In the meantime, I'll make sure we set aside a little time…uh…five days a week. I'll teach you to read and write and do your numbers. You can take time off from schooling on Saturdays and Sundays."

"I know what Sunday is," she bragged. "I learned about it from Mrs. Short. She kinda took me in as a helper when my brothers and me—that is, my other brothers that died and went to heaven—when we went into town to do some tradin' and get some supplies. She was real nice sometimes, but other times…" Jenny shook her head back and forth as if she was having a hard time believing what she was thinking, "She was *real* mean."

"Do you want to talk about it?" I looked at the last of the banana, took one more bite, and then offered the rest to her.

"Thanks," she said and bit off the last morsel. She chewed slowly, then suddenly stopped and spit the half-chewed mass into her hand. "Can we get the seeds out of this and plant them? We can have more custard fruit if we plant the seeds. Then we can have them every day!"

"No, no," I said, as I shook my head, refusing her masticated glob. "Go ahead and finish eating it. Bananas are different than most fruits. They don't grow from seeds. They grow from…" I paused, trying to figure out how to explain rhizomes and cuttings, "they grow from runners, and we don't have the main plant around here. So, just enjoy it while you have it, okay?"

"Okay. That means all right, huh?" she said, then licked off the slimy mess, bent over, and wiped her sticky hands through the fine soil at her feet. She rubbed her palms together and let the little grunge worms of food residue mixed with dirt fall onto the ground. She briskly dusted off her hands, turned them over for closer inspection, and then wiped them on the back of her skirt. She had apparently adapted to her earlier soap-less environment and found a way to keep from becoming grimy and tacky. I'd have to remember to teach her to use soap and water after her little dry cleaning routines.

"Do you still want to know about Mrs. Short?" she asked, then bit her bottom lip in mildly suppressed anticipation. She and I hadn't had much alone time, and she wanted as much of my attention as she could get.

"Sure, tell me all about her while we walk a little." My body needed exercise, at least something other than lifting or bending over babies.

"Well, she started out real nice. She saw me in town with my brothers—my other brothers…" She looked at me to make sure I understood. I nodded, so she continued. "Well, I don't think she liked that bag I was wearing for clothes. My brothers didn't have any pants 'cept the ones what they wore. For me, they just cut holes in old flour sacks for dresses. I had two of them," Jenny said proudly. "But Mrs. Short said I needed somethin' proper. I was a young lady and deserved more, whatever that meant. I mean, I didn't pay for nothin', so why did I deserve somethin'?

"Well, anyhow, she asked my brothers—my other brothers…" she looked up again, and I nodded again, "she asked them if it was all right if I stayed with her a while. They said they had some trappin' to do, and if she wanted, then I could stay with her for the whole winter. Well, that was all right with me 'cause it got real cold when they went out in the woods like that. They did their best to keep me warm and made me a coat outta some of the skins from the muskrats that got torn up in the traps. Those were the pelts that were spoilt and not worth much. But the coat was stiff. I couldn't move very good in it and well, when she said I could stay with her for the whole winter, and that she had a nice big fireplace, and I could sleep by the hearth and everything… Well, I asked my brothers…"

Jenny looked up at me, and before she could say 'her other brothers,' I nodded for her to proceed.

"Well, my brothers thought that it was a good idea, too. But they asked her if she could give them some bacon and flour for me since she would have me workin' for her all winter. I don't think she liked that much, but still, she gave them some.

"She was real nice at first, and I didn't have to do much. She let me sweep the floors for her and even let me put soap in a bucket with water and scrub down the hearth one day when it wasn't too cold.

"And she had this basket that she said she got from an Indian woman. It had lots of pieces of bright cloth in it. And, well, she said it was time I learned how to sew. She said her eyes weren't too good anymore, but she could still teach me what to do. So she gave me a little box and it had some needles in it. And then she showed me how to put the thread through the *eye*," Jenny looked at me to make sure she was using the right word.

"Yes, the eye of the needle is where the thread goes through. Go ahead. We still have some time, but I think we should head back to the porch. I didn't know I'd tire so easily."

Jenny grabbed my hand in an attempt to help me walk. It didn't make a difference as far as the walking went, but the emotional support was priceless. She was a chatterbox for sure, but she was our little chatterbox.

"So, I got to thread every one of her needles. I'm not sure how many there were, but at least ten." Jenny let go of my hand momentarily, brought up both her hands and displayed all her fingers. "Ten," she repeated.

"See, she had me put the needle in her hand so the sharp end wouldn't hurt her, and she showed me how to do a runnin' stitch and a backstitch and a overcast stitch. Well, I guess I wasn't as fast as she thought I should be, and sometimes she'd holler at me if my stitches were too big or too messy. You see, her eyes weren't too good, but her hands could feel just fine. She'd run her fingers across my stitchin' and could tell if I messed up. If I did, she'd make me tear it all out and start all over again. That is, after she smacked my hand for bein' lazy or careless or whatever else she felt like callin' me that day.

"But she wasn't always mean. I think it was just when her head was hurtin' real bad. She had some tonic that she drank for it, and I don't know if it helped or not, but it did make her fall asleep after a while. She called it a tonic, but I think it was just whisky. I've smelt whisky before, and that's what it smelt like.

"So I sewed all sorts of bits and pieces of the cloth rags together, and then she said that since I was such a good girl—you see, she wasn't hurtin' that day—that she would help me make my own dress. She showed me how to measure myself with a piece of string, and then stretch it across the cloth. Then she even let me use the shears—all by myself. Well, she said that her hands wouldn't work the shears anymore, but still, I got to use them all by myself," she repeated with pride.

"So, you made your first dress all by yourself?" I asked, proud of her youthful accomplishment.

"Well, yes, I guess so. At least, I did all the cuttin' and sewin'. I made one bad cut, but she didn't even get mad at me. She said that I just had to fix it myself and learn from my mistake. Every time that I would see that bit of extra stitchin', I'd remember to measure twice and cut once. But that was the dress that I lost at the mill last week. The one that the mean man made me take off and…"

"And now you have another one, and maybe we can make you one more. And since you already know how to measure and sew, maybe you can help Grannie make one for me, too?"

I was trying to make her feel better about her talent, but I also wanted to help her forget about that vile Captain Asshole who had attacked her at the mill. Hopefully, the soldiers had taken him before whomever, and a fair judgment and punishment was ordered. Well, I knew what the punishment was supposed to be, and it wasn't up to me whether he was hanged by the neck until dead or exiled to Elba or Timbuktu. As long as Captain Atholl MacLeod was out of our lives, that was fine by me.

Chapter 8: Evie and Wallace: Together at last (H'PJ Ch 2)

Sarah aimlessly fussed about in the kitchen area, intentionally avoiding eye contact with me, lifting each stack of diapers then setting it down, rearranging the cups on the shelf, shifting the chair back against the wall.

"Are you all set here for this evening? Do you have enough clean clouts, at least for tonight and tomorrow morning?" she asked.

"Yes, I'm fine, thank you." I narrowed my eyes in suspicion. "Where are you going?" There was something afoot by the tone in her voice and the attitude of her movements. She hadn't looked at me when she spoke, and that meant she was hiding something. She seemed to be investigating the room half-heartedly, but for what I didn't know.

She took a deep breath, then said a bit too casually, "Oh, Jody, Jenny, and I are going on a little trip." She kept her eyes low and brushed off a bit of transparent food or soil or whatever from her apron. "Will you and Wallace be okay by yourselves?"

"Of course, we will. He can take care of anything that I can't. And where... Oh!" I paused a moment, realization hitting me like a door slamming me in the face, "You'll be gone overnight, which means my husband and I will be here without any—shall we say?—chaperones."

Sarah blushed. She hadn't been as sly as she thought. She shrugged and said—this time looking me in the eye, "We'll just be in the barn so Wallace won't have to take care of the animals this evening or in the morning. We'll see to the feeding and such. Now, unless you yell *too loudly*, we won't disturb you, all right?"

"Well..." I said and giggled, "Don't come if Wallace yells *too loudly* either." Then I turned around and did a bit of blushing myself.

***

Later that evening...

"Come on, Jenny," Jody hollered, "we're gonna have a little party tonight, jest the three of us—ye, yer Grannie, and me."

"But what about Mommy and Daddy? Don't they want to come, too?"

"Well, we're gonna leave them alone tonight, aye? Sometimes a mommy and da jest need to be by themselves. Besides, I have a game I want to show ye."

"But who will help Mommy take care of the babies? She needs me, she told me so," Jenny argued, obviously hurt at not being able to stay the evening with her new siblings. "And don't Mommy and Daddy want to play the game, too?"

Sarah looked over at Jody and decided he needed a little help with the precocious little interrogator. She squatted down to Jenny's level and brushed the stray hair out of her eyes. "Well, they…um…have other things to do and really don't need our help for that. Besides, your daddy was helping Mommy with the babies before they got you. I'm sure he hasn't forgotten how to change a clout or burp a baby. Now, I have your quilt. Let's build a bed for you right over here on the clean straw. Grandpa and I will be right next to you in case you get scared."

"I don't get scared," Jenny declared strongly, and then remembered the fright at the mill last week. "Well, not much," she admitted. She looked around and saw that Grannie had already spread her quilt on the straw. "You mean we're going to be out here *all night?*"

"Aye, we'll have lots to do. I dinna think ye'll find it irksome." Jody opened out his fist. "See what I got fer ye."

Jenny peered into his huge hand. "Can I touch it?"

"Go aheid; its yers." He used the tip of his index finger to flip the bone-handled penknife onto its other side. "It's time ye had one of yer own. I'll show ye how to use it for work and…" He drew out the anticipation of the rest of his explanation by opening the folding knife and balancing it on the back of his hand. "I'll show ye how to play a game, jest in case ye happen to have a spare minute or two between tendin' to yon bairns, aye?"

He quickly flipped his hand over and caught the penknife flat onto his palm. "But I think we'd best be tryin' the first few rounds with the blade shut. Jest until ye get the feel of the weight."

"Can I make arrows with it like the Indians do?" she asked, bouncing on her toes in anticipation.

"Weel, I think yer mommy would rather ye start by carvin' knittin' needles and what she calls crochet hooks. They're better tools fer a lass yer age to have."

Jenny's response of, "Hmph!" was a guttural blend of 'why?' and 'I don't think so!'

Her face changed moods several times while she studied the small-bladed instrument. "Well, I guess I can do that, but I'm gonna notch the ends of my knittin' needles and put a feather in 'em anyhow. Then maybe when I'm bigger, like next week, you can help me build a bow. I'll shoot bows and arrows at the bad Indians and keep them away for good!" she said, chest out in pride.

"Weel, the only Indians I've seen around here are the good ones, so I hope ye dinna plan on shootin' anyone. And mind ye, ye shoot the arrows, not the bows. Maybe we can build ye a target to practice yer aim so ye can knock some of those nasty crows out of the garden next month when the corn starts gettin' ripe. They always seem to be the best judges of when it's time fer the harvestin'."

Chapter 9: Wedding Night (H'PJ Ch 3)

My wee three were all fed, burped, bathed, and put down to sleep. They were almost six weeks old and now looked like babies, not preemies. Their little arms and legs had filled out quickly, and their cheeks were pleasingly plump. The boys were still bigger than Wren, but she was closing the size gap quickly.

They were still too young to sleep through the night, but they stayed quiet for longer periods now. I didn't have a watch or clock, but my chest could tell time. My breasts filled at a constant rate, and if they weren't emptied at a regular interval, then I'd get uncomfortable. I knew from somewhere—probably from when Leah was a baby—that my body would adjust to more feedings during the day and fewer at night. I doubted I could last eight hours straight without nursing at least one baby, but I'd be willing to try for a four or five-hour stretch of uninterrupted sleep.

"Do you need a hand with anything?" Wallace asked as he put away the dishtowel. He had done the dishes after dinner, which left me free to give the babies their baths. They weren't 'dirty,' but a thorough rinsing freshened them up, cooled them down, and tired them out.

"No, thank you," I said, then quickly changed my mind. "On second thought, wait. I'll let you help me undress, so *I* can take a little sponge bath."

It wasn't the most romantic overture, but I didn't have much time alone with him until the next feedings. I didn't want to spend what precious little time we had alone being coy.

Wallace gulped, then grinned so wide, I thought his bottom lip would disappear altogether. He approached me slowly but decidedly as if I was the chocolate cake he had been denied his whole life. Whoa, wait... I guess I really was like that—a real dessert, a forbidden treat—now his.

I twisted and lifted the hair off of my neck and shoulders with one hand, using the other to work the button loose on the neck of his shirt. He hadn't asked, but I was going to do a little exposing, too. "Can I see you without your shirt?" I asked.

He crossed his arms and pulled the shirt off over his head. I inhaled deeply. At last. He was mine. And we were alone. Well, alone except for our three youngest, but they were asleep.

He put his hand on each side of my gown. "May I?"

I nodded, looked up, and then gave him the same lip-disappearing smile he had given me.

He gently opened out the dress and slid it down over my shoulders, carefully lifting the left side away from my beige-colored 21st century adhesive bandage.

"It's okay; it doesn't hurt much. As long as I'm careful, we can do just about anything." I glanced up and saw that he wasn't looking at the bandaging, but my plump and perky nipples, dark brown and hard with excitement.

He caught my eye and an immediate blush rose on his cheeks. "They don't look the same without a bairn's head in front of them," he said softly.

"Hey, they're yours, too…just like the rest of me."

"Aye? Oh, aye!" His hands rose to my cheeks. "Mrs. Wallace Pomeroy-Hart, my beautiful, wise, and wonderful wife, Evie," he bent down to share the first of—hopefully—many wedding night kisses.

After a very thorough smooch, he whispered, "Evie. Is that short for another name?"

"Um, no." I grimaced. I didn't want to spoil the mood but felt I needed to answer the question. "It's the name Ian gave me. I didn't know my name—or even who I was—when I found and rescued him, so he decided to call me Evie. I like the name just fine, though. It feels," I shrugged my good shoulder, "*comfortable.*"

"Hmm, I gave you the name Pomeroy-Hart when we married, but can I make a suggestion?" he asked, one eyebrow raised in hope.

"Yeah, sure," I answered, unsure of where this was going.

"Evangeline. I like the name Evangeline. We would still call you Evie, but you would be *my* Evangeline."

I felt my eyes light up. "Wow…yes…I mean, sure. I like that name! Cool. That's a gift no one can take away from me, and I'll have it as long as I live. No, wait—I'll have it even after I'm dead! At least, for as long as anyone remembers me." I was flattered with the gift of the new name and giddy at the prospect of immortality.

"Well, we'll just have to write stories so the life and times of Evangeline Pomeroy-Hart will be passed down through the ages—to our heirs, and to anyone else who's interested in life in a young America. You did say America will still be around in 200 years, right?"

"You know I did, silly. And I like the idea of a journal. I'm sure I can figure a way to get it handed down to Leah, so she can find out all about you and her siblings and the rest of her family here. I felt so bad having to leave her but," I exhaled sharply, "I made my decision and I'm glad of it. Now, how about we seal—or would that be dedicate?—this new name with a little friction."

Wallace looked puzzled, so I helped him out with a one-armed grab around his neck, pulling him down for a long, wet kiss. "I think I'd be more comfortable lying down," I suggested, and ran my hand down the side of his neck to between his pectorals.

"Oh…OH!" he exclaimed when he realized what I meant. He put his hand on mine and led me to our—well, really Jody's and Sarah's—bed.

"I've been saving it as a surprise, but," he pursed his lips and made the decision to tell me now, "I'm making a bed for us. We may not have our own home yet, but we'll have a bed for it when we do."

"Well, this will do for tonight." I snuggled into his chest and breathed in his male essence. We had only been close, physically close, a couple of times, but had never been skin to skin before. "Would you touch me, I mean, touch me all over? I've been aching for your hands… Oh, yeah…" I gasped as he began, then relaxed, and let him explore.

Wallace started at my face, air-glided his hand above my still tender shoulder, then settled his hand on my waist. He let it rest there for a moment and used his thumb to gently stroke my belly. He brought his fingers together again, then brought them down my hips to the outside of my thighs.

"You don't have to be bashful. My body is yours, too," I said and guided his cool fingers back over to my belly. "It's still kind of mushy from being pregnant, but it'll tighten up again."

I continued the guided tour to my intimate parts. "Right now, I'm kind of moist there because I'm so excited. It makes…um…everything go in easier," I said with a bit of embarrassment. I didn't want to be a little miss know-it-all, but I did want him to know some of the nuances that he probably had never heard about. Sarah had let it slip that Jody had a 'talk' with him. I appreciated the heads-up, so I wasn't too bossy in my instructions.

Wallace took control from there, his bashfulness overcome by a healthy combination of curiosity and excitement.

"Mmm," I moaned as my knees parted to let him explore further.

"You're so soft down there," he said, "like a padded pillow."

I giggled, "Yeah, a furry padded pillow. I guess that's so we don't bruise our pelvic bones when we…um…"

I didn't finish with words but decided it was time to do some of my own petting and pawing. I wrapped my hand around the shaft of his very ready cock and pulled down gently on the skin. He gasped and let out a gentle moan. "Just making sure you healed right," I said coyly.

I really was checking. I was afraid that he may have lost too much foreskin after he had been slashed in the groin area and I had to perform a little impromptu field circumcision after Pyle's Massacre last spring. I had heard horror stories about men who had been circumcised and had too much foreskin removed. It actually caused the men pain to have an erection. By the purring that Wallace was emitting, though, that wasn't the case with him.

Wallace still had his hand on my *pillow*, cradling it as if it was his prized possession. He let his thumb slip down a bit, and ever so gently touched and then rubbed just the right place. I gasped at the intense but very pleasurable sensation. I hadn't been touched there by anyone—including me—for an incredibly long time. I looked at him, swallowing hard with the excitement he had caused, and saw that he was chuckling.

"How…how…how did you know about that spot?" I stuttered.

"Oh, I got a few pointers. That one was easy to find. Now, should we see if I can find another?" He pulled his hand away and started to get up on one elbow, his other arm crossing over me to assume the missionary position.

"Uh huh," I nodded. It looked like Wallace was going to take to the more intimate duties of being a husband just fine.

Chapter 10: Jenny and the mumblety peg (H'PJ Ch 4)

Jenny lay on her quilt, flat on her back, pretending to be asleep. She rolled over toward Grannie and Grandpa Jody and listened. They were finally asleep. At least, they weren't whispering or giggling or telling each other to shush anymore.

Maybe if she was real quiet, they wouldn't wake up and she could go back where she belonged—to the house with Mommy and Daddy and the babies.

She had had a nice time—well, actually it was a whole heap of fun—spending the evening with Grandpa and learning how to play mumblety peg. But she missed her babies. And no matter what Grannie said, she was sure that Mommy needed her help. When the babies woke up at night with bad dreams, she was the one who rubbed their backs until they fell asleep again. It was only when they were really hungry, or had messed their clouts, or had a big burp that they were really awake. Even then, she could do everything except feed them. She needed to be there to help, so Mommy wouldn't have to work so hard and her shoulder could get better.

Jenny lifted her head and looked to make sure Grannie and Grandpa were really asleep. She couldn't see their faces, but they were very still. Only their backs were moving, in and out slowly with their breathing. Now it was safe to go back to her own bed. She tried to take her quilt, but the straw beneath it shifted when she tugged on it. She'd have to sleep without it tonight. That would be all right, though, because she only needed to sleep on top of it. She could do without it for one night. After all, she was a big girl now.

The moon was bright and lit the path to the house. She wasn't afraid of anything—not now, anyhow. All the bad men were gone, and the bears and pumas didn't come near the house, at least, not lately. Jenny looked around quickly, suddenly afraid of mountain lions, bad men, and bears, oh my!

"Eek! What are you doing up, Grandpa Jody?" she asked, twitching with embarrassment at being caught sneaking away.

"I was fixin' to ask ye the same thing. Yer supposed to be sleepin' in the barn with yer Grannie and me tonight."

Jody stood in front of her, arms across his chest like a Roman centurion, waiting for her answer.

"Um…um," she mumbled, twitching nervously. She couldn't tell him that she was sure Mommy needed her help. He had already told her at least ten times that Mommy and Daddy were fine and could do without her for one night.

"What's wrong?" he asked, noticing that she was uneasy, dancing from one foot to the other. "Do ye need to use the privy again?"

Jenny nodded frantically, then bent forward and squeezed her knees together in an exaggerated mime of urinary urgency.

"Weel, git to it. Come back to the barn as soon as yer finished. And no sneakin' back to the house, d'ye hear?"

"Yes, sir, Grandpa Jody," she said, then ran to the privy. She quickly shut the door behind her and climbed onto the seat to look through the little crescent-moon hole. She needed to make sure Grandpa was returning to the barn and wouldn't see her go back to Mommy and Daddy.

Shoot. He was still there. It looked like he was going to wait for her. Jenny decided it was time to for another tactic. "Ooh," she moaned. "Ooh! Uh, I think I'll be in here for a while, Grandpa Jody. I think I ate too many of those boiled peanuts. Ooh…" Jenny moaned and groaned dramatically for almost five minutes, or so it seemed.

"Do ye think ye can make it back to the barn by yerself? That is, when yer finished?"

Jody wasn't sure whether she really had a bellyache or not. She had eaten quite a few of the boiled peanuts, but then again, she might be trying to sneak back to the house. He'd let her be but would listen for her. He had never told her that she shuffled her feet and made a distinctive noise when she walked. It was a good way to keep track of where she was, and—by her long, foot-dragged tracks—where she had been.

"Uh, I'll be okay. But don't wait up for me. Ooh…" Jenny put her hand to her mouth to stifle a giggle. She had fooled Grandpa Jody!

Jody walked back to the barn, stomping his feet to make sure she knew he was walking away. It looked like he was going to be on sentry duty until she decided to come out.

***

150

Jenny looked out and saw that now Grannie had come out and was talking to Grandpa Jody. His back was turned away, and it looked as if he was going to kiss Grannie again. Good! Grannie sometimes made little noises—kind of like a kitten—when he kissed her. Hopefully, she would this time. Then he wouldn't hear her open the door and run to the house.

Jenny saw her grandparents were almost—no, wait, now they were—kissing. She stepped down off the privy seat and opened the door. She took two steps away and listened. Yes, they were *still* smooching. They sure liked to kiss a lot. She picked up her feet and walked on her tiptoes, being careful not to make any noise.

Just to make sure she made it to the house before they stopped kissing, she ran the last ten yards, almost stepping on the garden hoe she had forgotten to put away. Phew! Daddy was right! Someone could get hurt if the tools were left out. She'd put it away, but later, probably tomorrow. Right now, she needed to go inside and be with her babies and Mommy and Daddy.

The front door was open, but there was a blanket tacked across the middle part of the doorframe. Mommy said the cool air could come in at the bottom, and the hot air could go out the top if they hung the blanket up like that. She didn't like to sleep with the door open, but it had been too hot to bolt it shut. A big animal would make a lot of noise trying to come in, but she said it would stop if it couldn't see past the blanket. Wild critters didn't like going into the unknown.

Jenny got on her hands and knees so she could crawl under the blanket without knocking it down. Then she heard that noise. It didn't sound right. Mommy sounded like she was hurting. She was saying 'Oh, oh, oh, oh.' And Daddy was making noises, too. But she knew that noise. Kind of. It sounded like her brothers when they used to play rooster. They always made her leave, or at least cover her head with a blanket, when they did that.

Jenny cautiously threaded her neck under the quilt and saw Daddy on top of Mommy. He didn't have on any clothes and neither did she. She quickly crawled back out onto the porch, stood up, and tiptoed back toward the barn. Now she knew why they wanted to be alone. They wanted to play their own game.

"I'm okay, now," she said dejectedly as she walked up to Grandpa.

151

He had been walking toward the privy and met her halfway.

She was sure glad she hadn't taken the shortcut back. She had fooled him—he thought that she had been in there the whole time with a bellyache. She didn't like lying to him, but she had to make sure that Mommy, Daddy, and the babies were all right.

Why didn't they just tell her that they wanted to play by themselves? She would have understood. She rolled over on top of her quilt and thought about it again. No, she would have wanted to play with them, too. But if they had just told her that they were going to play rooster, she *knew* she would have left them alone. She didn't like that game.

Chapter 11: The Game of Rooster (H'PJ Ch 5)

Jody hadn't say anything when Jenny came back to the barn, but he could tell something had happened. She must have slipped out of the privy while he was talking to Sarah. How could he have let her get past him? He snorted. He knew how, but didn't want to admit to himself that he had been so engrossed in the little sexual fantasy he and Sarah were sharing—and the kiss that lasted longer than most—that Jenny had escaped the toilet and sneaked back to the house. Hopefully, she hadn't seen anything but came back because she saw that nothing was going on. Hopefully, but not likely.

He had to let Wallace and Evie know that they may have had an audience last night. He should probably tell them both. It would be easier to only tell Wallace, but Evie was the one who would wind up with the chore of explaining what Jenny possibly—rather, probably—had seen.

No one knew Jenny's age, but she was old enough to know the facts of life. At least, according to Sarah she was. He had to agree with her on that one. The discomfort of giving and receiving last minute wedding night explanations that he—and then later, his son—had to go through was enough to make him swallow his conservative views on what a lad or lass should know at such an early age. It would be much easier on everyone down the road if when the time came for marriage, the newlywed had received at least a preliminary talk as a child.

Jody stomped his feet as he walked up the steps to the house, the heavy footfalls announcing his arrival. The quilt had been taken down, and the sounds and smells of a full-fare breakfast came tumbling down the boards. Hopefully, Evie had made enough for everyone, he thought, then realized how selfish he was. His stomach overrode the guilt of his covetous desire, though, and roared with greed. It didn't care if it was intruding on a wedding breakfast or not. The smell of bacon and coffee would rouse anyone's appetite.

Wallace had Leo over his shoulder and was rubbing his back. It looked as if he had just been fed and Daddy was burping him while Mommy was turning the bacon.

"I know, I know, I should be cooking outside, but I didn't want to go through the bother, and it's still early enough that the heat will dissipate," I rationalized. "Besides, I love the way it makes the house smell for the rest of the day. And I made enough for everyone, so you'd better not be mad at me, or I'll eat your share." I walked up to Jody and gave him a quick peck on the cheek. The previous night's excitement hadn't totally worn off, and I was still perky.

I pulled back and noticed that Jody was wincing as if either his collar or his shoelaces were too tight. Since he had neither, I asked, "What's wrong?" Wallace had noticed his grimace, too, and was concerned, asking with his scowl to, yes, please explain.

"I...um...think I may have failed in my task last night," Jody said. "Jenny may have sneaked over here when it was late. Ye see, she said she had a knot in her wame, and I waited fer her by the privy fer quite a while, and then I got a bit distracted..." Jody didn't know what else to say but knew he had to try. "I dinna ask her if she came by, and she dinna offer an explanation. It was the frown she wore. She seemed what ye call mopey. I think maybe ye need to have *the talk* with the lass, Evie."

Jody hung his head in shame, let out a big sigh, then lifted his face and said, "Wallace, both of ye, I...I am so sorry."

I looked at Wallace and shrugged. "Well, if she did see something, then I can explain it. That means that *maybe*," I stressed with exaggerated exasperation, "we can have a life like the Indians do where having sex—making love—can be considered a natural part of life and not something to be hidden."

Wallace and Jody's heads snapped up, shocked at my words, but quickly returned to normal. I could tell they were both relieved. Well, at least the part where I said I'd do the investigating and explaining.

So, it turned out that all of us ate our big breakfast on the porch, the men sitting on the steps, the babies in their playpen snuggled under a light blanket, and the womenfolk sitting on chairs or benches, all of us with plates of bacon, scrambled eggs, and coffee cake balanced on our laps.

I could tell Jenny was uneasy, her head down, and nothing but a, "Yes, please," or, "No, thank you," escaping her tight lips. She had definitely seen something the night before. We could all see her reserve, but we certainly weren't going to address it at the family breakfast.

When we were done, Sarah and Jody offered to take care of the dirty dishes. Wallace looked as if he was going to say he'd help, also, but realized it would be too crowded with all three of them inside at the same time. Instead, he excused himself to the garden. "I think I'll go see how the corn is coming along. It shouldn't be too much longer and those first four rows will be ready. I've never heard of planting it in stages, but Evie was right. That small, early planting was a gamble, but we'll have roasted corn before anyone else."

That left me with two on-site caregivers for the babies and the opportunity for a discreet facts of life talk. "Jenny, let's go for a little walk," I said. "I found some raspberries, and I want you to come with me and see if they're getting ripe."

"I think the raspberries are already gone—the birds got them all," she said dejectedly. She saw my eyes shift, side-to-side, and knew that I didn't want to talk about raspberries. "But I'll go with you if you want me to," she sang out happily. She didn't have a clue about the reason for the walk, but the fact that she was going to get Mommy to herself for a few minutes didn't need an excuse.

I knew we didn't have much time. The babies still needed to be fed every couple of hours. Since I was their only source of nourishment, I couldn't be gone for too long or stray too far away. I had to cut to the chase and get the conversation started, figured out, and finalized as quickly as possible. But I also had to be both gentle and thorough.

"Jenny, did you leave the barn last night and come back to the house?" I wasn't looking her in the eye, but she was a lousy liar. I was glad of that and hoped she never learned.

"Yes, ma'am, I went to the privy," she replied with a half-truth. She also didn't know how to bluff.

"I didn't ask if you went to the privy. Did you come to the house?"

"Yes, ma'am," she answered softly, chin-to-chest, embarrassed that she had been caught.

I wanted to jump all over her for not doing as she was told, but because of the delicacy of the situation—at least, on the part that she may have seen me, her parent, engaged in sexual intercourse—I didn't want to put her on report. I bit off the 'why didn't you do as you were told!' scolding and instead asked, "What did you see?"

Jenny didn't answer immediately but instead went to the raspberry bush that was picked clean of fruit. "See," she said, "the birds ate them all before we got here. If I'd lived here with you back when they were ripe, I'd 'a made sure I got them all before the birds did." She looked back at me with a smile of pride at her declaration of devotion to help provide food for her family. It faded quickly when she saw that I was still waiting for the answer to my question.

"I saw you and Daddy playing rooster," she said flatly. Then she turned the tables on me and asked accusingly, "Why didn't you just tell me you wanted to play rooster? I woulda understood and covered my head or stayed out in the barn with Grannie and Grandpa Jody. Really, I would have."

What could I say? "Rooster?" was all that escaped my lips.

"Yeah," she said slowly, "at least that's what I called it when my brothers—my other brothers, the ones that are up in heaven—used to play it. They said that I couldn't watch and that I would have to go outside. Except in the winter when it was too cold, then they said that I could just cover my head with a blanket."

I shook my head but didn't know what to say. She looked at me to make sure I knew what she was talking about and then noticed that I didn't have a clue. She assumed the Mommy role and started her explanation to me—the dumbfounded child in the conversation.

"Clyde and Clayton," she said with assurance—I think she had finally decided that it was easier to call them by their given names rather than explain which brothers they were. "Well," she began anew, not sure of how to tell me, "they liked to, well, get happy together."

She looked at me and saw that I was starting to understand, at least a little. "Well, I…um…saw them playin' it outside once, and they said that I couldn't sneak up on them like that anymore. I guess they did it all the time, but they said I couldn't play it with them because I was just a girl. But, then after our daddy died, that's our first daddy…"

She looked at me and saw me frown. She realized that I knew who she was talking about, so resumed. "Anyway, they said that they could play by themselves inside now since he was gone, but that I had to cover my head when they did because it wasn't for little kids or babies. Actually, they always called *me* a baby, and it made me mad because I really wasn't a baby…"

I gave her the 'look' and she stopped babbling about being called a baby. "So, they'd tell me to cover my head every once in a while at night, and then they'd make happy noises, and then one of them would 'ooh ooh ooh rah ooh!' like a rooster, so I called it the rooster game."

I breathed a deep sigh of relief. She saw that I felt better and came over and gave me a big hug around my hips. "Mommy, it's okay if you and Daddy play rooster. I'll cover my head, but please, don't make me sleep outside. I liked being with Grannie and Grandpa Jody, but I felt like you didn't love me anymore and didn't want me around."

"Oh, honey," I cooed and bent down to wrap my arms around her shoulders. "I will always love you, and do want you around, but…" I cleared my throat and said a quick prayer for inspiration. She looked up at me, knowing that she would hear something profound. "God made mommies and daddies and gave them *gifts* to share with each other. And," I shook my head rapidly, trying to Etch-a-Sketch erase the image of Clyde and Clayton joined with anyone, "it is not a game called rooster."

Jenny tilted her head to the side and waited for further explanation. "You see, it might look like we were doing the same thing as them," I cleared my throat, "but it's not at all alike. You know that boys and girls are different; that Leo and Judah have a penis and Wren, you and me, well, we have a vagina. When you grow up and find someone you love and want to be with forever, then, Lord willing, you'll get married. And then, and *only* then will you get to share your gift. In the meantime, the vagina and penis are just used for, well, bodily functions."

"You mean like peein'?" she asked.

I didn't want to get deep into female anatomy and explain the difference between a vagina and a urethra, so simply nodded. "And you'll have changes happen in your body as you get older. You're already having some changes," I said, and pointed to her little budding breasts, "and here in a couple years, you'll get some *major* changes. But we can talk about that later. I think we still have a while before that happens and only a few more minutes before the babies start waking up. But, just so you're clear on this…"

Jenny brightened up and offered her synopsis of my mini facts of life lesson. "You and Daddy don't play rooster, but you do share your gifts, and no one else is supposed to watch. So if you want to do it, I have to go out to the barn or cover my head with a blanket."

"Well, we won't make you go out to the barn again. That was as much for you and your grandparents to have a little party of your own as it was for your Daddy and me to have…er…um…our party. But if you wake up in the middle of the night, and it looks like your Daddy and I are sharing our gifts, please, don't say anything. And yes, it would be very polite for you to cover your head and go back to sleep. Okay?"

"Okay," she replied simply, as if we had been making something big out of nothing. "Ooh, look, under here. The birds missed some berries. I'll put my hands out and you can knock 'em in."

I looked under the tangle of branches and saw the overloaded clusters. "Here, I'll put my hands underneath and you knock them down with a stick. My hands are bigger and can hold more. And I don't want you getting your hands scratched. It looks like we can have berries and cream for dessert tonight!"

Chapter 12: Who did it? (H'PJ Ch 6)

"Did you do it or did Daddy do it?" Jenny asked as she peered around my elbow while I changed Wren's diaper.

"Do what?" I answered as I continued to wipe the mustard-looking poopy mess from between the folds of the baby's vulva.

"Cut it off," she said simply.

"Oh, the little umbilicus just dries up and falls off after a week or so. See, it's still a little red, but she has a pretty little belly button. Would you hand me that cloth, please?"

I looked down at her as she placed the damp rag in my hand. There was something amiss with her. "What's wrong?"

"I didn't mean about her belly button. I mean the other thing—the peanut."

I choked back a laugh. "The penis, you mean? She's a girl and never had one. She was born like that, and you and I and Grannie were, too. Remember how I told you that boys and girls were different? Well, that's pretty much the main difference. I mean, we all have a heart and lungs." I looked down and saw that I was losing her. "We all have arms and legs and a head and eyes..." I looked at her again to make sure she was following.

Jenny was nodding her head thoughtfully. "So nobody chopped off my *penis* to make me a girl," she said, stressing the word carefully to make sure she had it right.

I nodded slowly three times, looking her in the eye to make sure she understood.

"They lied to me!" she carped, then sniffed and ran out the door, leaving me with a fistful of crappy clout and a delighted Wren, happy to be bare-assed.

Chapter 13: Why did they lie to me? (H'PJ Ch 7)

I found Jenny hiding—well, sort of—by the woodpile. She was whittling something, but looked very angry, as if she were pushing her rage through the little penknife's blade into the toilet paper roll-sized piece of pine.

"What's wrong?" I almost asked if it was something I had said or done but knew that she'd tell me the long version when she was ready.

She put her carving aside, wiped the blade on her skirt, and folded it up. Then she put the knife on the back of her right hand and flipped it over, caught it, then repeated the trick with her left hand. Grandpa Jody had shown her how to play mumblety peg only last week. It looked as if she was already pretty good at it.

She stopped showing off, and without even looking at me, asked, "Why do people lie?"

I sat down on the chopping block next to her. "Look at me, please." She did, but I wasn't sure I wanted to see *that* face. I didn't know that my sweet young girl could mix up anger and sadness so thoroughly. Shoot, I didn't know anyone could. But she was right. Why did people lie?

"I don't know for sure. I mean, it's not as if there's a book of instructions where you look up a question and the answer is right there. We have a Bible, and it has many great teachings in it. It says we're not supposed to lie, but I don't know if it says *why* people lie. I guess everyone has his own reasons. I mean, if I don't know the answer to a question or a problem, I'm not afraid to say, 'I don't know,' and ask someone for help, and you shouldn't be either. But some people believe they would be admitting that they're weak—as in not as good as another person—if they don't understand. Do you understand?"

"Yes, I understand that I don't understand everything, if that's what you mean. And it's okay." Jenny gave a silly grin and wagged her head like a bobble doll. "It's okay that I don't know everything because I'm still a child."

"Yes, but I'm an adult and I'm still learning. Granny is a great healer and has been to school for many years to learn ways to mend people's bodies, but she'll be the first one to tell you that there's so much she still doesn't know…and that many times she learns from people who aren't as schooled as she is. Just because you're older or have been to

160

more schools, doesn't make you smarter."

"So smart people lie, too?"

"Jenny, too many people lie. There have been times I've *not* told people things that I thought they didn't need to know, but I promise you, I have always tried to tell the truth." Uncertainty suddenly kicked in. "You haven't been lying, have you?"

"No. My brothers lied to me. I didn't even know what lying was for a long time. Sometimes they'd tell me one thing, like the sun always came up in the east because that's where the sun birds stayed in the mornings, and it was their job to carry the sun across the sky. Other times, they said it was because the sun was a great big candle and it floated from one side of the mountains to the other and then big giants blew it out for the night. They never told me how it got back again, though, or what sun birds looked like, or where the giants slept."

Jenny's frown was back. "But when they lied to me, they made me feel like there was something wrong with me because I was a girl. They said I was born a boy, but that part got chopped off because I wasn't smart enough. That's why I had girl stuff, because my boy stuff got chopped off. Well, they called what you pee with *stuff*, but still, it's okay *not* to have a penis, isn't it?"

"Oh, good Lord, yes! Honey, *all* animals, and even some plants, have either female or male *stuff*—that is, parts. And in the case of animals, there *have* to be both males and females—like boys and girls, men and women—in order for the world to continue; that is, so new babies can be made."

Jenny still didn't look convinced. I whispered, as if sharing a secret, "Didn't you notice the boy horses were different from the girl horses?"

Jenny covered her mouth and whispered from behind her hand, "They got real big penises, huh?"

"Yes, but that's because they're big animals. And if they didn't have them, the girl horses couldn't have babies. No one chopped off the penises on half the animals in the world to make them girls." I paused, then added, "And they didn't fall off by themselves, either."

Jenny giggled. *She had put that question in Mommy's head just by thinking it real hard. Mommy had answered it without even hearing it.* She swallowed her smirk and said, "So you won't lie to me, and if I think maybe something I learned from my brothers, or maybe someone else

161

like Mrs. Short, is wrong, I can ask you or Grannie or Daddy or Grandpa Jody about it..."

"Yes, and if none of us knows, well, then probably no one knows. Let's go back in the house and make a cake. We have enough sourdough starter for biscuits in the morning *and* cake tonight."

Chapter 14: Jenny's Gold and Gems (H'PJ Ch 8)

The day was bright and sunny—but not too hot—with random breezes just strong enough to keep bugs off and sweat evaporating. Perfect for laundry. Jenny was helping me with it, but she was unusually quiet. I could feel her eyes on me. She was staring at me, but every time I tried to catch her, she'd turn away. Her energy level was also low. No one I knew had been sick, but I guess it was possible that a flu bug had hit the area.

"Is there something wrong?" I asked and handed her a basket of clean clouts to wring out.

"What are those bumps hanging around your neck," she asked, bashfully pointing with one hand, clutching the basket close to her chest with the other.

"That's my necklace and these are gold nuggets," I said, fingering the largest one in the middle.

I hoped I didn't have to explain where it came from because I didn't remember. I had arrived in this 18th century world with a backpack, the clothes I was wearing, and a gold nugget necklace. What I didn't have was a memory of who or where I was...or when. I soon found out I was in 1780 North Carolina, but it wasn't until almost a year later that I found out I was a time traveler, that I had been born in the 20th century, and that although I seemed to be barely twenty, I had an adult daughter living in the 21st century.

"Are nuggets like dried-out grapes or currants?" she asked.

"No, these are special rocks that were dug out of the ground and put on a necklace. See, feel them. They're pretty hard, but not as hard as quartz. Gold is a rare and precious metal found in the earth. It's used for currency—that is, money—for decorations, and a few other things." *That was good enough for her. I certainly wasn't going to explain wiring, dental work, and the reflective coating on astronaut's visors to her!*

"Hmm, so if they make money out of gold, and gold is in rock nuggets, then maybe I can dig some out of the ground, so we'll have money. Then we can buy more stuff, like a better plow for Daddy and more cloth so you and my brothers and sister can have new clothes. I'll bet I could dig for gold after all my chores were done. Would that be okay?"

Her eagerness to be allowed to help resolve our financial situation was evident in her fast blinking, sparkling eyes. That sweet and pure look of longing was priceless.

"Well, I think we'd be better off if you…well…um," I paused, hoping to find the right words to say. "I appreciate the offer," I stalled, "but I know you like to do other things like carve and crochet and…" Jenny's bottom lip was pouched out in frustration. Here she had come up with a plan of how to 'make' money, and I was trying to dissuade her. "Okay, you can dig, but how about if you start your gold mining where Daddy's planning on putting the next privy. That'll help him, and if you find any gold, you can have it all."

"Okay," she replied, jumping up and down in place, "I'll find enough to share with everybody!"

***

"Daddy, I want to help you dig the next privy. Mommy said I could dig for gold wherever you're going to put it since we needed a hole there anyway and it would actually help you and I want to get some gold so we can use it for money and buy you a new plow and some cloth for new clothes and maybe another pot and if I find lots of it, maybe you can buy other stuff I don't even know we need."

"I appreciate the help, and don't let me stop you, but gold is usually found near creeks and rivers. If you want, you can go down to our little creek and dig near the edge. But don't dig in the stream…and keep your dress clean. I don't want your mother scolding me because I let you get in the mud."

Wallace knew Jenny worked hard helping with the household chores, gardening, and watching her younger siblings, but she needed some time to herself, too. It would be nice if she had another change of clothes that she could get dirty. He never got the chance to make mud pies when he was little and would like the chance to do it with her at some point before she grew up too much. Hmph. Jenny wasn't too far from puberty, but her innocence was that of a six-year-old. He'd see if he could talk Evie into letting Jenny have a 'dirty clothes' day where she could play in the mud just before it was laundry time.

***

"There wasn't any gold, but look what I found," Jenny told Wren. She held up the six rocks with red stones imbedded in them. "I think

164

they're pretty and I'm going to keep them forever and ever. I think if I use Daddy's hammer, I can knock off that gray rock around it."

Wren grabbed for the rock with the colorful bits. "No, no, you can't eat this. I have to take these to my special hiding place." Jenny put the rocks in her pocket and hoisted the baby over her shoulder. "Come on, I'll bet it's almost dinnertime."

***

"Lass, what can I do to turn that frown upside down?" Jody asked.

Jenny's lips pursed as she tried to figure out his riddle, then her smile grew as she realized what he was asking. "Well, you can tell me an easier way to find gold. I went to the creek, but I didn't find gold, just some pretty rocks. Is there an easier way, like when you make funny noises to call in the turkeys?"

"Well, I dinna ken of a 'gold call,' but I do ken that gold is heavy and it gets washed down creeks. That's where it's easiest to find. Ye may want to look about the edges of the rocks in the creeks, maybe even lift some of the lighter ones, and see if there's gold trapped underneath. Oh, and make sure ye check the rock on the leading side of the creek's flow. Fishin' in the creek is the easiest way I ken." He chuckled, then added, "After dinner, do ye want me to go with ye and show ye what I mean? It'll still be light out, and maybe yer da wants to go, too."

Jenny nodded rapidly, too giddy to speak. She reached over and gave Grandpa Jody a big hug. She looked up at him and sighed. She loved her mother and her Grannie whole heaps and loads, but she really did like being with the men more, especially when they were building things or figuring out how to make something work. Maybe someday, maybe next week, she could find a book that had lots of drawings in it about how things worked. Yes, she *knew* there was a book out there like that. But she'd have to wait for it.

***

"That was a mighty fine dinner ye made, Evie. How ye can accomplish anythin' with havin' three wee bairns about is amazin'," Jody said.

"Well, Jenny's a big help, and the garden is overflowing, so there's lots of variety. This winter might be tough, though, and the fare limited. Hmm, maybe I can figure out how to make freeze-dried meals so all I have to do is add water."

165

"Freeze-dried?" he asked.

"Actually, I don't think I'll have to freeze anything first. I can put together a food dehydrator in no time with Jenny's help," I patted Jenny on the head. "Yup, we can dry all sorts of fruits and veggies and then, hmm. I'll have to figure out a storage system and containers, so they won't get dusty..."

"It's always something, isn't it?" Sarah said. "I mean, sometimes I miss having freezers and, oops." Sarah had forgotten that Jenny was in the room, and she couldn't speak of the luxuries and conveniences of the 20th and 21st centuries. "Jenny, would you refill the ewer, please?" she asked to change the subject.

Jenny grinned, said, "Yes, Grannie," and grabbed the pitcher. She didn't want them to know that she knew their secret. She didn't understand why, but she knew Grannie and Mommy weren't the same as everyone else. Mrs. Short had talked about fairies—maybe that's what they were. She didn't know what a fairy was, and Mrs. Short was having another 'headache day' when she was talking to herself about them. She had wanted to ask her about them later, when she felt better, but that's when her other brothers, Clyde and Clayton, came and took her back.

But it really didn't matter if Grannie and Mommy were fairies or not. They were her family. She loved them and they loved her. It was all right that where they lived before, they could ride in carriages that moved fast on the ground, and even faster in the air, and they had books that talked to you with pictures that moved. They were still the same people. It was just the things they had in their lives before that were different from the things they had now. Just the things.

Chapter 15: The Trip to Town (H'PJ Ch 9)

"I'd like to take Jenny into town with me today. The cabinets I modified for Mr. Gibson are finished. I'd like to see if I can get a few things for us in exchange for my labor. I'd also like to get Jenny a peppermint stick. She deserves it. I doubt any parent has a child as eager to perform chores as she. "

"Sounds like a plan to me," I said.

Wallace tilted his head to the side, wordlessly asking, 'Please explain.'

I clarified, "That's a great idea. And bring back some candy for me, too." I chuckled. "I *really* don't know when the last time I had any was."

Just then, Jenny popped in, her hair freshly braided, her face spotless. She looked down at her hands, gave them a quick inspection, then presented them to me, showing off how she had washed them—with soap, this time—and had even cleaned under her fingernails.

"Looks like you're ready to go somewhere, dear. Do you have plans?"

Jenny tried to hide her grin by lowering her head, but her excitement was too great to contain. Her smile bloomed as she looked up at her father. "Do you need some help today? I mean, if you need to go somewhere, I'll come with you and help. That is, if it's okay with Mommy."

"As a matter of fact," Wallace said, drawing out the tension, "I was planning on taking the wagon into town. Would you like to come with me?"

Jenny bounced up and down on her toes, her head nodding just as fast, "Ooh, ooh, yes, yes. I want to go."

Wallace bent down and gave me a quick kiss. "I guess we're all set. We'll be back before dinner."

"Have fun, but stay out of trouble, you two," I said. They were so cute together. The tall and short of it. The mellow and the hyper. Who would have thought that two such diverse personalities would get along so well? Hmph. I guess the same could be said of Wallace and me. Nah! We were very different from each other, about 250 years apart in education, customs, and many experiences in general, but we complemented each other. Yin and yang, sweet and sour, tall and short.

Yup, we were a perfectly balanced couple. And a very happy one, too.

**

It probably would have been easier for Jenny if she could have run beside the wagon rather than ridden in it. She had boundless energy and it was hard for her to sit still. "I haven't been to town in a long, loong time," she said. "Did you know that I used to live there a long—maybe even a longer—time ago?"

"I think your mother mentioned something about it to me. Did you like living in town?" When Jenny didn't answer, he looked down to make sure she had heard him. She must have. She was pondering her answer, her bottom lip stuck out in deep and confused thought. "Well, did you?" he asked again.

"I liked being warm in the winter, and the food was all right. I didn't mind working, and sometimes Mrs. Short—she was the lady who sorta bought me from my brothers, my other brothers who are in heaven…" Jenny looked up to make sure he understood. He nodded, so she continued. "Sometimes Mrs. Short was mean, but I think that was because she hurt all the time. But her son, he said some real mean things to me. I don't miss him at all!" She looked up. "I'm sure glad I have you and Mommy now. And the babies, and Grandpa Jody, and Grannie, and Grandpa Julian, and José, and their pretty horses, and the goats…"

Wallace grinned as he flipped the reins, urging the sturdy draft horse along. *Just like her mother…she'd rather concentrate on the good parts of her life than the past. One of these days, the right man will come along for her. He'll be very blessed to have her as a wife. As long as he can get used to her chattiness, they'll be fine.*

**

Wallace hoisted the redesigned display cabinets out of the wagon and brought them into Gibson's for inspection. Jenny stayed at his elbow, her eyes wide, gawking at the inside of the store she had never been allowed to see by her former guardians.

The men were immediately busy, inspecting the workmanship and talking about angles and chamfers, shelving and drawers, so after an hour—or so it felt like to her—Jenny stepped outside to look at the town, the trees, and the cluster of buildings from a new perspective.

She wasn't a servant girl now, kept on a short rein, not allowed out of the house by the woman and her son who never let her forget that she was there as a favor, that she had to earn her meals and the right to sleep warm at night. Yes, she had a real family now, and never had to worry about a cuff to the ear or missing a meal because she talked too much or said the wrong words. It felt good to say what was on her mind. And if she pulled an apple off a tree to eat because she was hungry, she wouldn't get smacked.

She walked to the front of the wagon, reached into her pocket, and grabbed a handful of oats for the big Belgian. Xerxes wasn't her pet—he was a work horse—but she liked to think of him as a big dog that just didn't know how to fetch or roll over. *Slurp!* But he sure could lick the treats out of her hand.

"Well, if it isn't Ha'penny Jenny," called a voice from behind the wagon.

Jenny froze. She knew that voice. And there was only one person who had ever called her that. Her eyes darted side to side. She didn't see him, but he must have seen her. *Quick! Find Daddy!*

Jenny ran toward the store but was intercepted by the grizzled and stinky old man. "Well, if it isn't Ha'penny Jenny," he repeated with a sinister laugh. "I guess your brothers didn't want you after all, eh?"

"Da…"

Jenny's scream for her father was cut off by a grimy hand to her mouth. "Were you going to call for your daddy?" he asked. "You and I know your daddy died a long time ago. What I think is that you're here to rob the store. And then take all the goods to the devil. You're *his* child now, aren't you?"

Dick Short was back, causing trouble, but this time, his intended victim was too small to fight back.

Or so he thought.

Jenny stomped down on his foot and turned around and head-butted him in the crotch. She ran from his clutch, not paying any attention to which direction she was headed.

Dick bent over, stunned, in too much pain to even attempt to draw a breath. He fell forward onto his knees, his forehead breaking his fall. "My stuff! You broke my stuff!" he whimpered when he found his wind. He rolled over onto his side, tears falling and nose running, and curled up like a dried-up earthworm in the dust and dung of the narrow country road. "You broke it…"

169

Jenny stopped running when she saw the creek. She slowed her pace, looked side to side, then behind her, and saw that she hadn't been followed. Her ears stung, as if they'd just been boxed, but she knew they hadn't. Just his voice, taunting her with that name, made them ring. She stepped carefully into the edge of the creek and splashed water on her face. "He's a bad man, but he isn't in your life anymore. Just walk away, just walk away…"

Sudden terror hit her again. She turned back. Mr. Short was still there, lying on the ground, but now her daddy was there, too, looking over him. Her head shook back and forth, fear keeping any thoughts from forming. Back and forth, don't let bad thoughts come in. Back and forth. Keep it empty. Back and forth.

"Jenny! Jenny! Are you all right?" Wallace hollered as he ran, scared that the man on the ground—obviously suffering from a well-placed punch—had done something to hurt his Jenny. "Jenny! Jenny!"

Jenny looked up, her head still moving back and forth. She mustn't forget: words weren't allowed. Only the devil's words came out of young girls.

"Did he hurt you?" Wallace asked, holding her at arm's length, inspecting her for cuts and bruises. He turned her around and saw nothing amiss. "Look at me." Jenny's head stilled. She let him lift her face to his, her eyes not looking at him, but through him, stunned and emotionless. Wallace pulled out his silk handkerchief and wiped away the grime from around her mouth. He knew it had been spotless when they left.

"He hurt you, didn't he?"

Jenny remained mute.

"Well," he said and wiped her mouth again to remove the last smudge, "I think you hurt him a lot more than he hurt you. At least, on the outside. Now," he locked eyes with hers, "remember, you have a mommy and a daddy now. No one is going to hurt you. And just to make sure that someone doesn't hurt you when we aren't there—which I hope won't be often—I'll teach you how to fight."

One corner of Jenny's mouth turned up, and the sparkle came back to her eyes.

"And I know that you know I know how to fight. It's very important *not* to fight, but when someone tries to hurt you, and won't listen to reason, then it's all right to protect yourself. Understand?"

Jenny sighed, the other side of her mouth turning up by itself. "I understand."

"Great! Now, let's get back to the store. I think Mr. Gibson has removed Mr. Short from out front. I don't know what this town's going to do with that man. He seems to cause a lot of trouble with just his words."

"But words can hurt more than fists, huh?" Jenny asked.

"Yes, dear, they can. And the scars they leave can last a lifetime. Please, don't let anything mean people like Mr. Short say, bother you. I don't think he's right in the head. Even if he thinks he means what he says, I don't think he *knows* what he says. Does that make sense to you, or should I explain it another way?"

"It's like he's holding a rock and telling you it's an apple. Just because he says it's so, doesn't mean he's right, huh?"

"That's very right."

"So, will you tell me what a ha'penny is?"

Wallace started to ask what that had to do with anything, but knew it probably did, at least in the long run of Jenny's thinking. "A ha'penny is another way of saying half penny. That's the lowest denomination of coin minted by the British government." He realized as soon as he saw her face, that she probably didn't understand half of his words. "It's a low-value coin, a piece of metal that isn't worth much."

"Oh."

Jenny knew that her daddy knew that she hadn't been to school and didn't know much, but he wanted her to learn, so if she asked him questions, it was all right. He wouldn't make her feel bad about not knowing something.

"So, when Mr. Short called me Ha'penny Jenny, he was saying I wasn't worth much?"

Wallace choked back a cough. He had wanted to laugh at the humor of the little poetic piece, but also growl at the heartlessness of the man who would call a young orphan such a cruel name. "Jenny, you are priceless. And priceless means that you are worth more than all the money in the world. "

"You mean like a whole pound sterling?" she asked, mouth and eyes wide.

"At least a hundred pounds sterling," he said. "But I wouldn't take the whole state of North Carolina in trade for you, Jenny. Not even the whole North American continent."

Wallace hugged her close, making sure she couldn't see the store. Yes, Mr. Gibson was leading Dick Short back to his house. He'd give him a few minutes to get him situated before they went back. "Come down here with me. Lets' wash up a little and get a drink before we go see Mr. Gibson again. I want to get your mother a surprise."

Jenny's eyes brightened. She knew what the surprise was. Sorta. She had heard about candy but never had any.

It was supposed to be better than a honeycomb. Her brothers—her other brothers, who were up in heaven—once had given her part of one they had found while hunting. She smiled as she remembered how much fun they all had, sucking on the little holes, chewing the wax to get the last little bits of sweetness out, licking the sticky mess off their fingers when they were done. She was sure glad she didn't have a beard like her brothers did, although they used to joke that they could still taste the sweetness days later. It was one of the best times she ever had with them. But they were with God now. He had wanted them with Him. And now they could have all the food and honey they wanted, and be warm all the time...

"Jenny, are you ready to go back to the store, or do you want to wait a little longer? Mr. Short is gone, if that makes you feel better."

Jenny sighed. Everyone was where he was supposed to be. "Okay. Let's go. Hey, how come mommy talks funny? Like the word okay. She says it means all right, but why doesn't she just say all right? Do you know what country she *really* comes from? I don't want to ask her, but I think its America. Do we live in America? I thought we lived in North Carolina. At least, that's what Grannie told me, and I know she wouldn't lie to me. So how can I live in America and North Carolina at the same time?"

"Greetings again, Mr. Gibson. Now, as far as settling for the modification of your cabinets..." Wallace didn't want to be rude and ignore Jenny's questions, but he wanted to get the business transaction finished and get back to the rest of his family. He could explain geography later, possibly even on the ride back. It would be easier to do with a map or a pen and paper, but she was sharp and would probably follow a verbal description of states within countries. Of course, he wasn't going to explain why Mommy spoke differently. He barely understood time travel—it would be easier to explain gravity to the precocious girl, and he didn't understand that, either.

"I've got salt, sugar, flour, coffee, some newer yard goods, and even a bit of that other commodity you were asking about." Mr. Gibson ended his stock list with a big grin and a glance at Jenny.

Jenny smiled back. She wanted to tell him she knew what he was talking about, even if she didn't know what the word commodity was. Maybe that was a fancy word for candy. Sometimes, it was better to say nothing, even if she didn't *have* to be quiet.

"I'll tell you what, I'd like to keep it on account, if it's all right with you."

Jenny's smile evaporated, actually turned upside down like grandpa said. Did she do something wrong?

Wallace continued, "Except I'll be taking a bit of that *commodity* back with me." He had been watching her face and was glad to see she was positively radiant now. She was such a great guesser. She knew he was getting something for her.

Mr. Gibson reached under the counter and brought out the big apothecary jar. "Go ahead and point to which one you want," he said. "How about that big one there?"

Jenny's eyes shifted back and forth, undecided. She wanted the big piece—it would probably last her a whole year, maybe even a month. She looked up and asked her daddy, "Can we get that big one for Mommy? I know she'd like a piece of candy, and because she has to eat more so she can feed my brothers and sister—that is my new brothers, and I never had a sister, but I always wanted one, so she's my only sister ever—I'll take a smaller piece and can she have the biggest piece?"

"How about if Mr. Gibson pokes around in that jar and sees if there are two big pieces—one for you and one for Mommy?"

Jenny bounced up and down on her toes. "Ooh, ooh, really? I mean, thanks! I'd like that. And I'm sure Mommy would, too. You're the best daddy in the world. Well, I haven't met all of them, but still, I *know* you're the best daddy in the *whole* world! And thank you, too, Mr. Gibson. You're the best storekeeper in the *whole* world, too!"

***

The trip home was much different than the one in. Besides the fact that there was no weight in the back end of the wagon, so the ride was bumpier, it was also noisier, but in a different way. The creaks, rattles, and squeaks of metal on wood, wood on wood, and wheels on rocks and packed dirt were audible now. Jenny was quiet but in a good way. Mr. Gibson had given her a small length of new cloth to wrap around her peppermint stick.

"That's to keep your hands from getting sticky," he said. "And when you're done licking on it, you can wrap it around it to keep off dust, flies, and ants. But make sure you stop licking a few minutes before you wrap it up. Otherwise, it will be like glue and the cloth will stick to it. You don't want to have to rip it apart the next time your daddy says you can have your treat, now do you?" Jenny shook her head, her mouth wrapped around the top of her white peppermint stick. "Now, your daddy told me you're a good helper, that's why I gave you that pretty cloth. That and it matches your eyes. Get along now. I'm sure your mommy misses you. And don't forget to help her, every chance you get."

Chapter 16: Please don't go (H'PJ Ch 10)

"Don't go. Please, Grandpa Jody, please don't go," Jenny said, her eyes red and brimming, her tears almost—but not quite—spilling over.

"I'm not goin' anywhere, lass." Jody reached down, picked her up, and swung her in a tight circle. "I have to stay here and teach ye how to dance."

"Promise me you won't leave, please. Pretty please with honey and candy and flowers and sugar and please, please…"

"What's the matter, lass? I'll always be here fer ye. Yer my family—my granddaughter."

Jenny shook her head, trying to get the bloody image to go away, but it wouldn't leave. She sniffed. She couldn't tell grandpa that sometimes she 'saw' things before they happened. She'd never tell anyone *that* again. She shivered with the memory.

"Now, dinna be afeart of somethin' bad happenin' to me." Jody gave her an extra hug of reassurance. "Ye canna go through life afeart of what's on the other side of a door, or down the road, or…"

Jenny nodded rapidly, but even as he spoke the words, telling her not to worry, she saw him lying in the road, covered in blood. She squeezed him around the neck, almost choking him. "Well, *if* you have to go somewhere, be *verra* careful and don't go anywhere alone, okay?"

"All right, I promise. Now, loosen yer grip about my neck so I can show ye the proper way to dance. That is, with yer feet on the ground and yer hand on my shoulder—if it'll reach that high."

Jenny slid down his body until she was on tip toes, then reached up as high as she could with her fingertips. "I'm not tall enough yet, but I will be. Mommy said I'll grow tall and pretty if I eat my greens every day. But I can't eat too many, or I'll get a bellyache, huh?"

"Aye, lass. Too much of anythin', save lovin' yer family, is seldom a good idea. And I'll be verra careful whenever I leave yer presence. Oof! I need to stay around long enough to give ye a few more dancin' lessons, at least. Yer next partner's feet may nae be as tough as mine."

Jenny looked up at him again, squinting hard. Maybe he'd be okay now that he promised not to be alone.

But maybe not.

The sadness was still there.

But now there was hope. And help.

Someone else was coming to their home, maybe next month, maybe next week.

And maybe he'd bring a big sister for her, too.

Conclusion of Ha' Penny Jenny

Extended Excerpt from

Aye, I am a Fairy

The Fairies Saga Book One
(Author's suggested reading order)

Copyright © 2014 by Dani Haviland and Chill Out! Books
ISBN 978-1-950592-16-6

Chapter 17: Too Much Fighting (AYE Ch 49)

The wilds of North Carolina
August 17, 1781

Captain Asshole tugged at the hem of his jacket, obsessively adjusting the dusty and ripped red coat as if he were preparing to meet the king. He twisted the kinks out of his neck to compose himself further, looked down, and his haughty smirk grew.

It had taken three sleepless days to track him down – and one more to capture and subdue his pint-sized prey – but he finally had him. He strolled around his captive twice, eyes narrowed, giving him his best intimidating glare, his upper lip curled into a silent snarl. He stopped in front of the boy – just outside of striking distance – and squatted on his heels. His prisoner was wide-awake now, naked except for his breechclout and moccasins, securely bound with strips he had made from tearing apart the boy's threadbare shirt.

Cursing and wriggling as he tried to get free, the young half-breed was well-thrashed, but not spent. The captain watched and waited while the bare-chested boy struggled up to his knees, then chuckled and kicked him, shoving him against the ant-covered sweetgum tree.

"Did you like bein' able to give that war yell? Made you feel like a real man, eh? But you're not a man, not for quite a few more years…that is, if you live that long."

Pah-toie! The boy spat in the face of the ragged and physically torn-up man who had kidnapped him from his father. "Yer dead meat!" he snarled.

The captain wiped the spittle from his Y-scarred cheek, then poked the boy's bare hip with the toe of his boot – not to hurt him, but to show dominance.

"Well, I never had a boy, but I might just see how it is, you know? Fresh meat, either way, might feel the same." He leaned in, his face just inches away from Wee Ian's. "But whether it feels good to me or not, one thing's for damned sure…" He snorted, ran his tongue over his stained and split upper lip, "I'll make sure it doesn't feel good to you." He pulled back and ended his lecture with a closed-fisted punch, sending the pink calico-bound lad face first into the creek bed.

Wee Ian rolled over and glared at him as he spat out pebbles and grit. "Weel, it'll be the last thing ye do. I'll make sure of that."

The sham British officer reached out, grabbed his captive by the wrist bindings, and dragged him face first out of the creek, through the coarse gravel and scrub. He flipped him over onto his back and laughed as the struggling irate man-child swore and squirmed, trying to free himself from his cloth handcuffs and shackles.

His laughter grew to a roar; this was almost perfect. The more the boy wiggled and writhed, cursed and grunted, the more aroused he became. He untied the laces on his own pants and grabbed his cock, pulling on it in anticipation of a new form of sexual diversion. He leaned forward, wary, but still hoping to get close enough to the boy to rub his dick on the nubile body, to feel his hot, young flesh beneath him. Let the boy yell – no one would hear him. Besides, the screaming and resistance was the most exciting part.

***

James and Leah ran as fast as their lungs and new shoes could take them toward the source of the shouting – someone was definitely in trouble.

The air was blue with the curses from either a young man or a woman. Some of the words were English, although strung together with a creative flourish and in a thick Scots accent. "Get your filthy hands offa me, ye mangy fox fornicator."

There was a pause – then a grunt. The livid person started anew. "That'll be the last time ye have enough cock to hold in yer hand. I'll carve it off, piece by piece, stuff the bits up yer nose, and cram yer balls down yer throat 'til ye canna breathe." Foreign words that sounded as if they would be just as colorful if translated followed the tirade. They were certainly said with as much fervor.

Suddenly, there was a loud smack, a crunching sound, and then nothing.

"That'll teach you to mind your manners." The captain had had enough foreplay. He was ready for action.

James and Leah sensed a change in the conflict. The sudden silence, an uncomfortable stillness, was frightening. When they heard the man speak again, it was worse.

"Ooh, such nice smooth skin you have there, boy. It's just as pretty

179

as a lass's. Now, do you want it in the mouth or the ass first? Oh, you can't speak for yourself with your head cracked up like that, can you?" he mocked in a sarcastic tone. "Well, too bad," he added with a sinister laugh, "I wouldn't be giving you a choice, anyway..."

James and Leah repeatedly screamed, "Stop! Stop!" as they ran toward the man standing over the motionless, semi-nude child on the ground. Hopefully, he was only unconscious and not dead.

The man in the tattered British officer's uniform looked up at the shouts. He paused, seeing the two strangers rushing in from nowhere, shook his head in confusion, and yelled, "What the hell? Who are you?"

The pair arrived at the site of the commotion, breathless from their frantic rescue run. They gasped, frozen in momentary shock at the drama they had just interrupted. Leah saw the soldier's redcoat jacket and swore softly, "Oh, shit. We're here and in a handbag."

James heard her but didn't respond. He, too, could see that this ugly, torn-up man was from the Revolutionary War era. He didn't look like a friendly, either, with his semi-clothed posture over the unconscious boy. His nose was puffy and red, and it looked as if the end of it had been bitten off. He was also missing his left ear, the result of a recent savage wound that hadn't completely healed. It was red and infected, maroon streaks radiating away from where the ear used to be. James's legs were shaking with the knowledge that he and Leah had just journeyed back 230 years in time and were now interrupting the rape – or near rape – of a young, adolescent male.

James ignored the uniformed man's request to answer who he was. Instead, he said with as much wind and anger as he could muster, "Get away from the boy, NOW!"

"Oh, I don't think so, *muffin*," the captain replied coolly. "You see, I have this sweet little pistol here." He whipped out a silver-toned single-shot pistol from behind his back. He turned it over in front of his face, admiring its luster while still keeping one eye on James. "Oh, and I keep it loaded, you see, just in case an idiot like you shows up and wants to spoil my fun. You wouldn't want me to waste a bullet on you or your lady friend, now, would you?" He leaned sideways, trying to see behind James to get a better look at Leah.

The captain's eyes widened with shock and recognition at seeing her. "Who *are* you?" he asked. "And how'd you get here? I thought you were dead…" He suddenly realized he was showing confusion, so covered his weakness with impudence. "You're a long way from home and all those babies, aren't you? Oh, and it looks like you got yourself a new man, too," nodding to James. "It didn't take you long to get rid of that big sissy."

Captain Asshole took a step back and stroked his empty hand across unconscious Wee Ian's bared fanny, the breechclout yanked aside. "Does this get you excited?" he asked James, ending the question with a perverted leer, his lips widening to a smile that revealed stained and rotten teeth. "There's sweet meat on the other side, too. Nice, sweet…"

James drew and aimed his revolver at the Captain, holding back his smile. *He had just been given the upper hand. The degenerate's pistol had a plug of dirt in the end of the barrel – if he pulled the trigger, it would backfire in his face. He, Leah, and the boy were safe.*

"I will admit that I've never killed a man before," James said coolly, "but I've dispatched many an animal. I think you are about two clicks below animal grade, and so it will be of no consequence to remove you from this earthly plane. Now, get away from the boy or I. Will. Kill. You." James spread out his last words for emphasis, but also to steady his hand, sighted in on the man who was less than 20 feet away.

Captain Asshole snorted in defiance, squatted down, and grabbed the boy's butt cheek.

James flashed rage and squeezed the trigger with an immediate, visceral response.

It struck him before he could bring up his pistol. He felt a sharp, quick burn – like a hot ember on exposed skin – as the bullet struck him just above the clavicle. His gasp brought no breath. His esophagus had been blown apart and he had no airway left. His eyes widened in disbelief at the sight of blood still spurting from his gullet. He wouldn't get out of this mess alive. No strength to run for cover nor wind for excuses. He was dead.

James watched as the captain's head wobbled on the remains of his neck. Its upright support lost; the heavy skull submitted to the pull of gravity and dropped forward, pulling the lifeless body with it, collapsing atop the boy.

James quickly thrust his pistol through his belt, rushed over, and pushed the corpse off the child.

The impact of the fallen body had awakened the boy with a start. Still face down and mistaking James for his assailant, he began anew with his foul words and furious kicking.

James stumbled wordlessly as he backed away, out of range, as Leah screamed, "Leave him alone. He didn't do it."

Hearing the urgent plea from a female's voice, the boy stopped his thrashing, craned his neck around, and stared at the unknown woman who had suddenly appeared out of nowhere. She was pointing to a bloody corpse on the other side of him. He growled in recognition, then inhaled deeply, hawked up a big wad of phlegm, and spat it at the contorted face of his would-be molester, lying dead in the dirt.

A string of words flew out of his mouth, none intelligible. He paused, then stared up at the man beside him – his rescuer – the questioning look of 'Who are you and why are you here?' evident without words.

James pulled out the blade from his Leatherman multitool and held it flat in his palm to show him what he had. The boy accepted the gesture with a nod, rolled onto his back, and offered his bound ankles. James quickly sliced through the cloth. The boy scrambled upright, turned around, and nobly presented his bound wrists.

"Do you speak English?" James asked, as he cut through the twisted cotton handcuffing. Both he and Leah had heard him speak it, but it was as good a question as any to start a conversation.

Hands now free, the boy straightened out his breechclout and turned around. He looked at James, one eye narrowed in suspicion, then down at the strange pistol. His near-glare softened to a half-grin. This man was different. He could tell that he had nothing to do with those *other* men.

"I speak it well enough." He pulled back his shoulders, puffed out his skinny chest, and stood as tall as his youthful body could reach. "Thank ye fer comin' to my rescue. I owe ye one. Now, I need to go find my da. This," he kicked the contorted corpse in the ribs with his moccasined foot, "pile of shite trapped him and left him with three others to…to… Weel, I dinna ken what they were gonna do, but I'm sure they meant to kill him when they were done. Now, if ye'll excuse me…" He nodded and turned, heading into the unknown to rescue his sire.

"Wait! What's your name?" asked James. "And can we help?"

He stopped and called back. "The white man calls me Wee Ian, and if ye care to follow and can bring that wee cannon of yours, I willna send ye away. They're this way. Jest follow the creek." He pointed upstream, then resumed his swift pace.

"I'm James and this is my wife, Leah," he called after the boy, not knowing if his lame introduction was heard or not.

James bent over, grabbed his bag, said "Let's go," and didn't even ask whether she wanted to be involved in this mysterious mess or not. It was the right thing to do, and if he knew it, she did, too. Sometimes it was good to have a wife who was a mind reader.

Wee Ian was young, strong, and unencumbered, so was soon far ahead of James and Leah, who were still burdened with their packs. After several minutes, James stopped to let Leah catch up. "Here, give me that," he said, reaching for her backpack. "Remember, I'm the one with the broad shoulders. Sorry, I should have taken it before we left. Are you okay?"

"Yes but wait just half a minute." Leah reached around him and pulled the water bottle out of the side pocket of her pack, took two gulps, and offered it to him.

He took a quick swig. "No more. You'll get a cramp if you drink too much. Come on, let's go."

Leah saluted him with the bottle, letting him know that she'd keep it with her. She gathered her skirts together and bundled as much as she could in the crook of her bent right arm. "Cursed long dresses," she hissed, then took off running.

They ran without stopping or talking, James leading the way, until it became too much for Leah. She slowed to a walk – she was getting an ache in her side and didn't want to make a scene by throwing up or falling down, but still wanted to make forward progress. James turned around and noticed her clutching her side, so stopped and waited for her to catch up.

Then he heard it. Now that he wasn't running, he could hear the sounds of confrontation.

"Put it down, and no one will get hurt." The man's voice sounded as if someone was reciting a line from an old western movie. No, the voice sounded like Billy's…but the *tone* was just like a marshal calling out the bad guys in one of those old TV westerns.

James grabbed her hand and pulled her to the shelter of a large sparkleberry bush. He recognized it from Colleen's book – tall bush, low hanging branches, perfect for a temporary hideout. "Stay here," he said and dropped both packs at her feet.

He pulled the pistol from his belt and checked the safety, making sure it was still locked. "Stay here. Get your gun, too. Take the safety off and keep an eye out. But don't shoot anyone. That was Marty talking. I'm going over there to see what's going on. Wee Ian's around here, I'm sure. I'm *positive* Marty's not one of the men who took his father. He's probably trying to help, and that's why we're supposed to be here. Are you okay? You look a little pale."

"Yeah, well, so do you. I'm fine. Now, get out there," she whispered hoarsely, "It's show-time!" Leah puckered up, blew him a kiss, and then looked beyond him to the source of the disturbance.

James bent low and did his best to move noiselessly toward the fracas. Wee Ian popped out from behind a bush, put a finger to his lips, and directed James ahead to the next vantage point.

Marty's voice boomed out, "I'm serious now. I don't want to hurt you, but I'll shoot if you don't…" He stopped his threat at the same time as the sound of an involuntary yelp pierced the air.

"Ha, ha, hah…" someone laughed menacingly.

The cruel guffaw was quickly silenced by the crack of a gunshot.

The bushes beside James rustled. He looked over and saw Wee Ian flying through them, totally disregarding stealth or discretion. He followed suit, pausing only long enough to take the safety off his gun.

When he got there, Wee Ian was already astride the man – evidently his father – a skinny, broad-shouldered white man dressed as an Indian. The boy's small hands quickly pulled the hatchet from the fallen man's neck and tossed it into the trees.

The father was a bloody mess. The man-child held his hands over the wound, trying the stop the spurting, but his efforts and the foreign words he was chanting, obviously prayers, weren't slowing the bright red flow.

Pop, pop. The sound of two black powder rifles firing struck the air. James looked toward the sound of the shots and saw two men busily cramming rods down their rifles, reloading to shoot again. He looked back. It didn't appear Wee Ian or the bloodied man in native garb had been hit. They were safe for now.

Wee Ian had said three men. The third man was dead, or nearly so, less than two feet from the boy. James's gut instinct was to call Leah from the brush to help, but he couldn't do that with two muskets loaded and ready to fire on him or anyone else helping.

"Which one do you have, Marty – the one on my right or my left?" he called out loudly, as much to frighten the two skinny, musket-loading mobsters as to know which was his target.

"I got the right, you take the left. Glad you could make it here, son," Marty hollered, still in the brush and not visible. "I hope you remembered the medical kit. These two can't shoot faster or straighter than we can. The lad's father doesn't have much time…"

"I'm on it," shouted Leah, as she quickly took the initiative. She put the gun's safety back on, dropped it in her backpack, and grabbed the valise. Her hands were full – a bag in each one – so she employed them like giant baseball mitts, gathering her skirt in front of her so she didn't trip over it as she ran. "Grrr." A growl escaped her lips as she stumbled, despite her efforts.

She knelt beside the two males in breechclouts and moccasins. "Wee Ian, I'm going to see if I can fix your da. Keep doing what you're doing there while I get some cloths."

Leah pulled open her bag and grabbed one of the chamois cloths she had bought for just such a circumstance. Unlike terrycloth, these wouldn't shed into the wound, but were still small, absorbent, and reusable. She carefully slid her hand under Wee Ian's and held pressure on the wound as she made a quick assessment of the damages.

The dead assailant, shot and killed by Marty, had wielded a hatchet on her patient's neck, trying – and gratefully, failing – to separate his head from his shoulders. As she examined him, blotting away blood to find the actual site of impact, she saw that his protruding collarbone had deflected the blade. Her patient didn't have much in the way of body fat. He wasn't quite emaciated, but seemed to be built solely of hard muscle, sinew and bone, and unfortunately now, very little blood.

The bleeding had slowed down, but that might be because he had lost so much of it. The human body only had about five quarts of blood, and he had lost at least two by the looks of the mess covering his shirt and the ground around him.

Marty called out to the soldiers, trying to encourage them to make life easier for everybody. "Now, you boys saw what I can do with this gun here. How about if you two just drop your muskets, and we'll take you back to camp? The officers there told me that they'd give you a fair trial. Now put them down easy…"

Evidently they weren't interested in that offer. Leah could hear them mumbling back and forth, but couldn't understand what they were saying, nor did she try. She was concentrating on her task. She was going to have to sew up the nick in her patient's carotid vein. Fortunately, it hadn't been severed. It was a difficult repair for a surgeon with a microscope and bright overhead lights, but even more so for a recovery room nurse with only rudimentary micro-stitching skills and a pair of secondhand high-magnification glasses.

As she was guiding Wee Ian's hand back over the wound, she recognized a few of the men's words. "And I'll get the boy."

She looked up and screamed, "They're going to shoot us!" just as the renegades turned and readied their guns.

Marty and James hadn't heard the armed men's discussion but had been following their eye and shoulder movements. They watched as the rogues turned, ready to shoot the unarmed medics in cold blood. Their muskets were halfway to their shoulders when Marty and James fired, both of them killing their targets with single shots to the chests.

Leah panted quickly three times, composed herself, and then was back to her medical dilemma. "James, if you're done there, I need some help."

He was by her side in a flash, his face set in a grim scowl, ready to work. He could reflect on taking another life later. Right now, he needed to help save one.

"Would you get me the flashlight and those goofy goggles? I'll need them for this close-up work. Get that brown bottle and a long swab, too. I'll need you to pour alcohol over my hands so I can get the needle and suture ready."

James set the magnifying apparatus on Leah's head. The headpiece looked strange, but it was what she needed: ultra-magnification goggles with a built-in light. She had been able to buy it used from her dentist. She looked like a bug-eyed alien, ready to devour the bloody mess in front of her. She didn't want to scare anyone, but right now, the only one who might be frightened was the boy, and he had eyes only for his father and his wound.

"Wee Ian, put your hand right here and don't move it." He gently slid his hand under hers. She looked at him and saw that he was probably in shock. Well, at least it was a functional shock. He was her extra set of hands right now, even if they weren't sterile.

James gave her what she called her sewing kit. She took what she needed, turned towards him, and let him pour the alcohol over her hands, the hemostat, suture and needle. He opened the bottle of iodine antiseptic solution. "Take the cloth off, lad," he said, then performed a quick, but thorough swabbing of the injury site.

Leah closed her eyes in prayer then started to work. Despite the high-powered magnifying glasses, James saw her struggling to see. He retrieved the mini flashlight and squatted down at her left side, providing a small spotlight on her work area.

"Thanks," she said. "Grab a few pieces of that gauze, too. When the blood starts oozing up after a stitch or two, wipe it away *gently*. You won't be able to see what I see, so don't do anything until I tell you to."

As it turned out, there was so little blood left in the man that leakage wasn't a problem. The wound on the left side of his neck was relatively easy to mend. Now what was needed was more blood in his body. Evidently that's why Marty had sent word through the ages for the IV needles and tubing.

"Are you sure you want to do this?" Leah asked James. "It's going to be awkward, and he's lost a lot of blood, more than I think you should give. But right now, any would be better than none."

"Hey! Remember? I signed up for this. Just tell me where you want me. Oh, and before you get started, I want to tank up on water."

James got a full water bottle out of the backpack. He felt conspicuous drinking out of the clear plastic container, but it was all he had. Two weeks of planning and the one thing both of them had forgotten was a canteen. It was a good thing they had those water bottles in the truck. It would have been suicide to go out in the heat of a summer's day without water and a way to transport it. One more blessing that was unexplained. That brought it up to about 1,512, James reflected...not as if he was actually counting.

He guzzled it all down and was ready to put the bottle back into the bag when he noticed Wee Ian staring at it. "Here, do you want to look at it?" *Better to have the boy hold and examine it than suspect it was diabolical – or whatever it was the Indians believed.*

Wee Ian took it warily, twisted the cap off and on, then off again, and sniffed the opening. He frowned when he realized there had been nothing but water in it and handed it back.

"Would you do me a favor and refill it. It's the only way I have to carry water. I...um...lost my canteen."

Wee Ian nodded then headed downhill to the creek. James realized that he hadn't heard him say a word since his father had been attacked. If he didn't pull through, the boy might be an orphan. It didn't look like these two were from a tribe. It was more like they were their own tribe. Scots-speaking Indians: now that was a combination.

James looked over and saw Leah had moved aside some rocks and was using a broken tree branch to knock away the smaller pebbles, essentially sweeping a place for him to lie down.

"It would be better if you were higher than him. Gravity is a big help in pushing the blood through the tubes. The heart is a strong pump but wasn't made to transfer fluids outside of the body and through plastic lines. Maybe we can have you lie on top of the backpacks. Oh, crap. I didn't think about this. What can we use?"

"Well, it may sound morbid, but I can stack the dead bodies, and James can lie on top of them. I can cover the men with a blanket, so it won't be so messy. Hi, you must be Leah. I'm Martin Melbourne, but you can call me Marty."

"Oh," Leah shook her head, trying to separate the thought of using a stack of slain murderers to support her husband, the blood donor – and how should she greet the man who had arranged for him to help with this in the first place? She repeated, "Oh," then took a deep breath. "Or I could call you Dad. I'm your daughter-in-law now."

"You are? I sure didn't see that one coming!" Marty exclaimed. Literally taken aback, he shuffled two awkward steps in recovery, as if he had been knocked backward by a soft blow.

A split-second after regaining his composure, Marty was back into problem-solving advisor mode. "Well, you two are the ones to say yeah or nay on the corpse cart. Which is it?"

"I'll help you drag them over. Glad to see you, sir." James said, and slapped his father on the back, forgoing any other conversation until later.

What would, or should, he say to his newly discovered father? It was strange, but now that he knew Marty wasn't his grandfather, somehow the man looked different. It appears we'll have a long time to catch up. God willing. That's about number 1,513, isn't it, Lord?

The men grabbed their kill and dragged them by the heels to the fresh swept area next to Wee Ian's father.

Leah decided she should distract herself and the boy from the Melbourne men's gruesome ministrations of shoving and tugging the corpses into position. She turned away from their construction zone, walked several feet away, and squatted down, motioning for the youth to join her at creekside. "So, what's your father's name," she asked.

"Ian, Ian Kincaid," he said succinctly. "But he's also called Star Walker."

"Oh," she replied, then subconsciously held her breath. *She blinked rapidly in shock – she recognized that name. He was from the later Lost historical novels. Mom never mentioned anything about him!*

She finally remembered to breathe, glad that she was already near the ground and not standing. She was light-headed and afraid that she was going to fall over backward. Wee Ian saw her start to swoon and rushed to her side, grasping her shoulders to keep her upright.

"Do ye need to put yer heid between yer knees?"

Leah shook her head, rocked back off of her heels, and as gracefully as she could – which wasn't much – plopped down onto her fanny. She didn't care if the dress got dirty. The fine dust would probably just brush off anyway. She leaned forward and brought her knees up to her face. "Can I have a drink of that water, please?"

Wee Ian gave her the bottle and wordlessly waited by her side to make sure she was all right. *He seems to be protecting me – quite a gentleman for being such a young person.*

James and Marty finished their body building, and then draped a horse blanket over the pile of three. They had put the two skinny ones on the ground and laid Ian's attacker, a heavyset man, on top of them.

Leah hadn't watched on purpose. It was morbid but necessary. She had to move quickly and didn't have the luxury of time for the men to build her a table, or even to scout out a sizable fallen log. Ian Kincaid needed blood, and he needed it now.

189

"Use what you have and be grateful," she admonished herself softly. "At least you have help." She turned to face her support crew. "I'm ready. Are you?" she asked with as much courage as she could garner.

James started settling himself onto the lumpy body of Ian's attacker. *Thank you, Lord, for the blanket. Number 1,514.* "Marty, could you come over here and make sure I don't start slipping. This is very uncomfortable and a little shaky, too."

Marty came to one side and Wee Ian, without being asked, came to the other. Leah swabbed the site on James's arm with alcohol and inserted the trocar, using a short length of surgical tape to secure it to the site. "Don't move," she said. "It's just a plug right now. I have to get him stuck, too."

Leah slapped and moved Ian's arm around, trying to get a vein to pop up.

"Can you put it in his leg?" asked Marty.

"Yes, but I'd rather not," Leah replied, frowning with concern. She exhaled sharply, squeezed her eyes shut in exasperation, and said a quick prayer.

Wee Ian had been watching and decided to take matters into his own hands. He moved over to the arm that Leah had been rather gently – or so it seemed to him – slapping to get the vein to pop up. He did a rapid fire rat-a-tat-tat drum roll with the flats of his hands, making the area scarlet red and bringing up a vein. "Like that?" he asked.

Leah grabbed the trocar and quickly inserted it on the first try. "Like that," she said. "Thanks. Now I just have to connect these guys, so your father will get a fill up – or at least a partial refill – of the blood he lost. Do you want to watch?" she asked, knowing full well the boy would not leave his father's side.

"Aye, I'll stay. Yer a good woman, and I wager a good healer, too, but I'm still his son. I'll stay to help take care of him. He hasna been doin' a verra good job of it himself, jest the noo."

The blood transfusion was slow, but without complications. As Leah removed the needles and tubes, she heard James say, "Thanks. Number 1,515."

"What's that?" she asked.

"Oh, you said something about God, and how He works in mysterious ways, and how many blessings we have, but that we never take the time to count them or thank the Lord… So, well, a few days ago, I started counting. You don't realize until you *do* pay attention, just how full life is of little miracles…every day."

"And big ones, too. I think Ian here is going to make it," she said.

* * *

Leah continued to clean up and put away the tools of her field trauma center. After a couple of minutes, she whispered, "James, you never read beyond the first *Lost* book, or *Through the Stones* as your UK version was called, did you?"

"No, I was meaning to, but with all the other excitement, studies, and tasks we had to do in the last two weeks… No, I didn't read beyond the first one. Why?"

"Ian Kincaid here is Jody Pomeroy's nephew, his favorite nephew, if you will. Mom said in her letter that her new last name is Pomeroy-Hart. I would suspect there's a connection there. Do you mind if I ask him if he knows where the Pomeroys are when he wakes up?"

"You could do that, or you could just ask me," Marty said. "Sorry, I didn't mean to eavesdrop, but I was coming over to talk to you two about quite a few things, and that just happens to be one of them."

"Can we wait a while for any discussions?" asked James. "I feel a little sapped," and smiled at his own pun.

Marty nodded, then helped James off the platform of bodies and shoulder-bolstered him to a shady spot under the nearest tree.

It was hot, and the corpses under the blanket were starting to get ripe. Like all dead men, these three had lost their bowels at death and weren't very clean to begin with. Yes, the odor was horrific, and the bodies needed to be moved away quickly. Hopefully, Marty was feeling strong. James was weak and didn't have enough strength to help.

Leah could help if needed, but right now she was feeling a little drained, too. Whether it was from the intense emotional stress of the procedures she had just performed, or from the excitement of the time travel, or from seeing firsthand four men being shot, one hacked, and a boy nearly raped… Well, she was exhausted.

Yes, she'd pass on helping with the clean-up detail. She'd stay put and help James hold up the other side of the tree. She smiled. After all, they didn't want it to fall over now, did they? She sat next to the trunk, arranged her skirts about her, and then leaned back. She reached over for

191

her husband's hand, picked it up, and laid it on her soft, green calico skirt. Even though she wasn't holding his hand, she felt linked to him on a higher plain, their bodies and spirits joined with their pinkie-to-pinkie connection. Leah was completely at peace with herself and the world for the first time in nearly a year. Her disappearing, time traveling mother was just around the corner, figuratively speaking.

She hadn't planned on falling asleep – and didn't realize that she had – until she felt a tapping on her shoulder. She jerked away by reflex and opened her eyes to see Wee Ian's face a foot in front of hers.

"I think he needs ye," he stated without emotion, then waited for her response, eyes blank, forehead furrowed. She saw the sun was now high in the sky. She must have slept for two hours. She scrambled to her feet and was at Ian's side in the three long steps it took to get to him.

Ian was thrashing side to side, elbows flying, trying to sit up, and quite possibly undoing all of her stitches. She looked around to see who could help her restrain her hysterical patient. Marty was nowhere to be seen. She looked back and saw that James was still asleep. Awake or asleep, he couldn't help her either. She hoped she hadn't bled him too much. If she had, there was nothing she could do about it now. Nothing but pray, she scolded herself. "Lord, please heal these men and help us all in everything. In Jesus's name, amen," she prayed softly, swiftly, and sincerely.

Her tone and attitude changed quickly as she addressed her restless patient. "Hey! You! Knock it off! Lie still or you'll tear out my stitches, and then I'll be pissed!"

Her scolding him like an irate gunny sergeant seemed to work. He didn't move a muscle. Well, not exactly. He frowned as much as he could without aggravating his neck.

Leah continued in her stern voice, "Now, I'm going to give you some painkillers. You'll feel better, but that doesn't mean you can do anything. Do you promise not to move?"

"No," he replied, and remained stone-faced, his glare almost dense enough to mark a path to the sun that was now directly overhead.

"Well, then, I'm not going to ease your pain." She paused and then snorted testily. "Why do you feel like you have to move?"

Ian remained mute but didn't try to move.

Wee Ian came to Leah's side and held her hand. She looked down at him, and he just shook his head. Neither of them spoke and neither felt the need to. They stood there in silence, watching the grim-faced patient until they heard a noise. Leah tensed, but Wee Ian squeezed her hand in reassurance.

It was Marty coming over the rise. His dusty tri-corner hat was black around the middle from sweat. He took it off, wiped his brow with the back of his forearm, and set it back on his head. "Well, that's done. I didn't have a shovel, so I just threw them in a heap and piled rocks on top. That should keep the stink down for a bit. The wild animals will be out to feed on them soon enough, but for now, they're downwind and out of sight. How's your patient doing, Leah?"

"Oh, he's trying for the most stubborn male of the year award. I offered him painkillers if he'd promise not to move, but he said no. It must be a macho thing about being told what to do by a woman."

"What's macho?" asked Wee Ian

"Well, that's when a man thinks he has to be tough – even when he doesn't have to be – only because he doesn't want other men to think that he's weak. It's okay to be careful when you're wounded. I mean really, if he doesn't take care of himself, or let you or me take care of him for the next few days… Well, then Marty will just have to throw his carcass on top of those other three," Leah said sarcastically.

"What other three?" Ian asked, his voice soft, but only because that was the only volume level available in his weakened condition. He couldn't have hollered angrily if he had wanted to.

"Well, there's the one who tried to take off your head with a hatchet, and then the other two who were going to shoot me because I was tending to you. Marty tossed their bodies down that way. Oh, and that asshole who kidnapped and hurt Wee Ian, well, his rotting corpse is a few miles up the road. There are only us good guys left. So, since you and everyone else here is safe, would you lie still and let me give you a painkiller?"

"Aye, I'll let ye," he whispered hoarsely, "but I'd rather have a bucket of whisky. Is there anythin' to drink?"

Wee Ian was at his side in a flash. "Here, mind yer heid, jest let me pour some in yer mouth." The son was careful, dribbling in just enough to fill his father's mouth without choking him.

Leah saw the effort it was taking and decided she needed to modify the accommodations for her prone patient. She opened her medical bag and cut off a one-foot length of the flexible tubing. "Here, let's try this," she said and held out her hand for the bottle. She put the soft, clear plastic 'straw' into it and handed it back to Wee Ian. He frowned at the new arrangement then looked up at her.

"It's like a reed. He can suck through it. This way he can control how much he gets. But wait." She took two Percocets out of her pocket. "Open up, Ian. I want you to swallow these. Your son has the water."

Wee Ian did as he was told and held the water bottle for his father. Ian swallowed hard and almost choked but managed to suppress his gag reflex and kept the pills down.

"I still say whisky woulda been better," he mumbled hoarsely. He squeezed his eyes shut in discomfort, settled his shoulders back into the ground, and seemed to accept his lot as an incapacitated patient.

Leah could only hope that he was really trying to rest. He was such an angry man. It appeared that it had been a long time since he had truly relaxed.

***

Wee Ian showed himself to be a clever and resourceful young man. James watched from his shady earthen bed under the tree as the bare-chested boy toiled. He had gathered leafy tree branches while he and Leah had napped and was now back to his project.

No one had told him what to do, but the lad had taken it upon himself to build his father a shelter from the sun. He had gathered as many bush and tree branches as he could, then realized they needed a supporting framework. He went to the edge of the clearing and retrieved the hatchet he had thrown away in disgust after pulling it from his father's neck. He set it on the ground and rubbed dirt onto the blade, scouring the blood from it. After it was clean enough to pass his inspection, he walked toward the creek with it, head down, looking at the ground. He stopped, picked up, and then discarded several stones until he found just the right one: a fine-grained rock to use as a hone. He spit on the stone, then drew the edge of the hatchet across it in a wide semi-circle, stopping every few strokes to check the sharpness by touching it to his thumb.

When he was finally satisfied with the result, he went to the creek's edge to study the drooping tree branches overhanging the flowing water.

He cut down four bowed limbs best suited for use as arches, then came back to his father, dragging the timber behind him like a proud, miniature draft horse. He assessed the site, moved a few rocks out of the way, and then began digging post holes with another piece of wood he had chosen for his shovel.

Leah watched the young man's ministrations from the shade of the healing tree. Wee Ian was determined, not angry or frustrated by his lack of tools or by the magnitude of the project. He was simply getting it done. Leah felt a hand on hers. James was awake and had also been watching the small Hercules create a temple for his wounded father.

"I'd help him if I had the strength – or thought he needed it," he said softly. "I could only hope to have a son as resourceful and devoted as he is." He patted her hand a couple more times, the taps echoing the little prayers he was sending up that he *would* be a father one day.

Marty had disappeared again, or at least was out of Leah's line of sight. She wasn't concerned. After all, he would show up when he was ready. That seemed to be his style. "Are you hungry or thirsty?" Leah asked James.

"Yes and yes. Did you bring any watermelon?" he asked, grinning.

"Yes, as a matter of fact, I did. But it'll be three months before they're ready," she said, referring to the fact that what she had were watermelon *seeds*. "Would you settle for some granola and water?"

"Actually, I'd like some of that jerky. For some reason, I have a craving for red meat. Hmm, must be I'm a little anemic..." he drawled.

"D'ya think!?" Leah replied with a laugh. She started digging into the bag, handing him the other water bottle as she searched for the beef jerky. "Wee Ian, are you hungry?"

"Aye, I could do with a bite. After I finish this, I'll catch some fish fer our dinner. I'll have to wait until the sun sets a bit, though. The fish ken not to come out when it's so hot."

"Only mad dogs and Englishmen go out in the noonday sun," James said, quoting Rudyard Kipling. "But this Englishman will pass until the sun goes down a bit. It's been a while since I went fishing. I'd like to go with you this evening, if it's all right with you."

Wee Ian shrugged one shoulder, then went back to work, trying to get his arched beams set into their foundation holes.

Leah saw that no matter how clever the boy was, he needed

assistance. "May I help you? You helped me, and I'd like to return the favor."

It took her half a minute to manage her skirts so she could stand up – she'd figure out how to be graceful *and* decent later – and then went to his side. "Four hands are better than two, or something like that," she said, as an excuse to both help him and to see if her patient really was getting rest.

The arches were great and had just the right angle, but the wisps of river grass he had been trying to use to secure the frame walls at the apex were not working. No one had any rope as far as she could see, and the only leather thongs were holding up the Ians' loincloths. As if Wee Ian were reading her mind, he looked down at his waist in a quandary.

"Wait," she said, as he started to negotiate the knot. "I think I know what we can use."

Now it was James who could see what was going on. "Do you really want to do that?" he asked softly. Leah nodded and looked in her bag.

"Here," James said, handing her the duct tape. "It was in mine. Use it well and save some for later. I might get warts."

She smiled at his joke about duct tape for wart removal. "I just need a little bit of it. Drink more water and have another piece of jerky. I think I took too much blood out of you. I am *so* sorry."

James shrugged, grinned, and fished out the high-iron-content snack. His first mini-meal of jerky and water had helped, but he still felt he was only at 20% operating efficiency.

"I hope you don't need a building permit for that," he said, nodding at the new shelter. "It'd never pass inspection."

"Right," she drawled, and walked away, the roll of duct tape around her wrist like a fat, gray bracelet.

Wee Ian was still trying to use the lengths of grass to hold the north and south walls together at the top. "Just hold them there for a minute," Leah said, "I've got some stuff here that will work."

She shook the roll off her wrist and used her teeth to pull the end loose. ZAAAPPP. The noise of duct tape being pulled off the roll was loud and coarse, and made Ian the elder jump. But it was an involuntary reflex. He was in a deep sleep.

"Oh, shit," Leah said softly. Hopefully, he wasn't in a coma. If he was, she couldn't do anything about it except let him come out of it naturally. After she and Wee Ian got the shelter framed, she would offer him more water.

Wee Ian held the arch segments together while she wrapped the tape around the ends. One more ZAAAPPP – another length of tape torn off – and then another section of the framework was secured. Now it was time to set the top beam and tie the two together.

"Do you think we need more of the tape?" she asked Wee Ian. It was his project, after all. She was just a consulting structural engineer and tape puller-offer.

"Aye, I think we'd best use more of that zap. Da will jest have to bide with the noise of it comin' off the band."

Leah tore off two more pieces – this time, one right after the other – and put them on her sleeve for easy access. She returned the roll to her wrist, and with the help of Marty – who had just appeared – the shelter frame was completed.

Wee Ian looked at the two of them in turn, said a quick, "Thanks," and returned to the next step in the project: breathing walls. He wove the brush into the twigs of the tree branches that had now become the studs and roof, creating a porous ceiling and walls. The shade factor of his creation was high, but still allowed for a cooling breeze to pass through.

"Nice work," Leah said. Wee Ian backed away to inspect his construction, looking for faults by the frown on his face. Leah interrupted his evaluation. "Can I sneak in here and offer him more water? We need to get as much as we can into him."

Wee Ian turned away and came back with the bottle of water and the plastic tubing straw. He crawled into the little hut and held the straw to his father's mouth. Leah could see that Ian wasn't drinking, or at least not sucking.

"Here, let me show you something," she said. Wee Ian scooted back out and handed her the bottle. "Look." While it was still in the water, she put one finger over the tubing, then pulled it out. She tilted her head back, opened her mouth with the straw held above it, then let her finger off the end. The water dropped all at once into her mouth. She swallowed, brought her head back up, and smiled.

"Now, don't force the water into his mouth, just dribble a few drops into it with it held high like I did. Keep your finger on the end, and just let him have a few drops at a time. He'll probably wrap his lips around it and eventually get the sucking reflex going again. If not, we'll have to do the wet washcloth trick. I'd rather use the straw, though, because we can get more fluids in him that way. When you're done, come get that snack. You've been working hard."

James was tired but awake while they worked, content to stare out at the creek, at peace with himself, and looking forward to fishing for dinner with the young man.

Leah went back to the shade of the tree and pulled the backpacks to her. She hadn't realized how hungry she was until now. She chuckled to herself as she realized that she hadn't eaten in over 230 years. A little bit of the granola would tide her over until the men caught fish for dinner.

The men – all of a sudden, she had four men in her life: three good, hard-working men and one ornery patient. Well, at least the numbers weren't reversed, and it wasn't three ornery patients and one good, hard worker. Small blessing number 1,516.

Wee Ian came over to join them in the shade, bringing the water bottle and straw with him. "I got him to drink a bit. I think he's in the deep sleep. I dinna ken what ye call it, but he may be that way fer a few days. His body is healin' itself. I'll mind him if ye have other places to go. I sure appreciate the sewin' and gettin' more blood into him. I never saw that done." Wee Ian turned to James, obviously confused. "Does that mean he has some of yer spirit in him?"

"Well, first of all, it's called a coma. Hopefully, he's just in a deep, repairing sleep and not a deep coma. But either way, you're right – I'm sure his body is healing itself. And as far as the spirit goes, I don't know. I've been told that blood is just blood – red water that carries fuel like – well, like wood for a fire. It helps the body burn brighter, but sometimes I wonder…"

Leah cleared her throat hard – twice – to get James to stop talking. *He must be loopy from the blood loss. The boy's bewildered as it is, and he's confusing him even more.* "Would you *like* some of his spirit to be in your father?" she asked.

Wee Ian leaned over and looked at James cynically. Then he looked at Leah. "He's yer husband?" he asked.

"Yes, and a very good man. He's smart and kind and, well, practically perfect. No, I think he's a perfect man, and I'm glad he's my husband," she said, chest out with pride.

"Weel then, if it's all right with ye two, I'll hope that a bit of Mr. James's spirit got into my da. He ran out of perfect parts and pieces a long time ago. He can use all the help we can find him… What's that?" the boy said suddenly, staring at the large plastic baggie of granola he had just noticed.

"It's a mix of good foods to help you stay strong, or in your case, grow strong. Here, put out your hands, and I'll give you some."

Wee Ian reached out and accepted a fistful of the fruit/oat/chocolate-chip/nut mixture. He crossed his legs 'Indian' style and placed the bounty on his breechclout flap. "What are these?" he asked, holding up a tan bit.

"Well, that's a cashew, a nut. There are other foods in there that I'll bet you've never seen, either. But they're all good for you. There's pineapple and coconut, oat bits, pretzels, and chocolate chips. Well, chocolate is a little bit good for you, but it tastes *real* good."

"What's this one? It looks like a wee black turd."

Leah nearly choked on her mouthful of granola. "That's the chocolate that I told you tasted so good. Go ahead and try it. If you don't like it, put the rest of them aside, and I'll eat them. They're great."

Wee Ian picked up a piece and inspected it, turned it around, sniffed it, and still wasn't sure he wanted to eat it.

"It'll melt in your hand if you hold onto it too long. Just eat it – trust me."

Wee Ian huffed in uncertainty, then put it in his mouth – he trusted her. His eyes widened and a grin of satisfaction grew to a full smile as he quickly licked the melted remains off his fingers.

"I told you so. I wouldn't lie to you," Leah said and chuckled. She didn't have a radio or television, but she was definitely being entertained.

"You wouldn't lie to me?" Wee Ian asked, suddenly somber.

"Of course not. Why, what do you want to know? Oh, your father. I'm sure he's going to be all right. If we hadn't done all the sewing and the blood transfusion, he might have died, but now he has a great chance of recovery." Leah's voice and attitude changed into head nurse mode as she stressed her most important warning, "As long as he stays still long enough for the wounds to heal."

"That's not what I meant. I figured ye were a good healer, and I'm sure ye did the best ye could. That's what healers do. But," the boy paused, looked down at the partially eaten food in his lap, then decided to ask, "Are ye my kin?"

Leah was both shocked and guarded. She had briefly thought about the Pomeroy-Hart relationship when she talked to Marty before her nap, but there didn't seem to be any way she could be related to Ian Kinkaid. "Why do you ask?"

"Not why do I ask. Are ye my kin?" he repeated, his hard stare letting her know he wanted – no, needed – her answer.

"Shoot, I don't know. I don't know your mother, and I don't think there is any way your father and I are related. So, as far as I can tell, no, we're not related. *Now* will you tell me why you think I'm your kin?"

"Yer dress and yer face. Ye look jest like Evie and yer wearin' her dress. She's my kin because her... Weel, she said to jest tell people we're kin."

"Oh, shit," Leah mumbled.

"Yeah, oh, shit," James echoed.

"Ye ken, I can hear pretty good. Why do ye say *oh, shit*?"

"Well, yes, Evie and I are kin – very, very close kin. But how are you kin to her?" Leah asked, both confused and very curious.

"Weel, since ye are her kin – and I ken ye are, jest by lookin' at yer face and seein' how kind and helpful ye are – I guess I can tell ye. Her babies are my siblings – that's the right word, I think. My da was the sperm donor."

"James..." Leah's voice squeaked.

"Come here," he said, reaching out for her, but without the strength to get up for her. "Let me hold you."

"He's my stepfather," Leah whispered, as she leaned into him. "Ian Kincaid is my stepfather?"

"No, he's not. And Wee Ian can hear you. Can't you, lad?"

"Aye, I can. Are ye a fairy, too?" he asked. "Both of ye?"

Marty walked into the scene, saving James and Leah from having to answer immediately. He looked down at Leah, glanced at James, and then winked. "What's going on here? Is everybody taking an afternoon nap? Scoot over and let me have some of that shade. What's that in your lap there, lad? Looks like you have some of what I call trail mix. What ya got in there, Leah?"

"It's granola with cashews and chocolate chips. But I guess I shouldn't have used the chocolate. It melts in your hands before you can get it into your mouth. Do you want some?" Leah's heart was beating rapid fire. The appearance of Marty and his chit-chat were only delaying the need to answer Wee Ian's question.

"Sure, how about if you just put a tad into this handkerchief." He reached into his front pocket, took out the red bandana, shook it out, and held it open to receive a little afternoon snack.

Marty sat between Wee Ian and his son and daughter-in-law, munching on his morsels, making inane comments to fill the air with words, but not information or knowledge. It got to be a waiting game after about ten minutes. Marty wouldn't move and Wee Ian didn't know if he could speak in front of the older man. It was becoming uncomfortable. James reached over and held Leah's hand, squeezing it in a request for a little visual tête-à-tête.

The glances back and forth between them confirmed that they were in accordance – Wee Ian could be told they were 'fairies.' James looked over at his father and gave him a quick eyebrow lift that said they wanted some alone time with the young man.

"Well, I guess I'll go down to the creek where it's cooler and do something creative," Marty said. "Or maybe I'll see if there're any huckleberries upstream. At least, the color of the bushes looks to be about right. Does anyone need anything before I leave? Any…ahem…well, anything?" He had almost said, 'Any dead bodies removed,' but thought better of it considering the precarious health of Ian Kincaid.

Leah heard – or sensed – the words that Marty had cut short. He seemed to be an impetuous and garrulous man but did think at least *two* words ahead before he spoke.

"We're fine," she said, answering his request about needs. "Just don't get lost. It was a lot of trouble finding you this time. I wouldn't want to have to go through that again."

"I'll mind," he said, "and thanks for coming. We'll all sit around and catch up this evening when it's cooler. So long, for now." Marty grabbed the reins of his gray mare and walked down to the creek bed, following it upstream to the hoped for stand of wild berries.

James quietly watched his father leave. He wanted Leah close, but it was too hot to snuggle. Instead, he moved his hand next to hers, barely touching it. She tapped him back with her pinkie, letting him know that she could feel him. That small bit of tactile contact they shared was enough, though. There was no rational explanation for it, but he could practically feel her energy trickle charging into him. And right now, he needed her strength.

"Now, as to your question," Leah returned her attention to Wee Ian, "would it make a difference if we were fairies?"

Wee Ian cocked his head and thought about it for a full minute or more, and then explained. "My da said that Evie was a fairy. He said that's why he couldna stay with her. He was glad his cousin – his name's Wallace – could be there for her, though. They're probably marrit now. She's a nice lady, but still a fairy. Da said he was afraid she'd leave him and go back to her own time and her own people. He said he kent other fairies before, and they always left. Except one, and he wouldna tell me who she was. But he did say that even though she left once, she came back again, but it was a long time later. I think I ken who it is, but I dinna want to ask him. It makes him sad to talk about it."

Neither Leah nor James spoke. They could tell there was more to his story, and he was still working up to it. Finally, he asked, "It's all right to be a fairy. It's not like ye can change bein' one or anythin'…can ye?"

Oops! Now it was time for an explanation. "Would it be all right with you if I was a fairy…and my husband, too?"

"Aye, it's all right with me. So, I guess that means ye are, right – the both of ye?"

James felt compelled to speak for the both of them. "I never thought I'd hear myself say this, but aye, I am a fairy, and my wife, too."

Leah giggled then tried to regain her composure. James continued, "And since you believe in fairies, do you think they're bad or evil?"

"No, why would I think that?"

"Just making sure," James said, "Just making sure."

Wee Ian started picking at his granola again. "What's this one?" he asked and held up a twisted yellow triangle.

"That's dried pineapple," Leah said, letting James regain his strength by staying mum. "It's real juicy and messy when it's fresh, so they dry it out like you do jerky or apples. I don't think you can grow it around here, though."

As soon as the words were out of her mouth, she regretted them. If it didn't grow around here, then where did she get it? Ergh! Watch what you say, woman!

But Wee Ian hadn't paid any attention to her remark. His mind was elsewhere. "Does that mean my da is part fairy now?" he asked, then took a small nibble of the pineapple ort, trying to make it last.

"Uh," James and Leah chorused softly and awkwardly at the same time, then looked at each other.

"I don't think that changes with blood," James said without much conviction.

Leah looked over at him and was glad that he hadn't expounded on the subject. This one was definitely a good topic to be left as a mystery. But either way, Wee Ian didn't seem too concerned. He was having a good time playing with his food, content that, at least for now, his father wouldn't be getting into any more trouble.

Chapter 18: A Second Injury (AYE Ch 50)

August 17, 1781
Later that afternoon

"I think he has another wound," Wee Ian said. "But I think that maybe James should help me with this one," and looked from her to the man dozing under the tree.

"What? He's not a doctor. I'm the nurse, rather healer." Leah saw the look of both embarrassment and worry on the boy's face. "Oh, my God, did they...?"

"They must have done it jest after they sold me to that Captain. He wasna missing any parts when I was with him." He huffed, then kicked a stone into the brush away from their little campsite, frustrated. "Bring yer bag if it willna bother ye to look," he said and led the way.

Leah grabbed her backpack then paused. "James, come with me, please. I..I'm not sure I need your help in a medical sense," she stammered, "but I think I do for moral support."

She wrapped her hand around James's inner wrist, then pulled back hard to help him stand. Earlier, he had hastily whittled off side-shoots from a stout stick for use as a walking cane, but she insisted he steady himself with a hand on her shoulder, too. It was only a few feet to Ian's custom-built hospital ward, but he appreciated her help.

Wee Ian waited for them, his dark eyebrows furrowed with concern. His father was modestly covered, but the bloody breechclout was untied, just lying across his loins.

Leah growled in self-loathing. Because of the urgency to repair Ian's neck wound, she had never even thought to check if he was injured anywhere else. She bit her bottom lip then squatted next to him. "Lord, give me strength and wisdom and everything else I need for this."

The words were soft but heard by both of her assistants. "Amen," James said.

"What he said," Wee Ian added.

Leah reached for the water bottle. Wee Ian had been watching her closely, and anticipating her need, placed it in her hand. "Thanks." She poured the now lukewarm water onto the terrycloth washcloth. She pulled back the breechclout and saw that his thighs, pubic hair, and scrotum were matted with brown, clotted blood. She placed the cloth over the entire area and dribbled more water over it. She needed to soak off the dried blood and wipe the area clean to see what the damage was. She dabbed the area to make sure the wet cloth was in contact with the skin, sighed deeply in frustration, then looked up to see two pair of worried eyes staring at her.

James and Wee Ian were there for her emotionally and would do anything asked of them, but there was nothing to do but wait and be ready when she needed help.

The only positive side of this scenario was that Ian the elder was unaware of what she was doing. What had been done to him was brutal and horrendous. But having a strange woman wipe and prod around his privates while he was awake and aware would have added humiliation and shame to the atrocity. Sometimes a coma could be a blessing.

Leah used the edge of the cloth to start the cleansing. Ian flinched when she first tugged the skin to wash it, but he never woke.

"James, hand me the goggles again, please, And Wee Ian, the water bottle…"

She irrigated the wound by exerting slight pressure on the sides of the squirt top bottle. It wasn't sterile water, but it would have to do for investigating the wound. Without asking, Wee Ian and James each grabbed one of her patient's knees and spread them out, affording her a better view of the injury.

Leah put the magnifying goggles on her face and leaned in close to see the cuts. She sighed in frustration: she was in her own shadow. She stood up and moved to let the sun flood the area to be examined. When she was able to focus, she saw that the hackers had stopped short of any permanent damage. Apparently, the bloodletting had been enough for them. Or someone or something had made them change their plan. Ugh! Or they were in a hurry to kill him. Leah shuddered at the horrible thoughts that were streaming into her head. "Stop that," she said under her breath. She wanted those images to cease and commanding them verbally to do so was the only way she could think of to do it.

"Stop what?" James whispered.

Leah looked at him, pursed her lips, and gave the slightest of head shakes. Now he could tell what she was trying to do: clear her bad thoughts. He gave a quick, soft snort to let her know he understood.

Wee Ian looked back and forth between them, scowling. He could see that they were both aware of what had happened, but he wanted to know, too. This was his father who had been hacked and knifed…and possibly more. "Stop what?" he echoed.

Leah didn't want to lie to him. He'd probably be able to tell the difference, anyhow. "Stop the evil deeds, the killing, maiming, all of…all of this senseless… Ergh!" she hissed in exasperation.

Wee Ian nodded like a bobble-headed plastic dog – he understood. "So, is he still a man?" he asked softly, his words breaking apart and losing substance as they hit the air, his whispered fear and terror as audible as a scream.

"It looks worse than it really is. I mean, his penis is still intact. It looks like they tried to castrate him, but they didn't get the job done…thank You, Lord. He has several slices to his scrotum and inner thighs, a deep stab wound in his left testicle, but they missed severing the tendons securing the testes. I need to clean it with more than just plain water, though. Wee Ian, will you bring me that other bag over there? It has more of my supplies."

Wee Ian placed the bag in her hand without comment, only giving a nod that seemed to say, 'Here ye are, ma'am,' without a noise, and then returned to his surgery-side observation post.

Leah used the sponge-tipped swab to clean the cut areas with the orange-colored antiseptic solution. She dug into the medical supply section of her bag and found the adhesive tape. "A butterfly bandage would probably be better than stitches. I mean, he isn't going to be moving around for a few days. This way, no stitches need to be removed. He can pull the tape off by himself in a week. I'm sure he'll be awake by then and be glad that he won't have to have someone else remove his sutures."

Wee Ian leaned in to get a better look at Leah's ministrations. She saw that he was interested, so moved aside for him to get a better look. "See, the plumbing is all intact and the testes – the balls – look like they're going to be fine. Although…"

Leah didn't finish her thought, and that fact wasn't lost on either James or Wee Ian. "What do ye mean 'although'?" the son asked suspiciously.

Leah glanced over at James and gave him the 'just trust me on this' look. "Well, since you know I'm a fairy, I'll tell you that there were some 'fairy deeds' I saw before I came here." She realized as soon as the words were out of her mouth, it was the wrong approach. She changed her explanation but still fumbled with her new choice of words. "You, see… I mean… Oh, shoot. Do you know what a surgeon is?"

Wee Ian nodded. "He takes out teeth, spills yer blood into a pan, and puts leeches on ye. He's kinda like a healer, but nae as good."

"Well, yes, they usually heal with cutting, and there's blood around, but the surgeons where we're from are better than the ones around here. There's a procedure that I watched, actually assisted in…" Leah looked over and saw she was losing Wee Ian. "What I mean to say is that he may not be able to make babies again, but the…the…"

"Ye mean the cock'll work, but there willna be any more sperms?" Wee Ian asked.

"Exactly!" Leah exclaimed, then exhaled in relief. The bandaging was done and so was the explanation.

"So, you've assisted in a few vasectomies?" James asked with a sly grin.

"Yes, I have," Leah answered with a modest shrug. She straightened up and added, "And that's why I would say that even though he's been stabbed in the testes and sliced in a crude attempt at castration, the ligaments are still intact. The vasa deferentia may have been severed, but men don't need to have that little vessel intact. Shoot, they pay good money to have it cut! If he ever settles down and gets rid of that anger, I'm sure he'll make a good husband and be able to serve his wife well. But hopefully, he's already had all the children he wants."

"Well, he's had at least one great son. He couldn't ask for anyone smarter or more loyal, that's for sure." James looked at Wee Ian. He was sitting cross-legged in front of his father, head bowed – a young lion cub protecting his battle-scarred and ravaged elder.

The boy couldn't help but hear James. He knew he was smart enough – smarter than many boys his age – but it was nice to hear someone praise his father for having a good son. He lifted his head and smiled as sweetly as a skinny, half-naked, worried boy of eleven could. "Thanks." He swallowed hard and sniffed twice. "I'm sure he woulda appreciated hearin' it. I'll let him ken ye gave him the compliment when he wakes."

Chapter 19: Finally Here (AYE Ch 51)

The three of them returned to the shade of the tree and enjoyed an encore of their light repast in silence, no one feeling like the subjects of fairies and blood needed to be expounded upon or explained. Ian was sleeping soundly, an occasional snort coming from within his brush-walled castle. Marty came up to the little gathering, set down his handkerchief full of huckleberries next to the trail mix bag, then leaned back against the tree next to James, letting out a long, contented sigh. The world was at peace for all of them.

Well, almost all of them. Leah was happy that they had made it to their destination safely, and that Ian looked as if he was going to survive, but she was still eager to find out where her mother was. She knew it was too late in the day to head out, no matter where they were. James still needed time to recuperate, and there was Ian to consider. But, whether they were going or staying put, she still wanted – needed – to have a plan; something to look forward to, at least.

She looked over at the pensive boy and asked, "If we leave, do you think you can take care of – I mean, see to – your da's needs with Mr. Melbourne's help?"

"Oh, he can call me Marty. I'm more comfortable with that," Marty said. He gulped as he realized that he had just interrupted Wee Ian's answer. "Oops, sorry. That was rude."

Wee Ian looked at the gray-haired man from head to toe, literally. He was an older man, to be sure, but looked strong. He was nice, but just a wee bit silly. The boy nodded his head. "Aye, I can handle Da with or without *Marty's*," he stressed the name, "help. He's welcome to stay if he likes. If Da stays asleep for the healin', he willna be much trouble." He turned back to look at his comatose father, the man's mouth hanging lax, eyes squeezed tight, as if in pain. "I think he'll be asleep for another day or so. He's drinkin' water from the reed, and if I can get a squirrel, I'll make some broth." Wee Ian frowned in recollection and looked over at Leah. "Do ye happen to have a spare pot to cook in?"

"Uh, no, we don't even have one for us," James answered. *Damn, one more very important item they had forgotten. Maybe Gibsonville was nearby and they could buy one there.*

Marty piped in, "I have a pan and I'd be more than happy to share it.

And I even have an onion for the stew or broth or whatever you decide to cook. Or I can cook." Marty was about to say more, then realized that he was being too chatty again. "Um, I think I'll go down by the stream and look for some watercress. Mighty tasty stuff," he said in parting, then trundled downhill toward the creek.

"Don't take too long," James called after him. "I still need to talk to you."

Marty didn't turn his head but waved his hand in acknowledgment that he had heard him. He'd have to face him soon enough.

There was an awkward silence among the remaining group, but it didn't last long. Out of the blue, Leah suddenly asked, "What happened to the horses that belonged to those bad guys?" She scrambled up from the ground and stood on tiptoes, as if she could search better with the extra couple inches that that afforded. She looked beyond the trees and scrubby bushes, then turned and checked behind her in all directions, wearing a slight frown, as if she was merely searching for a mislaid coffee cup.

Wee Ian's eyes sparkled at hearing the question. He hadn't thought about that! Still seated, he looked at his immediate surroundings. He pursed his lips as he stared at his father's deep sleep, then changed focus to his new friends – the heroic but weakened James, leaning against the tree; Leah the healer doing the detective dance; and down the rise, the helpful but talkative Marty, his broad-shouldered figure disappearing into the landscape, foraging for food again. He shifted his eyes as he tried to justify his request with himself before voicing it.

Leah could see the thoughts spinning in Wee Ian's head. He had some serious decision making ahead of him – maybe she could make it easier.

"If you want to see if you can round up the horses, I'll keep an eye on your father. If you need help, I'm sure Marty would be happy to join you. I think James better stay put for a while, though."

The relieved youth stood up straight and tall to answer, addressing the couple with carefully worded solemn respect. "Ye have been most kind and helpful to me and my father in this…this mess, and if ye could see to stay by his side a wee bit longer, I'll get the horses. I only need to get the one, and then the others will follow." A grin of realization appeared on his face, and his voice brightened up. "And I'll wager there's at least one pot in the saddlebags that *used* to belong to those three." He tilted his head toward the burial mound and added, a full, white-toothed smile now shining bright, "They willna be needin' their goods anymore, that's fer sure."

Ian stuck his nose in the air and turned around slowly, sniffing for the direction of the horses. He chuckled as he caught the scent, shuffled down to the creek, and stood on an oversized boulder at the edge, about thirty feet downstream from Marty.

"I'll be quick about it then," he shouted, and waved to James and Leah, then over at Marty.

The little half-naked Scot-Indian headed out to capture horses, foodstuffs, and cooking utensils, happy to be of assistance to the fairy people who had rescued him and his father.

Marty watched the young boy tread lightly, quickly and quietly, down to the streambed. He was both fleet and clever, a credit to his father. He looked back up the ridge and saw his son. Right now, he was weak and hardly able to stand up straight by himself, but wise – and humble – enough to use a stick as a makeshift cane to help prevent a fall. He was also generous. He had given up his safe and secure life, and all the wealth and comforts of the 21st century, to come follow his addlepated grandfather into the wilds of Revolutionary War era North Carolina for no other reason than he had been asked.

Marty sighed deeply. He wondered if James had found out yet that he was really his father, not his grandfather. He was a very bright boy – man, he corrected himself – but the paths to discovering his true heritage had been cleared of clues and hints for years.

There were only two people alive who knew the truth since Bruce, the acknowledged and legal father of James, was dead. Bibb had promised not to tell, and he knew that she could be trusted. He snorted. How could she even start to tell him? There was no connection between the two of them. They were on opposite sides of the Atlantic Ocean, and he couldn't think of any reason for them to meet either socially or for business. No, he had wiped away any possibility that they would haphazardly become acquainted. Unfortunately, that also meant that telling James the truth of his parentage was going to be all the harder. But he had to tell him and tell him soon. He had lived the lie for too many years. James deserved to know that he loved him more – if that were even possible – because he was his real, biological, son.

And he should also know that he had another relative here besides great-uncle-many-times-over Lord Julian Hart.

How could he even begin to explain why he sent for him? 'Son, we needed to protect a person – your ancestor – so you will live, rather, be born.' Marty shook his head like a dog with a bug in his ear. The paradox sounded crazy to him, even inside his head, but James definitely needed to know who this ancestor was. But how in the hell was he to start the topic?

"Just jump in with both feet like you usually do, Melbourne," he said under his breath. "No reason to start pussyfooting around now."

He gulped in a deep breath for fortitude and approached James, who was awake but prone under the shade tree. "We have to talk," Marty declared with a feigned sense of bravado.

James rose onto one elbow and said, "I agree. But I don't think I know as much as you think I do."

Marty winced and shut his eyes but didn't say anything. He'd let James finish.

"I was only able to read the first letter in the bundle. And the map and the note about bringing the IV tools were just email copies that were sent to my phone. I never got to see the originals. If there was something on the back of them or…" He shook his head, eyes closed, apologizing without saying more.

Marty let out a deep sigh of relief and managed to utter, "Oh." He was rarely at a loss for words, but right now, he was stumped about how he could – or should – reveal their true biological relationship. He huffed again and looked over at James. His son wasn't waiting for him to reply, though. He was composing his own thoughts, getting ready to say more.

"The MacLeods were after the treasure," James said. "They broke into Leah's apartment because they thought she had it but came out empty-handed. One of them followed me to the motel and got into my valise while I was out of the room." James bit his lip, hoping he wouldn't be asked to go into detail, then sighed and continued. "That's where they found the letters, in the side pocket. Leah and I had only read the first one; we hadn't had a chance to look at the others. Eight – that is, Atholl MacLeod the 8th – poisoned his own brother as a diversion to sneak into the room to get them."

James's jaw tightened as he recalled the episode and the frustration he felt when he couldn't even dial 911. He started to say more, then stopped. Marty didn't need to know that he and Leah were sharing a room, nor that she was in the shower when that asshole broke in. He snorted, then grinned, glad that the scary story had a happy ending. "The treasure was right there in the bag the whole time, but he didn't see it." James patted the bag. "I brought it back with me."

"What do you mean 'it was right there in the bag'?" Marty asked. "What treasure would that be?"

"The jewels, of course."

Neither one of them spoke. Marty shook his head, amazed and dumbfounded. A mischievous grin grew, along with a sense of irony.

"What? That was the treasure you were talking about, wasn't it?"

Marty's head still rattled back and forth. "No," he said slowly, then stopped to look James in the eye. "*You* were the treasure."

"What? I mean," he lowered his tone and volume, "what *are* you talking about?" Wee Ian was probably too far away to hear, but he still didn't want to appear to be out of control.

Marty sighed, shifted positions, and proceeded haltingly. "I got caught up in doing genealogy. I mean, the Melbourne line was already well-researched and documented to almost the beginning of time – or so it seemed. The mystery of the Hart break in the family line was fascinating, so I began investigating it. I went – rather, came here – to North Carolina because it was the last place he was known to be alive. I researched the museums and universities and churches and graveyards…" Marty stole a glance at James to see if he understood where the story was going.

"And you found nothing, so decided to go home and look at those letters to see if there was anything in them, right?" James accused more than asked.

Marty shrugged with admission of guilt and continued his story. "At first I wasn't going to, but then…well, yes – I cheated. What can I say? I went back home, debated – argued – with myself about it for nearly a year…" Marty huffed in frustration, "but I couldn't stand the temptation. I was weak and curious and bored. I read them – read them all – and then was back on the plane to North Carolina within days. There really was something in those, for me, for us. But only a small part of it related to

Lord Julian.

"That second time, my friend helped me with the research. While we were working on it, we found a story – more a legend than written word – in this friend's history about an ancestor who was saved by a fairy. It wasn't Great-uncle Julian – he was in my friend's family line, too, but indirectly – but it was all so fascinating that I didn't want to stop the research.

"Yes, I got distracted." Marty rolled his eyes – James knew that it happened to him frequently, too. "The legend was about a fairy who put his blood into a warrior's father's father's body and saved his life. It never said how many generations were involved, but my friend and I did more investigating and traced it back to this time, the time when Evie was here.

"You see, Evie – the woman who had written the letters – would be considered a fairy, so I thought maybe she had something to do with this. By the way, there are tales of fairies as far back as lore goes. Fairies – that's the name they gave to people who just showed up without explanation, in strange clothes, speaking strange dialects – time travelers. Well, fairies and witches. The witches were the ones who weren't smart enough to shut up and adapt, but kept insisting…well, you get the picture."

James nodded. Yes, he got the picture. The only Lisa Sinclaire book he had read explained it well enough. And now he and Leah were here as fairies; and his father, Marty; and Leah's mother, Dani – or Evie, as she liked to be called – were, too.

"So, I think my friend's ancestor needed a blood transfusion to survive, and well, I wanted to make sure he got it, so I sent you the map and the note."

"Yes, how *did* you do that?" James asked.

"Well, I had seen the 'Back to the Future' movies where Professor Brown sent *Marty*," he winked at saying the name, "a letter because he knew where he would be on a certain date. I was sure you would be in London for your birthday, so did some creative mailing and forwarding, and yes, I even used Western Union at one point. You obviously got the letter or you wouldn't be here with the IV equipment." Marty looked pensive then added, "But I sure didn't see Leah coming. I guess everything isn't foretold or predestined."

"Yeah, well, the letter almost didn't get to me. By all rights, it should have been intercepted, but fate – no, God – was still in control. If it is meant to be, He will make sure there's a way to get it done. If I hadn't brought the IV tools, either Ian would have not been hatcheted or would have survived regardless of the transfusion…or maybe another fairy would have shown up and done the deed."

"So, it looks like Ian will live…" Marty looked around nervously, then changed the subject quickly and awkwardly. "I wonder what time the moon comes up."

"What the…?" James started to ask what was going on but clamped off the question as soon as he realized what it was. He looked over at Leah and saw that she had figured it out at the same time. Or had read his mind, or whatever – it didn't make a difference. They both knew why Marty was uncomfortable. The truth was so close, but he wasn't ready yet to admit that there was a genetic connection between Ian and James.

Now is as good a time as ever to let him know that I know. James sat up straight and cleared his throat. "So I'm the treasure and Ian is my ancestor, right?" He focused on Marty, eyes narrowed, letting him know that he was on to him. "And therefore, Bibb's, too."

James and Leah giggled at the wide-eyed, slack-jawed expression on Marty's face. The old man had been found out and hadn't seen it coming.

"Leah said she was my daughter-in-law," he mumbled in recollection. "You knew?" he asked haltingly, "You know that I'm your father?"

James nodded and grinned broadly but sobered up quickly when he remembered there was still another family member he had to talk to Marty about. "And yes, I know Bibb's my real mother," he said plainly, then shook his head to rearrange his thoughts. *Yes, I know Bibb's my mother, but you need to know that you have another son. But that subject will have to wait, or you'll never tell me why you sent for me.* "Please, continue your story."

Marty tipped his head in a tacit apology, wondered for a quick moment how James had found out, then continued. "Bibb's got a lot of Cherokee blood in her. That's where you get those high cheekbones and ruddy complexion. Anyhow, I asked her about it when I went back to visit when you were six. That was the one time I insisted Bruce stick around and spend some time with you. Anyway, Bibb and I went to the Cherokee Reservation and did research together. I'm not sure how excited she really was about researching her heritage, but she liked spending time with me. Shoot, she'd have been happy to dig through dung piles with me."

Marty's contented, glassy-eyed half-grin of recalling the conjugal times spent with Bibb evaporated when he saw James frowning, looking down his nose at him, giving him a non-verbal scolding to get on with the story.

He sputtered, "But it wasn't on paper – what we were looking for – so we went and talked to the elders. They were the ones in charge of keeping the tribe's history, but that part wasn't written; it was an oral history, a family's story not in any book. For the life of me, I can't remember the old woman's name, but she was a distant relative of Bibb's. They both had old Colonel Parks as an ancestor. He was one of the good American soldiers on the Trail of Tears." Marty noticed James was frowning at him again, so stopped rambling.

"Okay, okay, I'll try to focus. Bottom line, Bibb – and therefore, you – wouldn't be here if it weren't for the fairy who put his blood in Ian Kincaid, also known as Star Walker, because *he* was the father of Scout Kincaid who married a Janie or Junie or Genevieve Pomeroy-Hart. And *they* are your great-great-grandparents, however so many times over."

There was an awkward moment of silence. Neither James nor Leah commented on the revelation. Everyone looked at each other, and then Leah spoke up.

"Mom's name is Pomeroy-Hart, and as you know, she had triplets. Wee Ian just told us that Ian was the biological father of them, that they are his siblings. So far, the only children with Ian Kincaid's *blood* are her three and Wee Ian. And since he's now incapable of siring more children... Shoot, I'm sure those four didn't, or won't, intermarry or breed. I mean, they were, are, siblings, after all. And I'm not even sure if one of the triplets is a girl. There *is* no Scout Kincaid, and because of Ian's injury, he won't be able to sire any more children. Something is wrong with this scenario, or James wouldn't be here. I...I...I don't think we needed to come."

"Yes, we did," James said adamantly. "No matter what this story about a Scout Kincaid and a girl by the name of Pomeroy-Hart has to do with me, we are still, God willing, going to see your mother. And remember, except for that *one* relative back in Greensboro," James glanced over and winked at Leah – he'd let his father think he was referring to Bibb – "we don't have other family anywhere except for your mother and," James grinned and nodded acknowledgment, "my father."

Leah squinted her eyes and almost glared at James, backing off just enough not to be seen as mean or rude. "Oh, shit," her husband moaned softly when he realized the reason for her expression.

"Is Bibb okay?" Marty asked, the look of concern changing quickly to one of fear. Was there something wrong with that one relative back in Greensboro?

James closed his eyes, but before he could speak, Leah answered, sparing him the discomfort she knew he was feeling. "Yes and no," she replied, then quickly added, "She was attacked by Asshole MacLeod the 9th, but was recovering just fine when we left." Leah looked at Marty and saw he was biting his bottom lip, waiting for her to finish her explanation. "And no, because she has cancer – liver cancer."

"Is that a type of cancer the doctors can treat? Does she need a donor? Couldn't you help her? Is she going to be okay? Should I go back? Well, tell me!" Marty was practically – actually was – screaming by the time his questions were finished, his eyes wide in frustration with, and anger at, James for leaving Bibb when she was ill.

"Sit down, will you?" James suggested sternly, then added, "Sir." He wasn't sure how to address his father yet. Dad didn't feel right, but he didn't want to be disrespectful to him, no matter what the circumstances.

"Hmph!" Marty snorted, but sat down and was mute for about two whole seconds. "Well, spit it out, son," he grumbled, then added, "Damn, that feels good to say, knowing that you know and...well..." Marty shook his head gently, then said softly, "Go ahead, I'll try to calm down and not interrupt."

"The cancer is treatable, and she has an excellent chance of recovery. As far as going back to see her, yes, I think you should. You two have spent too much time apart, and it's obvious to me," James tipped his head to Leah, "and to my wife that you both care about each other. But there's something else you need to know, and it's another reason why you should go back."

James looked up to make sure that Marty was going to be able to comprehend – or accept – what he had to say next.

"Well, get on with it! I'm listening." Marty's back was board straight, as if he slouched or relaxed in the least, his powers of hearing would be compromised.

"You see, the reason she's going to be fine is that there's another donor for her. Actually, he's a better match than I am for the liver transplant."

"Bibb m...m...married?" Marty babbled in shock. "I mean, yes, I didn't talk to her as much as I should have, but I'm sure she would have told me if she had met someone else, and they got married and had a child together. Or didn't get married," Marty rolled his eyes and continued, "and still had a child. I never saw one around last time I saw her, and that was only three years ago."

Wrinkles and scowls of fear, hurt, and pain all rolled into one horrid emotion covering Marty's face – and it looked as if it was getting ready to be swamped with saline. His eyes were brimming with tears at the lost romance, the failed relationship that was his fault because he didn't want to have an American wife.

James laid his hand on his father's leg and brought him out of his self-imposed hell. "No, she never remarried, but I have a brother. And you have another son. She got pregnant the first time you two got together. She thought she would never see you again. She didn't want you to marry her out of guilt for having a love child, so she gave him up for adoption. He's a great guy and was actually Leah's best friend. He became my best friend several days before we found out that we were related, actually full-blooded brothers."

"When...who...his name?" Marty wasn't entirely speechless but couldn't manage to put a coherent question together.

"Billy Burke was born on the fourth of July 1984." James leaned back again and shut his eyes as he related the short biography of his brother. "He's a police detective – and a darn good one – for the Greensboro Police Department and looks a lot like me. Actually, he went to see Bibb in the hospital right after the attack by Niner. She couldn't see – her eyes were swollen shut and, well, she was in real rough shape – but she could hear just fine. When Billy spoke, she thought it was you. She thought she was telling you about your son who she had given up for adoption because she didn't believe she could rear a child by herself. Can you imagine the surprise when he found out that *he* was that child? I mean, he had the same birthmark and birth date and was dropped off at the same hospital…"

James opened his eyes to see his father's reaction to the story – and wasn't surprised. He was actually proud of him. Marty was crying, sniffing and snorting, and had resorted to wiping his runny nose on one sleeve, blotting his eyes with the other.

"Here," James said, and gave him his red handkerchief, "it looks like you donated yours to the berry basket cause."

"Oh, and here, I have a picture of the three of them I snapped just before we left." Leah handed Marty the small, laminated photograph. "Bibb still looks rough, but she's going to be just fine. And I know she'd like to see you. She asked if we'd send you back. I think it might be a good idea for you to acknowledge your other son, too. He and James did blood tests for Bibb's transplant and the DNA was so close…. James wanted him to legally change his name before we came back so all was in place for inheritances and such, but Billy was hoping you'd return, and then he could get christened with you there. I mean, I know it would mean a lot to him."

James paused, then felt as if he needed to add clarification. "It's not as if he's in it for the money – he's not – but I wanted him to be a steward for the funds, even if he didn't want any of it for himself. You couldn't have asked for a better son."

Marty started to giggle. Leah and James looked at each other – they didn't see anything funny in what had just been said. Marty's giggle turned into a big belly laugh.

"No, I didn't ask for him, but according to you two, I got one. And yes, I will acknowledge him, for sure. Although," the laughing stopped suddenly, "I don't know how I'll go about explaining *you*. Hmm, see where lying gets you? You need to keep making up more lies to keep up the deception."

"Oh, don't worry about kicking Bruce out of the family lineage. If Billy is my legal uncle rather than my brother, I won't mind. I'm not going back. I guess Leah and I disappearing can just be another unsolved mystery, and one that I would prefer not be investigated. Anyone who matters to us, knows where we are, so let's just let the genealogical inaccuracy about me stay in place. I'm proud of you, whether you're my father or my grandfather. Always have been and always will be. At least, for another 230 years, anyway."

Chapter 20: Food Finding Foray (AYE Ch 52)

Wee Ian walked proudly up the creek, leading the mare by her halter, the other two horses following behind her by instinct, not rein. Capturing them had been an easy task – well, sort of – and the rewards were great. Now he had a horse for his father to ride, and Leah and James could have one, too. Hmm, the mount that had belonged to that captain might still be back at the site where he had been attacked. He shook his head. No, he didn't want to return there, even if there was a horse to be had just for the taking. He didn't want to go back there for anything. He'd rather walk barefooted for the rest of his life! His father was all that was important, and now he was safe and healing back at the camp, being watched over by the fairies.

He knew James and Leah were fairies, and the man, Marty – well, he was probably one, too. Why were there so many fairies around all of a sudden? Hmm. At least they were helpful sorts and weren't trying to hurt anyone. It was just the opposite – his father was alive because of them and their fairy healing.

The outlaws' saddlebags didn't have much in them but was still more than he had. Well, no, not really, he argued with himself. He and his father were still breathing, and those degenerates were all dead. Each one only had a short ration of flour, oats, a bowl and a spoon, and there was but one pot between the three of them. He'd give that to James and Leah, and accept Marty's offer to stay and help cook for his father. It seemed that he wanted to stay, anyway.

Wee Ian could see their camp now. Marty was wiping his eyes and face, as if he'd been crying. He couldn't hear what was being said, but all three of them sounded cheerful. If the talkative old man was happy, then why was he crying? White men, hmph! They cried when they were happy and laughed when they were scared. He'd never understand them if he tried his whole life. But he wasn't going to try. Hopefully, he and his father would find a tribe that wouldn't mind having two more males. At least, they both were good hunters – or his father would be again after he healed.

"Hey, whatcha got there?" Leah called out when she saw Wee Ian and the three horses approaching. She glanced over at Marty and saw him swiping his face with James's red bandana, sniffling and snorting, doing his best to compose himself. She looked back at Wee Ian and saw that he had chosen not to stare at the emotional older man, but was busying himself, tying the horses to a tree.

Wee Ian pulled the single, overloaded saddlebag off the mare and stood up under it, shouldering the weight of the consolidated goods. "They dinna have much, so I put the better bits and pieces in here. There're some foodstuffs, bowls, and a pot. Ye and James can have the pot," he said, and nodded to Leah. He changed his attention to Marty. "Is yer offer to help make a broth fer my da still open?" he asked politely.

Marty sniffed one more time, then answered with more cheerfulness than the question deserved. "I'll help with anything you need, lad. I see you got the horses. If you want to go check on your da, I'll try to scare up a squirrel or some other tasty meat for his soup."

"Aye, I'd appreciate it," the boy replied with a courteous nod, then half-ran, half-skipped over to check on Ian the elder.

His father was still asleep and didn't appear feverish, but Leah had said he needed plenty of water. Using the little drops of water on the lips trick that Leah had taught him, Wee Ian managed to get him to take one long sip through the straw before he groaned and turned his face away.

Wee Ian sat back on his heels and surveyed the damages to his father's body. The neck wound hardly looked serious now that it had been cleaned and stitched. The breechclout was still stiff and stained with blood, but that was no problem. He'd take it off and clean it later, but after the others went to sleep.

It looked like his father was going to live now. Hmm. He had better not tell him that he wouldn't be able to make more babies, though. That would probably upset him, and he didn't want him to have another reason to be mad at anyone – even if they were already dead. At least all the pieces were there, and Leah said that the prick part would still work. He'd just tell him that he was fortunate not to lose his balls and would heal soon. Besides, his father didn't need any more children. What he needed – what they both needed – was a home, or at least a tribe, to call their own.

Wee Ian peered at the horizon. It wouldn't be too long before the sun would be low enough to catch fish for supper. He remembered that James wanted to go with him. He subconsciously nodded his head. Yes, he wanted to spend some time alone with the man – the fairy, he reminded himself. He had a few questions he needed answered.

***

James was in the same location, now seated, propped up against the tree, shoulders bent forward, intent, focused on his project. Wee Ian stared wordlessly at the diaphanous array on his lap.

James looked up, aware that he was being watched, and explained. "I was just putting the line back on the reel. It came off and made a mess. Here, would you pick out a couple of flies that you think these fish would like?" He smiled as he handed him the little tackle box. "I've never fished here in America. I don't know if they like the same flies as English fish."

Wee Ian took the little wooden box that held the flies stuck into a roll of yellow flannel sheeting. "These," he said, and pulled out two tiny twists of black and green. "They look like mayflies."

"Great. Here, I smoothed these down while you were out after the horses." James handed him two fairly straight poles that he had knocked the branches and rough bark from, offering him his choice of fishing rods. Wee Ian took one, looked hard at the end of the pole, then at the middle section. James had screwed in little brass eyelets to run the line through.

"It's called a fly rod," James explained. "Here, I'll show you." He struggled to stand up. "On second thought, I'll show you when we get there. If you don't mind, would you carry the poles? I think I had better use this walking stick. If I don't, my wife or father will beat me with it!"

Wee Ian gave a weak smile in return, then let it grow into a full grin. He shook his head. What a difference a few hours made. This morning, he and his father were near death – or worse – and now he was fishing with a fairy, using a fairy-made rod.

"I'd be glad to carry the rods. Ye can lean on me, too, if the walking stick isna enough."

The two of them took their time getting to the pool of still water they both agreed was their best bet for getting dinner.

"Here, like this," James said, and threw a perfect cast, flicking it back and forth a few times over the water to get the attention of the fish he was sure were waiting for their fly-by dinner. It had been a long time since he had been fly fishing and was glad he hadn't tangled the line. He was used to his lightweight carbon rod, perfectly balanced, and with a

222

foam grip. This was a crooked, roughly-finished sapling, but the fish it caught would taste just as good. "Do you want to try with this or use the other one?"

Wee Ian pursed his lips and looked back and forth, evaluating the rods, then picked up the one that hadn't been used. He put it in his right hand, found the balance point, looked over the loops with the line running through them, and fingered the roll of extra line stuck into the notch at the end of the pole. "Is this fairy string?" he asked, as he ran his finger along the top of the thin nylon line.

"Um, yes, it is. It's thin but very strong, and hard for the fish to see. Here, let me step back and you try."

Wee Ian took the little loop of extra line out of the notch, unwound it, and held it in his left hand. He grasped the rod with his right, inching his fingers up the pole until he found the balance point again. He stood back, surveyed the area around him for low lying branches and fairies, flicked the rod a few times, and let the line play out just above the surface of the pool. He snapped it again and again, as the fish leaped out of the water, trying for the little fly tied on the end of the invisible line. Finally, one trout found the lure. Wee Ian set the line quickly, and pulled it in, grasping the line, bringing in his dinner, hand over hand.

James saw the familiarity the boy had with fly fishing. Evidently, this sport had been around for a quite a while. No, not sport – method of procuring sustenance, he reminded himself. He watched as the trout was landed with ease. Hopefully, he would be as adroit when he caught a fish.

Wee Ian looked up at him, gave him a nod of thanks, then scanned the upriver edge of the pool. He indicated with a shift of his eyes and a nod that he would head up there so James could stay where he was and fish. The new arrangement would eliminate the chance of combat fishing – lines and elbows crossing – and give them both enough casting and flicking room. The courteous and agile Wee Ian – truly a gentleman, despite his youth – had offered to take the high side.

James held back the urge to shout with victory when he caught his first fish. He didn't want to seem like a greenhorn who had never caught one before, but he *was* in a way. He had never caught an 18th century fish with 21st century line. Shoot, he hadn't caught any fish in over ten years. Yup, this was the first of many fish to be caught, he assured himself. God willing, he prayed silently.

He caught two more fish in short order. He looked up and saw Wee Ian walking toward him with a stick strung through the gills of four fish. Seven fish and four people eating solid food. It looked like a hearty meal for dinner tonight.

Wee Ian sat down next to him. "Do ye have a knife with ye? I'll do the cleanin' if ye do."

James handed him the Leatherman tool he had used to remove his bindings earlier in the day. He grunted softly as he realized how much had changed in such a short time.

"I said, is this a fairy knife?" Wee Ian asked, apparently not for the first time.

"No, actually it's American. But I guess you could also consider it a fairy knife if that makes it easier for you. Sorry, I'm a little fuddle-headed. One of these days, I'll explain it all to you if you and I meet again… Shoot, where *do* you live?"

Wee Ian shrugged one shoulder. "Right now, here," he said plainly. He was glad that James was fuddle-headed, though. Maybe he could get an unguarded answer out of him. "Leah's your wife and a healer, right?"

"Yes," James answered warily. The boy already knew it to be true.

Wee Ian, watching him carefully for his reaction, asked, "So how come she said my father was her stepfather? Does that mean that Evie is her mother?"

"Oh, shit," James exhaled in frustration.

"Why is everything 'oh, shit'?" Wee Ian asked. "Is she or isn't she?"

"She is," James said with exasperation. Sometimes he wished he could lie, but now was not a good time to start practicing.

"So, my da is not her stepfather, but my two little brothers and sister are *her* brothers and sister, too," he stated, but almost asked as a question.

"So, the triplets are two boys and a girl? Cool. Leah always wanted a little sister. Oh, yes, the answer is yes, but I wish you wouldn't tell anyone about it. I mean, just because something is the truth doesn't mean you have to share it with everyone."

"Aye. Evie said almost the same thing. She asked that I refer to her babies as my kin, not my sib…siblings," Wee Ian said dejectedly then brightened up. "But, can we be kin, too – or almost kin?"

"Absolutely! Come on, *cousin*, I'll show you how to open this knife, and then I'll let you clean the fish."

Tom Sawyer would be so proud of him, he thought as he pulled out the knife blade for his newly discovered brother-in-law. So proud.

Chapter 21 A New Name (AYE Ch 61)

Several days later
Pomeroys' Place

Wee Ian finished brushing, feeding, and watering the nag that had carried his father to Uncle Jody's. It had been a long trip for all of them. There was no doubt in his mind that his father would have headed to Uncle Jody's house, with or without his help. At first, he had hidden the horse from him and said she had strayed, that he couldn't find her. He knew his father didn't believe him, but he didn't argue. Instead, he reached into the framework of the shelter above him and tugged and pushed at a sturdy piece of branch, working it free to use as a crutch. He ran his hand down its length, checking it for cracks or breaks, tore off the small branches protruding from it, then speared the ground, clutching at the middle of the staff, working his way up, hand over hand, struggling against gravity and his body's weakness to get up to a standing position.

"Wait! I think I ken where to find her," the son squeaked in desperation. "And I'll help ye get on her, too." He glowered, then huffed in resignation, "At least it'll be easier on ye than walking."

Before he went for the horse, though, he tried one more time to convince his father to stay, "Why canna ye jest wait fer two or three more days until yer healed?"

Ian didn't answer his question with words but glared in response at the suggestion. He didn't want to talk. He needed to save his breath and his strength for the trip to his uncle's house. No one else in the world – at least, in the American colonies – had cashews. It had to be Evie – or her fairy twin – who had come to help him. Could there really be two of them? Could this woman who Wee Ian had said tended to his wounds be the mysterious Danny? He had to know and was willing to die trying to find out.

Getting his father on the horse was the easy part. Keeping him on her was the real challenge. He was still weak from his injuries and had trouble staying mounted. The wounds to his manly parts were painful to sit on, so he assumed an awkward, tilted position. Wee Ian didn't have the luxury of simply walking beside his father and the horse for the trip – he had to run from one side of the pair to the other, shoving his father

226

back into an upright position – or catching him before he hit the ground as he slid from the old mare's bare back.

Wee Ian stumbled out of the barn and stretched his spine like an old man, one arm in the air, the other on his tender lower back. He looked up and saw his father asleep at the base of the big tree in front of the house and shook his head. His father's stubbornness had got him here alive, but there was no telling how much life was left in him. He walked over to him, dropped his rucksack, and plopped down on the ground next to the pale and winded shell of a man. Wee Ian was tired but afraid to fall asleep. His father might not be alive when he woke up. The lad bit his bottom lip and tried not to think about what his future would be if his father died.

***

I looked out and saw the Kincaid men under the tree. I told Leah to stay put. I'd take over the nursing duties and see how Ian was doing. I wanted her and James to conserve their strength.

I didn't know if my recent high energy level was because my body had finally healed or because I was so happy that I had so many family members around. But either way, I felt like a superhero. I was ready to tend to the infirm, counsel the sad, feed the hungry, and change the poopy. I could take care of everyone and everything today.

We still had at least forty-five minutes to wait until dinner was ready – a watched pot never boils and all that nonsense. While the kettle was getting up to temperature, Jenny helped me get the babies to sleep. It was one of those glorious times when all of them were down at the same time. "Are you *sure* there's nothing else you want me to do?" she begged.

"No, no, I'm fine. Why don't you go outside and play?"

"All right," she said dejectedly. She looked around and saw that there were now two people under the tree. She walked up confidently to the small one.

"Who are you?" she asked brightly of the young boy with the sad and dirty face. "I've never seen you before."

"Weel, I've never seen ye either, so we're even," he said tartly. He was concerned about what he would do if his father died and didn't feel too friendly, especially to a girl.

I overheard the two of them as I walked up to check on my ex-

227

husband, Ian. "I think your da is going to be fine," I told Wee Ian as I brushed the dark brown hair out of his eyes. He looked so much like his father. "I gave him some very good medicine, and I'll bet you won't even know that he'd been hurt after he wakes up. But he needs to sleep now. Why don't you and Jenny go over to the water trough and wash up? And make sure you don't get any soap in it. Use the little bucket for the soapy water, all right?"

"Yes, ma'am," he replied, and reluctantly scooted away from his father's side.

"Yes, Mommy," Jenny sang as she bounced around the tree, waiting for the young boy to get up so she could go with him.

Jenny skipped to the barn and Wee Ian trudged along behind her. He was sad and scared. Evie told him that his father would be fine, but even though she thought she was right, and he wanted to believe her, he couldn't.

Ever since he had met his father several moons ago, he looked as if he was dying a wee bit at a time. One more accident or fight, and he would be dead. And if his father died, then where would *he* go? His mother's husband made it clear that he didn't want him around their house, or even their village. His grandmother was dead, which was why he was now with Star Walker. Ian Kincaid was his name when they were with the white man, he reminded himself. He liked being here with Evie, Wallace, and the bairns, but all of a sudden, there seemed to be too many people around. And now there was this obnoxious wee lass, dancing around him, blabbering all the time. Yes, if his father died, he'd like to live with his little brothers and sister, Evie, and Wallace, but he hoped the little yellow-haired girl had someplace else to go. She was already annoying him, and he hadn't even been here an hour.

"So, what's your name?" she asked. "I don't know who you are except that sick man under the tree is your father, huh? My mother said he's gonna get better, so he will. She doesn't lie to me or anyone else. Do you know her?"

"Do ye ever shut up?" he asked, then dunked his head into the horse trough.

She waited until his head was out of the water. "I just shut up, but you didn't hear it because your head was underwater. Why won't you tell me your name and why do you talk funny? You sound like my Grandpa.

That's my Grandpa Jody, not my Grandpa Julian. They both talk English, but they don't sound the same. My Mommy speaks English, too, but it sounds even different from them, and she's gonna teach me to read and write. Can you read and write?" Jenny paused for a breath. She looked at him, waiting for him to answer at least one of her questions.

Wee Ian turned and looked toward his father again. All of a sudden, his stomach hurt. The thought of being alone was like a dirk in his waim. He clutched his gut and walked into the barn, head down, the emotions of fear and depression battling for dominance within him.

Once his eyes adjusted, he took in his surroundings. The floor was swept, there was fresh straw laid out in the stalls and – he inhaled deeply – it smelled of leather and hay. It was also cooler in here than outside. A simple, yet glorious refuge.

"Aah," he sighed, reveling in the first sense of peace he had had in ages. The straw looked so inviting. Evie had told him he would have to let his father sleep. Well, if Da had to sleep, he'd take a nap, too. He found a shady spot, kicked the straw to make sure there weren't any varmints in it, and then lay down. He would only sleep for a wee bit. Just a few minutes for a rest, then he'd go check on his father. Evie was a good woman and Leah a good healer, but Da was his responsibility.

Jenny watched the boy go into the barn. She wanted to talk to him, but he didn't look like he felt too good. She washed her face and hands, making sure she didn't get soap in the water. Her father had said it gave the horses a bellyache if they drank soapy water, so she was extra careful. She didn't want to hurt a horse but really didn't want to make Daddy mad. She had seen him mad the day her other brothers had died, and that was real scary. She knew he would never get that mad at her, but she could also tell that he didn't like getting mad. He had cried and cried after he got angry and beat up that other man. But that might have been because her brother had just been killed. He was sad about that just like she was, even though the two of them didn't used to like each other.

Jenny sighed. Thinking about her brothers dying made her sad again. She tried not to think about them because she couldn't do anything about it. Mommy had said that when God took someone away from the earth, it was because He needed them up in heaven. And when God took her brothers, He made sure that He gave her a Mommy and Daddy, two more brothers, and a little sister, too. Jenny walked over to the barn, still sad, and looked inside. The little boy was asleep in the corner. He had been sad, too. He looked real lonely. She'd go over and hold him like her Daddy held her when she felt that way – that should make both of them feel better.

Jenny took one step onto the straw pile and Wee Ian popped up into a crouch, his dirk pulled, ready to defend himself.

"I'm sorry, I'm sorry," Jenny squealed, "I didn't mean to scare you. I just wanted to make you feel better." She wanted to say more but remembered the boy had said she talked too much. Instead, she bit her bottom lip and stared at him, waiting to see what would happen next.

"Ye dinna scare me," he said defensively. He looked hard at her, then realized that she was the one who was frightened. At least, she wasn't blabbering. "Are ye all right, lass?" he asked. He did need to use good manners, even if she was just a girl.

Jenny really was afraid. No one had drawn a knife on her since those bad men at the mill had threatened to cut off her clothes. Knives didn't scare her. She liked cutting with them. Men with knives scared her, though.

The young girl stood in front of him, arms slack at her side, paralyzed, staring at his dirk. Since she hadn't said a word, she must be terrified. "I wouldna hurt ye with it," he said. "Honest."

Jenny kept staring, bug-eyed and silent. "Here, ye can touch it if ye want." He held out the knife to her, hasp first, but that didn't work. She wouldn't budge. Yes, she was a pest, but he still didn't want to get in trouble with Evie for frightening her.

Evie – she had called Evie her mommy. That must be fairy speak for mama. "Is Evie yer mother?" he asked, trying to engage her in conversation.

Jenny smiled and nodded. She realized that if she didn't talk, then he would. It was hard not to talk, though. Hmm. She could pretend her lips were sewn shut. She clamped her jaws then squeezed her lips together – forcibly keeping them tight so she didn't start talking – and nodded again.

"Oh," Wee Ian replied. "Does that mean the bairns are yer brothers and sister?" He knew they must be, but he was hoping she'd start talking again. He wanted to check on his father but didn't want to leave the girl silent and alone in the barn. If she stopped talking altogether, someone was sure to notice, and then he might get blamed. He didn't mind getting in trouble for deeds he had done, but he hadn't done anything to her, not really – just pulled his dirk on her when she had startled him from his nap.

Jenny wanted to tell him all about her little brothers and sister, Wren, but pressed her lips together tighter, settling for a rapid head nodding. She liked him and hoped he stayed around. Maybe she could have a friend her own age!

She seemed to like it when he talked about her brothers and sister. He wished he could tell her that they were his family, too – even that they were his blood family – but he had told Evie he wouldn't, that he would only refer to them as his kin. "Did ye ken that I gave Wren her name? She's my kin, too?" he said proudly, still hoping she would speak. Was it just a few minutes ago that he couldn't get her to shut up?

"You gave Wren her name? And if you're her kin, then you're my kin, too!" She couldn't contain herself or her mouth. She jumped up and grabbed him in a big bear hug.

"Watch the dirk!" he yelped and dropped it. He pulled out of the unwelcome embrace and held her an arm's length, checking to make sure he hadn't stabbed her. "Are ye all right? Did I cut ye?"

Jenny dropped her elbows to her side, clutching one hand with the other, holding tight to the excitement of having more family, finally someone her own age. She opened her mouth to tell him all about her other sister, but suddenly recalled how he had treated her when she had talked too much. She looked at him coyly, dipped her head down, and went back into mute mode.

"Yer bleedin'!" he exclaimed and grabbed her arm. His knife had cut her just above the elbow. "Quick, I need a cloth to stop the bleedin'. Oh, I'm so sorry. I dinna mean to hurt ye." Wee Ian found a rag hanging on a peg in the wall, shook it out, and held it on the bloody spot, applying direct pressure like Leah had told him to do for his father.

"Now will you tell me your name?" she asked, not paying any attention to her wound. It didn't hurt, and if she didn't look at it, it wouldn't bother her.

"The white man call me Wee Ian," he said, giving her the standard monotone reply he always used when asked his name. He inhaled quickly and returned to his normal voice, "Ian Kincaid is my father's name, too. He's the one who's ailin' under the tree." All of a sudden, she wasn't such a pest.

"Wee Ian? Like Wee'un, Pee'in'?" she asked. He nodded a short affirmative, but she couldn't stop herself from adding, "That's *awful*!"

He glared at her. Maybe she was a pest. A big-mouthed pest.

Jenny realized that she had made a mistake. "I mean, I can think of a better name for you, I'm sure I can." She paused, and added, "Did you really give Wren her name?"

He nodded again. He didn't feel like talking anymore.

"I *like* that name!" She felt his hand on her arm, still holding the rag to her wound. "Is it bad? I don't want to look. Blood makes me sick. Well, it does if it's mine or somebody's I care about," she added softly.

Wee Ian pulled the rag away and saw that it was just a small scratch that had bled profusely. The bleeding had already stopped. If she didn't bump it, it would be fine. "Ye'll be all right. It's naught but a scratch, but ye scarrit me. Can we go outside now? I want to go check on my da."

"Doc or Scout?" she said, then crossed her arms across her chest in a gesture of confidence.

"What?"

"Your name. Are you a Doc or a Scout? You just doctored my arm, so that's why I said Doc, but you seem like a Scout to me. I'll bet you always like to lead the way, making sure it's safe for everyone else to go ahead, right?"

"Scout. I like that. All right, ye can call me Scout," he said, smiling at getting a name that seemed to fit better than the hand-me-down name his father had also used when he was a child.

"And you can call me Jenny," she said, with a full-dimpled smile. "Come on, let's go check on your da, and I'll *try* not to talk too much. That is if you'll *try* not to stab me again," she added with a wink.

The two walked side-by-side out into the sunshine, then Jenny smacked him on the arm and said, "Tag, you're it," and ran to the big family tree. She had someone to play with, at least for a few more hours.

Chapter 22: You Were Wrong (AYE Ch 62)

Ian was awake and obviously feeling better. At least, he could sit up by himself now. He was my husband's cousin and the sire of my three babies, but also the orneriest, least-forgiving man I'd ever met. He gave me up – dropped me at Jody and Sarah's doorstep when I was pregnant – so he could go on a vengeance quest.

I turned out fine – finer than fine since I wound up marrying his cousin, Wallace – but *he* was still a wreck. I looked around. I finally had a chance to talk to him without a large audience. Wee Ian, the ever-vigilant caretaker, was at his side, and it was actually better for me that he was. He needed to hear this, too. I was ready to let his father have it with both barrels.

"You lost a wife and three children because of your hate and need for revenge. Wallace let the Lord take care of vengeance, and you know what? He gained a wife, three, now four…five children and a son-in-law. What do you have to show for doing it your way? You were inches from death, and if it weren't for the goodness of…of…the lass, Leah, and her husband, you and your son would both be dead."

I bit my tongue just before claiming Leah as my daughter. I had inferred it but didn't feel like going into that discussion!

Ian's head stayed low. I wasn't sure if it was shame or if he was trying to find words to refute my explanation. Either way, he wasn't ready to talk.

"And where is Rocky?" I asked. I wasn't ready to stop the conversation, and I really was curious about the huge masked-faced dog that was as much Ian's canine brother as a traveling companion. "He wasn't with you when you came last time, either – when the tax man was here."

"He's deid," Ian said flatly, humbled – or was that humiliated? – head still bowed.

Wee Ian added to the somber statement. "I dinna believe in the vengeance, but what they did to that dog was…was…" Wee Ian's eyes teared with the memory. I put my hand on his shoulder to let him know that he didn't have to recall or relate the story to me – I still understood.

"Okay, then you lost three children, a wife, and your best friend in the whole world. Do you think maybe you've learned something from

233

it?"

"Aye, if I'm gonna be vengeful, I'd best be quick about it."

I couldn't help myself. I slapped him hard on the back of the head. "I hope you get a big headache from that, too. And you're lucky I didn't have a pot or a crappy clout in my hand when I did it. Ergh!" I stomped off in a huff before I lost control and started kicking him.

Wallace came over and sat down next to Ian. He handed him a cold stone bottle of ale. "That's not to drink," he said. "It's to put on the lump that's sure to start rising."

Ian accepted the drink with a nod, then brought it up to the tender spot, wincing as the cool hardness hit the already sore area.

Wallace settled back against the tree. "You know, Evie is a pretty even-tempered person most of the time, but you sure know how to rile her. What did you do this time?"

"Ach, she was doin' her preachin' about vengeance and God, and how ye got her and all the bairns and a few more in yer family because ye let Him," he tipped his head up to the sky, then realized how much his head was hurting. He started again, "Ye let Him take care of the vengeance. If that's true, then why did she hit me so hard?" Ian brought the bottle down, examined it casually, and then decided the cool ale would be better inside of him. He opened the bottle, took a long swig, and sighed in satisfaction.

"Well, maybe she figured God needed an extra hand right now, and she'd help Him out. I mean, you don't seem too keen on listening to reason." Wallace looked over at Ian to make sure he was listening. Ian glanced up and gave him a blank stare – he heard the words but didn't feel like they pertained to him or this situation.

Wallace could see that he wasn't getting through to his cousin. He drew himself up and said plainly, "She's right and you're wrong. It's as simple as that. I'm with her. I'd like to see you have a happy life, but from what I've seen of you lately, I'd say you actually enjoy being miserable."

Wee Ian came up and smacked his father on the back of the head, almost in the same spot Evie had. "See, he said the same thing I did – ye like bein' miserable. Dinna ye ken yer supposed to be settin' a good example fer yer son? Do ye want me to wind up like ye: alone, hatin' and killin', always fightin' with someone about them doin' or sayin' somethin' agin ye or yer kin? I may be yer…yer son by blood, but I'd rather wind up like Cousin Wallace and Evie – with a house and a family and a dog that nobody wants to kill jest to spite me, aye?"

Ian looked over and glared at his son. "Yer not supposed to hit yer da," he said, totally ignoring what the boy had just said.

"Yeah, weel, if that's the meanest I ever get, I'll be glad," he said, and stomped off to the barn, not caring if he was stirring up dust or not.

Chapter 23: The Promise (AYE Ch 64)

"Can I see your knife?" Jenny asked.

"What?" Wee Ian replied, his voice squeaking in shock. "That's a private matter and none of yer business."

"Well, I got a knife. Do you want to see mine?"

"You canna have a knife. A girl has the other kind. Only men and boys have knives," he said.

"Oh, yeah? Then what's this?" Jenny reached into her pocket and pulled out the penknife Grandpa Jody had gifted her.

"Oh, *that* kind of knife – you mean a dirk." He had been thinking of the 'other' kind of knife. "Oh, sure, here." He unsheathed the blade he had recovered from his father's assailant's belongings and handed it to her, hilt first.

She turned the knife over in her hand, found its balance point, held it up to the sky to see if it was crooked or if the edge had nicks in it, then gave it back to him. "What kind of knife were you talking about?" she asked, her head down, concentrating on the geometric designs she was creating in the dirt with her big toe.

"Weel, like I said, it's kind of private, ye ken, the other knife." He slipped off his moccasins and decided to play in the fine, silt-y dirt, too.

"Huh?" Jenny looked up at him, nose wrinkled and mouth opened. She didn't have a clue as to what he was talking about.

He knew by her unblinking stare that she would pester him until he told her. It was better to tell her and get it over with. "Weel, the Indians refer to a man's…ye ken," he mumbled, and looked down at the front of his breechclout, "as his knife. That's why I said ye canna have a knife."

"You mean your stuff?" she asked.

"Stuff?" he echoed. He had never heard it called that.

"Yeah, stuff." She dusted off her hands and said, "Hey, if you show me your stuff, I'll show you mine. I got two hairs on my stuff now. Do you have any hair on yours? I know when you get to be a real man, you get hair down there. But you're not a real man, so you probably don't have any hair, huh?"

"Weel, I got a little," he admitted shyly.

"Can I see?"

He could tell that she was just curious but his answer was still,

"No."

"I think you're lying," she teased.

"No, I'm not," he replied adamantly, and crossed his arms. He walked away from their dirt drawing canvas and sat down next to the big chokecherry bush.

"Then what are you afraid of?" she said, then added gently, "I won't laugh."

"Why would ye laugh?"

"I don't know." She shrugged and came over to sit down next to him – a little too close, he felt – then almost whispered, "Why won't you show me?"

"Because it's private," he said with conviction, although he didn't really know why he couldn't show her.

"Why?"

"Because it is," he declared with a tone of finality.

"Why?" Jenny didn't believe the subject was closed. Everybody had one, so why was it so personal? He should know that without her saying so.

"Because yer only supposed to show it to yer mate – ye ken, the one yer marrit to," he said with exasperation. *There, that ought to shut her up!*

"Okay, let's get married then," she said, grinning from ear to ear.

"No," he huffed, then looked around to see where he could hide. She was too close, though, and would see him wherever he went.

He looked over and saw that his father seemed to be resting peacefully. At least, Evie was smiling at him now, even if he was asleep. He tried to recall if he had ever seen her smile at him before. If she had, she hadn't done it for very long. She looked happy, and that was a good sign.

"I said…why can't we get married, or marrit, or however you say it? It means the same thing, right?"

He nodded and said, "Because." Evidently, she had asked him at least once before. He hadn't heard her the first time, but that didn't seem to slow her down.

"Because why? Don't you like me?" she asked sadly.

He realized that he felt sorry for her. She must be an orphan because she wasn't with Wallace and Evie a few weeks ago. It wouldn't hurt him to show her a little sympathy. "Weel, yes, I like ye – sort of – but ye talk too much."

"If we get married, I promise I won't talk too much," she said, her eyes searching his to see if her pledge had made a difference.

He peered, unblinking, into her face to make sure she knew what she was saying. "Promise?" he asked, then noticed how long and soft brown her eyelashes were, perfect for setting off the sky blue of her bright, shiny eyes. She had a few freckles on her nose, too – little spots of happiness, he thought.

"I promise. You'll have to show me your stuff then because we'll be married, huh," she said, nodding her head, making sure he understood his part of the obligation.

"So, if we're marrit, I'll show ye my stuff, but then ye willna talk too much, aye?"

"Uh-huh," she said quickly, trying to make her answer as short as possible for him.

He was beginning to like this. She was already talking less. Maybe she *would* make a good wife. "All right. Just say that ye want me fer yer husband, then that's all there is to it." *At least, that's how he thought they did it back at his village. He wasn't sure how the white man did it and had never really talked to his father or mother about it. But this was good enough for a girl.*

Jenny remained still – just looked at him – not saying a word. Was it working already? "But ye have to say ye want me fer yer husband first, and THEN stop talking so much."

Jenny nodded.

Scout leaned into her face and glared at her. He was beginning to get exasperated with her and wasn't going to remind her again that she had to ask him to be her husband. She didn't need to be his wife if she would stay quiet without it.

"Will you be my husband?" she asked slowly, timidly.

She must know what a promise is. She sounded as if she was thinking about each word before saying it, not jabbering like a jay. Maybe she really will be a good woman, especially if Evie is her new mother. And she sure is pretty. "Aye, I mean, yes," he said, then leaned forward and gave her a quick kiss on the cheek.

Jenny didn't say a word, but shook her head 'no,' and pointed to her lips. She wanted her kiss on the mouth.

Scout, the boy formerly known as Wee Ian, sighed then leaned forward and gave Jenny Pomeroy-Hart, his child-bride, a kiss on the mouth. Before he could pull away, though, she grabbed him and pressed her mouth to his, twisting and turning her head, keeping a hard pressure on his lips with hers.

"Ow! Yer teeth hurt me. Yer supposed to do it soft, like this," then showed her how gently he could touch her mouth with his. He pulled away and grinned. He just might like being marrit.

Jenny started rearranging her skirts. She pulled the green calico up and held the bundle to her chest with her chin. "See," she said, pointing to her newly discovered pubic hairs.

"Oh," is all Scout could think to say.

She dropped her skirts. Neither of them spoke. She finally looked up at him, then stared down at his crotch. He followed her gaze, shrugged his shoulders, and shifted aside his breechclout. "See," he said, and pointed to his sparse dark hairs, suddenly feeling braver. "I got more than ye do, but that's okay; ye'll get more. And yer breasts will get bigger so ye can feed bairns when I plant my seed in ye. But I think we ought to wait for that until I can build us a home of our own. Do ye think it will be all right if ye stay with yer mother and father a while longer?"

Jenny nodded. She wanted to be married to Scout but didn't want to leave her new parents yet. She had been with them less than a lunar month. She knew her mother still needed her, even though she now had another daughter to help with the cooking and cleaning and babies.

"You can stay with us, too, if you'd like," she said, hoping she hadn't spoken too many words. Then she leaned in and kissed her husband again like he had showed her. She liked having a husband to kiss.

Chapter 24: Another Mystery (AYE Ch 65)

Leah stroked James's forehead with the pink terrycloth washcloth her mother had given her – a keepsake from Mom's trip to the 21st century and Leah's former place of employment, Moses H. Cone Memorial Hospital.

They were both exhausted – it had been a long day for everyone – but it was still too hot to sleep. They lay on a quilt on the floor, taking turns swiping the moist cloth across each other's face and neck. The evaporative effect was temporary, but welcome just the same. She dipped the cloth in the clay bowl, swished it around to suck up more of the cool well water, squeezed it out, and began lightly brushing it across his chest, zig-zagging down slowly to his belly button.

"Now, how is it that your Uncle Julian is related to you?" she asked, resisting the urge to flick his firm, dark nipple.

James grabbed her hand before she followed through with her impish prank. "My turn," he said. "Hand me the cloth."

Leah stood up but held the rag tight. "Shoot, it's too hot even for this." She pulled the Mickey and Minnie Mouse nightshirt off over her head and tossed it on her pile of skirts and shoes. "I know, I know," she replied to James's unspoken admonition, "life starts early in the country. I'll wake up earlier still and throw it on again before Jody or Wallace or Julian come in. If the chickens wake them up, I'm sure they'll wake me up, too."

"It's the roosters, not the hens, who are the alarm clocks. Here, give me that cloth before it gets too warm in your hand."

Leah twirled the pink remnant from her mother's former robe in the air like a lariat, then tossed it at his head. He reflexively put his hand in front of his face and grabbed it before it made contact. "Not quite a pillow fight," he said, then dabbed it on the back of his neck, "but definitely cooler. Lie down before I change my mind and go to sleep."

Leah gracefully transitioned from standing to reclining on her back. "Lots of yoga," she said. She put her hands behind her head, presenting her entire nude torso to him. "And no fair tickling, either. I want to relax enough to sleep."

James used the corner of the washcloth like a stylus, dragging it across her collarbones then down between her breasts. "More cloth," she mumbled, eyes shut in concentration. He opened it out and, using both hands, draped it down her chest, switching it back and forth sideways to cool the underside of her still perky breasts.

She opened one eye. "I'm glad I don't have big, saggy boobs. I'd get a rash there for sure…"

James distracted her with a kiss to her tummy. He couldn't help it. She had absolutely beautiful breasts, but her belly mound seemed to be calling for his attention. "How long do you think it will be before we have children?" he asked, trying not to sound too anxious.

"I don't know. I might be pregnant already and we just don't know it yet. I mean, we were sure going at it enough…"

James continued his gentle kisses, the cloth laying unemployed between her breasts. "Hey, hey, hey," Leah said. "It's too hot for that. And like I said, I might already be pregnant."

James sat upright, a scowl on his face. "If you think the only reason I want to make love to my wife is to get her with child, you are sincerely mistaken."

"Good Lord, I hope not. And the operative words in that statement are 'make love,' not have sex or carnal knowledge, or…or…" Leah looked over and saw that James was giggling like a child. "Yeah, you got me," she said, realizing that he had been joking.

"I certainly do," he said and planted a quick kiss on her belly. "And as for Uncle Julian, his brother, my great-grandfather Anthony, was the start of my line. Or at least, the continuation of the line from the early 1700s. Uncle Julian's line stopped with his stepson, Lord Urquhart, Viscount Cavendish – that would be Wallace. It was assumed he died in the war since he simply disappeared while in His Majesty's service."

Leah reached up and stroked the sparse, dark hairs on his chest. "Bibb told me before she left that her genealogy chart, as far back as she had been able to trace it, was in the safe that the MacLeods broke into. They didn't find any money or deeds in it, so tossed everything in a trash can and set it on fire, laughing as she pleaded with them not to, that there were important, precious papers and family photos in there. She didn't have the family tree memorized but said there was something about a Scout and Genevieve in the late 1700s. She also said she was pretty sure their last name was Pomeroy-Hart…"

James sighed deeply then lay back beside her. "I don't know the connection, and I forgot about asking Marty about it before he…he…left." He gulped back his feeling of abandonment, then continued. "There is a small fortune in a safe deposit box in London. Only the first-born males in the family line know about it. Hmm, I don't know if Bruce knew about it, but since he was Marty's first born from his marriage to Teighlor, he probably did. It's in Billy's care now. Anyhow, I was made aware of it at a relatively early age, probably to encourage my curiosity with the Hart part of the name. You did know that Marty manipulated me on purpose, right? Made me curious about Julian Hart and his line?"

Leah nodded, lips pressed tight, so she didn't tell him to knock it off and get over it. He continued. "I wound up getting married, briefly, but not briefly enough. When that skank of the female persuasion cleaned out all she could and then tried for the rest of the family assets through the courts, I never became desperate. Shoot, even if I had been left with nothing but my skivvies, it would have been better than having *her* in my life. But I digress. I always knew that no matter how much money was gone, I still had the Pomeroy-Hart fortune."

Leah's eyebrows raised, but she remained mute. *The Pomeroy-Harts have money?*

"I know," James said and matched her eyebrow movement. "They sure don't look like they have much now. I can't be sure they're the same Pomeroy-Hart line, and that I am a long distant relative of your mother and therefore of you. No, we're not kissing cousins," he said and gave her a quick 'cousinly' kiss. "I don't know when the funds were first deposited. I didn't ask nor did I have a reason to. I don't see any Genevieves or Scouts around, either." He sighed. "I guess if it *is* this family that becomes rich, it will be a generation or more down the line. In the meantime, we'll all work hard, hopefully eat well – and keep out of musket ball range – and live long, eventually prosperous lives."

Extended Excerpts from

The Great Big Fairy
The Fairies Saga Book Six

Before you start The Great Big Fairy, a brief introduction…

18th century-born Benji Pomeroy is stuck in the 21st century. The 6'7" big-hearted man discovers a way to go 'home' but has to wait a year before he can travel back in time to be with his beloved grandfather, Jody, and grandmother, Sarah, another time traveling 'fairy.'

Benji finally makes it back to 1783 and winds up the owner of a very tall, very stubborn black female slave. Life has never been easy for Benji, but his bright attitude and physical strength change the lives of many he encounters.

Chapter 25: What's a woman to do? (TGBF Ch 8)

Late spring, 1782

The months went by quickly for the lady in waiting. Sarah never puked once, although she admitted she got queasy when she smelled bacon or sausage cooking. "Okay, we're having grits and eggs in deference to the babies," I announced then laughed. I added, "I wouldn't doubt that those kids—I mean children—you're carrying will want a pet pig instead of a dog. The smell of cooked pork seems to upset them."

I designed and constructed a day coat, sort of a dress, for Sarah. "See," I bragged as I pointed out the extra seams. "This will grow as you grow. Just a few snip, snips, and the gown will be one size larger. I've allowed for four increases. I hope it won't be too bulky in the side seams for now, but I guarantee it's going to make you feel better later. Shoot, you probably won't even have to cut the seams—they'll probably pop apart by themselves. I only used basting stitches.

***

Sarah was now well into her eighth month. She asked me several times a week, sometimes even a couple of times a day, to listen for the babies' heartbeats. Of course, I always obliged her. I knew all was well with the physical aspects of her pregnancy, but her mental health was just as important. Her confidence level was definitely under the influence of hormones. "Would you check again," Sarah would ask, always using the same words and same gestures, a nod to the rolled-up parchment, then a weak, insecure smile.

"Okay," I replied again this morning. I spent the next five minutes playing submarine hunter, using the improvised stethoscope as a sonar detector. "I can hear two rapid heartbeats, clear as a bell. They're both strong, but about half a beat off of each other in rhythm. That one little guy sure moves around a lot. You ought to name him Neptune. He's sure at home in the water. And no, one of the beats isn't yours. I checked your pulse, and it isn't nearly as fast as theirs."

"Well, it least that part's normal," she said with *reliefignation*, her own custom mixed emotion of relief and resignation.

"Duh! Everything is normal *and* healthy with this pregnancy. Now, your body was 'rewound' enough to get pregnant," I began again with the same speech I gave every time…

"And stay pregnant," Sarah added with a voice of confidence, her lines spoken like a pro.

"And stay pregnant," I continued my part of the speech, "so I'm sure the delivery will be a snap. Come on," I said, taking a break from my 'it's all going to be fine' routine, "do you feel good enough to take a walk? It's a beautiful day out."

"Sure," she replied as she put her hands on the arms of the new rocking chair Jody had crafted for her. She leaned forward and I remained at her elbow, ready to help her stand. "Uh, I feel a draft," she said as she stood up all the way. "Oh crap, I think my water broke."

"No, it's too early," I argued, "I mean, it's only March, right?"

"It's April first," replied Sarah dismally.

"Right," I said, "April Fool's Day, hardy har har…"

"No, really," she explained, "I have the lower back ache and…"

I moved behind her to look at the back of her skirt. "Oh shit, I mean, oh amniotic fluid," I said, and then started to giggle.

"I can't have the babies yet—it's too soon!" Sarah whined, as if she begged me for it not to be so, then it wouldn't be.

"Let's see, you got pregnant about August 20th. Subtract three months and add five days so…May 25th due date and crap, Sarah: today is the last day of April, not the last day of March. You're only about three and a half weeks early. That's not too bad for twins. But, you stay put, just the same, and I'll get you some clouts. I remember how irritating, I mean frustrating, it was to have that mess dribbling down between your legs…"

"Is Grannie gonna have her babies today?" Jenny asked as she popped in the door, "'cause if she is, I want to help. I never saw people babies comin' out, just dogs and goats and baby chicks."

"Chickens are hatched, not born," I corrected.

"Well, they sure come out makin' a lot of noise, more than baby dogs…"

"Puppies," I interrupted in order to correct her.

"Uh, huh, that's right. I forgots. Hey, can Grannie have the babies without Grandpa? Isn't he supposed to be here? I mean, I'm sure he'd want to be here…"

"Well, he was here for the most important part," Sarah said, softly enough for me to hear, but hopefully not by my little Miss Perception.

"Did he share his present with you?" Jenny asked. "Is that why you're gonna have the babies?"

The look of innocent awe and wonder on her face was priceless. Sarah took a deep breath, hoping to say something profound, or at least convincingly evasive. She looked into Jenny's inquisitive eyes and was deflated by her pure and undemanding curiosity. "Yes," she said simply. "Now, would you get me a drink of water?" she asked. "I'm real thirsty all of a sudden."

"Yes, Grannnie," Jenny trilled, then grabbed a cup from the sideboard, and filled it from the ewer. "I'll get some more water, too." She hustled out of the room but paused once outside and carefully shut the door behind her so she didn't wake the babies.

"How long do you think it would take you to ride to Julian's?" Sarah asked, "I mean, if you rode as fast as you could?"

"Shoot, I don't know, an hour and a half, why?" I looked at Sarah, but she wouldn't lift her head to look at me. "Why?" I repeated firmly. Now I was playing the role of doctor and big sister.

"Because I think he can be of help here. He did great with you when I burned my hands and, and…"

"And you don't think I can handle delivering you of twins while watching out for my three plus Jenny? Duh! Remember, Jenny is the helper in this. She can do just about anything I can with those babies but nurse them. And they all can sip from a cup and are doing a great job with eating solid food. Shoot, I only nurse them three times a day anymore. And that's for birth control as much as anything. I mean, I gotta admit, I like the way it feels, and the bonding is nice and, crap, I'm rambling. Sorry. What I *can* do is have Jenny ride over to get Leah and James. I don't think he wanted to go into town with the other men since she's so close to her time, too. If she can ride in the wagon, she can be here in fifteen minutes, tops. Now do you feel better?" I asked, although I could already see that she did.

"That damned town hall meeting!" Sarah cursed. "Why did it have to be now? I swear those, those, *assholes*," she whispered the designation, "set up the election for now. They knew we were having a baby."

"Babies," I corrected with a grin.

"Well, Jody didn't let on that we were having twins…"

"At least," I interrupted with a laugh at the slim possibility she was having triplets, then backed it down a notch. "No, I'm sorry, I shouldn't make light of it. I'm positive everything will be fine. And, I doubt the next generation of Pomeroys will be here too soon. I mean, I would guess you're going to have at least six hours or more of labor. You haven't even started the real thing yet, have you?" I asked, although I was pretty sure I was correct. I could see her belly firming up with fairly regular contractions, but she didn't look miserable enough to be in true labor yet.

"No," she said crossly. "I want to get it over with, but I want Jody here, too. He wasn't able to be with me with the first two…"

And then Sarah broke into a thousand pieces, each one wetter and more trembling than the other.

"All I can do is help with the clinical aspects, but I'll send Jenny to the Melbourne's right away," I said. "If James believes that Leah can ride in the wagon with Jenny for assistance, then he can go into town and get Jody. I'm sure Wallace can speak for the two of them, if needed. I doubt there is any political issue in this new America, or in the world, or anyone or, or *anything,* that would keep Jody from being here with you for the delivery, *capisce?*"

"Capisce," Sarah agreed then started to compose herself, wiping and sniffing away her outward signs of weakness.

"What's *capisce?*" asked Jenny as she walked in with fresh water and a basket of eggs. She set them on the sideboard and waited for our answer.

"Do you understand," I answered, meaning that was the definition of the word.

"No, I don't understand. That's why I asked. What's *capisce?*" she asked again, this time with a slight tinge of frustration.

I was beginning to feel like I should start the 'who's on first' dialog with her a la Abbott and Costello. "Depending on what inflection you use, *capisce* means 'do you understand' or 'yes, I understand.' *Capisce?"*

"Capisce!" Jenny declared. "Oh, and I got the eggs before my brothers could get them. Leo and Judah found one this morning and were trying to eat it, shell and all! But don't worry, I got it before they could

put it in their mouths or even break it. But they sure cried when I took it away," she explained.

Before Jenny could catch her second wind on the tale of the two toddlers and the egg, I interrupted. "Would you ride over to your Big Sister Leah's and ask her to come help me with Grannie? And, have your Big Brother James go to town to get Grandpa Jody."

I liked to use family designations with the given names whenever I spoke with Jenny. She never dimmed in her delight of having a family. Pride may be a sin, but in this case, it was pure happiness, was based on the love of her new family, the close-knit group she had been deprived of in her younger years.

"Okay, I'll take Prince Charles and ride over as fast as I can." Jenny ran to me and grabbed me around the waist, "I love you, Mommy," she said, then bounced over to Sarah. "I love you, Grannie." Then she put her face down to her grandmother's belly and spoke to the wee inhabitants within, "And I love you, too, my little aunts or uncles!" She waved broadly, grabbed a cookie off the plate on the table, saluted us with it, and bounced through the doorway, pulling the door shut softly in consideration of her napping siblings.

In all of about thirty seconds, Jenny was back. "Mommy, Mommy! Grandpa Julian is here, and he brought my sister Leah with him!" she shouted, obviously forgetting about her sleeping brothers and sister.

I scurried down the steps to intercept Julian and my eldest, and very pregnant, daughter. *What was I thinking when I asked Jenny to go get her? Leah was huge and looked ready to foal at any time, too.* "Leah," I scolded aloud, "you shouldn't be out riding!"

"Well, maybe not horseback riding," she puffed as she approached the steps, "but I thought a wagon ride would be acceptable. I had Wesley ride over to get Julian so he could bring me here." Leah looked right at me, and then I could see there was another reason she was here. "I wanted Sarah to, um, check me, that is if she's up to it."

Julian helped Leah to the porch bench seat then took the break in conversation as an opportunity to excuse himself. "Well, if you don't need anything else, I'll be getting back to the ranch. I sent Wesley back to Leah's place since James is with Wallace, and Jody's in town. He can take care of their stock while they're gone. I don't want to leave José by himself. We have two nannies ready to kid."

"Well, I'd appreciate it if you'd stay here, for a few hours at least," I asked. "Sarah's water just broke, and I might need a hand. She's ready to 'kid', too!" I joked nervously.

"You didn't burn *your* hands, did you?" Julian asked, recalling his forced indenture as midwife at my delivery when Sarah burned her palms. She had grasped a hot pot while I was in labor. Julian, the man with the smallest hands among my three attendants—Jody and Wallace being the other two—was drafted into helping me bear two of my three babies that evening.

"No, my hands are fine. But four hands are better than two," I argued.

"Yes, and you have Leah here to help you," Julian countered as he watched Leah move awkwardly from the bench into the house.

"Yes, and with her we have the potential for another 'kid' popping out real soon. Now really, Julian," I argued, "How close do you think she could get to Sarah to pull out a baby? Did you see that gut, I mean baby belly? She's almost as big as Sarah, and she's only having one!"

Julian sighed, "Okay, once again, you've won me over with one part logic and two parts passion. I'll stay."

I walked with Julian to the barn to unhitch the wagon. Neither of us spoke nor needed to. I was glad I didn't have to convince him to stay and that he hadn't argued that he should be allowed to return home. I put out some hay for his horse while he took off the leather and brass accruements. "But, understand this," he said suddenly, "I'm only here as the backup. I'm sure that between you and Leah, you'll be able to take care of this. I'll just boil water or help Jenny with the babies. Where is my godson by the way? I haven't seen him in a month, at least."

"It's only been two weeks, but he misses you, too. James let him have that laminated photo of your portrait. He showed it to him when he was fussy. It calmed him right down. But, when he took it away, Judah screamed and cried so much that James let him have it back. He sneaked it away when he was asleep, but you're not going to believe this, Judah searched for it when he woke up. 'Poppi, Poppi,' he screamed, and wouldn't stop. I finally had Jenny ride over to James's place to get it back. I made him a little pocket in his blanky to keep it safe. I'd like to take it out and put something less intriguing in its place, but he'd know the difference."

"Yes, he's pretty bright," bragged Julian as he leaned on the ledge of the wooden half door, looking out at the corral.

"Yes, bright and passionate, just like his Poppi," I replied with a smirk.

"Evie…" Julian scolded, his voice stretching the two syllables of my name into a mini lecture on propriety and good manners.

"I know, I know," I replied, then moved over to plant a big kiss on his cheek. "But there isn't anyone here but the two of us. Now," I whispered close to his face as I looked around to make sure that my second-generation silent spot, Jenny, hadn't crept in without notice. "I want you to know that if I had come here as a gay man, I would have given José a run for his money…" I said lustily and smacked him on the behind.

"Evie!" Julian blurted out, totally surprised and shocked. He hadn't expected flirtation from a woman, any woman, much less his daughter-in-law. Julian had long ago accepted that I was unpredictable and had a very progressive set of morals, totally alien to this time period. But, I guess I had stepped over the line with the much too familiar fanny fanning.

I turned away from him, not wanting to hear a lecture or even see the stern look that would be the abbreviated version. "Julian, you're hot," I said sassily. "I just thought I'd remind you in case José hasn't told…"

I froze. "I'm sorry," I whispered as I paled, suddenly aware of what I had just said and done. I turned around to beg forgiveness, my mouth moving open and shut but the words stuck in my throat. The tears started to flow. "I, I don't know why I said that. It was totally inappropriate. I, I guess I'm stressed. I mean, I meant what I said, but I shouldn't have said it. I guess the filter on my brain mouth connection failed. Will you forgive me?" I asked with complete sincerity, my hands clutched together under my chin, essentially begging from a foot away, slowly lowering myself into a kneeling position.

Julian looked around and saw we were still alone and that I was not only distraught – I was panicked. He reached out and pulled me up from my half-lowered position, unclenching the hand I had tucked in front of my neck. He placed one arm lightly around my shoulders and pulled me close, but a respectable distance close. I heard my father-in-law tell me, "I don't know why, but yes, I forgive you." He released his open aired hug and looked me in the eyes, bringing up his thumb to gently wipe away the tears from my cheeks. He didn't add anything to his words but leaned in again and placed his left hand on my right shoulder. This time, it was my peer who wiped the hair off my brow and gave me a firm and, if it was possible to be given there, passionate kiss on my forehead. His hands dropped to his side and he stepped back, ending his gesture with a nod, a wink, and a smile. I think he felt the same way.

***

"I'm sure glad Leah decided to come and visit today," Sarah told me when I came back in. She had set out a tray of fresh clouts, medical alcohol, and a small jar of oil on the little table next to the window.

"You forgot; Leah *knows*. She's faster and more reliable than a cell phone. At least her powers aren't affected by sunspots," I added with a smile. "Now, if you think you could bend over low enough, would you check her? That's why she came, or so she said. I've never done a pelvic and don't know what to feel for."

"Go get her," Sarah instructed with a shrug. "She's out there with Jenny and the babies. I'm doing fine, but I'm definitely feeling the contractions now." My eyes opened extra wide at the new revelation. "But I'm not ready for the breathing yet," she answered in response to my slightly fearful stare.

I didn't have to go far to find all of my girls in one place. Leah was making over the cute little spit curl that Jenny had put in Wren's hair. "Jenny, I need to have Leah come with me. Now, she's probably going to spend the night here, so you'll have lots of time together, okay?"

"'Kay," she replied as she picked up Leo and ran her fingers through his sparse hair, obviously evaluating the chance of getting his hair into a fancy 'do.

"Okay, up here, young lady," Sarah called to Leah when we came in. "This is where your mother had her babies and where I'm going to have mine, God willing, and yours, too."

"Well, I hope you have yours first," Leah remarked as she adjusted her skirts. "I'm not ready for this, I mean…" Leah looked over to me with absolute terror in her eyes as she stopped in midsentence. I saw that she was 'reading' again.

She had done it many times before and told me about it just days after she got here. "It's spooky, Mom, knowing 'stuff' about people. I

252

don't want to 'peek' into the private parts of their lives, but it's just 'there.'"

"But it happens to you all the time, doesn't it?" I knew Leah was psychic to a degree. Of course, there was no way I could know what it was like for her.

"I subconsciously tune out most everything, but this is different." She leaned in to tell me what I already knew. "I 'read' about her in books!"

I nodded and added, "I did, too. I remember everything, I think. The first memories I had when I got to this house were of her and Jody, just like I had read in the Sinclaire novels."

Sarah hadn't noticed Leah's insecurity. She had other concerns. She sighed and said in exasperation, "Now, if you'll excuse me a moment, I thought I was ready. I'll be right back. Damn, that'll be the best part of not being pregnant. I'll be able to hold my water for longer than twenty minutes at a time!" She steadied herself on the doorframe, then walked toward the privy with an exaggerated waddle that I was sure meant that one of the babies had dropped down further into the birth canal.

"What's wrong," I asked Leah when I was sure Sarah was out of earshot.

Leah said, "I almost asked her about her first delivery. God, I didn't want her to have to recall it!"

"Well, she probably already has. I mean, she's been frightened about this pregnancy ever since she found out about it."

"Well, I definitely didn't want her to know that I knew about the first one!"

"Yes, but since she knows that you have 'the sight,' she wouldn't be shocked, at least not much, if you did know. Now, relax, okay?" I said and helped her lie back on the chaise.

Sarah came back from her potty break. "Sorry for the delay. Looks like you're ready." She placed the stool at the end of the chaise between Leah's raised knees. I held her hand as she sat down carefully.

She was willing, but not necessarily able, to perform Leah's evaluation. She bent forward and found that her belly was in the way. She stood up again and nudged the stool with her foot to the side of the chaise where I helped her sit down again. She sat parallel to Leah, then reached in sideways, finally able to perform her awkward pelvic exam.

I stood at the head of the couch and looked in awe at Leah, my eldest, and very pregnant daughter, as she got checked. I didn't remember her as an infant, but the bond was still there. And, now she was going to make me a grandmother. I watched as her hazel eyes widened in shock. I followed her stare. She was looking at her midwife doctor, Sarah.

Sarah never could hide her emotions, ever, and right now, she wasn't even trying to.

"What?" I asked. "Don't tell me you found a fist!" I hissed in fear. That had happened to me. Judah came out fine, but that wasn't always the result.

"No, no fist," Sarah said slowly, "but we have a lot of centimeters, about five."

"How much effaced?" I asked.

"Um, fifty percent, I'd say. It's kind of hard to get in there just right. I'm not used to doing an examination sidesaddle," she said as she wiped off her hand.

"But, I could stay this way for days," Leah argued, but with no one save herself. "Shoot, for all we know, I've been this way for days, weeks even!"

"Have you been having sexual relations?" Sarah asked clinically, her eyes unblinking and callous.

If I hadn't heard the change in her tone, and seen that Sarah hadn't moved, I'd swear another person had come into the room and swapped bodies with her.

Leah blushed, gulped, looked at me in embarrassment, and then up at Sarah.

"Never mind," Sarah said coldly. "It doesn't make any difference now, does it? But I hope you enjoyed it at least six weeks' worth, because that's the last time your husband's..."

"Sarah!" Leah and I screeched at the same time, interrupting the completion of her description of James's genitalia and report on their recent intimacy.

"Oh, I'm sorry," Sarah said, then froze.

"Did I really just say that?" she asked after a very long moment, her face still scarlet in embarrassment.

"Well, you started to..." I replied, then paused, filling the air with an awkward emptiness. Evidently, I wasn't the only one who had an alter ego taking over with the stress of babies coming.

I took a deep breath to recover. "Hey, Leah, get up," I announced to change the theme and atmosphere of the conversation. "Turnabout's fair play, eh, Sarah? Let's see if she can check you. I mean, Leah, you see how dilated and effaced, or whatever, she is, then scoot over and I'll see, or rather feel, what all this measuring stuff is all about. I mean, I know what a centimeter is, and effacement is the thinning of the cervix, but I need a baseline…"

"Ugh," Sarah carped, "the ultimate indignation: having my yah-yah felt up by my daughter-in-law and granddaughter."

"Or sister and niece," I suggested, "depending on which hat I'm wearing today. Actually, I'm feeling more sisterly than daughterly," I said, then punched her in the upper arm.

"Well, that makes it easier. I forget sometimes that you're really the same age as me."

"Yeah, well try it from my point of view," Leah interjected. "She's my mother, my 'biological, I came out from between those thighs' mother, and she looks like she's my little sister!"

"How about if I grab a few pieces of charcoal and draw old age wrinkles on my face, and maybe a wart or two; would that make you two whiners feel better?" I asked.

Sarah and Leah shared a look with each other, nodded, then answered, "Yes," as one. Leah waddled over to the fireplace and kicked out a small piece of burnt wood. She leaned to the right, then to the left, and then tried to squat down to get it.

"Forget it!" I said after stifling my giggles for a full half minute. She looked like a monkey in a fat suit trying to reach a handful of nuts on the ground. "You'll just have to remember who I am, because I am *not* painting on a mask. We don't want to scare the babies when they come out now, do we?"

Leah tried one more time to squat down and grab the charcoal, then winced and yelped, biting off a scream of pain.

"What happened? I asked.

"I think I pulled a muscle. I can't move. Oh, shit! That's what I get for trying to make you put on the mask. Shit, shit, shit! I can't move!" she cursed through clenched jaws.

"Hold on," I said. I ran to the door and called, "Jenny, come here, stat!" then came back to Leah's side to see if I could help her move to the chair.

"No!" she screamed. "Sorry, I'll just stand. It's just a muscle spasm; it'll pass."

"How are you going to check Sarah then?" I asked.

"Uh, ooo, shit, I mean shoot. Jenny, what are you doing here?" she yelped, embarrassed at being caught cursing in front of her little sister, the great 'appearing act,' who had suddenly popped into the room.

"Mommy called me and told me to come stat. That means right away. I know lots of words. Mommy and Daddy teach me new words all the time. Daddy's even teaching me Latin and José teaches me Spanish. "¿Como estas?" Jenny asked, showing off some of her new language skills.

"Tengo dolor, mucho dolor," Leah replied haltingly. "That means I'm in a lot of pain. Would you help me to the chair, la silla?"

"Okay," Jenny said, and moved in next to her arm. "Are you okay?" she asked. "Your face looks funny. Is the baby hurting you? Grannie says her babies kick her something fierce. But they don't hurt, not really."

"No, my baby isn't hurting me any more than usual. I just bent over the wrong way and pulled a muscle. Help me sit down over here, would you?" Leah asked haltingly in between yelps of pain.

It took Jenny and me a couple of minutes to get it accomplished, but Leah was finally seated. "Nobody talk for a minute, please," she asked, her face flushed from the pain. She shut her eyes, cautiously straightened her back, then carefully set the back of her hands on her knees, or as close as she could get to them. She touched her middle fingertips to the ends of her thumbs in the classic yoga pose of peace. "Ah ohm, ah ohm," she chanted between deep, calming breaths.

Jenny was standing by the door, both of her hands clasped over her mouth to contain the giggles that were trying to squeeze out. I didn't know which one was more comical, Leah or Jenny, but they were both cute.

Leah finally stopped her mantra, took what I recognized as her final deep cleansing breath, and then smiled, evidently pain-free, as she opened her eyes. "Doing yoga breathing for practice?" I asked. "You know, it won't be too long and you'll be doing the Lamaze breathing," I added.

"Yeah, I know, don't remind me," she answered with a face contorted between a grin, grimace, and a glare at me for bringing up the inevitable.

"Hey, you're only bringing one into the world. You have it easy. And speaking of bringing into the world, do you think you can check Sarah now?" I asked.

"Climb on board the BBB," Leah intoned like a cartoon character train conductor, adding a mimed elbow pull of the train whistle. "The Baby Birthing Bed, two babies, coming up!"

"At least!" I added in a high-toned comic voice as I held onto Sarah's elbow.

"Can I watch?" Jenny asked, unintentionally bringing the silly mood back to seriousness.

I looked at Leah, then we both looked at Sarah for the answer. "Come up here by my head," Sarah said. "You can watch from up here with me. Besides, I want you to hold my hand," she added, and put the back of her right hand on her shoulder in an invitation for Jenny to join her at the head of the chaise.

"Okay," Jenny chirped, and we all relaxed, the tension released.

"Alrighty now, how close are your contractions?" Leah asked Sarah as she arranged the skirts over her knees.

"I don't know. I wish I had a watch with a second hand. Every time I start to count, I lose track. Ooh, there's one now."

Leah's hand had been on Sarah's belly. She felt the contraction and immediately moved her hand up between Sarah's legs to check her cervix.

"Shit, I mean shoot; that hurts!" Sarah yelped.

I snorted but didn't say a word. Her eyes cut to mine. "You're enjoying this, aren't you?" she said sternly.

"Oh, yeah," I drolled, "but you told me that you 'had' to check for dilation during a contraction, right?"

"Yes, right. Leah, why don't you change places with your mother? She needs to see, or rather feel, what's going on. How many centimeters am I?"

Leah replied with widened eyes, "Five and about fifty percent effaced."

Sarah's face fell as fast as mine did, I'm sure.

"What's five and fifty mean?" Jenny asked.

"That's, uh," I stuttered in shock, "Um, that's how 'ripe' your sister and Grannie are. I mean, how ready their bodies are to let the babies go. They're both going to be ready at the same time, I think," I answered aloud, then prayed silently, 'but I hope not.' "Would you go check on your siblings?" I asked in order to dismiss Jenny. I didn't want to field any more female physiology questions.

"Isn't this where we make bets on who pops first?" Leah asked, a false lilt in her voice.

"Yeah, a pool with bets on times, weights, and genders. Although, we have more possibilities to bet on than people to bet," I said.

"I still say you're going to have a girl," Sarah told Leah. "Didn't you say that there hasn't been a son born to any of your maternal ancestors since…"

"Since anyone can remember, at least until my baby brothers," Leah said.

Sarah saw the sad look on my face and said, "Sorry, I forgot that you don't remember."

"What?" I mocked brightly with feigned jocularity. "You forgot that I forgot? Ah, don't worry about it," I said sincerely. "It's true. I don't want to know anything about my past life, but anything before that, like ancestors who I never interacted with personally, is fine. No, Leah is mine, and that's all I need to know. The life the two of us share as mother and daughter started a year ago, and that's good enough for me."

"You're afraid to remember, aren't you?" Leah asked gently.

"Hey," I said defensively, "how would you like it if you suddenly found out you had an adult daughter, an ex-husband, and God only knows how many skeletons in your closet, that someone else knows all about them, but you don't, and probably never will? How do you think James would take it? Aren't you happy now? With this new baby coming, a new home, a… a…"

"Sorry!" Leah blurted out. "I wasn't trying to bring up old shit…Jenny! How do you do that? I swear," Leah huffed when she saw that Jenny was back.

Sarah and I nodded in agreement: yes, Leah swore too much. Leah saw us and shot the two of us a dirty look then continued. "I think, I think…that every time a cuss word comes out of my mouth, you pop up," she said to Jenny.

"Grandpa taught me to be real quiet. At least he told me about me dragging my foot. He said that being quiet might save my life sometime." Jenny giggled. "But, he said sometimes it was good for other stuff, too, like hunting and fishing, and catching Grannie sneaking cookies…"

"I did not!" Sarah blurted. "Well," she admitted, "maybe just a few. The babies were hungry."

"So, Leah," I asked, in order to change the subject, "how about you do the counting so we can find out how far apart Grannie's contractions are?"

"I wish I had a watch with a stopwatch function, even a second hand would be nice. I left mine…" she said, then stopped suddenly before letting on where the watch was: back in the 21st century.

"Is the second hand the little skinny red one on Brother James's watch?" Jenny asked.

"Yes…" all three adult women answered at the same time. "Why?" I asked.

"Because he let me borrow his watch for a science experiment. See," she said, and pulled it out of her pocket. "He wanted me to see how fast I could run back and forth from the porch to the barn and back again. I'm supposed run every hour to see how many seconds it takes. I'm supposed to write it down here." Jenny took out a scrap of paper and a small pencil like the ones they gave out at miniature golf courses. "I'm supposed to let him know if I'm faster before or after I eat, or earlier in the day or later. Then he says he's going to show me how to make a graph or gaf; I can't remember the word exactly."

"Yes, the word is graph, but could you do the science experiment later?" I asked. "We need to use the watch."

"Here," Jenny said, holding out James's Rolex. "Do you need me to help? I can time stuff. I timed how many drops of sap came out of the trees in the spring so we could figure the rate of flow. I also timed how fast a stick floated from the big rock to the bridge. That was measuring speed or rate per second. Brother James said I'm real bright with some of my studies."

"Okay, you can time Grannie's contractions. Now, when her tummy

259

gets hard, you note what time it is, including seconds. Here, she's having one now," I said and nodded to her to check the watch.

Jenny placed her hand next to mine on her Grannie's belly, and then announced, "She's all done," at the end of the contraction.

"Fine, do you remember what time it was?" I asked.

"10:30 and twenty seconds," Jenny said. "Now what?"

"We wait for the next one. The time that it starts is what we need to know. From the start of one contraction to the start of the next one is the time between contractions…how far apart they are. They usually start at about fifteen or twenty minutes apart, and then get down to one minute or less."

"There it is!" Jenny announced when she felt Sarah's next contraction start. "It's 10:35 and 25 seconds. That's, um, five minutes and five seconds apart, right?"

"Right," I said. "Now, Leah, are you having regular contractions yet?"

"I don't know about regular, but yes on the contractions. I thought they were just Braxton Hicks, though," she said.

"Braxton hiccups?" Jenny asked, her face contorted in amazement.

"No, let's just call them false labor pains," Leah said. All three adult women realized that misters Braxton and Hicks, or was that Dr. Braxton Hicks, probably weren't even born yet.

"Labor pains?" Jenny asked. "Do they hurt?"

"Not yet, but they probably will later," Leah huffed.

"Most likely will," Sarah said dejectedly. "I never had a spinal, and I know it's not possible now, but a small part of me would like that option."

"I agree, but I'll pass on the needle and take the discomfort, not pain…remember, that's what you always said about labor, Mom. Oops, sorry."

Leah grimaced, realizing too late that she had just brought up my past life again.

"I mean, I'll take the discomfort for a few hours rather than be away from you and you and here," she said, proud of all her female family members gathered in the room.

"So, am I the designated nanny?" Julian asked as he walked into the house, Judah in his arms, toddling Wren and Leo clutching his pant legs.

Julian was smiling, radiant with love at being in the presence of his grandchildren. He saw the apprehension about the coming events in the women's eyes, and his face fell. He recalled the difficulty Evie had delivering Wee Julian who had decided to come into the world fist first. He gave his godson an extra squeeze of thanksgiving and said a silent prayer that Sarah's twins would arrive without complications.

"If you don't mind, yes, would you and Jenny see to the wee three?" I asked. "It's going to be a long day. I'm not sure, but it looks like you're going to be a great-grandpa today: Leah might be in labor, too. Only time will tell, but she's not going to be a lot of help here."

"Sorry!" Leah blurted out angrily, then added with absolutely no sincerity, "I didn't do it on purpose!" She sniffed back the tears she hadn't planned on shedding, then added humbly, "At least delivering early. I did want to get pregnant. I just didn't think that it would happen so quickly, both getting pregnant and then going into labor."

We were all stunned by Leah's surprisingly emotional eruption. I walked over to her and held her diagonally, my belly pressed to the side of hers, our faces close to one another. "Honey, I think we're all going through a very stressful time here today. I mean, your little outburst, Sarah's, ahem, personal remarks, and even I haven't been myself today," I said.

I glanced over at Julian and gave him another look of apology. He nodded that he understood, and I took a deep breath. "So, if Poppi will watch the babies, I'll get my little crash course in midwifery. Maybe we'll have a couple of babies, or more, by sunrise."

"What about me?" Jenny asked, her face full of frown. "Don't you need me?"

"Of course, we do," I said. I brought her over to her sister's other side and we shared the Leah sandwich hug. "You get to run back and forth, to be the expediter, and can even help Poppi cook."

"We still have some potatoes left. Can I chop them up and make hash browns? Huh? Can I?"

"You can talk to your Poppi about the menu. In the meantime, would you time your sister Leah's contractions? I want to see if they're consistent."

"Okay. Are you ready, Leah? I have to wait for the contraction before I can time it," Jenny said with administrative authority.

Well, Jenny waited and timed Leah's contractions while I took Sarah for a walk. Sarah's labor was progressing rapidly. At least we didn't have to worry about timing her. I never got my lesson on what to feel for with dilation and effacement, but it really wasn't too hard to figure out. Sarah got to the huffing and puffing stage, and even the foot massages weren't helping. "We have to wait for Jody," she shouted, "Shit, this hurts!"

"Shut up and breathe," I ordered. "In, out, in, out. Focus."

"Focus, schmocus, son of a bitchin'…" she huffed.

"Shush! Jenny's here," I said. "If you talk during a contraction, you'll pay for it in pain. There, it's done," I told her when her belly softened. "Now, next time, listen to me. Here," I bent down and picked up the elusive charcoal piece that Leah had tried to retrieve earlier in the day. "When a contraction hits, I want you to breathe in and out slowly, and concentrate on the dot inside of this circle." I drew a small circle within a bigger one on the hearth then wiped my hands on a cloth. "Jenny, how's your sister doing?"

"She says she's all over the charts, whatever that means. She can't talk now because she's having another 'traction," Jenny said.

I hastily poured alcohol over my hands and rushed to her side. "Let me check you," I said, pushing her skirt back over her knees.

Leah continued her huffing and puffing. Her concentration so intense that she never acknowledged my presence. She realized I was there, though, when the extra pang of pain caused by my finger on her cervix brought forth the word, "Shit!" from her mouth.

She finished her breathing regimen and blew out a quick sentence. "None of my contractions are consistent, some are ten minutes apart, and some are like now," she groaned, and started again with her Lamaze breathing.

She was having a rough time, so I went to her feet and pressed in on the labor-easing pressure points. I could see the relief in her eyes immediately. "Sarah, how are you doing?" I called back.

"We're doin' fine," Jody announced. "It looks like yer a bit busy there, so I'm doin' the coachin' here. How much more time do ye think she has?" he asked, his hands quickly moving to press her feet to counteract Sarah's pains.

"I don't know, but I'll check her on her next one. Leah's whippin' right along here. She's at eight centimeters already. Did James come back with you?" I asked as I washed my hands in another alcohol rinse.

"He'll be in soon. My horse was faster than his. We left Wallace in town to do the speakin'. There's talk of turnin' the regulatin' of the town over to the Crown. I dinna think it'll take much convincin' fer the townsfolk to realize that we're better off takin' care of our own needs right here. Oh, here, she's done fer a minute. Go aheid and do what ye need to do," he offered as he got up from the stool by her side.

"Am I too late? Is the baby here yet?" James blurted out as he pushed open the door. His intensity toned down as soon as he saw Leah. "How're you doing, sweetheart," he said tenderly.

"Ugh, I'm not sure why women keep getting pregnant after they've been through this once, much less multiple times," Leah carped.

James sat down next to her and used a cloth to wipe her face. "God, you're beautiful," he praised. Leah huffed and gave him an exaggerated frown. "I know, I know, you feel rotten," he said, "but you are positively radiant. Is there anything I can do…and don't tell me I already did my part."

Leah's face contorted between a grin at the fact that he had read her mind, a sneer because that really was how she felt right now, and a frown because she knew that many more contractions were imminent before their baby arrived.

"I feel lost at sea. Sarah's over there, having contractions regular as clockwork. Or at least like a clock that's gaining half a minute every hour or so. Me, I don't know when they're going to hit. I just told Jenny to take a privy break. She's been at my side for four hours, at least. She was supposed to help Poppi with the wee three but didn't want me to be alone. I mean, Mom's here, but she's doing double duty with taking Sarah for walks, cleaning up messes, oh, shit…"

Leah quit talking and immediately started her breathing. James knew what to do; he had been taught well. He didn't say a word but went to her feet and immediately applied thumb pressure.

I was performing a pelvic exam on Sarah while James took care of Leah's needs. "Shit, shit, shit!" Sarah screamed as I touched her inside.

"Sarah, it's going to hurt more if you talk. But I don't think you have too many more contractions in you—it's time to push. Jody, get behind her shoulders and help support her. Baby number one is crowning. I can work his shoulders out, but I want you ready with a swaddling cloth."

"It's a boy? Ye can tell already?" Jody asked as he positioned himself behind Sarah, excited at hearing me refer to 'his shoulders.'

"No, not yet. You can push with the next contraction, Sarah." I could tell by the feel of the soft spots that baby number one was face down, the correct position for delivery. I put my hands inside and urged him out. "Baby's a red head and…." I slipped the shoulders out, then pulled him out the rest of the way, "It's a boy. Here, Jody, take him and clean him up, would you? Sarah, just chill a moment. The other guy isn't in position yet. Lord, help us and bring him face down, too."

"Amen," James, Leah, Jody, and Sarah chorused as the youngest Pomeroy added his own squall of agreement.

"Can I see him?" Sarah asked, and turned her upper torso toward her first son.

"Aye, he's a good-lookin' lad and hearty, too."

"Mom?" Leah called urgently through clenched jaws.

"Dani, I mean, Evie, I think she wants to push. She doesn't know if she can yet or not. Can you see if she's at ten centimeters?" James asked.

I gulped at his Freudian slip of calling me Dani, my older 21st self who he first knew me as. Evidently, his inner-self wanted an older person to take charge, not the very young-bodied me. He was also speaking for Leah. She had told me they had developed quite the psychic communication rapport just before they married, his latent ability showing itself as soon as she opened up to him. I shook my head and snapped out of my momentary trance. I felt Sarah's lower abdomen: the second baby wasn't down in the birth canal yet.

Before I had a chance to answer James, Jenny popped in the room. "Do we have any babies yet?" she asked, bouncing up and down of her toes.

"Ye have an uncle here. And, he has red hair jest like yer little brothers and sister. Here, do ye want to hold him? He's a wee 'un but seems to have a good set of lungs."

"Jody, keep track of Sarah and baby number two. I'll be right back," I said, and scooted away to kneel down at the foot of the pile of quilts that Jenny had put together for Leah. She refused to lie on Jody and Sarah's bed lest she stain it and insisted that Sarah have use of the chaise since she was having twins, and it would be easier for me to help the babies come out.

"How ya doin', honey," I asked as I put my left hand on her belly, waiting for it to harden before checking her.

"I was tired, but all of a sudden, I'm wide awake. At least, it feels like it's time…" Leah stopped talking, immediately started panting, and then held her breath.

"Don't hold your breath! That means you're pushing." I was multitasking, lecturing as I felt to see if she was at the magic ten centimeters dilation. "Ho Kay…go ahead and push; you're ready. It'll probably take a while because this is your first one."

Leah's contractions were coming on top of each other. She pushed and she pushed but got nowhere. She was in tears, and James was getting weepy, too. "I'm sorry, I'm sorry," he kept saying over and over, trying to comfort her, but unable to find a place to touch her that didn't result in her shaking her head 'no' and shrugging away from him.

"Try squatting," Sarah called breathlessly from her birthing bed. "And Evie, can you come over here for a quick second. I…" Sarah stopped talking and started panting.

"Oh, brother," I puffed as I stood up and rushed to the foot of the chaise.

"Or oh, sister," Jody joked. "I think the other one is ready to come out."

I got in position on the stool and spread Sarah's knees apart, letting Jody support her shoulders. "Number Two is in the chute. Great work, Sarah, this one's face down, too. See, I told you the delivery would be perfect."

Sarah took a deep breath and pushed hard enough to get another child out to the shoulders. One gentle tug, and baby boy number two was announcing his arrival to everyone in the room.

"Wow!" Jenny exclaimed.

With all of the excitement, none of us had remembered that she was in the house, much less that she was standing quietly behind me, cuddling her uncle, bouncing him gently to keep him quiet. "Another boy; he looks just like this one, only bigger, I think," she said as she looked back down at the bundle in her arms.

"Uh, a little help over here, if you can," James called. "I think the baby's stuck."

I looked away from the happy grouping of Sarah, Jody, Jenny, and the two small, but perfect, baby boys and saw the terror on both James's and Leah's faces.

"I can't do it, Mom. She won't come out; she's too big."

"No, she's not; you're just too small. Here, James, lay her back down for a minute. Jody, hand me that oil, please. I am so sorry. I forgot to use the oil and stretch you out. Will you forgive me?" I asked as I pulled back her privacy cloth and lubed and stretched, trying to work around my dark-haired grandchild's head that was crowning.

"I'll forgive you as soon as she gets out. Oomph, here we go again…"

Leah was having a major contraction. She wanted to push but was doing her best to control the urge. "No, no, no, not yet, no, no, not yet," she puffed, her own chant to try and control her body. The contraction subsided, and the baby pulled back up just a little, at least enough that I could get a finger inside to tug rather than rub the opening.

"Okay, James, let's try to get her vertical again before the next contraction. Squat like the squaws do, Leah."

"Huh?" she asked but assumed the position just the same. "Oh, yeah, 'Dances with Wolves,' right. I don't need an Academy Award for this performance, just my baby," Leah said, then tried to laugh, her chuckle interrupted by another contraction. "Oh, shit! Here she comes; catch!"

I flopped down on my side and looked up to half pull out, half catch, the baby. "Cloth, please," I asked as I cuddled my white vernix-covered granddaughter to my chest.

James reached over, grabbed the swaddling cloth, and wrapped it around her, taking care not to touch the umbilicus. "When do you cut it," he asked.

"Oh, boy," Leah breathed softly, forgoing her customary curse word. She stood up halfway and let the placenta drop to the pile of quilts beneath her. "Oops, sorry," she said about the mess she had just made.

"Here, you can cut it now," I told James. "Cut it right here and Leah, don't worry about the mess," I said and handed her an oversized clout to put between her legs. "Everything's washable. Man, for being early, she sure is big. You were, too; eight pounds, four ounces. James, how big were you?" I asked, then suddenly realized what I had just said.

"Ten pounds," he answered, his eyes narrowed, asking me without words how I knew how much Leah weighed at birth: I didn't remember her early years, or so I had told everyone.

"Leah, you never mentioned how much you weighed to me, did you?" I asked. "I mean, I just popped out with that weight. I don't even know if it's right or not, or even if you ever told me. At least, I don't recall talking about birth weights."

"Yes, you're right, and no, I never told you. So, do you remember if she looks like I did?" Leah asked cautiously.

I beamed at my granddaughter as James brought her over to her mother to see. I looked over Leah's shoulder. "Oh, yeah; gotta be. Either that, or I've known what she's going to look like forever. I mean, she sure looks familiar. And don't worry; she won't be bald for long. If I recall, you were bald, too."

Chapter 26: Too Soon for Babies (TGBF Ch 9)

Summer, 1782

"When can I have a baby?" Jenny asked.

"When, when, when you're as tall as your father," I stuttered. I was busy preparing green beans and she took me completely off guard. I didn't expect to hear that question from her for years!

"But you have babies and you're not as tall as Daddy," she argued. "And Grannie has babies and she's not as tall as he is either. Or does she have to be as tall as Grandpa 'cause he's their dad?" Jenny stopped justifying and started calculating. "No, wait, that can't be or no one would have babies. No woman is as tall as Daddy or Grandpa, or even Brother James. 'Sides, Rachel had babies and she was little. Hannah said they was the same age as each other, too."

"Were the same age," I corrected.

Jenny didn't say a word, which was a relief. I was uncomfortable with the topic of conversation. However, one look at her face and I could see it was because she was waiting for me to answer her initial question.

"Okay," I answered reluctantly, "you can have a baby after you're married..." I looked at her to make sure she understood that very important requirement. She must have; she was positively radiant at that prospect.

"But no babies until after you're married and have finished school, okay?"

"Okay. And you told me that school was out in a few days because we had to work more outside in the gardens? So that means I can have babies real soon!"

"No! No, you can't. You're still too young. Besides, I said 'finished school' not just out of school. You'll be 'out' of school in a few days, all right, but you won't be 'finished' with your schooling until you know as much as your father, or at least me. And that includes reading and math, *comprende*?"

"What's math *comprende*?" she asked.

"Well, if you knew, then you'd be closer to being finished with your schooling." I looked over at her pensive face and added, "And remember, you have to be married, too. Don't forget that. And a good man isn't that easy to find. Just because there are a lot of good ones around here, doesn't mean that all men are worthy. So don't just marry any man so you can have a baby, okay?"

Jenny smirked and nodded her head. I didn't know what that meant and didn't know if I *wanted* to know. I put down the bowl of snap beans and put my index finger under her chin. "Promise me," I commanded with a serious tone and look that I had never used with her before. I wanted to make sure she knew how important this life lesson was.

"Mommy, I promise you that I will not marry a man just so I can have babies. And I promise you he is, I mean, will be a good man," she answered sincerely.

I could tell she was telling me the truth. It looked like she accepted that lesson easily enough.

***

"Well, look at what the cat dragged in," James said as he walked up to the longhaired youth coming in from the mill road. Wee Ian was back, and it looked like he was traveling solo.

"I think ye have it wrong, *cousin*," Wee Ian said with a grin. James was his secret brother-in-law, but they referred to each other as cousin. "The cat dinna drag me in, but I *did* drag a cat in," he said as he lifted up a leather pouch with a kitten paw reaching out. "I brought Jenny a gift. But I think I should ask Wallace first if it's all right. I mean, with all the mice in the barn, I dinna think there'll be any reason he'll need to feed this wee critter, but it is his home and his, um, daughter," he said, stumbling on the last word.

"You like her, don't you," James teased when he saw the uneasiness. "You brought her a cat just so you could see her..." James stopped the silliness and said plainly, "Hey, she's a great girl. If I were your age, I'd want her for a girlfriend."

Wee Ian blushed at the revelation. He wasn't going to deny it. He wasn't going to acknowledge its truth, either. Instead, he changed the subject. "Where is everyone?"

"Oh, here, there and everywhere. Wallace and Jody are clearing some more land south of here. We're planning on putting in more crops next year since I'm here to help. So, are you going to stay for a while? You're welcome to stay as long as you want. There's plenty of work to spread around."

The young man sighed wistfully. "I'd like to, but I want to see if I can make somethin' of myself first. I mean, I want to be a man of worth," he said as he stood tall, his skinny chest stuck out in pride.

"There's nothing wrong with being a farmer," James said. "I've had money and 'worth,' back before I got here," he nodded and gave Wee Ian a wink and a 'look' to remind him that he had a life in a different world before he came here, "and believe me, *this* is better."

"Aye, but ye still have to have money or goods to trade fer the land, the tools, the stock, the seed, and anythin' else ye happen to be needin' to get started."

James heard Jenny out in the back garden, calling to her little siblings to get out of the carrots. He noticed Wee Ian look dreamily toward the sound. He grinned and said, "Boy, you have it bad, don't you?"

A frown replaced the young man's smile. "Have what bad?" he asked as he checked his chest, arms, and legs like he was inspecting himself for lice.

James laughed. "I mean you *really* like her, don't you? Is she why you want to 'make somethin' of yerself'?"

The boy inhaled sharply, but didn't reply with words, only nodded dejectedly.

"And stay there!" Jenny scolded as she put Wren in the enhanced playpen that looked like a low-profile corral with vertical slats added to keep the toddlers from free ranging into places they weren't supposed to be. She looked over and saw James talking to a stranger. No, not a stranger: it was Wee Ian, the one she had renamed Scout.

"Scout!" she screamed as she ran toward the men. She threw her arms around the smaller man's waist, picked him up, and hugged him fervently, spinning him around at the same time.

"Um, put me down!" he grunted with a mixture of embarrassment and annoyance.

Jenny did as she was told, and then put her arms down at her side. She bowed her head slightly then bobbed it back up. She opened her mouth as if to speak then shut it quickly. James noticed that she was breathing in and out so rapidly that it looked like she was panting. She was a good-natured child, but he had never seen her so radiant and bubbling over with joy.

Scout looked over at James with full on embarrassment then back at Jenny with what could only be described as adolescent desire unwillingly held in check. "Go ahead and kiss her," James teased, certain that he wouldn't.

Scout leaned in and gave Jenny a brotherly kiss on the cheek then pulled back, chagrined, but obviously wanting more.

"Whoa," James said, "I was only joking."

Jenny looked at James, gave him a mischievous grin, then took one step closer to her secret husband, and put her hands on his shoulders. She looked Scout in the eye then shook her head. She brought her right index finger to her mouth, tapped her lip then moved the finger away and pointed it at his face, wagging it in admonishment. Wee Ian/Scout glanced over at James as if to ask, 'what should I do?'

"Go ahead and kiss her again," James said, "I won't tell anyone."

Scout looked deep into Jenny's eyes, slipped his hands around her waist, and held her close. He leaned in and gave her a kiss that would make any high school senior jealous.

"Uh, I think that's enough," James interrupted. "I mean, it's not as if you're married."

Jenny and Scout broke off the kiss and looked at James as one, both of them grinning with the smile of a shared secret.

"Scout?" James asked, suddenly recalling the name she had screamed when she had seen him. "You called him Scout, didn't you? Oh, shit."

Scout took one hand off of Jenny's waist, looked at James with mild disgust, and asked, "Why is everythin' 'oh, shit' with ye?"

James shook his head. He was looking at his ancestors. The mystery of who Scout Kincaid was had been answered. He had traveled back in time last year to assure that Ian Kincaid was saved, or at least that was what he thought. He only knew for sure that he was to ensure the life of a Scout Kincaid, the man who would marry Jenny Pomeroy-Hart, his great-grandmother many times over. James shook his head as disbelief whipped into realization. "You married her last year, didn't you?"

Now it was time for the young, innocent couple to blush. "Aye, we did it the Indian way," Scout explained.

"But we're still married or marrit or however you want to say it," Jenny blurted out then added, "oops, sorry." She didn't want to start talking too much again; her husband didn't like that.

"Well, I won't tell anyone about it, and I don't think you two should either," admonished James. "And don't go making any babies; for a few years at least, quite a few. I mean, she's still my little sister-in-law, even if she is your wife. You haven't been 'doing it' have you?" he asked.

Scout straightened out his shoulders and answered, "Nae, we will wait until I can build us a proper home. I willna be plantin' my seed in her until her breasts are big enough to feed babies, and I can put a roof o'er our heads."

Jenny looked down at her slightly budding chest and stuck it out with pride. Scout saw the gesture and shook his head at her: no, not yet. She sighed in resignation then giggled in relief. Good, she wasn't ready to share her gift yet. Mommy said she had to finish school first. She'd make sure she did that. Maybe by then Scout would be able to build them a home.

"Well, you two lovebirds," James said then saw the look of confusion on their faces. He shook his head in the universal sign language of 'no, never mind; it's not important.' He started again. "Well, Mr. and Mrs. Kincaid, please don't let anyone else know about your marriage. I don't think your parents or grandparents would be as understanding as I am. As long as you're, um, keeping your private parts to yourselves, then it's nobody else's business. And DO NOT go sharing those parts, okay, little brother and little sister?"

They both nodded to James, and then looked at each other. Scout's face lit up. He bent his knees slightly, wrapped his arms around Jenny, and spun her like she had spun him. He set her down and they shared another long, but more reserved kiss. They pulled apart and smiled at each other, both of them glowing all the way down to their curled toes.

"And don't go kissing each other when anyone else is around, all right? And if, or when, you *have* been kissing," James said as he looked down and saw that they were now holding hands, "I suggest you think of sad things before you see anyone else. Those smiles you're wearing will give you away, for sure."

James opened out his arms, walked up to the couple, and wrapped his arms around his many times over great-grandparents. "I sure love you two," he said, a tear dribbling down his cheek. "Now let's get down to the house. I'm sure that Evie would like to see you again, 'Scout.'"

272

Chapter 27: They're Huge! (TGBF Ch 26)

August 25, 1782
(Benji has Jane in his life now)

"Grandpa, Grandpa," Jenny screeched as she called out in all directions, trying to find her absent mentor. "There's a man here who looks just like you only bigger. And, he has a Negro woman with him, and she's huge, too!"

I heard the commotion and came outside to see what all the excitement was about. I heard her say the words bigger, huge, and Negro. Well, at least someone taught her some manners along the way; I wouldn't have to teach her not to say the 'n' word. There weren't very many slaves in this area, and we didn't associate with anyone who had them, but what was it that she said?

"See, I told you so," Jenny bragged when I came out to see the giant-sized, red-haired man in Carhartt jeans, and the stunning black woman, wrapped in a blue calico sarong, who was nearly as tall as he was. "Where's Grandpa?" Jenny asked excitedly, jumping up and down in place. "He has *got* to see this!"

"I'm sorry," I said to the visitors as Jenny ran off to find Jody. "She gets a little wound up sometimes. We don't get many visitors here. May I help you?"

"Evie?" the ginger giant asked as he stared at my face, trying to place me as someone he knew.

"Benji?" I answered. There could only be one man that tall, that red haired, and with those same, baby blue eyes…except Jody himself. "If you're not Benji, then Jody has a lot of 'splaining to do!" I joked in a Desi Arnaz, Cuban accent.

I walked up to him and shook his hand heartily. "Come in and have a seat," I said, then led the stunned couple up the porch steps. "I'll get some fresh water. I'll bet you're both thirsty."

The two of them appeared to be both overheated and in shock. I'd wait until after they got something to drink for proper introductions. I pointed to the kitchen chairs and table, grabbed the ewer and excused myself, and was headed down the steps to the well when I heard it.

"Eeee haaaaahhh!"

I followed the squealing noise with my eyes and saw that Jenny was on her way back from her scouting mission. The hyperactive, blonde bomber had found her grandpa, grannie, and infant uncles and was leading the fast-paced parade back to the house. Jody was taking long strides to keep up with her running pace. He held Wee Julian to his shoulder with a wide, one-handed clutch. Sarah was following behind him at a fast clip—half-running—and carrying Raymond in the same snuggled position but using both hands.

Benji stepped out of the house to watch their enthusiastic approach. He hesitantly walked down the steps and into the yard to meet them, unsure if he was dreaming or awake.

Jody didn't need to be told who the male stranger in his front yard was. He shook his head in astonishment, unbridled tears now flowing down his cheeks. He shifted his infant son to the right side then reached out and grabbed Benji to him, squeezing as hard as he dared with his left arm. Benji reached both arms around his grandfather's back and sobbed, "Yer here, yer still here."

"Aye, I am, and so is yer Grannie." Jody and Benji untangled their arms, but stayed close together, turning around as one to see Sarah rushing towards them, her beaming face streaked with shiny tears.

Benji sighed deeply at the sight of her, his eyes weeping anew. He moved into her, bent his knees, and picked up both Grannie and the bundle of baby she was clutching close to the middle of her chest. "Ye have no idea how happy I am right now," he laughed, crying at the same time with joy.

I watched the greeting and was overcome myself. I looked over and saw my babies contentedly playing 'who's got the rag dog' game in their oversized playpen under the family tree, tugging or biting on a cloth leg or ear of the oversized, remnant stuffed, quilted spaniel. Then I looked back at the porch and saw that someone was left out in this reunion: Benji's traveling companion. The beautiful and statuesque ebony woman was watching the reunion with a reserved smile, her glow reflecting her happiness, even if her reticent posture did not.

"Hi," I said as I approached her. "I take it your Benji's friend?" I asserted and asked at the same time.

She dipped her head briefly in acknowledgment but didn't look me in the eye.

"Would you like to come in for that water now?" *I didn't wait for an answer, but turned and walked into the house, hoping she would follow me. She did, but only came in as far as the doorway. I poured a cup of water and handed it her.*

"They'll be in shortly," I said to start the conversation. "If I know anything about these men, it's that they'll be in for, shall we say, liquid refreshment soon? And I don't mean water. Come to think of it, we might want to go to the springhouse right now." I grabbed a basket out of the corner and saluted her with it. "I'll need this for the refreshments. Come on," I said brightly, as I gently touched her elbow in an invitation to follow me.

Jane tensed at the familiar touch of someone she didn't know. She looked down at the smallish, dark haired, perky young woman. The nice lady must have felt her arm jerk away in reflex, but she hadn't responded to it. She acted as if they were good friends, peers at least, and that performing a chore together was normal. Maybe she was like Benji, from the future.

"Evie?" Jane asked tentatively, although she was pretty sure that was her name. If this really was Evie, the time traveling fairy, she wouldn't mind that a slave had been so bold as to speak without being spoken to first.

"Oh, I'm sorry, I didn't introduce myself. Yes, I am Evie, Benji's, um, kin," I explained awkwardly.

I didn't know how much she knew about us and didn't want to divulge any big secrets to someone I had just met, especially someone who I was sure had been born and raised in the 18th century. I had noticed the array of fresh and old lash scars on her back, and her posture was definitely one of servitude.

"We don't believe in slaves around here," I added softly, as if I was sharing a family secret. I returned to a normal speaking tone as we continued our walk. "You must be a good person or Benji wouldn't have brought you here. Although, I think it was rather rude of him not to introduce you right away."

"I think he was a bit distracted," Jane said in an apologetic tone. "He's been talking about finding his grandfather ever since I met him. Oh, I'm sorry; my name is Jane," she added with a nod of introduction.

"Glad to meet you, Jane," I said and paused in our trek to greet her face to face. Rather than attempt an awkward handshake with my right, basket-holding hand, I patted her on the back with a 'welcome to the family' gesture with my free, left hand. Jane winced at my touch, then sucked in air, stifling a yelp.

"I'm sorry; did I hurt you?" I asked.

"Oh, I'm just a little tender on the right side. I have a wound and it's not completely healed. I'll be fine. Benji tended to it, and I'm sure he did a good job. He did say his Grannie is a healer…" she began, then bit back any more words. Maybe she was speaking too much, she thought. These people were Benji's family, but they might not feel the same as he did. She didn't want to embarrass or shame him.

I noticed Jane biting her lip right after she had spoken. I realized she was between social castes, and even though I had whispered that we didn't believe in slaves, she still didn't know her place. "Are you okay? I mean, you can speak your mind around here. Your opinion is just as valid as anyone else's."

Jane didn't remark on my comment, but did look me in the eye and raised her eyebrows to ask, 'Are you sure?' I replied with a grin and a nod. She then gave me a warm smile that said 'Thank you.'

We continued walking to the springhouse in a comfortable silence. When we got to our destination, I made sure I had a good look at her face then asked, "How much did Benji tell you about me?"

Jane grinned. She liked this lady. She was just as open and comfortable as Benji. "I didn't let Benji know that I understood English when we, we first met. He talked a lot about his life and family and I listened. Then I slipped and forgot to play ignorant. He found out that I could understand him without his silly hand language." Jane smiled as she moved her left hand in rapid, nonsense gestures, mimicking the made-up sign language Benji had employed. "I think he was a little *scarrit* when he realized that he had been telling me all about," Jane eyes squinted as she tried to recall the right words, "planes, trains, and automobiles."

I nodded and grinned in acknowledgment that I knew what she was speaking of. "Did he tell you how he got here?" I asked, looking at her for illumination.

"Yes. He said he was born here," Jane replied simply and smiled courteously.

I guess my face showed the discomfort and frustration that I was feeling because Jane added softly, "But he did tell me that he left here and then came back. He said he followed you here from, well, *you know when*. You do know *when* you're from, don't you?"

Jane didn't want to give anything away and was being cautious which I appreciated. Evidently, Benji hadn't planned on telling her his time traveler status. I bet there was a very interesting story about how those two met, but that wasn't important now. What we needed was to bring in the cheese and cold ale for the men.

"Yep, I'm a fairy," I boasted with a smirk of pride. Jane laughed at the remark, or at least how I had said it, and brought her left hand up to cover her chuckling mouth. "What, am I too big to be a fairy?" I asked lightly, grinning at my enchanting new acquaintance.

"No, I don't think so. I mean, I don't know. It's just that I didn't know there were women fairies. I thought Benji was the only one."

"Uh, no," I said somberly. "Although, I suggest you never ask anyone if he or she is a fairy. It's pretty much a secret. There are a few of us here, but not everyone in the family knows about the other ones. My daughter Jenny's too young to know about it. I mean, I could probably tell her, and she would accept it and would be fine knowing about it, but I'm afraid she wouldn't keep her mouth shut. Loose lips sink ships and all of that stuff." I saw the confused look and reworded my concern. "I'm afraid she'd tell the wrong person and then someone might think we, I, was a witch or from the devil." I shook my head, recalling both Sarah's close call with witch hunters in Scotland and James and Leah's close call with Dick Short.

"You're too pretty to be a witch," Jane said, then gasped in embarrassment at her familiarity.

"Thank you," I said. "But I'll bet you're a smart woman and know that looks are deceiving. Pretty is as pretty does, right?"

Jane nodded in answer. Her head felt odd with the movement. Her eyes felt like they were trying to fall out. She brought the back of her hand up to her lips. Yes, she had a fever.

I saw Jane check her temperature by pressing her lips to the back of her hand. I could tell by the momentary shock in her eyes that she had detected a fever. Her wound was probably infected.

"Come on. I'll carry this." I quickly threw a big cheese and as many bottles of ale as I thought I could manage into the basket. "Let's get back to the house. You need rest and water. I want Sarah to look at your owie."

I looked up at her to make sure she had heard me and grinned at the dumbfounded look on her face. "Owie is what I call a wound. You have a fever, don't you?" Jane nodded. "Smart woman, you know to check up on yourself. Hold on to my shoulder. I don't want you to fall down."

Benji looked away from the glowing faces of his grandparents to see Jane and Evie walking toward the house from what must be the springhouse, a small building on the backside of the barn. Evie was carrying a basket, and Jane was a step behind, her hand on Evie's shoulder for support. "Excuse me," he said, "I…I…oh, Lord," he whispered in self-admonishment. How could he have forgotten about Jane?

"Looks like the lad forgot about his lady friend," Jody said to Sarah as he put one arm around her shoulder, guiding her to the house.

"By the look of shame on his face, she's more than just a friend." Sarah looked up to Jody to make sure he knew what she was implying.

Jody's eyes widened in surprise as he realized what she was insinuating. "A slave?" he whispered in disbelief.

Sarah shrugged. "Love is colorblind, and he *was* reared in the 20th and," she inhaled deeply as she said the exotic words, "21st centuries. Skin color isn't really much of a consideration in modern times."

"Aye, it may not be *then*, but *now* is where the two of them are today." Jody said dejectedly, "I'm glad to have him here, but if what he feels for her is one tenth of what I feel fer ye, they're gonna have a rough go of it in 1782 North Carolina."

"I'm sure they'll be okay. Just look at what we went through, and we turned out fine."

"Ach, finer that fine." Jody swiftly raised Wee Julian in the air, the gesture that always elicited a giggle from him. He smiled and said, "Although, I wouldna choose to do any of the bad parts over again. If I had a choice, I woulda passed on jest about everythin'."

"Passing up helping those in need is not your style, Jody Pomeroy. You'd do it all over again, I'm sure you would."

"Weel, ye would be right if my motivation was to have and keep ye and our family and friends safe. Aye, I'd do it all over again, but," Jody looked up to heaven, "I'm not volunteerin' fer any new tasks, Lord."

"And, our little family keeps getting bigger and bigger, too." Sarah looked over at the tall couple plus Evie, now on the porch. "Benji has himself a woman. Whether she is his *mate* already or not, I could tell by the look on his face when he looked at her, he wants her to be."

"Aye, I think it's *not* though. I dinna think he'd have relations with a woman who wasna his wife. By the looks of the scars on her back, she's a slave and dinna come back here with him. Aye, I'll wager she's from this time."

"Good Lord, Jody!" Sarah exclaimed. "Of course, she's from 'now.' Why in the hell would he bring a black woman *back* here to this time?"

Jody shrugged his non-baby laden shoulder at Sarah, then shifted Wee Julian, turning him around to face Mommy. "Here, ye take him back to the house, and I'll catch a couple of chickens fer supper. Or maybe three—Jenny was right. Benji really is huge, and his lady friend isna much smaller."

***

Benji bounded up the steps behind Jane and me. "Oh, Janie, I am so sorry I forgot to introduce ye to everyone. They'll all be here in a minute. Can ye forgive me?"

Jane nodded 'yes' then added a weak, "Of course." Her head kept nodding, as if she was falling asleep, but her words were finished. Her neck snapped taut as she came to with a start.

"Benji, go get your Grannie," I said. "I want her to check Jane's wound. She has a fever and probably an infection."

"Yes, ma'am," Benji said. He rushed out the door, and nearly knocked down his baby-laden grandmother as she came up the steps. "Whoa, there," he said as he steadied her. "Evie says she needs ye to look after Jane."

"Sarah, this is Jane," I said in introduction. "She has an owie, and I think it's infected. Do you want her in the surgery?"

"Yes. Here, Benji, take your uncles. Evie, help her get settled on the examination table, please. Glad to meet you, Jane. Come on in here and tell me where your owie is." Sarah smiled at the word owie. She noticed the big woman had grinned when I said it, so repeated it. Jane smiled for her when she said it, too.

"What do I do with them?" Benji asked as he lifted one then the other baby-bearing arm.

"Take them for a walk," Sarah said flatly. "Let them show you around the place. We've only been here a few years, and it's not as nice as our place on The Point, but it has potential."

"Will ye be okay, Janie?" Benji asked as he walked over to her, now seated on the long, tall table.

"She'll be fine," Sarah said, and shooed him then me out the door. The doctor was in and we were out.

Benji did what his Grannie told him – took his uncles for a walk. They were very small – he didn't know how to estimate babies' ages since he hadn't been around too many – but they were old enough to hold up their heads. "Uncles," he said in amazement. He thought his Grannie was too old to have babies, but evidently not. "I guess I'll have to wait to find out yer names. Until then, yer Uncle One and yer Uncle Two." He continued his stroll toward the barn, chatting with the little red headed boys who were enthralled with his voice and face.

And then he saw her: the little blond girl who had announced their arrival. "What are ye doing there: looking for gold?" asked Benji, although it was pretty obvious: she was drawing with a pointed stick in the fine, silty dirt.

"I'm making pictures," she said with pride. "See, that's you and her and that's me. Who *are* you? I know you're kin, but am I allowed to know how? Grandpa and Grannie and Mommy and Daddy don't tell me everything because they say I talk too much. But, I just want to know who you two are. Is that okay?"

"I'm Benji. Your Grandpa is my Grandpa, too. My mother – Mona or Ramona – is his daughter." Benji wanted to ask her relationship to Grandpa but figured that she'd probably tell him in a minute or two. She seemed to bubble over with enthusiasm with whatever she said or did.

"My Daddy is Grandpa's son, and so are Raymond," she pointed to the child in Benji's right arm, "and Wee Julian," and pointed to the left. "Raymond is named after Grandpa's father Raymond, and so is your Mommy. Wee Julian is named after my other Grandpa, Grandpa Julian, but I call him Poppi. The other babies, that's my brothers Judah and Leo, and my little sister Wren—her real name is Danielle—but my, my other kin," she blushed, unsure if she should say more about Scout, her other kin, "gave her that name. Anyway," she said as she took a deep breath to continue the family genealogy, "Those babies call him Poppi, so now I do, too. And Evie is my Mommy and she's Grannie's sister, sort of, not by blood, but they say sister's close enough. They get along real good even if Grannie's her mother-in-law, too. And Leah is my sister, and she and James—that's her husband—live a little ways down that road," she turned to indicate the dusty path that led to an odd shaped abode, "and they have a little girl, Bibb Elizabeth Melbourne," she crowed the name with pride. "She's my niece, and she's *exactly* the same age as my uncles 'cause they were all born on the same day. So, who's the lady who came with you?" she asked, suddenly changing the theme and tone of voice, obviously suspicious of the tall, dark woman.

"She's Jane, my fiancée. That means we're going to get married. Soon, I hope," he added softly, although he knew she could hear him.

"Oh," was her short reply, as if his answer was enough; now let's talk about something else. She picked up a wide, narrow slat of split firewood and wiped through the dirt, erasing her first picture, preparing her earthen slate for a new one. He watched silently as she drew another, very much like the first one, this time adding in what looked like a baby.

"Who's that?" he asked, as he sat down next to her, using his outstretched uncle-toting arms as leverage to sit down on his bottom with a grace that didn't see possible for such a large man burdened with babies.

"That's *your* baby," she announced with pride, then added. "You don't know about him yet, but I still drew him. If I had real paper and coloring sticks—Mommy calls them crayons—then I could draw you better. I could make Jane black, and make your hair and the baby's hair red, and mine yellow, and, and my dress green, and Jane's blue… Hey, are you my uncle or my cousin?" she asked, quickly changing topics again.

"Weel, since yer father and my mother are brother and sister that makes us cousins. But, if yer mother is my great aunt then I guess," Benji counted on his fingers, looked up as he tried to account for the lineage, then huffed in defeat and declared, "that's why it's easier to jest say we're all kin, aye?"

"Aye!" Jenny announced proudly in agreement, then bent back to her drawing, adding a cloud to the imagery's background. "It's kinda hard to tell who everyone is because this stick isn't as good as a pen, and

I don't have any paper. Mommy said that paper costs a lot, and that we can't make it, but that her sister-in-law, that's your mother, knew how to make paper. She made some before she left, and we still have a few pieces of it, but they're special. Mommy lets me hold onto one of them sometimes. But, I have to wash my hands *real* good because she doesn't want them to get dirty. They smell good, too, because your mother put flower petals in the mast. I think that's what she called it."

Benji interrupted, "That's mash, not mast. I think I remember how she made it. Do ye want to make some paper?"

"Uh, huh," she chimed, her head bobbing rapidly. "Yes, yes, yes!" Jenny screamed as she sprang up like a jack-in-the-box, continuing to jump up and down. "Can we do it today? Huh, please, please, puh-leeze..."

Benji looked around and didn't see any tasks that needed to be done. Being a guest at Grandpa's was nice, and he hoped he would be allowed to help, but everything appeared to be caught up right now. "I canna see why not. First, I'll have to talk to yer Grannie and see if she has some of the chemicals we need. Then, we have to get some old rags and sawdust, and maybe we can throw in some flower petals, too. But we dinna do that part until we're almost finished."

"What's chemicals?" Jenny asked, as she picked up a rotted piece of wood, examining its potential as sawdust.

"Well, that's like askin' 'what's food?' Both can be a wide variety of *stuff*. Chemicals can be what ye use to wash clothes, or to spray for bugs, or etch glass. Usually, they're in a solution, but they can be solid, too."

Jenny's eyes widened. "I know how to wash clothes, but I don't know what etch glass is, and why do you want to spray bugs?"

"Poison; ye can spray a poison on bugs so they die, but we dinna want to do that. The bairns might get a hold of it and it would hurt them. Etchin' glass is done with an acid, somethin' that burns even though it's a liquid, like water, but ye canna, or shouldna, drink it. Gee, Jenny, I guess I shoulda paid more attention in school. Science wasna my favorite class, ye ken."

Jenny dusted off her hands on the back of her skirt and reached for her uncle. "Here, I'll take Raymond." Benji handed her the dozing child and stood up, letting her lead the way.

"Now dinna be botherin' Grannie right now. She's busy doctorin' Janie. We have to keep these guys busy. We canna do the paper makin' until later, maybe tomorrow. Fer now, why dinna ye show me where ye keep yer animals."

Benji was glad to have her around for a distraction. With her cheerful chattering, he wasn't dwelling on what would happen with him and Janie now that they were here. It wouldn't be an easy life being married to a black woman in this time—if it were even possible. He'd waited too long to get here to his grandfather to give up right away and go back; that is if he could even find a way to go back to the future. But he'd waited just as long to find a woman to love and care about. Hopefully, he'd be able to have his wife and life here, too.

Jenny led the way to the little goat shed, holding her Uncle Raymond with finesse, almost as if he were a part of her body. "Shush," she admonished when he started to get fussy. "We have to let your Mommy work. She'll feed you when she's done working on Cousin Jane." She turned her attention back to Benji. "These are my goats. Leah named them Sarah P and Todd. She calls them that because they do whatever they want to do. You can't make them mind you. But, they're nice and follow me wherever I go because I love them, and feed them, and really, they're smarter than a horse and prettier, too. They're still babies, but they'll get lots bigger. Poppi, that's my Grandpa Julian, and José, that's his partner, gave them to me. I'm supposed to take care of them, but they said it's okay if Daddy or Grandpa, that's Grandpa Jody, help me. They're Angora goats, and when they're older—like maybe next spring—Poppi will help me cut off their hair. José knows how to spin the hair; I mean the wool, into yarn. Mommy knows how to crochet real good, and she showed me how, too. I even made a hat, but it's too hot to wear it now. Hey, are you gonna live here?" Jenny asked, suddenly distracted from her dissertation on the evolution of the cap she had made.

"Aye, I'd like to," Benji said over the squalls of wee Uncle Raymond. "Are ye sure he'll be okay? He looks like he's ready to eat his fist right off his wrist!" He knew the baby was probably fine, but he didn't want to talk about his future housing arrangements with the young lady. His cousin was charming, but the two of them wouldn't be able to solve the dilemma of whether he and Jane would be able to stay here and be married. He'd rather save the emotional investment to spend with his grandparents or the other adults in the family. He was beginning to feel like Wee Raymond: ready to scream in frustration. "I'm gonna take him to Grannie. Ye mind Wee Julian fer me, aye?"

"Okay," Jenny replied brightly, then turned her attention to the quiet twin. "Do you want me to draw a picture of you?" She sat down and prepared a lap for the boy next to her dusty drawing area. "I'll draw you when you're all growed up and a doctor like Grannie."

Benji took long strides to the house, singing a medley of Beatles tunes to Wee Raymond on the way. "They're gonna put me in the movies," he began, then shuddered. "Oops, wrong song, lad. Ye dinna want to be in any movies, at least the kind I was in," he groaned. "Okay, 'Help, I need somebody; help, not just anybody. Help, I need a milky booby to feed my empty belly…help!" Benji improvised as he climbed the steps to the house.

"My uncle," he said again. "Weel, at least I ken where I get my urges from. It seems that age dinna make a difference to either of them. I sure do look like yer Da—too much like him," Benji said to his young uncle. As soon as he stopped talking, though, the little boy started fussing again. "So, how does a man sixty-years-old look so young, and his wife have a baby when she's even older than he is? Weel, Raymond, did he tell ye? Do ye think he'll tell me? Do ye think it matters? Weel, neither do I," he said in resignation. It was a mystery that didn't make a difference to anyone.

Raymond started screaming again, this time Benji's words unable to quiet him. "Time to find yer mama," Benji said as he reluctantly opened the surgery door a crack.

Hopefully, Grannie was done with the doctoring so he could be close to Janie and help her with the healing—or at least feel like he was helping. She hadn't been in his life even a week, but now, being away from her for less than an hour, it felt as if it had been half a lifetime. Yes, he'd move wherever he needed to be with Janie, but as her husband. He'd settle for nothing less. She was worth it. And, by the way the rest of his family had received her, they felt she was family, too.

***

"Now, where is your owie?" Sarah asked with a big smile, hoping to get another one in return.

Jane beamed back at her. Sarah was Benji's grandmother and

another very nice lady. She was probably a fairy, too, since she was treating her like a person, not a slave. Jane lifted up her right arm and pointed to the site of the wound with her left hand. "Do you want me to take this off?" she asked, referring to her sarong.

"Well, it would make the examination much, much easier," Sarah joked, then offered her a hand to help her stand.

Jane stood up and Sarah followed her height with her eyes. "How tall *are* you?" she asked in awe before she could think.

Jane put her left hand on top of her head then pulled it straight out in front of herself. "So big," she joked. "Taller than most men, but not Benji. He's this much taller than me," she said, and indicated a three-inch span with her index finger and thumb. She began unwrapping her sarong but kept it close to her belly to hide her lower body. She was used to wearing clothes now and was beginning to feel bashful.

Sarah removed the ribcage bandage made from the same cloth as Jane's Polynesian-style dress. "Good Lord," she gasped at the sight of the vicious gash sewn together neatly with what appeared to be dental floss. "What happened here?"

"I was stabbed in the ribs, and the knife blade broke off in me. Benji pulled it out with his *Leatherman*," she said, making sure she said the word correctly. "He cleaned it out and put on some *antibiotic* and stitched it with *tooth floss*."

"Dental floss," Sarah corrected. "He did a fine job, but by the looks of this, part of the blade is still in there. That's why it's swelled up and infected. The body is rejecting the foreign matter." Sarah saw the confused look on her patient's face and clarified, "I'm going to have to open it up and get the fragment out. It's going to hurt, but we have to do it now or you'll never get better, or maybe even worse."

Jane's eyes opened wide at 'even worse' then nodded and said, "Yes, please, go ahead and do what you need to do. But, um, do you have any *Ibuprofen*?"

"Yes, as a matter of fact, I do. Wait, you know what Ibuprofen is?" Sarah asked, dumbfounded.

"Benji brought some with him," Jane said. "Can I lie down for this? My head feels too heavy."

"Yes, lie down on your left side and get comfortable. I'll scrub you up, and then take out his stitches. But first, I'll give you a couple of

Ibuprofen. I'll let it start working before I start poking around."

Sarah brought Jane a couple of the little brown pills and a cup of water. Jane carefully put them at the back of her tongue, then hurriedly gulped down the water, grateful that they went down on the first try and that she hadn't gagged. She smiled. She was glad she knew what a pill was and how to take one. Even though she could tolerate pain, she didn't like it.

Jane settled onto the long, elevated table next to the window, while Sarah assembled the tools she would need onto a tray. The healer then went to her basin and scrubbed her hands for what Jane thought was long enough to wash off the skin. She finally finished and came back to the table, skin intact, and put a clean cloth along each side of the wound.

"Now, try to relax. I don't have anything to numb you," Sarah said, watching her patient to make sure she understood. Jane's face went blank at the word 'numb.' "Deaden or completely stop the pain; I don't have anything like ice or Lidocaine or… The Ibuprofen will help but won't stop this from hurting. Please, don't move. Try to think of a happy thought," she added.

Jane's body went limp as her feelings of peace and security relaxed her. Her happy thought was Benji, and he was outside, visiting his Grandfather. And, his Grannie was in here, taking care of her wound, treating her like a white woman. A rich, white woman, she corrected. "Is this good enough?" Jane asked, very comfortable with her many happy thoughts.

"You're doing fantastic," Sarah praised, as she dabbed some of Leah's antibacterial soap on a square of clean cloth. "We'll get this done as soon as possible. I'm sure everyone wants to meet Benji's, um, Benji's friend."

Jane was a model patient. "Now I want you to take a couple of slow, deep breaths. You've been helping me out by breathing shallowly, but I want you to tank up with oxygen." Sarah saw the confused look on Jane's face and said, "Just breathe for me. I'm not ready to probe yet, but it's going to be uncomfortable when I do. Once I find all the fragments, I can sew you back up. Then you shouldn't have any more problems."

Jane did the breathing as instructed while Sarah swabbed her with the Betadine solution. "Okay, this is the most uncomfortable part. Hold very, very still and no more deep breaths, okay?"

"Okay," Jane whispered and sunk into the hard bed.

After several minutes of probing, pulling, and producing sharp pains for her patient, Sarah grasped the shard and pronounced, 'Got it!" She flushed the site with a antiseptic solution, blotted away the excess blood and pus, then said, "Now all I have to do is to sew you back together." She grabbed the sterile suture and bent to the task. "shit," she whispered just as she was ready for the first stitch.

"What's wrong?" Jane asked softly, trying not to show with her voice the fear she felt.

"I'm leaking; leaking milk," Sarah said in frustration, looking down at the wet spots on the front of her blouse. "It's time to feed one baby, at least, but he'll just have to wait until I'm done here."

Just then, Benji came to the door, peeking into the room with a squalling baby on his shoulder. "Ye did say this is my uncle, aye? I mean," he said, not waiting for her answer, "I think yer son is hungry, and I'm not equipped to feed him."

Sarah took a deep breath of annoyance, not knowing whether to scold her grandson—couldn't he see she was busy—or should she suggest he ask Evie if she could play wet nurse.

"Can I hold him?" Jane asked.

"You can't move," Sarah said sternly, then saw the sadness on Jane's face. "But, if Benji will put him next to you, and you don't move, then yes, he can lie down with you. But, if either one of you moves while I'm stitching, then you, young man," she said in mock scolding of Benji, "need to take him for another walk until I'm done here, okay?"

"Yes, Grannie," Benji said obediently, and walked up to his prone and slightly bloody fiancée. He gently lay Wee Raymond down alongside her, then took a step back to admire the sight. She looked so right with a baby lying next to her.

The infant boy immediately hushed at seeing the strange new face, forgetting to resume his crying. Instead, he grinned, cooed, and patted her chest, knocking at the sterile drape Sarah had around her work area. Jane's left arm was crooked up next to her body. She moved her hand out from under her chin and was able to hold onto his little fist with her long fingers. "He's very handsome."

"He likes you," Sarah said as she appraised her new situation. "Are you going to be able to control him with that one hand?"

"Aye," Jane said, totally relaxed at the proximity of the red-haired baby boy. "Is this what Benji looked like when he was a baby?"

"Very much so," Sarah said. "Benji, why don't you see if your grandfather needs some help?"

"Yes, ma'am. I willna be far," he said to Jane, then walked out the door backwards, a big smile on his face at the sight of her holding a baby.

"Now, just a little more pain, and then you're home free," Sarah said to Jane.

Jane didn't move a muscle other than the ones that focused her eyes. She peered up at Sarah, asking her wordlessly what she meant. "Oh, 'home free' is a phrase where I'm from. It means were out of the woods, no longer in danger…" Sarah babbled, finally deciding it was better to shut up then continue the awkward definition.

Sarah felt a miniscule twitch from Jane, but other than that, both she and Wee Raymond were quiet and content. Jane hummed a little song to the baby and both of them—all three of them counting Sarah—were soothed by it.

"Did he fall asleep?" Sarah asked as she piled all of the surgical tools onto the tray table. She took them to the sink; she'd clean them later.

"No, he's awake. I don't think he was too hungry; I think he just wanted to suck. Can I move now?"

Sarah was back to washing her hands again. "Yes, you can move, but don't sit up too quickly. I don't want you passing out, that is, fainting."

Jane stuck her finger into Wee Raymond's mouth and broke the suction. A little bit of bluish white fluid slobbered out as she did. She quickly wiped it away, trying to mask her shock at seeing it: mother's milk! She grasped him with her good left hand and brought him up over the left shoulder, rubbing his back with her pinky.

"Suck!" Sarah squawked as she realized what Jane had said. "He'd do that? I mean, Leah and Evie have nursed him for me a few times; he's comfortable with them, but you didn't just have a baby, did you?"

Jane shook her head quickly. "No, I've never had a baby. I'm sorry; I didn't think I was doing anything wrong." Jane sniffed and bit her bottom lip. She was only trying to help calm him. And besides, it felt so good.

"No, no, you didn't do anything wrong," Sarah soothed. She thought for a moment, then added, "Well, I guess you've already been acknowledged as one of the family by the youngest member. If you don't mind me asking, what is your relationship to Benji?"

Benji stepped forward. He hadn't spoken and wasn't sure if Grannie knew that he had come back into the room, but now he could lay claim to her. "She's my fiancée. We're to be marrit as soon as I, or ye, or Grandpa, or someone, anyone, can figure out *how*. And," Benji added with a comical full body twitch, "the sooner the better."

Benji felt a firm hand clasp him on his shoulder. "See, what did I tell ye?" Jody said to Sarah, "I told ye he'd wait. Now," he added with a sour tone, "we'll have to figure out how to get it done right."

"Excuse me," I said as I walked into the now crowded surgery. "I think we have more family showing up. Leah, James, and Bibby just arrived. You have more kin to meet! So, Benji, after you do the meet and greet, would you help your grandfather pluck those chickens? Yer long fingers have to be good fer somethin' besides pickin' yer nose, aye?" I mocked.

"Come on, lad. A few introductions then we can leave the ladies be. We'll go out and do the women's work of pluckin' chickens while they chatter," Jody said as he herded Benji through the door. "Uh, I dinna need to give ye the talk about the facts of life, as Evie calls them, do I?" Jody asked with a mix of mirth and apprehension once they were out of earshot of the others.

"Ach, no," Benji began, then changed his mind as soon as the first words had escaped his lips. "My father did have a talk with me a long, long time ago. Now, which parts go together?" he asked in jest, then burst into laughter, smacking his grandfather on the back. "But he never did tell me how ye make a bairn..." he continued with a grin.

James had just finished unhitching the horse when he saw the two men heading to the barn. He walked up to join them, very curious about the man who looked like Jody on steroids.

Leah and a squalling Bibby were already out of the wagon and on their way to the house. Jody paused and introduced his grandson to the pair.

"Oh, so *yer* Leah!" Benji exclaimed. "Ye sure look like yer mother.

289

Ye ken, I missed ye by this much," he said, as he put his thumb and index finger apart by a scant quarter of an inch. "I meant to come back with ye last year. But I'm sure it was meant to be that we dinna travel together. I met, and got to be good friends with, yer brother-in-law, Billy, and his mother—Bibb the First, would that be? Ye did say this was Wee Bibb?" He stroked the fussy, bald-headed, little girl under her chin. The child thrashed her head side to side in frustration, trying to decide if she wanted to be tickled and cajoled by the nice man, or scream because she was in a poopy diaper.

"Yes, this is Bibb Elizabeth Melbourne, and she is in desperate need of a clean clout. So, if you'll excuse us, I'm sure we'll get a chance to talk more later. But!" she said before he could turn to leave, "how are they: Bibb and Billy?"

"Last I saw them, Bibb, Billy, *and* Peter were all doing fine," he said, making sure she understood that Peter and Billy were still a happy couple. "And no cancer," he added, realizing that that was probably what she had been referring to.

"Great, glad to hear it," she said over the now screaming baby Bibby. "Later, dude," she called back familiarly over her shoulder. He seemed like a very nice man.

***

"Mom, where can I put her down to change her?" Leah asked when she walked into the kitchen, forgetting even to say hello to her mother. "She's a mess and could use a butt bath if you have any water warmed already. Oh, hi," Leah said in surprise when she saw Sarah and an unknown, very exotic looking woman come in from the surgery.

"Jane, this is my eldest daughter, Leah. Leah, this is Jane, Benji's fiancée. Benji's your sister-in-law Mona's oldest son, or only son. I don't know if she had any more or not. Oh, and Jane knows about me," I explained, referring to my status as a woman from a future time.

Jane would probably figure out on her own that Leah also wasn't from 'now' after talking to her for about ten seconds. This was my hint to her that she didn't need to be subservient around her either.

"Glad to meet you, Jane. And, this is my stinky butt daughter, Bibb Elizabeth Melbourne. Her father is out there with Jody and Benji. I just barely met him, but," Leah shook her head, "we've sure heard all about him. I don't think there's an antic or caper that boy ever did that we

290

haven't heard about at least three times. Of course, he's a man now, but he sure had a colorful first five or six years living near Grannie and Grandpa. Mom, a little help here, please."

I brought a pan of warm water, a rag, and a clean clout and held Bibby Liz's legs while Leah did the dirty work. Leah wrapped the clout through her daughter's legs then secured it with a shiny diaper pin with a pink plastic duck-shaped cap. I looked up and saw Jane's eyes blink in shock at the colorful apparatus. "Real handy little items," I explained, then let the subject drop.

"How old is she?" Jane asked, as she admired my granddaughter.

"She's the same age as her uncles. They were all born within an hour of each other. Now that was a *very* busy day," I said, bobbing my head in recall. "At least, she's easy to tell apart from them, with or without the diaper," I said as I rubbed her bald head. "Yep, she'll have dark hair when she finally gets it. Just like her mother, me, and my mother before me."

I watched as Jane lifted up her head and looked out the door. She was watching Benji talk with Jenny, my blondie. "That's Jenny, my adopted daughter. My other children are under the tree, tearing apart their dog." I saw her eyes open wide at the remark. Those big, dark orbs didn't make a sound, but they sure said a lot. "It's a toy dog; a rag stuffed doll that they don't ever seem to tire of. Yes, I really did break the mold with those three: all red headed."

"Three—at the same time?" Jane asked.

"Yup, I'm a tough old broad," I said, then looked over at Leah. "Tougher and older than I look," I added with a squint that said, 'Just believe it; don't question it, okay?'

"I still say you're pretty," Jane answered with a blush that, although I couldn't see in her skin, I could tell by her demeanor.

"So, what brings you and Benji here?" Leah asked without preamble as she settled back on the chaise, legs up and breast bared, to feed her voracious little vixen.

"Benji wanted to see his grandpa," Jane answered, "and…I…um, came along with him," she finished, looking back and forth in embarrassment.

I spared her a detailed explanation by announcing, "I'm sure Benji will tell us the whole story at dinner or whenever he's ready. I'm going to feed my little ones first, so anyone up to it, grab a baby, a biscuit, and I'll bring the noodles."

Jane helped me feed my three. I could see her fascination with their hair. "It's not common. I mean, red hair in white people is unpredictable unless both parents have red hair. If that's the case, their children will positively have red hair. Were you born in Africa?" I asked.

"I think so," she replied. "I know that my mother said I was a very small child when she came over on the boat. I didn't have any teeth yet. They let her keep me because I didn't need to eat food. She was suckling me. They said they wanted her to keep the milk coming. Um, wet nurses," she said as a question, as if she wasn't sure of the polite term, "were at a premium. I kept her milk coming in so I could stay with her. She was always feeding someone else's child," she said reflectively.

"I just asked because if you never had a white parent, you probably won't have any red-haired children with Benji, although, depending on whether there is a white parent in your children's spouses, you might have red headed grandchildren. I'm not an expert, but that's what I remember from school. It has to do with recessive genes, and, by the way, are you right-handed or left-handed?"

Jane looked down, turning over first one hand and then the other, confused at the question. Duh! She probably didn't know how to write—how rude of me. "Um, when you pick up a spoon or fork to eat with, which hand do you use?"

Jane reached down and picked up a twig with her left hand and held it like a spoon. She set it back down and picked it up with her right hand. "It feels better with this hand. I know I throw with the left hand," she grinned in recollection of her hidden assaults with rotten eggs when she was younger.

"Well, then there's a good chance you and Benji will have left-handed children. That's another recessive gene that kind of pops up, but it's not as predictable as red hair. And, they'll probably have brown eyes, but I think he'll like that. You have beautiful, expressive eyes."

Jane had never felt better. Benji wasn't here—he was still visiting with other family members—but the women were so kind. "So, where's their father?" Jane asked me, trying to, and succeeding at, overcoming her shyness.

"He's in town, but he should be back any time now. He's Jody's son and Sarah's stepson, but we don't use that four-letter word *step* around here." I saw the confused look on her face when I said, 'four-letter word.' "You see, we're all related, by blood, choice, or marriage around here. And, you will be, too. It's just easier to say kin. I mean, Sarah's my sister, sort of, and Wallace is Jody's son, but his biological mother died when he was one week old. Maybe later on, my husband, Wallace, will bring his," I whispered the word, "step," then continued, "father, Julian, here. He reared Wallace. Now that my husband's a father too, Julian and Jody are both considered the grandfathers to our children; no distinction is needed or desired as to whose blood goes through whose body."

"So, Sarah is your sister, sort of, and Leah is your daughter, and those are your babies, and Jenny is adopted, and Benji is your…" she asked by not finishing the sentence.

"He's my nephew which means that you'll be my niece. And that little blond bullet over there, bending his ear, is his cousin, your cousin. I'll bet you never thought you'd have a blond cousin, did you?" I laughed.

"I never thought I'd ever have any cousin, or a husband," she said, then started to waver, even though she was seated.

"Here, drink more water, and hand me that baby. You need to lie down."

"Oh, I'm fine," Jane replied, although she did pass Judah to me and leaned back against the tree.

"Drink," I said as I gave her my cup. Her eyes flashed fear at taking a drink from my vessel. "What, do you think I have cooties?" I asked. "The only germs I have are good germs, here," I insisted.

Jane took a long drink then handed back the empty cup. "I still think I'm dreaming, but I don't want to wake up. I like this," she moved her left hand around to indicate everything around her, "and these nice people. Is it always like this?"

"Uh, no, sometimes it gets scary," I said as I recalled the incident the year before with Captain Asshole MacLeod, knives, threats, and assorted mayhem and bullets. "We've been through some very rough and dangerous times, and I agree that this, my dear, is as good as it gets. Good food, good company, a healthy family, nice weather…gee, pinch me; I think I'm dreaming, too," I said with a laugh.

Just then, James, Benji, and Jody walked up to join the ladies and babies. "Are ye sure they're my uncles?" Benji asked as he bent over to pick up Raymond. "They look a wee small. And how old are ye now, Grandpa? Ye look to be about my age. Grannie, yer lookin' mighty fine for an elderly lady."

"My wife, yer Grannie, is not an elderly lady, she's, she's…" Jody fumbled for words that didn't sound harsh to describe his mate. He certainly wasn't going to explain in mixed company that their dosing a year earlier with the Fountain of Youth tonic had not only rewound their biological clocks, it had brought Sarah out of menopause, acted as a fertility drug, and allowed her to have a perfect pregnancy and deliver twins at just over sixty years of chronological age.

"How about an older woman?" I suggested. "Being older is fine but being elderly sounds gray and wrinkled. And Sarah, you are definitely not wrinkled, and the gray just highlights your brown hair. Although," I said as I reached over and moved the tips of my fingers through the curls around her ears, "I don't see much for gray hairs."

Sarah looked a little embarrassed at the revelation in front of her grandson that her gray hairs had disappeared. "It must be the henna and egg wash I used last time I shampooed my hair. I must have used too much henna."

"Um, yeah," I fumbled, "that must be what it is. And I hear that the henna won't wash out, that you'll have to wait for it to grow out. I guess you're *stuck* with it for a while."

I looked over and saw the men were in different states of eye rolling. Jody was relieved that the topic was over, James was enchanted with his mother-in-law's babbling and quick recovery, and Benji just wanted to talk about something other than women's hair care.

"Excuse me; I think I'm needed, um, somewhere else, I mean, elsewhere." I nodded to each of the men, picked up my skirts and walked as fast as I could without running to get away from there. Next time I'd shut up and just nod. At least if I dipped my head, my feet wouldn't find their way into my mouth!

Chapter 28: Back home with Grandpa (TGBF Ch 27)

I hid my embarrassment in the kitchen, which was a good place for me to be: dinner wasn't going to cook itself. Leah was tending to Bibby, Jenny was watching her little brothers and sister, and Jody was in charge of his young sons. Sarah had come inside to clean up her tools or whatever after performing the minor surgery, and Benji and Janie were taking care of each other. Everyone was basking in the joy of family and peace. All that was needed was a big dinner to make it a perfect day. That was going to be my job.

James had followed me inside, carrying the three plucked and cleaned chickens for our supper. "Well, since there are enough caregivers out there for all the babies and wounded, I figured I'd volunteer for KP duty. Do you need any potatoes peeled, corn husked, ale brewed?" he joked.

"Ale," I said, "I probably didn't bring in enough, but how about some snacks to go with it? Got any ideas?"

"I'm on it, and I'll bring back a little something special, too," he said, then headed out the door.

I grabbed three good-sized onions and a couple of garlic bulbs. I trimmed and peeled, then stuffed them into the heavily buttered and salted birds. I had three clay pots, one moderately chipped, but still serviceable, so employed them all. I scrubbed a dozen potatoes and threw them in a basket. I had baked bread the day before and held back a couple of loaves from the men, planning to make French toast. Well, it looked like we wouldn't be having that for tomorrow's brunch— sourdough pancakes would be fine – but I had the bread for dinner. I could glaze a couple dozen carrots in Jenny's maple syrup and bring out a rum-soaked fruitcake for dessert. I couldn't have accomplished a finer Thanksgiving dinner if I had worked on it all day.

Jenny popped up at my side at just the right time. Sometimes I think she has the sight, too. She and Leah both seem to anticipate my needs, even before I have them. "Daddy already has the fire going outside," she informed me, then asked, "Can I poke the potatoes into the ashes, huh? I know I was supposed to clean them out today, but I thought we still might need them for baking, so I left them for just one more day. But I promise I'll clean them out tomorrow, okay?"

"Yes, you may set the potatoes in, and yes, tomorrow will be fine, but let's put the clay pots in first. And leave room for the Dutch oven. I used some of your maple syrup for glazed carrots. It's a good thing we can cook outside. I don't think I could fit this many pots and potatoes in the hearth."

Jenny helped me ferry the food to the cook fire while the rest of the family visited. I shrugged off their offers of help. I had all I needed with Jenny, and then I let her go, too.

She sat next to her Grannie, both of them looking like spectators at a ping pong match, watching Benji speak, and then their eyes bouncing back to observe Jody's reply.

It was uncanny how much those two men resembled each other. It's a good thing Benji's hair was short and his clothes were different, or we wouldn't be able to tell them apart from a distance. Benji was at least four inches taller than his grandfather, but proportionately, they were built the same, and even moved the same. Both of them had the same regal bearing and walked with long, confident strides, as if they knew where they were going, and you'd be wise to follow them. Yup, they were both natural leaders.

I went back inside one more time to clean up my mess and heard James pull up with the promised snacks. He came in the doorway with a couple of crocheted sacks of what looked like small potatoes set on top of a basket filled with bottles of ale. "Will these do?"

"What do you have there?" I asked as I helped him unload. I opened the sack and grinned. "Salted peanuts? Salted in the shell peanuts and cold brewskies? I'd better hide one of the bags or everyone will fill up on these and won't have room for dinner."

James set a couple of linen dishcloths on top of the bottles then used the ewer to douse them with water. "These were already chilled, but this will help keep them that way. I haven't quite got the refrigerator to the point where it can freeze water, but I'm working on it. I really miss having ice cream, especially on a day like today."

"What d'ya mean?" I drawled, "We have ice cream here in the 18th century." James gave me the 'what you talkin' about, Willis?' look, and I continued. "But, only in the winter." We both laughed at that one. "Ice cream in the summer, though," I sighed longingly as I took out a bottle of ale for him, then grabbed one for myself. I saluted him with the brew, said, "Cheers," and then chugged down almost half the bottle at once. "Yes, ice cream would be nice, but having a cold beer is good, too. Although, I think we're going to have to work on a recipe for root beer or sarsaparilla for the young ones. This isn't fair to them."

"I already beat you to it," James said. He moved aside a couple of bottles. There were three half pint bottles sealed with the same little latch top caps. "I put some root beer in here for Jenny. Um, I hope you don't mind that I didn't bring enough for the wee three. I thought they were too young for soda."

"You're right there, although I might take out one of these and mix it half and half with milk for a treat for them. I just remembered doing that when I was young." I shook my head and explained, "I just flashed another memory: a poor man's root beer float. Hmm, another unrequested, but friendly memory pops back in."

"Does it bother you," James asked gently, "not remembering?"

"Actually, no, it doesn't. I have such a good life now, and what had to be the best part of my past life, Leah, is here. I hate to say that you can't miss what you can't remember, but it's true. I didn't miss Leah until she wound up as my nurse at the hospital last year and I realized that she was, had to be, my daughter. I didn't miss you because, even though I had found that business card of yours in my backpack, I didn't remember who you were. Hell, I didn't even know that I knew you."

"Well, we had only met briefly that one time. You had a whole lifetime—hers at least—with her, and less than an hour with me."

James gave me a slight grin of discomfort, letting me know that he wanted to change the awkward subject. "So, now that Benji's here to help with the harvesting and everything else, it looks like I might be able to spend more time with my, ahem, inventions."

I looked down my nose at James and shook my head in admonishment. "Okay, okay," he clarified, "I'll be able to spend more time on my re-creations. Is that better?"

"Yes, my number one son-in-law. Let's see, the chickens and potatoes are baking, carrots are glazing, I think I've scrounged enough plates and bowls for everyone, and gee, we're set." I stuck my head out the door and called to my family outside, "Why don't you bring it inside? I want to hear the latest gossip, too. And I think those babies need a nap out of the weather."

I set out the peanuts and poured more water over the towels covering the bottles. It wasn't as good as an electric refrigerator, but evaporative cooling was all we had at our place. Sarah and I already envied the solar hot water heater and ceiling fans James had put in their house and were eager for him to build them for our homes, too.

The men, women, children, and babies all filed through the door, bits of their stories still floating in the air. "And then I found out I had to wait one more year!" Benji declared.

I gave Benji a bottle of ale and let him continue. He toasted us with the homebrew, took a long draught, and set it down on the kitchen table. I wasn't sure, but I think his revelations about his challenges getting back *home* were making him feel like a part of the family again, and not just a visitor. His whole demeanor had brightened with his story telling. I set down a bowl of the peanuts for him to munch on while he continued his soliloquy, and we waited for our dinner to finish baking.

"I took on all types of jobs to keep me fed and sometimes housed. Ye see, I can operate pretty much anythin' that has wheels, wings, or tracks," Benji boasted. "Although, when it comes to flyin' those Super Cubs, I have to take out the front seat. They are'na made for anyone over five foot seven, or so it seems. Bein' a foot over height made fer cramped quarters even with the front seat removed. And of course, I couldna take anythin' other than my lunch with me because I was right close to maximum load with my clothes on. And I sure wasna gonna fly naked!" Benji paused then amended his statement. "I wouldna minded *flyin'* without my clothes, it's jest that I wouldna thought it proper to leave the plane without them."

"Ye flew a cub, a super cub? What kind of cubs fly—bear cubs?" Jody asked in total sincerity.

"No, no, it's jest a name they gave to a wee bit of an airplane that can take off and land in short areas. Its verra good fer sites with lots of trees or next to creeks. I've landed and taken off from little sand bars no longer than…than from here to the barn." Benji saw the confusion on his grandfather's face. "I'll tell ye what; I'll build ye a little model out o' pieces of scrap wood. It's much easier to see how one of these things flies than to explain drag and lift and air pressure coefficients."

I watched Jane as Benji spoke of modern technologies. She didn't seem shocked which surprised me. Then I remembered what she had said. He talked to her about planes, trains, and automobiles when he didn't know she could understand English.

It was a good thing Jenny had fallen asleep with her siblings. She knew about her brother James and his inventions. He had all sorts of ideas and incorporated several of them in his modernistic home. His fancy venting kept their home relatively cool in the summer, and he had even fashioned a solar water heater. But it was his story of his trip to America that could have been trouble. He had covered his slip of the tongue about his nine hour 'flight' from England by saying it was a dream; that he had dreamt he could fly over the water to America in a coach that sailed through the air rather than in a ship that took a month or more to cross the sea. She had accepted it as a good idea and incorporated it into some of her tales she used to entertain Judah, Leo, and Wren.

Well, at least I thought Jenny was asleep. She walked up quietly beside Benji as he was speaking about his days building roads with Caterpillars. "They're really called Caterpillars, but we always referred to them as Cats. And we who ran them were called Cat skinners," he said.

"Eww, that's awful," Jenny said, suddenly making herself known to Benji the entertainer. "You didn't really skin a cat, did you?"

"No, no," he explained, then thought fast, picking her up and setting her on his lap to buy more time to fabricate a cover story. "Ye see, we had tools – great big, huge tools – that we used to build roads. We called them Cats. And when a man, or woman, used the big tools, they were called Cat skinners. No animals were hurt or killed in the making of the roads using Caterpillar equipment," Benji added in a monotone as a comedic disclaimer. Of course, only James, Leah, and I laughed at his mockery of the movie industry, but we howled.

"Uh, oh," I said as I realized we had awakened the two youngest red heads. "I'm sorry," I apologized to Sarah. She was snuggled into Jody and nearly asleep. Or so I thought. I realized that she was actually in a deep sleep when she snorted then nodded, a sweet smile crossing her face. I may have inadvertently awakened the babies, but she could use a bit more rest, at least enough so she could finish her pleasant dream.

"Here, let me," Benji offered. "Jenny, do ye want to go with me while my uncles show me some more of the property?"

Jenny sat up straight – she was still on his lap – and nodded briskly. "I want to show you something special," she said in a voice so soft that only he could hear, or so she hoped. It was still a secret.

Benji and I looked at Jane. I could see that she was still in pain. Before he could ask her if she wanted to go – and I knew she probably *wanted* to go – I ran interference. "Janie, I think you might want to stay here and rest a bit before supper. You can take a nap in the surgery or lie down over here," I said, nodding to the cramped little corner where Jenny had been lying with the still slumbering Pomeroy-Hart toddlers.

"The surgery will be fine. Thank you," she said with her mouth, her eyes adding, 'thank you very much; I'm beat!'

Jody gently laid Sarah's head down, allowing her to finish her nap on the floor. "I think I'll jest go out to the garden and check on the traps I set. That raccoon is smarter than I am at getting out of one."

Wallace piped in, "I didn't know you got trapped? I didn't think it was big enough for you?"

Jody groaned at the joke and James spoke up, "How about if I look at it? I saw a humane trap for foxes once. I might be able to adapt yours."

"Come on, men," Jody said softly, "let's see if three big men can figure out how to catch one verra intelligent raccoon. And if we canna figure it out, we'll send fer ye, Leah."

Leah grinned at the compliment. "I'll hold down the fort while you're gone. Actually, I think I'll claim a spot on your bed, if you don't mind."

Jody pulled his neck back in mock indignation. *"Mi casa es su casa, mija.* Anything I have is yers. Help yerself."

Chapter 29: Hey, there! (TGBF Ch 28)

Jenny and Benji took their uncles for another walk, babbling idly as they meandered around the grounds. Ten minutes into their getting acquainted trek, Benji spotted six riders approaching at a fast clip, a cloud of dust kicking up and blowing ahead of the horde. "Come on Jenny; let's take our uncles into the house. They dinna need to be breathin' in the dirt," he said with concern. But, it wasn't the air quality that had him worried. There were too many people on horseback and riding in too fast to be bringing good news. "Here, on second thought, give him to me; I'll take them both in. Run ahead and tell yer Grandpa and Da that we have visitors."

Jenny passed Raymond to him then sprinted toward the house, screaming, "Grandpa! Daddy!" at the top of her lungs. If they were within a quarter of a mile, they'd hear her.

***

Benji entered the house and handed one uncle to me, one to Leah, and nodded his head as he counted babies to make sure that my three and Leah's were all here. "What's wrong?" I asked seeing his dour expression. He hadn't said a word, which was my first clue that something was amiss; he was always chatting. His lack of humor and furrowed brow were the other indicators.

"I have this itchin', crawlin' feelin' that somethin's wrong with these men comin' this way. How about ye, Leah?" he asked as he looked her way; he knew she had 'the sight.'

She had perceived the ill will, too. The uneasy look on her face was unmistakable: danger was imminent. "Um, do you have a gun?" she asked nervously, glancing at the door, looking for her little sister Jenny. "Mom, does Wallace carry his gun? I know James does; he never leaves home without his equalizer. These men are armed and emotional, Benji, so don't be bashful about showing off what you have."

Benji patted his sporran in answer to the gun question. He opened it, pulled the contents from the top section, and set them on the sideboard. Then he lifted out the false bottom and took out the revolver, flipped out the chamber, made sure it was loaded, peered down the barrel checking for obstructions, popped the chamber back in position, and set the gun into his waistband. "And Jenny's with her Da and Grandpa," he said, making sure we knew she was safe.

"Carhartts?" Leah asked, suddenly realizing that the pants he was wearing weren't era correct.

"Aye, yer the first one to say anythin' about them. If anyone else noticed, they dinna mention it. Come to think of it, do ye have any extra knives around here?" he asked as he put his thumb in the self-fabric loop on the outside of his thigh. "I think I'll dress up a bit. A little intimidation goes a long way, aye?"

"Oh, yeah," I said dryly, and grabbed the butcher knife out of the block, eyeing the carving fork, finally deciding he could take that, too. "Here, let them know you're not afraid to carve 'em up," I joked, then laughed nervously.

I didn't have a gun, didn't really feel comfortable with one, and wasn't very hot on the idea of stabbing anyone either. But then again, with so many male kin around who could, would, and had taken care of me and my children, I didn't feel the need to be armed.

Jane walked in quietly from the surgery, not saying a word, but very aware of the tension. Benji could see the fear in her eyes that mirrored his own. "Janie, ye stay inside with the other women and the children. And dinna come out here unless *I* call ye; no one else, aye?" Benji commanded stressing the word I.

"Aye," Jane answered meekly, sniffing back a tear.

Benji took two long steps over to her and gave her a hard kiss on the mouth. "It'll be okay, I promise," he said, and held her firmly by the shoulders. He turned back to look at Sarah, Leah, and me, making sure we had our end under control. We all nodded in silent answer. He forced a smile, then went out the door to investigate the gathering of riders.

Jane stood petrified. Her eyes followed Benji's exit, then looked to me for direction. At first, I couldn't understand why, and then realized that I was the first one here who had shown her friendship, treating her as a peer as we shared the chore of fetching refreshments, moments after she had arrived.

Jane was idle—without a chore to perform—and in a new environment. The person she cared about most had just left to face a possible mob. Leah, Sarah, and I were all in our element and had our hands full with children and household responsibilities.

"Can you sew?" I asked, hoping to distract her from the brewing commotion outside and the uneasiness inside. She nodded that she could. "Great, I could use a hand with some of this mending." I saw the concerned—hell, terrified—look on her face, and told her, "Don't worry, the men can handle anything that comes their way. We won't be thinking about what's going on out there if we keep busy…"

I was interrupted by the 'pop' of a musket firing.

"What the fu…?" Leah screeched as she bolted to the window to look for the source of the boom. "It's okay. Some idiot either missed or just fired in the air, I guess." At least, I don't see anyone on the ground or grabbing his shoulder," she said with a raised eyebrow to me.

Leah had been my recovery room nurse last year when I had been shot in the shoulder with a musket ball, then sent back for a one-day hospital trip to the 21st century, courtesy of Master Simon. It was a lame joke and didn't even get a groan out of me. "Get away from the window," I said brusquely, "and shush. I want to hear what's going on."

I pulled the door ajar and Sarah, Leah, and I gathered next to it, making sure we were out of sight. I looked back and saw Jane had practically become one with the back wall, a large, *bas relief*, black-fleshed and blue calico clad clump of wallpaper. "Good idea," I whispered to her. "Better yet, sit on the floor in case they get close and look in a window."

I paused to think about what I was going to say next—which didn't happen all the time, thinking first, that is. I made up my mind and decided to pose the delicate question anyway. "You're not an escaped slave, are you?"

Jane shook her head rapidly. "Benji has papers for me," she said meekly. She shut her eyes tight in embarrassment and admitted uneasily, "He owns me."

"Yeah, well, he may have papers that say that, but I'll bet you a million bucks—even if I don't have it—that he does *not* feel like he owns you." I ended my remark with a snort, "Hmph!"

Jane could tell I meant what I said and nodded that I was right. At least, that was what Benji had told her even before he knew she could understand him. Even before they had kissed, he hadn't felt like he could, or should, 'own' another person. It was the others out there who were the problem.

***

The group, all six of them white males, came to a halt in front of Jody and Benji, the two tall red headed guardians, their arms crossed in front of their chests in a united attitude of defiance. If Wallace and James were aware of the situation, they were keeping a low profile.

The wind was coming toward us, so we could hear the confrontation. The fat man with the sweaty tri-corner hat smashed too far onto his head yipped more than barked his words. "Hey, there!" His squeaky voice tried to sound tough but failed almost comically.

He paused, and waited for the other horses to settle down, then started again. "We've come to take her back." He shifted in his saddle, pushed the toes of his boots down into the stirrups, so he was actually standing up, trying to appear taller than he was. "The boss's brother was killed by her, so she's to be burned at the stake," he shouted in his off-key soprano voice.

"There's no one here who doesna belong here," Jody said, shoulders back, eyes squinted, as he studied the men, assessing their hunger for battle. It looked like Mr. Tinny-voice was in charge. Right now, words were the only weapons being used. The young man at the back of the group had dropped his musket to the ground, causing it to discharge. He hadn't meant to fire, so that shot didn't count. The lad was terrified and looked like he was about to piss his pants, either in fear, or in shame at his gaffe. Either way, he, too, was a threat because he would instinctively follow his leader, like a hungry cat after a rat through a burning briar patch. But Jody knew these men were also joined together by a cause. Whether it was a righteous one or not, didn't make a difference. They were a mounted, armed mob, fueled by a passionate pip-squeak of a man. Jody knew he would have to take him down a few notches. But first, he'd hear him out and let the joker supply him with intimidation ammunition.

"We know she's here. The old man down the road said that he sent him," the mashed-hatted leader pointed to Benji with his chin, "to your place, Pomeroy. He told us he called himself your grandson. The old man said he saw him leave with the Negress." The man changed from his accusing voice to a snide, belittling tone and added, "Holding her hand."

"Like I said, there's no one here who doesna belong. Now, I'd appreciate it if ye'd leave jest as fast as ye came in," Jody said with confidence and poise, hoping that there wouldn't be any more gunfire, intentional or otherwise.

"Oh, she's here all right, and she's a witch. I wasn't there, but she hexed Samuel – that's Mr. Jonathan's brother-in-law – making him stab him, his own sister's husband! We have witnesses! And she's a thief, too. She stole the silver whiskey flask right out of the dead man's jacket!" the ringleader shouted, his voice getting louder and higher pitched with each accusation.

Benji stepped forward and addressed the petite prattler, ignoring all the others. "Weel, if ye are'na a witness, then where are they? Ye see, I *was* there, and I saw it all. The lass never laid a hand on anyone. It was me on the ground who Samuel was goin' fer. If he hadna tripped and fallen over his own big feet, Mr. Jonathan would still be alive today."

Benji was supposedly explaining the scenario to the vigilantes but was really using the revelation to relate what had happened to his grandfather. "So, if there had been a problem with her, if she was guilty of anythin', the witnesses would have said so before they left. No, since there's nothin' but hearsay on yer part about poor Mr. Jonathan's accident, I suggest ye all leave." Benji slowly stepped back to stand next to his grandfather, spreading his shoulders wide to make sure the men saw his pistol, and realized that there were two very large men and one shiny gun they would have to overcome to get to the house.

"And I don't think that pointing that gun at them will do you any good," James said, as he came out from the trees in front of and to the side of the riders. "Right, Wallace," he said loudly, announcing his father-in-law's presence to the trigger-happy horde.

Both Wallace and James had seen the man readying his shot. The vigilante had used the younger man beside him to hide his waist high aim at Benji. When he heard James's warning, he lay his pistol down across his lap, but kept the smug look on his face. He wasn't going to give up his weapon—he'd just put it on hold until a more opportune moment arose.

"Now I dinna think it very neighborly of ye to come to my house, armed to the teeth with pistols and muskets, accusin' my guest of murder and witchcraft. So, I'm askin' ye nicely now: turn around, go home, and if there's any truth to yer story, we can have a trial. But it willna be without every one of the witnesses who were there and the magistrate to hear the story. Now, good day to all of ye and farewell," Jody said graciously, but with the tone that his dismissal of them was not up for discussion.

Vernon was tired of hearing the banter. He wanted his boss's murderess now. It had been a long time since he had a chance to use his whip, and his hands were yearning for the feel of its hilt, the wrist action of flicking the cat-o-nine tails, the tremor that passed up the strands when they impacted skin, breaking up and splaying bits of bloody flesh with each lash. If he shot from where he was, he was bound to hit one of the two big red headed men. Sure, there'd be a melee, but then he and the rest of the men could go right up to the house and find her. He had seen someone at the window, heard women talk and a baby cry. Yes, they were probably hiding that tall, murdering slave in the house with the women and babies.

"If you raise that gun again, I'll shoot first and ask questions later. Do I make myself clear?" James announced to the man who had lifted his pistol again, this time a scant four inches off of his lap.

Vernon set his gun down gently, cut his eyes to his brother, the swiftly lifted the pistol, and pulled the trigger.

Bang, pop: the two sounds were almost simultaneous.

James fired his pistol. He had seen the twitch and eye signal. He knew the man was going to shoot, to try to hit either Jody or Benji. He probably didn't care which one as long as he created chaos. Hopefully, he hadn't waited too long.

Benji and Jody ran for cover in opposite directions at the shots. Benji ran to the goat shed, his pistol drawn to cover his grandfather's hasty retreat to the backside of the outhouse.

Vernon had fallen forward, and now slumped over the horse's bloody mane. His eyes were frozen, forever wide in shock at what he had last seen while alive; his own throat blown apart, the red fluid spurting out, his lust for another's blood causing him to lose his own.

The horse reared at the loss of his rider's control and the shift in weight. Hal grabbed for the reins to subdue the high-strung steed as his brother's corpse dangled from one side, the lifeless foot caught in the stirrup. The horse continued to rear up and dance around Vernon's slack body, trying to rid itself of the awkward encumbrance, the smell of fresh blood like a hot poker up his nose. Hal finally jumped off his ride to free his fallen brother's boot from the stirrup, to release the corpse tether, allowing the body to fall to the ground. Now Hal's horse caught the scent of carnage and backed away frantically, pulling the reins out of his hand. All at once, both horses were gone, running back in the direction from where they had come, getting as far away from the smell of blood and death as their long legs and riderless backs could take them.

Hal stood petrified in the midst of the unplanned calamity, slowly turning his head side to side. This wasn't how it was supposed to happen.

"Now, I dinna want any more blood to be shed. Jest take the man's body and get out of here." Jody called out from behind his privy citadel. "If ye have a valid claim, send someone—unarmed mind ye—with a notice of when the magistrate wants the trial to be held. We'll do this the right way, aye?"

"Get him up on your horse," squeaked the squatty leader to the young misfiring rider, instructing him to load Vernon, the dead would-be assassin, onto his horse. "And you double up with him," he said, and pointed from Hal to the other slim built vigilante. He looked around to make sure his orders were being followed, then allowed himself the indignity of wiping his brow. He was sweating profusely with fear, partially blinded by the drops in his eyes. "We'll deal with you later, Pomeroy. And your grandson, too, if he even is one."

"I'll be sendin' ye a bill fer the cleanup of the mess ye made here today," Jody said as he walked out bravely and pointed to the bloody area on the ground. "And dinna be comin' back here without papers from the magistrate, or yer the one who'll be in court."

Benji walked up and stood next to his grandfather, watching the pathetic posse ride away, the two double-ridered hoses struggling to keep up with Master Toad's swift retreating pace.

"Dinna ye think the magistrate might side with them, I mean, that he might be swayed a bit with them sayin' a slave killed a man?" Benji asked softly before James and Wallace joined them.

"No, no chance of that, lad," he said with a chuckle. "Ye see, as of last week, I'm the new magistrate. Those idiots jest dinna ken it yet."

Jody looked over and saw that Wallace and James had paused in their short trek to join them. James was bent over at the waist, his hands on his knees, Wallace standing mute beside him a respectful six feet away.

"Are ye ailin' there, lad?" Jody asked as he rushed over to him.

"Oh, God," James said, then threw up. He wiped his mouth then kicked dirt into his mess. He looked up at his mentor and shook his head in embarrassment. "I didn't think I'd ever have to shoot a human being and now I've killed two in one year. The first one, I'm ashamed to say, didn't bother me. He really, really deserved it, and would have been dead in a few days anyhow, but him," James paused and shook his head and looked over at the bloody area where the man had fallen.

"Weel, if it was to be him, me, or Benji, then I'm glad it was him," Jody said simply. "He was a bad man and was killin' fer sport. Ye were killin' to protect yer kin. I canna say that there's a more honorable way to take a life. It was to protect yer own, aye?"

"Aye," James replied then looked over at both Benji and Jody in shock, suddenly realizing there was more to the incident. "Did he hit either one of you?" he asked in embarrassment. "I could have sworn he had a chance to get his shot off. I didn't want to wait until the last moment, but...but...I thought I had, did."

Benji reached over with his right hand and pulled his shirt from away his left arm. "He ventilated my shirt a bit, but no harm done. Janie can fix it fer me. Oh, shit, I mean, excuse me." He nodded quickly to the men. "I'll bet she's scarrit sh.." he started to say, then shut up quickly.

"Yes, I'll bet she's scared shitless," James finished for him. "I'll be there in a sec. I want to clean up a bit before I greet the ladies. Can you help me here a bit, Jody?"

Wallace picked up on the subtle hint that James wanted to speak with Jody alone. He had noticed long ago that there seemed to be an odd bond between the two men. Leah had told him that James had been reared by Marty Melbourne—the man he thought was his grandfather. The two were very close despite the age difference.

It wasn't until just a few days before Leah and James left their own time that James had found out that his grandfather, Marty—at that time missing and presumed to be in the 18th century—was really his biological father.

Last year James traveled back to 1782 with Leah. They caught up with Marty the day they arrived. James was only able to have one day with his dear grandfather—his newly acknowledged father—when the patriarch made the difficult decision to leave James and return to the 21st century. James told him that his newly discovered biological mother, Bibb Stephens—the woman Marty should have married—had cancer.

James knew it was the right thing for his father to do: make up some of the time lost with the woman he loved but hadn't spent enough time with.

James was still pained, though. Evidently, he still had an empty spot in his soul that only an older man—one more experienced in the horrors of the world—could fill. Legally, he was James's stepfather, but biologically, was a few years younger. He understood and didn't begrudge his son-in-law feeling more comfortable with the grandfather persona.

"What do ye need help with there, Wee James," Jody asked when the others had left. He only called him that name when they were alone or with family. He did it because he got a smile from James every time he said it. James was the shortest man in the family at six foot even.

James gave Jody the grin he knew the man was expecting by calling him 'wee.' "How do you do it? And how long does it take?" James asked weakly.

Jody cocked his head and asked without words, 'please explain?'

James elaborated, "How do you get that look, those looks, out of your head. That first one: when he's shot and realizes that he's death waiting to be fulfilled, and then that blank stare when you see that his spirit is gone."

"Aye, there are two moments when a man dies. It's only when yer up close when takin' a man's life, as ye were today, that ye see both of them. The first time is the soul separatin' from the body, not really wantin' to leave—that's the shocked look ye see, the one with the blink. But, it's the second face that's jest as bad. That's when the soul is gone and only the shell remains. That's why it stays with ye: it's frozen, like a portrait carved into yer brain where ye canna run from it. Ye see that face in yer heid and part of ye believes that it willna ever leave. It never really does, but with a good life, it doesna come to haunt ye as much. It may help if ye realize that the body that stays is jest a hull, like a walnut picked clean and left behind. The rest is either one place or the other. And in this case, I would suspect he's havin' to answer fer his bad intents. He was sure to wind up with the devil sooner or later. Ye jest sent him on his way a bit earlier, and kept him from doin' more harm to others, with yer clean shot. It's not much to brag about—and I ken ye wouldna—but the man dinna suffer, and neither did Benji, Janie, or me because of what ye did today. If it helps, when that man's face comes to try and haunt ye—and it will—think of the three of us who are here, now, because ye did the right thing. And fer yer own sake, pray that the Lord has mercy on the man's soul. Ye canna be damnin' him more than he already has been, aye?"

"Aye," James said. "Would you make an excuse for me not coming back to the house right away? I want to go home for a bit. It may sound—no, you probably understand this—I want to, need to, be by myself. And I want to take a bath and scrub this horrible feeling off of me."

"It willna scrub off, but the washin' does help. That and the solitude and prayers to the Lord, askin' to help repair yer soul. What ye did today wasna a sin, but it wasna an easy task either. I'm verra glad ye did it and so is my grandson. Dinna take too long. I'm sure yer wife wants ye to be with her and the bairn. And that's another part that will help the healin': bein' close to yer wife." Jody moved his shoulders uneasily, trying to decide how to word it.

"Do you mean being intimate with her?" James asked softly.

Jody nodded. "Aye, it will help, and I'm sure Leah would want to help ye with the healin'. That's what she does."

"All right. I won't be too long then. At least, now I have something to look forward to. Thanks for everything," James said, then bowed his head to take his leave.

"Oh, 'tis me that should be thankin' ye!" Jody said and planted a hearty pat on the distressed man's shoulder. "Take care now," he added and returned the farewell nod. He headed back to his own home, his wife, and the rest of his family who were safe today because of the reluctant warrior.

Chapter 30: Make room (TGBF Ch 29)

"Sarah, do ye think ye can let Jane sleep in the surgery tonight? Benji can have the barn," Jody announced when he came into the house, totally ignoring the topic of the shooting death that had just occurred. He didn't want to talk about the altercation right away. That could wait. The women had probably seen more than they wanted to anyhow. The bad men were gone and his family plus one were safe. Right now, that was all that was important.

Before Sarah could answer him, Benji protested weakly, knowing full well that what Grandpa said was how it was going to be. "But we've been sleeping together on the road for the last week. We'll be fine," he said, just in case the arrangements hadn't been finalized.

"Ye willna be sleepin' with a woman unless yer marrit to her. Ye'll be apart as long as there's at least one room and a barn or a shed or the open sky to separate the two of ye into. Leah," he called to change the subject and address his concerned granddaughter, "James will be along soon. He wanted to clean up a bit. Now, where is that bald-headed great-granddaughter of mine?"

"Jane has her. She was being fussy again—Bibby, not Jane—so she took her into the surgery. I don't know what it is about that woman, but she starts singing, and the child is enthralled. Can you hear her?" Leah asked then looked toward the closed door of the surgery.

***

Jane walked slowly around the small room addition, trying to soothe the baby cradled in her arms, singing her mama's love song to her. Little Bibby's mother—Leah was her name—had just fed her, but the baby acted as if she was still hungry. Maybe she just wanted to suck, too. Jane had never wet-nursed a baby before—intentionally, at least—but she felt something strange when Wee Raymond had suckled her. His tiny mouth pulling on her didn't feel the same as when Benji kissed and sucked and licked. And then there was that bluish white fluid the baby had in his mouth when she pulled him away. She'd seen it in the corner of babies' mouths before when her mother wet-nursed them. Could she have milk? She'd never had a baby, but maybe that didn't make a difference with people. She enjoyed the sucking—too much if that was possible. Just thinking about it made her feel warm and moist in the junction between her torso and her legs and made her nipples tingle.

She looked down at little bald-headed Bibby snuggled in her arms, gnawing her fist in hunger, and sympathized with the child's frustration. She had felt that discomfort many times in her life, too: the belly that didn't have enough food in it to be satisfied. At least she could let the child suck. It would feel good to her, and the baby; well, maybe, just maybe, if she really had milk in her breasts, then she would be able to feed the child.

It could be that she was like her mama that way. She was the only baby her mother had birthed, but Mama nursed other babies for years, sometimes even when she hadn't had one sucking on her for months. Maybe the milk was a gift like singing. Mama had told her that her voice was a present from God. Her mother could sing and nurse other people's babies. Maybe she had received both gifts, too. Jane loosened her sarong, bared her right breast, and offered it to Bibb, continuing her song of joy to the bright-eyed little girl.

Wee Bibby rubbed her nose back and forth on Jane's nipple, making it rise in response. As soon as she felt its firmness, she opened her mouth and started sucking, getting a taste of the sustenance that she had not been getting for the last few days.

Jane felt it; the same feeling she had the moment after Wee Raymond had latched onto her. It was a warm, comforting flush of relief. Her milk had let down, she knew it had; just as it did with cows and goats. When she milked the farm animals, only a small amount of milk came out when she first pulled and squeezed on their teats. Then, all of a sudden, the milk would let down and flow by itself. That must be what was happening to her. She put her finger in Bibby's mouth to release the suction and pulled the nipple out to check. Milk sprayed out from at least twenty points and onto the baby's face. Jane gawked at seeing her suspicion confirmed. Wee Bibby didn't wait to be proffered it again, but bounced her mouth back onto its target, latching onto the nipple, stimulating the flow with a gentle but insistent tug, swallowing the milk and sucking gently to keep it flowing, not relaxing lest its source be removed again.

Jane's shock disappeared quickly as her gentle song of grace resumed, a little more grateful for the added blessing she had just discovered. The rocking chair in the corner was empty. Normally she

312

would never think of sitting on a white person's furniture, but these people were her new family. Her mother would let her sit in her chair if she was tired; Sarah probably would, too. She pulled the rocker away from the wall with her foot and sat in the chair that, just like all the others, was too small for her. Her legs were too long for the seat, but her bottom wasn't too wide. She lifted her heels as she sat back in the chair, rocking the both of them to sleep.

***

Evie and Leah continued dinner preparations for the extended family while Jody and Wallace played chess. Wee Raymond had fallen asleep on his father's shoulder during the game. "See, if ye hadna taken so long to move yer man, he'd still be awake," Jody said. "Yer little brother weel be walkin' and talkin' before we're finished with this game."

Sarah went into the surgery to nurse Wee Julian. Maybe she could get him down to sleep early, too. The surgery was the one place she was sure to get some quiet time. She also wanted to check on Jane and Bibby; the singing had stopped. The odd couple was asleep in her rocking chair—baby Bibby's lax mouth hanging away from Jane's milky breast.

"oh kay," Sarah whispered and walked over to the straight-backed chair in the corner, selecting it as her nursing chair. She got Wee Julian to start feeding, and then moved her upper body back and forth in the stationery seat, as if it were a rocker. The movement was to soothe and relax her as much as it was for him. Between the pseudo rocking chair and his gentle sucking, Sarah found her inner peace and clarity of mind.

She had never taken obstetrics classes in medical school. All she knew about babies was from her own real-life experience, but she was pretty sure that a woman had to have a baby before getting milk. But then again, that's just what she thought, not what she knew to be fact. If Jane's oxytocin hormones had been triggered by suckling, then they could have responded to the call for milk without the need of a pregnancy. Or maybe she had a miscarriage… No, the way she shook her head at the suggestion she had a baby was not how a woman who had just lost a child would have reacted. And, by the way Benji was so anxious to be married, he hadn't had sex with her yet. But Benji was his grandfather's child and may have been getting familiar with her in other ways, ways that may have involved stimulating Jane's lactating

313

hormones.

Oh, well. Jane and the baby looked to be at peace. She'd have to have a quiet talk with Leah when she was done feeding Wee Julian, though. If Leah had just fed her daughter and she was still fussy, and then Jane fed her again and satisfied her enough that she had fallen asleep, it would seem that there was something amiss with Leah's milk. Or she was pregnant again.

Sarah fed Wee Julian until he was asleep then sneaked out of the room to put him down in his bed, letting the two dozing females stay zonked out in her rocking chair. She really didn't want Jane to know that she knew her secret—yet.

"Jody, may I have a word with you?" she asked the frowning chess master.

"Aye, might as weel. I'm not doin' any good here. Oh, Raymond, I'll put him to bed," he offered as he stood up and took one more look at the chessboard, trying a different view to get a new perspective on the stagnant game. He followed Sarah to the corner, set his son next to his sleeping brother, and asked, "What's on yer mind?"

"How's James doing?" she asked softly.

"Nae too good; I told him all the ways I kent to recover from takin' a man's life, and he's takin' it to heart. It would be nice, mind ye, if he and Leah could spend some time alone together. I love wee Bibby, but she sure has been fussy. Is it too early fer the teethin'?"

"Yes and no," Sarah answered. "I think Leah might be pregnant..."

Sarah saw Jody's eyes widen as he asked her the silent question, 'what about you?' "No, I'm fine. I'm taking precautions. I think she's relying on nursing alone to be her birth control. I don't think it's working, though. She's nurses Bibby but says the child's always hungry. It happens with babies during a growth spurt – eating more frequently to bring in more milk – but I don't think that's the case here. She also has the first trimester fatigue syndrome going on. I wouldn't know for sure without checking her, and even then, it might be too soon to tell. But, Jane, um, has milk and she just fed Bibby. Do you hear her crying?"

"Bibby or Jane," Jody asked, and then realized he had unintentionally made a joke. "Oh, I see... Or I dinna see. Did she jest have a bairn?"

"No, I don't think she needed to. She evidently had other

314

stimulation." Sarah cocked her head and grinned. "Hey, he's your grandson, aye?"

Jody shook his head, trying to keep the visual representation of what had apparently occurred on at least one occasion from slipping in. "So, it willna make a difference if Leah has Bibby with her tonight; her milk isna good anyway. And that means," Jody's face brightened, "that maybe she can help Wee James heal in the other way." His head kept nodding in acceptance of Sarah's undeclared plan. "Janie can spend the night here, in the surgery, away from our randy grandson, and keep Wee Bibby fed and happy."

"Sounds like it's a good plan for everyone all around," Sarah said with self-assurance.

"Except fer Benji. He'll have no one but the goats fer company, but I'm sure he'll be fine." Jody sighed deeply as he remembered the other dilemma: finding a way for Benji and Jane to marry. "We'll talk about the other problem at dinner. Maybe someone will have an idea of how the two of them can get marrit and stay here." He shook his head in sadness. "But I dinna ken how it could be possible."

***

James Melbourne stomped up the steps to announce his arrival, walking through the door with feigned self-confidence, his hair still wet from his prolonged bath. The sunny day and his roof mounted solar water heater had assured him of plenty of hot water. He had soaked in his custom-built wooden tub for nearly an hour, at least until the water got cold. He couldn't scrub enough, so didn't even try—at least not too long. Jody had been right, though. Soaking in the water had helped, although he did feel guilty for using all of the available hot water. They'd just have to heat water at the hearth for the baby's bath tonight. He sighed then grimaced. It would be nice if he could get the other part of the cure Jody had suggested. But that probably wouldn't happen.

Bibby had been fussy for the last week and was now sleeping with them in their bed. Leah was tired from taking care of her day and night. Just one good night's sleep would help. A thorough romping would be better still, although he'd settle for another one of their late night sneaky pokes. He grinned in recall. At least, Leah didn't protest if he took the initiative, and Bibby didn't seem to mind the bumping around her mother got while she nursed. Maybe the two of them could leave the baby with

315

Jane and Benji for an hour or so. A little privacy, unrestricted, uninhibited… Oops, change the subject before you get too wound up, Melbourne!

"Weel, look what the wind blew in," Jody said when he saw James enter. Leah sauntered over to him, snuggled into his chest, and looked up at him like he was her hero. She pulled back and sighed in appreciation of her brave man, then moved in for another full body hug.

"Where is everyone?" James asked, although it was obvious that the only two missing were Jane and Bibby. Jenny was sitting in the corner with her little brothers and sister, telling them a story about giant flying birds with people inside them, using her hands and exaggerated facial gestures to accentuate the strange sounds of her monsters and heroes. I was finishing the gravy for the chicken and baked potatoes, and Wallace was setting the table.

"Looks like ye have a babysitter fer the night if ye'd like," Jody said with a twinkle in his eye. "Yer Bibby and her Aunt Janie have a real good arrangement goin' on there. Janie sings to her and Bibby puts her to sleep. They'll be out when they wake. Leave them be fer a bit."

"Well, I guess it's good that she's sleeping, although I would rather Bibby slept all night rather than all day," Leah said, her face furrowed in frown. "I'm up feeding her every couple of hours, as it is."

"We got it covered," Sarah said, looking quickly at Jody then back to me. "I think we have enough wet nurses around here to cover her for one night. How about everyone goes and washes up, then we'll have Jody say grace? Benji, would you see if your fiancée is ready to wake up?"

Benji didn't have to be asked twice. He was up and almost running before the end of the request.

I looked at Sarah to see if she was going to let me know what was going on but saw that she was doing her best to busy herself, putting on an unneeded apron. She must be stressed. I've never seen her try to wear two of them at the same time. She'd either tell me later, or I'd find out about it myself. Either way, a thanksgiving meal was being set out, and I needed to help Jenny wash up the youngest of the Pomeroy-Hart clan.

***

Jane was fast asleep, baby Bibby at her breast, both of them totally relaxed, mouths hanging open. "Janie, are ye awake?" Benji asked softly.

Jane started at her name. The momentary panic she felt being caught asleep was quickly replaced by a smile of contentment. It was Benji calling her, calling her by the name he had given her. "Oh, I see ye got a little nap there. Are ye hungry? We have a fine chicken dinner, and all we're missin' is ye and little bit here," Benji said.

Jane suddenly remembered the baby she had been nursing. She scooted the rousing baby over her shoulder, effectively covering her bared breast with the child's body.

Benji was all smiles at seeing her, and she was happy to reflect them back to him. "I'll be in there shortly," she said, and looked toward the door, asking him subtly to go back without her.

Benji left quietly and Jane got up. She set the baby down on the surgery table and rewrapped her sarong. It didn't look like Benji had seen that she had been nursing, or at least allowing the baby to suck on her breast. She wanted to keep her blessing of having milk a secret for now.

"Come on, sweet child," she said to Bibby as she lifted her up over her shoulder, "there's nothing wrong with feeding and caring for you, so I won't feel bad about it. But, I'll bet your Mommy and Daddy miss you."

Bibby replied with, 'braat,' a healthy, dry burp, and almost a giggle then nuzzled her face into her cousin's shoulder. She was full, warm, happy, and ready for Daddy's snuggles.

***

I saw Sarah stare at Benji as he came out of the surgery. She was definitely looking for a reaction from him. I followed her line of sight and didn't see anything except the overly perky tall man coming over to the table to pick up his cousin Wren and attempt to carry on a conversation with the one-year-old. If he had seen anything unusual in there, he was keeping it a secret, and wearing his poker face. Oh, well, it must not be important, at least not yet.

317

Chapter 31: The teen years (TGBF Ch 30)

We all gathered together at the small kitchen table. It was time to eat our Thanksgiving meal. "We thank ye Lord fer the food, the friends, and family. Thank ye fer keepin' us safe today and fer the new member to our family. Bless us, O Lord, and gives us Yer strength and wisdom in all that we do; in Jesus name; Amen." Jody looked up from the blessing he had just invoked and smiled at his family: safe again, at least for now. "Okay, eat hearty everyone, there's plenty fer tonight and we dinna need to save any fer tomorrow. *Mangia!*"

"That means 'let's eat' in Italian!" Jenny declared although everyone but maybe Jane and Benji knew it. "And Grannie said I don't have to use a fork or knife when I'm eating chicken, but I have to make sure that I use a napkin. I put some extra ones out in case anyone's hands get too messy and hey, I wanted that piece," she carped as Leah took a drumstick.

"Don't worry about it—Grandpa and I fixed three chickens. That means there are how many drumsticks, Jenny?" Wallace asked.

"Six!" she announced with pride. "And, if Leah and I both eat one, that means there are four more drumsticks for everyone else."

"And lots of other pieces, but if ye dinna stop talkin' and start eatin', ye'll miss out on yer fair share," Jody admonished then passed the plate to Benji.

"Ooh, a nice juicy breast," Benji said as he stuck his fork into the golden roasted piece of meat, "my favorite part."

Sarah and Jody snorted at the same time then turned to look at each other. "I'm sorry," Sarah said at the same time Jody said, "Excuse me, something went down the wrong way," as lame explanations for their guttural responses to Benji's preference for breasts.

Benji shrugged with a sheepish grin. His slightly off-color joke was made for the wrong audience. To apologize for it would draw more attention to it, so he decided to drop the subject. He took a big bite. "Mighty fine fare here, mighty fine," he praised as he chewed the chicken that tasted just like Mom used to cook, more than happy that he didn't have to eat grubs wrapped in grape leaves anymore.

After dinner I nursed my babies then put them down on a quilt covered pallet in the corner, letting Jenny snuggle up to them so they would settle down and hopefully go to sleep. Leah sat as close to James as humanly possible with clothes on as he cuddled Bibby to his chest, his gratefulness to be alive and have his family with him evident in his Mona Lisa smile of peace and contentment. Jane took Sarah's advice and went to the surgery to lie down. The rest of us paired off and found chairs, stools, or fat quilts to settle onto to get comfortable for an after-dinner conversation with my nephew, Benji, the great big time traveling fairy.

"Ye see, I was, had been, a prisoner of Sept—that is Atholl MacLeod the Seventh—since I was nigh on twelve-years-old. He came to me at school, tellin' me that my mother was in trouble, and needed my help. Hmph! I was so gullible. Imagine, someone askin' a child fer help rather than goin' to my father or a police officer."

"Weel, at first he and his gang called me their hostage. They were gonna make a lot of money when my parents paid the ransom. Months later, when they couldn't get anybody to give them what they wanted, they called me a prisoner. Hmph. Prisoner woulda been a step up; I was more a slave than anythin'. They sold me to anyone to do anythin' from cleanin' out shitters, I mean privies, to shovelin' coal or other, um, stuff. And they werena verra nice to me either – not that I was verra nice to them. But, no matter what they did, I still wouldna tell them where they were or what was in them, The Letters, that is." He shifted his position on the hard stool, then sighed. "They thought I was deid."

"Who," I asked, "your parents or the men who held you prisoner?"

Benji didn't answer my question but continued with his narrative. "The bad men werena too smart and were sendin' their ransom notes to the wrong place. Ye see, I wasna too cooperative in givin' them the right address, and they relied on the postal system to get the letters delivered. Sept could read and write and made sure I wrote the notes jest like he said. I had only seen him write his name, and it was all scribbled, like he had held the pen in his mouth. So, rather than writin' the notes himself and them bein' illegible, he had me take down his words then he'd read them and make sure I wrote what he told me."

Benji wriggled his shoulders like his shirt was too tight. "Although I wished I had known he could read before I wrote the first note for him. He took a switch to me and laid me open fer writin' 'It's been a hard day's night and I've been workin' like a dog' instead of his request fer gold and gems fer my safe return."

Benji snorted then continued his story. "We dinna have any gold or gems. My parents werena rich. They had to work like everyone else. And if there *had* been any extra money anywhere…"

Benji looked toward Jody, and I could swear he gave him a 'look,' then continued.

"I certainly dinna want it to go to the man who stole me, beat me, and threatened my family!"

"But, you said they thought you were dead: who? Everyone?" I asked again.

"Oh, weel, like I said, Sept could read, so I made sure I wrote the right words after the second whippin'. I was mad about the first one and wouldna do what he said no matter how much he… Weel," Benji sucked in his bottom lip, "I stopped bein' so pig heided and realized that since the letters werena goin' to the right place anyway, I would go aheid and put down the words like he said. I musta written six letters, each one a couple of weeks apart. I told him that it took a long time to get the letters delivered by post there in Scotland. It sounded logical to me and since he saw that I believed it, he did, too. He dinna tell me where we were, but I figured by the accent of the men, we were in England, not too far from London, maybe Soho district.

"Weel, after a few months and no answers, he and his boys packed me up and we all heided fer Scotland. He figured if he mailed a letter nearby, it would get to my parents sooner. He waited day after day fer the ransom of gold and jewels that was never delivered.

"We were stayin' at an old abandoned brewhouse there in Angus. It was winter and he was tired of feedin' me since he couldna hire me out: there wasna any work fer anyone. I wasna makin' him any money so he decided he'd jest take that letter to Garden Hall himself, leave me locked up there at the brewhouse, outta sight. He dinna want to chance me runnin' away, um, again.

"Of course, when he tried to find the address of Garden Hall where the letters were sent, he had a wee bit of a problem. He found out that there wasna such a house number, or even road… I wasna there, but I'm sure he was *verra* mad! He found a tavern, of course, and asked where this Garden Hall place was. The locals realized he was confused and set him right; told him exactly where Barden Hall was."

"Um, dead?" I hinted again, hoping to get him back on track.

"Oh, yeah," he said, and laughed out loud. "That Sept wasna too bright, and not careful about what went out, the mail, I mean. Ye see, I was able to post a letter jest after I found out that the man was wantin' to ransom me." He shrugged in embarrassment. "Weel, it seemed like a good idea at the time and maybe it was wise in the end. I'm sure it caused a lot of anguish over the years, though. Ye see, I, um, sent a note to the newspaper, the one I kent my parents read, sayin' that a young lad, identified as one Benjamin MacKay by a witness who wished to remain anonymous, had fallen into the smelter at Lochaber and was incinerated, leavin' nothin' but ashes behind. I was hopin' they'd publish it, maybe even verify that I was gone, ye ken, askin' my family when they had last seen me. Ye see, while I was with Sept, I never saw any newspapers around, never heard a TV or radio, so I was pretty sure he dinna keep up with current events."

"TV and radio are like watching or listening to books or newspapers; well, kinda," I explained or rather reminded Jody and Wallace. "Sorry for the interruption. Please continue."

"So, I was hopin' my family wouldna be vulnerable to Sept or his cousins. I was pretty sure they never got any of the ransom notes. If they thought I was dead, they wouldna be scourin' the countryside lookin' for me. But, whether I was missin' or kidnapped, I still dinna want them askin' around about me. So, I had to make sure they believed I was deid."

"But, dinna ye ken the pain and anguish ye musta put yer parents through? They thought ye were deid? If ye let the ransom note get delivered to them, at least they coulda found out where ye were and got ye back. I'm sure yer father coulda found a way to pay the note." Jody was twitching with discomfort, identifying with his daughter and her family's pain at the loss of her only son.

"But, they were gonna to kill me as soon as they had the gold and gems. That's what he said, 'yer jest a way to get the treasure. When we have it, yer...' and then he," Benji took his index finger and mimed slitting his throat. "Ye'd be too much trouble to hang, and cuttin' yer throat is a bit messy, but weel make sure we're not wearin' our good clothes when we do it,' he said. And I dinna have a reason to doubt him. I'm pretty sure that if he or the others got close enough to my mother, they'd try to get her, too. They had this unnatural hatred of red heided people."

"Or jest my kin," Jody said. "Ye see, Sept, as ye call him, is Atholl Grant MacLeod the Seventh. His ancestor, Atholl the first or," Jody dipped his head as he said the name softly, "Captain Asshole," then returned to his normal stature and voice, "was a verra bad man. He tried to kill yer Grannie and Auntie Evie there and do even worse to yer cousin Jenny. And he did quite a few other bad deeds that we needna speak of. But ye see, it was my testimony that got him sentenced to hang. As it turned out, he escaped, and it was yer cousin James here who shot him, killed him, before he did harm to another of my family, yer," Jody closed his eyes and counted on his fingers, "Yer second cousin once removed or, weel, your mother's cousin's son. The lad Wee Ian is still alive because of James here and his fancy gun."

"So, yer sayin' that these MacLeods I've been dealin' with since I was twelve years old were causing, are causing, will cause, problems because of what went on here, in what, 1782?" Benji asked in disbelief.

"Well, it actually started in 1781 when these guys were only about six weeks old," I said, pointing to the penned in trio plus one who were now asleep. "And I have the scar to prove that he tried to kill me. I mean the," I whispered the name, "Asshole," then resumed my normal voice tone, "shot me in cold blood. And he kicked your Grandpa in the head, threatened your Grannie with a knife, killed Jenny's biological brothers, and threatened even worse than that to poor Jenny herself..."

Jenny popped in, suddenly awake and involved in the conversation, "But Daddy whooped the tar out of him. And then he and Grandpa Jody made sure that after he was caught, he got a fair trial, huh, Daddy?"

"I thought you were asleep," Wallace said with a mix of embarrassment and agitation. He looked over at his nephew Benji and admitted, "I'm not proud of the, um, thrashing, but he had just shot, and I thought killed, Evie, my fiancée at the time. But it all turned out okay, right?" he asked Jenny.

Jenny nodded her head, sucked in and chewed on her bottom lip, but didn't say anything. I could see she was remembering her 'other brothers,' Clyde and Clayton, who Captain Asshole had killed. Rather than call attention to it, Wallace opened his arms and Jenny crawled right in – right where she belonged. She rubbed her head under her daddy's chin, then tipped her head back and gave him a kiss on the neck. "I sure love you, Daddy," she said, and nestled back into him, at peace again.

My quiet son-in-law James cleared his throat and looked around. It had quieted with Jenny's appearance, but it was obvious that he wanted to say something. "Yes?" Jody, Benji, and I asked at the same time.

"I think I should tell you, oh shoot, it doesn't really make a difference now but," James looked over at Jenny and decided to continue the thought. "My father told me that *I* was the treasure; that the letters referring to a treasure were just to make sure that someone came back to save Ian Kincaid so that his heir, me, would be born." James finished his report with his eyes on Jenny, his future great-grandmother. She wasn't paying attention to what was being said but was running her finger around the button on Wallace's shirt.

"But, but?" I asked as I saw him look at Jenny. *He shook his head quickly, and I took his cue to shut up. I'd probably – hopefully – hear about it later.*

"Weel, that's a relief, in a way. The treasure was a person, not gold or jewels. Hmm. It's a good thing they dinna ken. I dinna think they woulda been too pleased if ye were given up as the ransom," Benji joked, then slapped his knee. "If ye'll excuse me, I think I need to go see a man about a horse."

"A horse?" Jenny brightened up. "Are we getting a 'nother horse?"

Jody looked up at Benji, now standing in the doorway. Jody didn't say anything, but knew he was missing something.

"Um, I think he just wants to go make sure one didn't fall down the privy," I explained lamely, and then whispered to Jenny, "I think he needs to go pee."

"Oh," she said with a big round 'O' mouth, looked down in embarrassment, and hid in her daddy's chest.

"But, if I find a '*nother* horse wanderin' about, I'll make sure I give her to ye, okay?" Benji said to try and ease her embarrassment.

"Okay!" she said brightly and popped away from Wallace's pectoral comfort zone. "But if she's been down in the privy, I'd appreciate it if you washed her in the creek before giving her to me," she added, head nodding with excitement at the prospect of getting her own horse, even an imaginary one.

"Aye, I'll be sure to do it – that is if I find one…," he said with a grin and a nod in farewell as he headed to the wooden-seated personal comfort station.

Chapter 32: He'll clean ye up (TGBF Ch 31)

Jody remained mute as Benji finished the tale about his youth and how he had let – no, made sure – that his parents believed he was dead. He watched Sarah during Benji's revelation; he could see that she was as torn up inside as he was. He had to talk to him about it, but not in front of the others. An hour passed; "Let's walk," he said softly to his grandson, taking advantage of the break in the other family members' after dinner conversations with the garrulous and congenial fellow.

Benji was taken aback at the sudden change in tone of the party that his grandfather's request had caused. He looked over at Janie and saw that she, Evie, and Leah were all making a fuss over the cute, petite ribbon that Jenny had affixed in Bibby's hair, or lack of it. She had tied a bow and fastened it to the very top of the little girl's bald head with a dab of honey. Jenny was holding one-year-old Wren's hands, making sure the little big aunt didn't pull the blue adornment off of her niece's nearly fuzzless head. Wallace and James had gravitated to the window, both on them holding one of Wren's brothers. It appeared that they were discussing the next building they planned to construct; the movements of their arms and hands indicating roof slopes and intersecting room additions. The Pomeroy-Hart boys were enjoying the security of their man jungle gyms, climbing over their family's shoulders then retreating, batting at each other, slapping hands and giggling in glee. No, the general mood of the family wasn't dour; it was just his and his grandfather's.

The patriarch and his giant heir walked quietly onto the porch. Jody took a deep breath, turned and looked back into the house, and watched Sarah join the other women in their adoration of Bibby's hairless coif. She looked back and saw her husband, tried to smile at him, but only managed a half grimace. She knew he had a difficult discussion to undertake. If Benji were anything like Jody, convinced that what he had done was right, there would be loud words tossed around. Jody frowned back at her and realized that his persuasive conversation might wind up becoming a confrontation with loud, angry voices. Yes, he had better get further away from the rest of the family than the porch. This wasn't going to be easy. No doubt, an ego or two would be bruised.

"Let's check out the goats," Jody suggested, his hand heavy on

Benji's shoulder to guide him. "Ye sure got big there, lad," he said as he patted him gently. Hopefully, these weren't the last kind words he'd share with him this evening.

"What? Ye dinna have that ornery old spotted sow anymore?" Benji asked in jest. He knew that when he was a child, Grandpa and Grannie had a huge sow that seemed to be indestructible. It wasn't what he wanted to talk about, but he was fairly sure that speaking of long dead pigs was better than discussing what he feared his grandfather had ushered him outside for.

"Why'd ye do it, lad?" Jody asked somberly.

"Come here?" Benji answered brightly, "To see ye and Grannie, and maybe even a few of those cousins of mine. I dinna ken if they'd be here or not. Last I heard, Angus and family were in New Bern. But I was hopin' that maybe they took a bit of a vacation—that is a trip, out here to see ye and Grannie—and I'd get to see them, too. I decided to come even though I wasna verra sure of where to find ye, jest a general location," he joked then deadpanned, "North Carolina." He added a hearty laugh. "I had a bit of trouble findin' ye but..."

Benji finally stopped his inane banter. He thought it was a good ploy, but he knew Grandpa was a smart man and could see through anything, even if his chatter was only a dodge and meant to be transparent. "What do ye wish to speak of?" Benji asked soberly, hoping the words he would hear wouldn't hurt too much.

Jody tried to hold back his anger, but the passion was too strong to be held in check by reason. "Dinna ye ken that it jest about kilt yer parents to think ye deid?" he asked, his voice gruff and harsh, in spite of his effort at self-control.

"It was the only way to keep them safe!" Benji snapped back. "We were all a target, it wasn't jest me. I was jest the pawn to draw them out. If my folks had come forward with the ransom or The Letters, they'd be deid, jest as sure as ye and I are standin' here!"

"Dinna take too lightly yer mother and father and their skills," Jody argued. "I'm sure they'd find a way to get the Fool's Gold." Benji shook his head and Jody knew. "Ye never told anyone where the gold and jewels were, did ye?" he asked.

"Nae," Benji answered. "It's still there for what good it does anyone. But ye see, the MacLeods wanted me and my family deid jest as

326

much as they wanted the treasure. They were, are, vile, sharp, and resourceful."

"Aye, that may be, but I'd wager yer parents coulda found a way to turn over the kidnappers to the authorities. Kidnappin' is still against the law, aye?" Jody asked.

"Aye, but I dinna ken all the men involved. There were others Sept and his cousins spoke of. It was…"

"Letters?" Jody asked, suddenly realizing it wasn't just money and revenge the MacLeods were after. "What are these 'letters' ye and James and Leah have been talkin' about?"

"It seems they believed there was a map or directions to a treasure in the letters that were kept by our family. I think that James's family had valuable letters, too, because he was runnin' into the same problem as me. Maybe the MacLeods thought they were the same ones; I dinna ken and never cared to ask. I kent ye and Grannie wrote letters. They were, are, the biggest treasure of all fer my family. I remember waitin' fer Saturday nights. Da would bring out the box and we would all cuddle up on the couch and he'd read one. Or rather, he'd recite one. We had heard them all. Da and Mom used to read jest one a month, but after they'd been through them all the first time, it became a family tradition: sittin' on the couch with our cocoa or cider, listenin' to Da read the letters."

Benji grinned in recall. "I blushed every time he told about the antics ye recalled about me when I was a wee 'un. Aye, I turned red, but I was so happy that ye were so proud of me. I hope I have'na disappointed ye with the deception I had to do. I really dinna do it to be mean, but to protect my family. Da and Mom could take care of themselves, but what if they went after wee Becky?" he asked, his eyes begging for forgiveness.

Jody didn't speak. He wasn't ready to pardon him for the deception, at least yet. There also seemed to be more that he wasn't being told.

Benji sighed deeply and spit it out. "I'm alive, but so are they because of what I did. Ye dinna ken that MacLeod family. They were, are, will be, insane. They'd never give up tryin' to find the treasure. That's reason enough to stay away from my family, but," he said sadly, shaking his head in self-disgust, "I canna go back—ever. I've disgraced them."

"How's that, lad?" Jody asked gently. This wasn't a simple case of telling his grandson to go back to his parents. Evidently, there was more involved in this, and his grandson needed counseling, not chastising. "Certainly there's nothin' so horrid that yer family couldna forgive ye. I mean, ye have'na kilt anyone who dinna deserve it, have ye?"

Benji's eyes widened in shock and distaste. "No!" he exclaimed, then slipped back into his morose mood. "It's worse than that and I dinna care to speak of it," he said with distaste. Benji realized as soon as the words were out of his mouth, how harshly he had spoken. "I'm sorry. That was rude and uncalled fer. Its jest, it...it...well, it's humiliatin' is what it is"

Jody shook his head. "That's what family is fer: to turn to when there's no one else. We're here to support ye, forgive ye if need be, but always accept ye jest as ye are, perfect or full of bad deeds in yer past."

"Well, can ye keep this to yerself? I mean, not even tell Grannie?" Benji asked softly. Maybe confessing to his grandfather would help at least a little.

Jody inhaled deeply. This was a big request. But whatever it was that Benji was going to tell him was so hideous—at least, to him—that he had let his family continue to believe he was dead rather than admit to it. "Okay, until ye tell Grannie yerself or tell me that I can tell her, I'll not share yer secret." Big commitments sometimes meant big sacrifices.

"Weel, ye've heard about movies from Grannie and Mom and...ye do ken what movies are, aye?"

Jody nodded. "A bit like a play, but also like a picture on the wall; it's a story told, but the picture moves and talks."

Benji nodded and bit his bottom lip. "Except sometimes they dinna tell a story, but jest show, um, private acts: like those that are enjoyed by a husband and a wife when they're alone and feelin' full of love and..." Benji looked at his grandfather to see if he knew what he was talking about.

"Ye mean performin' sexual intercourse?" Jody asked. If that wasn't what his grandson was talking about, he didn't want to know. Or maybe he did. The boy—man he reminded himself—was quite conflicted.

Benji nodded again but didn't speak. Jody did, though. Now he was curious as well as shocked. "Do ye mean they have movin' pictures of people copulatin'?"

Benji kept nodding and was back to biting his lip again. He glanced up. "And I, I…"

"And ye watched them?" Jody asked, trying to help his grandson set the revelation free.

"That's not it," he said. He had watched some, but that wasn't his problem. Benji looked up, saw the confused look on his grandfather's face, and could tell the man wouldn't be able to figure it out without further explanation. The morals of the 18th century—at least as far his grandfather's life was concerned—evidently weren't as depraved as what he had lived with.

"So, if ye dinna watch them, then…" Jody was searching for words, but was clueless.

"I was *in* one," Benji blurted out, and then burst into tears. "I dinna want to be; refused them politely at first, but they wouldna hear anythin' of it. They did everythin' they could to get me to cooperate, offered me money and, and lots of other *stuff*." Benji wiped the tears from his face with the back of his hand, omitting the part of the story where he was offered drugs and more sex for participating.

"They used a machine to render me unconscious. While I was down, they bound me with straps that cut into my wrists. They asked me again when I woke up. When I still refused, they whipped me 'til their arms wore out and… and," Benji sighed, not knowing how to explain a taser, then decided to bypass the instrument's details.

Benji straightened his back, hoping that the physical movement of trying to show some spine would actually help him relate his confession. He shook his head side to side and decided he would have to tell the story as a narrative and try to take his personal feelings out of the chronicle.

"They beat me with rubber hoses; soft sticks that wouldna leave bruises, but I still wouldna do it. So, they used a machine that paralyzed me so I couldna move but was aware of everything bein' said and done around me. They took a handful of these pills…" Benji shook his head, trying to disassociate himself, but the disgust was creeping back in, backing up like vomit in his mouth. "They have these pills fer men that canna, canna get an erection." Benji glanced over at his grandfather to see if he understood. Jody frowned with uncertainty, so Benji elaborated with common dialog. "They have wee tablets that can make a man's cock hard, whether he wants it to be or nae." He grunted with disgust.

"One pill is enough to, um, serve the purpose, but these men wanted to make sure I could, could *perform,* so crammed a whole fistful of these down my throat, nearly chokin' me to death in the process.

"Weel, the pills worked," Benji continued dejectedly. "Whether I felt kindly to the lass or nae dinna make a difference. But I dinna want to do it and she was, weel, she dinna care about anythin'. It was like she was drunk, but without the slobberin'. They gave her bad drugs and had her wantin' more. She dinna ken right from wrong; just wanted more of the drugs. She'd agree to do anythin' to get what she needed – nae, not needed – wanted. She dinna need them but thought she did."

Benji shook his head again. He had to continue what he had started, no matter how awkward or difficult it had become. "I told them again that I wouldna do it after I was recovered from the taser, that is the paralyzer, and my mouth would work again. Since they had either stripped or cut off all my clothes, they could see that the pills had, um, done their job, and even if I wasna willin', I was able. They even put a gun to my head, but I still wouldna do it.

"Ye see, I had…hmm, other incidents, encounters, whatever, in the past when I was younger, much younger, that made me decide to, to…" Benji blurted out with exasperation, "Well, anyway, I had vowed not to *be* with a woman unless I was marrit to her. I was gonna keep that vow, even if I had to die keepin' it. When they saw I was not to be persuaded with pain, or even my own death, they turned the gun, that is, the pistol, on the lass. If she saw it, she dinna realize what they meant to do, either because she thought it was part of the *movie* or because she was so drugged up."

Benji found the nerve to look into his grandfather's face. His grandfather wasn't judgmental in the least, but was stone-faced, waiting for his little four-year-old grandson in the grown man's body to finish his horror story. Jody nodded his head and let him know that he could proceed with the tale: he was following the sequence of events and understood the strange words and concepts of the 21st century.

"Grandpa, it wasna jest the pistol. They had a whole box full of tools, a brace bit with electric power, punches, awls, hammers," Benji shook his head, beginning to feel lightheaded, but continuing the movement, just the same. The story was incredible to him, and he was there and knew it was true. "They were going to punch holes in her body, everywhere, until she was deid, and film it, that is, make a movie of it! They were gonna kill her a little bit at a time and make money from showin' it to other people if I dinna," Benji snorted, then said, "have relations with her."

"So ye saved her life doin' somethin' that was against yer wishes, yer vow?" Jody asked, although he knew that was what he had just heard.

"Aye," Benji said with closed eyes, relieved that he had been able to finish his confession.

"I gave up a part of me to keep yer Grannie safe, to save her life, and weel, keep other parts pure, before yer mother was born. Ye wouldna be in this room with me if I hadna done somethin' so vile and disgusting to me that it still makes me ill to think about it. But no matter how horrid it was," Jody shuddered as he recalled being cut, beaten, and sodomized by two soldiers nearly forty years earlier, "I still have yer Grannie, four children, many, many grandchildren, and even a great-granddaughter, because of my sacrifice. It really isna my business, but the lass, was she harmed?"

"Nae, she was fine last I saw her. They tried to make her do more, um, sinful deeds in order to get the drugs. But I did a bit of an intervention there. Ye see, they dinna have that taser, the paralyzer, handy, and I broke the arm of the man who was gettin' ready to shoot the drugs into her body. Ye do ken what an injection is, aye?"

"Aye," Jody said, as he rolled his eyes. Sarah had given him injections on several different occasions in their life together. Even though each time was to save him from dying from either an infection or blood loss, he would chance recovering on his own rather than get another needle poked into him.

"I broke the man's wrist, the wrist of the man holdin' the drugs. I told him if I ever caught him givin' drugs to *anyone* ever again, I'd break his neck. Weel, I think he believed me. At least, I scared him so bad – or maybe it was from the pain of the broken arm –that he pissed himself. When he did that, I'm sure he lost the respect of his minions. I took the lass with me and left that place, his lackeys runnin' all over each other, tryin' to get away from me."

"The lass…" Jody prompted.

"I took care of her fer three days and made sure the drugs were out of her system. I told her to go home and get back to her family; that they would take care of her." Benji saw the look in Jody's eyes, the wide-eyed look that meant he was getting ready to tell him to do the same thing. "But I agreed with her that family wasna always the best place to go, dependin' on the circumstances. So, I gave her a note to go see the constable in the next town over. He wouldna ken of her past with drugs or the other, um, stuff she'd been doin'. The police, as we call them, are pretty well connected. I mean, a police officer may not be able to help her, but he could contact an agency – that is a group of knowledgeable people – who *could* help her."

"Weel, at least it was one lass and not two men," Jody said flatly. He sighed deeply and saw that maybe it was time to share some of his pain. "Come here and let me hold ye like I did when ye were a wee lad and scarrit of the thunder and lightnin'." Jody reached over and Benji cuddled into his arms like their sizes were of no importance because emotionally, they really didn't matter.

Benji started sobbing into his grandfather's shoulder. Jody kissed him on the top of the head and started his revelation. "Believe it or not, I ken how it is because of the, um, sacrifices I made, too. Ye made a gift of yer body, not to the man who made the movin' picture, but to the lass who ye saved from the drugs or bein' kilt or whatever. Ye see, I had to trade my body to save yer grannie's, but I had to give it to two men. It was me or her," Jody shook his head and shuddered with recall. "But she still loved me and I'm grateful. It isna easy to give up that part of your body under duress. It's supposed to be given in love, not taken against yer will."

"How did ye get over it," Benji asked as he sat up, feeling better for crying in Grandpa's arms like a young child.

"At first, it's minute by minute, then hour by hour until, weel, until ye brought it up, I hadna thought of that, um, time fer nearly a year. But ye canna take yerself away from yer parents. If ye have a way to get back to them, weel, I'll miss ye, we all will, but…"

Jody was without words. He had lost Sarah for 20 years, and then she had returned. It had been awkward at first. He couldn't, hadn't dared, tell her what he had done while she was gone. She found out about it, and then all hell broke loose. The two of them got over it, but this wouldn't be the same for his grandson. Benji was the man-child returning to his parents, the prodigal son. And then he had the words to share.

"Ye do remember yer Bible, aye?" he asked.

Benji shrugged his shoulder. "There werena many churches where I was, and I wasna allowed out by myself. After I got away, I dinna feel worthy of being in the house of the Lord. I do remember a lot from when I was younger, about what is right and wrong, the Ten Commandments, and most of the Lord's Prayer." He shook his head. "Nae, I have'na seen a Bible since I was at home and a lad."

"Two things I have to share with ye. Jesus said, 'Come to Me as ye are.' That means even if ye have a lot of sin, come to Him and He'll clean ye up. And ye need to read the story in the Bible of the prodigal son. It's about a lad who leaves and, even though he does some bad deeds, the father is glad to have him back. He even kills the fatted calf and has a big party in the young man's honor. Of course, the Bible says it better than I can. I have a wee Bible I can give ye. It should fit in yer sporran and ye can read a bit every day. It will feed yer soul and, from what ye tell me, it's been starved fer quite a few years."

Chapter 33: Don't tell my mother (TGBF Ch 32))

August 26, 1782

"Do you ever reread the letters you've written to Mona and Gregg?" I asked. "I mean, I looked back at what I wrote last year, and I sounded sappy, but I left it the way I had written it. I mean, those *were* my real feelings at the time…"

"I know what you mean, and that's why Jody and I agreed not to reread ours. Once they're folded and in the box, they're off limits. They belong to our heirs at that point, not us."

"So, what are you going to say about Benji coming back?" *I had heard the raised voices the night before. You definitely didn't want to get between those two red headed giants when they disagreed. Theirs were the only two opinions that mattered, and arbitration or anyone else's suggestions weren't even a consideration.*

"I was *asked* not to say anything. Benji doesn't want Jody or me to write anything in our letters to his parents about him being here. I guess he's afraid that those MacLeods will get our letters and will use them against his mother. It doesn't make any sense to me. If I could just tell them that Benji was here, safe, and not to worry about him: that he was alive and didn't die in a smelter accident when he was just a child…" Sarah put her head in her hands and started sobbing. "I can't imagine the grief she must be going through; believing that her son is dead…"

"Sort of like when you thought that Jody had died in the war?" I asked. "You went on though, didn't you? You had to let it go, as best you could, and raise Mona, I mean rear Mona, to be a good person. You had a full life even, with his loss."

"No, I didn't," Sarah said with a heap of hostility in her voice.

I didn't take her attitude personally. I could tell she was reliving her past life, or bits of it, in the 20th century. I stayed mum and let her continue.

"I never got over the loss of him, never felt complete again until I was back here, in his arms, in the 18th century. If I had found out earlier…"

"Well, what would you have done? Would you have left Mona with Fl.., with your first husband?"

I gulped as I realized that I knew the name of her first husband was Floyd – and for no known reason why. She had never mentioned his name that I was aware of. I only knew his name because I had read about him and her and everyone else in her family in Lisa Sinclaire's 'Lost' novels. I spoke quickly in what I hoped was a good cover story.

"Would you have come back, traveled through the stones with her as an infant or small child, and subject her to the intense pain?"

"Did I tell you how much it hurt?" Sarah asked. "And how did you know that I didn't find out about Jody until much later?"

"Shit, I mean, shoot, I don't know," I said then bent over to take the lid off the Dutch oven to check on the bread, hoping that I would be able to continue this line of conversation without revealing my inside source. I already knew more about her, Jody, and their personal *history* than I felt comfortable with. I wasn't lying when I said, 'I don't know' – I didn't remember which book it was in.

"Well, the pain was indescribably horrific, all three times, and I know it hurt Mona and Gregg the first time they came through; they told me. Since they went back the same way, through the stones, I think they had to endure it again. I'm just glad there are other ways – or at least one other way – to travel that doesn't cause you to feel like your liver is coming out your nose and your hipbones through your ears."

"And you did that *three* times?"

"The first time was an accident. The second time was for my unborn child, Mona, to make sure I had modern medical help for delivery. The last time was to come back to be with Jody. I could do it for love, but there is no way I would have done it for anything, even anyone, else."

"Well, *you* can't write about Benji, but have no fear, you have a sneaky sister. Let's just leave it at that, okay? I mean, I wouldn't want to tell you anything you would have to keep from Jody. You can keep your word that you won't write about Benji being here to his mother or father, okay? Now, the bread is ready, but the crock is empty. Would you go out to the springhouse and bring in some more butter and another wedge of cheese? Oh, and don't hurry," I added with a grin.

Sarah sniffed, wiped away her tears, and let a smile of hope escape. "Did I ever tell you that you were my favorite sister?"

"Nope, but if you're saying it now, back at ya, sis. Oh, and you might want to see if you can scare up a little jam, too." I looked up at the cupboard where Sarah kept her writing supplies and the dishes. "I'll set the table," I volunteered, "and do anything else that needs doing."

"I'd appreciate it. I'll be back in *a while*," she added with a nod and a wink, and took her leave, humming brightly as she closed the door behind her.

I opened up the cedar chest in the corner and pulled out my 21st century jacket from the back corner. I dug into the front pocket and found it: my ballpoint pen. I kept it stashed along with the zippered coat to keep questions from my middle daughter down to a minimum. Jenny was just a little too perceptive at times.

Writing with the ballpoint pen was faster by far than the dip, stroke, stroke, dip of the quill and inkwell. I absconded with a piece of Sarah's precious homemade paper—an odd shaped remnant of the batch of paper made by Mona when she lived here with her parents and Benji was a baby.

I hastily wrote out:

Mona, Gregg: Benji will disappear, but he's fine. He's here with his Grandpa and Grannie. Do NOT look for him or you will endanger him and yourselves. Take care of each other, Evie (your sister-in-law).

"There, that ought to do it," I said softly. I folded the note and stuffed it inside the second to the last epistle that Sarah and Jody had written. This way, the script wasn't obvious. The steady flow of ink made by the ball point pen made the format look glaringly different, but now it was enclosed inside another letter. If Jody did happen to go through the folded letters, he wouldn't see it. And, since Sarah said Jody didn't reread his letters, mine was as safe as if it was inside a double sealed envelope. Integrity is such a wonderful concept, and I hoped I wasn't compromising mine with the little deception. Nah, probably not, since I didn't feel guilty about it.

Chapter 34: Genealogy lessons and questions (TGBF Ch 49)

"So, yer a Melbourne," Benji said to his new brother-in-law, "but not from America, I take it."

"Nae, I'm from the line that originated with a James Melbourne who sailed from Great Britain over to Australia on *The Alexander* way back in 1788. He was one of the first white men over there. What a claim to fame: my ancestor arrived with The First Fleet, but he came over as a convict, not a marine or an officer. How ironic," Big Jim added dryly.

"Um, am I missin' somethin'?" Benji asked.

Big Jim snorted, "I'm a cop! Go figure. I mean, it canna be in the genes; I'm descended from a criminal," he said and chuckled.

"Weel, the Melbourne I ken in America is a cop, too. Hmm, I wonder if his adopted son – he's my godson, Mac – will be a cop? Genetics are only part of the equation. Environment makes a big difference. Was yer Da a cop, too?"

"Not really," Big Jim said solemnly, not wanting to speak of his father. Instead, he changed the subject. "What's that ye have there, Bibby?"

Bibby picked up her yard-long bundle of yellow yarn strands and set it on her Uncle Benji's lap. "Mommy made this for me so I could learn how to braid. Can you braid?" she asked.

"Aye, but I'd like to use this fer something else. I want to talk about my family with this." Benji looked up and saw the confused looks on everyone's face, including the little seer Bibby. He definitely had their attention.

"Most people have a family tree but keepin' track of our kin requires somethin' with more flexibility than wood. So here," Benji illustrated as he held up the bound end of the yard-long strings of yellow yarn, "the start of our kin, fer my purposes today, begins with Grandpa Jody's father Raymond."

"That's who Nana's named after, huh?" Bibby interrupted. "Oops, sorry," she apologized when she realized her rudeness.

"Aye, and one other, but I dinna want to get ahead of myself. Here's Grandpa Raymond. He had two children who lived to have bairns of their own," Benji split the hank down the middle, "Jody Pomeroy and

Elly Kincaid."

Benji smoothed out the long pieces and continued. "Elly had four children who lived to have children of their own," he said as he split one section into four, "and Grandpa Jody has had five children, two of them who I ken have had children." He pulled out two strands and set them out.

"Five!" Gregg, Mona, and Becky all exclaimed at the same time.

"Weel, the first one, Hope, dinna make it. Then there's ye, Wallace, and the twins. But, I dinna ken about them havin' bairns; they were too small to be marrit when I left." Benji saw the shocked looks and realized that they didn't know about his wee uncles. "Ye dinna read about them in The Letters?"

All three heads shook back and forth slowly. "Ach, those must be The Letters they had in the second batch. Grannie did say somethin' about not putting all her eggs in one basket. Quick answer is ye have two more brothers: Wee Julian and Raymond. They're the same age, or were when I left, as Jim there. Zodiac twins, right Bibby?"

Bibby Liz bobbed her up and down rapidly; they had spoken of her wee uncles earlier.

"Over on this side, yer Great Aunt Elly's side, we jest want to be concerned with one of her children, Ian Kincaid." Benji pulled out the clump of yarn representing him and tossed the other tresses back. "And here is his son, Wee Ian."

"And, over on Grandpa Jody's side we start with Ramona and her daughter Becky and her two children, Bibby and Jim," he said, and wiggled the one strand that represented Bibby, winking at her. "Then her son, me, but I dinna have any bairns yet."

"Except for your godson, huh?" Bibby Liz interjected.

Benji shared a quick look of shock with Jane. She put her head down quickly and squeezed her eyes shut. Benji took a quick breath, ignored the remark, and then continued, "And, accordin' to ye, Miss Bibb Elizabeth, yer Aunt Janie and I will have six children, but we're not concerned with me and my line right now," he said, dismissing her embarrassing revelation.

Benji saw the look of shock on his mother's face and subtle smirk on his father's; they both knew something was up but were genteel enough to stay mum.

"So next here," he said as he pulled out another length of yellow yarn, "yer Uncle Wallace who is marrit to Evie. They have, or had when I left, three bairns a little over a year old, an adopted daughter, Jenny, about eleven, and a grown-up daughter, Leah, who was, is, marrit to James Melbourne."

Benji watched Big Jim's face fall as he made the revelation. During his little genealogical lesson, Big Jim was polite, but hadn't been rapt like the rest of the family. After all, they weren't his blood kin. Or so he thought.

"Melbourne?" he squeaked in shock, then cleared his throat and tried again, this time an octave lower. "James and Leah Melbourne?"

"And ye see," Benji started grandly, then took it down to almost a whisper as he asked his sister, "he *kens*, right?"

"He's been *told*," Becky said with a slight tinge of disgust and a glance at their parents. They nodded in agreement with what she was saying, "But he doesn't believe."

"He thinks we're a bit dotty," Gregg said with an eye roll and sneer. He didn't like being tolerated, but at least his son-in-law accepted that they believed in time travel and didn't try and make them feel small about it.

"Actually, James and Leah went *back* to Grandpa and Grannie's from this time, a little over a year ago. Their first child, Bibb Elizabeth Melbourne, was born six months ago in 1782. And since James and Leah were born in the mid-1980s, that means they were, what, negative 200 years old when she was born?"

"James Melbourne, my great-great however so many times grandfather, was born in the 1980s?" Jim asked softly, then pulled in his neck and scoffed. He had believed Benji for a split second, but no longer than that. This line of reasoning was creative fabrication, homegrown science fiction with a twist that included his family name in order to try and drag him into the fantasy.

Benji cleared his throat and looked first at his parents, and then at Jim. Gregg and Mona both had furrowed brows of recollection. They remembered the horrific pain they had endured traveling through the stones, the Stonehenge-type formations that were the portals to the past. They had gone through them to be with her 18th century parents, and then went through again to come back to the 20th century.

339

Big Jim looked curious but was not convinced. Yup, he was probably a good cop, Benji reckoned, because he *wasn't* gullible. Hard evidence would be needed for this man.

"Yes, and that same James Melbourne's brother is the father of my godson back in North Carolina. So, how do you explain that one?" Benji asked with pride. "What kind of uncle is he to ye: yer great-great however so many times over, or just a plain uncle?"

Benji shook his head, dismissing the concept, then returned to his original subject. "Dinna fash; that's not what we're tryin' to show ye with the yarn. So, here we have Jenny, aye?"

"I know Jenny; she's real, huh?" Bibby asked, looking to Benji for validation. She knew her mother believed that she had a special connection with her – that she was real – but her father still believed Jenny was her imaginary friend.

"Aye, Jenny's real all right. And," Benji picked up the thread he had set aside as Wee Ian, "Jenny marrit Wee Ian. At least, that's what Wee James Melbourne told me."

Benji saw the curiosity in Big James's face and continued with a big grin. "Grandpa Jody called him Wee James because he was *only* six foot tall. That's as tall as yer Grannie, rather yer Nana as ye call her," he said as an aside to Bibby.

"Weel, Wee James traveled from this time back to 1781 to save a life. His wife, Leah, came with him because she loved him so much. It turns out it was the life of Wee Ian who was his great-great HSM times," Benji looked over at Jane and said, "that's short for However So Many," and then looked over at Jim, "grandsire's life. Ye see, if someone hadna saved Wee Ian, Wee James would have never been born. The story of *the fairy* that came and saved the elder Ian was in the Cherokee—that's Native American Indian—legend. But the story should have been about *the fairy* that saved Wee Ian—or Scout, as Jenny called him."

Benji picked up the Wee Ian yarn from Elly Kincaid's side and joined it with the Jenny Pomeroy-Hart strand from Wallace and Jody Pomeroy's side. "And these two wound up being the HSM great-grandparents of my good friend James Melbourne. It's a bit of a Möbius strip. He had to be there—or at least he *was* there—so he could be born two hundred years later."

"Hmph," Big Jim snorted, suddenly ashamed that he had believed any of the tale, even for a moment. "Fairies, time travelin'… Weel, I guess if that's yer family's legacy, I'll not be one to dash it."

"So, where does yer family start? It may jest be coincidence that yer name is the same as my cousin's husband. Where did yer James Melbourne—the one who went to the penal colony in Australia—come from?"

Big Jim shut his eyes and sighed in resignation. He really didn't want to be a part of this discussion, but he was the host to his sister's newly found family members. "He was an American colonist, from North Carolina, who was arrested for – well, that part's fuzzy – in London in 1787. Rather than hang him, they let him go with Captain Arthur Phillip on the prisoner transport ship Alexander to New South Wales. He had skills. He had been a farmer and also knew how to read and do his numbers. The Captain petitioned to take him along. Word had it that his wife and three small children followed later and caught up with him in Parramatta in the early 1790s." Jim shrugged and said, "That's the short story of my family's heritage, at least on the Melbourne side."

"Shit!" Benji exclaimed, then looked at Jane who appeared to be just as upset as he was.

Big Jim was taken aback by the harsh remark. He hadn't expected that. He looked over at his wife to see her reaction to her brother's cursing in front of their young daughter. What he saw was an expression twin to her brother's. He turned to his in-laws and saw that they were nearly as devastated as his wife. "Did I miss somethin'?" he asked, truly confused.

"Benji, there's nothing we can do. And, even if we could, you couldn't go back and warn him…" Becky said, then stopped in her explanation.

Her father picked up the thought. "Because if ye did, then Big Jim and my grandchildren wouldna, well, they wouldna *be*. It's already happened."

"Well, first off, I think you all know that I don't believe in predestination," Mona said firmly, rising to take on the moderator's role with her hands-on-hips power woman stance. "And, I'm sorry if Wee James had to go through those trials and tribulations or whatever, but Leah did find him, right? I mean, didn't you just say that your great-grandmother Leah Melbourne followed him to Australia?" she asked

Jim.

"Aye, but what does that have to do with anythin'? Yer not making any sense, any of ye," Big Jim replied with huff, trying to keep his rage in check.

"We were with James, Leah, and young Bibb Elizabeth Melbourne jest two months ago. They were alive and well in 1782 North Carolina. Leah had jest found out that she was with child again. Ye may not accept it, but we've all seen it. My wife, yer wife, and I were all born in the 18th century. I dinna ken how we can prove it, but it *is* true. And I ken the first of the James Melbournes. He is, was, a fine person and a more honorable man, I've never met."

"Ho kay. I think I'll go outside and make sure the gates are closed or the chickens are in or, or, excuse me; I need a moment," Jim said, and dashed out the door.

Now two more people in his life believed in that time traveling nonsense. It was a good thing he loved his wife so much. He'd tolerate her and her family's madness, even if they ate nothing but potato chips and dressed in purple polka dotted pajamas. It could be worse: at least they were all discreet with their insanity, and no one knew about it but the immediate family. After all, it wasn't as if he didn't have skeletons in his closet.

End of Jenny and Scout's presence in THE GREAT BIG FAIRY. To find out more about Jane, Benji, and the others, read that mega-novel in its entirety and BIG MAC.

Complete Novel

Chasing Christmas

The Fairies Saga Book Eleven

Copyright © 2017
by Dani Haviland and Chill Out! Books
ISBN 978-1-950592-12-8

Early winter 1783, remote North Carolina: Rejuvenated time traveler Evie and her family have little in life except each other, but they're content. When her husband rescues an abused young Native American woman and brings her home, she's welcomed into the humble home.

Chapter 35: Amateur Surgeon (CC Ch 1, NTY Ch 5)

Late spring 1783

Dinner was finished, my two-year-old triplets had all used the privy and were in bed, and now I was answering a different kind of call of nature: that of midwife to my adopted daughter Jenny's pet Angora goat. My husband Wallace had come out to help after he and Jenny finished with the after dinner and before bedtime routines of washing dishes and a bedtime story for the three little ones.

I had been in the barn with Sarah P, the partially pregnant goat, for at least two hours. The first kid came out without a problem. However, the second one was stuck inside her. I had been trying to maneuver it in utero, kneading and manipulating the nanny's belly to get the baby's head down so she or he could be born, but the pushing and urging did nothing. The kid was still crossways in the womb; I couldn't get either the head or feet pointed to the exit.

I huffed and grunted in frustration, but that didn't help either.

"Wallace, I have to do something for her! I can't stand to see her suffer. Good grief, if Sarah was here, she'd know how to do it."

"How to do what?" he asked, busy with a fistful of straw, wiping the birth fluids off the first kid—a pure white female—that I had just delivered.

Still seated on the milking stool now repurposed into a midwife's bench, I set my chin in my hands. "Perform a C-section," I said glumly.

"What's that?"

"It stands for Caesarian section. That's where the mother's belly is cut open and the baby is pulled out. Supposedly, that's how Julius Caesar was born. Anyway, it's quite common when I come from, but I haven't done anything even remotely like that before. Only qualified surgeons with anesthetics and antibiotics would even attempt it."

"But, you just said that Julius Caesar was born that way. They didn't have anas…anasteth…well, they didn't have what you're telling me you need. But, I'm sure they had sharp knives. That's pretty much the most important part, right?"

"Yeah, well, Caesar probably wasn't born that way, but I *know* they've been successfully delivering babies by C-section for well over a hundred years, and all over the world, too. Hmph, I can't see how she'd be in any more pain if I cut the kid out of her than if I left it inside. If we—or I—don't do something soon, they'll both die."

I shifted position and turned toward the house. "Jenny," I hollered. "Oh, there you are. Honey, I need to do a medical procedure on Sarah P so would you get me the…"

Jenny brought her hand out from behind her back, revealing my chair-side sewing kit. "Can we help?"

I looked behind her and saw Scout holding up a bottle of whisky. He grinned and shrugged his shoulder but didn't say anything.

"What are you doing with that whisky?" Wallace asked, slightly indignant that the young visitor had helped himself to the family's liquor.

"Jenny said ye'd need it. I mean, she said Evie wanted it. And this, too." He brought out the paring knife from behind his back. "Ye did want them, dinna ye?" he asked uneasily.

Just then, Sarah P bleated in agony, sounding so much like a woman that it gave me the chills. "Yes, you two brought me everything I need. Now since you're both here, I'd like your help, too. Wallace, would you bind Bristol, that's the first kid, in a blanket and put her in the corner? I need you to hold one end of Sarah P. Scout and Jenny can hold the other end while I make the incision. On second thought, Wallace, you're stronger; you get the back legs."

Everyone grabbed a leg or two and I said a quick, "Lord, guide my hand and help me help her and the baby within; in Jesus name, Amen." I poured whisky over the blade of the paring knife and neared the nanny's bloated belly. "Shoot!" I said, glad that the expletive had changed into a verb on its way out. "I wish I could knock her out."

"Here, let me try," Wallace said. He released one of her legs, letting it pump air in pain and frustration, and used his free hand to place direct pressure on the side of her neck. She melted like an ice cube in summer, limp as cooked lettuce.

"Cool, the Spock grip," I said. "Let's get going. Keep hold of her legs, though, just in case she wakes up."

"Spock grip?" Wallace asked. "I think it's the carotid artery I put pressure on so the oxygen to her brain was depleted, causing her to lose consciousness. Oops, sorry; you need to concentrate."

I glanced at him and gave a combination grin and grimace, and then bent to my work. The first cut bled a lot but didn't get down to the uterine wall. Jenny took a rag and wordlessly, without prompting, wiped the blood from the cut. "I have to cut deeper," I said to myself as much as to them. They all watched intently, concentrating on what I was doing, as if it would help me perform my task. Actually, I think it did help. At least, I wasn't distracted.

Another firm cut and I was in. I turned away as the water from the second birth sac squirted in my face, then wiped it away with my shoulder. I quickly set the knife down and pulled out the second kid—this one male—and handed him to Scout. "Here, hold him while I sew her back up. Wallace, get ready to zap her carotid if she starts moving again."

Jenny handed me a threaded needle, anticipating my need before I even asked for it. Well, at least she lets me *think* it first. "Thanks," I said, then bent to the task: cross stitching on a nanny goat's belly.

***

Jody and his wife Sarah, my mother-in-law and the most popular healer in our part of the state, came back the next afternoon. "I'm impressed," Sarah said after checking on my patient.

I shrugged my shoulder in modesty, then smirked and asked, "Impressed with the job I did or that I even did it at all?"

"I'm impressed with the job. You always seem to come through, ready and willing to perform whatever task needs done, whether you think you're capable of it or not. Or whether you believe you have the correct tools or environment. But, the stitching is nice, too. It's a good thing she's young. She'll heal quickly, I'm sure. I'm curious though, where'd you dig up such odd names for the kids: Bristol and Track?"

"I don't know; they just popped into my head. They must mean something, though, because Leah howled when I told her the names. James didn't know what was so funny, so I think it's something from my past life. If it's that hilarious, it's probably something embarrassing, and I don't want to know about it. Nevertheless, the names just sounded right for the first two offspring of Sarah P and Todd. Leah said I used to know them; a married couple named Sarah and Todd but didn't say any more about them. Either way, the goats will both produce beautiful, soft fleece, and we can shear them twice as often as sheep. I guess they must be Scotch angoras—mighty thrifty critters."

**

A few days later, Scout's father—who also happened to be my ex-husband and the sperm donor to my triplets—showed up with a satchel filled to the brim with hostility and nothing else. "Let's go," he said to Scout. "Gather yer belongings. Ye've bothered these folks long enough."

"He's no bother," I said, waiting for the glare of anger that had fueled our rift three years earlier.

And there it was. Brown eyes narrowed, jaw thrust forward, nostrils flared. There was no doubt in my mind that he was holding back words and actions that nearly gagged him. He swallowed hard to compose himself then counted to five under his breath. "He's my son and my responsibility. We have many miles to travel, so I'd *appreciate it* if he gathered what is his and came along."

Wallace had been plowing in what we called the south forty and had seen Ian come to the house. He shimmied out from under the harness he wore to turn the soil—we had no mule—and sprinted to the edge of the yard, walking the last bit to catch his breath. "Good day to you, Ian," he said with what I knew to be feigned courtesy. When Ian showed up, discomfort was sure to be close behind.

"Good day to you, too, cousin," he said. "I've come to take with me what is mine. Wee Ian is in need of education; one better than counting, reading, and shucking corn."

Wallace's eyes opened wide in shock at the insult, then narrowed in disgust. *"Scout,"* he said, stressing the name that all of us, including the boy, preferred, "is old enough to make up his own mind about where he'd like to get his *education.*"

"I'm his father, and I'll decide where he goes and what he learns," Ian growled, his face red with barely contained rage, his bulging eyes positively scary.

Wallace took two steps closer to Ian. He was a full five inches taller than his cousin, and although he wasn't a violent man, he wasn't above intimidation.

"Yer height doesna bother me. Now, where is he?"

"I'm right here. I was just gatherin' a few items to take with me and

348

sayin' good-bye to Jenny." He turned and looked back at Jenny, her cheeks wet with tears, her eyes red and swollen. "Ye ken I'll be back soon, right?"

Jenny nodded, wiped her face with her sleeve, then ran to the barn so she didn't have to watch him leave.

"Ye'll be back when I say ye can," Ian said plainly, the rage gone now that he was certain he got his way.

I ran up to Scout and gave him a big hug. I whispered in his ear, "Did you take some food? It doesn't look like he has anything in his bag."

"Aye. Jenny gave me all those pro-teen bars, as she calls 'em. She said she could make more. Dinna worry about Da and me. I'll do my best to make sure he doesna get in *serious* trouble."

"You do that. And you know you're welcome to stay with us at any time, right?"

"Aye, but someone has to watch out fer him. Maybe by spendin' some time with Da, I can teach *him*."

"We can only hope and pray," I said, and kissed him on the cheek.

Wallace came up and shook Scout's hand. "Be careful out there. We'll be praying for you."

Ian rolled his eyes and snorted. "Let's go. We've tarried here long enough."

And then they were gone, neither of them looking back, although Scout did slip his hand behind his back to give me a surreptitious wave good-bye.

Yes, Scout would be fine. It's that father of his who needed to learn a lesson or twelve.

Chapter 36: Not So Modern Communications (CC Ch 2)

Late November 1783
Backwoods North Carolina

Clunk! Clunk!

"What was that?" I called out the door.

Jenny popped her head around the corner. "I was trying to put my telegraph wire up on the eave, but the end I tied the rock to keeps falling down. I didn't have any wire, so I used rope. Then," my blonde pre-teen daughter sighed in exasperation, "I didn't have enough rope, so I used pieces of rag that I tore into strips so I could make my own. I thought I had enough to reach the whole way," she added a snort of frustration, "but it's still too short. James said that where he was from, you could send messages over wires, but since we don't have any wire—he said that's made of copper or some other kind of metal, albumen, I think—I have to use what I can find around here."

"I think you mean aluminum. That's very resourceful of you, sweetheart, but I think that it needs to be real metal wire, not cloth or sisal."

I saw her scowl of frustration wasn't going to vanish by itself anytime soon, so I tried to think of a way to bring a smile back to my very own 18th century Pippy Longstockings. And, boom, just like one of Jenny's rocks landing on the roof, there it was.

"We may not have wire, but since you've already strung the rope and rag cording from here to James and Leah's, all you need to do is tie a bell onto each end. If you need to get their attention, just pull the cord on your end and their bell will ring. If they need you, they can do the same thing. But we'll need two bells."

"Really? Oh, oh!" Jenny exclaimed, bouncing up and down. "And I can still use that Morris Code that James has been teaching me. Do you know it? It's dots and dashes, he said, but they're actually just short and long noises. We can use clangs and claa-angs. I almost have the alphabet memorized already!"

"First, it's Morse code and second, I think you'd be better off having short signals. How about we only ring the bell when we want someone from the other house to come give us a hand. Your father can be one clang, I'll be two, and you can be three. When we call over to their house, James can be one clang, Leah can be two, and I can't see a reason why we'd need to ring for their babies. Most likely, they'll be ringing for you. Now, how many clangs would that be?"

"Three! But we're going to have to find a couple of bells first. I don't think we have any around here."

"Well, I'm sure your father will find something. Or James can make something."

My daughter Leah and son-in-law James had arrived from the twenty-first century two years ago and now lived shouting distance away from our humble home in 1783 North Carolina. I'd been here almost a year longer than they had, and they had adapted quickly, too. James was handy with re-creating modern conveniences with what we had on hand. Ceiling fans and solar water heaters were his greatest achievements, but he bragged that he was just getting started.

"Are you sure you'll be all right watching all these babies by yourself?" Jenny asked, bringing me out of my reverie on how so much had changed in such a short time.

"Yes, dear. I was doing most everything by myself before you came into our lives. I mean, your father helped me and so did Granny, but I think it's time you got a break. Think of it as a Daddy-Daughter date."

I was having a difficult time convincing my precocious adopted daughter that I could handle three toddlers for half a day. Actually, Wallace was doing me a favor. Feeding and keeping track of our triplets was a breeze compared to playing the living, breathing internet search engine of 1783 for the most inquisitive girl in the state. She pretty much grew up without parents, and her now deceased elder brothers who had reared her had been about one shoelace shy of being feral. There was plenty for her to learn, and she was a quick study, but I wished she wouldn't try to achieve a college-level education less than a year after learning simple math and how to read.

"What's a date for daddies and daughters? I've never heard of it. I know Daddy is my daddy, and I'm his daughter now, and I know the date of Christmas is in fourteen days, but no one told me about a Daddy-Daughter date. Is it a holiday? Oh, and am I supposed to make him a gift or do something special for it?"

Saved by the clomp, clomp of my husband's boots coming up the porch steps.

"How's my favorite middle daughter doing, Jenny?" Wallace said and braced himself for her linebacker hug.

When it didn't appear, he knelt down to accept a more sedate hug and squeeze from the forlorn Jenny. He stood up and looked to me, then nodded toward Jenny. 'Is there something wrong?' I shook my head, 'She's all right,' so he turned his attention back to her.

"Are you ready to go to town?" He stroked her head from the crown down to her ear. "The weather is clear, but it's still cold, so grab an extra scarf."

While she rummaged through the box of scarves and mittens, my husband turned to me. "Are you sure you'll be all right watching all these babies by yourself?"

"You two! What? Did you get together and memorize lines or something?" I looked over at the two of them, standing elbow-to-shoulder, blank looks on their faces. "It's like memorizing Bible verses or poems or something. Yes, the young ones and I will keep each other entertained, I'm sure. If nothing else, we'll take that rag ball you made and go outside and play catch until they're worn out."

"Or you're worn out. I'm sure glad they're still taking naps. I'm hoping Mr. Gibson gives me a good price for the chest. It's going to be tight…"

"But we always manage, right?"

Wallace leaned down and kissed me on the lips, ignoring the tittering giggles of Jenny. "We'll manage, I'm sure. Now, if he's in a good mood and his arthritis isn't bothering him, I may have a couple extra coins. Is there anything you need or want, other than the flour, salt, and cornmeal?"

"Surprise me," I said. "Whatever you bring me will be appreciated."

Chapter 37: Skunky Slippers (CC Ch 3)

Wallace stepped outside and looked up, gauging the weather by the breeze on his face one last time before they left. The air was still dry and barely moving. Fair weather for another day, at least. Two weeks ago, they had experienced an early snow, but all that remained of the six-inch fall were wind-polished icy patches in the shady spots under a few trees and dense bushes.

He climbed onto the buckboard seat next to Jenny. "So, are you ready to go?" he asked. "And will you be warm enough?" and tucked in the two cream-colored woolen blankets she had laid over her lap.

"I'm fine," she answered and scooted closer to him, "but you need to keep warm, too," and proceeded to rearrange the woven coverings to include his legs, too.

"Thank you,' he said. "Now, the sooner we leave, the sooner we'll be back to rescue your mother from your siblings." He flicked the reins over the horse's back and headed into town to sell his latest creation: a sugar chest.

The cherrywood locking cabinet on stubby little legs would serve a dual purpose for its new owner. Not only would it make a secure storage area for both white and dark sugars in the two-compartment chest itself, the top was slanted to provide a writing desk. He might be able to get more money from it if he could wait to find the right buyer himself, but Joseph Gibson, the storekeeper, had a better chance of selling it in a hurry. Christmas was nearing, and although they had everything they needed for the next few months, provisions would be meager or non-existent if they had a late spring.

"What's a Daddy-Daughter date?" Jenny asked, gazing up at him, sure that he could explain it better than Mommy had.

"I'm not sure, but it sounds like it could be fun."

"Mommy said that's what we're doing now, going on a Daddy-Daughter date. Does it have to be today, or can it be on any day?"

Wallace rolled his eyes. Evie usually gave him forewarning when she told Jenny about a subject or event that was from her previous life in the 21st century. Right now, he'd just 'wing it,' as she called it.

"*Any* time you and I are alone together, especially away from home, can be a Daddy-Daughter date. Now, after I get paid for the sugar chest, we may have a few extra coins. I was going to buy a gift for your mother, but I don't know what she wants or needs. Can you think of anything?"

Jenny tipped her head from one side to the other, sighed, started to speak up, then sighed again. "She keeps telling me she has everything she needs. Every once in a while, she says she wishes she had another set of hands, but then she says that's what you and I are for."

"I'm sure we'll find something. If not, we'll save that money for later. You do remember what we told you about money, right?"

"Money isn't everything, but it's necessary when we can't barter or trade, build or scavenge, hunt or fish for what we do need." Jenny paused and cleared her throat. "Is that a good enough answer?"

"Yes, I think you have it down." He looked down at her and saw she was grimacing in discomfort. "Are you all right?"

"It hurts my throat when I talk 'cause the air's so cold." She re-wrapped her scarf around her neck. "I guess I'll just stop talking then."

The two rode along in a comfortable silence for an hour, Wallace designing another piece of furniture in his head, this one a kitchen cabinet with a removable basin in it, with room for a hand pump at the side.

"Hey, look! What kind of animal is that?" Jenny asked, pulling on his coat sleeve to get his attention.

Wallace leaned forward and squinted to focus on the creature traveling on the wagon wheel-rutted path that was considered the road to Gibsonville. It appeared to be a massive bear, but the fur was mottled and the gait was that of a stumbling man. "I think someone is carrying a large load. Maybe we can offer him a hand."

"Or a ride," Jenny said and scooted closer to him to make more room.

The man beneath the bulk of bundled furs heard the crunching of the wheels on the road and stepped aside to allow the wagon to pass.

Wallace slowed the horse, then pulled up beside him and stopped the wagon. The Native American man was about the same age as he was, broad-shouldered, but thin, and definitely ready to collapse. "Hey there, friend. Are you in need of assistance?"

The man nodded, then grimaced as he shifted his load.

Wallace jumped down and helped remove the rawhide-tied bundle of furs from his back. "You're welcome to ride in front with my daughter and myself. The bench is wide and we were just about to have a bite to eat. We'd be pleased if you'd join us."

Jenny had anticipated the scenario and had already removed the satchel of food from the storage chest under the buckboard seat, or 'bonnet' as James called the modification he had made. She held her bundle close, making sure the tall man had room to sit.

It took two tries before the traveler could pull himself up to the bench seat. Jenny looked at her father and he glanced back, glad that, for once, Jenny didn't make a comment about the obvious. The man was probably weak from hunger and exhausted from toting the heavy load.

After the man was settled in, Jenny pulled the second blanket from her lap. "My name is Jenny, and I think you'd be more comfortable if you wrapped this around your shoulders. I'll bet your back is cold now that you don't have all those furs on it, huh?"

"Thank you, Jenny," the blue-lipped man said, unable to cover the quiver in his voice. He settled into the blanket, still warm from her body heat. "My name is Samuel."

"And this is my daddy, Wallace Pomeroy-Hart. He wasn't always my daddy, but he is now. We're on a Daddy-Daughter date today, but it's all right if you come with us. Sometimes a party is more fun when you have other people, especially new people. We live that way," she said, and sat forward so she could point behind her. "Where do you live?"

Wallace opened his mouth to tell her to let their new friend rest but remained mute when he saw the gentle man smile. He squinted and looked up at the sun to get his bearings. "A few days walk in that direction. I've come to trade for food for my tribe."

"I'm sure Mr. Gibson will be fair with you. I'm bringing that chest in to him," Wallace tipped his head to point to his creation. "He won't be buying it for himself, but he is acquainted with some of the more affluent families in the area. He said that sugar chests are becoming very popular but are hard to find." Wallace saw the confused look on the man's face. "Sugar is quite valuable, so the families who can afford it, keep it under lock and key to keep servants, or whomever, from stealing it."

Jenny saw the confused look on Samuel's face. "I couldn't figure it out either. Who would want to steal? I mean, if a man's working for someone, and he stole from him, wouldn't they ask him to leave because of it? And then he wouldn't have a job or *anything!*"

Samuel smiled and nodded, then pulled the blanket closer around his neck.

"Hey!" Jenny said, sitting upright and turning toward the wayfarer. "I just remembered something. My brothers—not the brothers I have now, but my other brothers who are in heaven—used to take their furs to the man who lived just before you get to the store. I'll show you where 'cause we're going to ride right past it. But I think we ought to let you off there instead of going to the store. You see, Mr. Gibson—he's the storekeeper, remember?—sells the furs you trade to him to someone else. His name is Karl Something-or-other, but Mr. Karl's good enough. Now, the first price he offers you is not the price you want to take. He gives you a low price right away, but he doesn't expect you to take it. Just shake your head when he says it and frown. Tell him you know you can get a better price."

Jenny paused in her instructions, realizing that Samuel was not likely to haggle when it came to prices. He barely spoke at all. "Maybe you'd better just shake your head and walk to the door. He'll get the idea. He really wants skins. Not many folks have skins for sale this time of year. They're going out trapping now, not selling. Asides, I saw that you had quite a few furs in there that were already stretched and tanned. He'll pay more for them. Or he should. Don't let him cheat you. I know you need the money for food for your mother and sisters and all those other folks in your tribe. You can tell him that. Or just shake your head and walk to the door. He'll give you the money, and then you can come to Mr. Gibson's store to buy what you need."

Samuel looked down at Jenny and said, "I didn't tell you about my mother and sisters…"

"Jenny has a vivid imagination sometimes," Wallace said, and gave her a stern look, letting her know she had just revealed too much of what she 'saw' about Samuel. "But she's right about the tanner. See him first."

"Oh, and we have about," Jenny looked up to the sun, then shut her eyes as she calculated the time of day from the sun's position, "another hour to go before we get there." She reached into the satchel on her lap and took out a napkin and spread it on her lap like a tablecloth.

"I made sandwiches for everyone this morning before we left. We make flatbread sometimes, and put cheese and shredded cabbage on it, then roll it up! It's really good. Here's yours," she handed the tortilla-wrapped meal to Samuel, "and here's yours, Daddy. And here's mine. It's smaller than those two because my hands are smaller. Actually, my whole body is smaller, so I don't need as much food to stay warm and strong and I think I'd better stop talking and eat."

Wallace could tell by the confused look on Samuel's face that he'd never eaten anything like the 'wrapped' sandwich. "A bit different, but easy to handle when on the road," he said, then bit into it.

Samuel copied Wallace, biting into the end of the meal rather than starting in the middle as he thought he should. He chewed the unusual textured concoction, then smiled. "Good. Very good," he said. His stomach growled in agreement, and they all chuckled.

"Here's your drink, Samuel, and here's Daddy's and here's mine."

Jenny passed around the stoneware vessels that held some of the pressed apple cider she had helped put up two months ago. "*Slante!*" she toasted, then toped back a dribble. She put the stopper back in her bottle, then returned it to the lunch bag. "I'll finish it later," she said, then leaned closer to her father, and fell fast asleep.

***

Wallace pulled up to the small log cabin in front of the large clapboard structure that was the tanner's. The sudden cessation of movement wakened Jenny from her deep slumber. "Oh, we're here already. Can I come in and say hello to Mr. Karl, Daddy?"

"Go ahead. I'll help Samuel split this load up so Karl can see that many of these are tanned skins and hides, not just pelts."

Jenny rubbed the sleepy dust out of her eyes, then wrapped her lap blanket around her shoulders as a shawl. She stomped her feet loudly as she headed up the steps to the house to announce her presence. "Hello, Mr. Karl," she shouted. "It's me, Jenny. I brought you some good skins."

The scraping of wood on wood indicated that a door bolt was being removed. "Jenny? I thought you was dead!" he said, then scratched his head. "No, wait. I remember now. It was your brothers that died. You went to live with the healer's daughter and her husband or something like that."

Wallace walked up with half the load of furs over his shoulder, Samuel a step behind him with the rest of the pelts. "Greetings, Karl. Yes, I'm Jenny's father now, and this is Samuel. We have some mighty fine skins for you to look over. I noticed that some of these are prime and are already tanned and stretched, so should bring top dollar with your buyers. Less work for you, too. I'm sure you'll give him a fair price, but I must warn you, Jenny's already instructed him on how to deal with you."

Karl half laughed, half snorted at the remark. "Jenny, are you trying to take away my profits?" When he saw the quizzical look on her face, he changed his wording. "Jenny, are you trying to take coins out of my pocket and give them to someone else?"

"Only if he deserves them, and he does. Now, if you're not fair to him, I'll tell my brothers up in heaven to give you nightmares and scare the grasshoppers into your fields and mice into your cellar and turn your cider into vinegar and…and… Well, all sorts of evils will come your way if you cheat this man. He does have a mother and sisters and a few others to take care of still."

Karl's eyes widened in shock at what could almost be called a curse. Wallace saw his distress and tapped her on the shoulder, bringing her back to his side. "I'm sure Samuel and Mr. Karl can work out an agreement. Come on, I want to get to the store. I don't think it's going to rain or snow, but I don't want to be coming home in the dark, either."

***

Mr. Gibson the storekeeper was all smiles when he saw Wallace and Jenny walk in. "Did you get that sugar chest finished? I think I already have a buyer for it."

"It's just outside. Come take a look. Jenny, go ahead and see if you can find something for your mother. We'll be back shortly."

Jenny took her time looking at the bottles that held colored glass beads, toggles and buttons, the trays of buckles, all three bolts of fabric, then stopped. She found what she wanted: the larger jars that held candies. There were so many of them: four! She knew what most of them were from years ago when her brothers had spent all the money they earned from trapping that winter on candy. The brown ones were maple sugar candy and molasses pulls; the pure white ones, peppermint sticks; the yellow pieces lemon sours, and it looked as if he even had marzipan. Her mouth watered in anticipation. She opened the door and looked outside at her daddy to see if Mr. Gibson was happy with the sugar chest. She jumped up and down with joy: both of them were all smiles. Maybe she'd get candy!

358

Samuel walked up to the two white men—Wallace, the tall, quiet young man who had given him a ride just as he was ready to collapse, and the other man, an older gentleman who must by the storekeeper, Mr. Gibson. He stopped ten feet away and waited for them to finish their discussion. They were transacting business and he didn't want to intrude or eavesdrop.

Mr. Gibson looked up from his inspection of the sugar chest and saw the half-breed Indian waiting patiently. "Wallace told me you'd be needing some supplies. Go on in out of the cold to wait. No use catching a chill. I'll be in shortly."

Samuel nodded that he understood, then walked up the two steps to the store, grinning. He had actually been invited in! Is this what it felt like to be an all-white man? Maybe he should have said thank you, but he didn't like to speak. He knew many English words, but still had trouble getting his tongue wrapped around some of their sounds. It was much easier to read and write their language than to speak it. He would, however, make sure he told Wallace how much he appreciated his help.

And Jenny. He'd thank her, too, for feeding him and offering him the cider that revived his spirit. And for warning Mr. Karl about the perils that would befall him if he didn't give him a fair price. The man was quick to give him more than he expected, then he swiftly amended it, offering him even more. Yes, with the hearty fare he had eaten and the cider, he now had the energy to return to the village with winter supplies. He suppressed a sigh of satisfaction but couldn't keep the corners of his mouth from lifting in appreciation. He might even be able to afford a mule if there was one in town, but he didn't think he'd be that fortunate. Still, it would make returning with the food much easier. It was a long walk back...

"Oh, hello, Samuel," Jenny said, then stepped away from the candies. "Karl did well by you, I can tell from your smile. He's a good man, but he gets greedy sometimes. Did you make a list for what you need or do you have it memorized?"

Samuel didn't understand all her words, but he did know what he needed. He held out his coins to show her how much he had received.

"Ooh, he was *very* good to you. Here, let me show you around. This is where he keeps the flour, and over here in this barrel is the cornmeal, and..."

359

Jenny's tour of the little store was interrupted by an angry voice calling back from the opened door. "Get yer lazy arse up here before I have to kick it up the steps."

The grizzled man with the slouch hat pulled down over sprawling, matted hair and a greasy beard spotted with heaven-only-knew-what reached out and grabbed the small dark-haired woman by the arm. "Were ye raised in a barn? Nah. Not that lucky. Get in here. Yer lettin' all the warm air out."

The petite woman in the patched ankle-length buckskin dress shuffled in, stopping in front of the pot-bellied stove that heated the single-room store.

"Get away from that! Let the white folks get warmed up first." He pushed her aside and turned his back to the heat source. He realized he wasn't the only one in the room and turned his attention to Jenny. "Good day, little miss. Is that yer father out there?"

Jenny nodded, terrified of the man she'd just met. She didn't have to be psychic to sense the evil that was all about him. She shook her head to erase the unwanted mental images overloading her mind, of him beating and mistreating the Indian woman with him.

"Well, what is it? Is he yer pa or not?" the man bellowed.

Samuel came out from the shadows and stood beside her. "He's her father," he said, and glowered at the short dumpy man, crossing his arms in front of himself to let it be known that he was the girl's champion, and that her white father, his friend, was within shouting distance.

"Ooh, yer a tall one. Yer pa musta been a mighty big white man, him bein' able to build such a tall buck with one of them wee little squaws. Now, move aside. I have some goods to purchase." He snorted in derision at Samuel, "And the proprietor will want to see to my needs first since I'm using real coin, not wampum."

Samuel clenched his jaws. It wouldn't do his family any good if he let his temper out. One good punch to the mouth and the man would lose the rest of his teeth. Or maybe he'd target the man's gut. One hard jab and he could push his fist all the way through to the man's spine. He'd reach in, pull it out, and strangle him with it…

Jenny looked up and saw Samuel's face had turned scarlet. She could feel his righteous rage but didn't want him to lose his temper and get in trouble. The white man was always right around here, even when it

360

wasn't fair or just. "Come help me figure out what kind of candies these are," Jenny said, and urged him away from the arrogant bigot.

"I think I want to get my mother a peppermint stick," Jenny whispered to Samuel, trying to distract him. "You see, if Daddy gets enough money for the sugar chest, then we can get two. Then I can have one candy and share it with my little brothers and sister and my mother…"

She stopped in mid-thought and sniffed the air. "What's that smell?" she asked, looking around the room.

The pork-bellied white man roared out loud, laughing so hard, he broke wind. "That's her shoes. See?" He pointed to the woman's black and white striped raw pelt slippers, bound around her feet with strips of coarse-cut leather. "She went and lost her shoes, so I made her another pair. Ye'd think she'd be grateful, but she wouldn't wear them 'til I threw her others in the fire."

Samuel's back straightened, his chest puffed out in anger, but he stayed where he was when he felt Jenny's hand on his arm, silently begging him to stand down.

The meek woman looked up at the handsome stranger, saw his rage, then said, "They'll do." She'd seen the man who owned her get mad before. It wouldn't do for him to get in another fight. And kill again. She glanced back at the man who was at least half Indian, ready to stand in her defense. Her master didn't fight fair, but he did make sure the other person would never come back at him again. She moved away from the door and inched closer to the fire.

"Ach, I guess ye can warm yer scrawny bones a bit. My arse is so warm now, it feels like it's afire."

Mr. Gibson and Wallace walked in and immediately started sniffing the air. "What's that smell?" the storekeeper asked.

The woman collapsed to the floor in tears. Jenny rushed to her side and started patting her back, telling her she'd be all right, to ignore everyone else in the room.

"It's her shoes!" Porkbelly said and started laughing all over again. He finally regained his composure and looked at Mr. Gibson and Wallace. "It gets me to laughin' every time. Now, I have a lot of goods I need, so let's get to it."

Mr. Gibson looked from Wallace to the tall, silent Indian and said,

"I'm sorry, sir. There are two gentlemen ahead of you. Wallace?"

"Here's the list of the foodstuffs," he said and gave it to Mr. Gibson, trying to ignore the crude comedian.

"What? Two gentlemen? I only see an overgrown farm boy and the leftovers from a soldier's carousing in the woods," then he began laughing again.

Wallace walked up to the crude, dumpy man, just inches away, and stared down, the man's upturned face a full head and a half below his. He had no intention of telling the man that he wasn't common-born, that until a few years past, he had been a titled landowner in England, but he would use his Lord of the Manor demeanor to his advantage. "Am I to assume that you intentionally shod this young woman with the untanned skins of polecats?"

"Aye," he crowed and started to laugh again. "Ain't that a hoot?" then his merriment faded. He wasn't afraid of the big half-breed Indian. He could, and had, gotten away with whatever he wanted as long as he was in civilization, but this tall white boy—who he had thought an underaged and overgrown dirt farmer—had the speech and manner of someone high born. He sucked back his merriment. This lad might be connected with the constables. It would be best to keep on this one's good side.

"Well, at the time, it was all I had," he said with feigned sincerity.

"Am I to believe that you provided your wife with fetid vermin pelts to cover her delicate skin?"

Porkbelly started to laugh aloud, then thought better of it, but couldn't suppress a chuckle. "My wife? This ain't my wife. I paid a full dollar for her upriver a year ago last spring. The chief said she couldn't get a babe in her belly, so was worthless. I could do what I wanted with her."

Wallace's eyes widened in shock, but he quickly blinked back his rage. He glanced over at Samuel and saw that Jenny was now at his side, her hand on his arm, effectively holding the livid man down with her gentle touch.

"I'll tell you what, mister," Wallace said congenially, then changed into his commanding officer tone when he saw the smug look on the ornery man's face. "Mister... I'm sorry. We haven't been introduced. However, names are not important in this case, so I'll just refer to you as

Mr. Smith. Therefore, Mr. Smith, since you paid one full dollar for this woman a year and a half ago, I'll relieve your burden by taking this woman with me and I'll give you back that full dollar. No deductions for the wear and tear she seems to have incurred," he looked down at her red swollen ankles, "and lack of proper footwear." He held out an uncut silver Spanish dollar and offered his other hand to seal the transaction. "Do we have an agreement?"

The man now called Mr. Smith looked at the money, then over to the squaw, huddled on the ground, the scrawny young blonde who couldn't be much more than twelve now back trying to comfort her. "Why not? She can't cook worth a lick, and she's not much better at keeping me warm at night. But be careful! She bites when really riled." He shrugged one arm out of his heavy coat, then pulled up his sleeve to show the viscous bite mark on his inner arm, thick red streaks going out in all directions from it.

Mr. Smith pulled his arm back inside his coat, then grabbed for the money. Wallace had seen the intent in his eyes and held the coin high. He vigorously shook the man's blood poisoned right hand to complete the deal in front of witnesses, then handed him the coin. "I hear tell that the ordinary in the next town has saddle of mutton and sweetbreads along with the finest ale in the state. You could buy yourself a *very* fine meal there."

"Aye, and maybe someone to keep me warm tonight." He looked at Mr. Gibson, the man who had denied him priority service. "And I'm sure their stores are stocked with more provisions there than you have here. Farewell, Annie. I'd like to say it's been a pleasure, but as you and I both know, it hasn't." He tipped his filthy slouch hat to the store owner and Wallace, then shuffled out the door, letting loose another of his raucous laughs.

The room was suddenly empty and silent. "Now, then," Mr. Gibson said to break the bubble of gloom, "Didn't you want to get a few more items, Wallace?"

"I was going to have Jenny pick out some cloth and threads for her mother, but I'm afraid my funds have dwindled. I think we'll have enough left over for some candy, though. Do you think she'd like that, sweetheart?"

Jenny looked up from the dirt floor, still holding onto 'Annie.'

"Mommy said she's always had a sweet tooth, so I think a peppermint stick will make her happy. Maybe Father Christmas will bring us some cloth."

"Oh, it's just as well that you wait for the fabric, Wallace. I had a shipment coming in from Calcutta by way of London, but it's been delayed. Check back after the first of the year," he said and winked.

Wallace turned to look behind him, trying to figure out why Gibson was winking, then sighed as he realized that his shipment would probably be in before Christmas.

"Here's the change for your purchases," the storekeeper said, dropping a few pieces of eight into Wallace's hand. He looked up and saw that his customer was about to protest—they both knew that he had given him the correct amount of money for the goods Gibson had gathered while the negotiating for Annie had transpired.

"You got the gentleman of the year discount for helping out the young lady there," Gibson said. He reached into the candy jar and pulled out three peppermint sticks and wrapped them in an old political flyer. "And here's a surprise for your ladies," nodding to Jenny and Annie, "and your wife. It's for…well, just because. Happy Christmas to you and your family."

Gibson turned his attention to the other man in the room, Samuel. "Now, sir, how may I help you."

"I'll be right back, Jenny," Wallace said. "I want to secure the food in the wagon, then I'll help you and Annie outside. Move closer to the stove so you can get extra warm. It's a long ride back and I think the wind is kicking up."

Jenny took the second scarf from around her neck and arranged it around the terrified young woman. "Welcome to our family, Annie. My mother said she wanted an extra pair of hands around the house, so I guess that's what she's getting. At least until it's spring. You don't *have* to stay with our family, but we want you to. Both my granny and sisters are healers, too, and maybe one of them can get the redness and swelling to go away on your feet. Oh, and here."

Wallace came in and watched as Jenny pulled her skirt up to her shins, unlaced and pulled off her boots. "I wore two pairs of stockings today because I'm wearing what my older sister Leah—she's not my blood sister 'cause I'm adopted, but she's my sister, just the same—what she calls hand-me-downs. They'll still fit me with just one pair of stockings, though. We can toss those polecat skins in the burn pile and you can wear my other pair. These are real woolen stockings. They kinda look odd because they had to be patched where my heal rubbed a hole in one of them, but they're still warm."

Jenny had been removing her socks as she recited the story of why she had a spare pair and what her relationship was to her older sister. "Oh, my! That's gotta hurt!" she said when she pulled off Annie's footwear. "Goodness! I didn't know toes could turn black."

"Go ahead and put your extra socks on her, Jenny, but be very gentle," Wallace said. "She has what's called frostbite on her toes. I'm sure your mother, sister, or Granny knows what to do for it. In the meantime, we'll keep them warm and covered."

Wallace waited for Mr. Gibson to come out of the back room with an empty flour sack for Samuel's order. "Thank you again, for your help, Mr. Gibson. I'll see you in a few weeks maybe."

Gibson winked and said, "Sooner might be better. Be safe, and congratulations on the new addition to your family."

Wallace watched as Jenny finished putting the stockings on the dark-haired young woman. Annie's eyes were wide and vacant, like the shell-shocked soldiers he'd seen at the front when he was an officer in His Majesty's Army. Suddenly, the glassiness faded and warmth came into her eyes. He followed her gaze. Samuel was looking at her, his eyes narrowed in concern.

Wallace walked up and placed a hand of reassurance on the man's shoulder. "She'll be safe, my friend. She's a free person, not a slave or an indentured servant, and may leave at any time. However, right now I think it's best that we take her to the healer. She'll be warm and safe with my family."

Wallace watched as Samuel breathed a big sigh of relief, then added a terse, "Thank you," and gave a nervous sliver of a smile to Annie.

"Would you help me get her to the wagon, Samuel? Just grab one elbow and I'll get the other. I don't want her feet to touch the ground."

The two men ported the scared, but unresisting, woman to the wagon. Samuel held her in his arms while Wallace got in the wagon. Wallace patted the side of the seat where she was to ride and Samuel handed her up to him. Yes, there was a definite attraction between the two, but he knew that Samuel didn't have much, if anything, to offer the young woman.

"Feel free to come visit her any time you'd like. Jenny gave you the general location of our home. We're not difficult to find. Just look for the building shaped like this." Wallace put his fingertips together to indicate the shape of the tepee that James was building as his final home.

"Before we leave, Mr. Gibson," Jenny said, "I want to thank you for helping us. I know you didn't have to buy that sugar chest…"

"Oh, pish posh. He's a fine craftsman and, mark my word, his works will be in great demand soon. But before you leave," he went behind the counter, reached into the candy jar, held all the peppermint sticks to the side, then poured the crumbs out onto a scrap of paper. "Here's some traveling sweets for all of you. The bits are too small to sell, but taste just as good."

Jenny accepted the treasure packet with a smile, a giggle, then a big hug. "Thank you!"

He leaned down and whispered, "You make sure you're nice to that young woman. She's had a rough time. This wasn't the first time those two have been in my store. The last time was summer, though. If you and your father hadn't said something, well," he rubbed his chin in deep thought. "I don't know what my wife woulda done if I brought home a full-grown woman to stay with us, but I woulda dealt with her fussing and hollering rather than let him keep abusing her like that. Not even letting her have a tanned hide so she could make her own shoes, and him having so many of them."

"We'll be good to her. Oh, and I didn't know what to do with those old polecat shoes of hers. They're still on the floor by the stove."

"Now, don't you worry about it. I'll have a bonfire going sometime soon. I'll toss them onto it when the wind starts blowing the right direction. Now git before your pa leaves without you."

"Yes, sir," Jenny said and bounced out the door. He was her pa and everyone in this town knew it. Finally, a real father.

And maybe another sister.

Chapter 38: When's Christmas? (CC Ch 4)

Late November 1783

"Mom, remember when I was little and always asked, 'When's it going to be Christmas,' and you'd say, 'There's no sense in chasing Christmas. It'll get here when it's time.'"

Leah's face fell as soon as the words were out of her mouth. "Crap. Sorry, Mom. Well, if you *could* remember anything, I'm sure that's one of the things you'd remember."

I chuckled at her embarrassment. "You know what? That's the sort of thing I really *want* you to remind me about. That's a sweet memory. Now, if you can give me enough like those, I won't care that I have amnesia. I doubt that the wee three or even Jenny will ever have that gimme-gimme attitude, though, because Christmas isn't a big commercial deal in this day and age…"

I looked back at her to see if she was smiling yet or not. She was. "Doesn't it sound weird? 'In this day and age.' How many people can actually claim to have lived in two centuries that were separated by a third one?"

"As far as I know," she replied, multitasking nursing her young son while corralling her daughter between her outstretched legs, "it's just you, me, James, and Sarah. But you do remember what a madhouse they made Christmas into, right?"

"Yup. Halloween costumes were barely off the racks and then colored lights, ornaments, and wrapping goodies fought for floor space with toys and gizmos that were gifted then tossed in the garbage after a month or less."

"If they were even used at all. And the clothes! Remember ugly Christmas sweaters? Who thought of that?" Leah shuddered, disturbing young River. "It's okay, sweetie. Finish eating. I want to visit with your grandma a while longer." She looked up. "When do you think Jenny and Wallace will be back?"

I looked out at the sun, setting low in the corner of the southern window. "I hope soon. Dinner's ready now, so if you want to eat early, go ahead. I had half a jar of pickles before you came over, so I'm set for a while."

"Mom," she asked slowly and gently. "Do you think you're pregnant again?"

I snorted and shook my head. "Nope. Period started today, just like clockwork. If you don't see a moon, that means it's my time of the month. I really don't *need* to have another child. I mean, Leo, Judah, and Wren are two-and-a-half years old now and potty trained, so a new one wouldn't be too hard to handle."

"Another one? Ah, come on, Mom. You had me as a single, then the triplets. Aren't you due for twins?"

"Bite your tongue!" I said, then took it down a notch. "No, whatever the Lord decides to give us will be fine. I know Wallace says he couldn't love you or the others any more, even if he had sired you, but I really do want to have one of his children. I can't believe my luck…"

Leah interrupted. "Blessing!"

"Right. I can't believe how blessed I was to find a father for them, even before they were born." I shook my head and images of my past relationship with my first husband rattled up, down, and sideways. "I really and truly can't imagine being married to Ian, what my life would be like now." I saw that she didn't know why I had brought it up. That part of my life had been over for more than three years.

"Ian came and took Scout away this spring," I said. "He's probably on another one of his vengeance quests and wants to train his son in the fine art of retribution. That poor boy. It shouldn't be the son trying to keep the parent out of trouble. And Scout's not even a teenager yet. Or at least I don't think he is. Still, he doesn't even have a whisker and he's trying to keep that…that ornery bugger…"

I looked around, back in the present, ready to dismiss the woulda-coulda-shoulda issues and control who and what I could. "What are my wee three up to now, anyhow?"

"James whipped up some pieces of thick paper then stitched a bunch of them together into a book. He colored the pages with all sorts of weird homemade inks. Your three are under that blanket in the corner, taking turns 'reading' it to each other."

"He put words in it, too?"

"Nope. He made images that we might recognize but told them they had to make up their own stories for the pictures. Seems to be keeping them busy."

Leah stood up suddenly, releasing her daughter from Mommy jail and bringing her son up with her to look out the window. "They're here," she said and sat back down. A split second later, she popped up to look outside again. "It looks like there's three of them, though. We got company. I'd better get myself together. Here, hold onto your grandson a minute. Oh, and he needs burped, too."

Wallace walked in, saw that I had the baby, and asked, "Leah, would you give me a hand?"

Leah looked around, made sure her daughter wasn't in harm's way, gave me a wide-eyed 'What now?' look, and left to help her stepfather.

The door had barely shut when Jenny burst in. "Mommy, Mommy! Oh, there you are. Do we have any hot water?"

"Um, it's winter. I always have hot water on. We don't have coffee or tea, though."

Jenny shook her head. "I don't mean to drink. I mean for a bath. Or a part of a bath. We got a new friend, maybe even another sister for me!" Jenny brought her boisterous attitude down to a whisper, "But she stinks. I think she wants to get rid of the polecat smell, too."

Jenny ran out the door, hollering to her father as she zipped past him. "I'll go get the washtub!" and disappeared, skirts hiked high as she sprinted to the barn.

"Thanks, Leah, I think I got her," Wallace said, then turned toward the house. "I just didn't want her to be frightened, a strange man carrying her inside a house she's never been to. I hoped that seeing another woman would make her less tense."

I stepped out onto the porch and saw my husband leaving the wagon, walking towards me, carrying a Native American woman in his arms, Jenny's scarf around her neck. Neither seemed to notice that her buckskin dress had slipped up nearly to her knees, revealing the brightly patched socks I had darned only last night.

"Well, I got you a surprise," Wallace said weakly. "Would you clear a place in front of the fire for her."

I rushed ahead of him and shoved the stools the young ones sat on at dinner into the corner and tossed down the 'sitting' blanket we used in the evenings during story time.

Clunk! Clunk!

Jenny hollered, "Can someone get the door?" and kicked it. "We got our arms full." She turned to her father, "You can go ahead of me, Daddy. She's heavier and I don't want you to drop her."

I opened the door and was overwhelmed by the stench. I swallowed my gag reflex, then stepped outside, away from the pair, and took a deep breath of fresh air before coming back in to the *eau de skunk*.

Skunk! I just remembered. Not a defining 'I got my memory back' moment, but another one of those random but welcomed facts that helped all of us, especially those who were born in the 18th century. "Jenny, before you take your shawl off, would you go to the cellar and bring up as many jars of tomatoes as you can?"

Jenny grabbed one of the baskets I had made before the wee three were born from the corner and asked, "Are you sure you want to bring as many as I can carry?"

"All right. Bring me four quarts. That ought to do it."

Wallace placed the small woman on the quilt at the hearth, waiting until I had finished my request before making introductions. I don't think it mattered, though. She looked like she was in shock. Or maybe she was just terrified. Either way, I was the hostess and even if I wasn't, I wanted this frightened person to relax and feel safe.

"Evie, this is Annie. Annie, this is my wife, Evie."

The fear factor dropped from a full ten to about eight at the word 'wife.' I saw it and so did Wallace.

"You've already met one of our daughters, Jenny. This another daughter, Leah, and her family: Bibby Liz and young River."

Well, I'll say one thing for Annie: she didn't have to voice a question to ask it. At this point, I decided not to elaborate on how I—who looked to be 20 years old—could be the mother of someone who was a few years older. Instead, I just smiled at her and nodded. "Yes, those two are my grandchildren."

The wee three had come to watch the addition to the household but were holding their tongues, figuratively. They were, however, holding their noses, literally.

"And these are my three youngest: Leo, Judah, and Wren. Say hello, children."

"Hello," they all mumbled through hands covering their noses.

"Let's go back and read," Wren said. "It's my turn because I wasn't finished when we came over to see… Mommy, what's her name?"

"I'm sorry. Children, this is Annie." I looked to Wallace and made a wild spousal supposition. "She's going to be staying with us for a while."

"All right," they chorused, then ran back to their corner, this time the blanket pulled over their heads.

I knew they couldn't 'read' in the dark, but they were quiet under the quilt and weren't asking questions. Wow! Two mini miracles!

"Will Sarah be back soon?" Wallace asked. "I'm afraid she has frostbite on her feet. I'm not sure what to do, but I know what not to do: walk on them."

"I got this," Leah said. She unconsciously put the back of her hand up to her nose. "Wallace, why don't you put the children in the wagon and take them to my place for a bit. James should be done with his project by now. The little ones already ate, and Mom and I can hold off for a while." She gave him a stern 'I'm the nurse in charge' look, but she really didn't need to. Getting the children out of the house was a smart idea.

Jenny pushed the door open and came in with her half-filled basket. "I got the saucy tomatoes. I didn't think you'd want the lumpy ones." She set them down next to the washtub, then moved closer to her father and the door that he had left cracked open to allow fresh air in.

"Come on, children. Jenny, would you help me gather everyone together. Let's jump in the wagon since the horse is still hitched to it. I'll unload the supplies when we get back. You can hold River and keep Bibby Liz in line. You other three are in charge of yourselves. Stay in the wagon and don't even look over the edge, all right?"

"Yes, sir," they chorused, then giggled. "Did we do that right, like we're in the militia?" asked Leo.

He rolled his eyes at their role playing. "Yes, soldiers. Now, march to the back of the wagon and prepare to deploy!"

Chapter 39: Cleaning Day (CC Ch 5)

It was an arduous task, trying to bathe an unresponsive person, but Leah had been a skilled nurse in her previous life in the 21st century and taking care of semi-lucid people was as she said, 'Just like riding a bicycle. You just have to know when to turn and when to stop.'

Leah poured one quart of the tomato sauce into a wooden bowl, then add two ladlesful of hot water to it. "Only time will tell if this will work. In the meantime, let's see if we can get the gag factor under control. Stink and small homes in the wintertime don't go well together. Even if this only works a little, anything is better than nothing. The poor dear."

Well, we soaked her feet in the tomato sauce bath, scrubbing as gently as we could to remove the traces of fur, dirt, grime, and essence of polecat from between her healthy toes, just dabbing around the blackened tips of her big toes, but the stench remained.

"I'm sorry we put you through so much discomfort, Annie," Leah said, as she rinsed her hands in the basin of clear water. "I hate to say it, but let's try good old-fashioned soap." She then turned to me and said under her breath, "Too bad we don't have new-fashioned detergent, baking soda, and hydrogen peroxide. That's what we used for the Boy Scouts that year they cornered a skunk. One spray doused eight boys!"

Clomp, clomp, clomp!

It was Jenny.

"Before you scold me for not staying with Daddy and my brothers and little sister, James said that he and Daddy were big men and could manage the five little ones by themselves. Then James said you'd probably do better with his new all-purpose body wash and shampoo than with tomato sauce." Jenny produced a spring-topped glass bottle with a creamy white product in it. "Oh, and he said you could add this to the rinse water, too. But just a drop or two 'cause it's real portent."

"Potent," I corrected, taking the small vial from her. "That means strong." I uncorked it and took a whiff. "Whoo-ee! He's right there."

"I can smell it from here. Where'd he get oranges?" Leah asked.

"I helped him gather the fruit down by the river. I told him we called them hedge apples, but that they weren't really apples, and that the squirrels liked to eat the seeds…"

Jenny noticed me shaking my head.

"I guess I'll tell you about our harvest trip later. So, if Daddy and James are fine taking care of the babies, can I stay and help with Annie? I know I just met her, but I sorta miss her already." She turned to Annie. "Did you miss me, too?"

Annie gave Jenny a weak smile, the first indication that we'd had that she understood any of what was going on.

Jenny took the bottle of shampoo/body wash and uncapped it, offering it to Annie to sniff. "How'd you like to smell like this?" she asked, pointing to the tub that she'd brought in, but we hadn't used.

Annie nodded, then scooted forward and lifted up her dress. "Burn it," she said, scowling. "It's not mine." She proceeded to pull the wretched garment off over her head, then flung it toward the fire, missing the flames by a foot.

The pungent aroma of a body that hadn't been washed in ages was far worse than the skunk odor. I realized that maybe it wasn't just the polecat slippers that reeked. Her body was streaked with dirt and grime. Either *he* hadn't let her bathe or she intentionally stayed dirty so he'd keep away from her. Regardless, she needed a bath.

She sat there, naked and unashamed, and stared at the sweat and dirt-stained buckskin dress, too far away from the flame to burn.

"Here," I said, and handed her the poker. "Go ahead and burn it now while the fire is high. Send your old life to hell."

Annie's eyes misted up and she sniffed back her tears. "Go," she twisted the torn and patched dress onto the end of the fire tool, "to," tossed it into the blaze, "hell," then repositioned it in the flame, jamming it between the two large ash-covered orange logs. She took a deep breath as the flames roared up, a new stink permeating the air. "Gone."

Leah poured some of the body wash into a bowl and added hot water. "Do you want to help, Jenny? I think she's more comfortable with you."

Jenny took one of the fresh cloths and swirled it around the water, bringing the sweet orange smell into our immediate area. "I'll get your back for you, Annie. Go ahead and watch all your bad old memories go to the devil...or whatever Indians call him. You're living with us now. We don't know anything about you but your name, but you're part of our family now and we love you and care for you and will protect you..."

Annie reached up and covered Jenny's hand with hers. "My name."

She looked to all of us in turn and began her narrative, using her hands to embellish her words.

"I'm called Annie. It sounds good when you say it, but that wasn't always my name." Eyes squinted and mouth pursed in anger, she suddenly spat into the fire. "*He,*" indicating a big belly, "made a joke about what the…the…" She paused, searching for the English word, then put three fingers behind the top of her head like a headdress.

"The chief?" Jenny asked. "The man in charge?"

Annie nodded. "Our old chief dead. The new one stupid. He much liked the white man's drink." She held her hand up, mimed guzzling liquor, wiped her mouth with the back of her hand, then sighed in satisfaction, a lopsided grin pasted on her face.

Then her clench-jawed anger returned. "*He* showed up with a big bottle of whisky, looking for someone to," she mimed a trap closing with both hands.

"Run his trap lines?" Jenny asked, then dropped her washcloth back in the basin to use both hands to talk. "Someone to set the traps, take the dead animals out, skin them, and get them ready for the tanner?" verifying all the steps in the process with both hands and words.

Annie nodded, then whimpered. "And keep him warm at night," hugging herself in demonstration. "Chief," she held three fingers behind her head, then nodded to Jenny to make sure she had the word right. Jenny gave her the go ahead, and she resumed. "Chief pointed to three women and ask which one he want."

"*He* said 'any' woman would do. That's why he call me Annie. But he say 'Eny.' The way you say it is pretty," she said and smiled. It wasn't pronounced the same, so evidently didn't bother her now.

Her smile left as she continued. "Chief pointed to me. 'Take her. She no good at making baby.'"

Annie pointed to the marks on her belly. "No baby for me," sad at her words. Then she straightened up, proud. "I no want he*'s* baby in me, but he try." She shuddered at the memory.

Jenny had finished washing Annie's back and arms and now knelt at her feet to wash her legs. "You'll have a baby one day," she said, looking up until Annie returned her gaze. "I know it."

Annie shrugged her shoulder in disbelief, then pointed to Leah. "The," she mimed mixing potions and applying them to her feet.

"Healer," Jenny and Leah said at the same time.

"Healer tried to make belly good for baby." She leaned back so we could clearly see the marks on her abdomen. Apparently, someone had 'cut' fertility symbols into her to increase her chances of having a child.

"Oh, my God," escaped my lips before I could stop.

"But now you're with us. You're safe and we won't cut you. But you *will* have a baby one day," Jenny repeated.

Jenny rinsed and re-soaped up the washcloth. "Here, you wash your lady parts," putting the cloth in front of her own crotch, then handing it to her, "And when you're done, I'll wash your hair," then flipped her hair back and forth like a shampoo commercial model.

Annie put the cloth up to her nose and smiled. "Stink good," she said, then her smile turned into eyebrow-narrowed determination, diligent in her cleansing ordeal, making sure the washcloth was thoroughly rinsed before dipping it into the soapy water. The closer she got to completion, the more relaxed her face and attitude. Finally, she rinsed the rag one final time, squeezed it out, then folded it neatly and set it on the tray next to the basin.

Jenny handed her a lap blanket to cover herself with. "Now, are you ready for your shampoo?" she asked, repeating her hair model swish and head turn.

Annie clutched the quilt to her chest and tried mimicking her, but she just didn't have the poise or the loose hair. All of us giggled, then felt embarrassed that maybe we were insulting her. Evidently not: she was stifling a giggle, too.

"I'll unbraid it first, then we can wash it and comb it out. Have you always worn your hair this way?" Jenny asked, flipping the end of one of her braids back and forth.

She nodded, then helped her new blonde friend unplait her hair, letting us know she was eager for a make-over.

While I looked for something more permanent for Annie to wear than a patchwork lap quilt, Leah dumped the basins of stinky water into the bushes outside the front door. It was too cold and windy to toss them any further. She came back in and set up the beauty salon, filling our drinking water ewer with warm water and setting the big washtub behind the stool where Annie sat.

Jenny hummed a Christmas carol—Angels We Have Heard on

High, I think—as she used her fingertips to work the first round of
shampoo in. It was wash, rinse and repeat twice to cut the oil and dirt
build up on her scalp. The washtub caught the rinse water she poured
over her head as Annie gazed at the ceiling. I never thought about it as I
stared up with her, but our finished ceiling was probably strange to a
young woman who was accustomed to living in mud structures or in the
open air. She did look content, though. I guess the soapy water helped
wash away her fear and angers, too.

While Jenny finished the beauty treatment, pulling a wide-toothed comb through Annie's long raven-black hair, Leah ran over to her house to check on the husbands and children. Or maybe that was just her excuse...

Five minutes later, she returned. She paused a moment to catch her breath, then looked at me with her impish schoolgirl grin before turning her attention to our guest. "Look what I have," she said to Annie who was now literally sitting pretty in front of the fireplace, wearing my clean cotton nightgown, her towel-dried hair hanging loose over her shoulders.

I'm sure Annie had seen a looking glass before, but I doubt she had seen her image lately. She really was beautiful. We watched as that slight shadow of a smile she had shared with us sporadically throughout the evening exploded into a full, ear-to-ear grin of appreciation. I really doubt she could have stopped it from getting so big, even if she had wanted to. She kept looking back at the mirror, touching her face and hair with appreciation, making sure it really was her.

"Pretty, huh?" Jenny asked.

"Pretty. Uh huh," she replied.

Clomp, clomp, clomp!

"Someone's here," I said, quickly scanning the room to make sure I had everything dangerous or spillable put aside and out of the wee ones' grasps. All we needed to do was empty the washtub. Wallace spotted the need as soon as he stepped in the door, and two quick air-testing sniffs later, had both hands on it, ready to take it away.

"They were hungry again and Leah said you were at the point where we could come back home." He sniffed the air again. "It actually smells good in here." He looked at Annie who had turned her back on those coming in the house, facing the fire, timidly avoiding any socializing.

"Is that our Annie?" he asked me, knowing full well that it was.

"Annie," he said to her, "Would you turn around so the children can see you? They told me they didn't get a chance to see you before we whisked them off to James and Leah's home."

Annie turned to face the three youngsters. "You're pretty!" Wren said. "I wish my hair was that long and pretty." She boldly walked up to her and sniffed her sleeve. "And you smell good, too." Wren turned to me, "Mommy, can I take a bath, too? I want to smell like Annie."

"Not me," Leo said, "I like smelling like a boy."

"Me, too," echoed Judah. "When can we eat? I'm hungry."

"You're always hungry," Wren said, "but this time, I'm hungry, too."

"Well, while you're feeding your babies, Mom, I'll go home and feed mine. I know James can put something together for Bibby Liz, but he's not equipped to feed River." She patted the top of one breast gently. "Yup, it's time to feed him, too."

Leah turned her attention back around. "It's been a pleasure, Annie. Welcome to the family. Oh, and Mom will fix something for you to eat, too. I'll see you soon."

Chapter 40: What's a woman to wear? (CC Ch 6)

It was a good thing that none of us were fashion conscious. We wore what we had, regardless of the latest trends. It wasn't because we were snobs, preferring to wear our traditional garb; it was just that we were pretty much destitute in the apparel area. If it was warm, at least semi-comfortable, and covered what society dictated that we should (legs from the ankles up, arms from shoulders to elbows), we wore it. All I had to share with Annie was my sleeping gown, the only spare outfit I owned. No big deal; I could go back to sleeping in my shift. I usually did that in the summer anyway. Besides, I had a reliable and easily accessible heater—my husband—to sleep next to. All Annie had was the pallet composed of our one and only spare quilt and the banked coals and retained heat at the brick hearth. Still, that bed was probably more suitable than what she'd had—in the recent past, at least.

Annie wanted to help around the house, but because her frostbitten toes limited her mobility, there really wasn't much she could do. She stayed at her station, the south-facing sunny window, weaving baskets. She seemed content in her tiny realm. Occasionally a frown would appear, but then she'd look up at her surroundings, and a sweet smile would scurry in and take its place.

Sarah and Jody had returned the day after her baptism of cleanliness. They liked her as much as the rest of us, and she was comfortable with them, too. However, now our accommodations were even more snug. We were all able to sit at the table, and had our own sleeping stations, but the children definitely had to go outside or over to James and Leah's to play. Occasionally, the wee three would gather beside Annie and share their 'picture' book with her. Her sweet smile was genuine, her gentle touch to smooth a child's hair out of his or her eyes really wasn't needed—I think she just wanted to touch something pure and possible.

I had to wonder what Jenny 'knew' about Annie becoming a mother that we didn't. She had the sight, not me, but either way, that little tidbit of ESP—or whatever they called it now—she had shared seemed to soothe Annie. Apparently, she really did want children, just not with the wrong man. Smart gal.

Today Sarah and I were making small talk about the recent trip she *had made to see a former officer in the Continental Army. Colonel Holt was still as crotchety as ever, she said, but having a major flare-up of gout didn't help. I appreciated getting her version of an 18th century news update, gathered from handbills, newspapers, and gossip she had heard during her trip to the coast.*

Sarah suddenly sat up straight, then leaned forward to share her inspiration with me in confidence, not that Annie was an eavesdropper.

"I have the perfect dress for Annie!" she said softly, containing her enthusiasm with clenched fists. "I had forgotten all about it until just now. It was a gift, rather a payment, from one of the ladies I attended last autumn, a chief's wife. She had broken her ankle when she was faced with the decision to either jump off a cliff or face a wounded bear. She decided she had a better chance with the rocks and trees than his long claws, sharp teeth and riled attitude, so she jumped. When I came back to check on her three weeks later, she had crafted a beautiful buckskin dress for me. It would have been an insult not to accept it, but as we all know, I'd really stand out if I wore it anywhere but here in the house. Even then, I'd have to be wary of unexpected callers seeing me essentially *déshabillé*."

Sarah was right. She had to be a bit more presentable since she was the traveling healer in this area of North Carolina, tending to Native American chiefs and children, dirt farmers and estate owners, wandering former soldiers now without a cause, and government officials on duty, far away from their private physicians. Anyone with an owie or a fever knew she was there to help.

"Now, where did I put that?" She went to her side of the main room and pulled the wooden chest out from under her high four-poster bed. "Ah, here it is, right on top."

Annie had continued her basketwork while Sarah and I carried on. If she understood our conversation, or had any idea about what we were talking about, it didn't show. Her hands continued to weave the split river cane in a never-ending, or almost so, concentric plate. I had watched her earlier, mesmerized by her magic and how she seamlessly brought up the sides into a bowl shape. It had taken her almost a full day to complete the first one, but she was more than halfway done with her second basket in just hours. I don't think she had a chance to practice her skill while with 'he,' but she was making up for lost time now.

"Annie, I have a gift for you," Sarah said and knelt down beside her.

Well, it was hard to tell which was rounder: Annie's eyes or her mouth. "Pretty!" she said when she saw the embellished dress. She set her work in progress on her lap and gently touched the soft doeskin. She quickly pulled back, her mouth closed in a polite smile. "You dress pretty."

Sarah turned to me and asked, "How are her feet? Can she stand yet?"

"Oh, she can stand, but she toddles a bit. She can walk short distances, like to the dinner table or the privy, but I discourage her from helping around the house. Besides, she already told me that she's making the baskets for Leah, Jenny, and me. I think she likes the strict orders to stay off her feet so she can get more of them made. Wallace just brought her a fresh harvest of cane and Jenny donated the honeysuckle vines she collected last spring. I guess it was a good thing that we didn't get around to cleaning out the barn. The raw material for her baskets was like an early Christmas gift."

"Then let's make it two gifts. Annie, I'd like you to stand up," Sarah told her, offering her a hand to help her to her feet.

Annie looked at me to be sure it was allowed, that she wasn't going against my wishes to stay put. "Go ahead. She wants to see if the dress fits."

She accepted the help up, but was still wary, her shoulders drooped and hands lax at her side, fingers twitching in uncertainty.

Sarah held the dress up to Annie's back, then looked down to check the length. "I don't know what the appropriate hem length is for a Cherokee woman's dress, but if it's too long, she can trim it." Sarah peeked out the window to make sure no one was on the way in.

"Coast is clear."

"Annie, reach for the sky!" I said, and raised my arms high. I looked and felt like a complete idiot. "You, too," I said, and dropped one hand to pull hers up. "Both of them, come on. You need to help me. You can take off my nightgown now because you got a new dress."

And there she was again: my wide-eyed and mouth opened in shock, Annie. "Me dress?" she asked.

"If it fits," I answered. "And if it doesn't, we can do some modifications." I could tell she didn't understand my long answer. "Yes.

Put it on."

Sarah finished the strip and re-dress procedure as I kept an eye out for unexpected family. Annie was barely cooperating, but I think she was still stunned. Not only a dress just for her, but a new one in the style of her heritage, too.

"I wish we had a full-length mirror so she could see herself," Sarah said as she shifted the fit across the shoulders.

"Well, I don't think Leah ever took hers back. I mean, it's just a handheld looking glass, but it's better than nothing." I reached up and retrieved it from the kids-free zone on the mantel above the fireplace. "Look, Annie. Sarah has given you this dress. Isn't it pretty?"

I held the handle and moved the mirror up and down like a wand held by a TSA security agent at an airport terminal. *Zap!* Another random 21st century memory. I shook my head to get rid of the pesky, no-good image.

"No?" Annie asked.

"Huh?"

"I think you confused her when you shook your head, Evie." Sarah turned her attention back to Annie. "Yes, the dress is yours. It, um, won't fit me," she fibbed. She took the mirror from my flashback-dazed hand and gave it to Annie. "Look for yourself."

Annie held it in front of her chest, then lowered it, and eventually turned around in place, trying to catch up to the image. "Thank you, Sarah," she said, concentrating on saying the new name correctly. "Very pretty."

***

Annie had been with us almost a week now. Her frostbitten toes were pretty much healed. The dead skin at the tips of her big toes sloughed off, and her walking improved. She was as sure-footed as anyone else in the family now. She still didn't have any shoes or slippers, though. She made do by stepping into my boots when she needed to go outside to the privy, but that was just a temporary situation. I only had one pair of shoes, and no matter how generous I tried to be, I wasn't going to give away my one and only, especially since they didn't fit her. She had tried to weave some slippers, but that didn't work out because we had the wrong materials.

"I had good shoes," she said, pointing to her feet. "From grass. One

381

day, *he* say he cold, so he throw them in fire." Her face reddened as she shared the story with words and hand language. "'These for you,' he say." She pinched her nose.

"That's when he made you wear the polecat slippers?" Jenny asked.

Annie nodded, her face still red.

"I'm sorry we can't get any grass so you can make more like your old ones," Jenny said, signing and talking at the same time. "But you'll get new shoes, I know it."

I rolled my eyes and looked up at Wallace. "Whatever she says will happen, will," he said to Annie. "I'd volunteer to set a few traps, but the whole process from trap to workable leather takes time."

"And chemicals or animal organs that we don't have," I added. "Jenny's right. I'm sure Annie will get some footwear for Christmas. She's already been blessed in so many ways. What's to make us think that the Lord won't continue?"

Suddenly, Jenny started jumping up and down, then ran to the window, peering out through the frosty pane. "He's here, he's here!"

We weren't expecting anyone, and Jenny didn't get that excited about James and Leah, so it was evident that Jenny had anticipated company.

Wallace opened the door and stepped outside, closing the door behind him. "Wait here," he called back to Jenny. He peered down the trail and saw a tall rider on a mule coming his way. He ignored the sound of Jenny's bouncing up and down, glad that Evie was telling her to hush and be patient.

A long minute later, the man Jenny had 'seen' came into our view. Wallace reached inside, grabbed his coat, said, "Wait here," than walked up to meet the traveler near the barn. "Greetings, Samuel. I see you found our house. Let's take the mule into the barn, then you can come inside and warm yourself by the fire."

Jenny moved out of the way quickly when the door opened. "Samuel! You found us! You found us! Come in and sit down. Can I get you something to drink? Ooh, ooh. I'll make you some raspberry tea."

Samuel smiled at the little blonde who was glad to see him, then looked around the room and saw someone he didn't know.

"Let me introduce you to my wife, Evie. Our three youngest children are visiting their kin," Wallace touched his fingertips together to indicate the tepee-shaped home, "and will be back later. Oh, and I'm sure you remember Annie."

Only, if only I had a camera! The look on the faces of those two was positively priceless. I swear, the air was golden with the excitement and shock and, well, maybe love was a bit premature, but it sure felt like that to me!

Wallace stepped up to Samuel and put a hand on his shoulder. "You two never did get a proper introduction, did you? Annie, this is Samuel. Samuel, this is our friend Annie."

Those two didn't look alike except for their coloring, but their expressions were identical. And their transitions from shock to absolute pleasure blossomed at the same rate, too. Looked like Annie was going to be a Mrs. Samuel soon.

"So, what brings you to this area of the woods, Samuel?" Wallace asked although it was obvious why he was had made the long trip: Annie.

Samuel's head shook as he came back from the world of Annie to the world of everything else. "Shoes. I bring shoes for Annie." He brought out a rawhide-tied parcel, then set it on the table.

"Come on over and see what he brought you, Annie," I said, and walked with her to the table, holding on to her elbow. She was a bit shaky on her feet, but it didn't have anything to do with the frostbit toes or pain. She was in I-can't-believe-my-dream-has-come-true land, for sure.

Jenny felt the excitement, too, but still managed to make a cup of tea for Samuel. "Here you are," she said, breaking his trance. "We don't have honey," and handed the starry-eyed man the crude baked-clay mug she had made last summer, "but it still tastes good. Can you stay for dinner?"

Jenny suddenly realized that it wasn't her place to invite company to eat at her parent's home. "I mean…" She looked up to her father with a mixture of 'I'm sorry' and 'Can he stay, please?'

"Yes, Samuel, we'd be pleased to have you stay for our evening meal. It's a long ride back. We don't have room in here, but it isn't too cold in the barn with all those goats inside."

I could tell that Samuel was trying not to smile, wanting to keep a stoic non-committal demeanor, but it wasn't working. He looked over at

Annie and gave in to the smile, but still held back the giddiness we all knew he felt. "Thank you. That would be good. Mule is tired."

"And you are, too, huh?" Jenny asked.

"Jenny!" Wallace and I shouted at the same time.

She looked at us and said, "But he is, isn't he? It was a long ride. And maybe he got lost once or twice, but he's here now. I'll go to the cellar and get some more potatoes and cornmeal. I know it's not Thanksgiving, but we can still celebrate!"

***

I'm not sure which excited Jenny more: having the spontaneous Thanksgiving meal or being able to use her new Morse paging system to call James, Leah, and family to the house.

"Why all the clangs, Jenny?" James asked as he stepped in the door.

Jenny looked behind him. "Where's everyone else? I clanged it six times, then added another three for River. I didn't think you'd want to leave him behind. 'Sides, he's invited to dinner, too. He likes smashed potatoes, even though he'd rather squish them than eat them."

James had been looking around the room, trying to get a direct answer without Jenny's dissertation on bells and baby food. I saw his confusion segue into an 'aha' moment.

"Yes, we have company for dinner tonight, James," I said. "This is Samuel. Jenny and Wallace met him the last time they went to town. You're all invited to eat with us, but I think you'd better go back and give Leah a hand in getting the two little ones over rather than pulling the paging rope a few more times. I hope she hasn't already fixed dinner."

"Nice to meet you, Samuel." James nodded in greeting, then took the shy man's hand and shook it, placing his other on top, letting him know he was genuinely glad to meet him.

"It's just chili," he said. "It'll taste better after cooking an extra day, anyway. I'll be right back. Jenny, if it's all right with your mother, would you come give me a hand?"

"Go ahead," I told Jenny, then mouthed 'thank you' to James.

Jenny's face fell into a frown. She wanted to stay with Samuel and Annie. She knew she wasn't supposed to tell Samuel and Annie things 'she knew' about them and their future, but just being next to this happy 'future' couple made her feel giddy and tingly inside, too.

***

Jody and Sarah were back on the road again, and it was a good thing. There was barely enough room at the dinner table for all the adults, but we managed. Jenny sat with Judah, Leo, Wren, and Bibby Liz, eating her meal with River trapped under her left arm, feeding him bits of mashed potatoes. She'd look up from her catering duty and gaze at the shy young couple, visualizing them as a happily married couple with a baby, then frown as an alternate future tried to sneak in.

Waaa!

"Sorry about that, River," she said and she fed him another bit. "I get distracted sometimes."

It was no accident that I put Annie and Samuel right next to each other and across from me. I guess I was a romantic at heart, and since I didn't have any chick flicks or romance novels, watching a real-life love affair bloom right before my eyes was a real treat.

"Cornbread, please," Wallace asked, nudging my arm.

"Oh, sorry," I replied, and handed him the plate of sourdough cornbread muffins.

"You know, I only bumped you to get your attention," he whispered in my ear. "I asked you three times. You'd better stop staring. Not that they'd notice…"

We both looked at the couple and saw they were still head down, smiling, as they ate their dinner. I was tempted to drop my napkin on the floor to look under the table to see if they were holding hands, but that would have been rude and probably an invasion of their privacy. No, definitely a violation of both privacy and courtesy.

"Samuel, in our culture, we celebrate the birth of our savior, Jesus Christ, every year on December 25th. We decorate a tree, maybe exchange handmade or inexpensive gifts, sing songs, and read the story of His birth in the Bible. We'd be happy to have you join us."

Samuel looked toward the door, the glow he had moments earlier now gone.

"Oh, I'm sorry. I'm sure you don't use our calendar. Two days after the next new moon. At least, that's what we call it: when no light comes from the moon. Two days after that is our celebration. Please join us. I know Jenny and Annie want you to come back soon."

"I would like that. If the weather allows, I will come. Much easier now because I have mule," he said, his eyes shining with pride.

Chapter 41: Bedding in the barn (CC Ch 7)

"You should be comfortable in here with the animals. If we had more floor space available, I'd ask you to stay inside with the rest of us. As it is, we've slept head to toe many nights. Our plans for a home separate from my parents keep getting postponed. At least, James and Leah have their own residence now, even if it isn't completed," Wallace said, then realized he was probably losing Samuel in his expanded discussion on why he had asked him to sleep in the barn for the night.

"I see you have a blanket," he said, continuing his tour with hand gestures. "Jenny and I changed out the straw," pointing to the hay, "just this morning, so at least it smells fresh in here," and sniffed. "I'm sorry I don't have another lantern to share," and held up the windproof oil light. "The children broke our second one and I haven't had a chance to replace it," pretending to drop it.

"At least you'll be protected from the wind." Wallace stepped out of the doorway and looked up into the dark sky, assessing the moist breeze as it blew across and chilled his bare face. "And from the snow." He motioned snow falling by waving his fingers. "I think we'll have snowfall by morning."

"This is good," Samuel said. He looked around the small barn with the caged chickens and two pens, one with four goats corralled, the other filled with the fresh straw that had been raked into a low mound, perfect for bedding. "Thank you."

"Now, don't leave without coming in for breakfast. I'm sure Annie would like to see you again before you leave."

"Yes. I will see you and your family before I leave," he said, then unintentionally sighed, "And Annie."

***

"So, do you think it's going to snow tonight?" I asked when Wallace came back in.

"If it does, it might give Samuel an excuse to stay another day." He peeked over the privacy curtain at Annie to see if she had heard him. She must have, he thought, because she was snuggling into her quilt, smiling.

"I may not remember Leah as a teenager with a crush on a boy," I whispered to Wallace as he slipped into bed with me, "but I'd say Annie was at risk of sneaking out to see Samuel tonight."

"I don't know the word crush, but if it means she's infatuated with the man, I agree."

"Well, they're both adults. Besides, Indian culture is different than ours. It might be perfectly acceptable for them to…um…form a union without courting, an engagement, a wedding…"

I suddenly became excited with the thought of a young couple, enjoying those first powerful flushes of 'infatuation.' "I think the babies are all asleep. How about pretending you and I are together for the first time?"

Wallace snuggled under my chin, kissing my neck softly as he worked his way up to my eager mouth. He took his time, his soft and almost lackadaisical kisses driving me nuts! Finally, I tapped his shoulder, letting him know to turn up the heat.

He pulled away and whispered, "I didn't know much our first time. How about if we pretend it was the next week, when I found all your *erogenous* zones," he whispered, purring the one word, then slipped a warm hand on my fanny, gently tugging up my shift.

I squirmed up, down, and around, helping him pull my shift off over my head, then lay back and giggled softly. "Just like the tenth time," I whispered. "I'll never forget that one!"

***

Annie could tell by the whispers and giggles that Wallace and Evie were joining. She knew 'how' to do it, but had never enjoyed it. Now she knew what was wrong, though. It had to be with the right man. She had seen three happy couples in the short time she'd been here: Wallace and Evie, James and Leah, and very briefly, Sarah and Jody. Maybe there was something spiritual about this part of the mountain. If so, she should visit Samuel in the barn and see if he wanted to be the fourth couple.

She burrowed deeper into the quilt. Even if this place wasn't sacred or spiritual, she still wanted to be with him. He couldn't come to her, though. There wasn't enough room for another person to lie down in this house unless he was lying on top of her.

The thought sent warm shivers and tingles to her lady parts. That must be what the other women in the tribe told her was the way to find out if a man was right for her or not. She thought of Samuel at dinner, telling Wallace that he'd come back to see her and Jenny two days after the moon went dark. Another wave of warmth flooded her nether regions. She'd go see him tonight, before he left, just in case he didn't make it back again. She looked up at the window. The moon was full. and even with the clouds, there was plenty of light to see the way.

Annie slipped on her new moccasins, then wrapped the quilt around her shoulders, stepping softly to the door. The little pants and giggles coming from Wallace and Evie's side of the curtain would cover any noises she made opening and shutting the heavy door. She lifted the wooden latch and let herself out, easing the rod into the carved channel so it didn't even scrape.

She sniffed the air. Snow was coming. She'd better hurry to the barn while the ground was still dry.

***

Samuel lay on the straw, his blanket covering him up to his chest. He moved his hand over the front of his breechclout and rearranged himself. He couldn't stop thinking about Annie, about how much he wanted her for his wife, and those thoughts had aroused his man parts. Maybe he should have remarried soon after his first wife died in childbirth, but now all the available women had either married outside of the village or had died of the measles. Even his mother was eager for him to bring Annie back. As soon as he told her about the polecat moccasins and how a white family had 'adopted' her, she told him that she would make a pair of marriage slippers for the woman. Go to her. If she accepted them, then she would be his.

His thoughts were interrupted by a scratching at the barn door. Something, or someone, was trying to get in. He rolled off the straw pallet and listened for the sound of a wild animal.

The soft grunts were human, a female trying to lift the door latch that had swollen from the moisture in the air. He tapped his side of the bar with the side of his fist and the door swung open. "Come inside," he said, glad that he could speak Cherokee again. He nodded to the bed of straw. "It's still warm."

Annie thought about bringing the quilt she had wrapped around her shoulders to his bed, then changed her mind, and instead folded it and set it on the milking stool. She didn't want to get it covered in straw. That would be a sure sign that she'd been out to see Samuel.

While her back was to him, Samuel got under the blanket. He untied his breechclout, but let it stay in place. He wasn't a virgin and knew it

388

would be easier to join with her if he didn't have clothing in the way.

"Do you like the moccasins?" he asked. She turned toward him and he motioned to her, asking her to come under the blanket with him.

Annie removed her fancy footwear and set them down near the bed. "They're beautiful. Did you make them?"

"No, my mother did. She said I was to give them to the woman I wanted to marry."

"Oh," Annie said sadly, thinking that she might have to give them back, then realized that he had given them to her for that very purpose. "Oh!"

"You might be more comfortable sleeping with me tonight if you took off your dress," he said, not even trying to hide his smile of anticipation.

Annie chuckled. "Then you, too. Here, hand me your clothing and I'll set them here. But hurry. It's cold!"

Samuel stared wide-eyed at her firm nipples, eager to make them warm with his mouth. He blinked as he pulled his shirt off over his head, keeping the image in his mind, then shimmied out of his breechclout, glad that he had already removed his leggings and moccasins.

Annie quickly folded his clothes and set them on top of hers, then scurried under the blanket. "You're so warm," she said, her hands held together under her chin.

"You'd receive more body warmth if you wrapped your arms around me."

Annie loosened her grip. "Please, make me warm all over. And I'll warm you, too."

***

The chickens rustling in their cage roused Samuel and Annie at the same time. "Good morning, wife."

Annie giggled, then rubbed up against the part of him that had made her his wife. "Good morning, husband." She squinted at the crack above the door frame. "It's nearly daylight. I should return before they see I came to you."

"No. Stay here." He ran his hand down the curve of her back, caressing her round bottom, then pulled her closer to him. "I'm sure Wallace knows where you are. If Evie hasn't figured it out, he'll tell her. And they'll both keep Jenny from coming out here. No. We'll stay for more of what the White Man calls lovemaking, then I'll go in the house with you. I will tell them you are coming with me, as my wife, to my village."

"Your wife," Annie said, the warmth of those words adding to the warmth of her woman parts. "Yes. I like lovemaking." She giggled. "I like the word *and* the act." She grabbed him by his happy husband tool. "Again."

***

It was no surprise that Annie wasn't at her sleeping station in front of the hearth when we got up. Jenny and the wee three were still abed, snuggled together against the chill. Wallace added more wood to the smoldering coals and awakened the fire while I poured more water into the kettle. We both smiled, not just because we knew what had happened, but because it had instigated one of the most passionate nights we'd been able to share with one another in ages. Maybe we had made a baby—or two, if what Leah said was right. I sure hoped so.

I was in the middle of feeding porridge with dried blueberries to my family when Samuel and Annie finally came in.

"There they are!" Jenny exclaimed. "I didn't say anything, but I knew you didn't run off in the middle of the night."

"Good morning, you two," I said. "I hope it wasn't too cold out there last night."

"Here, enjoy some hot tea," Wallace said, then offered the two mugs he had prepared for us to them.

The two accepted, visibly capturing the heat of the earthenware cups with their hands, their noses red with cold.

"Come sit with me, Annie," Jenny called. "You sure look extra pretty this morning."

"Yes, she does," Samuel said. "She is my wife now." He turned to Wallace. "I thank you and your family for all you have done for me and my wife. My tribe had…"

"Hard times? Wallace suggested. "No food, too much sickness? That's hard times."

"Yes, we had hard times, but now we have much food and meat. I make a shelter for my wife, too. She can ride mule back to my village. I have big bear skin to keep her warm, too."

"You'll still come see us at Christmas, won't you?" asked Jenny,

"Both of you?"

Annie put her hand on Samuel's arm, silently imploring him to grant Jenny's—and probably hers, too—request.

He looked down at his wife, then over at Jenny, her eyes shiny with unspilled tears. "If the weather is good, we will come. Two days after the new moon."

"Congratulations to both of you," I said. "I kinda, sorta thought you might be leaving together, so I put aside some food for your trip. It isn't much, just dried apples and some corn muffins. Let's eat some breakfast, and then you can decide what you need to take from here for your new life as Mrs. Samuel."

I didn't know if the Cherokee used last names or not, and I'm certain that Annie didn't understand everything I said, but I could tell by the way she watched what I said and smiled at certain remarks, like 'Mrs. Samuel,' that she had the meat of my meaning.

The two of them politely ate their fruit-sweetened oatmeal, then Samuel nodded to Annie, then looked toward the corner that had been her bedroom/crafting area.

"Excuse me," she said, having learned good old-fashioned table manners from me as I was teaching them to my youngest three. She stood tall as she walked to the corner, her bearing so much different than it had been when she was a single woman. She knelt to the floor and gathered all the basket materials, placing the coils of split reed and stripped honeysuckle vine neatly in the largest basket. The other baskets were already nested, stowed beside the cupboard. She placed these on top of the weaving products, then brought the bounty to me.

"This one is for you," she said and handed me the largest basket. "Jenny can weave now, but she must ask you when is good time. She has other chores, too."

"Please give this one to Leah, the healer." The second-largest basket had a woven ribbon attached to the side, something I'd never seen in baskets in this day and age.

"For Granny. I only saw her one day, but she's good woman for this family and gave me my dress."

The basket was just a bit smaller than the other two, but I think that was just so they'd nest. I didn't know she had made this many. I did remember seeing her make the smallest one, though.

391

"This is for Jenny," she said and handed her a basket about five inches long and three inches wide and tall. What made this one so special was that it had a lid and small clasp on the front of it, like a treasure or keepsake box. "For summer when you gather your pretty rocks by the water. Keep them here."

"All right," Jenny sniffed as she accepted the gift. "You remember to come see us for Christmas." She held up ten fingers, closed her hands, then added four more. "I *know* we'll have something special for you."

Annie nodded to Wallace, then me, and said, "Thank you for saving me. And for being my friend." She turned to Jenny and rubbed her nose on Jenny's cheek. "You are special. I no need gift. I have you and family for friends."

Well, the men shook hands, the kids came over and hugged Annie's legs, asking why she was leaving, did they do something wrong; you know, the usual farewell mayhem. They had finally made it out the door when I remembered that I hadn't given them their 'on the road' food parcel.

"Here, you stay inside with the children or Samuel and Annie will never be able to leave. I'll take this to them," Wallace said and grabbed the twined-wrapped package.

Samuel was adjusting the bear skin over Annie when Wallace caught up with them. "That's a big pelt. I don't think I've ever seen a black bear hide that big." Wallace looked it over, admiring the stitching at the edges when he saw the patched area.

"It looks like this bear was shot with buckshot."

"This is man-killer bear. It killed two men and chased down wife of chief from other tribe. She can walk now. Granny fix her leg. Now bear keep this chief's wife warm."

"Oh, so you're a chief? I should have guessed. You are an honorable man. I'm proud that Annie is your wife now. Be safe on your trip home." Wallace looked up at the sky. "Good weather for you."

"See you in," Samuel put up his hands to indicate thirteen, "days. We come one day sooner to surprise your Jenny."

"You do that. I'm sure we'd all appreciate having guests for an extra day."

Chapter 42: Faith (CC Ch 8)

Someone or something was frantically kicking at our door. It was the middle of the night and I wasn't going to answer it. That's what I had a husband for. Or one of the reasons I had a husband.

Wallace grabbed a poker iron with one hand and pushed up the latch on the door with the other. We didn't have a lock but did have a thick lath across the door just in case a wild critter smelled food inside and decided to come in uninvited.

I heard the contorted noise even before the door was opened. It was human. And the human was in pain, severe emotional pain.

"Wee Ian," I whispered hoarsely, "I mean, Scout. What are you doing out at this time of night and what's that?"

The son of my first husband, Wee Ian Kincaid—or Scout as he had been renamed by my daughter Jenny—was at the door with a wad of cloth held close to his chest. Tears streaked his dirty adolescent face. It looked as if he had been crying for hours by the redness of his eyes. "What's wrong," I asked, presenting him with a new question since he hadn't answered my first two.

"Can ye help her?" he asked, then thrust his rag-wrapped bundle at me.

I unwrapped the first layer of coarse feed bag and gasped. It was a baby, still alive, but by the rapid, shallow breathing, not for long. "Who...what...why..." I babbled.

"Can ye, will ye, please?" he begged.

I didn't bother asking for the history: the child needed fluids immediately. "Jenny, do we still have that bottle around here we used for Bibby Liz?"

Jenny was wiping her eyes and blinking them rapidly, trying to work the sleep out of them. "Um, I think so." She turned upside down and looked under her bed. "Oh yeah," she said in embarrassment, "here it is."

"Why, what? Never mind. Would you put some water on to boil and put the bottle, cap, and nipple in it, too? Wallace, go get me some milk out of the spring house. I only need about half a cup, probably less, but half a cup will be good for a start. Jenny, after you get the fire going, get the spare metal dipper and make sure it's clean. I need you to put the cup end of it into the boiling water, too, but only for a minute."

I looked up and saw Scout sniffling, still scared beyond his tender years with the responsibility he had just transferred to me. I gave him a weak smile, then a nod for him to join me in prayer. "Okay, Lord, you've kept this baby alive this far, I'm sure you didn't mean for him or her to die now. Please give the child all the strength needed and…um…maybe a little extra. Oh, and some wisdom for me, too, so I'll know what to do. In Jesus's name, amen."

I sighed, then pulled the cloth back again to make sure the child was still breathing, then urged it down a little more to do a quick gender check. "Well, Scout, from what I recall, girls are inherently stronger than boys, so she already has a better chance of survival. Come sit next to me and tell me what happened."

I sat down on the edge of the bed and dipped my pinkie into the water cup on my little night table. I put my damp digit into her mouth, trying to see if she had the instinct to suck. Her face moved almost imperceptibly as she checked out the *faux* nipple. Her mouth opened but didn't close. She was too weak to pull her little purple tongue back in, but I could almost swear that she sneered at the deception. "Hang in there, sweetie, we have some real milk coming soon."

Scout was still mum, but I doubt it was because he didn't want to interrupt me while I was talking to the baby. He was in shock. Or scared wordless. Or totally terrified. Or all three. Well, I wasn't in a nosy mood right now, and he and the baby were both breathing. I had something more important on my mind—I had to remember how to make formula.

Wallace and Jenny were taking care of sterilizing the lone bottle, cap, and nipple and the dipper. "Didn't you use sugar in Bibby's formula?" Wallace asked.

"Oh, shoot, I'm glad you remembered. We still have a little left, I'm sure. I can't use honey to sweeten the milk because the bacteria in it are bad for an infant's digestive tract…" I looked at my nightshirt-clad family and the scruffy adolescent savior and added, "I just have to make sure we use sugar until her belly's older."

The three of them made an 'aha' expression, then breathed a sigh of relief. I knew Wallace was aware of my 21st century knowledge when it came to science, but it looked as if Scout and Jenny were also onto me now. Oh well, I could only hope they knew. Now I wouldn't have to find a way to tell them. Either way, they trusted my judgment as the mother of the house. I was the authority on babies, at least until Sarah or Leah came in, and then we shared the mentor's mantle.

"Wallace, put the milk in the dipper and hold it over the fire to get it to scald, just so it gets a little film over the top of it. Oh, and Jenny, sterilize the spoon, too. That means…" I saw her all-knowing grin again. "You know what sterilizing is, don't you?"

"Brother James taught me. Besides, I helped my sister, Leah, sterilize the bottles for Bibby Liz. You want to make sure there aren't any germs on the spoon when you stir in the sugar, huh? And that all the germs are killed in the milk, too."

"Yes but heating also breaks down the proteins so they're easier for a baby to digest. Mother's milk would be best for her, but I'm all dried up. If she can tolerate this and get through the next couple of days, heck, if she gets through the night, she'll be fine, I'm sure."

"I hope so," Scout said sadly, softly uttering his first words since his panicked request for help at the door.

I looked over at Wallace and saw he had a peaceful smile on his face, one that I remembered from somewhere… Oh yeah! He had that same look of contentment when he helped bring my youngest daughter into the world. With the parental status of this wee little girl unknown, I think he's hoping that we had just painlessly delivered another daughter.

He wasn't the biological father of any of my children but claimed them just the same. Wren, Leo, and Judah were a lot smaller than this one when they were born. This one was smaller than Leah's babies had been, but she still had some chubbiness to her. If she was premature, it wasn't by more than a couple weeks. Hopefully, this new delivery would be as strong as Wren, my smallest.

Jenny knew the bottle drill and used a pair of wooden tongs to pull the bottle out of the water, making sure all the water was out before she set it on a folded cloth. She repeated the procedure for the cap and nipple. James was so sly, bringing them along in his 'science' kit from the 21st century. Leah had been insulted when she found out about them, believing that he didn't think she would be able to nurse a baby. He said he had honestly forgotten about it until they needed it. Well, I believed him. If he had thought about it, Leah would have read his mind and known about it, too. Regardless, when she found out she was pregnant with her second child and wouldn't be able to nurse wee Bibby Liz at the same time, that bottle was a Godsend. Or blessing. Or whatever. And now it was going to be put to good use again.

"I just adjusted the formula for this small amount. I verified my computations with Jenny," Wallace said and winked at her. She was sharp with math and just about all her other school work. She still needed some work with spelling, but at least she wrote the words phonetically so I could figure them out. She'd be a perfect student if she had a computer with spell check.

"It is okay if I cool down the bottle in a pan of cold water, isn't it?" Wallace asked.

"Yes, as long as the nipple isn't on it yet. I want to get some formula in her as soon as possible. If you haven't already filled it, only put about an inch in there. It'll cool faster and I doubt she can handle much more than that. I think this is her first food."

I looked down at Scout, still stunned at whatever it was that had brought him to our threshold. "She's never eaten before, has she?" I asked softly.

He shook his head. "Her mother, my stepmother, was deid when I…I…I birthed her. I could see Raven's belly movin' after her heart and breathin' stopped. I had to do *somethin'!* I remembered when you did the surgery on the goat, Sarah P. I…I ken how ye felt, but this time I couldna help the mother, only the bairn. I feel bad because I had to leave Raven's body there. I couldna take the time to bury her and still get the bairn to ye. There wasna anyone any closer, or at least anyone I trusted to ken what to do fer her.

"I dinna ken if my da was coming back soon or not, but I kent someone would be by eventually lookin' fer him. He managed to make some men mad at him again. I think they're the ones who did that to Raven—kilt her. She was alive when I got there. She kept tellin' me to take care of my little brother. She didna ken she was havin' a daughter. She wanted a son to make Da happy. But nothin' would make him happy." Scout shook his head. "And now he's gonna be madder still. It willna bring her back or help the wee'un, either. Maybe Wallace and I can go back in the mornin' and bury her. That is, if ye can watch the bairn. Would ye want another daughter? I dinna care to let my Da ken he had a daughter. I'd rather he thought that Raven and the baby died together. If we bury her, he'll never ken what she died of unless her killers tell him…" Scout's tone suddenly changed to anger, "because I sure willna tell him! There's too much hate and revenge in his life. He doesna need to have a reason for more."

Wallace had filled the bottle and brought it to me as Scout related his story. I checked the temperature on the inside of my wrist. "Perfect," I said, then touched the nipple to her cheek. Her eyes fluttered but didn't open. I touched it to her lips, but she didn't seem interested.

"Okay, here," I said and dripped a drop on my pinkie. "Now, this isn't water this time, little lady."

Still nothing.

"Okay, I think I know what you need." I snuggled her up to my chest, as if I was going to nurse her, and blew in her face. "Now, I'm your new mommy, and you have to eat so you can get big and strong and play with all of your brothers and sisters. *Manga!*" I commanded and brushed my milky pinkie on her bottom lip.

"Well, I'll be," Wallace said, as she opened her mouth. "You're listening to Mommy already. That's a good little girl."

The baby dipped her head and put her mouth on my finger and exerted a very faint but definite suction. I quickly swapped my finger for the nipple and let her try. Her mouth stopped. She didn't like the polymer prosthetic. "Okay, you win for now." I dripped more formula on my pinkie and trickled it into her mouth, allowing her to give a weak sucking motion to accomplish the needed swallowing.

After half a dozen small drops, she was done. She closed her eyes and panted erratically. I knew the effort had exhausted her already weak body. Hopefully, she'd only nap for a short time, then wake for a few more drops.

I looked up at my rapt audience. Wallace was still beaming. "Scout, you need to go to sleep, too. Lie down over there on Jenny's bed with her," he said, gently patting the tired boy on the shoulder, urging him to lie down on the bed rather than stay in his current upright and wavering position. "You'll both fit. I'm sure you want to be in the same room as your sister."

"Aye, I could do with a nap, but ye have it wrong, Wallace. She's my kin, my father's cousin's daughter, not my sister. And I ken a little of the Bible," he said with pride. "I have faith that she'll live until tomorrow, at least."

"Well, Scout, I agree with you to an extent. My youngest daughter, Faith, will live, but I'm sure it will be much longer than just until tomorrow. You see, I think tomorrow is already here—it's after midnight. Now, get some rest. Cuddle up to Jenny, and I'm sure you'll be slumbering soon."

A smile crept up the side of Scout's mouth, making its way toward his ear. "Aye, I'd appreciate some rest and comfort. It's been a long day and a half."

***

I settled into my nursing chair with Faith wrapped in one of my babies' old receiving blankets, a napkin folded up as a clout between her red, bowed legs. I doubt she had enough fluid in her to make a mess, but she might as well get used to diapers now. Besides, I knew that sometime in the first 48 hours, she'd have a bowel movement even if she hadn't nursed. I didn't want to ask if it had happened yet or not. Scout was already sound asleep, Jenny's arm wrapped around his waist, the smile of contentment on his face surpassed only by the one on hers.

I nudged the bottle's nipple to the side of her mouth, hoping she'd follow its pressure and latch on by herself. She did! I was so excited that I swear I felt the milk tingling in my own breasts even though I hadn't nursed a baby in ages. Well, after I made sure little missy was going to be strong enough, I'd let her try out my natural nipple. Of course, I'd do it on the sly. Sarah had told me about Jane, the virgin wet nurse. She had never had a baby, yet was able to put both wee Julian and Bibby to her breast and nurse them. Evidently the stimulation that her randy fiancé Benji had provided earlier had kicked in her lactating hormones.

If I could get her to stimulate mine, we wouldn't have to mess with sterilizing the bottle and mixing formula. And if nursing was going to stop me from getting pregnant... Oh, well. Wallace and I had been trying for over two years and nothing had worked. Well, if he couldn't give me a baby, God could. Little Faith's black hair would be a sharp contrast to blond Jenny and the wee three's red hair, but that just meant that with my brunette Leah, I'd have the full range of hair colors. And by the earlier look of contentment on Wallace's face, he didn't care if he got a ready-made child or had to wait nine months for a build-your-own. We had one more in the family and he couldn't be happier.

Chapter 43: Faux ham and friends (CC Ch 9)

The days before Christmas were filled with hustle and bustle and evergreen boughs. We had a bit more room since Annie had 'eloped,' but now we had Scout. I didn't mind him sleeping with Jenny that first night, but they were both getting older, and I didn't want to encourage any curiosity. Scout took over Annie's old spot at the hearth, but I think he liked that. When I got up to give Faith her bottle in the middle of the night, he stayed still—never uttered a sound or shifted position—but I knew he was awake. I could actually feel his gratitude. It was as tangible as the smell of a Damask rose: not seen, but definitely in the air and appreciated.

I had tried to nurse Faith a couple of times, hoping I'd get milk from the stimulation, but the little girl liked the bottle better. Leah admitted to me that she had tried to nurse her, too. She had milk, so that wasn't the issue. I think Faith just liked that firm silicone nipple and sweetened goat's milk. Besides, the formula helped her sleep longer. She was getting plenty of nutrition and sleeping for four hours at a time worked well for my schedule.

The younger children were intrigued by her two-inch-long, thick hair. "River didn't have hair when he was born. Is it because he's a boy and only girls get hair?" asked Wren.

"No, all of you were pretty much bald, just pink fuzz for you and your brothers, and Bibby Liz, River and even their mother, Leah, had just a hint of dark hair, not even enough to brush. I don't know about Jenny, but she was probably bald, too."

"I'm sure glad I have hair now," Wren said. "I almost have enough for braids like Jenny!"

***

Christmas day was getting closer. We all hoped that we would have meat for our Christmas dinner, but it looked like we were going to have a vegetarian menu. Our last ham had been supper for a family of mice. The cat Scout had given Jenny a couple years ago was either too full of vermin from the barn or was just plain lazy. Roast fowl was out of the question, too. There were few domesticated geese or turkeys in the New World, at least in our neighborhood, so my alternate plan to traditional fare was to have chicken. Unfortunately, that was on a fox's menu, too.

We were down to three hens and a rooster. Eating our breeding stock was not an option.

"I know, I know!" Jenny exclaimed, her excited bouncy manner still more the norm than an exception. Puberty wasn't slowing her down.

"You know what, dear?"

"I can make a fox ham. That is the word, right?"

I paused, trying to figure out what in the world she was talking about, and then it hit me. "F-a-u-x is pronounced foe. And how can you make a *faux* ham?"

"We still have lots of bacon grease in the crock, and loads of potatoes, bread, a couple of eggs and I only need one beet for this. Oh, and some pie crust, but that's easy to make."

We had two days to go before Christmas, so I figured I'd let her experiment. "But this is also going to be a lesson in using scientific methods. You have your hypothesis which is can you make a *faux* ham out of what we have here. You need to write down all the ingredients, how much of each one, and how to prepare the items and in what order. That's called a recipe, by the way. Women and men have been recording recipes for…for…as long as there's been writing."

Jenny rolled her eyes at me, a new gesture I know she got from her older sister Leah.

"Okay, I'll tell you why," I said, ignoring the fact that she hadn't voiced her 'why?' "If it turns out great, you want to be able to make it again, right? And if it's a bust, you want to find out what you did wrong and not make the same mistake twice. Or three or four more times, right?"

"Right. I'll go get what I need, including the notebook James made for me, and I'll be right back."

Two hours later, Jenny's creation was complete. She allowed me to make the pie crust, but she did the rest. I hadn't thought it would turn out so well or I wouldn't have fixed a big pot of peas for supper.

"I'll tell you what, Jenny. Since I didn't have any ham to put in the peas, and I think your *faux* ham will disintegrate in the soup, how about if we just let everyone have a small piece as an *hors d'oeuvres?*"

"Huh?"

"Samples, appetizers. We'll let the family know what it tastes like tonight and tomorrow we'll have it for a main meal along with some turnips and baked apples."

"All right. And if they like it, I can make it again and again because I have the recipe!"

***

"Where did you get the ham?" Wallace asked when he came in from chopping wood. "It smells delicious. I thought we were having peas."

"Your little genius daughter… Oops! Sorry, I forgot: no labels. Our sweet Jenny came up with the idea all by herself. It's essentially a meatloaf without the meat. Mashed potatoes, a beet, bread crumbs, a couple of eggs, and some bacon grease all mixed together then wrapped in a pie crust which becomes the rind of the *faux* ham. It sure looks and smells like the real deal. Pretty clever, eh?"

"Ham! Ham! We got meat!" Judah and Leo shouted as they burst through the door.

Wren followed her brothers in. "We don't have meat because of the fox and the mice and oh, my! We got meat!"

Jenny's chest was so puffed out in pride, I thought she was going to pop her buttons. She brought it down a notch and stood in front of her culinary creation. "This is for tomorrow night 'cause we're going to have peas tonight."

"Ah, peas again?" Leo carped.

"Yeah, peas again?" Judah echoed.

Wren didn't say a word, but her frown of displeasure made her opinion about dinner loud and clear.

"Don't worry," Jenny said. "I'll let everyone have a hot turd before dinner."

"That's *hors d'oeuvres,* not hot turd. There's a world of difference, believe me. Now, children, wash up for dinner. I'll let Jenny slice off one piece of her ham from the end so you can tell if it tastes as good as it smells." I turned to Jenny. "That's part of the science, too."

"The proof is in the pudding," Wallace added. "It not only smells great, but it's beautiful, too. What's that round bit in the center? It looks like a bone, but I know it isn't."

Jenny giggled behind her hands. "That's just the mashed potatoes, eggs, and breadcrumbs without the beet for coloring. At least we won't have to worry about nicking the knife on that bone!"

***

401

The faux ham hors d'oeuvres were a hit. The younger children wouldn't eat their peas until I told them that if they didn't eat their dinner tonight, they wouldn't get any of Jenny's creation tomorrow. The boys grumbled and Wren snorted, but they finished their supper.

"Do we have to go to bed? Can't we stay up for Sandy Claws?" Leo asked.

"Yeah, can we wait for Sandy Claws?" Judah echoed.

"I told you, tomorrow isn't Christmas," Wren said, her arms folded in front of her chest. Suddenly they dropped to her sides. "It isn't Christmas tomorrow, is it?"

"First off, it's Santa Claus, not sandy claws. That's what a cat gets when it walks down to the creek."

I could tell by their frowns that either they didn't get the joke or they weren't in the mood. I tried again.

"Wren's correct. Tomorrow is Christmas Eve. We'll bake some rolls, maybe another pie or three, and string some popcorn and bog berries together to hang over the boughs. James, Leah, Bibby Liz, and River will be here to help with the decorating. Later, we'll have a big meal, including Jenny's *faux* ham and turnips, read from the Bible, sing a few songs, tell each other what we're grateful for, and then, well, I guess that's about it. It's sort of like Sunday dinners, but with more singing and decorations."

"What about the presents and *Santa Claus*," Judah asked, making sure he said the name correctly.

"Well, Santa Claus and gifts don't always arrive, but that's not what Christmas is about. Christmas is a feeling, an invisible spirit that comes from within, but it's warm and comforting like...like a daddy hug."

I saw the blank stares and realized I needed to elaborate. Again.

"You know how you feel when you've helped someone and they didn't expect it? And they were so grateful..." *They were still lost.* "Even if they forgot to say thank you, you saw it in their eyes and felt it in your bosom, right?"

Jenny started giggling at the word. I shook my head, 'not now,' and she sobered up. Well, after one uncontained chortle, she did.

"Can you imagine how the world would be if each day, one person performed a random act of kindness for no reason."

"What's random?"

"That means for no logical reason, they weren't obligated. They weren't asked to do it, it wasn't part of their jobs, and it wasn't family or kin who was in need. You know, because it was just a kind thing to do, a good deed."

"Oh, I know! I know!" Jenny popped up. "Like when we helped Annie get all pretty and clean again and let her stay here until Samuel could come ask her to be his wife. She wasn't family, and Daddy and I didn't know her when we saw her at Mr. Gibson's store, but Daddy made sure she was safe and got away from that mean old man, *he,* even though he wouldn't let her come with us until he got money."

"And we did it because we wanted to. We took care of her because that's what people are supposed to do. Do you think Jesus would want her to stay with that horrid man?"

"Nooo!" the children chorused.

"Well, Jesus is the One who told us how to treat everyone. And we celebrate His birthday on December 25th, Christmas."

"One other time I helped someone and he wasn't family or kin and he wasn't even in a bad *tickerment* like Annie."

"You mean predicament?" Wallace asked. He took off his boots by the door, hung up his coat, and settled in next to the hearth. "Do you mind if I join in the conversation? Come over here and sit next to me, children. It's cold out there and you're all so warm! Go ahead with your story, Jenny."

"You know Mr. Flynn? He's kinda crotchety sometimes, but I know he isn't mean. He's got rheumatism in his back, and I know it hurts him. But anyhow, he was trying to get rid of a big tree branch that got broke by the wind and was ready to fall onto his house. He had a saw—and it was plenty sharp—but he wasn't tall enough to get to it all the way. He was reaching up like this," Jenny illustrated an overhead sawing motion, "but he couldn't get the blade started, so I asked him if I could help.

"Well, he kinda growled, said something about how I was just a girl, but I told him I was a strong girl and I could climb a tree, even in a skirt. I don't think he believed me. He just kinda snorted and went back to swingin' that saw up in the air, tryin' to hit the branch just right. So, I tucked my skirt up into my apron and climbed up that tree. 'Hand me that saw,' I told him.

"He looked kinda shocked or scared or something, but he needed to get rid of that branch, so he handed me the saw. Well, I sawed and I sawed, and then when it was almost cut through, I pushed on it with my feet and it dropped right where I wanted it. It didn't hit the eave or nothin'!"

Rather than chastise her for performing dangerous tasks without an able adult nearby, Wallace made use of her shared story. "It wasn't one of your chores and you didn't get paid, but you helped someone because he needed it. Mr. Flynn felt good about it, too. I remember seeing him later. Having that tree pruned so it didn't fall through his roof… Well, he couldn't have been happier if you bought him a new plow."

He paused, then amended his statement. "He couldn't have been happier if you'd bought him a new blade for his plow."

I put my crocheting back in the basket that Annie had made me, then took over the lesson.

"See, you gave a little of yourself and received a warm, wonderful feeling and so did Mr. Flynn. And you know what else? I'll bet the next time he sees you, he'll wave and say hi."

Jenny hunched forward and giggled into her hands. "He already did. And he said that next time we're coming near his place, he has a surprise for me. Well, I guess it isn't a surprise anymore, because when I asked him, he told me what it was. He gathered a whole bunch of seeds from his flower garden a couple months ago and he put aside some of them to share. He's going to give me a whole bunch of them. He said to make sure it was okay with you and Daddy before I start spreading them around, though. I mean, I don't think we want flowers growing in the cornfield and between the tomatoes and squash, but maybe in between the peas would be okay, I mean, all right."

Before anyone could reply, we heard the footfalls on the porch.

"I thought James and family weren't coming over until tomorrow," Wallace said and stood to unlatch the door.

"Happy Christmas," Samuel said, and held up two dead wild turkeys by the feet.

"Samuel's here? Where's Annie? He brought Annie, too, right?" The children said one after the other.

Annie walked out from behind Samuel and handed Wallace a bundle. "For your next baby," she said.

I moved the children back so the couple could make it into the

404

house. Suddenly, the baby started crying.

Scout walked up with wee Faith in his arms, wide awake, squalling like every other healthy, hungry baby. "I think the sound of excitement woke her. It's nearly time for her bottle, though." He looked up and smiled. "Why hello, Samuel. Greetings to you and your wife."

"Scout?" Samuel asked.

"Aye, 'tis me. I was wonderin' if they were speaking of ye when tellin' the story of the tall man named Samuel who took their new friend Annie as a bride."

Annie totally ignored the men's chatter and quickly made her way to my elbow. I gently bounced the baby to keep her distracted while Jenny, the formula chef, was scalding the milk.

"Your baby?" Annie asked. "How? When?"

Tears were now spilling from her eyes. Here I had all these beautiful children and she had none. Whether or not she really couldn't have a baby was moot. Here I was with a new baby—obviously Indian, or at least half—and I hadn't even been pregnant.

"Here, do you want to hold her?" I said and stood up to offer her the chair.

Annie felt for the chair, but never took eyes off the baby as she sat down. "Yes. Please."

"She's a bit fussy, but we have a bottle coming for her." I looked at Scout to see if I could figure out what I should do or say, and then realized that Faith had stopped crying. Her eyes were wide open, her jaw slack as she looked at Annie with what could almost be called recognition.

"Ah, crap," I said and turned away. "I'll be right back. You have this, right?" I asked Jenny.

Jenny didn't know what to say or do about me but did know she needed to finish the bottle and formula for Faith. She nodded her reply, then bent back to her task, the uncertainty in her eyes nearly as loud as the fact that she hadn't responded with words. That girl was never mute!

No one had to tell me. I knew it in my bones. Faith needed to be with Samuel and Annie.

Wallace followed me out to the porch. "I'd ask you what's wrong," he said, and handed me a quilt for my shoulders, "But it's obvious."

"You saw it, too?"

"I know we'd be wonderful parents to Faith, but as an adult, or even a young child, she'd be ridiculed and scorned because she's different. We'd accept her, but society wouldn't."

"Yeah, well, that's one thing that really sucks about the 18th century—the prejudices. I hate to say it, but when I left in the early 21st century, it wasn't perfect, but no one batted an eye if a kid was a different ethnicity than the parents. Or not overtly. I mean, they didn't deny schooling or restaurant service or…"

I broke down sobbing.

"I just had a baby and now I'm going to lose her! You saw Annie. And if what she told us is true, then this is the only way she'll have a child, by adopting one."

Wallace re-wrapped the quilt around me, then chuckled.

"What's so cotton-picking funny?" I asked, glad that I had stopped the blaspheme before it came out.

"I guess Jenny was right again. Remember? She told Annie she'd have a baby. I guess this is the one, although…"

I could feel the shudder through Wallace's body. I realized what it was and shuddered right along with him. What a horrid way to get a baby. First, the mother is murdered, then the brother—barely a teenager—had to cut it out of his dead stepmother to save it.

"Don't worry, Evie. We'll have more children. I may not have the sight like Jenny, but I know in my bones, we'll have more children."

"But…but…"

"But what? We were given the chance to save a woman from death, or worse, and now she has the opportunity to raise a child that probably wouldn't have made it into this world without the bravery of a very young man. Two lost lives found. They deserve each other. I don't know what Samuel's story is, but he seems a decent sort. And Scout knows him. If there was a character flaw, I'm sure I would have seen distrust or apprehension in Scout when they greeted. Don't worry, they'll be fine."

"Yeah, well it looks like Jenny's Christmas wish is coming true. She told me all she wanted was for Annie to be happy. Let's go in and make sure she is." I started to laugh and cry at the same time. "I don't think there's a reason in the world for Annie not to be happy when she finds out she just had a baby."

"Hmm," Wallace said, rubbing his chin. "I think we'll have to give them Sarah P as a gift. That nanny will have milk for at least a few more months, long enough until the baby is able to eat smashed people food."

Chapter 44: Farewell (CC Ch 10)

"I didn't think you'd mind if I let Annie feed Faith," Jenny said, her head tipped down slightly, indicating she felt a tinge of guilt.

I looked over at the new mother and daughter and couldn't help but be happy for them, the lone tear sneaking down my cheek one of joy, not sorrow, at the surprise addition to my family getting a new mother. I guess the tears of loss would come after Faith left with her new family.

"Pretty baby," Samuel said, stroking Faith's thick black hair. Milk pooled in her mouth as she looked up and smiled at him. Annie took the bottle away and wiped the overflow with the edge of the baby blanket.

"She needs a better home," I said softly, then put my hand on his arm. "An Indian home. I know you just got married, but could you and your wife handle a child, too?"

"My baby?" Annie asked, then clutched the baby closer, her eyes looking deep into mine, desperate to verify that she hadn't heard me wrong or that I was teasing.

I shrugged one shoulder and nodded. "If both you and your husband want her." I sniffed back another tear that had imposed on the conversation. "I guess Jenny was right about you having a baby. I just didn't think it would be so soon."

I wanted to turn away, run back to the porch—or further—wrap myself in my quilt and curl up in a corner, pretend this wasn't happening. But it was. No matter how I tried to justify keeping her, I always rebounded back to the fact that Faith belonged with this young couple.

"Ye don't have to keep her if she's a burden," Scout said. "By blood, she's my sister. I'd be proud if ye took on bein' her father, Samuel." He sighed and shook his head, thinking of his own—and Faith's—biological father. "Ye'd be a grand father. I dinna ken yer wife, but if ye chose her, I'm sure she'd be a fine mother, too."

"Easy choice," Samuel said, "even before you said she was your kin. Yes, we would be proud to be her new parents."

"Well, that's settled," Wallace said, his eyes red from the tears that were now on the back of his shirt sleeve. "I think we have a bit of time to spare before we have Jenny's *faux* ham for dinner. Who wants to help me pluck a couple of Christmas turkeys?"

"I do! I do!" All three little ones chorused.

"I can help, too," Jenny said softly.

We could all tell that she said it out of obligation, not desire. It wasn't her normal tone and was sort of scary.

"Would you rather stay in here and tell Annie all about Faith? You know, her routine, how to calm her when she rouses in the middle of the night, the best way to burp her? You've been around her just as much as I have. I…um…want to help get those turkeys ready for tomorrow's dinner, too," I said.

It wasn't exactly the truth, but I had an armload of wishful thinking, hopes that my mind would be completely occupied somewhere else, even if it was with plucking pin feathers out of a turkey's butt. Besides, Wallace needed my help. Those were big birds. It was a tough job without wrangling our three competitive toddlers who were sure to make it a contest to see who could pluck the biggest feather.

***

"Are Annie and Samuel going to take Faith with them?" Wren asked.

"Yeah, huh?" echoed Judah.

I inhaled deeply, trying to find the right words, but was spared the chore by Wallace.

"Faith was living with us for just a little while, just like Annie was. They'll always be a part of our family. It's just that they won't be staying with us."

"Oh, all right," Wren said, then stood at my elbow, trying to decide whether she wanted to grab feathers or just watch.

"Yeah, that's all right," the boys said at the same time.

"She's cute but kinda noisy," Judah said.

"Besides," Wren added, "We have River around if we want to play with a baby."

"Won't Grandpa and Granny be sad that they're gone when they come back?" Wren asked, her hands at her side, fumbling with her pockets rather than pitching in to pull out damp stinky feathers.

"Your Grandpa and Granny never met Faith, just Annie, remember? They've been gone so much this year. I was hoping they'd be back by Christmas, but since that's just a few hours away…"

I stopped talking and looked out the lone window in the barn at the starry sky. There was just a sliver of a moon. Clear and cold. No chance of a white Christmas this year. Still, we had a warm house and our family kept getting bigger and bigger, even without me getting pregnant. I shook my head, dousing the sadness that was trying to sneak in by counting my blessings. I had so much. Every year, we had more and more as a family. And we were all healthy...

"Are you all right?" Wallace asked, his breath warm and welcome on my neck.

"Oh, I'm very all right. We may not have money, but we're about the richest people we know, save James and Leah maybe."

"Yes, our family as a whole has so much..."

Wallace didn't finish his remark, instead stayed still, listening. "Be quiet for a moment, children. I think someone's coming."

"Sandy Claws, Sandy Claws," Judah squealed.

His words were literally clamped off by Wren's hand over his mouth. "Daddy said to hush," she whispered, then took her hand off and wiped it on the skirt of her dress. "Ick," she said softly.

I looked to Wallace just as he faced me. "Company," we said.

"Stay here with your mother, children. Let me see who it is and I'll be right back."

"Do you think it's Santa Claus?" Leo asked. "I said it right, huh?"

"Yes, you said it right, but I doubt it's Santa Claus. It might be your Grandpa Jody and Granny, though. Gee, I hope so..."

I really didn't know why I was hoping for more people in the house. I guess more distraction was good. Of course, I couldn't help but think of babies all the time now. It was my time of the month and I was hormonal enough without a major life change coming into the picture.

"It's Grandpa Julian!" exclaimed Wren. She beelined toward him for a tackle or hug or whatever it was. Julian could have stood his ground with just her coming at him, but he knew the other two were right behind her. He held onto the door frame and braced himself.

"Grandpa Julian, I'm glad you came! I'd rather have you than Santa Claus any day," Wren said and hugged his leg even harder.

"My turn, my turn," the boys said, shoving each other out of the way for access to Julian's other side.

"Okay, children, let me get the horse inside. I have a few items in the saddlebags. Maybe you can help me carry some parcels into the house." Julian looked up, saw me standing next to Wallace, and smiled.

"What are you two doing? Oh, it looks like someone got lucky and shot a turkey?" he stepped outside and led the horse in, the children guiding him as much as hindering him.

"Look again," I said when he returned. "There are two of them. Our friend Samuel gave them to us. And since when did you start saying 'okay'?"

"You and your mother are wearing off on me," he said with a sly smile.

Julian knew Sarah, Leah, James, and I were all from a future time, but we never spoke of it outright. Wallace and Jody knew, too, but only Julian treated it as a bit of forbidden knowledge, occasionally inferred, but never revealed.

"Then I guess you may have to wait to eat the ham I brought. I have a few other items that may interest you, too. How much more feather plucking do you have to do there, son?"

Wallace chuckled. "Almost done. I'd shake your hand, Papa, but I don't think you'd appreciate it. Boys, come over and help me finish this bird. The feathers are off, but someone has to pull out the innards."

"Me! Me! Me!" both boys chanted, jumping up and down in place.

"Not me," Wren said. "I'll take my turkey cooked, thank you very much."

"My, what lovely manners, Wren," Julian said. "I agree. Let the young men do the slippery work. Why don't you, your mother and I go in the house? You two can help me carry the parcels."

***

"Shhh," Jenny warned when we came in. "She just went to sleep."

Julian looked around and saw a couple he didn't know, a big Indian holding a very young baby in his arms and a beautiful woman at his side, leaning into him as only a happy wife would.

"Grandpa Julian!" Jenny exclaimed in a hoarse whisper. "I didn't see you coming!"

"Help me with these parcels, would you, dear, so I can give you a proper hug."

Jenny grabbed the ham out of his hand and set it in the middle of the table, then took the twined-tied bundles from Wren and me and set them

411

next to it.

"I made a ham, Grandpa Julian," she whispered. "It's not a real ham, but it looks like one. We're going to eat soon. Would you join us? Huh, please?"

"Come look," I said in a normal voice, and nodded for Julian to follow me. I lifted the lid off the Dutch oven and showed him the *faux* ham.

"You did this? All by yourself? And it's not meat?" Julian asked Jenny.

"Uh huh. Well, mostly not meat. It does have some bacon fat in it. Next time, maybe I can save some of the fat from your ham and cook it down 'til its runny and I can use that. This one tastes good, too, but it doesn't have a real bone, so it isn't good for soup or beans or nothin' like that. Hey! Where's Diego? He's not sick or nothin' is he?"

"Diego is fine. He's staying with the animals. One of these days, we may be able to hire some help, but for now, it's just us two old bachelors," he said and winked at me.

"You're not old and Diego is at least ten years younger than you," I said.

"Fifteen," he replied, "but who's counting."

Julian and Diego were partners in both life and the horse breeding business. They were devoted to each other and really didn't care to be the fodder for rumors so had never hired help. Their lifestyle was their secret alone. The family held that secret even more sacred and hidden than our time traveling.

Stomp! Stomp! Stomp, stomp, stomp.

Two big men, two little men, and one average-sized woman came up the steps to the door. Jody let the little boys and Sarah come in first, reminding them with a whisper that there might be a baby asleep.

"Eek!" I squeaked, stifling the 'yahoo' that had been on its way out my mouth when I clamped my teeth together. "You made it!" I said and ran into Sarah for a full-bodied hug. "Oh, and you don't have to whisper, Jody. Faith is a sound sleeper. She'll wake when she's hungry. But please, no sudden noises, children."

"Just a moment," Wallace said and brought his father forward. "I don't know if Evie made introductions yet, but Samuel and Annie, this is my father, Julian."

Samuel stood up and shook Julian's hand and nodded. *Another nice person had come into this house. No scowl or derision about his race in his features. The man shook his hand and even smiled at his wife and child. Good people seemed to be attracted to this place.*

"Good to meet you and your family, Samuel," Julian said, then backed away so Jody and Sarah could meet the couple.

"And you already know my other father and mother, Jody and Sarah, but they haven't met your daughter, Faith."

Sarah immediately transitioned into doctor mode, threading her way between Leo, Judah, and Wren to see the very young baby. "But Annie, just a few weeks ago you weren't pregnant, were you? I mean, she looks just like you, but...but."

"She's their miracle baby," I said. "I'll explain later. Just know that mother, father, and baby are all fine. However, I think they're getting a gift we hadn't planned on giving. Sarah P will be going home with them."

Samuel looked at Wallace with a 'What's she talking about?' expression.

"We're giving you our nanny goat. You'll need milk for the baby."

Suddenly, Scout emerged from the corner, rubbing his eyes. "Sorry. I musta fallen asleep. Greetings Julian, Sarah, Jody. I'm glad ye made it in time for Christmas. Now, maybe it's the sleep still in my ears, but did ye say that yer givin' Sarah P to Samuel and Annie?"

"And Faith," Wallace said. "Is there a problem?"

Scout's mouth moved around as he thought, the words staying put until he had them sorted. "It's jest that Samuel only has the one mule. He could let Annie ride on it, then lead the mule and goat, but I think it might be better if I accompanied them. If somethin' happened, I'm sure he'd appreciate another set of hands."

Samuel swallowed hard. He wanted to believe that he alone could take care of his new family, and he knew he could if nothing unusual happened. But all it would take is for the goat to get loose and he'd be in a bind. He couldn't leave his wife and daughter alone while he chased the baby's food supply. He didn't have a goat or milk cow in his village or even nearby. He took a deep breath of gratitude. This young man would never insult him or try to make him feel inadequate. He was a gentleman, despite his youth.

"Yes, Scout, I would like it if you came with us."

"I heard about some of the hardships ye had. I'm fair at building structures, so I can help ye with that, too. And while yer tendin' to yer new wife and child, I'd be glad to help with anythin' else that needs done. I'm fair at trappin' rabbits, too."

"No polecats, please," Annie said and shook her head vigorously.

Almost all of us laughed. Julian, his face pinched in confusion, started to ask why she'd say that when Wallace said, "I'll explain later,"

"No. I dinna care to trap polecats," Scout said. "There are plenty of possums, squirrels, and rabbits and if I'm lucky, maybe a deer or elk. It's been a while since I lived in a village, and as much as I like bein' here, I'd rather be where I'm needed."

"But I need you, Scout!" Jenny said, then ran into his arms.

Scout patted her back, consoling her like the hurt child she was, at least emotionally. "I'll be back. I jest need to get Samuel and his family situated. Now, if ye were in the same place as Annie, wouldna ye want someone like me to come and help?"

Jenny sniffed a couple times while she thought, then finally admitted through broken sobs, "Yes. But come back in the summer. Or spring. Or maybe even next month…"

Scout shook his head at her. "I'll be back when it's time," he said, then wiped her tears with his shirt sleeve. "And I always ken where to find ye."

***

Leah, James, and their two youngsters came over after the introductions had been made. I guess Jenny was supposed to 'Morse Code' them when we were ready for them, but she forgot. Regardless, their timing was nearly perfect: Bibby Liz missed out on stringing popcorn and berries onto the string. I guess that was good, though, because at her age she'd rather eat the holiday decorations than make them. The Melbourne crew was in time for the stories and singing, though.

It was impossible to fit everyone at the table, even when we excluded the under thirteen crew, so Wallace brought in the milking stool and volunteered to eat with the children, balancing his plate on his knee. How I ever landed such a generous man, I'll never know…but I'll always be grateful for him.

Jenny's faux ham, turnips, and apples were a hit. With so many of us, we didn't have leftovers. The young boys actually took turns licking the platter clean. Well, they pre-cleaned it for me, anyway.

Bedtime came quickly, or so it seemed. Scout, Julian, and the young boys decided that they'd 'camp out' in the barn. Jenny and Wren took over the spot at the hearth, while Samuel, Annie, and the baby snuggled into the area Jenny and my youngest three usually slept in. No one slept in Jody and Sarah's bed while they were gone, no matter how crowded it got. That wasn't their rule, that was mine. Tonight, like always, it was clean and ready for them. When the yawns outnumbered the topics of conversation, James and Leah graciously backed out, promising to come over in the morning to help with Christmas breakfast.

***

"What are you doing in here so early?" I asked Julian as he tip-toed in the front door. "I don't even have the fire built up yet."

He brought out the parcel he had kept near him ever since he arrived. "I want to separate these gifts in the house," he whispered. "Go back to what you were doing. There's something in here for you, too."

"Hi, Grandpa Julian," Wren said, moving in under his arm to grab a hug. "I'm so glad you came. I'd rather see you than Santa Claus any day."

"Santa Claus? Did Santa Claus come?" Leo asked, Judah right behind him.

"Well, it looks like your sneaking out skills have faded, Julian," I said. "Boys, go back outside and use the privy."

"We already used the bush," Judah said. "It was closer."

The level of chaos and confusion rose from there for the rest of the morning, people of all sizes not yelling, but raising voices in order to be heard, folks practically stepping on each other. Actually, I think one of the boys did suffer a bruised hand from a boot at some point.

Annie had Jenny watch her make the baby's formula all by herself to make sure she didn't make a mistake. She said she did have a pan for boiling water at her new home, but not a ladle. I decided that it would be best if my spare one went with her family. It wasn't much of a gift, but sterilization was definitely a necessity for a month or two.

I fixed a big breakfast casserole with eggs, onion, and a bit of the ham Julian had given us. It was tight quarters again when James, Leah,

415

and their two joined us for Christmas breakfast. Leah volunteered to cook one of the turkeys. They weren't as big as the commercial ones available in the 21ˢᵗ century but were still decent sized. I didn't have room to cook two at the same time, but we definitely needed both of them for our big crowd. Jenny was put in charge of the 'smashed' potatoes, and James said he'd bring his dehydrated green beans and bell pepper dish. With the apple and pumpkin pies Leah and I had baked two days ago, we were set for our afternoon feast.

"Breakfast is finished, dinner menu and duties delegated, did we miss something?" Wallace asked with a big grin.

"Presents! Presents!" the little boys cheered. "Did Santa Claus come?"

"I'd still rather have Grandpa Julian," Wren said.

"Me, too," Jenny and Scout added.

"Well, I may not be Santa Claus," Julian said, "But I did bring a few gifts."

Julian doled out spinning tops to the boys and little hand mirrors to Jenny and Wren. Leah, Sarah, and I got a bag of buttons each.

"James, Jody, I hope you don't think I'm being rude or disrespectful, but I thought you'd know better what you'd like or need than I, so here." He handed them each a full silver Spanish dollar. "Buy what you need or want and consider it a gift from me and Diego. I couldn't ask for a better son and friend," he added, a hand on each man's shoulder.

"Thank you, Papa," Wallace said and shocked his father by giving him a hug.

"Thank ye, Julian."

"I didn't know that you'd be here," he said to Scout, "but I've wanted to give this to someone special for a long time. You deserve it." Julian reached into his vest pocket and pulled out a ribboned medal. "It says 'for meritorious behaviour.' I think you deserve this. I've heard the tales of your brave deeds over the years. It's about time you got some recognition for it."

Scout wiped under his nose, his eyes sparkling with unshed tears. "A medal? For me? Thanks, Julian. This really means a lot to me." He held it up to the light coming in the window. "Is that a house or a shield? I canna tell."

"I believe it's a shield, as in you're a great defender, too," Julian said, adding a wink.

"My turn," Jody said. "We stopped in at Gibson's store on the way in. He said ye'd been in the store earlier, Wallace, but ye hadn't returned. He asked that we send this along fer yer wife."

Jody brought out a large folded piece of blue cotton calico. "I thought that maybe yer daughters would like some, too, so I bought a length of these fer both Jenny and Leah. Ye do like red and yellow, aye? Ye can decide amongst the two of ye which one."

The rest of the day just seemed to slip away. The boys played with their tops, Jenny showed Faith her image in the mirror, then Wren decided that she'd swap presents with Judah. Evidently, the top was more her style than seeing her reflection. I shared some of my fabric with Annie, and Julian gave Samuel part of the tobacco he had stashed in his saddlebag. The gift Annie brought for me was a soft woven blanket for the baby she knew I hoped for, not knowing about Faith. I asked her to give it to Faith instead. Her friendship and happiness was enough for me.

Dinner came together as planned, the turkeys finished roasting at the same time as the potatoes were done. James's contribution only took him a few minutes to rehydrate and warm, even without a microwave.

Full bellies, reflections on how blessed we all were, and pies finished off the perfect Christmas. Farewells were said, just in case someone overslept. Scout, Samuel, Annie and Faith were going to be gone just before first light. Sarah suggested that Annie make three times the normal amount of formula and keep the extra in a glass jar tied close to her body. That would keep the formula at just the right temperature for Faith. She could add the formula to the baby bottle with ease as they were traveling. They'd have to skip sterilization for a couple of feedings, but that shouldn't be a problem.

There still wasn't any snow, but the air felt warmer. Hopefully, Samuel and company would make it to the village before snowfall.

Life was back to normal. Sort of. Something was still wrong with Jenny. I think it was because she missed Scout so much.

"Why don't you go visit James?" I said. "He always seems to make you feel better. Or at least he has enough projects you can help him with that you'll be distracted."

"Okay," she said glumly, her bottom lip pouched out so much, it looked like it had been stung by a bee.

***

"Hi," Jenny said to Leah, then gave Bibby Liz and River a hug. "Is James here?"

"You know he is. Go ahead and go out to the shop." Leah looked at her closer. "Are you all right? You don't look like yourself."

Jenny frowned. "Then who do I look like?" She snorted as she realized that Leah had made a joke. "Oh, I get it. I'm just sorta sad. I'll be fine. I wanna go see James. He always knows what to say when I'm blue. Or sad. Or bummed."

"There's my little helper," James said when she came into his shop. He saw her dour demeanor and jumped right into trying to bring her back to her bouncy, perky, full-of-optimism self. "Okay. Tell me what's wrong so I can fix it."

"I'm glad Annie's happy and that Faith now has parents who look like her and that Scout can help Samuel rebuild the village and help bring them fresh meat, but...but... I wanted him to stay here and live with us!"

James hugged her and said, "You and I both know he'll be back, right?"

Jenny looked up at James and squinted, trying to read his mind.

James saw and felt what she was doing, so quickly started thinking of the prime numbers in order. 1, 3, 5, 7, 11...

Jenny frowned at him. "I know what you're doing," she said with a scowl, then sighed and relaxed back into her brother-in-law's opened arm. "I may not know what you're thinking, but you're right. It'll all work out, huh?"

"Yeah, huh, Jenny," he said, almost calling her 'Granny' instead of her name.

13, 17, 19... He'd better concentrate on prime numbers before she found out the secret he'd been hiding since he time traveled here over a year ago, that she was his great-grandmother so many times over.

Jenny grinned. She didn't know what he was thinking—this time— but she knew it was warm and wonderful and she and Scout were part of it. Just like chasing Christmas, time had to pass until that day came. But it would. And then it would all come together and be perfect.

Conclusion of *Chasing Christmas*.

More adventures featuring Scout follow.

Complete Book

Little Drummer Boy

The Fairies Saga Book 12

Copyright ©2016
Dani Haviland and Chill Out! Books
ISBN 978-1-950592-20-3
All rights reserved.

Could a mere drummer boy help those stranded in the worst winter storm of the 18th century?

Chapter 45: Scouting for a job (LDB Ch 1)

December 1784
North Carolina backwoods

Snap!

Scout cringed as the branch broke under his foot, its disintegration echoing in the narrow walls of the ravine. If his father had been with him, maybe he'd have cuffed his ears, or even worse, subjected him to that angry white man scowl.

But his father wasn't here.

Again.

He'd make do by himself as he had in the past. He huffed as realization hit. His life had been so much simpler without a father. When had their roles been reversed? He shrugged a shoulder and a faint smile crept in. Ever since he'd met him, three years ago. The smile grew and he allowed a small chuckle to escape. Yes, his first ten years of life had been so much easier, living with just his mother and grandmother in their Cherokee village. Finding his 'real' father was almost an accident, but whether Star Walker—the man the White Men called Ian Kincaid—was a nuisance or not, he was still kin. And he'd watch out for him.

When he was around.

And not on another vengeance quest.

But no matter what, he needed to find food and a way to make money, but not in that order.

He clutched his rumbling stomach. "Quiet, or we'll never get that rabbit."

The sand-colored critter sniffed the air, then hopped through the knee-high grass, making his own trail, his white cottontail taunting a silent farewell. Dinner almost got away, but the youthful hunter's bolo toss was quick and accurate.

"No matter how dire the circumstances, there always seems to be enough rabbits to feed a traveler."
***

"I canna stay with ye any longer," he said as he kicked dirt over the dying embers of his campfire. "If I do, I'll wind up as mean and ornery

422

as you. I can hunt and fish to feed myself, and trap and sell furs to save a few coins. Ye see, I have a wife now. Even if she's young and stayin' with her parents until she finishes school, Jenny is still my wife. Ye see, we married the Indian way, claimin' each other as husband and wife two years past. I want to buy us a piece of land and a few critters, build a house, plant a garden and maybe some fruit trees. I don't want to be like ye. I want to be settled, have a family that lives in a house, with glass windows maybe—not out in the wind and rain, watchin' out fer snakes and bears and all those enemies ye're always makin'."

Scout—the youth called Wee Ian by his father—tugged at the strap securing his bundle of blanket, pan, and corn meal, and then stood up again, searching the horizon for signs of his father. Or anyone else.

"Weel, that's what I'd say to ye if ye were here, but yer gone again." He shook his head in disgust. "What did someone say or do to make ye angry this time…"

Kaboom!

Scout spun around toward the noise. A puff of smoke rose from an area near the riverbank, a ten-minute trot away. "Let's hope it's not you that they're shootin' at," he said under his breath, then took off down the hill, ready to help or hide, depending on who was involved.

***

He could have come in beating a drum and still wouldn't have been heard but moving quietly came naturally. The clanging and slashing of axes and swords—knocking down trees and trimming off branches—wasn't as deafening as the intermittent cannon blasts but was sufficient cover noise. The smoke overwhelmed what little scent his small body emitted, so the horses weren't alerted to him either.

It looked as if the soldiers were trying to build a bridge of some sort. Their small axes—more like oversized hatchets—weren't making much headway in bringing down the trees, so the men had resorted to using their cannon to blast a couple of the larger pines to speed up the work.

Apparently this small company—thirty men and horses and one two-wheeled cannon—needed to get across the fast-moving yet deep river. They might be desperate or maybe just in a hurry, but either way, they were certainly ignorant.

Scout shook his head, holding back a snort of exasperation that probably wouldn't be heard, but he didn't need to be reckless. He had spotted a wide spot up the road, not even half a mile away, perfect for fording a wagon. Walking across it would only be thigh-high on a short man.

A warm smile of contentment bloomed on Scout's face when he saw the exasperated officer wipe sweat from his brow—he had been swinging a small axe, too. If this company had a competent scout, they would have known where to cross. However, it would be better yet if they didn't have any scout at all. He didn't want to make another man feel inferior. Sometimes a bruised ego never healed. Hmph. His father was a testament to that.

***

"Excuse me, sir," Scout said, making sure he stood back in case he startled the officer.

Just as he had anticipated, the colonel's short-handled axe swung out as he spun around to see who was addressing him.

The colonel prided himself with knowing the name of each man in his outfit and what he looked and sounded like—quite handy when searching for the source of gossip and out-and-out lies. This scrawny young man standing before him was a stranger. He blinked twice. And apparently a half-breed Indian. No wonder he moved so silently.

"I dinna mean to come uninvited, sir, but is it true yer lookin' fer a good scout?"

Scout wasn't lying. He was just asking a question. It was either true or false on whether they had a scout. If they did have one, it was true he wasn't good because he hadn't helped with today's dilemma. Either way, he hoped his boldness would gain him employment.

The colonel's face transitioned from shock at being caught unaware that an intruder had made his way past the sentinels into camp, to anger at how swift the tale of the misogynistic scout who had beat a sweet young whore almost to death had spread, to mirth at the ambition of the enterprising young man in front of him.

"Yes," the colonel replied, wiping away his smile and the sweat from his face with the back of his hand. "I am looking for a good scout. However, I was more interested in an adult, not a child."

Scout nodded to the men of assorted sizes and ages who had given up on contriving a bridge and were now trying to cobble together a raft from some of the like-sized felled trees. "I'm small, but a man jest the same. My mother was a wee woman, and I take after her. It looks like ye and yer bigger men could use some of my wee-bodied knowledge, though. I'm familiar with this area and could help with yer river crossing. But make no mistake about it, jest because I'm not as tall as some, I'd expect the pay ye'd give a larger man. After all, it's what's up here," Scout tapped his right temple like he had seen Evie do, "that's most important. Especially on a day like today."

Scout looked up at the dark clouds chasing the white ones out of the sky. "I'd say we're gonna have rain here in a few hours. The river will be even higher by morn'. By the looks of yon raft, I'd say it willna be finished by then, even if it could carry the load. That wagon looks heavier than yer cook," nodding to the lone man at the fire.

The hefty cook was bent over his pot of peas, stirring then fishing with his oversized fork, hunting for the ham bone. "Ah, there you are," he said as he stuck one of the two tines into the end of the bone. He held it up in the air, looked around to see if anyone was watching, and plucked a long strip of meat from it before putting it back in the pot. The colonel huffed at the minor theft of food. He put up with the extra portions Cookie gave himself because he was an excellent chef. In his past life, he catered to lords and ladies. He had won Cookie's services from a general in a card game and was forever grateful. Not many men, or women, could make such meager rations taste so good.

Both Scout and the colonel stopped staring at the ham-pilfering soldier and faced each other. "If you can show us the way across the river—with the cannon arriving safely and with no loss of man or horse—you can have the job of scout."

"At full pay?" Scout asked, his hand stuck out.

"At full pay," the colonel said and shook hands to seal the agreement. "And full rations, too. You may say you're a full-grown man, but it looks like you could use a few more meals, just the same."

"Aye, I could use a few more meals, but I dinna say I was full grown. I am a man, jest the same, though. Bring yer pony and I'll show ye the way from jest around the bend. We willna even have to climb a rise."

***

"Sorry, son. The paymaster regulations say I can't pay a half-grown man full scout wages, no matter how good he is."

425

The sergeant with the pock-scarred face wasn't the man in charge, but he was the one who handled the payroll for the company. Or so he had said.

"But the colonel said he'd pay me full wages, whether I was full-grown or not. We even shook on it! You'd all be swimmin' down the river if it wasna fer me."

"That's just the way it is, lad. Now, for someone your size, we can allow wages for a drummer boy…" The sergeant reached up, dug a booger out of his hairy nostril, and flicked it over the boy's shoulder, watching to see if he'd flinch.

Scout didn't so much as gasp at the insult, but did glare at him, shoulders back, chin out. "What's a drummer boy? And how much does he get paid?"

"He's whoever we can find to walk in front of the troops when we march into battle, bangin' the drum. You can't be scared of loud noises or musket balls flyin' past your head, neither."

"What good does makin' a lot of noise do? Isna finding the best place to cross a river or scouting a spot to surprise the enemy a better skill?"

"You can stay around and bang the drum for the troops—callin' them to order and what-not—as our drummer boy. And if you happen to see any Redcoats or other vermin while you're doin' it, I'm sure the colonel would appreciate a little notice before we run into them. But you're too small to be our scout. Asides, we already have one."

Scout brought his moccasined feet together, straightened his spine, then rammed his knuckles onto his hips, as if the effort would squirt a couple more inches to his height. "Where's the colonel? I will speak to *him* about this."

The sergeant snorted, then laughed. "The colonel's cleaning up after another one of Briske's messes. He's our 'real' scout. And he'll be back before you get a chance to learn how to strap on a drum."

He nodded to the tent behind him. "You'll find what you need in there. You do know what a drum looks like, don't ya?"

Scout's eyes narrowed, but he remained mum and didn't move.

"If you want to eat and get paid, you'll learn how to beat that drum. Now, either get outta here or fetch that drum and see how it works. I'm tired of lookin' at ya."

Scout ground his molars in frustration, resisting the urge to spew curse words that he knew wouldn't help his situation. "Aye, but they'd make me feel better," he mumbled to himself as he kicked at leaves and twigs on his way to the drummer's tent.

"Can I help ye, lad?" the elderly man in front of it asked.

"Aye, the sergeant said I'm to fetch the drum. I'm to bang it for the troops when needed."

The almost toothless man dressed in an overly-patched uniform laughed at him. Scout huffed, indignant that yet another 'big' person was treating him so rudely.

"I'm sorry. I didn't mean to insult you, lad. My name is Corporal Gunther, but you can call me Gunny. And your name?"

"I'm known as Scout," he answered and stuck out his hand to greet the man in the gentlemanly fashion he'd seen other men do. "The colonel hired me as the new scout, but the sergeant said I was only big enough to do the drumming."

"Ach, pay no mind to Dunbar; nobody else does. You see, drumming is a necessary task for the company. And boy has nothing to do with the drummer's age: it just means he's an apprentice."

"Apprentice?"

"You'll be the colonel's voice, signaling the troops, letting them know by your drumbeats or rolls whether to stop or go, turn right or left, engage the enemy, or my favorite: call them to meals."

"If the job is so important, why did he say it was only half wages?"

"I'm not sure that it is. You'll be the one who tells the whole company what to do. The colonel will tell you what to tell the troops, and then you repeat it using your drumbeats. You see, the men can hear the drum easier than a man's voice. But the best part of the job is the protection you'll have. Since you won't be carrying a gun, you're not a target for the King's men. Or the Hessians. Or whoever. I'm not too sure who we're fighting this week."

Scout inhaled sharply, biting off the retort, 'As long as it isn't Indians.'

Gunny chuckled. He could see the self-conscious blush. "No, the red man is our friend. Well, at least he's mine. See this?"

The corporal unbuttoned his cuff and showed Scout a savage looking scar. "I was caught in a bit of a local feud. I was strung up, left to die by some rather unsavory sorts, when a couple of Cherokee hunters found me. The leader cut me down, dressed my bleeding wrists with some chewed up herbs, bound them with strips of fabric torn from his own red shirt, and left me with a few pieces of jerked meat. I was able to get to water without a problem…you can hardly spit around this neck of the woods without hitting a creek or a spring… But I digress. It's not the color of a man's skin, but the intent of his heart that makes him what he is."

Scout nodded in agreement, then noticed the man's boot. Or lack of one.

"I wasn't so lucky a few years ago. I lost the foot to gangrene. Stepped on a rake. You wouldn't think it would hurt anymore, but I'll be stripped and dipped if I don't get the itchiest big toe sometimes. I scratch and scratch, but since there isn't anything there, it doesn't do me no good. But enough about me. Are you ready to learn the signals? I'll bet you're a fast learner."

"Aye, I am. Or so I've been told."

"Fine. So, listen here," Gunny lowered his tone and closed his eyes as he began his monotone recitation. "Each new recruit has to be taught how to put on his accoutrements and stand properly."

"Ack-what-a-ments?" Scout interrupted, shifting his weight from one foot to the other. "And is there something amiss with the way I'm standing?"

"I'm speaking of your soldier-ing position," Gunny huffed in exasperation, then returned to his drill instructor tone. "Stand straight and firm upon your legs with your head turned to the right so far as to bring the left eye over your waistcoat buttons…"

"Waistcoat? I have the shirt on my back and a vest. Is the colonel going to give me a uniform?"

Gunny wiped his nose, stifling a chuckle. "I don't think there are enough funds for uniforms this year. Just pretend you have buttons down the front of your vest. Now, place your heels two inches apart, turn your toes out, suck in your belly, shoulders square, hands loose at your sides with palms close to your thighs…"

Scout looked over his shoulder, shifted his feet, sucked in a deep breath, and nearly fell over. "How is this supposed to help me bang a drum?"

"Hmph. Since you won't be armed with anything but a pair of drumsticks, I guess we can forget those instructions. Just stand tall and proud, keep your mouth quiet, and listen for orders."

"When do I start banging the drum?"

"That's beat the drum. Go ahead and pick it up, and make sure the sticks don't fall out. We need to get at least a hundred paces downwind of the company so as not to disturb them. The colonel is in town, ahem, seeing to some old business, but I'm sure he'd want you to practice out of earshot of the troops. No use stirring them up, although I think they're all fairly worn out from this morning's relocation."

***

Scout and Gunny spent the next two hours going over the various beats and rolls on the old drum that had been sitting in the corner.

"Well, that's about all the cues I know," Gunny said. "How about we take a dinner break. And, if you're willing, you can sneak out and do some real scouting. No telling who's out in these woods. That so-and-so Briske was worthless for everything 'cept causing trouble. And we already have enough no-goods around here for any regiment!"

Scout looked over at Dunbar, the rotund sergeant who had demoted him without a word to the colonel. "Aye, I'll agree with that."

"And by tomorrow morning, I'll try to have a new set of drumsticks carved for you. The ones you've been using were old when I was a lad."

429

Chapter 46: Old Friends (LDB Ch 2)

Julian let the glow of homecoming settle about him. He inhaled the aroma of black hickory and cottonwood infused with the must of damp fallen leaves as he rode down the familiar trail. Gone were the suffocating smells of fish guts, tar, and man sweat. His extended sales trip to Charleston had been a success. All the Andalusian colts had been sold for top dollar, plus he had a long list of breeders interested in contracting his stallions for stud service. Financial security was something he never thought he'd have to worry about, but that was in his former life as a British lord. Now he was a North Carolina landowner in the newly formed United States of America. With his recent financial coup, he had money for food and feed until spring and enough left over to gift his son a plow.

He sighed as he recalled the handsome face of the man who would greet him when he arrived home. He hadn't seen his partner, José, in nearly a month. How did his daughter-in-law Evie phrase it? 'After long separations, the hellos and good-byes are extra special?'

He shook his head and chuckled. Where would he be without that wise older woman who had been rejuvenated and now had a teenaged body? True, Evie was a time traveler, but that only served to broaden her thinking rather than stifle it. She had come to his aid and helped save José from a lynch mob years ago. And, after she saw the mutual attraction between him and the sexy Spanish caballero, had decided to perform a 'ceremony,' blessing and uniting the two of them. Men were able to marry other men 'when' she was from, she said. Same sex marriages were just beginning to be accepted in the early twenty-first century. He sighed. It would take more than two hundred years for people to be able to live and love anyway they desired. *Thank you, my dear daughter-in-law Evie, for giving me my peace now. Sorry, everyone else, for the long wait you'll have.*

Julian's mind rambled as he rode toward the clutter of cabins that was the closest thing to a town this area had. His mouth was parched. He still had water in his canteen, but a glass of whiskey—or better yet, a tall ale—would slake his thirst and revive his spirit. If he tarried here a few moments, refreshing his body with bread and brew, he could be home by noon tomorrow. Another night under the stars wouldn't be too bad. At least the longest part of his journey was over. He glanced up and noticed that the white fluffy clouds were now thick and dark gray. Or maybe he should find a room for the night. No need to arrive early, chilled, damp, and with the onset of the ague. If he was to spend the next two weeks in bed, he didn't want to be ill, too.

Julian's reflections on whether warm food and dry bedding would be better than arriving in the arms of his partner ten hours sooner were interrupted by someone calling out to him. "Hart? Is that you, Colonel Hart?"

Julian gulped and subconsciously tried to sink into his plain clothes. He shouldn't be known as a British officer in this area of North Carolina. He had purposely kept a low profile these past few years, but apparently someone recognized him. He sucked in a deep breath and answered back in a sharp, military tone, "Who goes there?"

"You sly fox, it is you, is it not? Don't you remember me? It is I, William Saulnier. We attended Cambridge at the same time."

Julian's eyes widened so much, his lashes tickled his eyebrows. "Willie? But, but… But you're wearing an American uniform!"

"Patriot, colonial, American…" Saulnier's eyes narrowed in belated suspicion. "Where are your epaulets? You are still with His majesty's army, are you not?"

"I am not. I am retired. And it appears that you have, ahem, turned your coat inside out."

Saulnier's face split into a wide, gap-toothed grin. "I always knew you were an intelligent man. Retiring in the middle of an armed conflict is the same as turning coat, some say. Your departure was a clever mystery. I did not believe you were really dead. But the war is over and I'm glad to see you're alive. There was nothing for this old soldier to do—save fight in France—if I had returned to England with the others. Since I did not care to eat snails nor consort with poxed women, I decided to stay and wear a different array of colors. Regardless, neither of us need worry about shooting each other any longer. The war is over, but I am still soldiering. I am in charge of training a very green company of men just south of here. I refer to them as 'the reserves'."

"What does your wife think of you living in this godforsaken country?" Julian asked, rolling his eyes at the description often used by English aristocracy.

431

"She didn't say a word. Just packed up her jewelry and clothes and said she was leaving for Prussia. Lord help them… And yours? Did she follow you here?"

Julian shook his head, but before he could speak, Willie spoke up. "I'm so sorry. I forgot she passed before you came to America. So, do you live alone, or have you taken a new bride?"

"No bride for me! I'm just an old bachelor with a horse breeding ranch a few miles north of here. My partner and I were able to turn a profit with the Andalusian stock he brought from Spain. Wallace—my adopted son—and his family live nearby. I get to see him, his wife, and my grandchildren on a regular basis. Life is good."

"Well, it would be for me, too, if I could get and keep good soldiers. It seems the bad ones stick around, like a dog turd you can't scrape from the bottom of your boot. If you're stopping at that poor excuse of a tavern, I'll buy you a drink after I attend to discharging our scout. Or maybe I should have a drink or three first."

Julian really didn't want to reminisce about old times. It looked like his decision on whether to stay the night in town or resume his travels would be easier than he thought. "I think I'll pass. If that commotion down yonder is your company training, I'll be able to find you. Maybe in a week or two then?"

Bang, bang, rat a tat, tat, tat. Willie was suddenly aware of the staccato noise of someone learning to drum. Did Gunny find another drummer already? "Yes, Julian, old pal. Unless the Indians around here suddenly become angry and drive us out, we should be here for the winter." He stared up at the sky. "It may not be a white Christmas here, but it looks like it will be a wet one."

"Then keep your powder dry. Until later," Julian said. He tossed a casual salute with his right hand, then rode away.

"And I really am glad you stayed in America," Willie said under his breath. "Now if we could just send some of the riff raff back to good old Mother England!"

Chapter 47: Briske the Baddest (LDB Ch 3)

The bright mood of seeing an old friend quickly evaporated when Colonel Saulnier saw Briske's gelding in front of the clapboard building. He stole a quick nip from his flask for liquid courage, then set out.

"Where is that jackal?" he growled as he burst through the tavern door, arms swinging wide, heedless of the sot who fell backwards with his abrupt entrance. "I'll patch my tent with his hide if I catch him."

Bill wiped the smirk from his whiskered face with the back of his hand. He knew who the commander was looking for.

And why.

His stool screeched on the wood plank floor as he rose from the table in the darkened corner. "She deserved it," he hollered in defense of his cousin, Gerald Briske, the army scout. "He barely hit her. Asides," he strode forward into the fading daylight, hiking up his rope-belted pants to present a more determined demeanor and repeated himself, "She deserved it. He told her he'd pay her if he liked it and he didn't. Well, not much, anyways. He said she shoulda paid *him* for their time together. When she wouldn't, he just gave her a chance to reconsider."

Bill swatted the empty air back and forth in demonstration, then laughed at what he thought was a clever gesture, glancing at his drinking buddies to make sure they agreed with him. They did, but when he turned back to face the colonel, the officer's clenched jaws and scarlet face sent a shiver down his spine.

"It was just his open hand," he justified. "Well, at least, the first time. He only used his fist when she screamed out for Seymour, the shopkeeper." He paused and bowed his head. "He did quit punching her when she finally shut up, though," then looked up to make sure the colonel had heard his last whispered words.

"She was unconscious, bleeding from her ears, and almost dead!" The colonel snorted with disgust. "If I had my way, that man would be strung up for attempted murder! He broke her jaw in so many places, she'll never be able to talk again, much less eat solid foods. Now what's she going to do for a living?" Colonel Saulnier brought his shoulders back, stood tall, and took a deep breath to compose himself. He really had been fond of her—he exhaled softly as he realized that he still was.

"I've come to a decision. Briske is relieved of duty immediately.

I've already found another scout. No more 'just one more chances' for him. He's to forfeit all of his personal belongings left at the encampment and any pay due him. The lass can use those proceeds to start a ladies wear shop and seamstress service. I've seen her work; she has a delicate hand when it comes to stitching."

He swallowed and turned away from the patrons. *Delicate for other purposes, too. The paltry funds from Private Briske wouldn't do much more than buy a bolt or two of cloth, good shears, and a few needles. He'd contribute to the cause so she had money for food and housing...and drop by whenever he could and make sure all was well with her. They communicated just fine without words or had in the past. It looked like this Christmas wouldn't be so dreary after all.*

Chapter 48: Christmas is coming (LDB Ch 4)

Weeks later
'Reserves' campsite

"It's too cold to drill," Dunbar said, not even trying to hide his spoilt sauerkraut attitude. "Asides, no one wants to fight. The war's been over for..." The sergeant pulled his mittens off with his teeth and mumbled as he tried to count. "Well, we haven't fought anyone for months. I can think of better places to be than here. And asides again, it's almost Christmas."

The other men, still in formation but not at attention, grumbled in agreement.

The colonel briskly rubbed his gloved hands together as he tried to think of a valid reason they *shouldn't* take a break. As far as he knew, there weren't any conflicts brewing. The British had either left the country or, like him, had decided to stay in America on friendly terms. The Indians had better things to do than create a ruckus, and the farmers weren't likely to go any further than their cow barns in this weather. Everyone—red, white, or plaid—was too busy trying to keep warm to create havoc with one another.

"All right, all right. Today is December 22nd. You may leave the compound to visit friends or family, but must return here in two—no, make that three—weeks. That should give you enough time to travel, visit, and perform the necessary repairs your wives and mothers have saved up for you, and maybe enjoy a hot dinner or two."

"Or a hot wench or two," Dunbar added under his breath.

Colonel Saulnier groaned at the crass remark but didn't address it. "Three weeks, men, and then you're mine again."

***

"So, where are you going, Scout?" Gunny asked as he used a stick to scratch his imaginary big toe.

"I suppose I'm staying here with ye. Someone has to look out after ye. I told ye that new peg wasn't right fer ye. Has that stump healed up yet?"

"You go ahead and visit your family. I'll be fine here. See?" Gunny held up a bottle of whisky with one hand, a sturdy length of hard sausage with the other, then set them back down clumsily on the table, ignoring the question of his health.

"And who will fetch water fer ye and help ye change yer dressings?" asked Scout, the deep scowl on his forehead almost giving him wrinkles.

"Now don't be treating me like an invalid! Just because my leg is a little red and my crutch doesn't like the ice and snow doesn't mean I can't take care of myself." Gunny stabbed the ground beside him with the aforementioned crutch and tried to rise from his cloth camp stool, but his arms were weak with fever. He pulled his handkerchief out of his coat pocket and wiped his face, averting Scout's chastising glare. His intended show of strength had just proved the young man right. He was an invalid. Worthless. Without family. And he had spent his last coin on drink and meat. He would be better off if he did die of fever.

"Now, dinna go feelin' sorry fer yerself. I learned a bit about healin' and the one thing ye have to do is rest. Yer body can take care of a lot the repairs, but not if yer workin' or," Scout grabbed the bottle of whisky, "poisonin' yerself with fire water. I'll see if I can get ye some greens to eat. Or better yet…"

"I'm not eating anything you pluck out of the ground!"

"Then how about a bit of this?" Scout pulled an orange out of his knapsack. "Cookie gave me a present. He said there weren't enough fer everyone, but that since I was still a growin' lad, I should have it. But I'll share it with ye."

Gunny watched as Scout turned the orange over in his hands, rolling it back and forth between his palms to release its tantalizing aroma. "All right. If it will make you feel better, I'll let you share it with me."

"Before or after I change those dressings?" Scout sniffed audibly then wrinkled his nose. "I can tell by the smell that ye haven't been doin' it daily. Tsk, tsk," he chided. "Corporal Gunther, sometimes I think ye still need yer mother."

Gunny replied with a grunt, then straightened up and rethought the proposition. "I'll tell you what; I'll peel the orange while you peel the bandages. That will give me something to do with my hands…other than strangle you. But are you sure I can't have some of that whisky first?"

Scout wafted his hand in front of his face. "I can also tell by yer smell that ye've had more than a taste of it already." He grabbed the pot

436

of hot water from the side of the cook fire, removed the first sopping bandage from it with his knife, and spread it across the old dressing. "We'll soften it up first so it won't hurt so much when I remove it. I dinna care to hear ye yell any more than ye care to shout."

"You're too good to me boy. I wish I could give you something. I've worked all my life, and all I have to show for it is a missing leg and a bad attitude. The only money I get I waste on whisky and women…"

"Ach, yer feelin' sorry fer yerself again. Ye have me and…" Scout paused in his ministrations.

"Don't stop now, lad. I need distraction if you're gonna be pulling on that mess."

"Ye have me and ye have yer stories. Now, as ye may have guessed, I grew up the Indian way. My father was…is…a white man, but he's never been around much. So I'd like to ask a favor of ye. I'm afraid to ask anyone else, so would you tell me what all this excitement is about Christmas? I think it has to do with goin' to church and such, and since I've never been…"

"Be extra gentle there, and I'll tell you the reason everyone gets as wound up as an eight-day clock about it."

Gunny did his best to get comfortable, then spent the next hour telling Scout about Christmas and the birth of Jesus. "He was a special man, born to a woman as a babe, but also the son of God. His earthly parents was poor, as poor as you and me. They didn't even have a cradle for him. He slept in a hay trough—they called it a manger—but it was just the place where the farm folks put food for their big critters.

"Now, when Jesus was born, a big star appeared in the sky, showing everyone who cared to look up where he was. Well, three wise men had heard about the prophecy and the star, so when they saw that bright shininess, they knew what it meant. They decided to follow it to see the newborn king. You see, that's what they called him, Christ the King. These three wise men were also rich. They brought gifts of gold and frankincense and myrrh. I know you know what gold is, but that other stuff, well I'm not sure exactly what they are, but they're sweet smelling and expensive. And it wasn't just the three wise men who came, either. Lots of other folks came, too, just to see him and give him presents. But you know who else came?"

"No. I didn't even know about Jesus the king before now. And he was God—the Great Father's—son?"

"Was and is. But that's the rest of the story. For another day. Now, there was a young man who came to see Jesus. He was maybe the same age and size as you. I don't think he got much respect, either, but he was a good lad. He felt bad because he didn't have a gift to give the new king. But he did have a talent. That means he knew how to do something really well."

Scout nodded. He knew what talent was. He'd been told he was talented several times. But he didn't want to brag about it. Besides, he wanted to hear the rest of the story.

"He was a drummer. He had a drum his grandfather had made for him. He used it to comfort the sheep in the fields and to play music for his little sister. His mother had told him that it helped her sleep. Well, he asked Mary—that's the name of Jesus's mother—if he could play for the infant king.

"Well, she being a nice lady and all, of course she said yes. And you know what?"

"What?" Scout asked, wide-eyed, his last orange segment hanging in the air in front of his mouth.

"He smiled at him. Jesus, the Son of God, liked his drum playing so much, He smiled at him. So, you see, your drumming is good for ordering troops around according to the colonel's orders, but it also makes people happy. And sheep, too. Now, since all the others are gone, and it's just you and me out here, you can learn to play other tunes on that drum. Maybe you have talent like that other drummer boy."

Scout looked at the orange piece, then popped it in his mouth. "Maybe it isn't so bad bein' a drummer boy. Ye go ahead and get yer rest and I'll see if I can play ye a sleepy time song."

Gunny leaned on his crutch and hobbled over to his cot. "You do that, son. You do that."

Scout experimented with random taps and rolls on the drum skin until a pleasing tune came into being. He repeated the refrain until it felt comfortable, his hands automatically moving the drumsticks to tickle out the melody. Suddenly, a loud snort interrupted his solo sonata. Gunny was sound asleep, a full smile on his face. It looked like his song was a good lullaby for older folks, too.

***

Julian didn't like the idea of leaving, but he had forgotten to get a salt lick for the horses. With the cold winter winds, the herd was reluctant to drink. The lack of hydration could be serious. He needed to get his valuable Andalusian horses thirsty. The only place that might have one was the general store. It had limited inventory, but even it should carry salt. Besides, he had found an old medal in his carved rosewood treasure box. He had received the award for excellence in mathematics his second year at Cambridge. If it hadn't been for Willie Saulnier's tutoring, he never would have won it. They hadn't parted on the best of terms years ago, and their recent brief re-acquaintance was barely cordial. Maybe it was just the Christmas spirit creeping in, but he really did want to gift the token to his former best mate.

"We don't have a whole salt block here, but you can have this broken one for a penny. I've been chipping pieces off it for some of the poor folk coming through." Seymour shook his head. "Too poor to even buy salt. No one should go without that! I didn't charge them for it. It was a gift from God, I'd tell them. The smiles and thanks I got in return were payment enough. Plus, maybe the Lord will look past some of my old indiscretions, seeing as I was generous and all…"

Julian thought about adding another penny to the payment for the salt, then balked. That would be taking away Seymour's gift to the others. "Thanks for sharing with and caring for others. I'm sure He'll remember you when your time is up. Have a happy Christmas."

"And to you, too. Godspeed."

Tum de dum dum… Rat a tat tat…

Willie had been right. The camp was easy to find, and the drummer had definitely learned to play in a more proficient manner. Maybe too well. Troops needed strong tones to respond to. These gentle rolls and taps were worthy of being in a music house.

"Hey the troops!" Julian called out as he approached.

He looked around. It was deserted. Or nearly so. He could hear movement near one tent.

A small man, or large boy, came out, his hand outstretched with a sharp implement in it.

"Julian?" Scout asked, then dropped the drumstick to his side. "What are ye doin' here? Oh, and how is my, my… How is Jenny?"

"I was looking for Colonel Saulnier, and as far as Jenny goes, I saw her maybe a month ago. She was in good health. I had planned to visit her and the rest of her family for Christmas. What are your obligations here?"

"He's the drummer boy and a darned good one. Or maybe I should drop the boy part," Gunny said, as he hobbled over to greet the visitor. "Greetings. I'm Corporal Gunther, but you can call me Gunny. Oh, and we're on leave. Young Scout here decided to stay behind and make sure I was healing well." He pointed to the new bandage on his leg, a bright pink spot seeping through the otherwise white dressing.

"So, you're a healer now, too? What other tasks are you assigned in this company?"

"He's really the scout," Gunny said, parental pride shown in his voice and broad-shouldered posture. "He's filling in for me as drummer until I get healed all the way and can wear my new peg."

"So, Colonel Saulnier is gone?"

"Not quite," came a voice from the trees.

The three jumped at the sudden noise.

"Didn't mean to startle you. I just brought back a few men who were, shall I say, a bit too rowdy. If you don't mind, Gunny, these men will remain in camp as guards. You and Scout can take off if you'd like. I'm sure these soldiers can handle anything, or anyone, who comes this way with mischief on his mind."

"Yes, sir," two of the scraggly soldiers replied.

"We won't be making any more bad decisions, will we?" the third and tallest of the three added.

"No, sir," the others chorused.

"We like the army and want to make it our career. You can count on us, Colonel, to keep the camp clean and free of hostiles."

Colonel Saulnier held back the urge to roll his eyes. The only ones they had to look out for were skunks and possums and other scavengers...or maybe a coyote or cougar if rabbits weren't around. "All right. I'm counting on you three. The Boone brothers, you say?"

"Yes, sir," they replied and saluted, beaming with joy at being given another chance. Chasing the serving wench around with a hot poker had been a bad prank, especially when it caught the curtains on fire. They'd never take a dare again. From anyone! It was fortunate that the water bucket had been full and the colonel alert. Otherwise, the tavern would have burned down and they'd have to make reparations or whatever it was the owner had called out.

"What brings you here, Julian?" the colonel asked.

"I was in the neighborhood and thought I'd bring you a gift. I didn't know you had my, ahem, kin in your company. Scout Kincaid is a sharp young man and able to take on any task." Julian looked over and winked at Scout. "But if you've been around him for even a few hours, I'm sure you realized that."

Julian reached into his pocket and pulled out the medal wrapped in a clean white handkerchief. "Here's a little memento, Willie. To our youth. May we never lose our eagerness to learn."

Colonel Saulnier accepted the packet and gently unwrapped it. "Your medallion for excellence in mathematics? But it's yours. You earned it."

Julian gently urged Willie's outstretched hand back. "I never would have proceeded to the next year if it hadn't been for your encouragement and willingness to tutor me. You'll be glad to know that I can still compute the volume of a cube, and although I remember the formula, I've never found a practical use for quadratic equations."

Gunny, Scout, and the Boone brothers looked at each other, confused about the other men's conversation.

"Well then, I'll accept this as a Christmas gift. Did I hear you ask young Scout to join you?"

"Those may not have been my exact words, but yes, that was my intent. Scout is a part of my extended family. He and my granddaughter are quite close."

Scout's face blazed so hot at the remark, he thought he would break out in a sweat. Rather than force words that would surely come out as squeaks, he nodded and smiled.

Yes, he would love to visit his secret child bride and her family. He didn't have any money yet, but the promised income from the army plus the chance to make contacts for other work would keep him busy until both he and Jenny were old enough to live together and have their own house.

Scout's musings about his future were interrupted by a question. "Well, do you think you could help Gunny if we traveled? Sarah can't seem to find enough folks to heal in her own area. I'm sure that woman would be overjoyed at the opportunity to look at his wound."

"Aye, I'll help Gunny on and off his mount. It's a might late to leave, though. Yer welcome to stay with us until sunrise."

Julian looked over his shoulder. The lad was right. Not only was the sky darkening in a hurry, the temperature was rising. Those clouds could only mean rain or snow. With no moon, the trail would be hard enough to find. Yes, he'd delay his return until the morrow.

***

The odd crew spent the evening around the fire, sharing stories, water crackers, cheese, and slices of Gunny's sausage. Julian contributed a bottle of cider and Scout shared his latest drum composition.

"I don't know about the rest of you, but I'm turning in. Daylight isn't that far away, and it's been a long day for me," Julian said, stifling a yawn.

"You're welcome to share my tent tonight," Colonel Saulnier said. "I have a spare cot. It has been mended quite a few times, but I'm sure it's dry and much more comfortable than this rocky ground."

Julian looked from his horse to the tent. He had neglected to bring his daypack. No spare food or bedding. All he had for a blanket was the one still draped over his mount's back.

"And I have a few spare blankets, too. It looks like you weren't planning on staying out this late."

Julian grabbed the canvas bag containing the salt lick. "Just dropped in to get something for the herd and to see if you were around. Yes, I'd appreciate the hospitality."

"Since we have able-bodied men here to watch the camp, we should be able to leave at first light. Oh, I won't be going all the way with you because I have plans to visit, ahem, a friend." Colonel Saulnier looked away as he spoke the last words, trying to keep his private life and feelings just that: private.

Julian saw the blush. He'd heard the rumors. It looked as if Willie would have someone special to spend Christmas with after all. "Well, if you change your mind, you're welcome to join us."

Gunny, sober now but sleepy, called out to the others, "Secure the area, check the horses, bank the fire, and do your best to keep from snoring. I'm a light sleeper and need my beauty rest."

***

It wasn't Gunny's snoring that kept Scout awake: his mind was all atwitter. All he could think about was seeing his fair-haired young wife again. He could hold her hand and tell her all about his adventures as a scout, how he had saved the day for a whole company of men and their horses and cannon. Maybe if he brought his drum, he could play her his song. Her little brothers and sister were sure to like it, too. And maybe, just maybe, she'd kiss him.

***

"You still abed?" Gunny asked, poking Scout with the crutch he had manufactured from a scavenged piece of blasted pine tree. "We're all loaded up, ready to hit the trail. Hop to it and go water your tree. I'll bundle your bedding. No time for coffee or breakfast this morning. There's a snowstorm brewing and I want to be ahead—not in the midst— of it."

Scout rubbed the sleep from his eyes as he stumbled over to relieve himself. He didn't even remember sleeping. Sure enough, though, Julian and Colonel Saulnier were already securing their saddles. The Boone brothers were huddled around the new fire, encouraging the dancing flames with larger pieces of fresh cut wood. Snap, pop, pop, hiss. The damp pitchy pine burned unevenly, sending sparks of exploded bark into the fresh snow. The three jumped back when a flare flew up, startling the sleepy sentinels.

When Scout returned, the three seasoned soldiers were mounted, waiting for him, their steeds dancing in place, eager to keep their muscles moving to get warm.

Scout grabbed his pony's mane and jumped on her blanketed back. "What are ye waiting fer?" he asked brightly. "We have family to see and miles to travel before it's dark."

***

It should have taken less than an hour to reach town, but the storm had shifted directions and the troupe was now headed into, not away from, the first major winter storm of the season.

Colonel Saulnier motioned for them to stop. "This is where I leave you," he said. "I'd ask you to come join me, but I don't think you'd listen. I know you, Julian. Once you have your mind set, there's no persuading you to do else."

"Yes, Willie, but I wouldn't put us in harm's way, either. I'm sure

443

we'll be fine. Say 'hello' to your new lady friend for us. If she's as fine a seamstress as I hear, I'll have work for her soon. I'm in need of a few new shirts. The ones I have are wearing faster on the ranch than they did in the parlor."

The colonel pointed to Julian's knee. "And it looks as if you've worn holes in your knee patches, too. Shoeing horses, I presume?"

Julian blushed at the barely disguised joke about what Willie had supposed was the reason for the worn spots in his britches. "Some tasks are better performed on knees…such as repairing roofs and building water troughs. Yes, I think I'll be requiring new trousers shortly, too."

Scout paid little attention to their light banter. He wanted to leave right away. He sat up tall and instinctively sniffed the air. In limited visibility weather, the senses of smell and hearing were often more reliable than sight. He turned his head and listened again. Nothing now, but he could have sworn he had heard a muffled curse.

"Ready?" Julian asked the others.

The assorted nods and ayes weren't needed; they were already back on the trail that became fainter as the minutes passed.

"I thought you said you could find your way to the Pomeroys blindfolded," Gunny said.

"I never said that," Julian said just as Scout replied, "Aye, I did. I never said anything about during a blizzard, though."

Gunny's jaw dropped, his eyes wide with fear.

"Though I'm sure it willna be a problem," Scout added with feigned exuberance, hoping to allay his mentor's fear.

"Keep your mouth shut, Gunny, or you'll freeze your lungs," Julian chided. He knew it wasn't that cold, but he didn't want to be distracted by Gunny's whining. True, the trail was harder to follow, but between him, Scout, and the horses, they'd find the way.

Scout put up his hand, ready to tell the men to wait—something was wrong—then changed his mind. Yes, he had definitely caught a whiff of something, but now he recognized that tangy aroma. It didn't indicate fiend or wild animal. Not really. It was the scent of the liniment he had given his father for his horse's stone-bruised hoof. Ian Kincaid the elder was surreptitiously escorting them.

Scout had learned years ago that his father couldn't smell camphor. By giving him a 'cure-all' for his aging horse, he had intentionally given him a tracking device. True, it might create a dilemma if anyone else smelled it, but if his father was sneaking up on someone with ill intent, then that person certainly deserved a head start. And, if he was hunting game, then he was afoot, not on his camphor-scented steed, and it wouldn't be a problem.

Gunny decided he had stayed quiet long enough. "I think we're lost. I'll be tied and whipped if we haven't passed this same stand of trees twice before. And just because I don't see our old tracks doesn't mean nothing. The snow is falling so fast and thick; it would have already covered them. There's no reason for us to keep going in circles. I say wait until the weather clears so we can see where we're going. Besides, my leg is bothering me something fierce. We won't have to worry about me finding a healer: the stump is ready to freeze off!"

Julian looked at Scout. He was sure they were on the right path and, by the eye roll and shrug he received from the perceptive young guide, he knew it, too. "Gunny, whether you're right or not, it probably would be a good idea to hunker down for a while. We're not making much headway. And if your leg is bothering you that much, well, I don't want to be responsible for frostbite."

"Then I'm all for camping right here!" Gunny said, then slid off his horse. He teetered on one leg momentarily, then lost his balance and fell backwards, his head cushioned by a snow-covered bush.

Scout hopped off his pony and rushed to help his friend. "Now why'd ye go and do that? I told ye I'd help ye on and off yer mount!"

"Now that was a right conveniently sitty, situationed... well-placed blueberry bush," Gunny stammered.

Scout reached into Gunny's unbuttoned coat and grabbed the bottle of whisky. "Dinna I tell ye to lay off this...this...distilled horse piss?!"

"Ah, I do recall you grousing about it some, but it warms my insides and eases my pain," Gunny said softly, then passed out.

"It looks like we're spending the night here, then," Julian said. "Let's build a shelter."

***

"Do you think we'll make it?" Scout asked.

Snort, grumble, snort. Gunny wasn't intentionally responding but seemed to be. Scout gently placed his hand on the old man's forehead. Fever. There was nothing he could do for it now.

445

"I'm sure as soon as there's a break in the storm, we can head out," Julian said. "Between the two of us, we can get Gunny back in the saddle. You may have to ride behind him if he gets delirious. I'm not sure whether it was the drink or the fever that made him fall."

"By the stink of his breath, I'd say it was the whisky. I know he needs fluids, but I dinna want him to choke by making him drink. Too bad there aren't any reeds around. I could make him a straw."

"Fluids? Now you sound like Sarah. Did she give you training?"

"No, but Leah did. A few years back, when my father was ailing." Scout looked around, as if someone had stepped on his shadow. He hadn't heard what he suspected was his father since they started out, and he had heard that first mumbled curse. And he couldn't smell anything because of the strong scent of the pine-fueled fire in front of him. But he could feel him, as if he were a scratchy woolen shirt on his bare skin.

The two healthy men didn't get much sleep. The impromptu shelter made of a one-man sized tent strung between two trees in front of a rocky outcropping would have been sufficient, but the fevered man situated between them, tossing and turning and flailing all three and a half limbs, made rest impossible. Gunny was delirious and kept trying to crawl away to meet his one true love. "Helen, Helen, I'm coming for you, sweetheart," he kept calling, grasping for the doorknob that didn't exist.

Finally, as the first hint of light peeked over the southeastern sky, Julian gave up. "Give the horses a fistful of oats, then help me strike this hellhole of an inn. Any rest we get on the road has to be better than what we've had. At least it will be easier to keep track of this love-obsessed man on top of his horse. He can't crawl away when he's a-saddle!"

"I agree. Just sit on him for a few more minutes, and I'll have everything in order. I managed to get a few winks and nods in between his ravings."

Julian relaxed against the soldier, the fevered man's deep breathing indicating that he, too, was worn out. He was glad the young man was so eager to help. And did so without grousing. Oh, to once again have the strength and vigor of youth! He smiled and realized that an even more precious gift would be to have Scout's dedication and determination. Yes, he was glad his adopted granddaughter Jenny was sweet on the lad. Hopefully, their attraction wouldn't fade. Theirs seemed to be a perfect match.

Suddenly, Julian's face was chilled and damp. Scout had pulled the canvas from the trees, and fresh snow was falling on him. Julian shuddered as he realized he had dozed again; evidently he had fallen asleep for a minute or two.

"I'm ready fer yer help getting Gunny on his horse."

"Let's get to it, then," Julian said and rearranged his jacket and scarf to keep in every bit of warmth possible. "It looks like the snow has slowed a bit. You and I both know, I'm sure, that we've been on the right trail all along. I don't know that stopping for Gunny was the right thing to do, but what's done is done. Now, onward. I'm sure Sarah has a tonic that will check his fever."

"Aye, and I'm sure someone in the house will fix us a proper breakfast, maybe with some sort of stimulating drink. I do recall Leah saying something about brewing a coffee made from roasted dandelion roots."

"That sounds good to me. Now, let's see if we can get this done swiftly."

They each grabbed one of the slumbering man's elbows and pulled him forward into a semi-upright position, then Julian stood up under Gunny's armpit and acted as a walking crutch.

"Stay put," Scout told the horse as he wrapped the reins around a sapling.

"He's a seasoned war horse—he will," Julian said. "Now come help me with Gunny. Well-trained horse or not, I've yet to see a steed who will mount a rider on himself."

Oomph! Shoving Gunny onto the roan was easier than the two had anticipated, and they almost pushed him over the other side. Apparently the unconscious soldier's reflex to grab a fistful of mane and pull himself up was as much a part of him as swatting away a fly when sound asleep.

"I'd better take the lead," Julian said, reverting to his former commander tone. "I'm sure it's hard to see around your passenger."

Scout leaned around Gunny's upper arm to answer. "Aye, I may be a fair scout, but he's hindering my abilities to see the trail and hear or smell any danger." Scout wrinkled his nose and coughed. "Remind me to ask Sarah if someone can help me give him a bath when she's done with her healin' tasks. If he's still asleep, it should be much easier. I dinna think he's known a cake of soap since he was my age. At least!"

The casual chatter stopped as Julian rode ahead, leading the way to the Pomeroys, Scout's pony loosely tied to the back of his horse's saddle, Gunny's double-ridered gelding obediently bringing up the rear.

The morning calm was soon swallowed by wind and more snow. It was hard to tell if it was fresh precipitation or if the flurries were old snowfall, re-conveyed from the trees and drifts around them, driven by the erratic gusts of an unstable storm. Either way, the icy bits stung all exposed flesh and froze eyelashes on both two and four-legged creatures. Julian wiped what felt like a runny nose. He looked at the icy lump on the back of his glove. It was a small ice sculpture, made from his moist exhales that had frozen in place. He resisted the urge to wipe again. It was better to leave an ice patch as protection than expose more bare skin to the elements. He turned and looked back at the huge war horse tagging along behind him. Even though he was burdened with two riders, albeit one of them small, he was keeping up, snorting forcefully to keep his nostrils warm and clear of ice.

Scout peeked around Gunny's bulk and waved to Julian, giving him a thumbs up. Julian noticed the lad's face was pink with health and not iced. At least Corporal Gunny was a good heat source. He couldn't tell how the fevered man—shoulders slumped, his face nearly to his chest in sleep—was doing, but the chilly wind was hopefully keeping his fever in check.

Rowr!

The wild animal growl came out of nowhere, sending shivers down everyone's spine, four-legged or two. Julian clutched reins close to his chest and clasped his thighs tight as his steed reared up. He stayed astride, but the grasp didn't stay his mount. The stallion bolted, taking Scout's pony along with him. He galloped away from the feral threat, the path of snow-laden branches and tall snow drifts no deterrent to the equine's anxious escape that nearly de-saddled Julian.

Gunny's experienced war horse, normally placid in stressful situations, reared up, too. Men yelling, cannons firing, guns blasting and steel swords clanging he could handle. An angry cougar was another matter. Gunny, still unconscious, instinctively grabbed mane, leaned forward, and held fast. He was old, but his reflexes were seasoned and had only improved with the many years a-saddle.

Scout, caught unaware, grasped only the lost warmth of Gunny as he was abruptly dumped backwards off the ass-end of the horse. The young man lay flat on his back atop a snowdrift—helpless—the wind knocked out of him. He tried to gasp for air, but his lungs were unresponsive. He rolled onto his knees and let his stomach sag, hoping to ease what Evie called a spastic diaphragm. She told him once that if he could relax and do that, the air would find its way back in. It worked. But now he had a bigger problem.

The mammoth horse was above him, reared up, dancing in place, the semi-conscious Gunny still clutching tight. Scout's stunned brain scrambled to find an escape from the tumbling hooves that clawed the frosty air in panic. He couldn't see: a dense fog of fear created by the steamy grunts and whinnies of the frenzied steed obscured the area. If the cougar was near, Scout wasn't aware of it. That also meant the horse couldn't hear or see it, either. The horse would stomp on and thrash any movement, including his.

Scout rolled to the right, but the powerful kicks of the gelding followed him. A shoed hoof grazed his cheek, warming his flesh with friction from the scrape. "I'm not the fiend," he screamed, but his shouts went unheeded, his shrill call of fear fueling the horse's agitation.

Suddenly, Scout was no longer alone.

"Get back, ye mangy sow!"

The tall, lanky man dressed in roughly tanned hides waved his long arms broadly, deflecting the kicks of the started gelding. "I mean it. Get back or yer stew meat!"

Gunny's horse settled down. Either she understood the threat of becoming dinner or she had tired from the fracas. *Snicker, snicker. Snort. Snort.* She'd let him win this one. Not many men jumped under a startled horse.

"Wait. What?" Scout sputtered. "What are ye doing here?"

Ian Kincaid, the man known as Star Walker—and who also happened to be Scout's father—looked around. "Looks like I'm savin' yer hide."

"I can do fine by myself, thank ye verra much," Scout said, ignoring the proffered hand. He swallowed a groan as he rose, dusting off crackers of snow that had adhered to his warm woolen britches.

"Hmm. Weel, most times ye can. I was jest in the neighborhood and

449

thought I'd lend a hand. Or an arm or two. Looks like yer friend managed to stay on well enough, though." Ian approached the spooked roan, mumbled gentle noises to him, and grabbed the reins.

Gunny, still astride, briefly straightened his shoulders, as if aware of his surroundings, then slumped forward again, a brief snort and wheeze indicating he had never awakened.

Ian bent over and picked up Scout's brightly colored knit cap that had come off during the altercation. "Looks like yer skull's thick and tough enough to keep yer brains in. Ye have a lot of hair, but with this storm, yer likely to want this back."

Scout snatched the crocheted hat from his father's hand. "Thanks," he said and nodded, grateful that his departing gift from Jenny hadn't been lost in the *bhlàr*.

Ian grunted in acknowledgment, then looked away. The two stomped around the site, looking for either the cougar that had spooked the horse or Julian with Scout's pony.

Scout glanced at his father and saw that he was staring at him.

"What are ye lookin' at? Did I sprout another eye or somethin'?"

"Nae. It's jest I haven't seen ye this close up in a long time. Ye've changed. Fer the better. And it seems ye've been able to find yerself a job with the army."

Scout opened his mouth to speak, then turned aside quickly, crouched low, knife in hand, ready to meet the cougar.

Ian saw the move and mimicked it instinctively. Then he heard the noise, too.

"Scout! Scout!"

The faint noise became louder as Julian neared.

"Over here," the young man replied, waving his arms in the air.

"What or who is scout?" Ian asked.

Scout frowned at him. "It's my name. The name given me by Jenny, my wife. But ye needn't be tellin' anyone about her bein' my wife. She's young. We both are. But she's my wife, jest the same. I dinna think her parents need to ken about it yet, though."

Ian looked up and saw Julian had spotted them. "Is she white?" he asked quickly. "Her parents will skin ye alive if they find out."

"Aye. She's white and fair with blue eyes. But Wallace and Evie are her parents. They willna harm me."

Ian paled. Evie and Wallace were his kin. Sort of. He had been handfast to Evie but abandoned her when he found out she was pregnant. His cousin Wallace had married her and taken on the joys and duties of being father to their triplets. He sighed audibly. *Her* triplets. He hadn't been responsible at all. But how did they have a daughter old enough to be wed to his son?

Scout saw the sunken look on his father's face. "She's adopted," he said softly to him, then changed tones. "Looks like we weren't too hard to find," he said to Julian.

"I saw the cougar run off with something in its mouth, a rabbit, maybe. Looks like someone came to your rescue, though. I thought for sure you were going to be crushed to pie filling."

"Ian Kincaid," Ian said, then added, "Senor," and stuck out his hand.

Julian shot a quick glance at Scout. "Kincaid?"

"Aye," Scout said, then took a deep breath. "He's my father."

"Oh…" Julian said, then inhaled deeply and clenched his jaws. He had helped deliver the three babies this man had sired. He knew a bit of his history, too, but if Scout was still willing to acknowledge him as his father, then he couldn't be too bad.

"I was jest in the area and heard the cougar and horses. If yer all right, I suppose I'll be on my way…"

Scout saw his father's reluctance to leave and made a snap decision. "If it doesna bother yer plans too much, yer welcome to join us. We're on our way to visit Evie and family. I'm sure ye'd like to see yer kin. It's been how long since ye've seen the bairns?"

"Two years, four months and nineteen days."

Julian's realized his mouth was hanging open when he felt his throat get cold. "Would you care to lead or would you rather bring up the rear? It's difficult for Scout to watch for wild critters whilst making sure Gunny doesn't fall off. Although, after this recent altercation, I think he'd be able to stay on if hit by a six-pound cannonball."

Ian shrugged a shoulder, swallowed a grin, and said "I'll take the tail position," trying not to look too happy at being a part of a family again.

No matter how many years he had lived as—and tried to think like— an Indian, the Christmas season had always been difficult for Ian. The

451

Scottish Christmases of his youth were hard to forget. He didn't know what Evie and Wallace had planned for the wee three plus Jenny, but it was sure to be better than jerked venison and raisins around a simple campfire with cougars yowling in the background.

Chapter 49: What's a Christmas tree? (LDB Ch 5)

The Pomeroy Place
December 22nd, 1783

My fourth 18th century Christmas was in two days. Because I was from the twenty-first century, I still had much to learn about how locals celebrated holidays. My first Christmas was spent in a cave with my first husband, Ian. That was a rough time and one I'd just as soon forget.

Last year's celebration was North Carolina traditional with a bit of London influence thrown in by my second and favorite husband, Wallace. My first attempt at figgy pudding was flat, but sweet. It may not have been pretty, but there weren't any leftovers, either.

I still have amnesia for the most part, but a few flashes of memory pop in every once in a while. Or maybe those facts and events were so ingrained that I never forgot them, like knowing that 3.1417 is the value of pi, and its 'righty-tighty, lefty-loosey' when opening or closing a faucet. Oh, and I found out that 'deck the halls with boughs of holly' was a real 18th century—or earlier—holiday tradition. So far, that and reading the Bible are the only the 18th and 21st century Christmas customs I've found in common.

This year, I decided to add a bit of Later (as opposed to Early) American flair to our celebrations. Last week I, Evie Pomeroy-Hart, established the new old tradition of an ornament exchange party. I invited several of our nearest friends and family over to initiate it with a potluck dinner. Everyone involved had been asked to spark up their imaginations and create ornaments to adorn the evergreen branches they would bring inside for Christmas. Just freshly cut boughs was boring, I said. If they made a few extra of their pretties for sharing, we had a good reason for a party. Plus, it was a good excuse for them to get out of the house, tell stories, return borrowed pots, pans and tools, and to share food that didn't taste the same. Different households tended to use different recipes and ingredients. Besides, I was pretty sure Mrs. Donaldson had enough peach preserves left over to make some of her famous cobbler. I'd wade through swamp water to get just a bite of that!

I hadn't bothered to let any of our guests know that I was bringing in a whole tree—not just cut branches—for our Christmas decorating, either. We weren't going to cut it until Christmas Eve, anyhow. There was no way I could fit our friends visiting for the party, the tree the children had chosen, and us in the same house at the same time!

The arrival time of our guests was nearing. Jenny had told me that there would be lots of snow for Christmas, but it would be fair weather for our ornament exchange party. I believed her and was glad there wasn't a reason to postpone our celebration. After all, Christmas really did only come once a year.

Wallace and Jody brought in the saw horses and the old barn door that had been repurposed into a table; Jenny gathered every available chair, stool, and empty bucket for use as dining room seating, and my wee three—Leo, Judah, Wren—and their similarly-aged short legged friends and kin were 'treated' to the picnic area Jenny and I created by arranging an old quilt in front of the hearth.

"What's a coffee-teria?" Jenny asked, trying hard to make sure she pronounced the word correctly.

I couldn't help but stifle a chuckle as I penned in the children's area. I closed my eyes and tried to think of variations of the word she was sounding out. I knew she was psychic and she knew that I knew, but we rarely spoke directly about it and *never* mentioned that I was from another time. That didn't stop her curiosity, though.

"You know," she said, giving me a hint, "like where you eat."

"Oh, a cafeteria! Yes, that's a gathering place where food is served. Sort of like an inn or a tavern, but you choose from food laid out on a sideboard rather than have a server or maid assist you."

"All right. Then I can play cafeteria with the children after the other big sisters get their babies settled. Don't worry, though. We won't let them eat until it's really time. We have pretend food. It's a lot less messy. Plus, it won't ruin their tappetites."

"That's appetites, dear, and thanks for being so considerate."

***

December 24th

Four months ago, my children pre-selected our Christmas tree from a thick stand of loblolly pine across the creek from us and halfway up the hill. They marked it with a double-knotted bow made from a strip of red rag so it would be easy to find again. Back then, it had taken us three hours to get there, but that was before the autumn rains had come. Now, the ground was slick with rotted leaves and mud. I doubted the wagon could even make it up the hill. Add to that the dark clouds racing in, portending rain or snow. The trip was too much risk for my comfort. It looks like I'll be the bad guy and cancel this year's quest for acquiring the children's prime tree. They'd just have to settle for one closer to home.

"Mommy, when—I mean, where—you're from, what did they do for Christmas besides cut down a perfectly good tree before it was full grown just to hang fancy ordaments on it?"

"The word is ornaments, dear, but we also did a gift exchange. Some of the people let it get out of hand, though. They spent hundreds of dollars at the store, buying presents that weren't needed, just to make a good impression on the recipient."

"Hundreds of dollars? You mean pennies? And what's a recip…i…ant?"

I gulped at another faux pas. I still thought in 21st century terms when asked about my past. I ignored that part of her query and answered the last part. "A recipient is the person on the receiving end of a transaction. Here, let me give you a for instance. You did me a great favor this morning, letting me sleep in while you fed your siblings their breakfast."

"I fed Daddy, too. He likes dried blueberries in his porritch just as much as the babies do."

"Yes, that was very considerate, and I know you didn't do it just for me to give you my extra hair ribbon. You were the recipient and I was the giver."

"So, what does that have to do with Christmas? I thought Christmas was the birthday of Jesus."

"It is, honey, but remember the Bible story of the Wise Men? They wanted to honor our Lord—even if he was just a tiny baby—so they brought him gifts. Of course, his parents took care of the presents for him. He didn't have any need for frankincense and myrrh. But Jesus hadn't done anything—at least yet—to deserve the gifts. That premise, idea, is why we give presents to each other. At least, I suppose that's why…"

I really didn't know why we gave presents. 'It's a tradition' was the short answer, but since I didn't know when the tradition started, I decided to wing it. Besides, it sounded pretty logical to me.

Jenny started jumping up and down, doing a mini version of her happy dance, "Oh, oh! Are you going to give us presents for Christmas? And am I supposed to get gifts for everyone? I don't have hundreds of dollars or even two pennies, but I want to give people I love presents 'just because.'"

"Remember, it's not 'just because,' or it shouldn't be. We're doing it to remember our Lord on his birthday."

"Oh, oh, like when you made me the dolly for my birthday. Except we didn't know if it was my real birthday because no one ever told me what date it was when I was little, or littler, so we just chose a day and called it my birthday." Jenny stuck out her chest in pride. "And you gave me a date for my birthday as a present, too! I sure love you, Mommy. I'm sooo glad you and Daddy adopted me."

I never tired of Jenny's outlandish yet optimistic sense of reasoning and her unbridled love for me and her new family. She'd only been my daughter for two years, but I couldn't imagine loving a natural-born daughter anymore. This Christmas was going to be the best one yet.

***

"We didn't stop to eat our picnic lunch; we ate it on the road," Wallace said. "I wanted us back as quickly as possible. Jenny was right. There's a big storm coming in and I didn't want to get stuck in it."

"Were you able to get the tree?" I asked, then reached up to give my husband a quick kiss on the cheek.

"We got 'a' tree. I don't think the children would have let me leave without one. We left 'Kris Kringle' up the hill. I told them he'll be bigger for us next year. This one is just as pretty. At least it is on three sides."

"Uh, huh," Jenny said. "And it will fit inside the house better because the ugly side can stay against the wall."

"I already filled the bucket to put it in," I said. "We don't want the tree to dry out and start dropping needles all over the place now, do we?"

"Nuh, uh. Can we decorate it now?"

I looked at Jenny, all aglow with anticipation, and my three youngest, imitating her bounciness, their hands under their chins, mimicking her. "Did you get your naps on the way home? You sure don't look sleepy."

Thump! Thump! Thump!

I recognized those footfalls. It was my father-in-law, Jody Pomeroy. And I'd bet he wasn't coming alone.

"Greetings!" I sang out and gave him and his wife, Sarah, big hugs. "You're just in time for a light snack. Where are the children?"

"James and Leah are bringing all of the wee ones with them," Jody said. "James devised what he calls a camper for the back of his wagon. They have more comforts in it than I had as a lad. Or ever had until a few years past! Did ye ken that if ye set a pile of hot rocks in a clay pot, it creates a warming stove? It keeps the heat even so it's less likely to burn a hole in the bottom of the wagon."

"That son-in-law of yours," Sarah said with a grin. "Always creating wonders."

"Or re-creating," I said to her alone, my eyebrows raised, shoulders shrugged in defeat.

Sarah, my daughter Leah, her husband James, and I were all time travelers. Sarah was from the 20th century, so her knowledge of modern technology was a few years behind ours. The rest of us were from the early 21st century, but it was James who was a whiz at cobbling together everyday items here—in 1780s rural North Carolina—to re-create wonders that made our lives easier, or at least more comfortable. He had devised ceiling fans, hot water heaters, rubber hoses and seals, and evidently now, a camper with a heater in it.

"Anyone up for a bit of hot cocoa?" James asked as he walked in the house, a child in each arm, one on his back, and one in front of him.

"You have chocolate?" I gasped, nearly dropping the toddler—it was either Judah or Leo—from my arms.

"What I have is a great start for making hot cocoa." He saluted me with a ceramic carafe. "I did some trading with a man who had some pull at the port. I received both sugar and cocoa powder in exchange. Did you know the dock bosses mix those together with hot water for a brew for their laborers who unload the ships? It gives the men quick energy, plus they don't have to stop working to eat. Just drink and go."

I opened up the clay jar and inhaled the sweet smell of chocolate. "I never thought I'd smell it again," I sighed. "Not that I remember the last time I smelled hot cocoa, but who could forget chocolate?"

"Not me," Leah said and gave me a hug, taking Leo from my arms.

457

"I just about fell over when he woke me up last week with that heavenly aroma. I guess we finally have everything a person could want here and now."

I nodded in agreement, then headed for the tray with mini pastries laid out in a geometric pattern. "But we need to eat before bringing out the chocolate, gang. Hot ham and potato pies for everyone. And dried apple slices on the side. Thanks for making such a beautiful display, Jenny."

Both the food and the company were excellent. It wasn't our main Christmas dinner—that would be tomorrow—but almost everyone was here. Julian, my husband's stepfather, had sent word that he would try to join us, that his partner José would stay behind and tend to the animals, but it appeared he wasn't going to make it.

Dang.

***

Somewhere up the road

The foul weather didn't seem to care that it was Christmas Eve. It wasn't snowing, really—or at least not at the moment—but the winter storm set down and re-used the same icy crystals, blowing more than enough of them from the trees and snowdrifts to keep visibility down to maybe a few yards. Then, just as soon as the four men had their scarves adjusted to keep the wind from blowing down their necks, it would shift direction again, working at ice-blasting off whiskers and eyebrows. It got so rough, it even brought Gunny out of his whisky and fever-fueled fog. "Damn winter wind, anyhow," he groused, and grasped his collar, trying to keep it snug with his gloved hand.

Scout took Gunny's lucid comment as a sign he was ready to handle riding alone. He slid off the horse that had nearly thrashed him to oat dust, and jumped onto his own mount, quickly arranging the wrinkles in his pony's blanket to afford him a bit more warmth.

"What did I do to make you so mad?" Gunny yelled, shaking his fist at the sky. "I know I ain't been the best man around, but I'm not mean to horses, women, or other dumb critters. How about giving us a break? At least until we get to wherever the hell it is we're going." He pulled himself up in his saddle and turned around to see the others. "Hey! Where *are* we going?" he asked Scout, then did a double take when he saw there was now another person in their company, a white man dressed

458

as an Indian. "Who the hell are you? And what happened to your face?"

Ian glowered at the teetering old man but didn't reply. He was traveling with the group because he wanted more than anything to see the young children he had sired. He could handle a few people hanging around, but this worn-out soldier was light in the head, sour in the disposition, and already getting on his bad side.

"That's my father," Scout told Gunny. "And those are star tattoos. Like his name, Star Walker."

"I thought your father was an Indian. This man sure looks white to me. Are you sure he belongs to you?"

"Aye, I'll claim him," Scout said with a tinge of resignation. "Dinna worry about my family. I'll take care of him…"

Ian grunted in response. *The nerve of the boy. He had just saved him from being thrashed by the iron-clad hooves of a spooked war horse, and now he was telling the sot how he'd take care of him!*

Scout took a deep breath, straightened his back, and added, "And he'll take care of me. We take care of each other when needed."

Gunny's response was to reach into his inner coat pocket for a drink. He took out his flask and saluted the boy's declaration of devotion.

"And we willna be having any more of that whisky for ye or anyone else, either," Scout scolded.

Gunny brought the flask to his mouth, pulled out the cork with two of his good teeth, then dumped it upside down. "Not to worry. It's gone. Now please tell me that we're going to a place with a warm fire and lots of round and friendly tavern maids. You may think I don't need any of my medicine, but everything I can feel is aching. What I can't feel," he raised his rear end from the saddle, "I'm afraid already froze off."

Julian rode up in front of Gunny and pulled the whole procession to a stop. "Look, we still have quite a ways to go. You caused us a big delay yesterday because of your drink and arguments about being lost. We're on our way to our kin's house for a Christmas gathering and to see if my friend can help with your wound. Now, if you'll stop complaining, we'll make better time. Sit up, shut up, and let's make those last few miles before we lose what little daylight we have."

***

The rest of the trip was slowed only by the weather. Not one word was spoken, although an occasional snort or mumbled curse was heard from the disgruntled Gunny.

Suddenly, Ian clicked loudly to his pinto just as Scout kicked his pony in the flanks. The two of them passed Julian, each trying for the lead position. In the hubbub, Scout was knocked from his ride by an inconveniently placed and heavily snow-laden pine branch.

Crack!

The report of the broken limb brought Gunny out of his quasi-slumber and Julian to Scout's side. "What happened? And are you hurt?"

Ian, now twenty yards ahead, looked back to see that his emotional rush to be the first to see the family had unintentionally led to an accident. He faced forward again, ready to resume the homecoming. Julian was there; he could take care of the boy if he was hurt. Besides, he had fallen on soft snow. He'd be fine. He looked back again. His son wasn't moving and there was a large, freshly snapped-off tree limb stuck in the ground beside him.

Or had he been speared?

"Damn it all," he said to himself and turned back around. His first glimpse at the three young children he had sired would have to wait. Wee Ian—no, his son wished to be called Scout—was in peril. *He said we'd take care of each other.* "About time we started to think about family," he told his horse. "At least, I don't think I have anything to fear from him."

Gunny sensed his young apprentice was in trouble and rushed to his side. "Stay put!" Julian told him when he saw that he was preparing to dismount. "It would be too much trouble to get you back on your horse."

Scout wiped the snow from his eyes, nose, and mouth, sat up, then looked down. The branch had snapped off and the sharp end was stuck right between his legs, as if a giant snow monster had tossed a pointed caber, aiming to emasculate him. He quickly brushed the snow away from the planted end to make sure it hadn't pierced him or his privates, then let out a loud sigh of relief. His trousers were pinned, but he was unharmed.

He grasped the rough bark and tugged. "A little help here," he called up to Julian. "I can't pull this out by myself."

"Do ye need a hand?" Ian asked as he returned to the pair on the ground.

Scout frowned. He wanted to be the first to the house, but he knew

460

that his father did, too. He'd let him have this one. "Go ahead. Julian has this taken care of, don't you, sir."

Julian took a deep breath, looked the youth in the eye, and nodded. The emotional tension between the two Kincaids was almost tangible. Who was the adult and who was the impetuous adolescent here? It was suddenly obvious that Scout could survive this situation—or any other— with or without Ian the Elder's help. "Yes, I have this under control. We'll catch up to you in a moment."

***

Ian followed the path of various sized and styled footwear to the porch. Did he really want to open himself up to a crowd of people, even if most of them were certain to be kin, one way or another? Suddenly, he was surrounded by toddlers looking up at him. There was no turning back now.

He hadn't seen these little imps in over two years, but there was no doubt about who they were. The first one sported a crown of curly red hair, her smile so warm and radiant, it immediately warmed his chilled heart. His little girl. She may be Evie and Wallace's daughter now, but she was still his little girl. Two boys of about the same size were with her, obviously twins. Or rather two of triplets. They'd grown so much.

One of the boys came up and tugged on his leggings. "What happened to your face?" he asked, pointing to the star-shaped tattoos on Ian's cheeks.

"Oh, it's nothin' to fret about," Ian said, and turned away from the boy who must be his son. He looked for something, anything, to talk about to change the subject. Should he ask him his name? Now that he was here, he realized it was much easier to face cougars and startled horses than inquisitive children.

Wren grabbed his pinky finger and pulled him away from the boys. "Here, sit down. I'll fix it," she said, and patted a spot on the porch bench next to her.

Ian couldn't help but smile at her bossiness. Just like her mother. She knew what she wanted and would get it done, one way or the other.

Before Ian was fully seated, Leo was at his elbow, looking up, getting a closer look at the tattoos.

Wren nudged Leo away in a most ladylike fashion, then climbed into Ian's lap. She pulled up her apron, and then in a very *un*-ladylike fashion, spat on the corner of it. She did her best to scrub away one of the dark blue marks. "Hmm. I guess I need more spit."

Before she could continue her ministrations, Ian picked her up and turned her around, setting her on his knee. "They're there on purpose," he said. "It was done during a ceremony to make me a man."

"Our father is a man, and he doesn't have spots on his face," Judah said.

"Yeah, and our grandpas are men, too," Leo added, "and they don't have marks on their faces neither. I think someone tricked you because Grandpa Jody and Poppi Julian didn't need to get stars or anything else on their faces…"

"Or anywhere else," chimed in Wren.

"To become men," Judah finished.

I came out to the porch to see if Jenny had brought her siblings outside without telling me. The loud clammering of the young ones' games had disappeared. I learned long ago that when young children were quiet, it was because they were either asleep or in trouble.

I noticed Judah and Leo first. "How come you're out here?" I asked "It's cold and wet and you don't have on your coats or hats. And where are your sisters?"

"Good day to ye, Evie," Ian said, rising from the porch, Wren in his arms. "I have one, but I have'na seen their elder sister. Would that be Jenny?"

"Wait. What? How? How did you get here?" I asked.

"On a horse," Ian answered and nodded to the horse standing in the only clear area in the yard, under the big 'family' tree.

"That's not what I meant. And why…"

My earlier question and the one I didn't get a chance to ask were both answered by the arrival of Jenny riding in on a pony, seated in front of Scout.

"Mommy, don't get mad at me. The babies promised me they'd wait on the porch for just two minutes. I had to go see if it was true. I mean, I knew it had to be, but it was too good to be true. Scout's here! He's here for Christmas!"

I dropped the bowl in my hand as almost every muscle in my body went limp. *Thunk, thunk, thunk.* Thank goodness the bowl was made of wood and my legs hadn't failed me.

Ian squatted down to pick up the oranges that had fallen out of the bowl and nearly collided with his cousin—and my husband—Wallace.

"Good morrow to you, Ian," he said, the tone of his voice nearly as icy as the wind that I was suddenly aware of.

"Let's everyone come in the house," I said, wondering what I was going to do next. This was certainly not what I had expected for the holiday.

As I shuffled Ian and the last of the children into the house, I heard, "Do you have room for two more under your roof?"

I looked up and saw my old friend—and father-in-law—Julian Hart. "Julian!" I hollered, as I ran through the shin-high snow drift to greet him. "You made it!"

"Evie, this is Sergeant Gunther. He is a good friend and compatriot of Scout. I'm afraid he's in need of a bit of medical attention. Did Sarah come today?"

Julian dismounted, then approached the worn-out and thoroughly chilled soldier, still stride one of the tallest non-draft horses I'd ever seen. He reached up and helped him down to his feet. Or rather foot. There was only one of them. "Yes, Sarah's inside right now."

"Thank you, ma'am. If you please, you can call me Gunny."

"And you may call me Evie."

"Here, Father, let me take the horses to the barn." Wallace said, taking the reins from Julian's hand.

"Thank you, son. Good to see you. I hope all is well."

"It is," Wallace replied, then sucked in his bottom lip, trying to swallow the anger that had arisen unbidden at Ian's arrival. "Let's just hope it stays that way."

"Just remember, son," Julian said with a big smile, "it takes two to tango. If you don't ask him to dance, he probably won't ask you." Then, with Gunny under his shoulder, the three-legged duo made it up the steps into the warm and densely populated house.

Wallace looked over and saw Scout was already leading his and Ian's horses to the barn, Jenny's hand clutching the inside of his elbow as though if she let loose, he'd fly away. His tension dissipated. Ian the elder was nothing but a sperm donor when it came to his family. He was his cousin and kin. He was not—and had never been—the father to his three youngest children, though. Suddenly, he felt sorry for the disenfranchised bachelor.

Ian Kincaid had nothing.

He, Wallace Pomeroy-Hart, had everything.

Maybe by being a good host, he could make a great Christmas memory for the man who had missed so much over the years.

***

It did turn out to be a wonderful Christmas, although nothing like I had anticipated. Scout had found a moment when I was alone to come up and apologize for inviting his father to the Christmas gathering. He shook his head and said, "I ken I should have asked first, but he was so pitiful."

"Pbbt," I replied with a quick raspberry. "Don't worry about it. I'm just glad you and Julian could make it. I didn't even know you were in the area. You've been away for so long. Jenny sure misses you."

Scout blushed in reply, then composed himself and answered, "Aye. And thanks again fer yer generosity."

Sarah got her gift by being able to help someone. She always was aglow after ministering to someone in need, and Gunny was certainly one of those. He knew she was married, but thoroughly enjoyed her holding his hand after she had cleaned out his festered wound. Of course, some of that may have been due to the fact she had insisted he drink quite a bit of whisky before she began. "Don't bother with the egg," he told her. "Just make sure there's plenty of nog."

When she was done, it was time for dinner. It may not have been traditional in this area, but since Wallace had managed to capture several wild turkey chicks last summer, we now had our own little flock. Keeping them penned in and well-fed on grubs and grain had filled out their typically bony frames. Also gone was the gamey taste from whatever it was they ate when in the wild. The one thing I had insisted on was that the children were not allowed to give them names. Jenny had tried to teach a few of them to come when she called, 'Here, turkey, turkey,' but admitted defeat.

"You're right, Mommy. They really are dumb birds. And mean! I sure hope they taste good, especially that one with the fancy feathers. He tried to bite me for no reason!"

We all ate our fill of turkey, mashed potatoes, glazed carrots, and sausage and raisin dressing. None of this was typical fare, but my family

464

enjoyed eating my new-old traditional foods. I was saving the 'old' traditional dessert of figgy pudding for after our small post-dinner gift exchange.

Ian had stayed on the porch for most of the evening, whittling something or other, but after a bit of urging, agreed to join us for dinner. After a very inspirational prayer of thanks for family and good fortune given by Wallace, we all dug in. Ian sat on an upturned bucket, his back against the door, his plate balanced on his knee. I sneaked a peek or two at him and saw that he seemed to be hovering between panic and peace. One moment, he looked as if he was ready to bolt out the door, and then he'd see the children.

I guess it was more of a gaze than a sneak peek when I watched him watch Jenny tear strips of meat from her drumstick and share with Leo. Wren copied her actions and pulled her breast meat apart and hand fed pieces to Judah. I had to intercede, though, when she kept putting food in his mouth before he had a chance to chew and swallow. "Save room for dessert," I said, and they both stopped, then dropped their folded hands into their laps in anticipation.

I don't know how we managed to talk so much while eating just about every scrap and smear off of every plate, but we did. True, the volume level was high partly because we did have a few extra guests, but no one went deaf or hungry. Plus, now I wouldn't have to deal with the vast amount of leftovers I thought I'd have.

Sarah, Leah and I stacked the dirty pans and dishes and toted them just outside the door. We could wash and put them away later. We'd never done that before but decided that since we'd never had so many people under one roof at one time—and we had literally dirtied every dish in the house—well, storing them on the porch was a great way to make more room for the guests inside and put off until tomorrow the task nobody wanted to do today. And if some wild critters decided to stop by and lick the plates clean, I wouldn't mind too much…as long as they didn't break anything or steal the serviceware.

***

Julian, James, Jody and Wallace were once again in their comfort zone: standing at the hearth, holding their progeny and discussing future construction and horticulture projects: breeding and seeding, floors and doors.

Jenny and Scout were cuddled up on the other side of the fire, talking softly, giggling, and from the few words I overheard, making plans for their future. Uh, oh. Oh, well. They were both great kids. I was sure all would be fine, and I needn't worry about them.

Ian had disappeared on me again, but this time I was pretty sure where he was: back on the porch with the un-peopled air and dirty dishes. He had told me he'd pass on dessert, but I knew he was just anxious and wanted air and thoughts he didn't have to share with others. That was fine with me. I didn't know if he planned on leaving for home—or wherever he rested his head—right away, but I wanted to make sure he didn't leave until the storm had settled and there was plenty of daylight. I could tell by the top of the outhouse that we had accumulated at least a foot of snow in the past twenty-four hours. I knew it wouldn't cave in—my husband was very snow-load conscious when constructing even an outside toilet—but slogging in the dark through that much fluff wasn't healthy for horses or the dumb animals riding astride them, either.

"Your choice," I told Ian when I opened the door to stack the last pan on the pile. "You can sleep on the porch with the dirty dishes or join the critters in the barn. Hmm. Not too sure where Gunny and Julian will be sleeping, but I can tell you for certain, there's more floor space available out there than in here."

"Probably smells better out there, too," he said, then grimaced as he realized it might have been taken as an insult. "I mean..."

"I know, I know. You're not used to smelling people. Don't worry about it. I just want to make sure you're not going to take off in the middle of the night or do something else just as stupid."

"I canna guarantee I willna do any other stupid deed, but I'll stay the night. Are the children asleep yet? I wanted to see them before I went to the barn."

"We were going to have a small gift exchange. Then I think Scout had something special for everyone."

Jenny had already arranged the small children in a circle around the Christmas tree in the corner. "Christmas is about sharing our love," she said. "Jesus was born so he could share his love for us and wants us to do the same for anyone, I mean, everyone else. That means strangers, too, but especially family. And since we're all family here," she said, nodding to Ian who had just come in, "that's a lot of love to give and get. The Wise Men gave Jesus presents because they loved him, so I'm giving everyone here a present. But don't worry, it didn't cost me a hundred dollars, or even one penny, because I made everything myself."

Jenny allowed a little pride to show through, but she had worked so hard on her gifts after the wee ones went to bed, she deserved a little self-satisfaction. She reached under the tree and pulled out a small wooden box that had been stashed behind the water bucket. "Here's three for each one of you," she said, and doled out small clay marbles.

Judah immediately put one in front of his mouth, but Jenny was ready. "And don't try to eat them 'cause I made them out of mud."

Judah smiled; that was not a deterrent to him but made the marble even more attractive. He licked it and immediately spit and sputtered. Jenny handed him a cup of water. "Oh, and I put pepper juice in the mud so they'd taste really, really hot. So don't put them in your mouth, or pick your nose after playing with them, or rub your eyes…"

Wallace chuckled at her cleverness. "And remember to wash your hands after playing and before eating, right?"

Judah tipped the cup back, draining the last drop, then joined the others in saying, "Yes, sir!"

A few more presents were shared. Julian had brought small picture books for the younger children. Each one was different, and since there were seven under four here tonight, we could have our own little book exchange library.

Julian presented Jenny with a hinged box containing a dozen glass containers that held different colors of crushed powders. "Those are tints," he said. "You can make your own oil paints with your father's help. I'm sure he remembers how to mix them. You have a gift, Jenny. I want you to pursue your talent."

Jenny lightly touched the bottles of brilliant and earthy hues in the opened box. "Wow," was all my normally chatty daughter could say.

"It looks like we have still another use for some of that old sail canvas I wound up with last spring," Jody said. "It shouldna be too hard to prepare it on a frame. Now, for some of you larger folks, I have chits."

"Baby chickens?" Leo, Judah, and Wren asked at the same time.

"Nae. Chits. A bit of paper written out that is as good as the item, but a lot easier to carry. You see, I have a few animals who will likely be reproducin' in a few months. I've written the types down on scraps of paper. I'll let the adults draw one, and if they like it, they can keep it and exchange it for the critter come spring. If they dinna care for, say, another hen, they can swap with one another. Let's show ye how it's done."

We all knew what he was talking about, so played the colonial version of a Chinese auction gift exchange. He had included one for me, too, even though I usually didn't have anything to do with the livestock when it was breathing. My duties came after the eggs popped out or their necks were wrung.

"First pick of piglets," I read aloud. "All right. I already got a name for him: Wilbur."

Leah laughed at my reference to a book she had read when younger, but the others were confused. "Wouldn't you want a sow?" Wallace asked. "I mean, if it's a big litter, surely a sow would be more logical."

"All right. But I still want to name her Wilbur. Now, what did everyone else get?" I asked. "Not that I want to swap, but this is fun, counting our chickens and pigs before they're hatched!"

"Pigs. Hatched," Leah laughed. "Yeah, right. Oh, lookie! I get a calf!"

"Yum, yum." James patted his belly and sighed. "You're too good to us, Jody."

"Ach, I jest do fer ye as I would anyone else in the family." Jody looked over the group and realized that he hadn't brought enough chits to include Gunny and Ian.

"Don't worry about me," Gunny said, and saluted him with his tin cup of whisky. "You gave me some fine drink and great memories. I can't remember a finer dinner with more gracious hosts. Oh, and a mighty fine-looking healer, too."

"Here, here," replied most of the adults in the group.

Ian remained silent, but that was because he was deep in thought. The stillness of the moment was eerie and uncomfortable. I wanted to say something to break the tension but didn't have an idea of what could help.

"I have some gifts, too," he said softly, and bit his bottom lip. "For yer wee ones. Sorry, I dinna ken about the others. I dinna ken Leah and James had wee 'uns or that Uncle Jody and Sarah could have more bairns, but, but…"

"Miracles happen all the time," I said, glad that I had found an appropriate comment.

"Aye, they do," Ian agreed. "This Christmas is a miracle. I never thought I'd see the wee three again. It's not that I dinna think of them. I mean, they're my kin and I think of them all the time… But to be invited into yer home, and treated so fairly after how I was to ye in the past…"

"As you said, it was in the past. Let's keep it there," I said. "You're here now, with all of us. Now, what did you say you have for gifts?" *Phew, a distraction from talking about old 'stuff' and a redirection to something positive.*

"I made the three of ye whistles. I carved yer initials on the ends so ye didn't get confused. Here, this one with the 'L' is for Leonardo, the 'J' for Judah, and I wasna sure if ye went by Wren or Danielle, so I just carved a flower on yours."

"How did you know my name was Danielle? Everyone always calls me Wren," my youngest daughter said.

"Um, I came to visit ye when ye were only this big," Ian held out his hand and pointed from the tip of his middle finger to just past his wrist. "Ye were a wee thing but had a strong voice. My son, yer…kin, gave ye the name Wren."

"Yup," Wren said, and climbed on his knee again. "And I keep getting bigger and bigger. And louder and louder…"

"And prettier and prettier," Ian said, and gently kissed the top of her head.

I could see the tears well in his eyes and decided it was time for more distraction. "Didn't you say you had something for all of us, Scout?"

Scout had seen the emotional display and it had taken him off guard. "Aye, I did. Now, if ye care to sit where ye are fer jest a few moments longer, I'll play a song fer ye. If ye dinna already ken, I'm a drummer now. I was a drummer boy, but Gunny here taught me well. He said I'm no longer a boy, an apprentice."

Julian had anticipated his need and presented him with the well-seasoned drum and a new set of drumsticks, a gift from Gunny.

Scout stuck his shoulder under the strap and began his percussion sonata in rat-a-tat minor.

It wasn't long before all of us were humming the refrain he had composed, a comfortable tune that was sure to stay with us all year long.

I looked over and saw that Ian now had Judah and Leo leaning against him—sound asleep like their sister on his lap.

There was peace in the world—and more importantly—this family, again.

And all it took was love, forgiveness, and a little drummer boy with a caring heart.

~The End of Little Drummer Boy.~

Just a note that readers may find interesting: Gunny's words about how to stand and perform as a soldier are from a drill manual written by Inspector General Friedrich Wilhelm von Steuben in the 18th century. He wrote down and standardized military procedures thus bringing order to the early American military system.

Complete Book

Never Too Young:
True Love is Ageless

The Fairies Saga Book 13

Backwoods North Carolina, post-Revolutionary War:

Deceived and robbed of two years' wages, would the young Scout's wife want him if he returned to her empty-handed?

Chapter 50: Jenny (NTY Ch 1)

Autumn of 1783
Near Greensboro, North Carolina!

"What are those," Jenny asked, pointing to my necklace.

"Those are gold nuggets," I answered, hoping that I didn't have to explain to my recently adopted daughter where I got my jewelry, mostly because I didn't remember. I had arrived in this 18th-century world with a backpack, the clothes I was wearing, and a gold nugget necklace…but without a memory of who I was or where I was. It wasn't until almost a year later that I found out that I was born in the 20th century and had an adult daughter in the 21st century.

"Are they dried out fruit like currants?" she asked.

"No, these are rocks that were dug out of the ground and put on a necklace. See, feel them. They're pretty hard, but not as hard as quartz. I certainly wasn't going to explain wiring, plating, and the reflective coating on astronaut's visors to her!

"Hmm, so that's what Benji meant when he asked if I was digging for gold. If they make money out of it, then maybe I can dig some up so *we* can have money. Then we can buy more stuff, like a better plow for Daddy and more cloth so you and my brothers and sister can have new clothes. I'll bet I could dig after school and after all my chores are done. Would that be okay?" she asked, her fast blinking, sparkling eyes reflecting sweet and pure longing to be allowed to help resolve our dire financial situation.

"Well, I think we'd be better off if you…well…um," I paused, hoping to think of something to say. "I appreciate the offer," I stalled, "but I know you like to do other things like crochet and…"

Jenny's bottom lip was pooched out in frustration. Here she had come up with a plan of how to 'make' money, and I was trying to dissuade her. "Okay, you can dig, but how about if you start your gold mining where Daddy's planning on putting the next privy. That'll help him, and if you find any gold, you can have it all."

"Okay," she replied, jumping up and down in place, "then I can share it with everybody!"

"Daddy, I want to help you dig the next privy. Mommy said I could dig for gold wherever you're going to put it since we needed a hole there anyway, and it would actually help you, and I want to get some gold so we can use it for money and buy you a new plow and some cloth for new clothes and maybe another pot, and if I find lots of it, maybe you can buy other stuff I don't even know we need."

"I appreciate the help—and don't let me stop you—but gold is usually found near creeks and rivers. If you'd like, you can dig near the edge of our little creek. But don't dig in the stream…and keep your dress clean. I don't want your mother scolding me because I let you get in the mud."

Wallace knew Jenny worked hard helping with the household chores, gardening, and watching her younger siblings, but she needed some time to herself, too. It would be nice if she had another change of clothes that she could get dirty. He never got the chance to make mud pies when he was young and would like the chance to do it with her at some point before she grew up too much. Hmph. Jenny was very close to puberty, but her innocence was that of a six-year-old. He'd see if he could talk Evie into letting Jenny have a 'dirty clothes' day where she could play in the mud just before it was laundry time.

"There wasn't any gold, but look what I found," Jenny told Wren. She held up the six rocks with red stones imbedded in them. "I think they're pretty and I'm going to keep them forever and ever. I think if I use Daddy's hammer, I can knock off that gray rock around it."

Wren grabbed for the rock with the colorful bits. "No, no, you can't eat this. We'll get you something to eat in a little bit, but I have to take these to my special hiding place first." Jenny put the rocks in her pocket and hoisted the toddler onto her hip. "Come on, I'll bet it's almost dinnertime. Mommy said we're having chicken with Sister Leah, Brother James, and Cousin Bibby Liz at their house. We can wash up there and use hot running water."

Jenny washed herself and Wren, then let her little sister play with her baby cousin, Bibby Liz, inside her colorful playpen. Now it was time for advice. She sought out the smartest man she knew, James. She knew where he probably was: his workshop. He was always building or planning something and let her help when it came time for building – or constructing as he called it.

"Hey there, little sister," James said when she walked in. He saw her furrowed brow and knew she had a dilemma. "What can I do to turn that frown upside down?"

Jenny's lips pursed as she tried to figure out his riddle, then her smile grew as she realized what he was talking about. "Well, you can tell me an easier way to find gold. I went to the creek, but I didn't find gold, just some pretty rocks. Is there an easier way, like when you make funny noises to call in the turkeys?"

"Well, I don't know of a 'gold call,' but I do know that gold is heavy and gets washed down fast-moving creeks. That's where it's easiest to find. I mean, we don't have bulldozers to move the overburden off the … How about if you look around the edges of the rocks in the creeks, maybe even lift some of the lighter ones, and see if the gold got trapped underneath or on the leading side of the creek's flow. That's the easiest way I know of. After dinner, do you want me to go with you and show you what I mean? It'll still be light out and maybe your Dad wants to go, too."

Jenny sighed deeply. She loved her mother, her Grannie, her big sister Leah, and baby sister Wren, but she really did like being with the men more. She liked building things and learning how things worked. She had seen Brother James's book, he called it his codex, but he didn't want her reading it yet. He said that he would teach her what was in the book first, then later—maybe that would be next week—it would make more sense to her.

***

"That was a mighty fine dinner you made, Leah. How you can accomplish anything with that high-energy granddaughter of mine underfoot, I'll never know." Wallace was multitasking, giving Leo the last few green beans while wiping Judah's face with a napkin.

"Well, I only have one and you and Mom have three, Grannie has the two, so I guess I have it the easiest," Leah winced, then put her hand on her belly, "although it might be a different story here in a few months when this one gets here. I'll take all the help I can get. Maybe we can figure out how to make freeze-dried meals so all I have to do is add water."

"Freeze dried?" Wallace asked.

"I don't think we'll have to freeze anything first, though. I can put together a food dehydrator in no time with my little sister's help," James said, then patted Jenny on the head. "Yup, we can dry all sorts of fruit and veggies, and then...hmm. I'll have to figure out a vacuum system and containers, so they'll stay fresh..."

"It's always something, isn't it," Sarah said. "I mean, sometimes I miss having freezers and, oops." Sarah had forgotten that Jenny was in the room and that she couldn't speak of the luxuries and conveniences of the 20th and 21st centuries. "Jenny, would you check on your uncles for me?" she asked to change the subject.

Jenny grinned and said, "Yes, Grannie," nodded, and went into the back room. She didn't want them to know that she knew their secret. She didn't understand why, but Grannie, Leah, James, and Mommy weren't the same as everyone else. Scout had told her that they were fairies, but not to tell anyone else, especially them. She didn't know what a fairy was and didn't want Scout to know she was ignorant about them, but it really didn't matter. They were her family. She loved them and they loved her. It was all right that where they lived before they could ride in carriages that moved fast on the ground and even faster in the air and had books that talked to you with pictures that moved. They were still the same people. It was just the 'stuff' that had been in their lives was different from the 'stuff' they had now.

Chapter 51: I Read You Loud, But Not Clear (NTY Ch 2)

"What's this?" Jenny asked.

She had been rummaging through the cabinet and found the photo James had snapped of the portrait of his favorite great-uncle many times over, Julian Hart, the man who was now Jenny's grandpa, Poppi. James had had it laminated before he left the 21st century to ensure it would be protected from time and the elements. At one point, he had used it as a pacifier for his little brother-in-law, Judah—Julian's godson and grandson. It had been in this time era over two years now and was still in great shape, only slightly bent on the edges.

"Um," I stalled, trying hard to think of a way to explain that it was a laminated photograph, polyethylene—or whatever that synthetic product name was—shielded so it wouldn't wear or tear. My brain cramped up, so I took the easy way out. "Um, it's a picture of Poppi, can't you tell?" I answered, trying hard to hide my exasperation.

She rubbed her finger over the flat, smooth surface, brought it up to her face, and sniffed it. "It kinda looks like him, except for the nose, but is it part sheep?"

"What? Why would you think that?" Sometimes that girl asked the darnedest questions.

"I thought it was made out of a skinny baby sheep named Polly Ethel," she said bashfully with head down, not wanting to look me in the eye, instead keeping her face down, finger gliding over the photo's shiny surface.

"I know you mean something else. Just tell me exactly why you think it's a skinny baby sheep with a silly name."

Jenny brought her head up, and just before her eyes locked onto mine, she closed them and said, "Polly Ethyl lean and lamb end ate. But, maybe that's lamb, the letter 'n,' and the number eight; I'm not sure."

I winced. It looked like it was time for a real tough 'facts of life' lesson. "Okay, that's polyethylene and laminate. Your Brother James can explain it better than I can. He's the scientist, not me. I know it's a laminate, but don't know if it's really polyethylene—but it's something like that. We laminate 'stuff' all the time where we're from. It keeps photos and documents from damage, preserves them from water and wear and tear, or well, whatever. Does that make any sense?"

It was a big bomb to throw at her, but maybe this way, I could find out how much she really knew from her classes with James and how much was from her psychic impressions. By the skinny baby sheep question, I'd say she was 'reading' me.

"No, it doesn't make any sense. Is it made from sheep then? Is that why it's called *laminate*," she said, concentrating on the foreign—to her—word.

"I think laminate is from a Latin word. It's a description, mostly. The poly-whatever is the chemical that was used to produce it. Is that better?"

"I know what chemicals are. Sort of. When Benji was here, he told me. They can use chemicals to make paper, spray bugs, etch glass, and lots of other stuff, huh? But, we don't have that stuff here, just mostly where *you're* from, huh?" she said and grinned.

I could tell she wanted to tell me she knew my secret, but if she told me she knew, then it wouldn't be a secret anymore.

"Yes, we have lots of chemicals where *we're* from, but there are lots of chemicals here now, too—I mean, in Europe and England, and even some in America. It's just that they've been working with chemicals longer over there. They have a few in England that I'd like your Poppi to bring back next time he goes there.

"Speaking of England, did he tell you when he was going? I know he wants to buy a few horses to send back here for breeding stock."

Jenny's dimples deepened as she beamed her all-knowing grin. She knew I was changing the subject on purpose. Well, it was a gentlewoman's agreement, unspoken, but shared just the same. I knew something was going on, that she knew more than she wanted to admit. I was fine with it. I didn't want to assume she knew everything—Lord, I hoped she didn't—and she liked being a lady of mystery. Well, I liked being a woman of mystery, too!

Chapter 52: Science Projects (NTY Ch 3)

Jenny ambled from around the back of the house to the porch, swinging her greenwood basket, overloaded with milkweed plants, singing her ABC's.

"What are you doing with all those weeds," I asked.

"Brother James asked me to get as many as I could find. I kinda felt bad, though. I know these are the plants the orange and black butterflies like. I got as many as I could fit in here, but I couldn't pull them *all*. I mean, there were weeds *everywhere,* and since I'm not allowed to go too far from home, the butterflies will just have to find some *other* weeds to live in, farther away from our house," she explained with an unintentionally comedic exasperation.

"They're Monarchs," I said, reaching over to push a few of the stragglers back into the basket.

"Like kings and queens?"

"No, Monarch butterflies—that's what they're called. Now, why would James want weeds? Especially those—they're sappy and sticky and oh… I think I know what he wants them for. You'd better get them over to him right away before they dry out. Here, drink some water before you leave and don't stay too long. We still have lessons to finish, although I think my number one son-in-law already has his own science lesson planned, complete with a hands-on project."

"Will my husband be your number two son-in-law then?" Jenny asked softly, as if embarrassed about bringing up the idea of her being married.

"No, I think he'll be my second number one son-in-law. I'm sure he'll be just as great as James. Now, hurry up."

"Good, I mean, okay," she said, then slugged down her drink, the water dribbling down her chin as she tried to swallow with an oversized grin on her face. "Bye," she said, then skipped up the road to James and Leah's house with her overflowing basket of raw material for latex, her exuberance not affected by the afternoon heat and humidity.

There was definitely something going on with her and her fascination with getting married. We had more than the usual number of mother-daughter talks on the subject. She was almost obsessed with it. We hadn't got to the topic of sex yet, though. She had already received the most basic lecture: that she was only to share 'her gift' with her husband. Of course, I reminded her that he had to be worthy of her and the rest of our family. We spoke mostly about goals and homes and what was needed in the way of household goods when a couple got married—pretty much the nuts and bolts and foundation required.

If I didn't know better—and I didn't—I'd swear she had her cap set for someone. And that someone could only be my husband Wallace's second cousin, Jody's great-nephew, the son of my first husband: Wee Ian, the young man she called Scout. Well, not exactly a young man—he was still a child in my eyes. He had dropped by to visit a couple of times in the last year, the last time to give her a kitten. I caught the two of them holding hands, but didn't say anything to them or anyone else. James was there with me at the time. He told me not to worry, so I didn't. He had a look of total peace and contentment as he watched them walk away. I think he knew something about the two of them, but as her mother, I didn't want to know. She was still my little girl, even if she had only been in my life just over a year.

***

It looked like James was going to try and make latex. I remember reading something—somewhere, at some time in my other life—that it was possible to manufacture it on a small scale. Well, if it could be done, I'm sure James would figure it out. That is, unless he already knew the formula and had it jotted down in his little codex. Leah had a similar one she had transcribed from the book *The Way Things Work,* but James had jotted down some of his own ideas. He had fabricated both a solar water heater and an overhead fan for his odd-shaped house. The structure was pretty much a modified tepee. It was cooler in the summer and, hopefully, would be warmer in the winter, than ours.

Leah had never really enjoyed my passion for gardening in her younger years, but now that she wasn't distracted with television, music, magazines, and school, she had more time on her hands. True, she had a baby in a sling half the time and a bun in the oven, but she still liked going outside in the early summer mornings when the weather was tolerable. "If I work in the morning, then I don't feel bad about taking a nap later with Bibby Liz," she told me. "James offered to take the baby with him while he worked on the fan systems for you and Sarah, but I don't want her around all those sharp tools. She's little, but she's fast.

Besides, I don't think he could work wearing a baby sling. Men just aren't built right for toting babies: they don't have hips."

***

"Let me guess," I said to James.

He looked up from his mess of greens, spread out over his impromptu table. Jenny was standing by, ready to chop them with the chopper he had made from a broken hatchet head. He grinned in reply. "Yes, I want to see if I can make rubber, or at least latex. If I can waterproof fabric successfully, maybe I can build some hoses. Of course, there are only about a thousand other uses for rubber that I can think of…"

"You know, from what I remember, dandelions would be even better. I guess we'll have to start another garden just for them. At least we won't have to plant them—they're the first thing to come up in the spring."

"You remember?" he asked softly, then looked at Jenny to see if she was paying attention to him. She was, but not at his words. Her eyes were fixed on his converted cutting instrument.

I nodded then shrugged, not wanting to elaborate in front of her. "Here," he said to Jenny and handed her the curved-edged cutting tool, "You be careful. Just mash them enough that they start oozing the latex—the milky stuff—then throw them in the pot."

I walked over to the laundry kettle he had borrowed from me, bent over and sniffed what looked like plain water. "Vinegar?" I asked, blinking back the tears. "And, yes," I whispered, "I have random memories. I'm glad they're mostly impersonal bits and pieces, like the value of pi or that dandelions are an even better source of latex than rubber trees or milkweed. Plus, we can eat dandelion roots like turnips or roast them for coffee, eat the greens, or even make dandelion wine. Did you know they reproduce asexually?"

"Yes, it's vinegar and yes, I knew they reproduced asexually."

We both heard Jenny sniggering at the word as she continued chopping. She had keen hearing, but hadn't learned to be discreet. Yet. I was sure that was coming, but hopefully I had a few years left of being able to read her reactions. "That just means they have fancy flowers and don't really need the bees," I explained.

"Or birds," James added, then laughed. "Um," he said to change the

481

subject from pollinating, birds and bees to latex extraction, "We'll put the gooey stuff in here, stir it around in the vinegar water, and then the raw latex will adhere to the stirring stick. I can use heat to cure the product slowly. I think I'll spread some of it on this fabric and smoke it."

Now it was my turn to laugh. "Smoke it? Don't you need rolling papers for that? Oh, like smoking meat, low heat over a long period of time…"

"Yes, Mom," he said, then smiled. "One thing you've never lost, that's for sure: your sense of humor."

"Either that or I found one here. Nah, I probably always had one. This attitude feels like it's as much a part of me as…as…the two freckles on the back of my right hand."

"And I doubt that either the freckles or the humor will fade as you get older."

"Hmm." I looked closely at the back of my hand. "Or I guess both of them might increase. It looks like there's a third one now."

***

"Jenny, let me try this first," James said and stuck his finger in the pot of milkweed greens. He swirled it around, letting the tannish residue gather on his index finger. "Watch this," he said. He started at the base of his finger and rolled the film off, creating a rubber band that increased in girth as it got to the end of his digit. He pulled the flexible ring off and tugged at the edges. "Cool! My first homemade rubber band."

"What's a rubber band?" Jenny asked, bending over to look closely at the perfect, flexible circlet. "It looks like a ring, but you made it by cooking greens? Do you eat it?" she asked, as she warily sniffed it.

"No, you don't eat it, but I guess you could chew it like gum…"

Before he could explain further, Jenny asked, "What's gum? Is that some kind of food? Does it have vitamins and minerals in it, too?"

"No, gum is not a food. When…I, mean…where I came from, we used to chew what we called gum or—when I was a youngster like you—bubblegum. It was made like this…I guess. Actually, I never made it before. We bought it already wrapped up. It was mint or fruit-flavored and, after you chewed the sugar out of it, you could put your tongue in the middle of it like this," James mimed preparing a wad of gum for blowing, pursing his lips in an exaggerated manner, causing Jenny to laugh aloud. "And then you blew real hard, making sure you didn't blow

482

the gum out of your mouth." James blew and blew then caught the imaginary piece of gum as it blew out, then stuck it back in his mouth. "And then you made a bubble." James rolled his eyes and he put his hands around his imaginary oversized bubble.

Jenny was now bent over double, mimicking James, blowing imaginary bubbles, slobbering and wiping her mouth in between lip pursings and puffs.

"Don't tell me, you're teaching her to blow bubbles without the gum," Leah drolled, as she walked over to the pair, Bibby Liz snoozing over her shoulder.

"How'd you guess? Oh, yeah, well, I guess it's pretty obvious. I guess I'll have to see if I can add a bit of sugar and mint to the mix and see if we can get some big ones. But see, I made my first rubber band," he crowed in pride as he held his newest product in his opened palm.

"Trade ya," Leah said, as she snatched the band and handed him the baby. He took Bibby Liz and watched Leah bend over, smooth her hair forward, and twist the hair into a ponytail. She carefully parted the band and pulled the thick tress through it. "Cool! I mean, really, cool. A late anniversary present, but very much appreciated. My sweaty neck and I both thank you," she said, inching over to him to give him a gentle kiss on the mouth.

"Oh, wow; I'm sorry. I forgot our anniversary. I really didn't even know what day today was. I mean, it's almost harvest season is all I knew."

"Yeah, well, if I had remembered, I'm sure you would have, too," she said with a smirk then a nod at Jenny. She didn't want to say more than that. Leah and James shared a strong psychic connection. If either of them had remembered, both would have known.

Jenny grinned at both of them. She knew what they were thinking: that they both forgot. She knew what they thought about lots of times but didn't pay attention to their private stuff. The day-to-day tasks and some of the classes were easy to understand without words, but where they were from—Scout called it Fairy Land—there were so many strange people, places, animals, and things that it was hard for her to comprehend. That was okay, though. Brother James was a good teacher and she liked listening to him. Sometimes he told her more than he was supposed to during her lessons. Hopefully, one of these days, she'd be

483

able to tell him that he didn't have to stop when he got to the real
interesting subjects, like flying planes and the big caterpillars that made
roads. She knew he wasn't the same as her Daddy. But he and Leah and
Mommy and Grannie were all the same: fairies.

Jenny opened her mouth, allowing a bit of saliva to gather, then blew a big spit bubble. She tapped James on the elbow and got his attention.

"Like that!" he exclaimed. "Now that's a bubble. Come on, we'll spread some of the latex out on the cloth, and then we'll make more rubber bands. If we still have time afterward, we can make more, this time with dandelions. Then maybe we can have a real bubblegum blowing contest."

Chapter 53: Pumpkin Seeds (NTY Ch 4)

Summer 1782

Jenny reached into her pocket, pulled out her fist, then tipped her head back, opening her hand slightly to drop the food into her mouth.

"What're ye eating?" asked Scout.

"Pumpkin seeds. Do you want some? They're good," she said, offering him a fistful.

Scout tucked in his chin and put his hands behind his back, using his body language to refuse the offer, then asked, "Are'na ye supposed to plant them? I mean, I thought seeds were to put in the ground or if ye had too many, to feed to the pigs or put in the compost pile."

"Not these. We already have the seeds saved for next year, so we use these for snacks. Mommy soaks them in salty water for a couple of hours, then puts them in the roaster over low coals. I get to take off the lid and stir them every ten minutes, and then—when they're dried out *just* enough—I take them out, let them cool, then *manga!*" she crowed.

"Manga?" Scout asked. "What's *manga*?"

"That means eat hearty or something like that. Come on, try one. They're good for you—full of minerals and a good source of protein, too." She held her palm out flat, determined to leave it hanging out there in space until he took one.

Scout saw her clamped jaw and pursed lips—she wouldn't give in—so went ahead and picked up a seed. He held it by the edges, sniffed it suspiciously, and asked, "It's full of what?"

"Minerals and protein are kind of like chemicals. Everything is made of something—atoms and molecules, and cells if it's living or ever was—and well, James is teaching me all sorts of stuff." Jenny's voice lowered to a whisper, "But I'm not supposed to tell other people what he's teaching me because they wouldn't believe me, but I can tell you because you're my husband and we're marrit."

She ended her confidentiality clause explanation with a wink, then grabbed his hand with her empty one, swinging it widely in uninhibited joy.

"Aye," Scout agreed. "He's teaching ye fairy lore. I'm sure he believes it's true…" He looked at Jenny's face, her former smile now a scowl of disagreement. He changed his outlook on his brother-in-law's wisdom and reworded his remark. "I think James kens more than most men, or women either—except maybe yer Grannie and Leah. I think that fairies have to go to some special school or somethin'. Since yer not from where they're from, they're teachin' ye the lessons here."

Jenny sighed deeply and explained. "He's teaching me the truth. He wouldn't—they wouldn't—lie to me. It's just that they, they have more books wheh…I mean, where they come from."

Scout took a cautious lick of the seed and thought about what she had almost said. Maybe she knew about them, too; that they were from a different *when*. He bit the end off of the seed and chewed it. "Are ye supposed to eat the hull, too?"

"I eat the whole thing, but make sure you chew it all the way before you swallow and um…"

Jenny smiled, then decided not to say any more about her family from their future time. She knew that he was thinking about it. Maybe they'd talk about it later, but right now, she wanted to show him her gold and gem mining site. And then maybe they could do some kissing.

Spring of 1783

North Carolina

Chapter 54: Am I grown up? (NTY Ch 6)

"When will I be grown up?" Jenny asked.

I nearly dropped the pan of sourdough biscuits in shock. I didn't know how she managed to do it, but she was an ace at getting me completely off guard with her 'facts of life' questions.

I gulped and sputtered as I tried to collect my thoughts and re-balance the soaked-pine plank of dinner rolls. I shoved a wayward biscuit back in place, then set the new, old-style cookie sheet into the modified Dutch oven. By the time my buns were in the oven, I had her answer.

"You'll never grow up."

"Wait. What? How come? Is there something wrong with me? I, I…"

"No, there's nothing wrong with you at all. Actually, I think you're as perfect as can be. That's why you'll never grow up. Or rather, never stop growing. That mind of yours is fantastic, always searching for truths and how comes and why nots." I hugged her close. "You're already sharper than many adults. And your body has changed now, so you've become a woman physically, too."

Jenny hung her head and blushed. "I didn't know you knew…"

"Well, I still help with the laundry, even if you think you can do it all by yourself. You do a great job with getting out the bloodstains in your lady rags, but they're still lady rags and not something else, right?"

"Yes, Mommy. I didn't want you to be upset that I cut up some of the old clouts…"

"Well, if you remember…and I'm sure you do…I told you that is what they were for. Now, why do you want to know when you'll be grown up? You're not still thinking about getting married, are you?"

Jenny turned away, looking out the front door toward the family tree. She sighed deeply and answered with what I knew was the truth, "Not about getting married. About being married. About my husband and, maybe in a few more years, our children. But don't worry about me. We, I mean, I'll be fine. I guess I just have to wait…"

I remained mute. I knew something was bothering her and know I knew what it was. "Yes, James got a letter from Scout. It seems he now has a job with a survey company. They're making maps of the wetlands near the coast. He said it will probably be another year before he gets back this way."

Jenny's eyes dimmed. The younger a person, the longer time felt. One year must seem like centuries to her.

"Why don't you go ahead and go to see your sister and James now. He can share the letter with you. And I'm sure Leah can use some help getting the babies ready for our Sunday dinner. I should have sent you as soon as I put the biscuits in. Depending on how your niece and nephew are cooperating, dinner should be ready about the time everyone gets here. I'm so glad we live close together."

"I'm so glad that Grandpa gave me those five acres near the creek," she said, her perky attitude back. "I'll be close by for Sunday dinners when I have my family, too."

"But that won't be for a few more years, right?"

I squeaked in surprise at the sudden appearance of my son-in-law, James. He had taken the words out of my mouth—or at least shared them before I could.

"Sorry. I didn't mean to frighten you. Jenny, Leah is still back at the house. I walked up here a little early. Would you go help her bring your niece and nephew?"

"Yes, I will. Oh, and did you…"

"You know I did. I have it right here," James opened up his jacket and flashed the folded paper protruding from his inner pocket, "and I'll share it with you and everyone else after dinner."

Chapter 55: River (NTY Ch 7)

We were swamped with babies in our little niche in the woods, but we liked it that way. Each child was loved and considered a blessing by all of us. Jenny helped me manage the daycare tasks of my brood, her two-year-old triplet siblings: Leo, Judah, and Wren. Sarah had her hands full with twin sons, Raymond and Wee Julian, who, at eleven months old, were the exact same age as their niece, Bibby Liz. At least the wee uncles were easier to handle than she was… sort of. They still got into trouble, but they always did it together. Besides, two red-headed boys were easier to spot from afar than the one 'still-waiting-to-get-her-hair' very young Lady Melbourne, who was fond of hiding in the bushes.

Bibby Liz never really crawled, but that didn't mean she was ever slow. She mastered the sport of walking around furniture early, then progressed to sprinting. Well, at least it felt that way when I was watching her for her pregnant mama's after-lunch naps. Leah needed her late afternoon breaks even though Bibby Liz had decided that she was old enough to do without hers. I didn't dare so much as sneeze when I was in charge of her; she would be gone as soon as I blinked.

All the Melbournes and Pomeroy-Harts were gathered at the prime Pomeroy's home for our traditional Sunday dinner. It was a perfect spring day. The buds were bursting on the apple trees like pink popcorn. A slow, intermittent breeze spread the light scents of freshly sprouted grass and newly emerged sassafras and sweetbay leaves; it was if we were receiving a friendly 'hello' from our little section of heaven on earth with its reawakening. The paths to the barn and privy finally had dried out but were not yet dusty from the foot traffic.

Jody was teasing both of his adult grandchildren about their alacrity in naming their son. "Ye've had nine months and three weeks to name the lad," he said as he held the wide-eyed infant Melbourne in the air, turning him from side to side—inspecting him for defects, I suppose.

The male child was hefty—he must have weighed ten pounds at birth—and was perfect in every way. His pouty bottom lip hung lax as his dark grey eyes examined everything that came into his limited field of vision. Leah told me that he fussed only when hungry, then fed quickly, and went back to sleep. She toted him everywhere in the sling James constructed for her, holding him close while she did her chores or chased after little Bibby Liz. There was still a chill in the air, so she appreciated his warmth. I'm sure the feeling was mutual. Their arrangement wouldn't work in the summer months, but for now, he was easier to take care of than his rambunctious older sister.

Sunday dinner was a simple yet cherished ritual. We didn't have a church to attend, so Sunday was the day we shared a few Bible verses together, then had dinner. We had started our own Sunday school tradition last year. Rather than having the patriarch, Jody, choose and recite a scripture, we would all share in that honor. If a person was old enough to read or recite a verse, he did. Then he or she would lead the family in discussions for a few minutes, or more, afterward. We had intended to proceed by age, oldest family member to youngest, but made an exception with Sarah. She was a couple of years older than Jody but followed him in rotation since he was the head of their family. The order wasn't a hard, fast rule, but a matter of convenience. I guess we could have just as easily proceeded alphabetically, but this seemed easier.

Dinner was still a few minutes away. Most of us were gathered near the table, conversations at an amiable, dull roar, when we heard Jody bellow, "What kind of name is River?"

Apparently Sarah, trying to give him a heads up, told him his great-grandson's unconventional name ahead of the formal announcement. Unfortunately, her plan backfired. Her attempt at discretion blew up with her husband's loud exclamation, or would that be his question?

James stuck out his chin in defiance; this was his son's name being challenged. Jody saw the body language and backed down, dipping an apologetic nod to him, giving James an embarrassed half-grin that said, 'I'm sorry.' He softened his vocal tone and remarked sheepishly, "I've never heard that name applied to a lad, or a lass either, for that matter."

James chuckled at his wife's grandfather. He knew the man hadn't meant to insult him or the name chosen for his first great-grandson. "Weel," James drawled, mimicking Jody's accent, "with so many of the men in the family havin' names beginnin' with the letter 'J,' my darlin' wife and I decided to move down the alphabet a bit. Ye see, James, Joseph or Jody, Julian, Judah…" James sighed in a comic parody of fatigue, bent over with an imaginary load, and then arched his back, putting his hands on his lower back and smiling, as if he had finally rid himself of the burden. "We considered the name Xerxes, that bein' a powerful name of a great man from a time long gone, but it dinna feel quite right. Zorro was all the way down there, but I dinna think the lad cared to be called the Spanish name fer fox. Then I realized that one of the most powerful forces on this earth was water."

"And, he was so beautiful," Leah said, taking over the etymology of the name. "Not much is as lovely and serene as a flowing river. And, at the right time and place, when the air is still, it's like a mirror, reflecting all that is right in the world."

James picked up the dialogue, discarding his feigned Scottish brogue, returning to his native British accent that he had all but lost in his two years in North Carolina. "A river is powerful, too. It can change the face of the earth dramatically. Channeled, it has the energy and force to carve canyons, run mills, create electricity, and even cut steel." James saw Jody's confusion and amended his statement, "It can grind grains and cut metal if applied with the correct technology."

Jody rolled his eyes in defeat. He didn't understand the concepts as well as his 21st-century family members, but he did know that water power was one reason why there were so many mills in North Carolina. 18th-century technology wasn't very advanced, but paddles and wheels turned cogs and gears, and did the work of many farm animals without the food and upkeep that critters required.

"Aye, River is a grand name," Jody admitted. "And jest like his sister, Bibby Liz, I dinna think he needs to worry about there bein' another person who shares the name."

"Is it too late to beg a bite of dinner?" Julian asked through a crack in the doorway.

"Come on in. Ye needn't beg of anythin' in this house. *Mi casa es su casa, hermano,*" Jody said.

"Well, I did knock, but I didn't think you heard me. I didn't want to pound harder in case there was a baby or three napping. Where are those grandchildren and great-grandchildren of mine?" he asked, as he tiptoed over to investigate the cluster of quilts on the bed.

I guess it had started early, even before the first babies of the next generation were born. My three had shared the same womb for nearly eight months and, even after birth, were more comfortable sleeping snuggled together. They didn't like being separated except for maybe a few inches apart during the summer. When Sarah's boys came around, and then Bibby Liz, the bonus three spent many an afternoon nap, cuddled next to my three. In the evenings, Jenny lay down with as many as were in the house to tell them a story or two and get them settled down for the night. She often fell asleep with them for half an hour or so, and then was up again, socializing with the rest of the 'big people.' Now there was one more child to blend into the baby bed, at least when we were all visiting. Bibby Liz was used to her own cot but enjoyed the closeness of her kin when she was visiting. The group got along well, which was a blessing that all of us appreciated. I guess the early start in shared accommodations worked.

Chapter 56: The Letter (NTY Ch 8)

Jenny had sat attentively while James read the letter aloud to all of us after dinner. Later, when everyone split up into separate chat groups, she asked if she could hold the soiled and creased paper that had once been held by her secret husband.

"I'm sure he wrote a letter to just you, sweetheart. I mean, he does mention it, and I just *feel* that he wrote one to you and only you."

Jenny's eyes were brimming with tears. She nodded, the movement starting into motion a trail of wetness down her cheek. "I know he did, too. But it's not here. It got stolen before it even got to the carrier. But I know he loves me and still wants me and, and…"

The sobs began as the tears continued. James stroked her hair. Words weren't necessary with the two of them. He knew how she felt. She was his ancestor, even if she hadn't had any children yet. And Scout was her husband, also his ancestor. He didn't know if she knew that he was a time traveler or that she was his great-grandmother so many times over or not, but he didn't want to say anything and 'jinx' the time-space continuum or whatever else might be involved.

"I don't know when you two will get together, but I'm *positive* that you'll have a long, wonderful marriage."

As soon as he said the word 'marriage,' he gulped. Did he just jinx something?

"You know Scout's my husband, huh?" Jenny asked, wiping her tears with her apron, her sobs quieted by his reassurance.

James nodded, too afraid to say a word less it be wrong.

Jenny tipped her head, looking at James in a whole new light. He did look like Scout in the eyes. She knew he was from a different 'when,' so maybe that meant…

"Whoa!" she exclaimed, then stood up and spun in place. "You're, you're… How did you know he was my husband? And are you? I mean, you are, aren't you? You can tell me. Oh, please tell me you are my…"

"Yes, I am. Granny."

Jenny thrust the letter back into his hand, then crossed her arms in front of herself and jumped up and down. "Who needs a letter? I got you!" she squealed, then ran up to him and squeezed him so tight, he thought he'd faint.

James held the letter high and agreed. "Yes, who needs the letter. We've got each other."

Autumn 1786

Chapter 57: The Chore Becomes a Game (NTY Ch 9)

"Can we brush our teeth now? Huh, Mommy? Can we brush our teeth?"

All of a sudden, I had three little red-headed children pulling on my skirts and apron, begging me to let them brush their teeth. At least, that's what I thought I was hearing.

"What do you want to do?"

Little Wren, the undeclared yet acknowledged by fraternal attitude spokesperson for the trio, huffed in exasperation. She knew they were speaking clearly, and that I must have beans in my ears.

"Mother, we would like to brush our teeth, please," she said with exaggerated enunciation.

Evidently, she realized she had sounded rude and didn't want to upset me with her suppressed but unintentional sassiness, so pasted a sincere smile on her face at the end of her request and fluttered her eyelashes, the same ploy she often wielded on the older male members of the family when trying to get her own way.

"All right," I replied slowly, looking around and behind the trio to see if I was missing something. "Is there a special reason why?"

"Because we just ate lunch," Wren replied diplomatically, her head dipping into a nod as if speaking before a judge or member of royalty.

"Well, you know I only ask that you brush your teeth after breakfast and before bed. Is there a reason why you want to add after lunch to your regimen?"

"What's regimen?" asked Leo, his finger slipping up a nostril to pick a ripe booger. He saw me watching his action closely, then reached into his pocket and used his handkerchief to give his nose a quick swipe. He looked at the nose napkin to make sure he had snatched his target, grinned at the size of it, then wadded the cloth and shoved it back where it came from. He had plans for it later, when nobody was watching.

"That's your routine," I explained. "You wake up in the morning, use the privy, wash your hands, eat breakfast, get dressed, and brush your hair and teeth."

"But, not with the same brush," Judah said, "or you'll get hair in your mouth. 'Sides, it's kinda hard to get it in your mouth unless you open real wide." Judah opened his mouth and pretended to put in his sister's wide hairbrush. "And don't try to comb your teeth—that won't work either." He added a comedic parody of combing his front two teeth, then grinned up at me, seeking my approval for his mini stand-up routine.

"All right, you can add brushing your teeth after lunch to your regimen. Here, you go," I said, and handed them the cup that held their custom-made toothbrushes.

Actually, just about everything here was custom made. These, like so many other items in our house, were made by James. He had fabricated a personalized wooden handle for each family member. Each 'head' had a standard-sized opening. He had found that willow was soft and fibrous if treated properly. He could easily flay one side, leaving the other half of the nugget solid to be inserted into the brush handle. He bore a tiny pinhole on the flat side of the insert and threaded a short length of dental floss through it to attach it to the handle. Every new moon we changed out the 'brush' in our toothbrushes, doing our best to stay hygienic in our crude and detergent-less existence.

"Can we have the salt water, too?" asked Wren.

"Oh, that's right," I said. Your brother James said he used to use warm salt water as a mouth wash when…"

I stood there, wide-eyed and at a sudden loss for words. Why were they so excited about brushing teeth and using warm salt water for a rinse? Instead of questioning it, though, I portioned out a half teaspoon of salt in the palm of my hand, dumped it in a mug, added some near boiling water to get it into suspension, and then cooled it down to slightly warmer than tepid with water from the ewer. I verified the temperature with my finger, then handed the cup to a very eager Leo.

"It's my turn first 'cause I was born first," he said.

Wren and Judah's shoulders slumped in defeat. Any time there was something new to do, he claimed the right of the firstborn. In this case, I'm sure all would be fine. At other times, like getting the first taste of one of Wren's fabulous mud pies, it wasn't in his favor. All in all, it seemed fair. At least they were comfortable with it, and I didn't have to be a referee.

Leo led the way to the water station near the barn, his cup of saline held before him like a holy grail. Wren followed behind with the mug of toothbrushes, one arm wrapped around it, clutching the brushes to her chest, the other hand picking through them to make sure hers was there. Judah brought up the rear, tugging the booger-laden handkerchief from his pocket, carefully scraping a pale green gem away from the fabric, ready to savor its saltiness. "Don't even think about it," I called from the porch.

He looked back at me, said 'sorry' with his eyes, and then flicked the tasty morsel into the air, watching it arc into nothingness. I'm sure he'd get another chance at a fresh one when I wasn't watching. Sometimes I think that having a hanky didn't encourage him to blow his nose but spurred his body into producing more snot.

Leo set the cup of salt water down on the wooden stump near the barn. Wren followed suit, setting down the mug, then retrieved her toothbrush and handed Judah his. Leo proceeded to draw a line in the silty soil. Wren and Judah quickly stood behind it in anticipation, both ready for what came next. Leo stood tall, took his toothbrush and ceremoniously dipped it in the water, then handed the cup to Judah. Judah went through the same motions then handed the cup to Wren. This whole time, I was leaning against the porch post, fascinated with the little ritual. Good grief, they were just brushing their teeth, but you'd think that they were getting ready to hand out an Academy Award!

Wren gave the cup back to Leo, and then I saw what all the excitement was about. Leo took a big swig, gargled for a long half minute, swished then leaned forward, looked down to make sure his feet were behind the line, then spit as far as he could. He handed Judah the cup, then ran over to the furthest point of his spittle, standing next to his mark. Judah went through the same moves of slurp, gargle, swish, and spit, and then passed off the cup. Unfortunately, he had bad presentation and half his fluid went down the front of his shirt, the remainder only squirting out about three feet.

"My turn!" crowed Wren. She wiggled her shoulders, loosening up for her grand performance, took a healthy swill, gargled, paused as if to spit, decided that she needed more projectile fluid, took a short sip, gargled some more, and then let fly.

"Hah!" she exclaimed. She had out-spit her elder-by-a-few-minutes brother by at least two feet.

"Where did you learn to do that?" I asked although I was pretty sure

I already knew.

"Guilty," James said, as he came out of the barn. Evidently, he had been watching the performance, too. I had forgotten he was here to help Wallace trim the hooves of the goats.

I looked down my nose, waiting for the explanation I was sure he would provide.

"I just wanted to find a way to encourage them to spend more time with their oral hygiene. Brushing is great, but that extra time with the salt-water kills the bacteria that cause decay better than anything else we have here now. I thought you were already using a saline rinse for them. When the boys saw how far Bibby Liz could spit, well, I guess they had to see which of the Pomeroy-Hart clan had the best distance. Looks like the girls win with this talent."

I gave James a sidelong glance and snorted, "Hmph," with a reserved disgust. "Maybe they'll find other talents that will serve them better in life. I don't think there's a big call for women to put out fires at fifteen paces with a mouthful of water."

Chapter 58: The Dance (NTY Ch 10)

"Are you sure you don't want to visit the Creekmores? After the barn raising, there's going to be a big dinner and a dance. I'm sure they'd be happy to have your strong back when it's time for setting the walls. Donna's not fussy about who is doing the work, as long as it's getting done."

I could tell by Jenny's furrowed brow that there was another, more important, reason she didn't want to go, but I would let her tell me in her own time. I know that if our places were swapped, I wouldn't want my mother nagging me to go to the biggest–well, the only–social gathering of the season.

"*They'll* be there," she spat out, then huffed. "I'm sorry. It's not your fault. Those, those..." Jenny snorted, then stood up and shuffle-stomped the perimeter of the room for a full thirty seconds. "They're vile! Those Johnson boys are so rude and disrespectful and stupid and crush... Is that the word?"

"I think you mean crass," I said. "At least, if we had a dictionary, right next to the word crass would be a picture of Old Man Johnson's sons. Better not use that word, though. I don't think anyone around here knows it. They'll just think you're being pretentious."

Jenny rolled her eyes at me like a teenage daughter of any era.

I repeated it in simpler words. "They'll think you're trying to show you're smarter than they are. You *are* smarter, but there's no need to make them feel bad about it."

"You couldn't make those vermin feel bad about themselves even if you tried. Those brothers think they're God's gift to women. And men. They're always having spitting contests or arm-wrestling contests or, or whatever." Jenny tipped her head to hide her face, but her blush was obvious, her ears positively radiant.

"So that's how you got those bruises on your inner arm..."

Jenny shrugged her shoulder. "Daddy taught me long ago that arm wrestling was not about strength so much as it was about leverage and the ability to read your opponent's tells."

"Huh?"

"You have to throw him off guard both emotionally and balance-wise. When his eyes show he's ready to move in and use his muscle, that's the time to push him over. I tried it out with Silas Junior just because I was curious if it was true or not. When Buford, that's his big brother, saw him get whupped, he decided it was his responsibility to put the…" Jenny's face skewed up and she mimicked the ornery giant's squeaky voice, "Put the little woman in her place…on the floor, pickin' up scraps and sweepin'."

"So, you threw that air-headed bull's shoulder out of place? That's why he was at Sarah's last month? He didn't get kicked by a horse or fall out of a tree or… Gee, I think he gave her about four different excuses for his dislocated shoulder."

Jenny pulled her shoulders back and grinned so wide, I could see all her molars. "Yup, that was me." She took it down to a cautionary level and added, "But I'm not so careless as I'd tell anyone. I know Silas Junior saw his loss, but although he's dim, he's smart enough not to mess with his big brother's ego. That, and I heard Buford threaten to cut off his dangly man parts if he ever breathed a word of it to another soul, living or dead!"

"I know you don't want to see them, but you can't live in the shadows, afraid that you might encounter someone who might hurt you. There will be plenty of folks there. Those boys won't dare touch you."

"Mommy," Jenny said gently and stroked the side of my face, pushing the barrette she had made me back in place, "I'm not afraid of any man."

I sighed deeply and leaned into her hand. "Yes, I know, dear. And that's what terrifies me."

Chapter 59: The Pink Pony (NTY Ch 11)

On the road

It wasn't where Scout wanted to be, but Edgar had asked him to meet him inside The Pink Pony. His skin crawled at the idea of going into that shanty. The haphazard construction and tilted walls that seemed ready to fall down at any moment weren't what bothered him, though; it was the boisterous laughs and phony squeals of delight from women that turned his stomach. He'd wait up the road for his former boss and his sturdy red roan. They could speak in the open air, without any distractions. Waiting for him outside shouldn't be a problem. They weren't supposed to meet until tomorrow, the weather was fair, and he had plenty of jerked venison and dried apple to fill his belly. Plus, he didn't have anything better to do than carve another chess piece or two for Jenny's brother, James.

Another loud forced giggle pierced the peaceful melody of the twittering wrens. He'd heard the tales of wanton women. His nose twitched as he stifled a grunt of realization. Until a year ago, he'd never even heard the word wanton. When he asked Jubal what it meant, he said it was a word to describe a female who wasn't afraid to shake her lady parts in front of a man's face. Or do other deeds to make a man happy. Usually, but not always, for money.

"Yes, Scout, if you go into a bawdy house, make sure you have plenty of coin. They don't charge you to look, but to get up real close and touch those soft spots…" Then Jubal laughed and grabbed the front of his trousers, "Or do anything else you may want to ask of her, it'll cost you a coin or two. Oh, and they don't take script."

That last warning was the most important one Scout had heard from any of the men in his survey team. He'd been paid in government script for the last year and a half. Shoot, he had an oil-skin bag stuffed full of that paper currency. The other men in the expedition had opted for less money as long as they were paid in silver coin. Now he knew why. Outside of the government-run stores, the paper was worthless. He'd have to find a way to change his back pay into coin or he'd never have enough money to buy Jenny the house she deserved. Or at least a one-room starter home. He could build a basic shelter with timber from the land Jenny's grandfather had given her, then add on to it later. After he had the stumps pulled. And crops planted. And made sure he gave his wife all the attention she deserved as a 'real' mate...

Scout was awakened from his musings about his future with Jenny by the clanging of metal on metal. "Buy your pots and pans here. Pretties for the ladies, too. Books and plates and cups and other dainties that are sure to put a smile on your little woman's face..."

It was an enclosed wagon, much like the one his young wife's neighbor Diego had, but not nearly as pretty. This one was made from scrap wood of all cuts, colors, and thicknesses, hammered in place over a rickety frame, the gaping holes patched over with rawhide leather.

He had heard of peddlers but had never actually seen one. Maybe he could buy a small gift for Jenny, something pretty but not too large or heavy. He was still traveling afoot after the debacle with the Major last month. Maybe the traveling salesman would take some of his script for something small and lightweight. Then he could exchange it for what he really wanted when he got closer to home and Jenny.

Scout stepped closer to the vendor, then looked up and down the road again, just to be sure he still had a good view and wouldn't miss his meeting. Still no sign of Edgar. Well, he'd see him if he passed this way, whether he was a day early or three days late. The peddler had stopped in the middle of the dusty trail called Main Street. There was no way he'd miss the tall man and roan horse, no matter which way they came in.

"What pretties do you have that are small and easy to carry?" Scout asked the peddler.

The tall, gangly salesman started at the question, dropping the oversized skillet and lid he had been using as noisemakers. "Land sakes, lad! I didn't hear or see you approach. I'm sorry. What is it you were needing?"

"I have a pretty young wife who I have'na seen in over two years now. Her eyes are the color of cornflowers, her hair a bit darker than cornsilk. I'd like to take her a present, but something small and easy to carry. Ye see, I'm travelin' on foot for this part of my journey."

The sly salesman saw an easy mark with the young man. Two years past this young man was a boy. There was no way he had a wife back then. He must be wishing that the young lass from church or the next town over would take to him if he brought her a pretty. His smile grew as he realized young men like this were both naïve and proud. He'd want a big jewel for his 'bride' and would be willing to pay much more than it was worth for it.

"I have something for your pretty young *wife* right here," the man said. "But first, a gentleman always makes introductions, especially when there's business to transact. I am Cain McCain, but you may call me Cain."

"Scout Kincaid. Scout by name, scout by trade." He reached out, grabbed the man's bony hand, and shook it vigorously. "Glad to make yer acquaintance, sir. I mean, Cain."

"Scout. Hmm. Never heard that name, but it seems to fit you. Oh, and you do have cash, don't you? I don't sell my products for chickens or hogs or anything else with eyes or that require feeding."

Scout grinned as he looked under both arms, then behind him. "No, no chickens to trade," he patted his oil skin satchel, "but I do have quite a few chits. I worked for the government fer quite a while. They saw fit to pay us with chits, that is, this paper money, instead of silver. They explained that these were as good as gold, but not quite so heavy."

"It's easier to start a fire with those, too, but that doesn't mean they're valuable. No, son, I have no need for those."

Cain rubbed the side of his nose, hiding his smirk of deception, and waited for the young man to argue. He had a good source for changing the script into silver coin, but the rumor he had helped spread was that it was totally worthless. He'd grab as much of it as he could, then turn it into a shopping trip to France. A pocket full of coin could buy real dainties and pretties in Paris which he could then sell to a higher class of people. No more cheap imitations for the common folk. He was going to be both rich and respected!

"I'll tell you what, son," the peddler said, then turned away to the locked box on the side of his wagon. "I was holding this back for when I found a woman wonderful enough to be my bride." He coughed at the lie: he would never share what was his with a woman, even his name. "I'll lighten your load with this genuine diamond and sapphire ring. It would be much easier for you to carry. The stones are quite valuable, as is the gold that it's set in. Here, I'll even let you have the velvet pouch to keep it in."

Cain pulled the ring out of the dark blue purse and set it on top but kept everything in his hand. "Do you think this is pretty enough for your young," he gulped as he choked on the word, "young bride?"

"Ye say this is a genuine sapphire and those are real diamonds surrounding it?" Scout leaned forward and sniffed the item as slyly as he could. It smelled wrong, almost like vinegar, not like a metal at all. "And that metal is genuine gold?"

"As sure as I'm standing here. May the Lord drop me in my place if it isn't. Yes, genuine gold and those gems are the real deal, too."

"How much of my script did ye want fer this?"

"Oh, since it's such a burden for you to carry—and not worth a drink of clean creek water—I'll take it all from you. I was thinking of stuffing a mattress with it. I don't have the funds for goose down, and straw is too uncomfortable for my old bones." He stared at Scout's satchel and shook his head. "There might not be enough for my narrow cot, but may be enough for a pillow to lay my weary head on."

"May I hold it?" Scout asked, palm outstretched.

"Let me have your script, first," the shyster grunted. He realized he had dropped his 'you can trust me' persona, and quickly sweetened his speech. "Here, I'll hold your bag for you so you can use both hands to look it over."

Scout's fingers curled up into a fist as he pulled back his hand. Something was fishy here, and it wasn't just the strange odor from the ring. He paused and took a deep breath before pulling the bag from his shoulder. If what Jubal had said yesterday was true, the script was pretty much worthless. Anyway, he had changed some of the smaller denominations into five dollar bills and stuffed them in between the doubled cotton sacks that held his cornmeal. He didn't want to arrive with nothing to show for the last two years of work. If the ring truly was valuable, he might be able to sell it for real silver plus have enough left over to buy Jenny a simpler ring. He would still have some government script to show Jenny that he really had been working every day, saving everything he made to buy seed, tools, and livestock so they could finally live together as man and wife.

Cain's fingers itched to snatch the satchel from the young man, but he knew not to appear too eager. The boy was young but did seem to be sharp. Hopefully, his desire to impress a lass was stronger than his ability to spot a con in the making. He slyly slipped the ring back into the bag. He could still smell the strong tang of the paste the stones were made of. Every minute it was in the bag was another moment his deception wouldn't be noticed. He wanted to take care of this transaction right away. The boy was afoot, and he had a horse and wagon, but someone in the tavern behind them might give chase if Scout called foul and started a ruckus.

"Here you go, Scout," the peddler said, thrusting the velvet pouch just in front of Scout's hand, intentionally dropping it as he snatched the satchel the rest of the way from the boy's shoulder. "I'm sure the stone can never be as blue as you say her eyes are, but the sooner you get it to her, the happier you'll both be."

Scout bent over to retrieve the velvet bag, made sure that it wasn't empty, then stood up to glare at the man. "Ye ken that if ye've cheated me, ye'll have the devil to pay."

Cain snorted, indignant at the remark. "I'd never cheat a man, so I have nothing to worry about. However, I just remembered that I told Hildy, the lady in charge of the ordinary up the road, that I just acquired the sweet-smelling salts she's been after for over a year." He looked up to the sky, itching to leave. Nary a gray cloud, just a few white wisps tickled the blue sky.

"It looks like rain," he lied. "I'd best be on my way," then rushed to the side of his wagon and scrambled up. "Give my best to your bride when you see her," he added breathlessly, clutching Scout's satchel under one arm as he flicked the back of his horse with his frayed buggy whip, urging her up the road.

Scout fingered the smoothness of the velvet bag. She'd like it, too. Two presents for the price of one.

"Looks like you just made a transaction with old Cain McCain," Edgar said, startling Scout.

The young man gulped in embarrassment. Someone had sneaked up on him! And on horseback, too! How could that have happened? Oh, that's right. He was thinking of Jenny. Scout shoved the blue pouch into his vest pocket. He'd check it out later. Right now, he had a few other things to get squared away.

"Aye, sir, but we're done. I have the information ye were after. But just to be sure, there isn't revenge or vengeance or anything like that involved with finding this man, is there?"

507

Edgar laughed aloud. It was a true and pure laugh; not the ornery ones he bellowed just before pulling a prank and embarrassing one of his men.

"No, Earl is my brother. I haven't seen him since he was about your size. I was hoping to visit with him before I went to England. I have some business to transact and wanted to make sure he was not in harm's way. He has a bit of a hot head. A good man, but quick to anger and throw a fist...or a few words that aren't easily retracted."

"If by retracted, ye mean he canna, or willna, say he's sorry, or that he dinna really mean what he said, then aye, I ken what ye mean."

"Now, where is the ornery cuss? Is he a free man or in gaol? Is he healthy? Does he have a wife and family?" Edgar asked, leaning forward, not wanting to miss any word Scout had to share.

A grin widened across Scout's face. "Weel, if I had my doubts before, and I did, I dinna anymore. If he's not yer kin, at least yer fond of the man. He's hale and, save for the loss of the hair on the top of his head, seems to be all there. He has a wife and about six wee'uns runnin' around his print shop. Ye see, he owns a printin' press and bookstore. He says he took another's name to spare his family embarrassment. I take it he was a wild young man?"

Edgar's eyes filled with tears. He sniffed them back and nodded for Scout to proceed.

"He asked me to give ye this letter. And his wife said to give ye this." Scout took a deep breath, kissed his fingertips, then cautiously approached the big man. "Here," he said and tapped Edgar on the cheek. "She gave me a peck on the cheek and said to pass it on to ye. I dinna think ye'd like me kissin' on ye any more than I'd want to do it, so, weel, that's all there is. Oh, and yer invited to stay with them any time yer in Greensboro. It's gettin' to be a big town now."

Edgar held the wax-sealed letter up to the sky and grinned. He'd savor it later. Right now, he wanted an ale to wash the road dust out of his mouth.

"Here's a bonus for doing a fine job, Scout," and tossed him an entire silver coin. "Maybe you can put it toward buying a bull for your new homestead. But for right now, put it away where shysters like Cain McCain can't see it. And come inside with me for a bit of drink and squeeze."

508

"I ken what drink is, and ale does sound fine, but what's a squeeze?"

"Now, Scout, I know that you say that you're married, but I know for a fact that you haven't seen your wife in over two years. At least, that's what you say. If that's the case, you might want to spend some time with one of the ladies here. Give one or two of them a squeeze. Maybe they can teach you something new to put an even bigger smile on your wife's face."

"Sir!" Scout screeched. "I would never…" He sputtered and swallowed, but words wouldn't come.

"Now, now, son. What she doesn't know won't hurt her. I'm sure she'll be happy to have you back, whether or not you've been shared."

"No, sir. And as ye've said in the past, that subject is not open to negotiation. Good day to ye. May ye have a safe and pleasant journey. And if ye plan on sellin' that horse, please allow me to be the first to make an offer."

"Thank you, Scout. Safe journey to you, too. And no, the horse will be coming with me. He's the most valuable asset I own."

***

There were still a few hours of daylight left before he needed to find a place for the evening. Scout patted his vest, making sure his metal treasures hadn't slipped away. Nope, coins and jewelry parcel: still there, safe and sound. He hefted up his bag of cornmeal. It was still half full and he knew by the telltale crinkling that his five dollar bills were still in place. His confidence that all was well with the world—and that he would see his lovely bride in just another day and a half—gave him a burst of energy. His determined trek down the road turned into a lope.

"Yer legs are longer and stronger than last time she saw ye," he told himself, then concentrated on reaching one rise and then the next, before both daylight and his zip faded.

'Weel, now ye only have one day left,' he mused. He approached a barren spot off the road. The charred circle of rocks indicated that it was an oft used spot for weary travelers. There was even a fallen log, conveniently placed as a back rest or stool, depending on the ground conditions. He looked up at the sky. No rain tonight. He'd use ol' hickory as a recliner and re-read the letter Jenny had given him two Christmases past, the last time he had seen her.

509

In just moments, he had his evening fire ablaze. Normally, he'd break out the cornmeal and pan and fix some johnny cake to fill his belly, but tonight, he just wanted to rest. And dream of tomorrow.

Caw! Caw!

Scout awoke with a start. It was daylight already! He must have fallen asleep while sitting up. He didn't even remember curling up next to the dying embers, but that's where he was now, his bag of food under his head as a pillow, ravens pecking at it, searching for an easy meal.

Caw! Caw!

"Get away, ye mangy raven! That's my food. Go find yerself a field and pinch the corn that hasna already been ground!"

He grasped the bag. There was a small leak, but nothing that a bit of script rearranging couldn't fix. He opened the bag, shoved the contents to one side, positioned a five-dollar bill over the exterior pinhole, then set the bag up straight again, securing it with a simple knot.

"Looks like a dried apple breakfast with a clear water chaser today," he said aloud to keep the birds at a distance. "Ye'll have to look elsewhere fer yer meal. There are no scraps here. Now be off wi' ye. I'm on my way to see my wife!"

Caw! Caw! Caw!

It was almost as if the birds were replying to him.

It was a wonderful day.

Chapter 60: The Blonde Frenzy (NTY Ch 12)

Near Pomeroy's Place

It had been two years last Christmas, nearly three years now, since he'd visited the Pomeroy homestead. Scout knew he should have come back last spring, but the crew was headed out to a new area. If he had left then, he would have lost his job as scout for the survey team. It was a man's job, one that paid real money, not promises or sickly chickens.

When he asked to be hired for the position, he let Major Murphy believe that he was much older, saying he had been sickly as a youth and that it had stunted his growth. Of course, the fact that his hands were bigger and tougher than most his age—and that he promised he would and could do the same amount of work as any other man in the regiment—was in his favor. He didn't even have to explain his lack of beard; his Indian dress made it obvious that he wasn't all white man, if any at all.

The major wasn't as gentlemanly as his former employer, Colonel Saulnier, had been and teased and taunted him with words that still stung. Still, he paid a fair wage. That spring, his body began to fill out and shoot up. He grew over a foot in less than a year, so his actual age was no longer an issue. Not that the major cared how old he was. He was too wound up in his shady land grabbing dealings to pay attention to anyone or anything that didn't make him a quick sack of gold or silver.

Scout hefted his knapsack with his foodstuffs and hidden five-dollar bills, then patted the coins and jewelry pouch. Nothing rattled, but he knew he had money and a gift. With his experience and the reference he had received from the now General Saulnier, his first real employer, he should be able to find work closer to his wife. But, before he went anywhere else, worked for anyone other than himself, he had to see his Jenny.

Even if he hadn't been familiar with the roads, he would have known he was close to the Pomeroy's place: he could feel the pull on his heart. He still had almost a day's walk ahead of him, but he could literally feel the tug. His chest felt as if it were two feet ahead of the rest of his body, leading the way to the girl—no, she was a woman now—with whom he would spend the rest of his life.

511

His fantasies of a future with her as his full-time wife were interrupted by the sounds of conflict. The thuds of blows landing on solid flesh, eliciting unintentional squeals of pain—the puffing and panting of exertion by at least two persons—were unmistakable.

"Like that, is it?" grunted a winded, angry male. "I'll have you seein' it my way in no time, Missy."

Scout heard a thwack, an oomph, and then the sound of someone losing his—or would that be her?—balance, and then clunk, a body hitting the earth. Someone had been smacked to the ground and, by the angry, masculine call of, "Missy," it sounded as if a female was losing her battle with at least one male.

"Whoo-ee!" Scout whistled through his teeth. He couldn't run fast enough to the sound of the melee to stop the apparent onslaught, but he could divert the male's—or males'—attention, possibly giving the woman a chance to get away.

"Who goes there?" a man asked angrily, obviously upset at being distracted from the fracas with the female.

"Whoo-ee!" Scout whistled again; he'd save his breath for running rather than calling out. He sprinted across the uneven ground, jumping over boulders he normally would have walked around, to reach the rise above the brawl, a higher vantage point where he could see the disturbance below.

There was no way he'd go against an unknown enemy and unknown numbers—Scout was his name and his job. He needed information before he could devise a plan for rescue. He almost lost his life once because of being impetuous; he wasn't going to let anyone lead him into a mess like that again! He'd take care of this now, but he'd do it his way.

Yes, it was a woman—a busty, blond woman—who was on the wrong side of winning the wrestling match. Her long, unbound hair was wild about her head, completely covering her face, obscuring her features, but not muffling her feral-toned guttural protests. One man stood behind her, struggling to keep his grip on her elbows. Another dashed in to try and steal a kiss, then quickly backed away in fear. She kept her face down, rebuffing his unwanted advances with such vigorous, vicious head thrashing that it would make a rutting bull moose envious. The growl coming from her throat unsettled Scout, even from fifty feet away. He saw two more men on the ground, one of them cradling a bloody cheek. The other was writhing on his back, knees up, grasping his groin, moaning in agony, ultimately rolling to his side, puking from the intense pain.

Scout, shocked by the hedonistic quarrel, realized that he hadn't stopped to observe it, but had watched it as he moved down the hill silently, without conscious thought, and now was at the perimeter of the earthen fight are'na. He didn't have a plan yet, but there were only four of them, one still on the ground. One wily Indian scout and a rage-fueled woman could surely overtake the three remaining mangy males.

Suddenly, the kissing bandit slashed the air in front of the woman, apparently tired of her resistance, ready to make good his threat to kill her. "I'll have you as a corpse if you won't take me willin'. Yer hole will feel just as good—naw, probably better—if yer dead." He hiked up his sagging trousers. "At least you can't kick me in the stones if yer not breathin'!" he bellowed, then lunged at her, blade held low.

His first swipe missed her completely, instead drawing blood from the hand of the scared man trying to restrain her. The second thrust was closer but still didn't hurt her. It did, however, rip open her bodice and expose her full, round bosoms. The woman's chest was heaving in anger, not at being exposed, but at being restrained by another. It was obvious she'd fight to her last breath. She'd die before yielding.

Scout quickly pulled a rock out of his pouch, had it loaded and flung from his slingshot before the attacker could launch his third assault. *Thunk!* It found its target at the back of the unsuspecting knife wielder's head, sending blood and scalp flying in one direction, the projectile in another. *Thunk!* A mere second later, the bloated, hairy assistant trying to hold the blonde warrior's arms to her ribs sported a third eye, a dark cavity with a skid mark off to the side, marking the bloody furrow where the stone bullet had glanced off his forehead.

Omph! Thud! The two bodies fell simultaneously in opposite directions from each other. The third man, his face unevenly marked—a nail-raked bloody cheek on one side and a serious gash on the other— saw his brother laid out where he had fallen, the angry young woman kicking at his unconscious head. "Don't…don't hit him anymore…uh, please," he begged, as he tried to pull the fallen would-be rapist away from her furious feet.

Mr. Trounced Testicles was now up on his knees. "Stop, stop," he begged, as he crawled toward the other three. "We'll leave, we'll be gone. We was just havin' some fun, you know…" He groaned, as he stood up, gasped again in pain, and then grabbed the other hand of the fallen man. "Are you sure you don't want to go to the barn raisin' with him?" he asked sheepishly, nodding to the passed-out man who had just threatened to kill her.

"Raahr!" she growled, then bent down to pick up a softball-sized stone. "I'll hunt ye all down and skin ye, use yer hide fer lampshades, if ye ever so much as talk to me!" She pulled her arm back as if to launch the four-pound projectile, then hesitated, waiting for their reply. The men paused, apparently giving her offer a second thought. "Lampshade…" she hissed, palming the stone in her long-fingered hand. The two men quickly gathered their fallen comrades by the feet and scurried down the hill, not worrying about the bumps and brambles in their path, or the knocking about the passed-out males' skulls were receiving.

The young woman stretched herself up to her full height and twisted the kinks out of her neck, never taking her eyes off her assailants, verifying their exodus. She paused when they were out of sight, then tensed her back. She looked to either side without turning her head. Very gradually, she pivoted around, looking behind her. She realized she wasn't alone. She had been so consumed with anger that she hadn't been thinking. She hadn't been aware of anything but staying alive, and untouched—at least her personal parts. Now that the terror and anger were over, she realized there had to be someone else out there. Someone had thrown two rocks in very rapid succession and allowed her to escape her captors.

She took two slow breaths, calming her mind, emptying it of the negative emotions that enveloped her. She heard a raven call, then two more. Life was back to normal. Or nearly so. She brought together the fabric of her bodice, covering her exposed breasts, and realized that whoever was out there could see her. At least she could mend it right away. Temporarily. She reached into her pocket, still trying to rid herself of the tension from the last half hour and found it: the pink-capped diaper pin. She pinned her blouse together, then looked to the trees above her.

"Hello," she said in greeting, maintaining a speaking tone. Hopefully, he hadn't heard the tremble in her voice. She knew he could hear her without yelling. He was close, maybe just a few yards away.

"Are ye okay?" he asked, as he came out from behind a tree. "It seems ye are, though. At least, ye look to be in better shape than those men. Yer a tough one."

Scout walked down the path, keeping his eyes low. He had seen her breasts, they were beautiful, but they weren't his to appreciate. A man, any man, would be blessed to have a wife as strong, determined, and with as fine a figure. Yes, she'd be able to bear many children, take care of a farm by herself, if need be, and most certainly would make her husband happy at night.

"You don't recognize me?" she said softly, intentionally disguising her voice, although she probably didn't need to. She knew it had changed in the last two and a half years, as had many other aspects of her physical being.

"No, ma'am," Scout said, his eyes still low. He had seen her fumbling with her bodice and didn't want to look and see if she had been able to cover herself or not.

Jenny didn't say a word—her husband didn't like it when she talked too much—she simply looked at him. He was keeping his eyes low out of respect for her attire. She knew that, so she took the opportunity to look hard at him, to see how much he'd changed.

He had a beard now; not much of one, and it looked like it had been at least a week since he had shaved. It was just stubble but appealing just the same. He also had a few hairs on his chest. She could see because his shirt was open. It was too small for him, couldn't be buttoned up, and was tight across his broad shoulders. He was still too skinny, but she could fix that. She could also make a shirt for him that fit. She looked down and saw he was wearing leggings and a breechclout, not trousers like most men around here. His hair was long, pulled back in a queue. It was still dark but had blonde streaks in it from the sun.

She looked at his hands. It must have been a rough two years. He had a big scar across the back of his wrist, almost as if someone had tried to chop it off, but it still worked. She could see his fingers twitching, nervously tapping each other, unsure of what to do or say next. Jenny neared him, took one fidgeting hand in hers, brought it to her lips, kissed it, and set it on her rent blouse-covered left breast. "Still yours, and big enough to feed babies now?"

"Jenny?" squeaked Scout. He would have had that same, high-pitched shocked voice if any woman had made that same gesture, but this was Jenny, his wife of nearly five years. She had changed—grown up so much—that he hadn't recognized her.

"I…I'm sorry I wasna here to protect ye," he said, his head hung down in shame, voicing his simple, heartfelt apology.

Jenny put her index finger under his chin and lifted his head, so he had to look her in the eye. She shook her head slowly and, with her other hand, tapped her slightly swollen bottom lip.

He couldn't resist an invitation like that, even if he had wanted to. This woman, whose curvy body and luscious blonde hair he had guiltily been admiring, was his wife.

Chapter 61: Gold and Gems (NTY Ch 13)

"I'm sorry I'm so late in comin' to see ye," he said after a kiss so long, he thought he'd never be able to draw another breath.

"I knew you'd be back! I told those Johnson brothers that I had a husband, and they wouldn't believe me." Jenny shrugged one shoulder. "I really wanted to keep it a secret. I mean, I was so young and for so long, it didn't make a difference whether I was marrit or not.

"And then my body started to change. And menfolk took notice. Most of them were polite. Actually, all of them were except those Johnson boys. I'd call them men, but I don't think they'll ever be full-grown men, no matter how old they are. They think that just 'cause their daddy owns most of everything around here, they can take whatever they want. And since I didn't have a man following me around all the time like some of the other young women, they figured they could have me. When I finally decided it was time I told them I had a husband, they laughed at me and said they didn't see no ring. Hmph! As if a woman needs a ring to be married!"

Scout picked up her hand and kissed it, and then picked up the other one and kissed it, too. "Which finger does a wedding ring go on?"

Jenny's mouth twitched back and forth, trying to remember. "Leah wears hers on her left hand. This finger," and waved it back and forth.

"All right, then. Let's see if it fits on that finger."

"Wait. What? What fits on this finger?"

"Jenny, yer my wife and I've neglected ye fer nearly three years now. I was workin' hard, savin' every bit of money I could, only buyin' what was absolutely necessary. Sometimes, goods like cornmeal and blankets, I'd trade my labor fer. Other times, I had to use some of my pay. But most times I could hunt, fish, or harvest whatever I needed.

"But jest yesterday, I met a peddler man. He told me that my money, my Continental script, was only worth pillow stuffin'. He had a ring, though, that he'd been savin' fer a wife. I figured he'd never have one, and since I wanted somethin' nice fer ye… Weel, I traded most of my script fer this."

Scout pulled the velvet bag from his vest pocket and showed it to Jenny. "Here, let me open it up fer ye." He began picking at the double knot Cain had used to secure the parcel.

"It's a blue gemstone with diamonds. He said it's called a sapphire. I've never seen a sapphire before, but I guess that's what it really is." Scout grunted in frustration then pulled out his dirk and used the end of it to pry loose the knot. "It's a real pretty color, but not as blue as yer eyes. Oh, and the metal band is real gold, too."

Jenny held out her hand to accept the ring, then sneezed.

The smell was overpowering to both of them.

"Do sapphires smell like vinegar? I know Leah's ring is made of blue diamonds, and they don't stink."

Scout picked up the ring by the band and looked it over. The big blue stone was pitted, the smaller colorless stones disintegrating in the setting. He pinched the 'sapphire' and it crumbled between his thumb and forefinger. "Cain."

"That's the name of the man who sold it to you, right?"

He nodded but didn't reply. He'd been conned by Cain. The Continental script he traded for the ring probably had some value, too. He sniffed back the tears that wouldn't stay back.

"God's gonna get him for that." Jenny scooted as close as she could and whispered, "Besides, I don't need a ring. At least, not right away."

"But all that money! I have a wee bit held back: some pieces of silver and a few of what they call five dollar bills, but all that labor," he turned away from her so she didn't see his rage, "all those hours I coulda been with ye… He stole them from me!"

Jenny touched his elbow, then moved in front of him. She held his cheeks in her hands and inched closer to speak to him, her nose just inches from his. "But you have me now, right? He didn't get that. And maybe, just maybe, what he has is not worth what he thought. James has said over and over, 'What goes around, comes around.'

"What you've done is totally selfless. You sacrificed lots of hard work and time away from your," Jenny blushed as she got down off her tiptoes, "wife. Now you're here. With me. And you're going to stay. Right? I don't think you know, but Grandpa Jody gave me the five acres down by the creek. I overheard James tell him it was the right thing to do. It was insurance for the future, whatever that means.

"Anyhow, I've been working, too." Jenny reached into her pocket and pulled out a drawstring bag made of green calico. "Here. I don't know how to make these into pretties, but I'm sure they're valuable.

Julian said next time he goes to London he'll take them with him and maybe do some trading. Scout, these are real! Look!"

"These are gold nuggets, jest like the ones in Evie's necklace. And these…"

Jenny wrapped her arm around his waist as he looked at the fistful of gemstones. She picked up a raisin-sized clear stone, licked it, then bit it.

"See! No taste. Oh, and the red ones are rubies, unless they're blood red, and then they're garnets. The green ones are emeralds, and the blue ones are sapphires, and those clear ones… They're real diamonds! Julian said they're about the most precious gem in the world." She paused and thought about what she had just said. "Maybe he said they *were* the most valuable, but anyway, we're rich!"

"You're rich. All I have are a few silver coins and some script that may or may not be worth even the tiniest bit of gold there."

"No, we're rich. But your money will be easier to spend. James told me not to tell anyone about the gold and gems except you, and Grandpa Jody, and Grandpa Julian. I mean, I'm sure their wives know everything about it, too, but I'm not to say a word." Jenny pulled her thumb and finger across her lips, figuratively zipping them closed.

"I ken ye were a beautiful person when I married ye, even if we weren't full grown. I wanted ye fer my wife then, but not nearly as much as I'm glad yer my wife now. Beautiful, strong, and clever. What else could a man want?"

Jenny got on her toes to be nose-to-nose with him again. "How about a good kisser?"

Chapter 62: Am I My Own Ancestor? (NTY Ch 14)

"So, if Scout is my ancestor, and he and Jenny are already secretly married, and their children—yet to be born—will certainly have children, and they'll have children, and then *they'll* have children..." James mused aloud, counting on his fingers, "and typically there's about twenty years to thirty years per generation then..."

"Then what?" Leah asked. She had an empty laundry basket on one hip, baby River on the other.

"I'm just trying to pin down how many generations there are between Scout and me. I guess it's about seven, maybe eight."

"Unless, of course, all your ancestors were the firstborn children, and their fathers were young when they came along. I mean, we'll have to wait to see how old Jenny is when she and Scout have their first child. Lord, I hope we're all together when they do, living within at least a day's ride from each other. That would be so awesome. I mean, being able to meet, to hold as an infant, your own great-grandfather seven or eight times over..." Leah paused in her ramblings and brought River up for an unsolicited hug and squeeze, eliciting a delighted giggle out of the mellow boy who reached up and stuck a fistful of fingers into his mother's mouth and grabbed.

"And those gems and gold nuggets Jenny's been digging up from the area around the creek? Do you think those...?"

"Yes, my dear wife," James said as he lifted her left hand. He kissed the blue diamonds in her platinum wedding ring, "I doubt that these are the same gems that Jenny mined, but there's no doubt in my mind that the Melbourne fortune of precious gems was all started by the young girl who wanted to dig for gold to help out her family. Who would have thought that I'd ever meet her, in any lifetime?"

"Well, who would have thought that you and I – an American nurse and a British lord – would ever meet, much less get married?"

"And be fairies, as Scout calls us. Time travelers. Aye, the finest family of fairies in North America."

"Yes, dear husband, in North America. Because I don't think there's anything on earth that will get me on a boat to go over to your old Mother England."

"Don't worry, dear. I'm happy here. With you and all our children. And will be, Lord willing, with our children's children."

Leah snuggled up to her husband and gave him a kiss on the cheek. "But I don't think you could ever be your own ancestor. We're just pretty good at finding the ones you didn't even know you had."

**Conclusion of NEVER TOO YOUNG *and* JUST JENNY AND SCOUT: THE COLLECTIVE WORKS. The end of their youth and the beginning of the Melbourne Dynasty. **

Thank you!

Thank you for reading my collection of stories about Jenny and Scout. I've been writing The Fairies Saga for nearly twenty years now. Need I say I'm still not done? Check my website (danihaviland.com) for the latest releases. There are more adventures for this wonderful group of friends and family in the works.

I'd appreciate a review of this set – or any of the singles in it – on Goodreads, Amazon, or BookBub.

Read on for more links to stories from The Haviland Universe.

About the Author

Author Dani Haviland started writing late in life and has been making up for lost time with a flood of works from sports, gritty women's fiction, time travel, and Sweet and Sassy romances to Unforgettable romantic suspense, Cute But Crazy rom-coms, and cozy mystery stories – with some short stories thrown in to round out the reading experience.

Dani is also the owner of Chill Out! Books, one of the publishers for The Authors' Billboard. Follow her on BookBub to make sure you get her latest stories.

Contact information:
Website: danihaviland.com
Email: dani@danihaviland.com
Twitter: @dani_haviland @gr8authors

I love to hear from readers!
Sign up for my newsletter to get the latest information on new releases, free stuff, and contests here.

Awesome readers group!
I have a Facebook Page for folks who are interested in early excerpts and insights into my latest books and box sets plus the latest from some of the authors and box sets I publish under Chill Out! Books. I'd appreciate it if you'd like the page. Drop in and see if I've remembered to add photos and excerpts of my works in process. Search: Dani Haviland & Friends Readers Group.

More Books by Dani Haviland

THE FAIRIES SAGA SERIES
(Historical fiction/time travel, listed in order):

Kibbles and Bits: **FREE** ebook: Sample the early stories in The Fairies Saga stories with extended excerpts, and also find out how they got their crazy names.

Aye, I am a Fairy: (Book One) Young British lord finds himself entwined with a time traveling family and must decide if he should go back in time, too.

LOST: The Time Travel Romance That Started It All: (Book Two) The fun introduction to some of the very colorful characters from The Fairies Saga and Arlie Undercover. Find out how they're influenced by the fan-obsessive romance novel LOST by Lisa Sinclaire.

Naked in the Winter Wind: (Book Three) How does an older woman wind up as a young hottie in Revolutionary War era North Carolina?

Ha'Penny Jenny: (Book Four) More about the naïve and psychic young girl who was adopted into a time traveling family. Will her past catch up to her?

Dances Naked: (Book Five) Directionally challenged time traveler is rescued by Cherokee in 18th century. What must he do before the chief will show him to The Trees, the portal through time?

The Great Big Fairy: (Book Six) Very tall Benji grew up in the 20th century but was born in the 18th. When he finds a way to return to his grandparents in the distant past, he goes for it. Once there, he realizes he can't stay, but must return to the future.

Kidnapped! (Book Seven) The Scottish police officer would do anything to get his wife back...even trust the mysterious letter sent to him from his ancestor, a convict on The First Fleet into Australia!

Little Bear and the Ladies: (Book Eight) What's a bachelor trapper to do with all the females he rescues from the Hessian mercenaries? He'd better hurry and figure something!

Time in a Little Blue Bottle: (Book Nine) Elvis, Mark Twain, and the prime vampire are racing to get the bottle of Fountain of Youth water before sweet Bella and the youthful pickpocket. So why are time travelers Marty Melbourne and Master Simon interested?

Big Mac: (Book Ten) Fate and science said they should never have met but after that first touch, he knew he'd stay with her forever. Would the sudden appearance of the father he never knew be their doom – and the start of a pandemic?

Chasing Christmas: (Book Eleven) A young Cherokee is rescued from an abusive man and changes the lives of many in this 18th century America family.

Little Drummer Boy: (Book Twelve) Young Scout works to earn money for a home in post-Revolutionary War America but runs up against prejudices and snowstorms.

Never Too Young: (Book Thirteen) Scout and Ha'Penny Jenny have grown up, but will they be able to spend their life together, or will the past and ruffians get in their way?

Pool Boy Wanted: No Experience Preferred: (Book Fourteen) Young Benji has been a hostage and slave, but life gets worse when an older woman decides she wants him as her own.

Luke the Unexpected: (Book Fifteen) Love of classic motorcycles brought them together, but Luke and Holly have other challenges to face. Find out how their friend Benji got his stripes here.

TRIPLETS: THREE AREN'T ONE
(A potpourri of literary styles, all with strong characters)

The Set Up: Grace's story. A gritty Women's Fiction of how it all began.

Diamonds Aren't for Everyone: Vickie's story. A Billionaire Romance with mysteries and surprises.

That Magic Touch: Ria's story. A tender, heartwarming Medical Romance.

How Love Grows: Tori's story. A spunky young woman insists on doing everything her way. A Romantic Comedy.

They Call Me Sherlock: Silas's story. A young couple who met at Woodstock get a second chance due to creative use of time travel. Romantic Comedy.

The Whole She-Bang – Triplets: Three Aren't One Collection. All the stories in one set.

ARLIE UNDERCOVER SERIES
(Romantic suspense & Cozy Mysteries based in Alaska and Arizona)

A Stingray Christmas: (Book One) Anchorage detective on medical leave travels from Alaska to Arizona to see for the first time the son he'd fathered as an anonymous sperm donor. Great and rotten surprises await the cop with the smartest smartphone around.

The Biggest Heart Ever: (Book Two) When would Arlie learn that trying to do everything by himself could be deadly—and make Charlene a widow before they were married?

Always a Bigger Fish: (Book Three) Back in Alaska, Arlie finds out he's a target. Will vacationing detective Billy Burke (from THE FAIRIES

SAGA) have information to help nab the scalper?

How to Fix a Broken Life: (Book Four) When Arlie's very pregnant wife is kidnapped by pseudo terrorists, will he be the one to rescue her or will a surprise hero come in to save the day?

Because You Said So: (Book Five) Something's amiss at the Port of Anchorage. Will Arlie be able to solve it and still be back in time to wear the Santa suit?

Heaven and Heartbreak: (Book Six) Sharing her child with a gay father and his lover was the easy part. Finding a woman for herself seemed impossible.

Crazy Ladies in Capes Debut: (Book Seven) Louie witnessed a murder – or did he? Are the senior women downtown responsible?

Never a Dull Murder: (Book Eight) Arlie has too many people trying to help him solve the murder of the baker in Witness Protection. Will his new gadget – or a hungry bear cub – find the answer?

Arlie and Company: All eight books of the Arlie Undercover series in one place.

THAT TWIN THING SERIES
(Romantic suspense series)

The Midwife's Son: The midwife refused her selfish patient's request to smother the scrawny twin and instead took him home to bring up as her own. Years later, will the two young men wind up in each other's lives despite the midwife's efforts to keep them apart?

Phoenix I'm Not: Will the billionaire's spoiled son be resurrected from the ashes of his former life of drugs and mayhem by love or be tortured and eliminated by the assassin sent by his mother?

Lost and Found Family: Separated at birth, these twins find they have more than genetics in common: they're both the target of killers who are willing to risk everything to take them out.

Peter Elph: A supplement to the story of Lost and Found Family, this short story is about a member of the Wagner family back in 1886 Tombstone, Arizona.

That Twin Thing: The Complete Collection: All four books in one place.

STAND ALONE NOVELLAS
(Contemporary romances)

Kit Kringle: An Alaskan Tale: Kay moved to Alaska for the wrong reasons, then decided to stay and start her own business. What she hadn't planned on were prejudices and falling in love.

Be My Angel: Wyatt's dream to help save the wild mustangs began with the purchase of a rundown ranch in western Oregon. What he hadn't anticipated was being mesmerized by a sassy woman in a wheelchair.

Three Are One: The post chaplain tried to help the young widow adjust, but would his feelings for her and the search for his lost sister cause problems?

One Arctic Summer: That unforgettable summer of 1994 in Barrow, Alaska, and the touch she never forgot…If she goes back, will he remember her?

The Polar Xpress: Will the California chiropractor get a first chance at romance with the owner of Second Chance Kennels when he is stranded in Alaska?

Too Fast For You: Ten years after Little League, two talented professional baseball players wind up on the same minor league team. Will she remember him? And will their friendship be ruined if she does?

A Plate of Christmas Cookies: World War Two got between them the first time. Will his adult children stop his second chance at happiness? Based on a true story.

The Wizard of Odds: Four co-workers get closer than they expected on a cross-country tour to win a bet and rescue some exotic animals at the same time. A Rom-Com.

The Purebred and the Mutt: The British auto enthusiast TV star meets the caretaker and mechanic at his American ranch. Could this Southern gal hold her own when they're confronted by a crazed fan? A Rom-Com.

Splendor and Surprises: Alaska Style – The Singles Collection Set One: All of the Stand Alone Single Romance stories that occur in Alaska in one place. Includes Three Are One, One Arctic Summer, The Polar Xpress, and Kit Kringle: An Alaskan Tale.

Cookies, Angels and Road Trips – The Singles Collection Set Two: A potpourri of sweet and savory romances. From Love at First Sight to Second Chances, lots of surprises and 'ah moments' plus a few giggles and guffaws. Included are A Plate of Christmas Cookies, The Purebred and the Mutt, Be My Angel, Too Fast For You, and The Wizard of Odds.

Cast of Characters

Annie ~ Native American 'slave'

Captain Atholl MacLeod ~ evil, phony Redcoat officer, 18th c.

Clayton ~ degenerate 18th century man

Clyde ~ Clayton's degenerate brother, 18th century.

Curly ~ rogue British soldier

Evie ~ 20th century born older woman, transported back to 18th century, has amnesia, now in young body due to an overdose of Fountain of Youth Water.

Faith ~ rescued infant

Gimpy ~ bad guy with a limp, 18th century

Gunny ~ Friendly soldier

Hannah Althouse ~ helpful teenager, 18th century

Ian Kincaid ~ 18th century backwoodsman, Scout's father, Jody's nephew

James Melbourne ~ young British Lord, 21st century

Jenny ~ indomitable young psychic, 18th century

Jody Pomeroy ~ 18th century patriarch, Wallace's father

José ~ Spanish emigrant, 18th century

Julian Hart ~ British Lord, 18th century

Lady ~ cougar (the feline type), semi-tame

Leah ~ 21st century daughter of Evie

Leonardo da Vinci Sr. ~ time traveler, 18th and 21st centuries

Little Bear ~ white trapper, 18th century

Ma ~ 18th century backwoods woman

Mac Donaldson ~ 18th century farmer, father, patriot

Master Simon ~ strange man, time traveler 18th & 21st centuries

Mrs. Donaldson ~ 18th century homemaker

Mr. Gibson ~ 18th century storekeeper

'Mr. Smith' ~ horrible slaver, trapper

Mrs. Short ~ Jenny's former 'caretaker'

Richard Short ~ local troublemaker, 18th century

Samuel ~ Cherokee chief

Sarah Pomeroy ~ Jody's wife, 20th century-born time traveler, healer, living in 18th century

Skinny ~ rogue British soldier, 18th century

'The Fireman' ~ bad guy, 18th century
Wallace ~ 18th century British soldier, Julian's stepson
Wee Ian ~ also known as Scout, 18th c.
Wren, Leo, Judah ~ Evie's triplet children and Jenny's new siblings